The Riddle

of

THE LOST

LOVER

PATRICIA VERYAN

The Riddle

of

THE LOST

LOVER

ST. MARTIN'S PRESS
NEW YORK

Library of Congress Cataloging-in-Publication Data

Veryan, Patricia.
    The riddle of the lost lover / Patricia Veryan.—1st U.S. ed.
      p. cm.
    ISBN 0-312-19324-6
    I. Title.
    PS3572.E766R535 1998
    813'.54—dc21   98-21111
                                                 CIP

First Edition: November 1998

10 9 8 7 6 5 4 3 2 1

For Florence Feiler,
my agent and my friend

The Riddle

of

THE LOST

LOVER

Prologue

St. Jean de Luz, France
Winter 1813

Outside the building that was now Field Marshal Lord Wellington's headquarters the grey afternoon was made greyer by the unrelenting rain. Inside, Colonel the Honourable Hastings Adair waited uneasily in the passageway and jerked to attention as a door opened. A tall officer came out and nodded to him. "Go on in, Hasty. He's alone."

Adair half-whispered, "How's his temper?"

Colonel John Colborne grinned. "He's melting down his barometer!"

Groaning softly, Adair knocked as he opened the door.

The great soldier sat turned away from a littered table, and was rapping on the top of the tubular barometer that accompanied him on his Peninsular campaigns. He muttered something about not knowing why he bothered with "the stupid thing." A keen stare was directed over his shoulder and he added, "Well, sit down, Adair. You're wet. Damnable weather. But we're more comfortable here than we were in Lesaca. Food's better, as well. I suppose London's not bright and sunny, eh?"

"Cold and foggy, my lord. I wonder if I might take off my coat?"

His lordship turned the chair back to his table. "Do your best," he said dryly and, indicating another chair, added, "Throw it over there. I presume you've brought me something?"

"Yes, sir." Adair scrambled out of his coat, slung it aside and pulled several letters from an oilskin-covered bag. "From the Prime Minister; Sir Henry Wellesley; and Lady Wellington."

The Field Marshal stared at the letters as though he could see through the sealed paper then pushed them aside. "Very good. Now let me have your report. As fast as possible, if you please. I've left orders we're not to be interrupted but I can't give you much more than ten minutes. What the devil was Sir Kendrick Vespa about in Dorsetshire?"

Adair's brain raced, trying to reduce a twenty-page written report to a brief verbal account. "You knew that his heir, Lieutenant Sherborne Vespa, fell at the Third Siege of Badajoz, sir?"

"Since his brother John is—was on my staff, I'd be a dunce not to know it, wouldn't I?"

Adair reddened, and sidestepped the rhetorical question. "The thing is that an estate called Alabaster Royal, which would have gone to Sherborne from his maternal grandparents, thus passed to John, who was later severely wounded at the Battle of Vitoria, and sent home." He glimpsed the pit yawning at his feet and added desperately, "As you also know, my lord."

"I do not want to hear what I *know*, Colonel. Let us commence with what I *do not* know! This Alabaster Royal is a Dorsetshire estate that was of interest to Whitehall?"

"Yes, my lord. Sir Kendrick Vespa had approached several gentlemen in Government with a view to locating the proposed subsidiary arsenal on the property."

The dark stare pierced him. The voice was a rasp of anger. "One trusts that is not common knowledge! If word leaks out that we're even thinking of a secondary arsenal the newspapers

2

will scream that invasion is imminent and we expect Woolwich Arsenal will be captured!"

"No, no! It has been handled as Very Secret, I assure you."

"Yet Kendrick Vespa learned of it!"

"He is—was, a diplomatist, sir. At all events, there is an old quarry on the Alabaster Royal estate. No longer in operation, but it is located close to the village and at one time provided employment for—"

"Why and when was it abandoned?"

"It was closed down several decades ago. An underground river flooded some of the lower tunnels from time to time when there were heavy rains."

"Sounds like a stupid location for an arsenal, but they'd have picked a site away from this quarry, I fancy? Certainly, government surveyors would inspect the ground."

"Yes, my lord. However, Sir Kendrick Vespa discovered that the tunnels are far more extensive than was generally known, and in places descend to several levels. If this became known, he would lose the sale, and he stood to gain a pretty penny from leases and rights-of-way, and such, so—"

"But I understood you to say that the estate had passed to his surviving son, John Vespa?"

"It had, my lord, and that presented a large problem for Sir Kendrick. From what I've gathered, Sherborne, his heir, was easily influenced. When he was killed and John inherited, Sir Kendrick knew he had a different tiger by the tail."

A twinkle came into the eyes of the Field Marshal and the harsh lines of his face softened. He said, "Aye. Jack Vespa's a stubborn young rascal. But—good Lord, man! The family is far from purse-pinched. I've visited their Mayfair house, which is very nice, and I believe they've a fine property on the River at Richmond. The loss of one small estate is scarce likely to throw them into debtors' prison! Why all the desperate doings?"

Adair tightened his lips, then said reluctantly, "I'm sure the

Field Marshal is aware that Sir Kendrick Vespa was a remarkably handsome man, much admired by the Fair Sex?"

"Aha." The famous bray of laughter rang out. "Set up another mistress, did he? I wonder he could keep count!" He coughed and said severely, "A fellow has to know where to draw the line, Adair. Remember that! Too much dallying with the ladies has been the ruination of many a fine career!"

Well aware that Wellington had a reputation of his own along those lines, Adair managed to keep his face solemn. "Sir Kendrick had several—er, *affaires de coeur,* my lord. One of the more recent being with the young lady who—er, was to have wed Sherborne."

"The devil you say! That must have set the gabble-mongers by the ears!"

"Yes. But it appears, sir, that there was yet another—and secret—entanglement. This with a beautiful lady from India. Sir Kendrick was deeply enamoured. He planned to divorce his wife and marry his latest love. As you may guess, such a union would have been condemned both in her country and in Britain, especially in view of the scandal involving his late son's lady. Sir Kendrick was determined, and apparently did not feel bound by moral or legal considerations. He devised a plan to sidestep both. To succeed he had to raise a great deal of money, but his London property is entailed, and to have sold the Richmond house and liquidated his other assets would have taken time, besides causing more scandal and most probably a family uproar. He was not prepared to wait, so he planned to sell the Alabaster Royal estate to the Government at a much inflated price, no doubt. With the proceeds from the sale he meant to build a palace on a small island he had bought and dwell there with his lady."

For once rendered speechless, Wellington stared at him.

"So," went on Adair hurriedly, "he had the main quarry tunnel sealed off in such a way that it looked as if no work had ever been done beyond that point. It was then that his younger son,

4

John, was sent home, and to Sir Kendrick's considerable annoyance, decided to live down at his Dorsetshire manor."

"A deuced good thing, by God! John Vespa was one of the finest fellows I've had on my staff. I'm only sorry he was so badly mangled at Vitoria. He's not the man to stand still for any hanky-panky." Wellington said shrewdly, "Though I was of the impression he idolized his father—true?"

"Quite true, sir. Sir Kendrick tried very hard to steer John away from Alabaster Royal. Nothing worked. I'm told John's decision may have been prompted by grief. He and his brother had been very close, and the family residences likely held too many memories."

Curious, Wellington asked, "Do you cry friends with Captain John Vespa?"

"Er—not precisely, my lord." His colour a little heightened, Adair said, "We both admire the same lady, in fact."

"Aha. Go on. So John persisted in moving down to this Alabaster Royal, did he?"

"Yes, sir. And just as his father had feared, started to poke around."

"Of course he did! Bright lad, young Johnny! So his sire had to abandon his plans, eh?" Wellington took up the Prime Minister's letter. "He must have been addled to think he could pull it off. Once the surveyors looked over the place it would have been ruled out, at all events."

"They did look it over, my lord. And it was judged perfectly sound and eminently well-suited to—"

"*What?*" His heavy eyebrows bristling, the Field Marshal slammed the letter down again. "Were they daft, or what?"

"As I understand it, my lord, there was a—er, sizable exchange of funds. . . ."

"*Bribery?*" Outraged, as always, by any hint of misbehavior in government, Wellington's roar made Adair jump. "Now *confound* the makebait! Well, he'd never have convinced everyone. John must have known the true state of affairs, and the scheme would surely have been discovered."

"It was, my lord. It chanced that Preston Jones lived nearby."

Lord Wellington frowned. "Preston Jones . . . I know the name, but—I have it! The artist. Very clever chap. Lady Wellington is a great admirer. But—wait— Died, did he not? Fell, or something of the sort?"

"Allegedly—yes. Mr. Jones was fascinated by the manor house at Alabaster Royal. It's a quaint old place. Jones took to wandering about the estate, sketching. Sir Kendrick and a couple of neighbours who were partners in his schemes objected to Mr. Jones' trespassing. Violently."

"Are you saying Preston Jones did *not* fall accidentally? You surely don't hold Sir Kendrick Vespa responsible?"

"We know Mr. Jones discovered that the ground on the estate is undermined. If he had also discovered there were plans to build a large arsenal on such land and fill it with weapons and high explosive—"

"Which would be to invite disaster," growled Wellington.

"Just so, my lord. Especially since there is a good-sized village adjacent to the quarry. We believe Mr. Jones hadn't dared voice his suspicions until he was sure. The very day he had his proof he was seen, apparently under the influence of drink, being supported by two strangers. Next morning, he was found at the bottom of the quarry."

"Was he, by God! So Kendrick Vespa didn't draw the line at murder!"

"At several murders, unfortunately, my lord."

"It's past belief that a well-bred gentleman as widely admired as he could have sunk so low! Where was young John? Was he as gulled as everyone else? I cannot think he'd have been party to such treachery."

"He wasn't, sir. There were several attempts on his life, in fact, when he started to investigate. He thought he had identified the conspirators. He didn't discover until it was too late that the man at the top was his own father."

"Poor fellow." The Field Marshal shook his head sombrely. "What a devilish fix to be in! Poor fellow. Still, he did what he had to do. No one could fault him."

"Your pardon, sir?"

"No need to wrap it in clean linen, Colonel. It has been spread about that Sir Kendrick Vespa was swept away by an underground flood when he and his son surprised some ruffians in the quarry. I can see as far through a brick wall as the next man." Taking up the letter once more, Wellington said, "We must make very sure the tale dies here, is all."

Colonel Adair paused, then said reluctantly, "I'm afraid—it er, doesn't, though, my lord."

The stern lips tightened. "Why did I guess you were going to say that?" Tossing down the letter, Wellington leaned back in his chair. "Very well. Don't hide your teeth."

"As I piece it together, sir, things came to a head in the quarry. John went down there to test his suspicions, and his father offered his aid. The other plotters arrived and John learned the whole ugly business, and that the mastermind was his own father. Or—the gentleman he thought was his father."

The dark head jerked up. "He—*thought . . . ?*"

Adair nodded. "Sir Kendrick, it seems, had for four and twenty years accepted another man's child as his own. He was never faithful to his wife, as all London knows. Apparently, Lady Faith Vespa was so wounded when he set up a mistress only a year after their marriage that she gathered a court of her own." He shrugged expressively.

"And John Vespa was a child of her—indiscretion?" Grinning broadly, his lordship drove a hand against the table. "I'll be damned! Now that I think on it, John's colouring is fair, and Sherborne was as dark as Sir Kendrick. Come now, Adair. Do you say the man didn't *know* he'd been cuckolded?"

"Oh, he knew all right, and was enraged. But his pride wouldn't let him admit it publicly. He's not the first, sir, to accept a bastard as his own to protect the family name."

"No, by Jove. And he concealed it well, appearing to be the proud father. The boy gave him plenty of cause for pride, of course. When did John find out the truth of his parentage?"

"In the tunnel. Sir Kendrick showed his true colours and told John very explicitly how he had loathed and despised him all these years."

"By heaven but that was a wretched thing to do! The poor lad must have been shattered. Small wonder he retaliated!"

"He was not responsible for Sir Kendrick's death. Another man claimed that privilege after John had been shot down."

Wellington shook his head broodingly. "What a tragedy! Greed, and a woman—a deadly combination. I'm glad my fine aide survived. How is he, Adair?"

"Going along remarkably well, sir. Under the circumstances. And full of determination. They all are."

"Determination about what? Who?"

"His friends. Lieutenants Paige Manderville and Tobias Broderick. They were all sent home after Vitoria, and they're united in trying to help him in his quest."

"*Good Lord above!*" roared the Field Marshal. "*Will* you have done with all this roundaboutation! *What*—quest?"

"To find his real father, my lord. John had hoped to be married, you see, but cannot approach the lady without a name—or without at least knowing his parentage. He refuses to use the Vespa title or to accept the fortune or the properties. The only thing that keeps him from revealing the whole ugly story is his loyalty to his mother."

"He had *best* not reveal the whole!" Wellington sprang up and began to pace about the room. "We don't need a scandal like that breaking over our heads while we've Bonaparte to deal with! The men in government who took Kendrick Vespa's bribes will be

8

punished. But quietly, mind! And there must be not a *whisper* of our plans for a secondary arsenal!" He halted, head bowed and brows fixed in a frown. "By Jupiter, but I'd like to give young Vespa a hand. Does anyone know who was Lady Faith's side-door lover?"

"Yes, my lord. It explains to an extent why Sir Kendrick harboured such a hatred for John. Lady Faith gave her husband back his own—and more. She chose his most bitter enemy for her lover. And John grew up to resemble the man. Most people assumed that the boy took after the Wansdykes, his mother's family. But you may be sure Sir Kendrick was all too aware of the truth, and reminded of it each time he looked at John."

"Well? Well? Never back and fill! Who was the fellow?"

Adair leaned to take up the letter from the Prime Minister. "Perhaps you should read this, sir."

With a snarl of irritation, Wellington broke the seal. His eyes ran rapidly down the page. When he looked up, he was pale. "I cannot *credit* it! Of all the men in the world . . . !"

Adair watched him gravely through a brief silence.

Wellington folded the letter again and stared at it blankly. "I've a real sympathy for John Vespa," he muttered, as if to himself. "He's a fine young fellow and was a splendid officer." He looked up from under his brows and said with grim intensity, "A deuced ugly mess you bring me, Colonel."

Apprehensive, Adair said, "Yes. I apologize, sir."

The great soldier grunted and dealt the barometer a sharp rap.

Adair's apprehensions were justified.

"You shall have to tidy it up," said Field Marshal Lord Wellington.

1

London.

"Disgusting!" Jerking aside the heavy draperies that shielded her drawing-room windows, Mrs. Fortram scowled down into the rainy darkness and said in her elderly and irritable voice, "Here's *another* of 'em rattling up the street to shatter our quiet! Look at 'em, Hubert! Confounded idiots! There ought to be a law against routs and balls and musicales and falderals being carried on in this peaceful and refined neighbourhood!"

"Mmm," said her son, savouring another sip of his port.

For all her apparent frailty, Gertrude Fortram was not easily diverted from a Cause. Choosing to forget the many occasions on which her own parties and balls had disrupted the neighbourhood peace, she went on fiercely, "Cluttering up the streets at all hours of the night! Keeping honest folk from their rest! You'd think people could find better ways to amuse themselves than to put on clothes that belong more to midsummer than a cold wintry night, and drive halfway across Town to answer the summons of Esther Wolff, as if she were one of the almighty *ton* leaders! Which she is not, and so I've told her!"

Receiving only a sympathetic grunt in reply, the old lady continued, "It's not as if we were at the height of the Season. I'd thought London thin of company, in point of fact, but— Heavens! If ever I saw such a crush! Much good those special constables do! Lud, only look at how the carriages are obliged to wait in line! One might suppose Wellington himself was among the guests!"

Mr. Fortram settled his portly self more comfortably in his deep chair, stretched his slippered feet closer to the warm hearth, and turned the page of *The Times*. "In that case I would have accepted the invitation, Mama," he murmured, drowsily content. "I can only be glad that—"

He glanced up, startled, as his words were cut off by a shriek. "That wretched *cat!*" shrilled his mother. "The fur will fly now!"

His curiosity aroused at last, Hubert puffed and huffed, extricated himself from the chair and crossed to the window. "Who? Oh, Gad! The Hersh dragon! I thought she was in Bath."

"As she should be at this time of year. And— Look there! Lucinda Carden, and on Ted Ridgley's arm! Who's next? Ah, that horrid Phineas Bodwin escorting . . . I cannot recognize her, but she looks a trollop, which surprises me not at all."

"Gathering of the gabble-mongers," sneered Hubert. "I wonder whom they mean to flay tonight."

"Sir Kendrick Vespa, of course!"

Shocked, he protested, "Jupiter, ma'am! They can't flay poor Sir Kendrick. Dead, y'know."

"No, I don't know! Nobody knows for sure. And his son's not gone into mourning, I heard."

"What, is Jack Vespa in Town, again? Gad, but that was a fast recover. Last word I had was that he was at death's door."

Mrs. Fortram turned her attention from the window and eyed her son with rare interest. "Well, he's not there now, and I'm glad of it, for I like the boy. What else have you heard? The gabsters who usually know everything are suddenly like so many stuffed owls. Why all the secrecy?"

"Be dashed if I know. Paige Manderville was in White's yesterday, and all he'd say was that Jack and Sir Kendrick surprised some rogues hiding in an old quarry on Jack's Dorsetshire property, and—"

"And that Captain Jack was shot down and his father pushed into some sort of underground flood. Outrageous! Despicable! Dastardly! But that was weeks ago, and despite all the flurry at Bow Street and Whitehall, with Runners and Special Constables and dragoons galloping about hither and yon, what have they accomplished? Have the culprits been arrested? No! What mischief were they about down in that old quarry? No one knows—or will admit to knowing! Why is Bow Street mum, and the newspapers scarce mention the business? That's what *I'd* like to know!"

"As would we all, ma'am. It's a regular mystery, especially when you consider that Sir Kendrick Vespa is—was a distinguished diplomatist."

"True." Mrs. Fortram restored her attention to the window. "The thing is, they haven't found his body yet. Might never find it. Which will leave his surviving son properly in the suds, eh?"

"Mmm." Putting up his quizzing glass, Mr. Fortram admired the points of a fine chestnut team now pulling up before the great house across the street, and murmured absently, "I wonder if his poor mama knows of her bereavement."

"Poor mama, indeed! All Faith Vespa ever did was whine about Sir Kendrick's neglect of her. I doubt she'll grieve him, though she's missing a splendid opportunity to moan and wail and weep crocodile tears all over Town. I don't see how she could know of her widowhood, at all events. The silly widgeon ran off to some relations in South America, didn't she?"

Hubert pursed his lips and returned to his chair. "So they

say. I for one cannot blame her. All that scandal about her husband's lightskirts. Terrible embarrassment for the lady."

"Well, running away added grist to the gossip mills, which she'd know had she a particle of sense. Kendrick Vespa was too handsome, and that's always a danger. But had Lady Faith handled him properly . . . instead of which I'm of the opinion her complainings fairly drove the man to infidelity."

Again reaching for *The Times,* Hubert murmured, "Now we don't know that for sure, Mama. And the Vespas, after all, rank among our most ancient and respected Houses."

"The more reason for Sir Kendrick to have guarded his name against scandal! It's downright shocking that a fine old family could be thriving one day, and destroyed the next. That's what comes of— *Look!* Only look! The *Ottavio* woman! I haven't seen her for— Doesn't she live in Dorsetshire? I'll warrant *she* knows what went on down at Alabaster Regis—or whatever it's called."

Joining his parent once more, Hubert put up his quizzing glass. "You're right, by Jove! I remember the little lady. French, ain't she? A duchess or some such thing."

"Italian. She claims to be the duchess of Ottavio, but her husband died just before inheriting the title, and she is no more a duchess than am I! Whatever can have brought her back into Town, I wonder? Well, that bears off the palm! Lord, are you lumping back into your chair again? Come, Hubert! Up! Up! Rouse your lazy self! No use looking so hardly done by. The whole town's talking and with the gathering of gabblers across the way there's not a doubt in the world but that Sir Kendrick's escapades with the Stokely hussy will be the prime topic. I don't mean to miss it, and so I warn you! Change your dress. I'll be ready in half an hour!"

"But—mama," wailed Hubert. "You said you didn't want to go out tonight. It's raining! And besides, you declined the invitation."

"Well now I'm accepting! Half an hour, Hubert! Stir your stumps!"

14

Mr. Gaylord Wolff had instructed his architect to design a ball-room in the Grecian style, and the results of that talented gentleman's efforts were much admired in London Town. Despite the cold air outside and the abundance of marble inside, the impressive room was crowded and very warm, and when a quadrille ended many of the guests made their way to the cooler dining and reception rooms where an elegant supper was spread on long tables. Laden trays were borne off to adjacent ante-rooms whose smaller tables, chairs and sofas filled rapidly. The air hummed with polite chatter, aristocratic faces were variously sad or titillated, and on every tongue it seemed was the one name—Vespa.

Seldom had the *ton* enjoyed a more delicious scandal. Sir Kendrick Vespa had long been known to have a mistress in keeping, in addition to other ladies believed to have enjoyed his protection from time to time. What had not been known was that the much admired gentleman had lately enjoyed a secret *affaire de coeur* with Mrs. Esmeralda Stokely. The widow was lovely, but she was young enough to be his daughter, and, worse, had been on the brink of marrying his eldest son prior to the young soldier's tragic death in battle.

Mrs. Fortram and Hubert, having made their way to the supper rooms, gathered plates of delicacies and drifted unobtrusively from one group to another, their eagerly stretched ears gathering a choice harvest of gossip.

". . . and not to speak ill of the dead, my dear Lady Vera, but to think that *lovely* man could have been so *devious!*"

". . . poor Mrs. Omberleigh. She was never good *ton,* of course, but my heart bleeds for her."

"What did she expect? The Omberleigh was his mistress for ten years at least, and few gentlemen keep a fancy piece for that long. *My* sympathies are with . . ."

". . . *poor* Lady Vespa! She knew about the Omberleigh

woman, of course, but to then discover the *others!* My dear! And now . . ."

". . . is it truth that The Stokely was betrothed to his own *son?* If *ever* I heard of so shocking . . ."

". . . and that he was involved with the Widow Stokely even while poor Sherborne was *still alive!* Can you credit . . ."

Having at this point reached an especially fruitful source, Mrs. Fortram drew Hubert to a halt close to one of the sofas set about the fringes of the dining room.

Mrs. Anne Hersh, seated beside her friend Lady Grey, arranged her sharp features into what she supposed to be a look of piety and said with a sigh as deep as it was insincere, "Now Captain John Vespa is the one *I* sympathize with. First his brother, and now his father gone, and his mama flaunting off to the other side of the world!"

Not to be outdone, Lady Grey moaned softly. "How *alone* he must feel, poor boy. And there is no bride in the offing, as I recall."

"If there were, *you* would surely know of it! You always are so well-informed!"

Lady Grey smiled patronizingly. "Thank you, my love. One does not care to *gossip,* you understand. But when one is well acquainted—well, how can one refrain from . . . hearing things?"

"Exactly! So now, *do* tell me, *whatever* do you think of this latest ghastly *on-dit?*"

Her ladyship, who had been in the midlands visiting her mama-in-law, knew of no 'latest ghastly *on-dit*' and tried in vain to hide her chagrin.

Gertrude Fortram was also chagrined, for she could not quite catch the whispered confidence when Mrs. Hersh spread the good word.

Accustomed as she was to London's gossip mills, Lady Grey uttered a shocked squeal and dropped her fan. *"Another* one?"

"And a foreigner, no less! The hints are that she is very beau-

tiful, in an exotic uncivilized sort of way. At least, that's what—"
Mrs. Hersh stopped speaking, and turned around.

Mrs. Fortram returned Anne Hersh's haughty stare with an unrepentant display of brown teeth, then tugged imperatively on Hubert's arm and they resumed their enlightening stroll.

The orchestra was striking up for a country dance and the guests started to drift towards the ballroom.

"What now, ma'am?" asked Hubert, as intrigued by what they had gleaned as was his mother.

"Over there," hissed Mrs. Fortram. "Manderville. If anyone knows who was Kendrick Vespa's 'other one,' that impudent young rascal does. Come on!"

"If he does know, he won't tell you," warned Hubert. "He's one of Jack Vespa's best friends."

"Then we won't ask him, you flat," snarled his doting parent. "Come—*on!*"

———◦∾◦———

"It was the most horrid party I ever attended!" Miss Consuela Carlotta Angelica Jones twitched her cloak tighter about her small and shapely self and snuggled against the squabs of the carriage. "I wonder the musicians even bothered to play; the only reason people came was to gabble and gossip and giggle about the Vespas!" She was a little flushed, her blue eyes reflected her irritation and she pushed back a straying curl impatiently.

Seated opposite her, Paige Manderville reflected that although she could not be judged a beauty, Miss Consuela Jones was very pretty. Her disposition was sunny, her heart warm and her loyalties deep and unwavering. If she was also unconventionally frank, inclined to act on impulse (sometimes disastrously), and had a quick-flaring temper, those were qualities he found charming, so that he envied Jack Vespa, who was in love with her, and to whom she was devoted. He said an amused, "You look like an irritated little pouter pigeon, m'dear. I'll own it's as

17

well Jack was not present this evening, but considering the party was so 'horrid,' you did not want for dance partners. Indeed, had Jack and your gallant Colonel both been present, they'd have had small chance of writing their names on your dance card."

Even in the dim light thrown by the carriage lamps it was clear that those who named Manderville one of London's most handsome bachelors were justified, but Miss Jones viewed his dark good looks without rapture. "If by my 'gallant Colonel' you refer to Hastings Adair," she snapped, "you give me too much credit, Paige!"

"Since Toby and I are both lowly lieutenants and Jack a mere captain, whom else should I—"

"Jack is not *merely* a captain, but was one of Lord Wellington's personal aides, which makes him very special indeed! Furthermore, how could he possibly attend a ball when he is—or is supposed to be—in mourning for his—his father. Horrid, wicked creature that he was!"

The diminutive Francesca, self-styled 'duchess of Ottavio,' who was the third occupant of the luxurious coach, yawned, and demanded, "Well—and well? What have you expect, my meadowlark? Jack was shot, so people they sympathize. But now, he is recovered, and does he go into blacks? He does not! Does he use the title that is now legally his? No! Will he stay in the Vespa mansion in Town? No! Has he once set his feets into his great house at Richmond? No again!"

"You *know* why Jack refuses to use the title and the Vespa properties," said Consuela defensively.

"Oh, *si. I* know. *You* know. Lieutenant Paige and Tobias Broderick, they know. But does the *ton* know?"

Manderville inserted quietly, "Can't very well tell 'em, can he, ma'am? Not without disgracing his mama."

"So what does your *ton?*" demanded the old lady. "It seethe. It revel! It is *contissimo!* Rumour, she spread her feathers and fly like—like the tempest about this old town! I will speak of the silliness that *I* was hearing at this very silly ball. One—that Sir Kendrick Vespa is not killed in that quarry at all, but has run off to some secret paradise with his beautiful Indian lady. Two—that Lady Faith Vespa did not go out to South America to visit her cousins, but that Sir Kendrick strangled her. And, three—she is buried somewhere—"

"In the quarry at Alabaster Royal, no doubt," put in Manderville derisively. "Which is what Jack and Sir Kendrick were occupied with down there when they were attacked. Burying the poor lady."

"Exactly so."

Consuela gave a squeak of rage. "No! Surely, *Nonna,* they did not say such things!"

"I heard much the same sort of slanderous nonsense," drawled Manderville. "Only in even more lurid detail. Is it so much worse than the truth?"

Consuela frowned broodingly at the window. "They don't know the truth. So they make up things!"

"They've learned enough to discover that Sir Kendrick Vespa, the pattern-card of a British diplomatist, was at the least a womanizing rascal. He has betrayed the Code. They won't soon forgive him."

"Me," flared Consuela fiercely, "I shall *never* forgive him! For what he did to my beloved Papa, and to Jack, who loved him, he should have been taken and hanged by the neck till he was thoroughly dead! Dead without question! Nor need you pretend you did not despise him as much as I."

"True," admitted Manderville. "I'd enjoy to have called out the bas—er, to have had the gentleman in the sights of my pistol."

Lady Francesca said, "All of this it tells us nothing in the matters, saving that no one of us has learned anything of what our Captain Jack hopes to discover. I myself have try many careful ways. I did the giggle and gabble with the most spiteful of the *ton*

19

cats, and could learn nothing of the *affaires* of Lady Faith Vespa. That woman with the long nose, Gertrude Fortram, has learn that we are the neighbours to Captain Jack's Dorset lands, so she come and smile and coil around me like a dried-up serpent, as if I am not awareness that she have much despise for me. And why must you laugh so much, Lieutenant Paige? Have I perhaps lie in my tooth?"

"Certainly not," said Manderville unsteadily. "But your expressions, dear ma'am, are so delicious. Do tell us if this—this 'dried up serpent' of a lady was of any help at all."

Mollified, Lady Francesca said that Mrs. Fortram had been of no use save to confide that in her younger days Lady Faith Vespa was believed to have had 'some interesting liaisons.' She sighed. "Which we already have know. But the naming of these 'liaisons' gentlemen I cannot come at."

Manderville chuckled. "Phineas Bodwin managed to imply that he'd been Lady Faith's lover at one time."

"Pah!" said Consuela. "That one—he would say anything to be interesting! Oh, but it is all so discouraging! We try and try, and learn nothing. I had so hoped we might have some news to cheer Jack!"

Lady Francesca squeezed her hand comfortingly. "So had we all, my little one. And we will do this, I know it."

"The problem is," said Manderville, "It's a—um, delicate matter. Begging your pardon, ladies, but one can't very well go smack up to a likely prospect and say, 'How de do? We've just found out that Jack Vespa is a bastard. Might you be the fellow who really fathered him?'"

Consuela's giggle was drowned by Lady Francesca's squeal and her outraged declaration that Lieutenant Paige's language was 'vulgar in the extreme!' She paused, and added, "But he speaks truth. I have the fearing we must tread on the eggs and it will be difficult."

"But not impossible," said Manderville. "And Jack's not

20

downhearted. Only this morning he told Toby and me that he has every confidence he'll come at the truth. And with all of us to help—how can we fail?"

Consuela pounced forward and to his huge delight and her grandmother's pseudo-indignation, kissed him on the cheek. "You are a dear and good friend, Lieutenant Beau Manderville! Thank you for that! So—what do we do next?"

"All I have to do," he said with a grin, "is think up more ways to win such lovely approval. No, seriously, Jack's likely with his great-uncle this very minute. The old boy should know all about his mama's—er, peccadilloes."

Consuela said, "If he does find out something, Paige, you *will* come to Claridges and tell us the very first thing in the morning, please?"

"If I do, will I get another kiss?"

"You are of an impudence," scolded Lady Francesca without heat. "But—*si.* You will win a kiss. From me, you rogue!"

He laughed. "Then I cannot fail!"

———

"Of course I knew your mother well, she was my niece, wasn't she? Watched the pretty creature from the moment she left the schoolroom. One of the most sought-after young damsels in all of London Town, she was."

Sir Reginald Wansdyke refilled the two wine glasses and tried not to betray his impatience. He had always been noted more for his brusque and vigorous ways than for tact. His thick hair was grey now, but at five and sixty his complexion was bronzed, his back straight, and his shoulders as broad and unbowed as many a man twenty years his junior. He'd had a difficult day at the Ex-change, a tiresome confrontation with his youngest grand-daughter and the totally ineligible young rascal she wanted to wed, and a pleasant sojourn at his club had been spoiled by the arrival of Monsieur Imre Monteil. He'd never liked the Swiss, but not because of the man's jet black hair and eyes and 'pastry-white skin,' as Lady Wansdyke described it. In his opinion appearances seldom counted for much. But Monteil was known to have made his fortune in munitions, and his obvious gloating over this drawn-out war with France was repellent, especially in view of the appalling casualties. He himself had lost Sherborne, one of his favourite grand-nephews, to the terrible third siege of Badajoz; and John had been so badly mangled at Vitoria that they might count themselves fortunate he had survived.

The reminder softened Sir Reginald's irritation that the young man had insisted upon awaiting his return instead of postponing his call until tomorrow. He went back to the leather chair in the panelled and pleasantly cluttered room that was his study and looked speculatively across the hearth at his grand-nephew.

John Wansdyke Vespa had inherited neither the impressive height nor the dramatically dark colouring that had so distinguished his father and brother. Indeed, he'd been quite cast into the shade by the handsome Sherborne. Of the brothers, John had been the athlete, and Sherry the dashing Town Beau. No more athletics for John, sad to say. Still, he looked better than when he'd first been brought home after the Battle of Vitoria, and no one could say he was plain. His hair might be an undistinguished light brown, but it had a tendency to curl that Lady Wansdyke said was very attractive. And if the eyes, which she declared to be 'tawny' rather than hazel, lacked the sparkling jet that had made Sherborne's eyes so striking, they were clear and steady and could be warmed charmingly by a lurking smile. His features lacked the delicate carving that blessed most of the Vespas, but the mouth was firm and the chin strong. The scar down his left temple was less noticeable already, and his limp not as obvious. All in all, a fine-looking young fellow, thought Sir Reginald. And he'd certainly distinguished himself on the Peninsula.

Still, it was odd that having called at such an hour he seemed to want to discuss not the recent tragedy that had robbed him of his sire, but the early life of his mother. It was puzzling also that John, who had worshipped Sir Kendrick, had not yet gone into blacks. Very likely, Sir Reginald told himself, it was all too much for the poor lad. Perhaps he was trying to work his way around to speaking of the tragedy. Whatever the case, he was entitled to be handled gently. It was in a compassionate tone, therefore, that he said, "I presume you've notified my niece of your father's—er, death. Have you heard from her since she sailed?"

Jack Vespa had been quite aware of and faintly amused by his great-uncle's intense scrutiny, and could guess what had gone through the mind of this honest and upright gentleman. He knew that there had been no love lost between the Vespa and Wansdyke branches of the family, but he was also aware of Sir Reginald Wansdyke's fierce pride, and he replied cautiously, "I wish I had, sir. There are business affairs to be settled, and other matters on which I have a most urgent need to consult with her."

'So that's it,' thought Sir Reginald. Slightly disappointed, he said, "If it's a matter of your inheritance, I can likely advise you."

"I have a generous inheritance from Grandfather Wansdyke, sir. And Alabaster Royal."

'That dismal hole!' thought Sir Reginald. "True. But in view of—er, everything, I expect you won't want to continue living down there. You've the Richmond property, and the London house is entailed. Certainly the title will come to you, once—er, that is to say, after— In due time."

Vespa nerved himself and took the plunge. "Then you think I've a right to them, sir?"

Sir Reginald gave him a sharp look. "Why the deuce would you not have a right to them? John—I know this quarry business must have been a frightful experience, and I'd not distress you by referring to it, but—are you of the opinion that your father is still alive?"

"I don't know. That's why I asked about my mother. I'm a grown man, sir, and not blind. I'm aware my parents' marriage was not happy."

"Hmm," grunted Sir Reginald, uneasily. "I think it is not for me to comment on such matters. You must talk to your mama, though I'd have thought this was scarce the time to rake over old coals."

"Nor can I do so, since my mother is now in South America."

Lady Faith's flight from the gossip mill was a sore topic with her conservatively minded uncle, and he growled, "Worst thing she could have done! Kendrick had his faults, no denying, but running away don't solve anything." He caught himself up and said testily, "The thing to do, my boy, is to put it all behind you. Your health is much improved already. You can stay peacefully in that lovely house on the river till your mama comes home again, and if you're in need of the 'ready' meanwhile, I'm very sure your father's man of business—Skelton, or some such name as I recall—can oblige you."

"Felton, sir. But—"

"No 'buts,' dear lad. It there's any difficulty along those lines, you just let me know, and we'll come at the root of it."

"Well, there *is* a problem, Uncle. It concerns something Sir Kendrick told me just before—" Vespa paused, one hand clenching. "Before the tunnel—business. It has to do with the early days of their marriage and a friend of my mother's."

"Hmm. I didn't know all Faith's friends, of course. Still don't. Rather a silly lot of females, if you was to ask me."

"This was a gentleman, sir."

"A *gentleman?*" Sir Reginald's smile faded. "Now what the devil could your mother's friends, be they male or female, have to do with your drawing against your inheritance?"

"A great deal, sir. In fact, according to Sir Kendrick, any Vespa inheritance is not—mine."

Sir Reginald's face turned very red. Staring at his grand-nephew he demanded hoarsely, "What a'God's name are you bab-bling at, boy? Your father was mighty high-in-the-instep, but—"

"Was he, sir? That's what I'm trying to find out, you see. Did you know him?"

"What the *deuce* . . .? Of *course* I knew him!" Sir Reginald stood and faced the younger man in consternation. "My poor fellow! You're ill! It's that head wound you took at Vitoria, I don't doubt. You shall overnight here. Tomorrow, I'll refresh your memory about your father. You may ask whatever you wish, and—"

Standing also, Vespa said gently, "I have only one question, Uncle Reginald. Who *is* my father?"

Sir Reginald drew a deep breath and fought his temper. "Now—now, John, I can see you are not yourself. But this is all very . . . improper. If someone has been filling your head with rub-bish, I wish you will name the lamebrain."

"Do you know, Uncle, I wish with all my heart that I could be-lieve it was rubbish. Unhappily, I have no choice but to think he told me the absolute truth."

"Who—who did?" gulped Sir Reginald.

"Sir Kendrick Vespa."

"WHAT? Your—your own *father?*"

Vespa gave a wry shrug. "Evidently not. Sir Kendrick said that years ago, when my mother discovered he had set up a mis-tress, she took a lover to spite him. And that I'm the—the result of her . . . *affaire.*"

His face purpling, Sir Reginald snorted, "If *ever*— If *ever* I heard of such disgraceful twaddle! I can't *credit* it that—that even Kendrick Vespa would—would have *deliberately* said such a wicked thing! Be so good as to tell me, nephew—*when* did he kindly impart all this claptrap?"

"While we were down in the tunnel at the old quarry, sir."

"Indeed. This would have been before you were shot, then."

"Yes, sir. Just before he shot me."

Sir Reginald dropped his glass.

———❦———

"You may believe I am upset!" Pacing to and fro at the foot of his wife's bed, Sir Reginald flung one arm in the air to emphasize his vexation and declared untruthfully, "I'm sorry if I woke you, m'dear. Your candles were still burning, so I thought—"

"Yes. I was reading." Lady Paula drew her bed-jacket closer about her ample figure and sat higher against the pillows. "John is adept at concealing his feelings, but I sensed he was troubled, so I waited up for you."

Sir Reginald gave an explosive snort. "Troubled, you say? He ain't *troubled,* my lady! What he is—he's *daft!* Ripe for Bedlam! I vow if he weren't family, I'd have called in the Runners and had him taken away under strong restraint!"

"Good gracious! Now, my love, I trust you have considered that John is bound to be distressed at this time, and we should—Oh, *pray* do not stamp up and down, you'll wake the house. Have a glass of wine, it will settle your nerves."

Muttering ferociously, Sir Reginald did not argue with this sensible suggestion, but filled a glass from the decanter that was always left on the sideboard for him. He sat on the dressing-table bench and sipped the port, only to spring up again and say explosively, "When I *think* what a fine fellow he was before he went off to Spain! And now—whatever wits the poor lad has left are so full of maggots—"

"Yes, yes, Reginald, but you're spilling your wine. Sit here on the bed, dear, and try to compose yourself." Her spouse obeying with marked reluctance, she asked gently, "Whatever has John done to so discompose you?"

"Gone stark, raving mad," growled her husband not mincing words. "Have I not said it? The first looby in the family! *Egad!* I tell you, my lady, if that boy goes about London Town spreading the balderdash he hurled in my face tonight, our name will be—will be so tarnished we're like to never make a recover!"

This declaration alarmed Lady Paula. She said uneasily, "If it is balderdash, dear sir, how shall it tarnish us?"

Sir Reginald ran a hand through his already wildly dishevelled grey locks and groaned. "It's all so damned ridiculous. But with the rumours that are abroad . . ." His thick eyebrows bristled. He snarled, "Confound it! I always *knew* Kendrick Vespa was a potentially dirty dish!"

"Aha," said his patient lady. "So poor Sir Kendrick is at the root of the problem. I wonder why that does not surprise me. Now, my love, I beg you to tell me. From the beginning."

Her life's companion snorted and fumed, but in rather erratic fashion did as she asked. He was interrupted several times by her shocked gasps, and by the time he finished she had become very pale. When she did not comment, he demanded, "Did ever you hear so much fustian? Nobody will believe the stupid tale!"

His wife said nothing.

Sir Reginald watched her from the corners of his eyes. "You surely do not, Paula?"

By now very frightened, she evaded in a trembling voice, "Sir Kendrick was involved in some wicked plot connected with Alabaster Royal, and Jack found out about it?"

"That's what the boy claims, yes."

"Did he give you any information about the plot?"

"Your grand-nephew was not at liberty, he said, to go into details. Convenient, eh?"

"Did he imply then—that the authorities are handling the matter?"

"He mentioned— Dammitall! He says he's under—under orders!"

"The—*Horse Guards?* Oh, my heavens!"

"And—don't fly into the boughs—Wellington!"

Lady Paula appropriated her husband's glass and took a healthy swallow. She spluttered and coughed, but managed to say breathlessly, "I want you to be . . . honest with me, Reginald. If there is . . . any chance of this dreadful business being . . . *published* . . . in the newspapers . . . I must be prepared."

"Have I not said that it's all so much poppycock? Only consider, my lady. Was there ever a more proud and haughty creature than Kendrick Vespa? Can you suppose a fellow so puffed up in his own conceit would have accepted another man's by-blow as his own all these years? Fed and clothed and educated—"

"It is *exactly* what Kendrick would have done," moaned Lady Paula. "Especially if he knew who the man was. You know as well as I that there are many fine families among the *ton* with children born 'on the wrong side of the blanket,' as they say, yet who are acknowledged as legitimate purely to avoid scandal."

Sir Reginald glared at her and said without much force, "It's all fustian I tell you! The boy's ill. Mentally deranged from his wounds, and should be clapped up. For Lord's sake do not let that imagination of yours start running wild!"

Gripping her hands tightly, Lady Paula took a quivering breath, and as if he had not spoken, murmured, "What a vicious thing for Kendrick to have done! Much worse than having shot down the boy who loved him so. But I suppose it was quite logical for him to have hated John all these years." She smiled wanly into her husband's dark scowl, and nodded. "Oh, yes, I believe it, my dear. It all falls into place, do you see? Why Kendrick was so seldom at home. Why Faith was so neglected. And now, of course, I see the resemblance, so that I can only marvel I didn't comprehend long ago . . . John was so very unlike either Kendrick or Sherry."

"What *stuff!*" roared Sir Reginald, springing to his feet. "John takes after *our* side of the family! The fine Saxon side of his heritage! Whereas Kendrick gave his Norman characteristics to Sherborne! I might have known that, womanlike, you'd fasten onto such a melodramatic explanation! Well, *I* don't believe it! Not a word!" He began to pace up and down once more, carrying his glass and growling to himself, while Lady Paula stared into space and thought her thoughts and was silent. Checking abruptly, he demanded, "Who was it, then? Since you think you know."

She looked at him steadily. "Don't you remember? When Sherry was two years old and Kendrick was flirting with so many of the beauties of the day, and Faith began to form her own court? Think back, Reginald! She was very lovely then, and of all the men who adored her, who was the one Kendrick most hated? The man Faith *should* have wed, you used to say. The man she *would* have chosen for her lover. The perfect way to thoroughly humiliate her husband and give him back his own."

"My . . . dear . . . God!" Sir Reginald's eyes had become very wide. He collapsed onto the side of the bed as if his legs had melted under him. "I wonder Kendrick did not strangle her!"

His wife nodded. "You see the resemblance now."

"Yes. Jupiter! How could we all have been so blind?"

There was a brief silence, broken when Sir Reginald started and exclaimed, "Deuce take it, Paula! We're in a fine bumble-broth! John wants to marry Francesca Ottavio's granddaughter. Kendrick was instrumental in the murder of the girl's father, and the old lady knows the whole story. The *whole* story!"

"Oh, how dreadful! Then John must be equally unacceptable to her as Kendrick's heir, or as a man with no name. Lady Francesca will never permit the marriage. Indeed, I'm surprised he'd approach the girl, under the circumstances."

"He can't fix his interest, of course. But he thinks she cares for him, and he is determined to at least discover his real father's identity. Can't blame the poor lad, but . . . I hope you'll not be so unwise as to, er . . . ."

"As to tell him?" Lady Paula sighed and shook her head sadly. "If I had a grain of compassion, I would. But—no, dear. If he's to

29

learn that home truth, it must be from his mama; not from his great aunt."

Sir Reginald gave a sigh of relief. "Faith's off flibbertigibbeting around South America. I doubt she'll ever come back. And if she does, she'll never tell him. The very thought of more scandal would keep her silly mouth shut! I only pray that whatever roguery Kendrick was about don't become public knowledge."

"I wonder whatever it could have been? How dreadful to have real *wickedness* in our family! If the Horse Guards and Lord Wellington are involved . . ." Tearful, Lady Paula reached out both hands. "Oh, Reginald, I could not *bear* to be shunned by Society!"

"Now then, m'dear," he soothed, holding her hands firmly. "No need to make a Cheltenham tragedy of the business! We may never know the true facts, and if John does say aught of it, folks will surely set it down to the poor lad's cracked brainbox. If there was some really shocking dealing, the authorities may be as anxious as we are to sweep it all under the rug. Whatever the case *we* must keep silent, Paula. Our niece *did* marry a Vespa, so our honour is involved. For the sake of the family name you *must* keep your tongue between your teeth and admit *nothing*—to any-one! You promise?"

Sir Reginald's lady nodded and on a smothered sob gave her promise.

2

It had stopped raining when Captain Vespa left Wansdyke House. The night air was very cold and bracing and a half-moon imparted a soft radiance as it broke through shredding clouds. It was not far to his club, and although the Battle of Vitoria had left him with a marked limp, he chafed against inaction. Thanks to his more recent brush with death there had been little chance for exercise these past few weeks and he stepped out briskly, waving on the jervey who slowed his hackney coach and peered at him hopefully.

Lady Francesca did not keep very late hours, but it was doubtful that she would leave the ball before midnight. With luck, Manderville would escort the ladies back to Claridges and then join him at the Madrigal Club. With more luck, between them they'd have learned *something* of his mother's erstwhile admirers.

Few people were about on this rainy late evening, but when he turned onto St. James's he had to jump back to avoid being run down by a coach racing around the corner, the coachman very obviously the worse for drink. He shouted a protest and was answered by a flourished whip and a muddled response seemingly having to do with Christmas. Muttering indignantly, he walked on, his thoughts turning to the unhappy interview with his great-uncle. Lord, but Sir Reginald had been furious. For a while it had seemed likely that the poor old fellow would suffer an apoplexy. He should have anticipated such a reaction, but he'd counted on the fact that neither Sir Reginald, nor Great-Aunt Paula had been fond of his—of Sir Kendrick. He'd sometimes suspected, in fact, that they thoroughly disliked him. Obviously, he had underestimated their dread of scandal. He smiled a twisted smile. What a multitude of sins was hidden behind the fear of sullying a Family Name. Sir Reginald had all but threatened to have him put away if he dared pursue his enquiries. His jaw tightened. He was fond of the old gentleman and had no wish to upset him. Nor had he the slightest intention of giving up his search.

His introspection was broken as a link boy came running to offer to light his way. Between the moonlight, the occasional flicker of an oil street lamp and the flambeaux that still blazed outside some great houses, he had no need for the lad's services and sent him off with a groat clutched in one grubby fist, and a jubilant outpouring of wishes that 'milor' be blessed with health and good luck ever'n ever.

Amused, Vespa thought that his health was certainly much improved, and as to good luck—he had plenty of that, for there were loyal friends eager to help in his quest: his former comrades in arms, Toby Broderick and Paige Manderville; his Dorsetshire neighbours, the Italian 'Duchess of Ottavio,' and most importantly, her half-English granddaughter, little Consuela Carlotta Angelica Jones, the lady who gave meaning to his life and without whose vibrant presence there would be no life.

If all went well and he discovered that his real sire had been an honourable gentleman . . . Surely Mama would have chosen no less? But even if that were so, he must face the fact that he was illegitimate. The awareness still shocked him, and the hand on his cane clenched tight. All his life he'd believed himself to be the scion of a fine old family. He'd been proud of his name and lineage and especially proud of the brilliant diplomatist he'd thought was his father. He would have been enraged had anyone dared suggest that Sir Kendrick Vespa was a conscienceless villain who had suffered no qualm of conscience in destroying those who stood in the way of his schemes. At least three innocents had paid the supreme penalty for being in the wrong place at the wrong time. And when he himself had unwittingly interfered in Sir Kendrick's plans—

He closed his eyes briefly, fighting the grief that persisted against all logic, and was such a fierce pain. It was over. When Sir Reginald had been swept away by the flood that had raced through the quarry at Alabaster Royal, his schemes had died with him. Consuela and Manderville and Toby Broderick, and even Lady Francesca, had each tried in their own way to help him surmount the tragedy. They each had said with great kindness that there was a time to put the past behind; to refuse to think about it; to firmly dismiss it from his mind. Excellent and well-meant advice. The trouble was, it was easier said than done.

He shuddered, chilled by more than the icy wind as he crossed Piccadilly. He was greeted by two friendly but unknown young exquisites who, between hiccups, invited him to join them in the chorus of "She Was Only a Fishmonger's Daughter." Short of engaging in fisticuffs, his attempts to escape proved unavailing. His nature was not quarrelsome and it was clear that, however intoxicated, they meant no harm. Bowing to the inevitable he obliged, but stressed that he could not stay for encores. In the event, he was not asked for an encore. His new acquaintances were, in fact, quite ungrateful, and he left them, ignoring their hilarity over his vocal efforts. Grandmama Wansdyke, he thought indignantly, had always enjoyed to hear him sing. Toby Broderick had once been so uncouth as to comment that the lady must have been tone-deaf, but—

From the alley beside him came sounds of desperate conflict. The moonlight did not penetrate far between the tall buildings, but his eyes were keen. Three against one. Thieves, no doubt. "Hey!" he shouted, and gripping his cane firmly, limped into the fray.

It was short but sharp. Almost at once he realized that here were no ordinary footpads. There were no shouts; no curses. The three, armed with short cudgels, fought in a silent co-operation that spoke of experience. He had fully expected that with his arrival and his shouts for the Watch, the rogues would run for it. They did not. Their victim groaned and sagged to his knees. One sturdy bully bent over the fallen man, the other two plunged at Vespa. He countered a flashing cudgel with his cane, then swung it in a sideways swipe across the third man's ribs that evened the odds. A ham-like fist whipped at his face, and he ducked then brought his famous right into violent collision with a craggy jaw. His ears rang to the resultant howl of anguish. The first bully turned from their victim and joined the fight. Vespa flung himself to the side, but only partially avoided the cudgel that blurred at his eyes.

Through an instant of blinding pain he heard someone yell, "Here's the . . . Watch! Stand, you miserable . . . varmints!" The voice was unsteady but vaguely familiar.

He was being assisted to his feet, and he gasped breathlessly, "Are they gone?"

"Thanks to you, Captain, sir, they are. Oh, dear. I lied to the . . . poor clods. Our reinforcements ain't the Watch after all."

Vespa wiped blood from his eyebrow and saw two gentlemen weaving towards them, clinging to each other while peering at him blearily.

"Be damned," said one of the new arrivals thickly. "It's the—hic—poor chap who—who can't—hic—sing."

"Sho 'tis, dear boy," confirmed his friend. "Can—can fight, though. Jolly—jolly goo' show, shir. 'F I shay sho m'shelf."

"And you've my thanks, gentlemen," said Vespa. "You were—a good substitute for the Watch."

"Even if they can't see straight," murmured the man at his side. "Come on, Vespa. It's starting to drizzle again."

Vespa looked at him sharply. "I thought it was you! What the deuce are you doing here, and out of uniform?"

Colonel the Honourable Hastings Adair drew him away. "Not now. Those louts may return with more of their kind. Come!"

They hobbled on together, investigating their various hurts, and followed by the strains of the shockingly ribald third verse of "She Was Only a Fishmonger's Daughter."

"Going the wrong way," pointed out Vespa, halting. "I'm bound for the Madrigal."

Adair held a grisly handkerchief to his nose and from behind it urged him on. "I'm not. Now that I've found you. I thank you for your help, though."

Standing firm, Vespa scanned the colonel in the light of a flambeaux and noted glumly that, despite a darkening bruise across one cheekbone, a bloody nose, and a graze beside his mouth, and although civilian dress lacked the dash of his military scarlet, the dark-haired young officer was all too well-qualified a suitor for Consuela's hand. "Sold out, have you?" he enquired sardonically.

"You know better." Investigating, Adair muttered, "Gad, but I believe those varmints have loosened one of my teeth. Well, never mind that. For Lord's sake, will you move? I can't lounge about under this light."

They left the flambeaux behind. Lowering his voice, Vespa said, "I thought you'd gone back to France. Did Wellington send you to sniff around?"

"In a manner of speaking."

"You said you'd tell him the full story of what happened at Alabaster Royal."

"So I did. He was most concerned. He spoke highly of you and sent you this letter. . . ." Adair groped in his pockets. "Be damned! Those dirty bastards made off with it!"

Vespa would have prized the letter. "It was kind of the General to write his condolences."

"Field Marshal now, don't forget! And he wrote more than condolences. He wants something of you."

There was a note in the colonel's voice that triggered warning flags in Vespa's mind. He said warily, "For instance?"

"Stop poking your nose into—past history."

"Devil take it!" Vespa halted again. "I've a perfect right to make enquiries about personal matters. Wouldn't you, were you in my shoes?"

Adair hesitated, then said evasively, "You're stirring up more than you know, Captain."

"What difference does it make? The whole story will come out sooner or later. You can't stifle that kind of—of—"

"Treachery? I'm sorry, but there's really no kinder word, is there? And it *must* be stifled! There'll be no more of it in the newspapers, I promise you. Now why look so astounded? Forgive, but your late father—"

"Which one?"

Adair swore under his breath, then hailed a slow-moving hackney coach. The jervey grinned in triumph, and Vespa saw that it was the same coach he had refused earlier. Adair called an order to "Just drive," adding a curt, "Get in."

"Why?"

"Because it's freezing and we can talk in here without getting soaked. Don't be so blasted stubborn. I'll remind you that I outrank you, Captain!"

Vespa bit back an unflattering comment and climbed reluctantly into the coach.

"I'll remind *you,* sir," he said, when Adair had lowered himself painfully onto the seat beside him, "that I am not at the moment on active service."

"Really? And do you feel that entitles you to undermine the security of this nation? Or do you consider your personal affairs more important than King and Country?" Adair gripped Vespa's arm, and looking into his startled face, said in a kinder tone, "Through no fault of your own you've had a wretched year, and I'll own that had you not taken a hand just now, I'd be in a very sticky mess at this moment. I know you must wish me at Jericho, on more counts than one. Please believe that I don't like this. But I've no choice."

Frowning, Vespa settled back against the lumpy cushions and waited.

The Colonel said softly, "Sir Kendrick Vespa almost succeeded in selling the Alabaster Royal estates to the Government as the site of a proposed secondary Arsenal. He was perfectly aware that large sections of the property were undermined by extensive tunnelling, and that it would be dangerous to locate an arsenal on such unstable ground, so—"

"Thank you, Colonel, sir," interrupted Vespa, pale with anger. "Did you really feel it necessary to rub my nose in my family disgrace? I promise you, I'm sufficiently aware of it!"

"Damn your eyes! We know you almost lost your life when you refused to do as he wished. No—don't say it! You don't want my sympathy. But what *I* want—what *his lordship* wants—is that you look farther than your personal tragedy. Despite his cunning and his ruthless disregard of human life, none of it would have been possible had Sir Kendrick not first purchased the—ah—cooperation of several highly placed gentlemen at Whitehall."

Vespa gave a disgusted snort. "What you mean is that rich and powerful men took bribes to look the other way! Good Lord above! Do you say that Wellington wants me to also 'look the other way?'"

"He wants you to consider that we are in a state of war, *Captain.* At least half the people of this island believe a French invasion to be imminent. Many men behind the scenes of power struggle desperately to prevent a panic. Were it to become public knowledge that so respected a diplomatist as your late father was corrupt; that some of our leading citizens exchanged their integrity for gold—"

"It would seem to me," said Vespa hotly, "that the public has a right to know the truth about great men who abuse power! They *should* be exposed and held up to shame and to punishment!"

"The punishment will come, I assure you. But the shame would spread to some very famous families. Including your own."

After a short silence, Vespa muttered, "I don't know what is—my own, sir."

"You're splitting hairs. I know you're in the deuce of a fix. But you've your mother to consider still, and her side of your family. Speaking of which—how does Sir Reginald Wansdyke view the matter?"

"I just left him, as you evidently are aware. He chose to take the attitude that my mind is permanently impaired, and that I should be locked away."

"Natural enough." A pause, then Adair murmured, "He is not alone in such sentiments."

With a shocked gasp, Vespa jerked around to face him. "By the lord Harry, I do believe you're threatening me!"

"Call it a friendly warning. His lordship asks your cooperation is all. Just during the present national emergency."

It was too bland; too gently appealing. Vespa leaned back and said thoughtfully, "His lordship sent you home only to give me a 'friendly warning'? And you found it necessary to leave off your uniform—in time of war—for such a purpose?"

"I have several commissions for Lord Wellington," said Adair with wooden calm.

"Yet interrupted them to ensure that I was behaving myself? I was—that is to say Broderick and Manderville and I were—warned to keep our tongues between our teeth in the matter of the Arsenal, which we have done."

"Very good." The colonel inspected his handkerchief in the glow from the coach lamps. "Ah, my nose has stopped bleeding at last and—"

"The devil with your nose! Why should my search for my true identity cause the Field Marshal, or the Horse Guards, to be alarmed?"

"I'd think it obvious that your enquiries must provoke curiosity, to say the least."

"Not so! For my mother's sake I've been discreet."

"Yet your search has been noted."

"By whom? Whitehall?"

"And others."

"Rubbish!" Leaning forward, Vespa said intensely, "Do you know what I think, Colonel, sir? Those louts who attacked you just now were not run-of-the-mill street *banditti*. They were professionals. The fellow who brought you down had plenty of opportunity to put an end to you, but did not. They wanted you alive because they want information from you! And if you expect me to believe that one jot of it had to do with my search for my real father—"

Adair exclaimed, "Where the *devil* are we? Hey! Jervey! What are you about?"

The coach lurched to a halt. In a flash, Adair had wrenched the door open and sprung out.

Following, Vespa found that the hackney had stopped on a gloomy narrow street. He was able to distinguish that the coachman had vanished. A shocked cry rang out, and against the dim light from a dirty window he caught a glimpse of Adair, who appeared to have taken wing. Astonished, Vespa crouched, prepared for battle, his cane fast-gripped. The lighted window was blotted out. He had a brief impression that a giant loomed before him. The chances being slim that this giant was friendly, he did not pause to enquire, but with both hands and all his strength thrust his cane at the creature. It was as if he had attacked solid rock. A guttural roar deafened him. He was swept up in a crushing grip and hurled aside. With the instinctive reaction of the athlete he landed rolling. Short of breath, he crawled to his knees and tried to see who—or what—had attacked them.

A mighty hand jerked him up, then released him abruptly as a voice with a slight foreign accent snarled, "Not him, fool! The other!"

"Halt, or I fire!" Adair's voice.

Vespa hoped the colonel could see more than he could, and crouched lower.

A pistol shot shattered the quiet of the night.

Somebody screamed.

There sounded again that inhuman, guttural growl. "Honourable master light lántern? Cannot find—"

And then hooves were coming fast, rattles clattered, and a distant bobbing glow proclaimed the approach of law and order.

The foreign voice rang out. "It is the Watch! *Sacré nom de nom!* How did the imbeciles come so fast up with us? I cannot be seen in this!"

"Master go. I find—"

"Idiot! Come!"

"I bring Barto? Colonel man shoot straight. Barto dead I think."

"Then leave him."

By the brightening glow of the lantern, Vespa saw two men running toward a darkened carriage; one tall and thin, the other shorter, but massively built with long arms that bulged the sleeves of his coat. The carriage door slammed, the coachman whipped up his team. Sixteen iron-shod hooves struck sparks from the cobblestones, and Vespa had to leap for his life.

Adair came staggering up and helped him to his feet. "What the devil was . . . that?" he gasped in a shaken voice. "Did you see?"

"Not clearly, but enough to know I hope never to see it again!"

Two members of the Watch ran up, their lantern swung high. Vespa caught a glimpse of a red waistcoat and thought a surprised, *'Bow Street?'* He said thankfully, "You came just in time! I—"

"You best be movin' along, sir." A pair of narrowed eyes scanned him from under a low-crowned hat. "This ain't no neighbourhood for a gent like you to go for a joy ride."

"Joy ride! I'll have you know—"

" 'Alf a minute, sir." The Bow Street Runner bent above a still shape. "This one's stuck 'is spoon in the wall." He turned to Adair. "I reckernizes you, Mr. Brownley, and I'll take that pistol, if y'- please. Up to yer tricks agin, but I gotcha this time, ain't I! In the King's name I arrest you on a charge of murder. Let's 'ave the bracelets 'ere, North."

Seething with indignation, Vespa demanded, "Are you quite daft? *We* are the victims, you idiot! That coach you saw driving off holds the ruffians you want!"

"A *proper* idjut I'd be to believe that one, sir," leered the Runner. "I 'opes I knows when I got me man! 'Ere's our coach at last. We'll be orf, North. And let's 'ave no trouble from you, Brown- ley—*h'if* you don't wanta bump on the tibby!"

Adair murmured something in a despondent tone.

Vespa sprang forward and wrenched the Runner's hold from the colonel's arm. "You're out of your senses! I tell you we were murderously attacked, and you most *assuredly* have the wrong man! This gentleman's name is not Brownley! He's—"

"It's good of you to try, friend," interrupted Adair. "But it's no use. They got me proper." His very blue eyes met Vespa's levelly, and said a clear if silent, 'Keep out of this!'

A moment later, having mounted the box on the abandoned

hackney coach, Vespa took up the reins and sent the tired horse plodding after the Watchman's carriage.

———❦———

The office at the Horse Guards was not large and in the subdued light of this cold winter morning the presence of five gentlemen caused it to appear crowded. Although nobody spoke there was a distinct air of tension in the room. The youthful major seated at the desk appeared to be fascinated by the quill pen he turned in restless fingers; the rosy-cheeked and robust captain who stood leaning back against the front of the desk folded his arms and stared wistfully at a coat he coveted shamelessly; and the three young men who sat facing the desk exchanged incredulous glances. For several seconds the silence was broken only by the pattering of raindrops against the window.

Lieutenant Tobias Broderick's blond curly hair and cherubic blue eyes made him appear younger than his twenty-four years and masked a brilliant mind. He now said with considerable indignation, "In view of Captain Vespa's extraordinary military record, and the fact that he was chosen by Lord Wellington to be on his personal staff, I find it astonishing that you should question his word, Major Blaine."

"You are mistaken, Lieutenant." Major Blaine lifted a pair of cold brown eyes to engage Broderick's angry stare. "I do not question Sir John's account of what he believes to have transpired last evening, but—"

Vespa interrupted, "Your pardon, sir, but my name is *Captain* John Vespa! I do not use the title." Clearly taken aback, the major blinked at him and he took advantage of the pause to add briskly, "Also, I am perfectly *sure* of what happened last evening. As I told you just now, a high-ranking army officer was attacked on the street and later arrested, completely without justification, by an officious clod who called himself a Bow Street Runner! It was clearly a case of mistaken identity. I would respectfully sug-

42

gest that you get in touch with Bow Street at once and arrange for Colonel Adair's release."

"As should have been done last night, when Captain Vespa came here and reported the incident," murmured Paige Manderville, adjusting the cuff of his coat.

The large captain continued to gaze at that superbly tailored coat as he remarked, "And would have been done, Lieutenant, had we been able to verify Sir—er, Captain Vespa's—er, assertions, but—"

"Assertions?" said Vespa angrily. "Now see here, Rickaby, if you've been brought into the business to claim that my mind is still disordered from the knock I took at Vitoria, I'll have you know I am fully recovered!"

"And have recently taken another knock on the head, by the look of it." The military surgeon tore his eyes from Manderville's coat and moved to examine the cut over Vespa's eye. "When did this happen?"

"Last evening. While Hastings Adair and I were fighting off the thieves who attacked him. This cut is proof of what I've told you, so do not waste more time in trying to convince me that none of it happened!"

Major Blaine said gently, "But, my dear fellow, we have no intention of doing such a thing. We've already been in touch with the Bow Street Magistrate and have a full report of the occurrence."

"Then why did you imply that you doubted my story?"

"Only one aspect of the affair," qualified Dr. Rickaby. "You were apparently confused as to the identity of the man you went to help. Logical you would be, all things considered."

Through gritted teeth Vespa declared, "I was *not* confused! *Nor* concussed! *Nor* hallucinating! Adair had a nosebleed after the fight. We called up a hackney coach. He said he'd been looking for me, and we talked for a few minutes about a—a personal matter. If you say I was talking to myself, you're quite off the road!"

Major Blaine put in mildly, "I've no least idea of to whom you were talking, but I know damned well it wasn't the man you've named. Colonel Hastings Adair is at this very moment in France with Field Marshal Lord Wellington's forces."

"The devil!" exclaimed Broderick.

"Is he now," drawled Manderville cynically.

Vespa's jaw tightened. "I don't know why you would make such a claim, sir, or why Adair was rushed off to jail for some trumped-up reason. He's not a close personal friend. But he's a good man, and I'd try to help him out of a fix, even if I didn't have my own sanity to defend. Good day to you, gentlemen." He stood, his friends standing with him.

"Where do you think you're going?" asked Blaine, amused.

"To find Colonel the Honourable Hastings Adair," said Vespa, starting to the door. "When I bring him here, you may wish to make me your apologies."

The surgeon glanced at Blaine and volunteered with a sigh, "Very well. I can tell you where to find him."

Vespa turned back eagerly.

"He took a bayonet through the thigh during the Battle of the Nivelle," said Rickaby. "We've settled him into one of our charming field hospitals in Pamplona. I visited him there just before I started for home three days ago."

Blaine said reasonably, "So you see, Captain, poor Hasty Adair is quite unable to walk, much less to have left France and battled ruffians on a London street last night."

"Were I you, my boy," advised Rickaby. "I'd go down to that nice Richmond house of yours and enjoy a warm and cozy winter and forget all this unpleasantness."

It was really remarkable, thought Vespa, that so many people were eager to put him out of the way. He looked from one kindly smile to the other and shook his head in reluctant admiration. "I'll say this for you," he said, "you're jolly good at it!" He followed his friends and closed the door quietly.

After a glum minute, "Damn!" said Major Blaine, slamming his quill pen onto the desk disastrously.

Captain Rickaby sighed. "Stubborn fella, I'm afraid, Ed."

"So I was warned."

"It comes in handy sometimes. After Vitoria, for instance. He should've died. Wouldn't. He's a dashed good man."

"They all are. Broderick and Manderville can be dealt with. One way or another. But—Vespa . . ." the Major scowled. "His lordship's hand is over him. To an extent."

Rickaby murmured, "D'you know, Ed, if it was up to me, I'd tell him."

"Well, it ain't up to you," snapped Blaine, glaring at him. "And it ain't up to me. And how the hell could I tell him what I don't know myself?"

"You don't? Jupiter! I thought surely a man in your position— Then—who does know?"

"I don't know that, either. I only know it's not to be talked of, or whispered, or even, God save us all, thought about! So this conversation must not be mentioned outside these walls."

"Lord, man! I'm your cousin! You surely know I'm to be trusted?"

"Of course I do, you great clunch. Secrecy! It's a double-edged sword at best. The inevitable result of all these cautions and prohibitions is that everyone's wondering what the devil they're not to talk, or whisper, or think about!" Blaine scraped back his chair and went to stand at the window and glower at the rain. "It must be curst big, Rick, whatever it is. Did you notice there's been not one word in the newspapers about that fiasco last night?"

"Early yet, old boy. Besides, London's unhappily replete with robberies. Not surprising if one goes unnoticed."

"Is it not?" Blaine gave a snort of derision. "Yet another murderous attack on a popular young war hero who appears to have become a magnet for violence. Do you really suppose the news-

45

papers would not begin to ask why? Or that they would ignore such a story?"

"Humph. Well, perhaps they—"

"Besides which, Jack Vespa's sire provided the grist for a scandalous rumour mill. And to add to all this, another slippery customer has oozed onto the scene. A rogue we've been after for years, and never managed to so much as detain for questioning!"

Rickaby frowned. "I didn't hear about that. Only Vespa's report that there was a second attack."

"Just so. A second attack involving a tall man with a foreign accent and a giant for a servant who tossed Adair about like—"

"Oh—egad," gasped the surgeon. "You're never thinking it was—"

"Imre Monteil. The very shady Swiss munitions maker. And his monstrous Chinese henchman."

"Be dashed," muttered Rickaby. "If only half the tales one hears about that pair are truth . . ."

"I'll tell you one thing, coz," said Blaine after a brooding pause. "If Imre Monteil has a finger in the pie, it's a rich pie! A very rich pie indeed!"

3

I suppose I need not ask if the rain it still drips?" Lady Francesca lifted her eyes from the *Morning Post* to direct a mournful glance at Consuela who knelt in the window-seat, gazing down into the busy street. Her grand-daughter confirming her supposition in a rather abstracted fashion, my lady sighed. "A wretched climate has this small island."

"Then only think how fortunate we are," said Consuela, "to be comfortable in this lovely hotel instead of outside in the cold and wet."

Refusing to feel fortunate, my lady sighed again. "How I miss my sunny Italy. Can you wonder that I yearn to take you back where you belongings?"

"And where would that be, Grandmama? In the middle of the English Channel, perhaps? The Italian side of me facing to the south, and the British side to the north?"

"Do not be flippant, *signorina!* Your blood is of a royal Italian House and is warm, and your temper it blows hot, in the Latin manner! As for your British side—"

Consuela turned and smiled at her. "My British side loves

this funny old island, dearest. As it loved my adored and so very talented English Papa. And you know perfectly well that I mean to wed an English gentleman, so—"

"An English gentleman who does not even know his real name," snorted Lady Francesca. "No, do not send me dagger glances, miss! I know you are fond of Captain Jack Vespa, but—"

"Much more than fond, Grandmama! He is the bravest, kindest, most truly honourable gentleman I—"

"You will not interrupt, if you please," interrupted my lady, rattling the newspaper at her granddaughter. "For him to try and his interest fix with you, this it is not proper."

For some days Consuela had sensed that her diminutive grandmother was pondering something, and guessing what that something was, she knew this would be a serious talk. She left the window-seat, therefore, and came with her light dancing step to sink onto the footstool before Lady Francesca's chair, the pale pink velvet gown rippling about her. "He did not exactly declare himself, you know," she pointed out meekly. "It was more of a 'testing the waters,' Toby said. A 'supposing this,' or a 'supposing that,' and if such and such chanced, might I then consider him." She smiled tenderly. "Poor boy. He was very careful not to make me feel that we had plighted our troth, so that I could be free if other gentlemen offered."

"*If* other gentlemen offer? Of course they will offer! At the ball last night the beaux were fluttering around, and you have already today receiving two charming bouquets, is it not? Nor dismiss from your mind that very handsome young colonel."

"Colonel Adair is back in France with Lord Wellington. I doubt we shall see him again until the war is ended." Despite this assertion, Consuela knew she must be careful; she was sure her Grandmother really liked Jack, but if she set her mind against him, it would be disastrous. She said airily, "Besides, you may be *à l'aise,* dear *Nonna.* Romance, so they say, is capricious, and a lady seldom marries her first love."

Lady Francesca shook one finger under her granddaughter's small nose and said perversely, "This it is the talk of a flirt, *signorina,* and ladies who flirt have the reputations and sometimes end with nothing more!"

"What about gentlemen who flirt? John Vespa loved another lady once—"

"*Si.* Long ago. But you know very well he has eyes now only for you. And it is unkind in extremity to tease the young man."

Consuela asked demurely, "Then you think I should accept if he really makes me an offer?"

"No! And—no! A most strong *no!* You will accept him only in despite of my strict disapproval, child."

Startled by such vehemence, Consuela searched the old lady's face and found there a stern resolve. She said in dismay, "But—but, you are most fond of Jack!"

"*Si.* This it is truth."

"And when Sir Kendrick shot him you helped nurse him and grieved for his sake, and now we are helping him seek out his real father. Although," she added, forgetting her earlier caution, "I care not a jot whether his father turns out to be a well-born gentleman, or—"

"Or—what, Miss Rattlepate? A highwayman? A footpad? A murderer? Do you care not the jot if your children have inherit the consumptive habit? Or madness? Or the disease that brings sightlessness? What is in the blood will out!"

Consuela was silent. Then she muttered, "As if Lady Faith would have chosen such a one for her lover."

"Ha! Look who she chose for her husband! A pretty monster!"

"True. But her parents chose him, not she. Besides, can one really tell? Sir Kendrick Vespa was to all outward appearances a fine example of aristocracy: handsome and clever and elegant. And inside he was a cheat and a murderer several times over! An honest coal-heaver would have been a better choice for a husband!"

"This also is so. However, one is born to a certain station in life, *bambina,* and no matter what people may say, this it will never change. Was we all to become the coal-heavers there still would be the strongest among the heavers, or the one who sells the most coal would become the Aristocrat among Coal-Heavers and gradually he would pull away from the common herd. It is the way of the world. You loved your papa. Do you thinking he would countenance a marriage between Consuela Carlotta Angelica Jones, of the royal house of Ottavio, and a young English captain who has a haunted and decaying old country estate and expectations of the smallest?" Lady Francesca flung up one hand, silencing Consuela's attempt to comment. "I know what you will say. He was, and I admit this, a gallant and brave soldier. But he also is either the son of the wicked Sir Kendrick Vespa—who was directly responsible for your own father's death—"

"You *know* he is not Sir Kendrick's son," interposed Consuela fierily. "That evil man almost killed Jack as well as my Papa, and—"

"In the which case," overrode the old lady with a daunting frown, "your Captain Jack is the *natural child* of a mystery man about whom we know nothings at all."

"But we *will,* dearest! You and I and dear Toby and Paige, we all are trying to help Jack find the gentleman."

"And if we succeed, how then is it? Your fine captain is too fond of his Mama to shame her by refusing to any longer bear her name."

"Y-yes. Perhaps. But—but if we find that his real father is a fine and honourable man, then you can at least be easy and know what his—his background is."

"And Jack still will be no less of a bastard who will accept neither the Vespa fortune nor the title!"

"*Grandmama!*" Her cheeks pink with anger, Consuela sprang to her feet.

"*Signorina!*" Lady Francesca stood also and drew herself up to her full fifty-seven inches. In her stockinged feet Consuela was four inches taller, but her grandmother's head was thrown back regally, her fine dark eyes could still flash fire, and in that moment she seemed to tower over the girl.

"You will be quiet and pay me heed," she commanded, her voice harsh. "I am knowing of the great service Captain Jack Vespa made us in proving your Papa's murder. I am knowing of the fact that his life he risked and almost lost in saving yours. We are beholden. It is for this reasons I have allowing you to come to London with me, and that I will help him in his quest. He is a good man, *si*. But when *all* the facts are whispered about Town, as soon they must be, he will be a very much disgraced man. *Your* line it is proud. *Your* prospects they are most fine. I would be a poor *nonna* if I allowed you to be shamed by marriage to a man whose only hope for holding up of his head is to leave the country!"

"Oh!" Wrath rendered Consuela almost speechless, and to add to her mental turmoil was the awareness that the old lady loved her and wanted only the best for her. "H-how *can* you speak of him so?" she spluttered. "He is—is one of the most popular young men in London! *Everybody* likes him and has only good to say of him!"

In this, however, she was mistaken. The maid, who at that moment was admitting Captain John Vespa to the suite, neither liked nor admired him, and what she had to say of him to her intimates was far from good. Violet Manning, whose life was not unpleasant, might grumble, as was the fashion, about her 'fussy' employers, but she was also proud of them. She lost no opportunity to point out that although the Duchess of Ottavio was a foreign lady, she was highly born; that Mr. Preston Jones had been among the greatest of Britain's artists; and that his daughter, Miss Consuela, might have had an Italian Mama, but there was royal blood in her veins, and she could look as high as she pleased for a husband.

To Manning it was little short of tragic that her mistress must instead smile upon Captain Vespa. Miss Consuela was perhaps just a bit short of being judged beautiful, and she could get very cross very quick, but she was pretty and full of life and charm, and she had a lovely body. Captain Vespa had a scar down one temple, and he limped. People said he was a fine athlete before he became a soldier. He was not a fine athlete now. Worse, he was evidently touched in his upper works, for why in the world would a sane man refuse his rightful title?

She took Captain Vespa's hat and cloak and scanned without admiration the ally who trotted in after him. Another example of poor judgment. The captain could have adopted his father's bloodhounds; to have such creatures as Solomon and Barrister at his heels might have lent him a bit of interest and dignity. But— no! The great hounds had gone to live in the country with Lieutenant Manderville's father, and the captain was accompanied as always by 'Corporal,' a small dog with long greyish-brown hair and no consequence whatever. It was all of a piece, thought Manning resentfully, and opened the drawing room door to announce, "Captain Vespa, my lady."

Vespa sensed the tension in the air when he entered the drawing room. Lady Francesca looked vexed, and Consuela hurried to stand at the window and surreptitiously dab a handkerchief at her eyes.

"Good morning, ladies," he said as he crossed to kiss the hand of the little duchess.

"You are late," she scolded, tapping his cheek with her fan. "We have expecting you an hour since."

"And Paige did not come as he promised," said Consuela, gaining control of herself and turning to face Vespa.

He bowed and, meeting the ardent smile that was then levelled at her, she wondered how Grandmama could be anything but charmed by the hazel eyes so intriguingly flecked with gold, or the strong chin and sensitive mouth, and the way the thick hair— She gave a shocked gasp and flew to touch the gash above his eyebrow. "What now? You are hurt again! I vow I cannot let you out of my sight for one moment but you are into trouble! Tell me!"

"Che orrore!" Lady Francesca threw up her hands. "Have you none of the manners, Signorina Consuela? Ring the bell! First, we offer Captain Jack coffee and the politenesses. *Then,* he may tell us his tales!"

Consuela's 'politenesses' extended to ringing the bell, but her impatience could scarcely be contained, and the moment Manning had gone off to gather refreshments Vespa was commanded to tell them about his evening's activities. It was not an easy task, for he was interrupted frequently, but when he named the victim of the street attack both ladies were startled into silence. They did not recover their vocal powers until he described his interview at the Horse Guards, whereupon the duchess unleashed a flood of Italian during which her small hands were flourished about wildly and expressions such as *stupidita!* and *pazzia!* were so scornfully uttered as to leave little doubt of their meaning.

Unaccustomedly mute, Consuela at length said a puzzled, "But why would they lie about it? And why would Colonel Adair have behaved in such a strange fashion? Jack—you're *quite* sure it was him?"

"Quite sure. Though both Major Blaine and my army surgeon did their best to convince me I'm wits to let."

Consuela asked sharply, "Why should your doctor have been there?"

"That's what Broderick wanted to know. It seems Captain Rickaby is cousin to the major. Perhaps it was pure coincidence that he chanced to be there." He said with a wry smile, "I try, you see, not to let my imagination run riot."

"Well, I think it all most odd. And your surgeon claimed to have seen Hasty— I mean, Colonel Adair, in a hospital in Spain only three days ago?"

"Yes." Very aware of the quick correction, Vespa said, "Not that I believe a word of it."

At this point Manning returned with a laden tray. Lady Francesca poured coffee and when the maid had gone asked shrewdly, "What *are* you believing, Captain?"

Vespa accepted a slice of seed cake, and replied, "That Colonel Adair is most definitely back in England. I didn't imagine our violent encounters. Nor do I think my activities are his major concern."

Consuela said, "But he warned you to stop your search. So, surely, whatever he's about must be in some way linked to what you—we—are doing."

"Shall you stop—as the colonel he demand?" asked Lady Francesca.

"By George, but I won't! I did what I could for Adair and met a brick wall. I'm not on active service now, and barring a straight command from his lordship, I'll keep on."

Consuela nodded. "What about Sir Kendrick's man of business? Might he be able to help?"

"Very likely. But Felton's slippery as an eel. Every time I call at his offices he is very much 'out.' It's clear he doesn't want to see me, and if I did trap him he would likely talk in meaningless circles as those lawyer fellows love to do, so I see no point in wasting my time on him. Toby and Paige have gone off to Bow Street to try and see Adair. I mean to drive down to Richmond and see if any letters have arrived from my mother."

"Good." Consuela slipped a biscuit to the hopeful Corporal. "We have plans for this afternoon also, Jack. Grandmama and me."

He looked at her uncertainly. "You have both been so very good, but—"

"I know. We must not run into danger. You told me that once before."

"Yes, I did." His eyes darkened at the memory. "And had you paid me heed you might not have nigh got yourself killed!"

"Don't go into the boughs. *Nonna* and I mean to—"

"She calls me *Nonna* when she is trying to turn me up sweetly," interrupted Lady Francesca looking far from sweet.

In a stage whisper Consuela told Vespa, "It is merely the Italian version of Grandmama, and I use it because it pleases her. How unkind I should be *not* to want to please my dear little duchess!"

"You are a conniving minx!" declared Lady Francesca, but she could not keep the twinkle from her eye, and Consuela laughed, and went on: "We mean to do nothing more dangerous than to visit the biggest gossip in the southland. But, I had hoped . . ." She glanced rather wistfully at the window.

He said, "You had hoped to see more of London, instead of which you're spending all your time trying to help me."

Lady Francesca said, "You gave up a great deal more than time when you helped us, Captain Jack."

He smiled at her gratefully. "If you don't mean to call on your gossip till this afternoon, may I now take you both for a drive?"

"In the rain?" Lady Francesca shook her head. "For me, this is not!"

Consuela's blue eyes glowed. "Oh, I should so like to see some more of the city, dearest Grandmama. May I please go?"

"I'll take great care of her, ma'am," Vespa pleaded.

"It is unwise, this," said the duchess meeting his eyes sternly. "There must be no talkings of troths and promisings, you understand? No interest fixings. I will have your word, Captain."

He gave her his word, and said that he was in no position to make such 'talkings,' but his heart sank and he was reminded once again that even if he found his sire to be a most unexceptionable gentleman, his hopes of winning his lady were slim at best.

———

The dreary weather had kept many people from venturing outside but for Consuela it might have been a summer's day. She had chosen to wear a claret-coloured cloak and hood over a pale pink woollen gown and she came, or so thought Vespa, like a ray of sunlight into the coach. She had seen the more famous of the city's landmarks, and informed him that although she loved to watch the ships on the river, and thought the various parks beautiful, it was a pity more trees had not been planted along the streets. "It is such a sea of bricks and cobblestones. But it is a very exciting place to be, do you not think? All the shops and theatres, and the carriages, and so many people!"

"Less than usual today, because of the rain no doubt, which makes it easier for our coachman to get about."

"Papa used to say that in England if we wait for the rain to stop, we'll never go anywhere. But only look, it *is* stopping! How nice of the Weather Angel to bring the sun out for us! Oh, Jack!" She reached out impulsively and touched his arm. *"Do* look at that lady! What a remarkable bonnet! Are those the new colours? They seem awfully bright."

With difficulty he tore his gaze from the little hand resting so confidingly on his sleeve. The lady in question was indeed clad in bright colours and the umbrella shielding the feathers of her bonnet constituted a distinct hazard to other pedestrians. "A trifle too bright for propriety," he said with a twinkle.

Consuela gave him a questioning look, then chuckled. "Oh. I see. Well, you found a lovely coach for us, and *you* are behaving with great propriety, Captain Vespa."

The smile left his eyes. His 'propriety' was a constant frustration. To have this time with her; to see her vivacity and enthusiasm was delight. To long so to tell her of his love and know he must not, was torment. Her bright glance was fixed on his face. He said, "It was very good of the duchess to allow me to steal you away. She cannot be easy, knowing I— I mean— Oh, Jupiter!"

"What do you mean, Captain Jack?"

Her eyes were so soft, so glowing. Her hand was still on his arm. It was as much as he could do to refrain from seizing and kissing those soft pink fingers, but a gentleman did not break his given word. He wrenched his head away and said hoarsely, "Here—here we are at Cornhill already. You will have a fine view now, Consuela."

It was as well he did not see her tender smile. She said, "Yes, indeed! What is that tower? And why is it called Cornhill?"

"The tower is the Royal Exchange, and Cornhill is so named because it was at one time the site of a corn market." He drew her attention to the famous Tower of St. Michael and the numerous graceful church spires that could be seen. She was interested in everything, especially the fine shops, and the modern architecture of the large houses, and asked if this was a newer area of the city.

"Not really, but much of this section was destroyed during the Great Fire, and the new buildings were marked improvements over the old." He bent his head and leaned towards her side window to point out a fine lantern suspended from a sign that advertised the Manufacture of Writing Desks and Morrocco Dressing Cases. "Now we are turning onto Lombard Street," he added, and straightening found his lips scant inches from her chin. He drew back with a gasp. The voice of temptation hissed, 'Fool! This might well be your last chance to be alone with her, don't waste it!' He fought to shut out that all too persuasive voice, but it crept into his mind once more. Where would be the harm in simply begging her to wait? How could there be shame in at least holding her close, just for a little while? 'No one will see you in the coach.'

The struggle for control was won, but he could not keep the yearning from his eyes, and seeing it, and the way his hand trembled, Consuela repented and turned away. "Aha," she said gaily. "Lombard? Now there is an Italian name, no? Does some great family live here?"

Watching the velvety curve of her cheek, the way the light glistened on her dusky curls, he murmured, "What . . . ? Oh! Er, well, yes the Lombards were a great banking or money-lending family, long ago."

"Really? Then Grandmama will probably know them and may wish to pay a call."

"I rather doubt it. I'm afraid they were a rascally lot, Consuela, and did so much mischief that Queen Elizabeth sent them packing."

At once bristling, she said tartly, "From what I have learned of that lady, she made a habit of sending people packing! With or without their heads!"

"You prefer to believe the poor Lombards were pure as the driven snow, do you? Why? Are they kin to you?"

"I don't know. . . ." A new thought banished her irritation, and she clapped her hands. "But—oh, that would be very helpful, would it not? Then Grandmama couldn't very well—" She bit her lip and cut the words off.

"You mean it would be a case of the pot not being able to call the kettle black, I think. As if I would allow my own disgrace to touch you, little *signorina.*"

"You are *not* disgraced!" she declared, her eyes sparkling with anger. "Your war record alone proves you an honourable gentleman! Why should you suffer for what *he* did? You are not of his blood!"

Such fierce defensiveness warmed his heart. He said, "I

mean to prove that, just as fast as I can. To which end, Miss Jones," he tugged on the check-string, "I must take you home to the duchess, and get started to Richmond."

Consuela asked, "Must you drive all the way down there? Surely Thornhill can go and collect any letters that wait for you?"

"He's a fine valet, I grant you, but he has only worked for me a short while. Our butler, Rennett, has been at Richmond since I was a small boy, and there are questions that . . . well, that only I can ask him."

"Ooh!" breathed Consuela her eyes very wide. "What a very good notion, Jack. The servants know *everything!*"

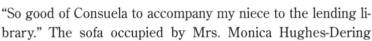

"So good of Consuela to accompany my niece to the lending library." The sofa occupied by Mrs. Monica Hughes-Dering creaked protestingly as she turned to select another sweetmeat from the box beside her. "I would gladly have gone with Minerva," she lied, nudging away the golden spaniel that had settled itself on her foot. "But my constitution is frail, you know, and I cannot like wintry weather. How fortunate that you should have chosen today to call upon me, Duchess. My little London house is close to everything, but I declare none of my friends will venture out in the rain, and I was like to die from boredom till you came. Now, with the girls gone, we can enjoy a comfortable cose."

The 'little London house' was a luxurious mansion located off Dover Street, and was considered by most people much too large to be occupied by one person. However, it had been for many years a Mecca for the *ton* and after her spouse had gone to his reward, the widow had chosen to remain. When she was not receiving her friends, she relied for companionship upon her numerous pets and, to a lesser degree, on whichever indigent relation she could bully into living under her roof. It was a rare afternoon that the elegant drawing room was not crowded with callers come to pay homage to the *grande dame,* and Lady Francesca counted herself fortunate to have found her quarry comparatively alone.

Now, surrounded by five dogs of varying origins, all anxiously watching the path of the sweetmeat, Lady Francesca also watched in fascination as it disappeared into the tiny slit of a mouth. If this tyrant of the *ton* was 'frail' she gave no sign of it. Always, she had been a large woman, but it was some years since they last had met and Lady Francesca was genuinely aghast to note that the dowager had more than doubled in girth. An initial suggestion that they share the sofa was a piece of empty rhetoric, for not even a small child could have squeezed in beside her. The chins that had once been double had quadrupled, neckline and waistline blended into one great bulk, and the eyes were small black beads, almost hidden by the swell of the rouged cheeks.

They were shrewd eyes, none the less, and, aware of this, Lady Francesca accepted the mumbled offer of a sweetmeat and stifled her yearning to enumerate the various means by which one might put off flesh.

Their 'comfortable close,' frequently interrupted by loving exchanges between Mrs. Hughes-Dering and her unruly pets, commenced with polite enquiries as to old friends and family members. There was a small disaster when a Pekinese jumped into the box of sweetmeats, precipitating a battle royal for the scattered pieces, but once a neat maid had provided another box the 'cose' resumed. The frightful morals of today's youth provided an entertaining topic, then Lady Francesca skillfully initiated a discussion of the terrible discomforts of travel, and 'chanced' to mention that she had come to town under the escort of a young officer. "I fancy you know of him, dear *Signora* Monica, for you know everybodys who is anybodys. Captain John Vespa?"

The beady eyes glittered with interest. "Jack Vespa? But of course I know him. Do you say he is in town already? Poor boy.

Such a dreadful thing when members of the aristocracy can be attacked and murdered by these dreadful revolutionary ruffians, for that's what they must have been, I am very sure. I suppose Jack will be sailing off to South America to fetch his mother home, eh?"

"This it would surprise me not at all. Only am I surprised the lady she have run off like that. Why do you suppose her to doing such things?"

Mrs. Hughes-Dering paused for another assault on the sweetmeat box. "Far be it from me, dear Francesca," she said, fending off the persistently optimistic spaniel. "Far be it from me to pay heed to the gabble-mongers. You know how unkind they can be. But—one must face facts. Once a widgeon, always a widgeon!" She lowered her voice and added confidingly, "To be honest, Duchess, I often wondered how Sir Kendrick could abide the foolish creature."

"*Si*. This I heard. But he was a handsome man, and they say Lady Faith is a lovely woman. Perhaps she was a credit to him?"

Around the sweetmeat her friend uttered a disparaging snort. "If he thought so, he hid it well! More than a little bit of a rascal with the ladies was Kendrick Vespa."

"Ah, but this, it is sad. The poor wife abandoned in the country alone and unwanted."

The dowager roared, *"Here, lads!"* and hurled two sweetmeats to the far end of the room.

Lady Francesca gave a gasp as a greyhound leapt across her knees. There was a cacophony of barking, scrambling claws, yelps, growls and more warfare. Nobody's fool, the golden spaniel sprang instead onto his owner's lap, or what might be assumed to be her lap. Mrs. Hughes-Dering caught him as he slithered down the slope. "Mummy's little rogue," she cooed, kissing him fondly, and then bellowed, "Elise!"

The maid hurried in, waving biscuits. The canine contingent followed their Pied Piper as though they'd not been fed for several days, even the spaniel abandoning his mistress. "Are they not the dearest creatures?" gushed Mrs. Hughes-Dering. "But they do love Mummy's treats, and I mustn't let myself spoil the little pets. Now—what were we saying?"

"Lady Vespa. Such a sad fate. I feeling for her." The duchess raised her brows enquiringly. "Unless . . . ?"

Mrs. Hughes-Dering giggled. "Oh, yes. There were some of those!"

"Is so? How much of a secret this was, for never did I hear of it. Do you say there was more than one—ah—"

"Side-door lover? Indeed there was, not that many knew of it."

"But you did, clever one!" Pulling her chair closer, Lady Francesca said avidly, "Living as we do in the country, I never hear such stories of romance. Do tell me—ah, but I am silly and these happenings of so long ago you will be forgetting, or perhaps you did not know *who* were these side-door peoples."

It was a challenge no dedicated gossip could refuse. Mrs. Monica Hughes-Dering sat straighter and said, "I *never* forget the *affaires* of the *ton!* Now, let me see. . . ."

4

The gracious house that sprawled along the banks of the Thames near Richmond had been quiet for weeks but today it hummed with activity. The butler, Obadiah Rennett, had set maids to bustling about with dusters and towels, and bed linen; the fireboy had awoken a fine blaze on the drawing room hearth and was now preparing another in Captain Vespa's bedchamber (Mr. Rennett having been advised that the captain would not move into the suite his late father had occupied); the chef sang happily in his kitchen; and everyone's spirits were lifted because at last the young master had come home.

Not since early summer had John Vespa set foot in this house, and no one could have been happier than the butler when the captain's post-chaise pulled onto the drivepath and he came limping up the front steps. He was unaccompanied, which meant this would be a brief visit. Rennett, who had served the family for most of his life, stifled a sigh and ordered a lackey to collect the Captain's valise, while the first footman was sent scurrying upstairs to serve as temporary valet.

Mr. Rennett had been fond of both sons of the house, and had often marvelled at their mutual devotion, for they were in his opinion very different articles. Mr. Sherborne had been the heir, of course, as handsome as his sire, full of fun and always ready for any prank or escapade no matter how outrageous. It could not be denied that there had been the trace of a 'wild kick in his gallop,' as the saying went, which had displeased Sir Kendrick Vespa, yet a more unaffected and good-natured youth would have been hard to find.

When Sherborne had bought a pair of colours and dazzled everyone with his splendid uniform before rushing off to join a crack Hussar regiment, Rennett had wished him well, and prayed his brother would not follow, for despite the affection in which he held Sherborne, it was Master John for whom the butler would have put his hand in the fire. John had followed, however, and the butler, waiting and worrying, had scanned every edition of the newspapers and trembled over the casualty lists. It had grieved his faithful heart when Sherborne had fallen, and he had grieved even more deeply when John had been brought home a year later, such a shadow of his former self.

It had been a bitter disappointment when the young soldier had elected to live not in London or Richmond, but in the lonely old ruin he'd inherited in Dorsetshire. Today, after one look at Master John's face (he *must* think of him as Sir John now!) the butler guessed the reason behind the prolonged absence, and the lack of mourning dress. The devoted young man was obviously clinging to the hope that Sir Kendrick had managed to survive and would be miraculously found alive somewhere downriver.

'A forlorn hope, poor lad,' thought Mr. Rennett, carrying a tray of decanters and glasses into the drawing room. He glanced about to see if everything was in readiness and swung around when he heard the door close behind him.

Corporal bounced across the thick rug, wagged his tail at the butler and took possession of the warmest spot before the hearth.

Vespa said with a smile, "Everything to your satisfaction, Rennett?"

"We all want to please you, Sir John, and—" There was a slight flinch and an involuntary movement of the master's hand, and Rennett knew he had not pleased. He wouldn't make that mistake again! He said hesitantly, "The staff and I— That is, I am sure you will know, Captain, how deeply we all sympathize with your loss."

"Yes. And I am most grateful." Vespa selected a fireside chair, trying not to see Sir Kendrick sitting in it. "Be so good as to pour me a cognac. Thank you. And now pour one for yourself and come and sit down. I want to talk to you."

Rennett's heart sank. Captain John was going to close this house. He was about to be told to dismiss the staff. He poured a small measure of Madeira and walked to a straight-backed chair.

"No, not there. Over here, man. And for mercy's sake don't sit on the edge as if you cringed before a tyrannical despot." The familiar and endearing smile was slanted at him, and his employer asked, "I'm not one—am I?"

"By no means, sir." Rennett leaned back and waited.

"This—chat must be of a most confidential nature, Obadiah."

'Obadiah!' Mr. Rennett's troubled heart gave a leap. "Of course, sir. If there is *any* way in which I may be of help? Is it about Sir Kendrick's death?"

"Yes. The authorities suspect that there was a—a sort of conspiracy. And I am trying to discover if my—father had any enemies."

The butler's honest eyes widened.

Vespa said hurriedly, "I know there may have been resentments, especially of late years, connected with his various romantic—er, entanglements. But we believe it goes farther back than that. Much farther back."

Thinking a great deal, the butler said with marked hesitation, "Sir—it is not my place to— Perhaps Lady Faith, or Sir Reginald Wansdyke . . ."

"I'm asking you to compromise your high principles, I know. But you see we cannot wait for my mother to come home. To say truth, we've not even heard from her as yet. Sir Reginald was—disturbed by my questions and I'm afraid he's of the opinion I am more than a touch cork-brained." Vespa smiled ruefully. "So I've come to you. I think we have always been friends?"

"I would not presume to—"

"Oh, for heaven's sake!" His patience wearing thin, Vespa exclaimed, "You're a man and I'm a man, and only an accident of birth prevents you being the master of this house and me the butler! Speaking of which, you'll never know how much I needed you in Dorsetshire, Obadiah. I apprehend it's the last place you would want to live, but—"

In an unprecedented interruption, Rennett said fervently, "I would go anywhere with you, Master John!" For just an instant the enigmatic eyes lit up, and the face of this man Sherry had laughingly referred to as 'Mr. Aloof' betrayed a depth of affection that astonished his employer. The butler looked down and a shy flush stained his cheeks.

Touched, Vespa said, "How very good of you. Then will you help me? I understand and commend your reticence, but this is of the utmost importance, and it is vital to me that you speak frankly."

"In that case, sir, yes, I know Sir Kendrick made enemies. As you say, he was very popular with the ladies, and there were gentlemen—several gentlemen—who resented his—ah, conquests. But none I'd judge so distressed as to resort to violence."

"Then let's try another tack. Do you recall anyone whom Sir

Kendrick particularly disliked? I mean *really* disliked. Perhaps long before I was born."

The butler blinked. "I'm afraid I'll be of small help there, Master John— Oh, your pardon! I keep calling you that, when I should say—"

"It's quite all right. You called me that for years. Just don't fling my title at me, if you please. I imagine it is difficult for you to remember what took place a quarter century ago."

"It's not that I cannot recall, sir. The thing is that I wasn't the butler in those days. Mr. Clipstone was still alive, and I was an under-footman, in which position I wasn't privy to—er—"

"To family secrets? Come now, Obadiah. Surely you'd have heard a few pieces of gossip; in the Hall, at least."

The butler met the whimsical grin that was levelled at him, and grinned in return. "Well, I'll have to think back, sir. Let me see now. . . . When Sir Kendrick and Lady Faith first married there were—there always are, you know—those who didn't exactly—ah, smile on the union. One gentleman I do recall was a Mr. . . . now what was his name . . . ? Dilworth! That's it. Very much enamoured of Lady Faith, he was, and even after the wedding he would send her odes and tragic poems and great bouquets of flowers. Sir Kendrick thought it hilarious."

"Whatever became of him, do you know?"

"Yes, indeed. He acceded to his uncle's dignities and became Lord somebody or other. I don't recall the exact title. Perhaps because he enjoyed it for so short a time. He bought himself a yacht. It sank on its maiden voyage, alas."

"With the new lord?"

"Unfortunately so."

Persevering, Vespa coaxed from the butler the identities of several other gallants who had aspired to Lady Faith's hand. One had since passed away, another had been killed during the retreat from Corunna. Rennett was aware of none who had suffered a broken heart or harboured a particular grudge, and to the best of his knowledge most had eventually married other ladies.

Stifling his disappointment, Vespa asked, "What about different forms of enmity? Political or economic strife, for instance. Do you remember anything of that nature? Anyone who might have seriously crossed swords with Sir Kendrick?"

Rennett racked his brains, but without success. Vespa called for their glasses to be refilled and changed the subject, and for an hour the two men chatted like old friends. The afternoon was fading to dusk when the butler stood and began to light candles. "I do wish I could be of more help, sir," he said regretfully. "I'm afraid, if you'll forgive my saying so, Sir Kendrick had such charm, he could win over the most angry men." He paused, frowning at the taper in his hand. "When he really cared to," he added slowly.

There was no more to be had from him; at least, for the moment. Vespa tried not to be downcast, enjoyed an excellent meal, sent his compliments to the Chef and, having leafed through several newspapers, went up to bed.

It had been a long day and he was tired, but Corporal was obviously uneasy in these strange surroundings, so he allowed the dog to come into the room and having commanded sternly that he stay on the bedside rug, fell asleep almost at once. He was awoken by a warning bark and a knock at the door. After the fashion of men who have slept under constant threat of attack, he was at once wide awake.

In answer to his call, a night-capped head, lit by the glow of a candle, loomed around the door. Corporal wagged his tail and accepted a caress.

Rennett said eagerly, "Sir, forgive, but I have remembered something. It's just a small thing, and likely of no help, but I thought I should tell you for fear I forget it by morning."

"Come in, man," commanded Vespa, sitting up. "You've remembered one of my mother's admirers, is that the case?"

The butler hurried in and closed the door. "No, sir," he said, advancing to stand beside the bed. "And, alas, my poor brain won't give me the gentleman's name. He may be dead now. But I remember being awed at the time, because our chef said that if ever there was a man Sir Kendrick detested, it was him, and that sure as check it would someday come to pistols at dawn for them! I never saw the gentleman, and I'd have forgot all about him, except that Mr. Clipstone was such a great one for fussy little details, and he asked Chef if he'd noticed that the gentleman's name had an interesting feature."

Vespa asked intensely, "You mean he was foreign?"

Rennett hesitated. "He may have been, sir. Mr. Clipstone pointed out that the gentleman had the same two letters in both his first and last names. Next to each other, if you take my meaning."

"You mean, if, for instance, his first name was Philip, and his surname Milbank—the 'il' would be in sequence in both cases?"

"That's it, sir. I only wish I'd paid more heed, but—it was so long ago, and I was young and empty-headed."

Vespa said he'd done splendidly, and might have provided an important clue, and the butler left, beaming.

Disappointed, Vespa lay back and stared at the ceiling. For a moment, he'd really entertained high hopes, but for all his efforts he seemed to be getting nowhere. Perhaps he never would discover his real identity, which would surely spell the ruin of his hopes. He sighed, which was a mistake because it alarmed Corporal who at once jumped onto the bed to console him. It was several minutes before Vespa was able to reassure the consoler and when he at last fell asleep it was with Corporal—having taken flagrant advantage of the situation—snuggled close against his feet.

***

Lady Francesca surveyed the magnificent tapestry that hung on one wall of the large drawing room, and nodded her approval. She proceeded to wander from the massive and elaborately carven stone chimney-piece, to the great bow windows that overlooked the back gardens of Vespa House. The marble statue of Venus and the jade collection on an inlaid table were viewed critically.

Consuela asked, "Well, Grandmama?"

"Is a fine *casa,* this." The duchess turned to Vespa who hurried to join them. "You will be foolish not to dwell here when you are in London, my Captain."

He bowed over her hand. "You know I cannot, ma'am." Crossing to Consuela, his eyes were a caress. "Forgive. The roads are all mud, and my coach was delayed."

Consuela surrendered her hand and said softly, "I am only glad you've come home, but I was surprised that you wished to meet here. This is difficult for you."

Difficult . . . Every room, every piece of furniture, even the smell of beeswax and burning coal, held memories of the brother he'd loved and the father who had made devotion into a savage mockery. He said quietly, "Yes. But we have things to discuss, and we must be private. Have Toby and Paige been here?"

"We are now, my pippin!" Tobias Broderick came briskly into the room, bowed to the ladies and went over to the hearth to make a fuss of Corporal, while complaining of the 'beastly cold wind.'

Paige Manderville followed, paying his respects with his customary easy grace and stunning them all with the splendour of a dark purple coat and lavender pantaloons that would have been vulgar on anyone else, but merely enhanced his good looks.

Under the supervision of Rennett, who had accompanied his master from Richmond, two laden trays were carried in. Corporal's attempt to investigate this feast was circumvented, and with a ceremony that amused them all the butler produced a likely looking bone and lured the dog to the kitchens.

"Well," said Vespa hopefully, as plates and mugs of hot chocolate were distributed. "Has anyone been lucky?"

Manderville exclaimed, "Custard tarts! Egad, but I adore custard tarts! You go first, Toby."

Shaking his head, Broderick looked glum and begged that his news come last.

Consuela sprang up, clapping her hands and almost oversetting a tray. "Oh, I cannot wait! Grandmama has been so clever, and has found out—"

"These tells they are *my* tellings!" protested the duchess indignantly. "Sit down, *bambina,* and try to behaving *correttamente!* So. *Now,* we proceed. I, Captain Jack, upon your behoofs, have visit my sometimes friend, Mrs. Monica Hughes-Dering, the queen of gossip, who has, I will say it, become *gross!* How this woman she can allow herself such a great stomach— But—that is neither heres nor theres. She knows *everything,* my dears, about *everyone!*"

Laughing, Manderville said, "Quite true. You went to the proper fountain, my lady, obese or no."

Broderick protested, "No, really, Paige! You cannot scramble syntax in so haphazard a way! I think you mean a well, not a fountain. And how could either be obese?"

"Oh, I don't know, old lad. I've heard there's a fall of waters in the New World that is enormously wide, much like the duchess' friend, so—"

Vespa interrupted impatiently, "Do you say, ma'am, that the lady remembers someone who was particularly enamoured of my mother?"

"No. But—from her I have one little thing learned. If we put it with another little thing, and then some other little thing . . . Who can say?"

"You can," said Consuela, frustrated.

"It is," resumed the duchess with a lofty gesture, "that this *grande dame* of the *ton* have boast and brag of her so *eccelente* memory, but when we put it to the test, pouff! Away it has go!"

"Memory is a fascinating area of study." The learned Broderick appropriated a custard tart and waved it about to emphasize his remarks. "Actually, even today little is known about it, though Aristotle was most interested in concepts formed by reason evolving from sensations which produce memory, and—"

"Unfair!" cried Manderville. "Unfair! We gave you first chance to take the floor, and you refused. So have the goodness to cease your lecturing!"

Vespa said through gritted teeth, "In about one second I'll strangle the pair of you! My lady, are we to understand that the— er, 'Queen of Gossip' had none to impart?"

"But of course she did! She was fairly bubbling over with it! To sort the 'meat from the staff' or whatever this saying is, I learned only one item that is of interest to us. Your Papa—and I mean Sir Kendrick, dear Captain Jack—he had the enemy. The bitter enemy."

"Rennett said as much." Vespa leaned forward. "Was this to do with my mother? Could Mrs. Hughes-Dering name the man?"

"No, and no. It was to do with behaviours. Politics. Ideals— or the lack of them!"

"Ah! Rennett said matters between Sir Kendrick and one gentleman were so strained that a duel was imminent. This sounds a likely customer. Could the lady tell you nothing at all of him? Is he still alive?"

"This she did not know, for the person was outside of England a good deal. Mrs. Hughes-Dering say he had an estate— in Suffolk, she thought, and a castle somewhere, but not in England. And that he lived in those places, when he was not hunting."

"Jove, ma'am!" said Vespa, delighted. "You've done wonderfully!"

Manderville dusted crumbs from his knee and murmured, "What does he hunt? Fox? Wild boar? Stag?"

"Let me tell them, *please,* Grandmama!" begged Consuela. "For it is not important, and so very funny." Receiving a resigned

nod from the duchess, she said, her eyes sparkling, "He hunts—
rugs! Is it not the strangest hobby?"

"Rugs?" Manderville shook his head. "Sounds as if he has a
vacancy in the upper storey, Jack!"

"Some rugs can be valuable," pointed out Broderick. "In
fact—"

"Desist, for mercy's sake," groaned Manderville. "A lecture
on rug-making we do not need. What we've to do now is try to put
it all together as Lady Francesca said, and see what we've got—
do you agree, Captain, sir?"

"I do, but I must tell you first how grateful I am for all the time
you've spent, trying to help me."

"Why not?" said Manderville. "We enjoy your hospitality."

Broderick declared, "I don't. Not for much longer, at all
events. Been recalled. I was at the Horse Guards this morning,
and the doctors say I'm perfectly fit again."

Consuela and the duchess greeted this news with mixed feelings, but Vespa said heartily, "Congratulations! That's good news
indeed. Are you for France, then?"

"Next week. I'm pleased, of course, but I don't much like leaving you in the middle of this bog."

"You may be *à l'aise,*" said Manderville. "I shall stand by Jack,
staunch and true, as ever. The Army won't have me yet." He
moved his arm tentatively. "Shoulder. Still stiff, y'know. And I
shall now contribute my *soupçon* of information, which really tells
us nothing, yet says a good deal, I think. While Toby was ensconced with the medical monsters, I called in at Bow Street
again. You will be interested to learn, Jack, that there is no record
of any street brawl the night before last involving your esteemed
self; that there was no murder done in London Town; and that
Colonel the Honourable Hastings Adair has not set foot on British
soil for the last six weeks, at least. In other words, friends, Ro-
mans and so forth, something very sticky is afoot, and Consuela's
colonel is up to his ears in the glue."

Vespa nodded. "Not much doubt of that. Certainly, they don't want us sticking our noses in whatever it is. Well, at least we tried to help Adair."

"Who is not *my* colonel," murmured Consuela pertly.

Vespa smiled at her, and went on: "Then we shall leave him to his own devices and do as Paige suggested. Please interrupt if you think of something I've overlooked. It seems to me that the most likely candidate we've found thus far is a gentleman much disliked by Sir Kendrick, and who is out of the country a good deal of the time. We have several clues as to his identity. One is that both his first and last names contain the same two letters in succession. Also, we believe he may have an estate in Suffolk. And, lastly, his hobby is to hunt—rugs. Not a great deal, I admit. But it's a start."

Broderick pointed out, "Your surest route would be to sail at once for South America and try to wheedle the truth out of Lady Faith."

"Oh, absolutely. But the courier my great-uncle despatched must surely reach my mother long before I could get there, and she may well decide to return at once. There is the risk that if I now sail, our ships may pass each other in mid-ocean, and—" he met Consuela's eyes steadily "it would take a year, at least. I think I do not want to wait that long."

Consuela blushed, and there was a small silence.

Lady Francesca, who had been frowning at Manderville's purple coat, said suddenly, "I cannot like that colour, and I have find something we forget, Captain Jack. It is the castle. Did not your man tell you this same gentleman have a castle some-where?"

"Yes. But he didn't know where, save that it was not in England."

"Still, it's a help," said Broderick. "We can go into Suffolk and enquire for a landed local gentleman who also owns a castle that may or may not be in the British Isles."

"Oh, oh!" cried Consuela happily. "We *are* making progress! And if the castle chances to be *somewhere* in Britain: Wales, for instance, or Scotland, it would . . ." She stopped suddenly, her widening eyes flying to Vespa's face.

Lady Francesca demanded, "What is it? What is it? Never become mute and stiff like the stockfish! If you have thinking of somethings, speak up, Meadowlark!"

Consuela moved hesitantly to stand before Vespa. He stood at once, and she touched his arm and murmured, "I am sorry to speak of that terrible time. I know you don't like to think of it."

His nerves tightened into knots, but he put a hand over hers and said, "Do you mean when we were down in the quarry? It's all right, Consuela. Tell me, please."

She closed her eyes for a second and could see again that dismal mine tunnel, and Sir Kendrick, pistol in hand, so cruelly taunting his son. She shivered, and looked up quickly. "He said," she blurted out in a rush, "Sir Kendrick said something about your having a stubborn Scots streak in your make-up."

Vespa muttered, " 'Miserably dogged Scots streak' were his words, as I recall."

"He *did* say it?" Broderick asked intensely, "You're sure?"

With a travesty of a smile, Vespa said, "Do you suppose I could ever forget that moment?"

"I have to admit he was right," said Manderville. "No offence, dear boy, but you *are* stubborn, you know, and—"

"Very true," agreed Broderick. "Thing is—have you also—"

"Or have the Wansydykes—" interrupted the duchess.

"Any Scots on the family tree?" finished Consuela, breathless with excitement.

Vespa stared from one expectant face to the next. "I know there are no Scots among the Vespa's. I'm not . . . not sure—" He gave an exultant shout. *"No!* I *am* sure! My grandfather, Sir Rupert Wansdyke, was a great one for tradition. Several times when Sherry and I were schoolboys he dragged us through the picture gallery in Wansdyke House and gave us a small lecture on each ancestor. We thought it deadly dull. But I remember that he said they all were of Saxon heritage, most having been born and bred in the Southland, and that not until his daughter—my mother—married a man of Norman origins had anyone from so far afield been brought into the family!" Jubilant, he seized Consuela and swung her around. "Clever, clever one! You've found the best clue of all! My father must have been a Scot!" He gave her a smacking kiss on the cheek. "Thank you! Thank you!"

Lady Francesca screamed and pounded him with her little fists, demanding that he 'unhand' her granddaughter at once, and when he did so, threw her arms around him and collected a kiss of her own.

Manderville and Broderick came to clap him on the back and share his triumph.

Broderick said enthusiastically, "Your puzzle is as good as solved, old fellow! We'll go up to Suffolk at once, and if we can't track down a gentleman who owns an estate somewhere in the county, besides having a castle in Scotland—why, I'm a Dutchman!"

"This, it is so?" asked the duchess, misunderstanding, but beaming at him. "And I am the Italian, and my Consuela is a bit of this and a bit of that, and Jack may be half of a Scot." She turned to Manderville. "You, dear Lieutenant Paige, it looks like is the only true Englishman of us all!"

He laughed. "And my many greats-Grandpapa ran afoul of Charles of Anjou in 1257 and had to leave Marseilles or lose his head, so I'm likely as mixed as the rest of you!"

His heart lighter than it had been for weeks, Vespa summoned Rennett and ordered champagne, and they all drank to Suffolk and success.

And never dreamed that Suffolk was just the beginning.

5

Although a pale winter sun broke through the clouds, the wind that swept in from the North Sea had an icy bite. Vespa drew the collar of his riding coat higher, glanced back along the winding lane, and whistled. Bright-eyed and ears flying, mud on the end of his nose, Corporal scampered from investigating a burrow.

"Keep up, you little scoundrel," called Vespa, and turned his hired grey horse to the west once more.

He had spent three fruitless days scouring the Ipswich area. Friendly inn-keepers, waiters, parlour-maids, blacksmiths, shop-keepers, a cobbler, two muffin-men, a pedlar, a fisherman and a constable had each been only too willing to pass the time of day over a tankard of ale or a cup of tea, but no one knew of any local land-owner who also owned a Scottish castle and was away a good deal of the time. He could only hope that Toby Broderick, investigating Bury St. Edmunds, and Manderville, prowling the area around Stowmarket, had been more successful.

In this eastern edge of Suffolk the roads were not as travelled as those in the Home Counties, nor the houses as numerous, but the villages were charming and the country folk kindly. The land was low for the most part, but not flat, rising into occasional gently rolling hills. On this bright morning Vespa followed a lane that was lined by thorn hedges and trees. It would have been deeply shaded during the summer months, but today most of the trees lifted obligingly naked branches that did not shut out the welcome December sunshine. He came to the crest of a rise dignified by an impressive flush-flint and stone church, and as he rode down the slope he entered what was more a town than another village: a prosperous wool town by the look of the people and carts bustling about.

He raised his hat to a lady and a little girl passing by in an open carriage. The lady looked away, and the child stared unsmilingly. He was accorded the same treatment when he nodded to two men loading a cart outside a mercantile warehouse, and an old gentleman in smock and gaiters positively glared at him. It was the first time he'd encountered an unfriendliness that bordered on the hostile. The folk hereabouts appeared to have a distrust of strangers; possibly they took him for a Riding Officer—certainly smuggling was widely practiced along this coast.

Corporal raced past, his little legs flying. Vespa caught a whiff of woodsmoke and cooking; a laden waggon rumbled by, the waggonner scanning him with cold suspicion. 'Brrr!' thought Vespa, and wondered whether the proprietor of the whitewashed inn up ahead would deign to serve him luncheon. The street dipped into a watersplash through which the grey horse trod daintily. Corporal had been obliged to swim across and as the street turned uphill once more he trotted towards a pump, at which point he paused and looked back for his master.

A young gentleman stood beside the trough, watering his mount. Vespa's glance flickered over the high-crowned hat tilted at a rakish angle, the fashionable riding coat and leathers, the gleaming boots and long-necked spurs, and came to rest on the tall chestnut horse. It was a handsome thoroughbred with a glossy coat and a long and waving mane and tail. It was also, in his opinion, a shade short in the back and too much inclined to twitch and dance about. 'All nerves and show,' he judged.

It was then that Corporal decided to shake himself.

For a small dog the amount of displaced water was remarkable. The young exquisite was liberally showered. He sprang aside and collided with his nervous mount which promptly shot into the air as if levitated, sending its owner into an ungainly sprawl. The elegant wet garments became muddy wet garments.

Noting from the corner of his eye that several grinning passers-by had stopped to watch, Vespa rode up and dismounted. "I'm so sorry," he began, limping to the rescue.

The victim fairly sprang to his feet. His well-cut features were scarlet and twisted with wrath. Cursing, he aimed one of his glossy boots at Corporal. "Damned little *cur!*" he howled.

"Hey!" Vespa's helping hand became a firm tug and the kick landed only glancingly.

"Is that—that apology for a dog—yours?" roared the victim.

As cool as the other man was enraged, Vespa drawled, "I see only an apology for a gentleman."

Somebody hooted.

The dandy's bloodshot eyes narrowed. His heavy riding whip flailed at Vespa's head.

A lithe sway, an iron grip and a heave, and the infuriated young man was flat on his back again.

"Cross-buttocked!" howled an exultant voice. "Limp or no, he cross-buttocked him, by grab!"

"Neat as ever I did see," confirmed another.

Vespa turned to take up the reins of his grey, and Corporal scuttled quickly to his side. Vespa bent to inspect him, but the little dog didn't seem badly damaged.

" 'Ware, sir!"

He straightened at the warning yell. The dandy had regained

his feet and although he tended to sway, was lunging into another attack. Growling ferociously, Corporal charged forward and got a good grip on a now considerably less glossy boot.

"Confound the—mangy cur!" The young man's hand plunged into the pocket of his riding coat and emerged holding a small pistol.

"Corporal—*up!*" said Vespa sharply.

The dog released the boot. The pistol shot reverberated in the small valley of the street, and Corporal flew into Vespa's arms.

A small crowd had gathered. There were shrill screams, cries of "Shame!" and "Play fair!"

A matron wearing a splendidly laced cap cried, *"Disgraceful* behavior! To try and kill a poor little doggie!"

"You're damned lucky I didn't hit you, fellow! Whoever you are," advised the dandy rather thickly, and with an uneasy glance around the ring of condemning faces.

Vespa set Corporal down. "If I weren't particular about my acquaintanceships, I'd give you my card." He took out his purse. "Your aim is as uncontrolled as your temper. But since my dog did dampen you a trifle, I'll pay for your garments to be cleaned." He tossed a half-crown contemptuously, and was mildly surprised when this unpleasant but undoubtedly aristocratic individual caught it with a quick snatch.

A ripple of scorn went up from the onlookers.

The dandy said ungraciously, "It's a small part of what you owe me. If you weren't—were not—crippled, I'd call—you out! Be damned if I—'f I wouldn't."

"You'd not get me out," said Vespa. "I only fight gentlemen, and never when they're 'up in the world.' "

Again, the reddened eyes were lit with rage. "I'm not drunk, d-damn you!"

"Go home!" shouted a youthful voice from the edge of the crowd, and other voices were raised:

"You ain't welcome here, Mr. Keith!"

"Go back to the 'big smoke'!"

"Maybe we should show 'un the way, mates!"

"Aye! At the tail of a cart!"

'Mr. Keith' glared at them, but it was clear their antagonism was growing. He swung into the saddle and wheeled his mount so hard that Vespa was almost caught by the chestnut's plunging head. With a snarled threat to 'have the law on the l-lot of you yokels,' the ill-tempered dandy spurred to a gallop and beat an inglorious retreat.

Vespa, however, found himself surrounded by now-beaming faces. He was patted on the back, informed that "We took ye for Mr. Keith's friend, sir!" and was borne into the White Horse Inn very much the conquering hero.

The tap was a cheerful place, mellow with age, and ringing with talk and laughter. Vespa's limp was not mentioned again, but his tidy victory over the evidently much disliked Mr. Keith was a cause for celebration. A tankard of ale was pressed into his hand, and he was begged to reveal his identity.

Before he could respond, a deep voice shouted, "Jack Vespa! As I live and breathe!"

A bronzed young giant with unruly red hair, a black patch over one eye and a broad grin pushed his way through the throng, and swept Vespa into a crushing hug.

"Calloway!" gasped Vespa. "Let be, you old warhorse before my ribs are powder! I thought you were dead! What the deuce are you doing up here?"

Lieutenant Sean Calloway, late of the 71st Highlanders, roared a laugh that rattled the casements. "Farming, Captain, sir! And if it's any consolation, I was *sure* you were dead!" In response to shouts of enquiry, he turned to the gathering and introduced "Captain Jack Vespa, who was an aide-de-camp to Lord Wellington."

Vespa's intent to remain incognito was foiled, but he could scarcely blame this old friend, and he reacted smilingly to the admiring and awed exclamations and the inevitable questions of the company until Calloway broke in to ask, "What the deuce have you done to have caused such a fuss in this quiet corner of England?"

"Cap'n knocked down that there Keith gent, Mr. Calloway, sir," supplied a very wizened little old man. "Wanted doin' for ages'n ages. Cap'n done it. Tidy. Eh, lads?"

During the chorus of agreement Vespa gathered that 'Young Mr. Keith' was 'proper high-in-the-instep,' that he had 'too much Lun'on in his ways,' and ordered folk about 'like we was dirt under his feet.'

Calloway laughed. "If that ain't just like you, Jack! Always up to your neck in some kind of imbroglio! Come over here and sit down, I want to know what you've been about since Vitoria. I got my come-uppance at that little rumpus, as you see."

"Yes. It must be a beastly nuisance for you."

"Oh, well. I'm alive, which is more than you could say for a lot of my poor fellows. Or for that fine brother of yours, eh? You must miss him."

Vespa stared rather fixedly at his tankard, then said quietly, "Very much. We're the lucky ones, Sean, even if you don't see quite as well nowadays, and I don't run quite as fast."

They adjourned to an inglenook by the blazing fire and for a little while enjoyed mutual recollections of their army days and the comrades they'd served beside. The local people relived and chuckled over the morning's encounter, the name 'Keith' being bandied about frequently. Vespa asked at length, "Who is this fellow who's made himself so unwelcome here?"

"Be dashed if I know. I'm fairly new to the county. My mama inherited a small farm here and has been good enough to hand it over to me. She thought I'd soon tire of it, I suspect, but I'm not a Town beau, and country life suits me. I did hear that Keith has a boat moored somewhere along the coast. Don't know if it's truth, but if it is he likely runs tubs or such-like and passes through here en route back to London. He's no local, that's certain."

"Know most of the locals, do you?"

"Most." The solitary blue eye slanted at Vespa shrewdly. "Why?"

"I'm trying to locate a gentleman. I understand he has an estate in the county, but the devil's in it that I don't know his name." Calloway stared, and he added, "It's a commission my mother sent me just before she sailed for South America. Unfortunately, her letter was rain-damaged and all I have is a most urgent message for the old fellow. I feel I have to try to deliver it, but I've little to go on."

"Gad! Your best chance, surely, would be to contact some of the local squires, or the clergy."

"It would, of course. But—well, to say truth, Sean, the matter's of a rather delicate nature, and . . ." Vespa shrugged.

"Ah. Family business, eh? Well, I wish I could give you an assist. Have you no other description at all?"

"Only that he also owns a castle in Scotland."

Calloway scratched his red head and frowned thoughtfully. "A castle in Scotland . . . hmm. Now what did I hear about . . . ? I know! It was my great-aunt! You don't know the lady, I think. Gad, what a chatterbox! Kindest heart in the world, mind you, but— Well, at all events, she was rattling on to my father about an old friend whom she and my great-uncle used to visit at one time. She was enormously impressed by his estate, which is up near the Cambridgeshire border. Delightful place, to hear her tell it, and with a superb rose garden. There was some sort of family trouble years ago, and the gentleman sort of dropped out of sight. Sounds to me as if he's short of a sheet. Hardly ever in England. I'm sure my aunt said he has a place in Scotland, but whether it's a castle or not, I couldn't tell you."

Jubilant, Vespa exclaimed, "It sounds very promising, Sean! Why do you say he's short of a sheet?"

"Well, it seems he don't spend much time in Scotland, either. Two jolly fine homes, and what must he do but waste his life flitting about the world searching for a mythical rug or some crazy thing. Poor old fellow must be in his dotage, or—"

"That's *him!*" cried Vespa, giving his friend a clap on the back that rattled his teeth. "You've found him for me, bless your clever old red nob! Do you recall his name? Or the name of his estate? Is he a Scot, d'you think?"

Calloway pushed him away and said with mock indignation, "Easy, you madman! I'm a feeble invalid yet! Devil if I know whether he's a Scot, though my great-aunt is, and I'd think she would have mentioned it if he were. Name's—um . . . Cragburn or Kincarry—something like that. Don't remember what his estate's called, but oddly enough the name of the carpet he's after stuck in my mind. It's called the Khusraw. Some Eastern fairy tale, probably. I say, is this your dog? What a nice little chap, but he looks hungry. Don't you ever feed him, you flint-heart?"

Vespa laughed. "I suppose you're hinting me to buy you lunch?"

"I suppose I am."

Vespa did; in fact he bought lunch for everyone in the tap.

A drop of rain fell coldly on her nose. Consuela halted and looked up. The clouds were pulling together now, the occasional glimpses of sunlight becoming less frequent. She had left the cottage to escape her grandmother. A large bunch of hot-house roses had been delivered to the duchess this morning; a gift ordered before his departure by Colonel Adair. Not one to let the grass grow under his feet was Hasty Adair, and knew which side his bread was buttered on. Predictably, the old lady had gone into raptures, singing the colonel's praises and envying the "lucky girl" who would become his bride, until Consuela had been driven to retaliate. A heated Italianate argument had ensued, and refusing the company of her maid, who suffered loudly from corns, Consuela had ventured alone into the chilly early afternoon.

When she'd reached the Widow Davis' Grocery/Post-Office in Gallery-on-Tang there were three letters and a parcel for the duchess and two letters for herself. The widow loved to talk and had told her that Captain Vespa had quite a pile of correspondence waiting to be picked up by his steward, Hezekiah Strickley. One of the captain's letters, she imparted, was from G. L. Manderville, Esq. "That'll be Lieutenant Manderville's father, I do expect, Miss. Likely telling the captain how poor Sir Kendrick's dogs are going on in their new home. And there's another letter, very important it looks too. From the Horse Guards. Do you know when the captain will come home again, Miss Consuela? Such a fine gentleman, and I'm sure we're all sorry for the terrible happenings out at the quarry . . ."

She had launched into a lengthy monologue, during which Consuela chose some wools for a shawl she was embroidering for her grandmother's birthday. Mrs. Blackham, the constable's tall lady, had come in with her booming voice and a long shopping list, and tucking her purchases and the mail into her basket, Consuela had managed to escape. Outside, she'd walked on, thinking wistfully of how she had first met Jack and of their desperate efforts to uncover the truth of her father's death. She was too lost in thought to notice that her steps had turned instinctively towards the old manor, and when the raindrop interrupted her musings she was mildly surprised to find herself far past the village and on the Alabaster Royal estate road.

She wandered along slowly, taking note of how much Jack had done to improve the property. The once pot-holed lane was now a quite respectable road; the grasses of the wide park, that had been a mass of weeds, were smoothly scythed, the yew trees that lined the drivepath neatly trimmed, the overgrown rose garden weeded and pruned. Her gaze went past the little hump-backed bridge over the stream, to the manor itself. Alabaster Royal. Long, two-storied, its entrance flanked by the twin round conical-topped towers that lent it an aura of strength and invincibility. The exterior was bright with new paint, the mullioned windows clean and sparkling even under the greying skies. 'Dear old house,' she mused, and with the thought heard hoofbeats on the road behind her.

Hezekiah Strickley was probably exercising some of Jack's horses, she decided, but on turning, saw that it was not the rather cantankerous steward. Instead, a luxurious coach drawn by four magnificent matched bays pulled up beside her. The coachman was one of the biggest men she had ever seen; not fat, but with a great spread of muscular shoulders and powerful hands that stretched the seams of his gauntlets. His hat was pulled low over his face, and his head was downbent, concealing his features. A window was lowered. An elegant gentleman with dead-white skin and lank black hair, leaned to smile at her.

"Good afternoon, my pretty," he said in a purring and slightly accented voice. "Have you far to go? There will be rain soon, I think."

Consuela thought indignantly, 'My *pretty?* How *dare* you address me so?' She was about to respond to his presumption when two things occurred to her. Firstly, that there was something about this man and his strange coachman that made her uneasy; and, secondly, that her windblown hair and the basket she carried, in addition to the fact that she was unaccompanied, had undoubtedly caused the creature to think she was a village lass. For no reason she could have explained, she bobbed a curtsy. "Good aft'noon, sir. I've just to go as far as the manor, if y'please."

"Then it is that you are a local girl," he said, with a flash of very white teeth, "and can be of assistance to me."

Consuela wondered if this was a French spy. Beginning to enjoy herself, she asked demurely, "How, milor'?"

He swung the door wide, and she drew back as he trod down the step. Goodness, but he was tall.

"There is not the need for alarm," he said. "It is that I have heard Sir John Vespa he seeks a friend of mine. I may be of help to him in this. Do you know if he is at home?"

She blinked at him. "Your friend, sir?"

"No, child. Sir John."

"I don't know, sir."

"But surely, if you are going to the manor you must know whether he is there."

"Oh, I know that, sir. There isn't no Sir John there. Just Captain Vespa, sir."

The black eyes widened a little. "Do you say he does not use his title?"

She wrinkled her brow and said with bovine density, "Most folks calls him Captain Jack, milor', be that what ye means?"

It seemed to her that suspicion came into those deep eyes. Perhaps she had overdone her little imposture. From the corner of her eye she saw the coachman turn and glance at her. It was a brief glance, but enough to show her a face the like of which she'd never seen. The complexion was sallow, the eyes narrow slits sunk into features that might have been carven from stone.

The tall man's hand reached out, a shilling on the palm. "This is what you want, eh? And, me, I am only glad to pay you for a simple answer, pretty child. I will speak slow for you. Is—Captain—Vespa—at—home?"

"Oh. No, sir. He bean't."

"Ah. We progress. Would you know where he can be found, little cabbage? He will be most pleased to hear what I will say."

Consuela hesitated. Perhaps this odd individual did have news that would help Jack in his quest. Perhaps she could help by telling him that Jack was in Suffolk. And yet—the manor was no more than a half-mile distant. Surely the most natural course would be for the coach to simply drive to the front door. "I did hear summat," she murmured. "The groom said where the master goed. I think . . . he said Caernarvon—or were it? Car—summat."

"In *Wales?*" he exclaimed.

"Be it, sir? No! Cardiff! That's it! Can I have me shilling now?"

He muttered, "Cardiff. I wonder . . ." then tossed the shilling.

Consuela caught it, and like a striking snake his hand flashed out to close around her wrist. "Such a dainty hand," he purred. "One might think it never had scrubbed a floor or milked the cow."

The coachman slanted another piercing glance at her. Consuela was suddenly quite frightened, and she started when she heard another vehicle approaching.

"Miss Consuela! Oh, Miss Consuela!" Violet Manning was perched on the seat of the Widow Davis' delivery cart. *"Here* you are! The duchess is fairly *beside* herself, and desires you to come home at once!"

Consuela jerked her hand free.

Anger glinted in the eyes of the tall man. His lips smiled, but it was a mirthless smile that made her forget her vexation with Manning. He said, "I think you have the little game with me. Is it not so, miss? I do not care to be made sport of. And I cannot but wonder why you should be so devious. Perhaps, next time we meet, this I shall discover."

"Perhaps you will not then be so impertinent as to address me as 'your pretty,' " she riposted haughtily.

A frown, a curt inclination of the head. With a swirl of his dark cloak and a shout to his coachman, he was inside the coach. The door slammed, the team swung in a wide turn and raced away.

The slow-witted youth who now made deliveries for Mrs. Davis said haltingly, "Dicky-Boy don't like that there genelman."

Manning, who had been temporarily bereft of speech, cried, "Goodness gracious me, Miss Consuela! Whatever were you *thinking* of to talk with such dreadful people? That coachman made me go gooseflesh all over!"

"He is Chinese, I think," said Consuela, still gazing after the rapidly disappearing coach. "I wonder what they really wanted with Captain Vespa."

The youth reiterated, "Dicky-Boy don't like him. Nor his master, neither. Cap'n Jack he wouldn't have no friend like that one."

"I almost thought the gentleman was *threatening* you, miss," wailed Manning. "I vow, 'tis all of a piece! Wherever Captain Vespa goes, trouble follows! It would be so much better if you—"

"If you were to say no more," snapped Consuela.

The lone pedlar had been amiable enough, especially after Vespa had purchased a small cloth doll from him. The Inn of the Black Lamb was 'just t'other side of the village,' he'd said, adding, "Can't miss it. Jest keep going straight, sir." The drifting mist was thickening to fog and reducing visibility so that it had become necessary to ride cautiously along the rutted lane, and Vespa was beginning to wonder if he'd missed the village altogether. Manderville, who had a more than nodding acquaintanceship with Newmarket, had suggested the inn, saying he'd once stayed there during racing season when all the better posting houses had been full, and that it boasted clean beds and a good cook.

"I wonder he could find the confounded place," muttered Vespa. "Of all the hidden-away—"

The grey horse shied suddenly as a lad darted across the lane. With consummate horsemanship, Vespa kept his seat. Ghostly cottages loomed into view. They had reached the village, at last. He whistled and Corporal raced up, tongue lolling, only to stop abruptly and growl at some menacing object on the ground. "Come on," called Vespa, and reined around.

The inn sign hung from a rail extended over the lane. Vespa

turned the grey into the yard, and a groom ran to take the reins and scream "House, ho!" in a high falsetto that sent the grey into another shy. Vespa swore and dismounted as a door opened sending a flood of light gleaming across the damp cobblestones.

"Welcome, sir," called the host, a big bluff individual, his ruddy features wreathed in a grin. "Ye'll be my captain guest. I knows ye by yer dog. What've ye got there, you little terror? His toy, is it, sir?"

Vespa's downward glance revealed that Corporal had retrieved something he'd not realized he had lost. He said with a grin, "I must have dropped it. Give it here, you scavenger. That's for little Molly Hawes. Much need you have for a doll!"

Having been advised that his friends awaited him in the parlour, he arranged for Corporal to be fed, then was shown up the narrow winding stairs to his room. It was a tiny but spotless chamber under the eaves, so low-roofed that he had to bow his head when he approached the latticed casement.

A rosy-cheeked maid carried up a ewer of hot water, and a lad hurried in with his valise. In short order he washed, brushed his hair, changed his neckcloth and went downstairs, his spirits rising as he breathed the heady scent of preparations for dinner.

He found the parlour, and his friends stretched out in chairs flanking a roaring fire.

Broderick stood to greet him heartily. "Thought you'd never get here, old lad. What's to do? Any luck?"

Manderville waved a tankard, and yawned. "Too tired to get up, *mon capitaine*. My efforts in your behalf have left me with a blistered heel and an unquenchable thirst."

"And that's all," appended Broderick, pulling up another chair. "He didn't learn a thing."

"Indeed, I did," argued Manderville indignantly. "There's a jug of ale on the sideboard yonder. We saved some for you, Jack."

Vespa filled a tankard, carried it to the fire and sank into the chair. The flames warmed his feet, the ale warmed his inside, and the loyalty of these good friends warmed his spirit. He leaned back, stretching out his long legs. "No luck, eh, Paige?"

"Some. Toby thinks he's bested me, but I doubt it."

Broderick said, "I know damned well I've bested you! All you achieved was to pick a fight with some poor fellow."

"Did you, though?" exclaimed Vespa. "What about?"

Manderville shrugged. "Nothing, really. I'd given up on the Stowmarket area and ridden east. I was making my little enquiries, polite as you please, to the most fruitful sources—"

"Namely—housemaids, dairymaids, nursemaids and pretty maids all in a row," inserted Broderick.

"Which is known as mixing business with pleasure," said Manderville with a grin. "At all events, this stupid dolt took exception. Called me a nosy foreigner, if you can credit it! I punched his head for him, I can tell you."

Amused, Vespa said, "One of your 'pleasures' was his, eh? These country-folk regard anyone from outside the county as foreign, and guard their women-folk from such threats as city men and especially from soldiers like us. You're lucky your 'stupid dolt' didn't come after you with a pitchfork."

"The devil!" exclaimed Manderville. "You make me sound a conscienceless libertine! I'll have you know, Captain sir, that I didn't touch the wench! And besides, he was no countryman. A slippery roué, more like, and didn't deserve her." He paused, looking thoughtful.

"Paige thinks he knows the chap from somewhere," said Broderick.

"Can't remember where." Manderville shook his handsome head and said that he must be getting old. "I've met him before, I'm sure of it. Oh, well. It'll come to me. Go on, Toby. Amaze our captain with your superior achievements."

Broderick leaned forward. "I think I may have solved your puzzle, Jack. Or part of it, at least. I discovered that there's a fellow named Lord Kincraig who owns an estate some distance from

Bury St. Edmunds. It's said to be a fine property, but the old fellow travels extensively and is seldom there."

"Jolly well done!" cried Vespa. "Did you chance to learn his given name?"

"Curse me for an addlepate! I forgot to ask. The business of the two successive letters, eh?"

Vespa nodded. "Never mind. My grateful thanks to you both."

Manderville said aggrievedly, "Dash it all, Jack! I believe you already knew."

"Some. Not all. But when we put it together— Now why do you look so glum, Toby? To my mind, between us we've done splendidly."

"Yes. Well, there's just one thing, dear boy. Splendid or not, I think we'd best hope this old duck is *not* your sire. Tell him what else you turned up, Paige."

Manderville said, "His lordship is said to be touched in the upper works. Has some—er, very odd fancies. Sorry, but there it is. Did you turn up anything?"

"Yes, I rather think so. I ran into Sean Calloway in Kersey. D'you remember him? Big chap with red hair. Lieutenant. 71st Highlanders. Lost an eye at Vitoria, poor fellow. He knew of a mystery sort of absentee land-owner with an estate up here somewhere. The gentleman is said to wander about Europe collecting carpets, but he's hoping to find one in particular." He paused as his friends exchanged sombre glances. "What now?"

Manderville answered reluctantly, "Then it must be the same gentleman. Did Calloway tell you the old boy is after a *flying carpet?*" He pursed his lips. "Not very promising, Jack."

"More like a fine case of senility," said Broderick.

"Or an artful dodge," murmured Vespa. They both stared at him, and he went on: "Well, only think, if this man really is a collector, he's probably too shrewd to go about advertising what he's really seeking."

Manderville said dryly, "If he's seeking a flying carpet he'd do well not to spread that about else he'll find himself in Bedlam with not so much as a dishcloth on the floor!"

"Very probably, but it would certainly prevent charlatans from trying to foist off imitations or raise their prices when he's in the vicinity, as they would if word got out that he's after something very special."

Curious, Broderick asked, "I suppose Calloway had no more details about this 'special' rug?"

"Only one. It has a name, apparently. I knew I wouldn't remember, so I asked Sean to write it down for me." Vespa tugged a crumpled piece of paper from his pocket and passed it to his friends.

Manderville glanced at the paper and remarked that it sounded like a Polish name.

Broderick however took one look and was galvanized. "The *Khusraw* Carpet? Lord save us all! Was Calloway quite sure of the name?"

"He said his great-aunt told him, and that it had sort of stuck in his mind. Why?"

"Then it's as we feared! I'm truly sorry, Jack, but this Kincraig must be mad as a mangle!"

"Is this as bad as the flying-carpet business?"

"Practically. It's a legend almost, going back to about the sixth century."

"Gad!" exclaimed Manderville. "The rug must be of better quality than the one my grandmama bought! Hers is only about fifty years old and already showing moth fang marks!"

"The Spring Carpet of Khusraw," said Broderick, fixing him with a stern look, "is of Persian origin and was made for the palace at Ctesiphon. It was said to have been designed to represent an elaborate garden complete with ornamental waters and pathways. And it had a religious significance, in that it also rep-

93

resented Paradise. By all accounts it was exquisitely beautiful, even apart from the fact that the 'dirt' was of woven gold, the border was of emeralds to resemble grass, and all the flowers and trees and what have you growing in the garden were of precious gems."

Vespa said incredulously, "And people *walked* on this treasure?"

"I don't know about that," said Broderick. "But you're right about the treasure part. It's believed to have been the wealth of the nation, and to have made a profound impression on visiting potentates of the time."

"It would have made a profound impression on me, I can tell you!" Interested, Manderville lost his lazy drawl and asked, "How large was it? Ten by twelve inches?"

"I think it measured about eighty-some square feet."

"Good Lord!" exclaimed Vespa. "It must have been priceless! Even if Lord Kincraig found it, I shouldn't think anyone now living could afford to buy the thing!"

"Well, you're right, of course. It was seized when the Arabs defeated the Persians in the seventh century. They cut it up. The Caliph is said to have been awarded the largest piece, and after him, a few other notables. The balance was distributed among their warriors, and you may guess their shares were not large. Most of them sold their pieces, but even then they were valued at about a thousand pounds each. Fact is, we're talking about something that ceased to exist almost twelve centuries ago, Jack. If any of the segments could be traced today, which I very much doubt, they'd likely be found in museums or locked away in the vault of some sultan or princeling!"

"Why on earth would any rational man go hunting something that no longer exists?" muttered Vespa frowningly.

"Said it yourself, old lad," said Manderville, watching him with compassion. "Best give it up, Jack. Our long-lost lordling cannot be a rational man!"

Broderick shook his head and sighed. "Mad as a mangle! One thing, though. Monteil's lurking about. He's after something."

After a pause, Vespa said, "I suppose it's possible Lord Kincraig really is on the track of a remnant of the Spring Carpet?"

Manderville said, "Anything's possible, but take my advice, dear boy. Let's go home."

6

Vespa and Manderville rode out alone next morning, Broderick having left them to visit his family prior to rejoining his regiment. The host of the Inn of the Black Lamb had contributed another piece to their puzzle, and they now had the name of Lord Kincraig's estate and clear directions as to its location.

The sky was white and the air frigid but Vespa was elated because he believed his search to be almost ended. East Anglia continued to impress him with its prosperous farms, large flocks of sheep and lush paddocks where thoroughbred horses grazed. "And I'd expected to encounter only desolate miles of fen and swampland," he told Manderville. "When you think that most of this is reclaimed land, it's a real achievement, don't you think?"

"Too flat for my liking," grumbled Manderville, shivering, "and too damp. Water everywhere!"

"It's not so flat as the Low Countries. And do you notice the light?"

Not at his best early in the morning, Manderville squinted about and observed that it was usually light by nine o'clock.

"But not this light. Everything seems so crystal clear. The Kincraig estates are well-named."

"Lambent Grove," said Manderville, and added cynically, "Let's hope it will shed some lambency on the whereabouts of your elusive rug merchant, since you *must* persist in this search for disillusion."

"Hold up a minute." Vespa drew the grey to a halt and dismounted, waiting for Corporal to catch up with them.

"He'd go along better if he didn't haul that stupid doll everywhere," grunted Manderville. "You should take it away from him."

"I did. Twice. But he manages to find it. It's in no condition to give to Molly now, so he may as well keep it."

Corporal arrived, puffing around the cherished toy that was firmly gripped between his jaws, and Vespa picked him up and deposited dog and doll in the shallow basket he'd tied to the pommel. Mounting up again, he said, "You've been a great help, Paige, but d'you know, I really think I've reached the end of my search. If you were to ride fast you could likely come up with Toby and be back in London tomorrow."

Manderville looked at him obliquely. "Trying to be rid of me, Captain, sir? Well, you'll not. I promised I'd stand by you, and we Mandervilles don't break our given word."

"Even if it kills you, eh? You've been in the doldrums since we left Town, don't deny it."

"I'm concerned, I'll own." Staring fixedly at his horse's ears, Manderville said, "I don't want— That is to say— Deuce take you, Jack! If you must have it, I've a strong feeling you're galloping straight to Point Nonplus! I wish you'd forget about this quest of yours. After all, these are modern times. Nobody gives a button about who was your actual father, or whose natural son you may be. You've built an honourable name for yourself, that's all that counts."

"Thank you." Taken aback by this cavalier view of the almost fanatical emphasis the *haut ton* placed on Lineage and Family, Vespa said wryly, "I'm grateful for the vote of confidence. But— if you had a daughter whom you loved dearly, would you permit her to marry a man who doesn't know who his father might have been? Or—worse perhaps—with a name that at any moment will be disgraced past forgiveness?"

"Nobody could blame you for Sir Kendrick's misdeeds. And Britain has countless 'Fitz's' and 'bar sinisters' who've become great men despite their—er, clouded parentage."

"A nice evasion, Paige. But Lady Francesca has made it perfectly clear that I'm not presently a *bon parti* for Consuela. She's right. No man in my position could in honour propose marriage to such a—a darling girl," He paused, then said huskily, "I won't bring shame to her. I must *know,* do you see, Paige? I *must!*"

Manderville scowled at his horse's ears, and after a pause grunted, "Well—there it is. You can see the chimneys over that stand of oaks to the—"

Vespa caught his arm in a hard grip. "How do you know? By God, you've *been* here! Why in the *devil* didn't you tell me?"

"I told you I think you're disaster bound. Besides, this Kincraig may not be your man, you know, and—"

" 'Morning, gents." A wiry individual with snow-white hair but wearing green livery watched them from behind tall and delicately wrought iron gates. "Oh, it's you again, sir," he said with a nod to Manderville. " 'Fraid I can't tell you no different today. His lordship's away. As usual."

Manderville met Vespa's enraged glare. "Now I'm properly dished!" he moaned and, spurring his horse, rode back up the lane.

Restraining the impulse to follow and strangle him, Vespa said curtly, "I've an urgent message for Lord Kincraig. Is there a butler or steward in residence who can tell me where to reach him?"

The elderly gatekeeper swung one gate wide while looking

curiously after Manderville. "Aye. Mr. Barnard's up to the house. He's the butler. The young master was here yest'day, sir, but I dunno but what he's gone already."

Vespa rode through, and said, "I only hope I've come to the right house. Is this the residence of Lord Peter Kincraig?"

"Nay, sir. Our master's Christian name do be Blair. A odd sorta name, bean't it? Now the family name be Keith—what sounds more like his first name. Only it bean't. Proper contrary—backwards, says I."

Vespa scarcely heard the words. Blair! And the 'ai' repeated in 'Kincraig'! His heart leapt. Another link in the chain? Or was he building too much on coincidence? "Blair!" He realized that in his excitement he had spoken the name aloud. The gatekeeper was staring at him, doubtless thinking he was properly dicked in the nob. Glancing down, his heart gave another lurch and he flung himself from the saddle.

The gatekeeper was deathly white. His hand, shaking violently, clutched at the grey's mane.

Vespa threw an arm about the frail shoulders. "My poor fellow. You're ill!"

The old man mumbled something.

Alarmed by the fear that he had suffered some kind of seizure, Vespa dispossessed Corporal and his doll then helped the gatekeeper into the saddle and led the grey along the winding drive.

The house was quite a distance away. It was a large Elizabethan structure of handsome brown carstone, the main block rising to three storeys, with a two-storey wing jutting to the west. The roofs were high-pitched and contained a row of oriel windows; the windows on the lower floors being tall and narrow. The chimney-stacks were also tall, and elaborate. All the wood trim and the balustrade that edged the steep flight of steps leading to the front entrance were a creamy white. Noting inconsequently that the house and grounds were very well maintained, Vespa eyed that long sweep of outside steps uneasily, and he was relieved when in answer to his hail a neat, darkly clad man appeared from the west side of the house and hurried towards him.

"Your gatekeeper's been taken ill," Vespa shouted. "Are you the butler?"

"I am. Come this way if you will, sir."

Vespa followed the path leading around the west wing and discovered another single-storey wing at the rear.

With the butler's help he guided the gatekeeper from the saddle and supported him into what appeared to be the servants' hall.

The elderly man sank onto a chair. "I'm all right . . . now, thankee, sir." He watched the butler who was pouring a glass of wine. "It were just . . . the shock, Mr. Barnard. Thought fer a minute I seed a ghost."

The butler handed him the glass. "Here you are, Shubb. I thank you for bringing him up here, sir. May I ask . . . what . . ."

The polite words ceased, and, again, Vespa saw a hanging jaw, and a pair of glazed eyes that regarded him in stark disbelief.

"Might I . . . ask your name, sir?" faltered 'Mr. Barnard.'

"It is Vespa. Captain John Vespa. Perhaps I am in the wrong place. I've an urgent message for Lord Kincraig."

Butler and gatekeeper exchanged glances. Barnard regained his composure, but his voice still shook when he said, "Rest here till you feel better, Shubb. Will you step this way, Captain?"

He ushered Vespa through an inner door, past a great kitchen where maids peeped curiously, and up a flight of stairs. They entered a long corridor where parquet floors gleamed, and finely carven chests and benches were spaced about the walls. Next came a very large and luxuriously furnished saloon, and then a smaller but even more luxurious drawing room with one of the finest plastered ceilings Vespa had ever seen. Lowering his gaze, he found the butler watching him intently, and he said with an apologetic smile, "I fancy you are accustomed to rude visitors who gawk at this ceiling."

"It has been featured in several guide books, sir." Barnard gestured towards the hearth. "The painting is also much admired.

Vespa was at first struck by the fine Queen Anne fireplace. A portrait hung above the mantel, and— He stood perfectly still then, staring at the lean face, the strong nose and chin, the sensitive mouth and the wide-set hazel eyes that might be described as 'tawny.'

But for the powdered wig, it might have been a portrait of himself.

The butler's voice seemed to come from a great distance. "You see why Shubb and I were so taken aback, sir. This is a portrait of the late Robert Keith Lord Kincraig, taken in his youth. You'll be—of the family . . . ?"

Vespa stammered, "I came here . . . hoping to—"

"What the devil? Are you gone demented, Barnard? Throw this fellow out! Or I will!"

The bray of a voice cut through Vespa's confusion. The arrogant dandy he'd been obliged to knock down yesterday stamped into the room. The handsome features were not flushed this morning; the hazel eyes were clear and they were of the same unusual shade as his own. Stunned, he thought, 'Jupiter! This impudent lout may be my half-brother!'

"You caught cold at that the last time you tried it, Keith," he said.

"Captain Vespa has brought a message for his lordship, Mr. Duncan," murmured Barnard.

'Duncan Keith,' thought Vespa. 'A Scots name if ever I heard one!'

"Then it should have been left at the kitchen door! Did you not tell him my father is off at his stupid wanderings, again?

There's no excuse for having allowed him . . . into . . ." Keith, who had been staring at Vespa, broke off and turned his frowning gaze to the portrait. "What'd you say your name was?"

"It is Vespa. Where may I find his lordship?"

"Vespa . . . I've heard that name before. . . ." Comprehension brought a shout of laughter. "By God, but I have! All London is buzzing with it! What's to do, Captain? Do you seek to escape your disgraced name by claiming kinship with us? So far as I'm aware we've no Vespas on our family tree." His grin became a leer. "Not—ah, legitimately, that is! So don't fancy to fill your pockets at my father's expense, or—"

His sudden leap to the rear was much too slow. Vespa's hand was fast-gripped in his cravat, his narrowed eyes blazed into Keith's alarmed face as he said gratingly, "What gentleman in his right mind would have the least desire to claim kinship with a slug like you? I came with—"

Choking for breath, and unable to tear free from that steel grip, Keith kicked out in desperation, his foot smashing against Vespa's injured leg. Vespa swore in anguish, but despite his injuries he was in far better physical condition than Keith, who obviously drank too much and whose athletic pursuits were probably limited to Mayfair saunters and an occasional afternoon ride in the park. With a lithe sway, Vespa eluded another kick and brought his boot heel down hard on Keith's toe. Keith howled and doubled up, and Vespa shoved him violently, sending him hurtling across the room to crash into a sideboard, the impact causing a fine Limoges fruit dish to shatter on the floor.

Gripping his throbbing leg, Vespa said, "I'm sorry about the dish, Barnard."

"Damn your . . . eyes! You'll meet me for this!" gasped Keith, making no attempt to rise.

"I've more important things to do," said Vespa contemptuously.

Barnard said, "I think you're hurt, sir."

"He'll be more . . . than hurt when . . . I'm done with him," raged Keith. "Come and help me up, curse you! You work for *me,* if you remember!"

"No, do not, Barnard," said Vespa. "If you help that creature stand, I'll just have to knock him down again." Ignoring Keith's profane response, he went on, "I *must* find Lord Kincraig! I don't mean to endanger your position in this house, but, if you can help me—"

Keith dragged himself to a sitting position and said with a breathless laugh, "Tell him, Barnard! Oh, by all . . . by all means tell him where my illustrious sire may be . . . found! With luck this . . . silly clod will go seeking him!"

The butler looked from his employer's enraged heir to the slim young soldier. The resemblance was undeniable. He thought 'if only . . .' and smothering a regretful sigh, he said in his quiet way, "Lord Kincraig is at the moment believed to be—in France, sir."

"France? But—"

"But we're at war with France," jeered Keith. "And you are likely thinking no . . . no sane Briton would attempt to enter enemy territory. Quite correct! But—but you don't seek a sane man, Vespa. My sire is a lunatic who hunts a *rug,* of all things! A rug that was destroyed a millennium since! He's the laughing-stock of Europe. But, with luck, old Boney will get him!" He glared at the frowning butler. "I'll be master here then, Barnard. Bear it in mind, if you want to keep your situation! Now—ring for my man, blast you, and kick this slippery bastard off the premises! I've a splendid five-bore duck gun I'd be happy to use on a mushrooming fortune-hunter. You'd best see how fast you can run, Vespa!"

"By all means stand up," invited Vespa coldly. "I'll wait."

Keith's jaws rippled as though he ground his teeth. He snarled, "You heard me, Barnard! And tell Wickes to fetch my new Manton."

Barnard bowed and tugged at an embroidered bell-pull.

Vespa stood there, gazing down at this sullen and spoilt man, and thinking of the gallant half-brother he had loved and lost.

"If you please, sir," murmured Barnard.

"He wants thrashing," said Vespa thoughtfully.

"You'd not dare," blustered Keith.

"For my sake," pleaded Barnard *sotto voce.* "This way, Captain."

Reluctantly, Vespa accompanied him across the saloon, and offered his card. "I've likely done you a poor turn today. If Mr. Keith's hopes materialize, or if you decide on a change of scene, you must call on me."

The butler thanked him and pocketed the card. "I'd fancied a change of scene long since, Captain. But—his lordship is fond of this house."

"And you're fond of his lordship."

Barnard flushed. "I've been in the family's service most of my life. Lord Kincraig is a fine gentleman. He worries for young Mr. Keith. I promised that in his absence I'd try to preserve both the estate and—"

A tall footman hurried toward them and eyed Barnard questioningly.

"He's in the drawing room," said the butler. "He wants Wickes."

The footman nodded and looked at Vespa, curiosity coming into his eyes.

"At once!" snapped Barnard.

The footman fled.

As they walked on Vespa said, "You've done very well with the house and grounds, at least."

Barnard smiled. "Thank you, sir. My efforts in the other direction were doomed, I'm afraid. The damage was done years ago."

"Indulgence?" asked Vespa, as they started down the stairs.

"A beautiful but unscrupulous woman, sir. Lady Kincraig trapped his lordship into marriage even after he'd told her he was devoted to—someone else. I collect she thought she could change him. When she found she couldn't, she chose to think herself ill-used. She was a woman of violent and brooding temperament. Her vengeance was to make her husband's life a hell on earth, and to turn their son against his father."

Surprised by such confidences, Vespa said, "You use the past tense. I take it Lord Kincraig is a widower?"

"Her ladyship was killed in a riding accident two years ago. There had been a particularly acrimonious quarrel. The lady demanded that they return to their home in Scotland. Lord Kincraig had some business to attend to, and would not agree. He urged her to go without him, but there was no reasoning with her when she was in one of her furies. At length he told her he was sailing for Italy that night. She insisted on accompanying him. He refused, and in spite of her threat to shoot him if he attempted to leave her, he drove out. Lady Kincraig followed, still wearing her dinner gown and slippers, and riding her favourite horse: a high-strung animal. There was summer lightning that night. The horse bolted and the lady was thrown." Barnard pursed his lips. "She was killed instantly. Mr. Duncan blamed his father."

They had reached the lower floor and as they entered the servants' hall Vespa said, "One would think that Lord Kincraig might have stayed with his son."

"He did, for a while. Mr. Duncan tormented and vexed him in every possible way until his lordship forbade him this house, set him up in a London flat and gave him a most generous allowance."

"But when Kincraig is away, the charming heir returns?"

"Just so, sir. His lordship knows. In spite of everything he still has affection for the young man, and I think he worries that having his mother's excitable nature, her son will meet a similar fate. He's wild enough, certainly."

Vespa leaned back against the long table. "Duncan Keith is not a pleasant fellow to work for, eh?"

"No, sir. But I promised his lordship. Even if I had not, I've an ailing mother, and Lord Kincraig pays me very well, and allows her to live on the estate."

"I see." Vespa said thoughtfully, "You don't impress me as the man to betray your employer's secrets, Barnard. Why do you tell me all this?"

The butler met his eyes steadily. "The resemblance is so strong, sir. I don't pretend to know how, but—of a certainty you are in some way connected to this family."

"You must have some idea what is that connection."

"It is presumptuous in me to—to dare hazard a guess, Captain, but—" Barnard flushed darkly and stammered, "But—forgive, sir. I—er, I do know that his lordship, who is a very gentle person, had an—an almost ungovernable hatred of—of one particular gentleman."

"Sir Kendrick Vespa."

"Yes, Captain. But—I never heard— I mean, her ladyship was half crazed with jealousy. If she'd ever so much as suspected—"

A distant voice howled, "My *gun,* you idiot! And fast!"

Barnard said, "You must go, sir!"

"Never worry. He'd not dare shoot down an unarmed man."

"There are four other menservants in the house. And he has *her* blood. After one or two glasses of cognac, there's nothing he wouldn't dare!"

He was pale. Clearly, he believed what he said.

Vespa swore. "I *must* have some answers! Can we meet? After your work is finished tonight, perhaps?"

"It will be late, and brief, I'm afraid, Captain. But unless Mr. Keith decides to leave for Scotland today, I'll try to slip out. Where will I find you?"

"I saw a fine stand of oaks up near the road. I'll bring a closed carriage and wait there. Quickly, now, is there a painting of Lord Blair Kincraig I can see? Perhaps a miniature I might take with me?"

"Regrettably, no, sir. There was a fine portrait of his lordship, but Lady Kincraig destroyed it in one of her tantrums and he refused ever to sit for another."

"Blast! Is there some feature that would help me recognize him?"

"Not any one feature, Captain, but you've only to look in the mirror and imagine a few lines, and some grey hair at your temples." The butler's eyes brightened; he asked hopefully, "Do you really mean to try and find him?"

"Possibly. He *is* in—er, in full possession of his faculties?"

"Oh, most certainly. A trifle eccentric, perhaps, but a highly intelligent gentleman. His interest in rugs and carpets, especially antique rugs, is of long standing."

"But why would a man of intelligence allow the rumour to be spread that he's searching for a *flying* carpet? That's so nonsensical!"

Barnard glanced uneasily at the door. "I couldn't say, sir. Except that his lordship has ever been a rather solitary man, and not one to care about the opinions of others."

"Is it true that he ventures into France on his expeditions?"

"He travels all over Europe and the Near East. And always alone. He's had some very desperate encounters, I know. It worries me excessively. His life has not been happy, and sometimes I fear . . ." The butler looked troubled and left the sentence unfinished. "I believe he has no set route. He goes wherever he hears of some interesting specimen. I'm sorry, but there is *nothing more* I can—"

"Barnard? Where in *Hades* are you got to?"

The enraged howl was closer and spurred the butler into hurrying from the room, turning back at the door to whisper an impassioned plea that Vespa leave Lambent Grove at once.

Seething with frustration, Vespa yearned to wait and face down the terrible-tempered heir. But it would result in a turn-up at the very least. Common sense whispered that he was not at the top of his form, and with several menservants to back Keith, he'd likely get himself soundly trounced. Reluctantly, he abandoned the prospect of such delicious but foolish heroics. He would see Barnard tonight, and learn as much as possible about the elusive Carpet Collector. He fought against becoming overconfident, but with the help of his friends he had learned so much. 'Consuela, my darling girl,' he thought, 'we may yet stand at the altar together!'

Outside, the elderly gatekeeper was leading the grey horse up and down the drivepath. He accepted the coins Vespa handed him, and relayed the information that the captain's dog had run off and that a gentleman was in the lane, throwing his toy for him.

An unseasonable sun was shining and the air was less chill. Corporal pranced gaily to meet his master. Manderville drew back, throwing up one arm protectively. "Do not strike me! Ah! I am reprieved! How much nicer you look with that dazzling grin, Captain, sir! You must have realized why I didn't tell you about your odd relations."

"Chawbacon! They may be odd, but you're right. There can be no doubt but that my father was Lord Blair Kincraig!"

"One look at Duncan Keith should have told me that, but I didn't realize till today why I thought I'd met the fellow somewhere." Manderville mounted up. "I hope you appreciated my tact in not accompanying you. He's the roué I had to knock down after I left Stowmarket. He don't much like me."

Vespa's smile was rather grim. "I'm afraid I didn't impress him, either!"

———— ❦ ————

Lady Francesca Ottavio's 'cottage' was actually a large house set back from the lane amid venerable old trees and pleasant gar-

109

dens. It was located a short distance north of Gallery-on-Tang, the Dorsetshire village that had once been part of the estate John Vespa had inherited from his maternal grandparents. The village was a delightful sight even under the gloomy skies of a December afternoon, and when Vespa had ridden along its single street he'd been welcomed with such warmth and affection that it had been some time before he could decently break away. Now, he was alone with the little 'duchess' in her comfortable drawing room, his nerves taut as he awaited her reaction to the news he'd brought.

She looked very small and frail in the great fireside chair, but he knew better than to judge her anything but formidable. She wrung her claw-like hands absently, and gazed at Corporal who lay on the rug.

"Why do you allow that he plays with that silly doll?" she demanded. "Is not the proper toy for a boy dog."

"I bought it for Molly Hawes, but he found it, and—"

"You mean he stole it. You should have beaten him."

He said meekly, "I thought I'd leave that to you, ma'am."

She gave him a sharp look and seeing the twinkle in his eyes, advised him that he need not think to bring her around his thumb with his flirty ways, adding, "Consuela you have telling all these things?"

"No, ma'am."

"Why? It might have won you the advantages."

"And had I told her without your approval I'd have been dealt a thundering scold—and deserved it, eh, my lady?"

She smiled suddenly, and patted his knee. "You are the honourable gentleman, and with honour you play the game. What do you mean to do?"

"Are you satisfied with my— I mean, would you think me more acceptable if Lord Kincraig is my father?"

"Acceptable, is it? Ha!" She threw up her hands and demanded, "What is this choosings you now offer me? My great-grandsons they must have fine men in the family to look up to. And what shall they look up to in either a grandpapa who was a murderous black-hearted villain; or an aristocrat with the bent brain, the mad wife and the half-mad son, and who wastes the life the Good God give him by roaming about seeking flying carpets! *Le gioia e della vita!*"

Vespa reddened. "I believe that remark had to do with joy, my lady?"

"*Si.*" She said in a gentler tone, "And me I am being the cynical, which is rude. Very well, you say you love my little Consuela. If I leave this decision in your hands, you would now with happiness make the offer for her—yes?"

He frowned, then said resignedly, "No. Had I been able to question the Lambent Grove butler privately, as I'd hoped, I might have sufficient information, but Duncan Keith took a sudden whim to leave for Scotland that very afternoon. So I still lack many of the answers I need. I must find Lord Kincraig, and see for myself what kind of man he is, and whether he will acknowledge me."

"Ah! This is good and I know you would doing it. Now—you really think he is in France?"

"I think that is where I must commence my search."

She gave a derisive snort. "Madness! What have the handsome tailor's delight he say to this?"

"Manderville? Oh, he's dead set against it. Says I could never hope to find his lordship. But we traced him to Suffolk, in spite of all the gloom-merchants." His jaw set. He said a vehement, "I'll find him!"

"Jack!" Consuela hurried into the room, her eyes alight, and hands outstretched to him. She still wore her cloak, and the wind had tumbled her curls and brought roses into her cheeks.

Vespa's heart gave its customary lurch, and he sprang up and took her cold little hands eagerly.

"Oh, but I did not know you had come home," she cried,

searching his face. "You must stay to dinner, must he not, Grand-mama? Is Paige here also? What news have you?"

"Sit down and your gabbling stop," commanded the duchess testily. "And you may sit next to my granddaughter, Captain, if you will be propriety."

Consuela allowed Vespa to take her cloak. Briefly, his strong hands tightened on her shoulders. She looked up, her sparkling eyes meeting his ardent ones.

Lady Francesca snapped, "No fondlings, no fondlings!"

They sat dutifully on the sofa, side by side and a little distance apart.

"I am so anxious to know," said Consuela eagerly. "What have you discovered, Jack?"

He glanced at Lady Francesca.

"He has lost Lieutenant Paige, who have gone wandering off about his own businesses," imparted the duchess. "And he have find this man he thinks may be his sire. Who is mad."

"Oh, never say so!" Aghast, Consuela gripped her hands tightly. "Are you sure? Who is he? Where is he? Have you met him, Jack?"

"He is Lord Blair Kincraig, and I haven't met him—yet. But—"

"How can he be meeting him when this lordling is gone to France? Which proves he is mad."

Dismayed, Consuela said, "To *France?* What on earth . . . ?"

Vespa smiled at her. "He is, I believe, eccentric. Nothing more."

"Hah!" said Lady Francesca. "Only that he hunts two carpets, *bambina.* One that fly like the bird; and the other made of jewels that was cut up more than a thousand years since! Eccentric, you say? Hah!"

Intrigued, Consuela demanded the whole story and listened raptly while Vespa told her of the Spring Carpet of Khusraw, and of his visit to Lambent Grove. "Good gracious," she said, when he came to the end of his account. "Lord Kincraig does sound a—a rather odd gentleman. Whatever do you mean to do now?"

"What would you suppose?" interposed the Duchess. "Our Captain John Vespa he follow this mad father to France, which it show the madness he has inhibited!"

"Inherited, dearest," corrected Consuela. "And, of course you cannot even think of going, Jack."

Her proprietary air warmed his heart. He said, "I must, but—"

"We will *not* hold the hands," warned the duchess.

Sighing, Vespa snatched his hand back. "My apologies. And I *must* go, Consuela. Heaven only knows how long it may be before he returns to England."

"I had sooner you wait than have you go to France and be shot as a spy!"

"Very right, and we will speak no more of foolishnesses," agreed Lady Francesca. "Now, Consuela has something to tell us, that she keep the big secret. Speak up, meadowlark."

Consuela said eagerly, "Oh, yes. I have wanted to tell you, Jack. I met an—er, admirer yesterday, who—"

Vespa stiffened. "Has that confounded colonel been slithering around you again?"

"Languages!" shrilled the duchess, clapping her hands over her ears.

Vespa apologized for his lapse, and Consuela said with a trace of annoyance, "La, sir, do you fancy I have but the one admirer?"

Hastings Adair was the rival Vespa most feared and his wrath cooled a little. "I can visualize regular armies of 'em," he acknowledged. "Nor could I blame the poor fellows."

"Why 'poor'? Perhaps you think their choice is ill-considered? I'll have you know—"

"Come down from the boughs, *Signorina* Consuela Carlotta Angelica Jones! Tell me about this latest of your beaux."

She was always amused when he reeled off her complete

name, but although she smiled, there was a look at the back of her eyes that disturbed him. His unease grew while she told of the strange man who had questioned her on the estate road, and at the end a cold fear gripped him.

Horrified, the duchess exclaimed, "Foolish, *foolish* child! You should have tell me this at once! Do you knowing these mens, Captain Jack?"

He frowned. "I hope I don't, but you'll remember I spoke of the very powerful fellow who tossed Hastings Adair about when we were attacked in Town. Toby thinks their descriptions would fit a fanatical Swiss art collector named Monteil. He has a very large Chinese servant, and a decidedly ugly reputation."

"If this it is so, then these are very dangerous peoples," said the duchess, wringing her hands agitatedly. "And now they make the threats on my meadowlark? *Dio ce ni scampi e liberi!*"

"That means 'God forbid,' Jack," translated Consuela.

"Amen," he said fervently. "But our prayers would not be necessary had you not seen fit to tease them."

Consuela had been eager to share what she had found out, and she gave a gesture of exasperation. "Oh! Is that the thanks I get? If it is not typical of a man to never give a lady credit where it is due! It does not occur to you that I was all alone when they came up behind me, and yet—"

"My God, but it occurs to me! You will persist in—"

"—and yet I managed to convince them I was a villager and—"

"If you had Manning with you, child, there would not have been the need to convince them of anythings," put in the old lady, her eyes glinting with a mixture of alarm and vexation. "Ah, *San Pietro!*"

"Saint Peter was likely helping me, *Donna,* for I'd almost succeeded in sending them off in the wrong direction. If that silly Manning had not come wailing up and spoilt everything—"

The picture of what might have happened if Manning had

not come, made Vespa break out in a cold sweat. "You might have got your pretty neck wrung!" he said harshly. "I'll not have you taking such chances, Miss Independence! It is as unwise as it is improper for—"

"*You* will not?" She sprang up in a flame. "What right have you to censure me, John Wansdyke Vespa? We are not betrothed— nor ever like to be if this is how you bully and browbeat a lady!"

His own cheeks flushed, Vespa stood and faced her. "A lady does not wander unescorted about the countryside, inviting the attentions of any womanizing makebait who chances her way, as—"

"In—*inviting? Oooh!* How—"

"—as I've told you before, ma'am. No! Be still! It is one thing, and a very dear thing, for you to want to help, but quite another to deliberately make mock of a man who you admit alarmed you."

She said with a rebellious little pout, "He was insulting, and deserved a set-down!"

"And you gladly administered one, did you not? The truth is that you plunged recklessly into another of your jolly adventures." He checked. She was angry now, and she had meant well, and was so young and sweet and innocent, and he loved her so much. His tone softened. "There are men, Consuela, with whom one dares not play games! Who are far less civilized than the deadliest jungle serpents. I'd hoped you had learned that lesson."

"From whom?" she riposted furiously. "Your father? How *frightfully* disappointing for you that I am such a widgeon as to try to be of assistance! Only think, Captain, you almost offered for a girl who is as—as stupid as she is *improper!*"

"That—will—do!" Lady Francesca's voice was ice.

Feeling beset on every side, Consuela half-sobbed, "You are as—as bad as he is! You both think I am a silly child, but I am *not!* I try to help. I *have* helped, but for all the appreciation I get, I had as well not bother!"

115

"What you had as well to do is go to your room, at once, *signorina!* I do not wish to be seeing your face again this day!"

Blinded by tears, Consuela was already running for the door.

The duchess turned to Vespa, who was as pale as he had before been flushed. "You will please not to heed her, Captain Jack. When she is angry—well, you know she do not always mean what she sayings." She shrugged expressively. "She is Italian."

He took a steadying breath. "And as she said, I had no right to censure her." He sat down wearily. "But—Lord, ma'am! She's as brave as she can stare, and so fearless there's no telling what she'll do next. Hastings Adair warned me that my enquiries concerning the—the rug fancier had been noted. Heaven knows I never dreamed I would involve Consuela with a man of Monteil's stamp! I'd sooner die than put her in danger!"

"She is a proud lady, and the Swiss man he was a rudesby. But I cannot really think he would harm her only because she have chastize him."

Vespa said gravely, "It's more than that, my lady. In Town I thought they were after Adair, but now here they come, very obviously seeking Lord Kincraig. They must know I also am searching for him, and now Consuela has tried to send them off on a wild-goose chase. I've no wish to alarm you, and I hope I am borrowing trouble, but you must be aware of the business—just in case."

"I *am* alarmed! Which it is as well. We should not keep the secrets, you and I. Is best to be prepared. Perhaps I need this man you set to guard us when those bad men steal our paintings?"

"Cobham. Yes, he's a good man. I'll hire him before I leave." Vespa ran a hand through his hair distractedly. "How *can* I leave? If I'm not here to protect her, she'll run herself into danger, sure as check! Almost, I wish her wretched colonel *was* slithering about!"

"Perhaps I should take her in to Town. Better yet—take her back to Italy!" The duchess was briefly silent, pondering. Then she exclaimed, *"Mama mia!* Now have I not the fine notion to which you must give your ears! If you follow your mad lordling you will surely be caught, for you have much too fair the hair and skins to pass for a Frenchman. Me, I am Italian, and a duchess. My name, my family, they are known and respectful. My wanting for many years has been to take Consuela to meet her relations in Italy. Now, who is to notice if while travelling across France I have on my coach a footman who does not speak—or do you have the French?"

Answering her in that language, Vespa exclaimed, "By heaven, you're as reckless as she is!" Reverting to English, he declared vehemently, "If you imagine that for one instant I would allow you, or Consuela, to accompany—"

At her most regal, the duchess came to her feet and interrupted, "Again, you have overstepping yourself, Captain John Vespa! Francesca Celestina, Duchess of Ottavio, is not spoke to in such a ways! You may apologize."

Standing also, Vespa faced her and said quietly, "I have the greatest respect for you, my lady, but I think you have not considered. I am a British officer. If I should be caught, out of uniform, in enemy territory, I would be tortured and eventually shot as a spy. If I was lucky, it would be over quickly. Forgive that I must speak of such things. But if you and Consuela were in my company, you both would merit the same fate, or worse. No, pray do not tell me of the fine French gentlemen you know who would never resort to such barbarism. I also have friends in France whom I value highly. But we are at war, ma'am, and although the war seems far away to most people in England, I promise you that suspected spies, male or female, are shown no mercy by either side. *No,* Lady Francesca! You are a very dear and brave woman, but—I'll have none of it!"

The little duchess blinked up at him. "Well," she said, for once at a loss for words. "Well, now . . ."

Paige Manderville burst into the room, grinning broadly and

obviously much excited. "Excelsior!" he cried. "How d'ye do, ma'am?"

"Pray come in," she said with daunting sarcasm.

"Eh? Oh, yes, well you must forgive me, for I've grand news! I came upon one of my sergeants, Jack. He's been sent home because he lost a leg. Had blisters on his heel and if you can believe— But never mind that. Thing is, he's a wheelwright now, and he told me he worked on a large cart yesterday morning. The cart was full of *rugs!*"

Vespa stiffened and the duchess uttered an excited gasp.

Manderville said, "The owner was a cultured gentleman but clearly wits to let. He claimed to have just come back from France, which so astonished my sergeant that he asked how ever the gentleman was able to travel there in these times. The rug dealer said he's well known to be a 'collector' and everyone knows him because over the years he has brought back some fine specimens!"

"By George!" cried Vespa, his heart pounding rapidly. "Did your man know where this 'collector' is going next?"

"Apparently the gentleman likes to chat, and while he was waiting for his wheel to be repaired he said he'd intended to stay at his home in *Suffolk* for a while, but—"

"*Suffolk!*"

Manderville grinned. "Yes, dear boy! Suffolk! But he's apparently learned that a *flying carpet* has been discovered near Antwerp, so he will go there as soon as he unloads his cart. It *must* be Kincraig, don't you agree? I mean, there couldn't be *two* of 'em!"

"Not likely!" exclaimed Vespa. "What tremendous luck!" He wrung his friend's hand. "Bless you, Paige! I'm deep in your debt!"

Manderville rubbed his numbed fingers and stared at Vespa in an oddly embarrassed fashion. "No, no, my boy," he protested, his face very red. "Glad to be of assistance."

Elated, Vespa scarcely heard the mumbled words. "I'll warrant Kincraig plans to sail from East Anglia. I'll leave at once!"

"Not now, you won't," said Manderville. "There's fog rolling in. It was all I could do to find my way here."

Vespa strode to the window. The gardens were wreathed in a white blanket. He swore under his breath. "I'll have to wait till morning then. But if he's driving a laden cart to Suffolk it shouldn't be hard to come up with him before he embarks for Belgium."

"I'm going with you," declared Manderville. "Wouldn't miss it for the world!"

7

Consuela's hope that she could enjoy her misery in private was doomed. When she reached her bedchamber she found Manning sitting before the fire, replacing a button on her dressing gown. Consuela hesitated in the doorway, and then realized the woman was fast asleep. Sighing, she crept in and sat on the bed.

Why had she said such a dreadful thing? Poor darling Jack had so much to bear, and for her, of all people, to turn on him, was inexcusable. It was her horrid temper: the bane of her existence. Try as she would, she could not seem to behave in a cool, poised and dignified way, as an English lady should. On the other hand, Jack and *Nonna* gave her no credit. It was the same as when she'd followed that horrid man into the Alabaster Royal quarry in September. She'd not *meant* to be caught. She'd been trying so hard to help. Instead of which . . .

Manning's snores were getting louder. Consuela looked at her maid resentfully. She could wake her, of course, but if she did she would either be treated to another homily on the unwisdom of a young lady talking to strange gentlemen, or endure a report on the condition of Manning's corns. If she sent the woman away, Manning would at once run to Cook and wail that Miss Consuela was upset, and Cook would tell Grandmama, and there would be a fuss. She suffered a guilty pang. Manning was often tiresome, but she was also loyal and impeccably honest. She had suffered a bad head cold last week, and she really did look tired.

There was no refuge up here, it seemed. She took her warmest cloak from the press and ran lightly downstairs. The drawing room door was closed but she heard the murmur of voices. Grandmama and Jack were likely discussing her shocking want of conduct. The entrance hall was empty. From the kitchen passage came a rattle of crockery and cook's merry chatter, interspersed by deeper male tones. Watts, their elderly coachman, had probably come in for a cup of tea.

Wanting only to be alone, Consuela went outside and closed the front door quietly. It was chilly this afternoon, with mist drifting about. A fine setting, she thought, for her gloomy mood. She wandered in the garden miserably, and was startled when something struck her foot. Corporal had deposited his doll on her shoe, and sat regarding her hopefully. She bent to stroke him. He picked up the doll, pranced away, and stopped, looking back at her. She smiled and dried her tears.

"You want to go for a walk, do you?"

His little tail vibrated, and a muffled bark came from around the doll.

"Very well," said Consuela. "But it must be a short walk, my friend. I think we are to have real fog, and I dare not get into any more trouble."

She set out, glad enough of the little animal's company, and throwing the doll when it was occasionally presented for her attention.

The stricken look on Jack's dear face haunted her. She had loved him very soon after their first meeting. It had been a tempestuous meeting. She and *Nonna* had moved into the then empty manor house at Alabaster Royal, hoping to discover what her beloved father had learned there—the secret that had led to his death. Jack had arrived and surprised her, and during her struggles to escape, *Nonna* had hit him on the head with the frying pan. She smiled nostalgically. Those had been adventuresome days. Dangerous days at times, but there had been gaiety, too. And comradeship. And by the time it was all over, her heart had been given completely and irrevocably.

The fog was becoming quite thick. She had given the dog a nice long walk, but now she must turn back.

There was no sign of Corporal. She called him repeatedly, but the fog muffled her voice. And then, from somewhere nearby she heard him whine. He must have heard her, but had not come. Usually, he was very good about— There he was, foolish creature! Why was he crouching down like that? She peered at him curiously. One might think he'd been turned to stone.

A feline voice rang out nearby. An orange and white cat trod daintily towards Corporal, its tail high-held in a friendly fashion. It was a very large cat. Not too long ago Corporal had been badly frightened by a similar creature and, even as Consuela called to him, he snatched up his doll and ran away, his little legs flying.

Consuela's calls and commands were ignored. The cat, having found a playmate, joined the game merrily, its pursuit lending wings to the terrified dog.

Exasperated, Consuela tried to discourage the cat while demanding that Corporal "Come!"

Refuge appeared when least expected. A large coach, apparently abandoned, stood at the side of the Alabaster Royal road, one door wide, and the steps down. Having discovered such a familiar haven, the dog sprang up without an instant's hesitation and vanished inside.

"Oh, my *goodness!*" panted Consuela, clapping her hands at the cat. "Now see what you have done, you bad moggy!"

The cat had lost all interest in such a silly game, and sauntered away with fine feline nonchalance.

Consuela peered about. Even though the brake was probably set, the owner of the carriage must not be far off. There was no sign of a coachman, but one of the four horses had been taken from the traces. It had likely thrown a shoe or gone lame, and had been led to Young Tom, the village blacksmith. She ran quickly to the carriage. Corporal was crouched, trembling, under the seat. She reached out for him, but he shrank away. "This is not your master's coach, you silly creature," she scolded. "The cat has gone, and you must get out at once, or we'll be in disgrace. Come!"

Instead, Corporal scuttled back. With a moan of exasperation Consuela hurried up the steps and tried to catch him, but caught only the doll. She threw it into the road, urging Corporal to "fetch!" but he only whined and looked at her soulfully.

She was stunned then as a vaguely familiar voice with a French accent declared, "That blacksmith, he is a slow-witted fool. I cannot wait about. This is a good enough animal. I shall ride ahead. Dyke will bring our hack."

"You finish with people here, master?" This asked in a frightening deep growl.

"It was a sorry waste of my time! The yokels would not have refused my money had they known anything. Save that young woman. *Certainement* she knew more than she pretended. Could I but get my hands on her . . . !"

Consuela gasped with fright and prepared to jump from the coach. It was too late. Their figures were already looming up through the fog: a very tall man mounted on a fine bay horse, and his companion, incredibly broad and powerful looking, striding at the stirrup. There could be no doubt; it was the same pair who had tried to question her on Wednesday afternoon, the Swiss whom Jack thought was very dangerous and his great coachman. She shrank down, expecting to at any moment be confronted by a dead-white face and piercing black eyes, and trying to think whatever she would say to him.

Another horse came up at reckless speed, almost colliding with the Swiss who unleashed a flood of profanity at someone named Lieven who was evidently a dolt and a clumsy block.

The newcomer panted in French, "A thousand pardons, Monsieur Monteil! It is that I am told to rush, and do not expect to find you here. Ah, but you have suffered a mishap with one of your hacks?"

"A shoe it is lost, merely. The animal is now at the village smithy. When you feel so inclined no doubt you will give me your message."

"Your pardon, monsieur. It is that the Big Bertrand has word of him!"

Monteil snapped, "Where? When?"

"He was seen in Belgium some time since, and again last week, near Rennes."

"Ah! How persistent he is!" Monteil's soft laugh held a chilling edge of gloating. "A long way for an Englishman to travel alone on French soil. And dangerous in the extreme. It were a kindness for us to assist him. Especially if he has found his flying carpet."

Consuela's heart gave a jump of excitement. Then these nasty creatures *were* looking for Lord Kincraig, just as Jack had suspected!

She heard a rumble of sound that might have been amusement, and then the growling voice of the coachman:

"Fog thick very far way, Lieven?"

"No, Ti Chiu. A mile or so to the south it is still clear."

Monteil said, "Then I shall ride on to the coast and find a boat." He issued crisp instructions as to the disposition of the various horses, there was the chink of coins, and he said, *"Adieu.* With luck, we shall sail tonight."

With luck, thought Consuela, her heart beating very fast,

she would now slip out of this coach and run home to tell Jack his quarry was in Rennes and that the sinister Monsieur Monteil and his terrible Chiu coachman were hard after him. Why that should be so was baffling. Horrid as he might be, this Monteil did not sound like an idiot. And who but an idiot would really believe in such mythical objects as flying carpets? Unless . . . Might they suppose the eccentric Lord Kincraig had actually found a piece of the ancient and legendary carpet—what had Toby called it? The Spring Carpet of . . . Poonah or was it Basrah?

Someone was riding away. Monsieur Monteil, no doubt. She peeped from the window, then jerked back with a shocked gasp. Only a few feet away the messenger named Lieven had dismounted and was unbuckling his saddle girths. He was a stoop-shouldered individual with a lined face that was set into a sour expression, and he grumbled that it was very well for 'Monsieur' to commandeer his horse for the carriage. "Much he cares that it is cold and damp and I've to trudge all the way to the village in these riding boots!"

The carriage lurched. Consuela saw Ti Chiu's bulk approaching. She crept to the left side and reached for the door. This would be her best chance, before they finished poling up Lieven's horse and while they were both on the right side of the coach. The latch was very stiff. Struggling, she gave a yelp of fright as something touched her elbow.

She whipped around. Corporal had jumped onto the seat and now panted at her sociably. "Little beast," she whispered. "You frightened me half to death! No, do not dare bark! Were it not for you, we wouldn't be in this terrible pickle!" She glanced at the far window apprehensively. The two men were beyond her range of vision, but she could hear them: Lieven grumbling, and the mighty coachman offering an occasional unsympathetic grunt.

She turned back to the door handle again. Hurry! She must hurry!

A breeze came up at about eight o'clock, strengthening to a wind that began to disperse the fog until, by nine, the evening was clear. It was very cold. A three-quarter moon sailed up the sky, threw shadows on the quiet village street and turned the river to a silver thread.

Slightly more than a mile to the east the manor of Alabaster Royal, bathed in its brilliance, seemed almost a fairy-tale castle, its twin conical-topped towers standing guard majestically on either side of the entrance. Several of the windows glowed with amber candlelight, including three on the upper floor, for Vespa meant to retire early so as to be ready to leave at sunrise. He was at the moment seated at his desk, writing a note to Consuela. Manderville had stayed on at the cottage, accepting the duchess' challenge to a game of chess. Lady Francesca had refused to reprieve her granddaughter, saying it would do her good to stay quiet in her bedchamber and let her temper cool. Nor had Corporal appeared; Consuela was fond of the little dog, and had probably kept it with her for company.

His hand slowed, and he gazed dreamily at the unfinished note. Her rages were usually brief, for her nature was too sunny for her to sulk or hold anger. She was probably unhappy at this moment, bless her, regretting her hasty tongue. Or perhaps she was asleep, if her maid had left her in peace. He smiled the fond smile of lovers and, taking up his note, put it down again as rapid hoofbeats clattered over the stone bridge. If this was Paige returning, he must be foxed to gallop his prized horse, Trouble, at such a rate.

Candlestick in hand, he limped to the stairs, unease touching him now, because the clamour of the bell was accompanied by Paige shouting his name. That was no drunken outcry. Something was wrong.

Thornhill, the large and majestic major domo at Alabaster,

hurried across the entrance hall and flung the door wide. Manderville strode in, shivering with the cold and clearly agitated. "Has the master retired, Thorny?"

"No." Vespa came quickly to join him. "What's amiss?"

Manderville searched his face in an oddly desperate fashion. "Is Consuela here?"

"Of course she's not here!" A part of Vespa's mind registered the fact that Thornhill was poking up the fire in the drawing room. The implications were obvious. Trying not to panic, he said, "Come. I'll get you some brandy. You look half frozen."

"Only half?" Manderville's laugh was short and strained. Pulling off his gauntlets he crossed the big room to warm his hands at the fire.

Vespa offered a glass of cognac. He was pale now and deeply apprehensive. Marvelling at the steadiness of his hand, Manderville said, "You staff officers! You're a breed apart!" He took a mouthful of the liquor and sprawled in a chair. "God! I'd prayed she was here!"

"You're quite certain she's not at the cottage, I take it?"

"We've searched it from cellars to attic. There's not a sign of her. That wailing woman of hers had fallen asleep in her room and didn't wake until Consuela's supper tray was carried upstairs an hour ago."

'Steady! Steady! Keep your wits about you,' thought Vespa, but his voice was harsh with strain when he said, "She was upset. She likely went for a ride and stopped to call on someone."

"The hacks are all accounted for. But her new winter cloak is gone, and— The dog, by George! Has Corporal come home?"

"No. If he's missing also I expect she took him for a walk." But if that was the case, she wouldn't have stayed out after dark. Unless she had fallen . . . The spectre of the quarry rose up to haunt Vespa. She wouldn't go there, surely? Not after the nightmare they'd all lived through in those ghastly tunnels!

Watching him, Manderville said, "We've half the village out

128

searching, Jack. I made a detour at the quarry on my way here. The tunnel's still boarded up."

"Thank God!" But Vespa was plagued by a dread vision of his little love lying somewhere, alone in the dark, hurt and afraid, needing him. He turned to tug on the bellrope, but glanced up to find his small staff gathered by the door. Thornhill, the tall and majestic former actor; Harper, short, bow-legged, ex-Navy, who had come close to starving before becoming Alabaster's manservant; Peg, 'fair, fat, and forty' as she described herself, and who had led the chequered life of a barmaid before joining the household as parlourmaid; and the very stout Henri, the latest addition to the staff, who had tumbled down a steep bank while poaching two rabbits and, fully expecting to be hanged, had instead been hired upon revealing that he had once been a chef '*Par excellence!*' The back door creaked open and hurried footsteps announced the arrival of Hezekiah Strickley, formerly the caretaker and now steward/head groom. The thin, harsh-featured man looked around the gathering and asked, "What's to do, Captain?"

"Miss Consuela is lost," said Vespa. "She was at her home this afternoon, but has not been there since about four o'clock. Have any of you seen her?"

No one had seen her.

Manderville said, "Corporal was with her. Is he somewhere about?"

Heads were shaken. Corporal had not been seen either. They all looked apprehensive.

"The village people are out and looking for her," said Vespa. "It's late and it's very cold outside, but there's a bright moon and we dare not wait for daylight. You men go and dress warmly, and we'll join the search. Hezekiah, we'll need lanterns and torches."

They dispersed at once.

Vespa stood motionless, his eyes blank. Manderville gripped his shoulder. "We'll find her, old fellow. Never worry so."

"I keep thinking . . ." Vespa's hands clenched hard. "I keep

129

thinking of that rogue who tried so slyly to pry information from her—about Kincraig. If Imre Monteil has—taken her . . . !" He drew a shaking hand across his eyes.

Manderville's grip tightened. "Steady, old lad! She needs you now."

"Yes." The bowed shoulders were squared, the fair head came up. "Thank you, Paige. I'll get a pistol."

"I have brought one, sir." Thornhill paced in carrying Vespa's cloak, boots and gloves. "Hezekiah is saddling up Secrets, and Peg is preparing hot soup."

"You are all—so good," said Vespa.

Settling the cloak carefully across his shoulders, Thornhill boomed with rare brevity, "We are your people, Captain."

Manderville thought, 'And they all would die for him! He hasn't got my looks, or Toby's brains, or a great fortune. How in heaven's name does he do it?'

"You'll stay at Alabaster, if you please, Thorny," said Vespa. "I want someone here in case Miss Consuela should come. Or Corporal."

The valet looked worried. "I should be with you, sir. Peg will be here."

"Yes, but I don't want her left alone. Ready, Paige?"

Thornhill swung the front door open. "God go with you, Captain!"

Consuela whispered, *"Nonna* is likely talking to Saint Peter by now, but I am asking *you,* dear Mama. How I fall into these dreadful scrapes I do not know, but if you could contrive to bring me safe out of this one, I would truly be very grateful!"

Her attempt to escape before the carriage drove away had failed miserably. The left-hand door latch was so stiff it might as well have been nailed shut, and all she'd achieved was to break three fingernails in her attempts to open it. Desperate, she'd taken off her boot and hit the silly thing. It had been the magical solution. As if cowed, the handle had yielded easily to her next attempt. Overjoyed, she'd started to open the door, only to hear Lieven's voice, very close by, saying he thought he'd heard something. Monteil's cold words, 'Could I but get my hands on her . . .' had seemed to thunder in her ears again, and she'd hidden under the rug. A moment later the carriage had lurched and started off. Helpless, she had hugged Corporal and prayed they would stop somewhere so that she might slip out.

It had begun to get dark, but they had left the fog behind and the team had increased its pace. The steady pound of hooves and the rocking of the carriage had made her drowsy. If they'd stopped anywhere she hadn't felt it, and had been bewildered to awaken to shouts and moonlight. Peeping from the window she'd glimpsed a quay where fishing boats bobbed and sails flapped and men ran about with lanterns or wind-whipped torches. A horse had been led past, and someone had shouted, "Look sharp, mates! We'll have the Riding Officers down here 'fore the roach can run!" There had been no sign of an inn or tavern. It had dawned on her then that the coach was to be shipped. Frantic, she had wrenched the door open. Corporal had jumped out and gone scampering off, but before she could follow, the big coachman and two rough-looking seamen had come clumping up, and she'd had to swing the door shut quickly. Men were all about the coach then, chains were being lowered, and she'd had to return to her refuge under the rug lest someone should glance inside and see her.

There had been a horrible lurch, a rocking sensation, howls of "Keep clear o' the mast, you stupid block!" and "Ye be too far to starboard!" and, more terrifying than the rest: "Careful, dang yer eyes, or ye'll swing right over the side!" Flung about dizzyingly, preparing to faint, Consuela had been plunged into deeper darkness, landing with a thud that had rattled her teeth. She'd huddled under her rug, trembling, grateful to be alive, knowing

131

that the carriage was now in the hold of some large fishing boat, probably setting off on an illegal run for France.

Now was her chance! The boat must have a captain. She could appeal to him for help, and Monteil would not dare . . . But seamen laboured all about the carriage, cursing and straining to load boxes and crates and heavy objects that shook the floor. By the dim light of a lantern their faces looked dark and villainous. In her agitated state she thought they were probably all smugglers who would fear she'd report them to the authorities and be more likely to throw her overboard than to help. Peeping out, she caught sight of the great Chinese coachman, watching. And she was too afraid to move.

For an eternity the uproar had continued. Before it eased the sudden jolts had settled into a steady rising and falling motion. With a sob Consuela realized they were putting out to sea. Her chance to get away was gone. She was all alone in this beastly coach, with not even Corporal to keep her company, and she was cold and very hungry and in great need of a room with a washbowl and towel—and other amenities.

It was chill and stuffy in the hold, the only light coming from a lantern that hung swaying beside a ladder, and was too far from her to do much to alleviate the gloom. Horses were stamping and snorting somewhere. She felt utterly helpless and for once her resolute spirit was daunted. She thought of her beloved Jack, so far away, and of Grandmama and Paige, and even Manning, all worried and searching for her, as they would certainly be by this time. Whatever was to become of her? Who would protect her? If that horrid Monsieur Monteil caught sight of her he would certainly either hand her over to the authorities, or kidnap her away. 'Could I but get my hands on her . . .' She shivered. And what possible chance would she have against him and his gigantic Chinese servant?

She found that she was crying. Disgusted by such weakness she dashed her tears away with the heel of her hand. One might suppose she had never been in danger before, that she must now turn into such a weak-kneed watering pot! Only a little while ago she'd been trapped in a hideous quarry with men who were even more evil than Monsieur Monteil—at least, she hoped they were. Whatever else, she didn't think Monteil had murder in mind. So why was she snivelling?

What she must do was behave as Grandmama and Papa would have expected. She had, so *Nonna* insisted, royal blood in her veins. It was time to start living up to it! First of all, she would get out of this revolting coach. She opened the door cautiously. Ti Chiu had gone at last and there were no other men to be seen. The hold was crammed with boxes and bales, great coils of rope, large barrels and smaller tubs. There was very little space between the coach and what appeared to be an empty horse-box with steel bars comprising the walls and roof. She squeezed through the coach door, and was trying to push it shut again when a warm breeze blew on the back of her neck. Paralyzed with fright, she stood utterly still. The breeze blew at her again. She thought numbly that whoever was behind her had very nasty breath. Perhaps, if she moved quickly enough, she could elude him. He said something in a growl of a voice. It must be that giant coachman, she thought with an inner moan of despair, and how could she run when there was scarcely room to move? If she bribed the great brute, perhaps he would take pity on her.

She gathered her courage, jerked around, and came nose to nose with a very big brown bear.

She was not conscious of having screamed, nor of having moved, but somehow she was kneeling on top of a bale, a good ten feet from the cage. The light was a little brighter here and she saw the bear drop down to all fours and mutter to itself disconsolately. Even as her heartbeat began to ease to a gallop she realized that there was something else alive nearby. Strange snuffling sounds were coming from below her bale. She peered through the gloom. A small figure lay writhing about on the floor.

"Good gracious!" she exclaimed. "Are you ill?"

There came a heart-rending wail. The small figure resolved itslef into a boy. Consuela climbed from the bale and bent to offer a helping hand. He sat up and leant back against the bale, drying his tears, and moaning feebly.

"Poor boy," she said. "I'll go and fetch help."

"I never . . ." he gasped, "saw anyone move so quick . . . in all my life!"

Indignant, Consuela drew back. "You are laughing at me! Horrid creature!"

"Well, anyone would. You were so—funny." He sighed, and dabbed at his eyes again. "Why did you stay in the coach? Are you a stowaway?"

"No. I am just hiding from—from somebody."

"Who? The Excisemen?"

"From a very unpleasant person."

"Oh. I thought I heard someone crying. I 'spect it was you. Girls are always crying about something or other."

"I'm afraid it was me. I've been in that horrid carriage for hours, and—I'm so cold and hungry, and—if I could just go to a cabin and wash and tidy myself, I think I could bear it." She knew she'd sounded forlorn and added quickly, "What are you doing down here?"

"Oh, I'm hiding too." He sounded miserable. "My uncle said he had come to my school in England to take me home to Paris, but I heard him paying a man to throw me overboard."

Horrified, Consuela exclaimed, "My goodness! We must tell the captain at once!"

"I tried to, but my uncle's with him. He's very rich, now. Till I grow up."

"Is he your guardian, then?"

"Yes. He wants my fortune. I've tried to tell them, but they won't believe me. He gets whatever he wants. He's a very bad man. I'm doomed."

134

"Indeed you are not," she declared, stroking his thick hair comfortingly. "But you must have some help. You're much too young to fight him all alone."

He said staunchly, "No I'm not. I'm—er, twelve!"

He looked more like eight. His coat was well-cut, his shirt gleamingly white. Lurid as it was, his tale might very well be truth. She said, "I'll help you if I can. But—would you be brave enough to help me first?"

" 'Course I would. Come on. I'll take you to my cabin, and I'll get you something to eat." He looked at her skirts dubiously. "You'll have to climb up the ladder. Can you?"

Consuela assured him she could, and followed as he went up the rungs with the nimble ease of childhood. At the top, he pushed back the hatchway with much huffing and puffing, and peeped out.

Consuela smelled sea air, cold and fresh, and heard voices, flapping sails and ropes and the thud of the bow slicing through the waves.

The boy turned his head. "What does your nasty man look like? There's a great big fellow hanging over the rail in the stern. I thought he was a pirate, but he can't be, 'cause he's seasick. My uncle says he's Chinese."

"Is there a very tall man with him?"

"No. But there was when we came aboard. He was all black and white. I 'spect he's in his cabin. Do you want to try it now? I'll help you."

Consuela nodded, and clambered up eagerly. There were several men on the deck, but they were farther forward and not looking her way. She held up her hands and the boy steadied her until she stood beside him looking forlornly at a great expanse of dark tumbling waves.

"Quick, now," he said, and guided her through an open door into a narrow passageway lit by two hanging lanterns. He flung open another door and announced, "This is our cabin."

135

Willy-nilly, Consuela was pulled inside. The cabin was large and surprisingly comfortable, with two bunk beds against the walls, a washstand with soap and towels, and a small writing desk. There was no other occupant, but some large portmanteaux were stacked behind the door, and there were shaving articles on the washstand.

She turned to question the boy and was momentarily struck to silence as for the first time she saw him clearly. He was the most beautiful child she had ever seen, with deeply lashed green eyes, auburn curls burnished in the lamplight, a pale and clear skin and finely etched features. She thought, 'Paige must have looked like this when he was a boy.'

"I'll go and see if I can get you something to eat." He opened the door, stuck his head back in and said warningly, "You best be quick 'fore my uncle comes. He's very wicked. Especially with ladies. There's a commode under the washstand."

Consuela's face flamed.

The boy shrieked with laughter and slammed the door.

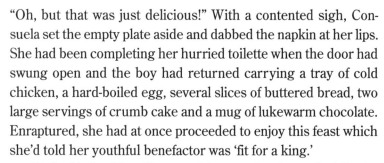

"Oh, but that was just delicious!" With a contented sigh, Consuela set the empty plate aside and dabbed the napkin at her lips. She had been completing her hurried toilette when the door had swung open and the boy had returned carrying a tray of cold chicken, a hard-boiled egg, several slices of buttered bread, two large servings of crumb cake and a mug of lukewarm chocolate. Enraptured, she had at once proceeded to enjoy this feast which she'd told her youthful benefactor was 'fit for a king.'

He had helped her dispose of the crumb cake, and while she ate had told her more of himself. His name was Pierre de Coligny. He was an only child and his life had evidently been a lonely one. At his birth his British-born Mama had extracted a promise from her husband that her son would be educated in England. He was seven years old when both parents perished in a fire and he was placed in the care of his uncle. That heartless individual had been only too willing to pack his unwanted charge off to school in England. Pierre had hoped to find friends there, but instead had been subjected to the endless beatings of the seniors, and the ridicule of the younger boys.

"Poor child," said Consuela sympathetically. "What a horrid time you have had, to be sure. But at least now you are going back to your own country."

"If ever I reach there alive," he sighed.

She put down the mug of chocolate and stood, shaking out her skirts. "I mean to make sure of that!"

"Where are you going?"

"To report this business to our captain." She clung to the end of a bunk as the vessel slid down a wave.

He stared at her. "Do you not feel sick? After eating all that, I would think you'd be green."

"Oh, no. I'm a good sailor. My father used to take me with him when he went fishing. Sometimes, it was very rough. Shall you be all right while I am gone?"

The boy stammered uneasily, "Suppose—he comes back?"

"Hide. Once I've told the captain about that wicked man, he'll never dare touch you, and if—" She paused, it occurring to her that the captain might be surprised to hear such a tale from a lady who had no ticket and was really no more than a stowaway on his vessel. Her heart jumped when somebody jerked at the door handle.

"Here he comes!" cried Pierre shrilly.

Consuela gave a gasp, looked around desperately for some kind of weapon, and snatched up a silver-handled umbrella.

The door burst open. A tall, handsome gentleman came in, taking off his hat and ducking his auburn head as he stepped over the threshold. His fine eyes widened as they fell upon Consuela, umbrella raised threateningly.

"*Qui êtes-vous, Madamoiselle?*" he demanded with a frown.

"Do not dare attack this child!" cried Consuela, swinging the umbrella higher.

Pierre screamed, "Papa!"

"What?" gasped Consuela.

The boy raced to throw himself into the newcomer's arms, shouting in French, "I found her hiding in the hold, Papa! She made me bring her here and buy her food! She is an English spy!"

8

Dawn crept in while the men were still searching. They were all tired and cold, but there was no thought of giving up hope. Vespa was scouring the wilderness area lying between his land and the preserves of Lord Alperson. He was hoarse from calling Consuela's name, and tormented by fears that grew ever more terrifying as hour after hour passed without a trace of her. Plunging into dense shrubs and copses had made riding impractical, and he'd been on his feet for most of the night, a lantern held high, his red-rimmed eyes narrowed, his ears straining to hear the faintest answer to his calls. Weariness and despair were ignored as was the steadily worsening pain in his leg. He refused Manderville's pleas that he rest, as the other men had been obliged to do. When his friend persisted, warning that he would surely collapse if he didn't at least sit down for five minutes, he swore at him, and strove on, driven by his overwhelming need to find her.

Little Signorina Consuela had come unbidden into his house, rearranged his life, and taken possession of his heart so gradually that he'd not realized for a time how much she had come to mean to him. She was not his first love; yet in a sense she was, because his love for her was so deep, so right, so much a part of him that he knew he had never really loved before. Certainly, he had never known a lady like her. He smiled yearningly, seeing in his mind's eye her sparkling blue eyes, the soft and often unruly curls, the lovely mouth that could be so wilful and proud, or so tender, the rich curves of her beautiful body. Consuela Carlotta Angelica Jones. Hot-tempered, impulsive, irrepressibly mischievous, prone to act in an outrageous fashion—and a perfect little darling, who he knew beyond question fully returned his devotion. If he lost her now . . . "Dear God!" he whispered. "Please . . . Please!"

As if in answer, Manderville came running, shouting his name excitedly, and flourishing something.

"Jack! See what we've found! See here!"

Vespa's hand shook as he took the ragged little doll. "Where?" he demanded.

"It was lying on the estate road."

"Show me!"

Together, they ran across the wilderness and through the park.

Vespa panted, "Have—have you had time to search the area where you found it?"

Also breathless, Manderville said, "I didn't find it. Your ex-Navy tar did. Sharp eyes has Harper, to have seen it with all this mist about. They'd started to search both sides of the road when I came to find you."

The light was brighter by the time they reached the spot where Harper waited. The bow-legged little man touched his brow and said eagerly, "Hezekiah's gorn over to that there spinney to have a look, but I knowed you'd want me to stay here, sir. Pure luck it was that I stepped on it. Lying right here, it were.

The dog musta been here recent, 'cause I see him carrying it yesterday."

Vespa slapped him on the back. "Good man!" He bent to peer at the ground. "There's been a coach here."

Manderville wheezed, "So there has . . . by Jove! And a heavy one at that."

"Stood here for some time, sir," said Harper. "A four-in-hand, I reckon."

"Someone rode off this way, alone." Manderville pointed towards the village.

Vespa said, "Yes. But the coach drove . . . south."

He felt icy cold and as he stood straight the world tilted and he reeled drunkenly. For a moment he lost touch with things. He heard Manderville swear, and found his friend's arm tight around him and a flask held to his lips.

"I warned you, damme if I didn't!" fumed Manderville. "Prancing about for hours on that game leg! And still not fully recovered from the pistol ball you took in September! Who the hell d'you suppose you are? Goliath?"

Vespa said brokenly, "They've got her, Paige! God help her! That miserable bastard's . . . taken her!"

"Lor' luvvus!" exclaimed Harper. "Gypsies, you reckon? Never say so, guv!"

Manderville tightened his arm about the stricken man. His own face unwontedly grim, he said, "Not gypsies, Harper. And we can't be sure it was him, Jack. But I'll go after the coach at once, and you can—"

"No!" Vespa pulled himself together. He turned to Harper. "You've done splendidly, and I know you need some sleep, but I'll ask that you first ride into the village. Go to Young Tom at the smithy and find out if he shod any coach-horses yesterday, and if he did, everything he can tell you about their owner. Come back as quickly as you can, please."

141

Harper nodded, and ran off to get his horse.

Manderville asked, "Do you mean to call off the search, now?"

Vespa shook his head. "I may very well be wrong, Paige."

"Exactly. That's why you should stay here while I—"

Vespa stopped that offer with one flashing glance.

As they started towards the manor side by side, the sun came up, painting a roseate glow on small scattered clouds.

"I understand, dear old boy," said Manderville kindly. "You mean to follow that coach yourself. I don't blame you, but have you thought this through? If you go haring off after Monteil, you'll lose Kincraig."

Vespa rounded on him fiercely. "Do you suppose anything weighs more with me than to find the lady I love?"

"No, of course not. Don't eat me! But—but this is your best chance to catch him, and I can follow the coach as well as—"

"Have done! I'll come up with Lord Kincraig after I've found Consuela."

"Be sensible, man! Look at yourself! You're properly wrung out. Most of us took a few minutes for a bowl of Peg's soup at least, but you haven't stopped once. Can't keep on like that. You'll fall over and lose the pair of 'em."

Chafing at the delay, Vespa bowed to common sense. "Very well. We'll breakfast while we wait for Harper's report. Then you can go on up to Suffolk for me."

"Devil a bit of it! I'm going *with* you! If it is Monteil and his Coachman Colossus, you'll need help."

Vespa gripped his arm briefly. "Thanks, Paige. There's one thing in our favour—the ground is so damp that the coach left a clear trail. With luck, we'll be able to follow it far enough to have an idea of their eventual destination." He scowled and muttered through gritted teeth, "Lord help that filthy swine if he's hurt her! I'll kill him!"

Watching that anguished face, Manderville did not doubt it.

Two hours later, Vespa's eyes searched the ground as he walked slowly back to where Manderville waited with the horses. "Confound that miserable bastard! He could have turned off half a mile back, or more!"

Manderville said, "They're heading for the coast, Jack."

"Small doubt of that. He means to carry her into France. But—why? What can he possibly hope to achieve by—" Vespa interrupted himself, groaning a frustrated, "Why do I waste time with such nonsensical questions? Perhaps we should just make a dash for Weymouth. It's pretty much in line from here, and we could start our enquiries there, though I dread the waste of time . . . if . . ." The words trailed off. Initially they had followed a poor thoroughfare, potholed and muddied by the rains, and not much travelled. The latter condition had helped them in their enquiries and several farmhands and a gatekeeper had recognized their description of Monteil's coach. They'd come to a busy crossroads then, and a better-maintained road. With the increase in traffic both their sources of information and the wheel tracks had disappeared.

Plagued by indecision he gazed along the road ahead. From a distant hill a farm waggon was crawling towards them. He tensed. "Paige!"

"What? I don't see—"

With an imperative gesture Vespa said sharply, "Listen!"

Straining his ears Manderville could hear only bird calls and, faint with distance, a dog barking.

Vespa walked forward, his eyes beginning to brighten. "By God!" he half-whispered. "I think— Hey!" He began to run.

Leading Secrets, baffled, Manderville followed, and then he too saw the small shape bounding past the waggon.

"*Corporal!*" shouted Vespa.

"Be damned!" exclaimed Manderville.

143

Another minute and the dog was close enough to hurl itself into Vespa's arms, writhing with joy and licking his chin frenziedly.

Hugging the little animal, Vespa looked up at his friend through blurred eyes and said brokenly, "Thank the Lord! Now we know which way to go!"

They lost no time, but having reached the coast and investigated several likely-looking coves, they had still discovered no trace of Monteil's coach. They were both very tired when they rode into the yard of a tiny cliff-top hedge-tavern to rest the horses. Manderville stumbled into the tap and called for luncheon, then had to be awoken to eat the thick coarse bread, sliced cold beef and pickles that were offered. He was dozing over a tankard of ale, and Corporal was fast asleep, when Vespa went outside, fretting against the delay.

There was a cold wind and the clouds were dark, but occasionally a ray of sunlight peeped through. 'Afternoon, already,' he thought wretchedly. The picture of Consuela forced to endure another night in Monteil's hands was like the turn of a knife under his ribs. Wandering across the cobbled yard, he sank onto a hay bale, and bowed his head in despair. Gradually, he became aware of a heated discussion nearby.

". . . wuz, Oi tells ye! Din't Oi see him, an' me Pa, too?"

"An' he were bigger'n a bull."

"Wiv a yeller face, an' no eyes."

Two of the country voices dissolved into laughter that was abruptly stilled as Vespa limped towards them. All three sprang from the fence where they'd perched. Hats were snatched off, and brows knuckled respectfully. They were youngish men, the eldest among them not over forty, their broad faces aglow with health, their eyes friendly.

"I heard you talking about a big man," said Vespa without preamble. "No—pray don't be alarmed. Which of you saw the fellow?"

144

Uneasy glances were exchanged.

Vespa lied, "The thing is, there's a reward for anyone with news of him."

"There be, zur?"

They crowded around eagerly.

"How much?"

"What's he gone and done, milor'?"

"The reward is not large, I fear." Vespa took a quick mental inventory of the funds he'd brought along. "Five guineas to the man who can tell me where he went."

"Cor!" Clad in the smock and gaiters of a farmhand, his bronzed face crowned with a shock of very blond hair, the youngest of the three exclaimed, "Five *guineas?*"

The older man, who appeared to be a fisherman, had been eyeing Vespa shrewdly. "Why?"

Clearly, to these simple folk five guineas was a vast sum even split three ways. Equally clearly, they were not sure of him. "I put it up myself," he elaborated. "My name is Captain Vespa. The big man you saw is Chinese. He works for a Swiss gentleman named Monteil. They have stolen an English lady. The lady to whom I am betrothed. I'm very afraid—" his voice cracked slightly "—I'm afraid they mean to carry her over to France."

The brief, shaken words won them over as no amount of involved explanations would have done, and provoked an outburst of shocked wrath. That a foreigner would dare to make away with an Englishwoman was as insulting as it was horrifying.

"Oi couldn't but notice as ye look proper pulled, zur," said the fisherman. "Nor Oi cannot blame ye. If ever Oi heered o' such wickedness! Oi be Ezekiel, zur. This here—" he pulled forward a small and painfully shy individual who appeared to be an ostler "—this be Ed. And the big lad wi' all the yeller hair—that's Samuel. Ye best tell the Cap'n, Ed."

Thus encouraged, Ed stammered that he had indeed seen such a strange chap. "Hugeous big, he were," he said, throwing

145

out both arms to emphasize his remark. "Nigh to seven foot tall, Oi do rackon. And broader'n Farmer Stowe's bull! Axed me summat as Oi couldn't no-wise make out. But me Pa were along o' me, an' he tells this here giant as how the other gent had rid through a hour afore."

Vespa's breath was snatched away. Then he gasped, "What other gent? Not a very tall man with black hair and dead-white skin?"

"Ar." Ed nodded.

"I see *that* 'un," the blond Samuel chimed in eagerly. "Riding of a neatish bay mare, he wuz."

"Bravo!" exclaimed Vespa, elated. "Was my lady with him? She is small and very pretty, with dark brown curls and big blue eyes and the sweetest smile anyone—" He caught himself up, feeling his face redden.

The loverlike description won sympathetic smiles. Samuel said with regret that he had seen no such lady.

"Me Pa says as the big giant fella axed fer Willy," supplied Ed, hopefully.

"That'll be Willy Leggett, zur," clarified Ezekiel.

"Willy were lying off White Cove yestiday, but—" Samuel stopped, looking scared.

His heart pounding with renewed hope, Vespa said quickly, "Never fear, I'm no Riding Officer. Mr. Leggett is a free-trader, I take it. Show me where his boat lies, and I'll make it nine guineas you can divide between you!"

———⁂———

Willy Leggett's 'fishing boat' was at the moment 'at sea.' George Leggett, his brother, conveyed that information to Ezekiel, who had accompanied Vespa and Manderville to the large quay that ran out from a cove that was as if tucked into the cliffs. Ezekiel had at first approached Leggett alone and had held an earnest dis-

146

cussion with him, during which Leggett's enigmatic gaze had shifted constantly between Vespa and Manderville, while the straw he gripped between his teeth jerked as constantly from one side of his mouth to the other.

He was a sturdy man of late middle age, his skin red and leathered from years of exposure to wind and water. At first suspicious and reluctant to talk to these strangers, he was much shocked by the tale Ezekiel told, and Vespa soon managed to win his confidence. He admitted that Willy was on a run to France, and had sailed with the previous evening's tide, bound for Brittany.

Startled, Vespa exclaimed, "Brittany! Do you know whereabouts?"

"Aye," said Leggett, retaining the straw.

"Was there a lady passenger? A very lovely young lady?"

"One or two ladies. I wouldn't 'zackly say 'lovely.' But that tall gent were aboard, and his gert hulking servant with him."

"You're quite sure the gentleman did not drive away in his coach?"

"Couldn't of. Coach went too."

Vespa glanced along the quay. Several fishing boats were tied up, and a good-sized crane was unloading bales from the hold of a merchantman.

Manderville said, "Jupiter! Your brother must have a large boat, Mr. Leggett."

A faint sly grin curved the thin lips. "Aye."

"Is she very fast?" asked Vespa anxiously. "Have I any chance of coming up with her?"

Leggett viewed him thoughtfully. "Might. The *Saucy Maid*'s heavy laden. Low in the water. Touch and go it were, whether she'd clear the sand bar. If Willy spies any Coast Guard cutters, he'll likely hide in the Islands 'fore going on."

"Which would give me a chance to catch up?"

"Might. If you wasn't 'bliged to hide as well. Either way, ye'd be needing a fast boat, sir."

"Only tell me where to find one!"

Leggett took the straw from his mouth and considered it. Once again his keen gaze flashed from Vespa to Manderville. "Both on ye?"

Manderville said quickly, "Both of us."

Turning to him, Vespa argued "Paige, this will be enemy territory. I'll not ask you to—"

"Both of us," reiterated Manderville.

Vespa clapped him on the back gratefully. "I must send off a letter to the duchess at once. And then—what d'you say Mr. Leggett?"

"Enemy territ'ry, right enough," said Leggett. "Risky. But if this here Frenchy stole your lady, Cap'n—well, we can't have that now, can we?" With an almost-grin he replaced his straw and started to stroll along the quay. "Foller me, gents, and meet my *Lively Lace,* the fastest yawl on this or any other water!"

The *Lively Lace* was fast, all right. Clinging to the rail near the aft mizzenmast and watching her mainsail and two jibs crack in the wind, it seemed to Vespa that the yawl fairly flew, her bow throwing up billowing clouds of spray as it sliced the waves.

George Leggett had been quite willing to convey them to the port on the Brittany coast where his brother would hopefully have dropped anchor. The fee was surprisingly low. George had said with a twinkle that since he'd not be carrying any contraband for once, if a Revenue cutter did challenge him, he could claim that he was simply ferrying passengers to the Channel Islands. "Put their noses proper out of joint, it will," he'd chuckled, as he showed them to the small cabin below decks. There were bunks in the cabin, and within minutes two were occupied. Vespa had slept for almost seven hours, awakening to the familiar pitch and roll of a ship and the heavenly aroma of frying ham that wafted from the tiny galley. A wash and shave and a hasty meal, then, leaving Manderville still sleeping like one dead, he'd come up on deck feeling a new man.

A bright moon escaped the clouds from time to time and was reflected on the endless expanse of heaving waters. The cold air blew salt spray in his face. He thought yearningly, 'I'm coming to you, my love. God keep you. I'll find you soon.' Leggett, at the wheel, had watched his approach approvingly and called that the captain had his 'sea legs' all right.

Vespa crossed to his side and shouted, "I've done my share of sailing. Can we hope to reach France tonight?"

"If this wind holds, sir, I'll have you in Brittany by dawn—give or take sunrise."

Vespa nodded and returned to the rail. Time passed, and he was joined by the tall yellow-haired Samuel, who Leggett had explained sometimes sailed as 'crew.' Samuel offered an oilskin coat with the warning that Cap'n Vespa would get 'soaked through' without it, because it looked like 'weather' was blowing up.

He was right. Within an hour, Leggett and Samuel were struggling to shorten sail while Vespa took the wheel. Manderville came reeling up, shouted something unintelligible, lost his balance and shot across the deck. Vespa gave a horrified yell, secured the wheel and ran. Manderville was hurled over the rail but somehow managed to clutch it. He hung on for dear life while Vespa dragged him back onto the deck.

Bracing himself, Vespa gasped out, "Devil of a time . . . for a swim, Paige."

Manderville clung to him and groaned, "What . . . I don't risk . . . in the name of . . ."

"Of—what?"

"Of—er, friendship, of course. And—curse you, you've torn my—new coat!"

"Ingrate," panted Vespa, staggering back to the wheel. "D'you want a turn at this?"

"Certainly not! I'm a soldier—not a damned merman! When dare we hope to reach—to reach dry land again?"

"Dawn—so Leggett says, if this wind keeps up."

"Wind? I thought it was a hurricane!"

Hurricane or not, when the pale fingers of dawn streaked the eastern clouds the *Lively Lace* was following the Normandy coast-line towards Brittany, just as George Leggett had promised. Vespa had seen several distant lighthouse beacons, but not so much as a glimpse of a Revenue cutter. The seas were treacherous here; great plumes of spray boiled up around offshore rocks, and the dark water surged in swift and deadly currents that only a skilled mariner could hope to navigate.

The wind having dropped, Manderville risked another climb to the deck. One glance at lowering skies, heaving seas and a great mass of black granite that suddenly reared up beside the bow, and he flung a hand over his eyes and retreated, moaning.

For Vespa it had been a night of backbreaking effort, but the battle against the elements, bruising as it was, had given him the chance to put aside, for the moment, his crushing anxieties, and he had the satisfaction of knowing his health was steadily improving and that he'd managed to be of real assistance.

Peering at the looming ridges of Brittany, he stood at the wheel beside Leggett, and asked, "Are you sure of your brother's destination? That coastline ahead looks very wild. I never saw so many coves and inlets, and each guarded by offshore rocks. Might he not choose an easier route?"

"He got no choice, Cap'n. With that there coach to off-load, he'll need a port with a crane, but he's got to take care. The French navy don't amount to much since our Nelson met up with 'em, but they got a few ships of the line and some Customs cutters, and Willy being English they'd be main glad to send him to Davy Jones' Locker!"

"I haven't seen much in the way of towns. This area's pretty sparsely populated, isn't it? Would it be worthwhile for French naval ships to patrol here?"

"Not in a reg'lar way, sir. But the more lonely it is, the more chance for free-traders and such to slip in and out." He shouted suddenly, "Hi! Sam! We're going in! Shorten sail!"

The yawl slowed, and turned landward. For some minutes Vespa had heard a dull roaring, and now, looking ahead, he caught his breath. Here again, the coastline was guarded by clusters of rocks like so many jagged teeth snarling against shipping, the waves thundering and foaming around them. "Good Lord!" he muttered.

Leggett's hands were strong on the wheel, his keen eyes fixed on the tumultuous seas. "If it weren't for that there dratted coach . . ." he muttered.

The *Lively Lace* began to buck and leap like a fractious horse. Vespa clung to the rail and marvelled at the skill of these men who could pick their way through such treacherous currents. Black-green water hove up along the side, then suddenly fell away; the roar was deafening, and for a heart-stopping few seconds the deck seemed to drop from under his feet and he was sure they were going down. A moment later the yawl drifted easily on a surface with scarcely a ripple.

Leggett shouted, "Good for you, Cap'n! Ain't many land-lubbers could keep their nerves steady through that. This is where I put you off."

"Here?" There was nothing in sight but a deserted beach backed by low, barren-looking cliffs. "I cannot see the *Saucy Maid* or any other shipping. Where are we?"

"As close as I can bring ye to Brittany, sir. Sam'll row you and Mr. Manderville ashore and set ye down on the beach. You see that headland, yonder? Go 'round that, and you'll find the fishing port. It's called La Emeraude, what means emerald, on account of when the sun shines on 'em, the rocks and the sea looks green.

151

Not today, they don't. But there's times they does. They got a nice deep harbour and a crane." He winked. "Cater to The Gentlemen, they do."

"Free-traders, you mean."

"Aye. Them. Likely, Willy will be already tied up and offloading. He's knowed here, and he's got plenty of Frenchies aboard what had no business going to England, any more than you got going to France. More'n I dare do to sail in right under their noses with two Englishmen aboard, and one of 'em a army captain! You take care, sir, and don't speak nought but French. It ain't exactly what they speak here, but better they should think you French than British. Been a pleasure having you on the *Lively Lace*. Good luck finding your lady!"

"Thank you. You'll be sure to send my letters off, and keep my dog safe till I return or my people call for him?"

Leggett gave his solemn promise to do as asked. Manderville came up in response to Vespa's hail, and having shaken hands with Leggett, they climbed into the dinghy and were rowed ashore.

"How do we get home, once we find Consuela?" asked Manderville, eyeing the departing dinghy uneasily.

"We'll arrange that with brother Willy."

"If he hasn't already sailed."

Vespa didn't respond. His thoughts were all on finding Consuela and settling accounts with Monsieur Imre Monteil.

The sun was up now, but concealed by a grey overcast. The air was dank but not as cold as it had been in Dorsetshire. They were both wearing riding boots which made the long walk tiresome. Manderville said morosely that he didn't believe there was a port at all, but Vespa's faith in Leggett was justified when they rounded the headland and a little forest of masts came into view. A moment later they saw the port. It was not much more than a village; some clusters of pale granite houses and on the outskirts quite a number of whitewashed cottages set well apart from each other, their steep thatched roofs and the unfamiliar shapes of the chimneys appearing alien to British eyes. On a nearby hill a church spire rose among sparse trees. There were few people on the cobbled street; an old lady wearing severe black except for the tall and snowy lace cap on her head carried a covered jug to a nearby house; three small boys were running down towards the quay, where Vespa's searching gaze had discovered several fishing boats and men already at work repairing nets.

Manderville muttered, "Don't see no *Saucy Maid,* do—"

"The crane. See—there!"

And there she was, a large two-masted vessel, with some half-dozen passengers gathering their luggage on the deck, and four or five children watching in great excitement as a fine travelling carriage was hoisted from the hold. Observing this procedure critically was a tall, elegant gentleman with jet-black hair and very pale skin.

"Hi!" cried Manderville. "Jack! Hold up, you lamebrain!"

He was too late.

With an inarticulate growl of rage Vespa was already sprinting up the gangway to the deck of Willy Leggett's *Saucy Maid.* In another instant an astonished Swiss gentleman was whirled around, an enraged young face glared at him murderously, a strong hand was ruining his perfectly arranged neckcloth, and a very British voice was snarling a demand to know what he had done with 'her.'

Unaccustomed to such treatment and considerably off-stride, Imre Monteil gasped a bewildered, "With—who?"

"You know who, you murdering bastard," raged Vespa, tightening his grip on the neckcloth. "Tell me, or so help me God, I'll—"

"*Jack!*"

However shrill, there was no mistaking that beloved voice. Vespa's heart leapt and he jerked around, whispering a prayerful, "Consuela!"

Her face aglow with joy, she rushed to him.

Monteil, half throttled, gasped, "Let . . . me . . . go, you curst imbecile!"

"So you *did* take her! Damn your eyes!"

Vespa's deadly right was brought into play and Monsieur Monteil ceased to complain.

Ignoring the resultant uproar, Vespa crushed Consuela to him and with his cheek against her silky curls half-sobbed, "Thank God! Thank God! My little love!" He held her away, scanning her frantically. "Did he hurt you? Did he dare to touch you?"

"No." Her radiant eyes searched his face. "I am perfectly all right. Oh, my dear, how ever did you find me? How worn you look! I must tell you that—"

His overwhelming relief turned perversely to anger. He shook her, and snarled, "If *ever* you deserved a good spanking! Wandering off alone again! Frightening us to death! After I'd *told* you—"

They were wrenched apart.

"Ma foi, but this one is of a violence!" cried a Gallic voice.

Two of the deck hands who'd been working with the crane gripped Vespa's arms, and told him in an odd French dialect that he was fortunate Monsieur's servant was a victim of *mal-de-mer* else he would assuredly by this time be very dead.

Manderville ran up beside a stocky young man who bore a strong resemblance to George Leggett. Several of the male passengers gathered around, ladies were shrill in their condemnation of such bestial behaviour, various saints were called upon for protection and the air rang with questions and expostulations.

Leggett waved his arms about and spoke loudly in the language that sounded like a mixture of French and Gaelic. It was hard to follow, but Vespa identified enough words to realize that the onlookers were being informed this was a simple case of mistaken identity, and that no great harm had been done.

The two deck hands released their prisoner reluctantly.

"This wild one he is *sans doute* from Paris," declared one.

His companion nodded scornfully. "There, they all are mad."

Vespa slipped his arm about Consuela's waist again. "I suppose you would be overjoyed if your lady was stolen," he said in French.

They stared at him, obviously taken aback.

The small curious crowd that had gathered began to disperse, and the deck hands carried the awakening Monsieur Monteil off—presumably to his cabin.

Willy Leggett said in low-voiced English, "They was right, sir. Your friend tells me as you sailed here with George. I can't hardly blame you for cutting up rough if he stole your lady, but you'd be wise to stay least in sight for a while. If I knows Monsieur Monteil, he'll be out for blood! Was you wanting to make the return voyage on the *Saucy Maid?*"

"Yes," said Vespa emphatically.

"No," said Consuela, even more emphatically.

Someone shouted urgently for Willy.

"You people best get below," he said. "And make up yer mind, sir. I don't stay hereabouts a second longer'n I must. The *Saucy Maid* sails with the tide."

He hurried away, Manderville following and enquiring uneasily as to the likelihood of interference by French port authorities.

"No, we cannot go," said Consuela, tugging at Vespa's arm and leading him into a narrow passageway. "Do come quickly. Oh, I wish you had not struck that horrid Swiss man!"

"I should have wrung his scrawny neck," he growled. "You're of an extraordinarily forgiving nature, Consuela."

"There is nought to forgive. Monsieur Monteil never touched me. He didn't even know I was on board." She flung open a cabin door. "This gentleman has been taking care of me."

Bewildered by her revelations, Vespa was more bewildered to face a steadily aimed pistol in the hand of a tall and distinguished individual.

"*You!*" he gasped.

"*Mon Dieu!*" exclaimed de Coligny, recoiling.

"Shoot him! *Shoot* him, Papa!" urged Pierre, jumping up and down in excitement as he rushed into the cabin. "He is English! I heard him when he knocked down that funny black and white man. He called him a murdering bas—"

Consuela clapped a hand across his mouth.

"Well, he did!" squealed Pierre, wriggling free. "He is a *spy,* Papa! Just like her! I told you—"

"You will cease to tell me," said de Coligny in a no-nonsense voice that silenced his son. He reached out. "My dear fellow!"

The two men exchanged a firm handshake, and de Coligny gestured to Pierre to close the cabin door.

"You are—acquainted?" asked Consuela, sitting on a bunk beside Vespa. "But—Monsieur Gaston, you never said you knew my betrothed!"

The Frenchman put the pistol aside and said with a twinkle, "It is, you might say, a passing acquaintanceship. Besides, Miss Jones, you did not tell me his name."

"I never thought my Papa would cry friends with a perfid'us Englishman," grumbled Pierre, disappointed.

"He is *not* perfidious!" protested Consuela.

"I believe that is from Napoleon Bonaparte's name for us," said Vespa. "Perfidious Albion." He glanced at the Frenchman's left hand, immobile and encased in a leather glove. "So you lost your hand, after all. Were you then exchanged?"

De Coligny nodded. "I was sent home. Did your shoulder necessitate your own separation from the army?"

"It was a—contributing factor."

"Ah—you fought together," said Consuela, the light dawning.

"But on opposite sides," qualified Vespa.

Pierre was sitting on the floor watching sulkily, but at this he sprang up, exclaiming, "Now I know, Papa! This is the British officer you told me of! The man who shot you!"

"Fair exchange, rather." Vespa turned to Consuela. "The Chevalier de Coligny was with D'Erlon at Vitoria. We encountered each other on the field, and were unhorsed by the same shell. Only one hack survived and, in the struggle to capture it, each of us was wounded."

De Coligny explained. "My shot took Jacques in the shoulder."

"And he shot off your hand," cried Pierre, scowling at Vespa.

"Not quite," said his father with a smile for that fierce resentment. "Although he was himself hurt, Captain Vespa was so good as to apply a tourniquet to my wrist. Else, my son, I should not be here now. Unhappily, the infection it set in." He shrugged fatalistically. *"C'est la vie.* And I am fortunate. I have not to earn my living, and with the help of my family and my good servants, I contrive. I am only glad, *mon capitaine,* that I was not responsible for your demise, for I had heard it that you were killed."

"Wars!" said Consuela, who could picture the battlefield scene all too well. "How utterly stupid they are. If women ran the world we would outlaw the silly things!"

"Perhaps, someday, you will," said de Coligny.

"In the meantime," said Vespa, still holding Consuela's hand tightly, "Will somebody be so kind as to tell me how it comes about that my lady seems to be—ah, travelling under your protection?"

Simultaneously:

Consuela said, "I was trapped in that horrid Swiss man's coach!"

Pierre said, *"I* found her, hiding with a bear!"

The Chevalier de Coligny said, "The lady slept in my cabin!"

"Did she, indeed?" Vespa seized on the final incomprehensibility. "I think you must explain that, monsieur!"

157

"Certainement, I must!" agreed de Coligny hurriedly. "But I pray you will not look upon me with such ferocity, *mon cher Jacques."*

"He is very ferocious," put in Pierre. "And he is an English spy also, Papa. What are you going to do with him?"

The two men looked at each other.

"Ah," murmured de Coligny. "Now that is the question."

9

The chevalier, who had begun to look grave, was much relieved when Vespa assured him that he was in Brittany only to retrieve his lady. Consuela told her tale with typical Latin drama. Vespa paled when she spoke of her "flight through the air" as the coach was loaded into the hold of the fishing boat, but was won to laughter by Pierre's exuberant description of her encounter with the bear. "So it is Pierre who has rescued your Miss Consuela," the boy boasted proudly.

"And it is Pierre to whom I am very deeply indebted," said Vespa, bowing to him.

"Such a terrifying experience for a gentle lady," murmured the chevalier, who was still not a little shocked by such behaviour. "I am very sure my dear wife would have swooned away."

Consuela stared at him. "She would? But it was a great adventure. Though, I'll admit I was a little bit afraid. Just now and then, you know. And I am very glad that Jack has come and everything turned out so nicely."

"Oh, are you?" said Vespa, feigning indignation. "I take it that you care not a button that I have knocked down an innocent gentleman!"

"Not the tiniest button," agreed Consuela, her eyes sparkling at him.

"And I must question the innocence of that particular gentleman," said de Coligny. "He has the reputation most unsavoury."

"Yes, indeed." Having kept her most exciting piece of news to the end, Consuela said, "And now you must listen closely, Jack, for I have learned something of the greatest importance, that you will be very happy to know."

He smiled at her tenderly. "I can think of nothing so important as to know that you are safe, my little Signorina."

For a moment there was silence as they exchanged glances that betrayed their love with more eloquence than mere words could have done.

Amused, the chevalier coughed politely behind his hand.

Vespa started and flushed with embarrassment.

Consuela said, "Oh, dear! Now what was I saying?"

"It cannot have been so very important if you've already forgot," said Pierre, bored, and went out onto the deck.

"But it is!" said Consuela. "Jack—Lord Kincraig is *here!* In Brittany! That's why Imre Monteil came. He means to find him!"

"What?" He said incredulously, "But are you quite sure? Manderville heard that he was gone to Suffolk."

"No, no! I was hiding in the coach when the messenger brought the news to Monteil! He said the 'Crazy Carpet Collector' had been near Rennes last week, and Monteil was very pleased! Isn't it wonderful that we've found him?"

"That *you've* found him, clever girl! And it's wonderful indeed, if—"

"So here you are!" Paige Manderville stepped into the cabin and closed the door quickly.

"Yes." Vespa stood, his mind a whirl of excitement and new hope. "Has Imre Monteil reported us to the authorities?"

"Don't think he found any to report to! He seems to think you've gone inland, and the silly clunch has taken his monstrous coachman and gone haring off after you. Jolly good luck to him! I've arranged with Willy Leggett for our passage home. I fancy you'll want to go ashore, de Coligny?"

The chevalier confirmed this, and Vespa also declared his intention of going ashore.

"Consuela has been telling me how she came to be in Monteil's coach," he explained, responding to his friend's astounded expression.

"The man is a scoundrel, no doubt of it," said Manderville. "But to follow and demand satisfaction would be the height of folly, dear old boy."

"I've no least intention of doing either. Though, I suppose he is entitled to a meeting. I did knock him down, after all."

"Stuff! You'd every right to knock him down. But if you don't mean to follow the villain, why do you wish to go ashore? Ain't much of a place, so far as I can see. No offence intended, de Coligny, but there's not much here outside of granite and sand and a lighthouse every few miles."

"There will be," declared the chevalier. "We've plans to improve roads and transportation and to plant crops to enrich the soil. Soon, this will be a grand agricultural centre."

"And besides, I found out that Lord Kincraig is here," put in Consuela. "Isn't it marvellous?"

Manderville gave a snort of derision. "Marvellous fustian! What on earth gave you that notion? Kincraig is in Suffolk—and likely even now preparing to hop over to Belgium. Someone's been filling your ears with treacle, Consuela."

"No such thing!" she argued fiercely. "I heard a courier tell Imre Monteil that the 'Crazy Carpet Man' is in the vicinity of Rennes! It is *your* informant who is wrong, Paige Manderville!"

"In which case," said Vespa, "we're closer than we've ever been, and I mean to lose no time in—"

"In—what? Running your head straight under the nearest guillotine? You're as bacon-brained as he is!" Exasperated, Manderville declared, "I tell you, Jack, Kincraig's nowhere near Rennes!"

Vespa said dubiously, "I suppose Monteil's man could have erred."

De Coligny said in his courteous fashion, "Forgive that I interfere, but may I know why you would wish to find this poor mad gentleman?"

Consuela and Manderville both looked to Vespa and were silent. He improvised quickly. "It is a family thing, Gaston. My mother believes this carpet collector may be her long-missing cousin, and she has charged me to find him."

"Ah," de Coligny nodded sympathetically. "It is a sad task, that. I cannot help, for I know very little of him. From what I have heard of Imre Monteil, his people would not dare to bring him false reports. But Lieutenant Manderville speaks truly, Jacques. Even had you the means, to venture into France would be to write your death-warrant."

"That does not appear to weigh with Lord Kincraig," said Vespa.

"No—because he is, you will forgive, demented, and knowing this, people do not pay him heed. With you, it would be otherwise. And of a certainty you must take Miss Consuela out of harm's way."

"Paige will escort her home for me, won't you?" said Vespa, turning to his friend.

"We both will take the lady home," argued Manderville stubbornly.

"You will do no such thing," said Consuela, her little chin setting. "Whatever you say, Jack, I know what you mean to do, and I am not going to be packed off home to worry myself into a decline while you rush out and get yourself slain! No, and no!"

His heart warmed by this declaration, Vespa said fondly, "You are very dear, but you must see that I can't drag you about all over France, with not the whisper of a chaperone. Even if your lovely head were not forfeit, your reputation assuredly would be."

"Look about you, Captain John," she commanded. "Where are the crowds? The leaders of the *ton?* The gabsters and gossips and rumour-mongers? Who will know I am here? Rennes is not very far away, and you certainly do not mean to journey through France wearing a scarlet uniform—"

"Blue," corrected Manderville absently.

Consuela swept on, "—you will go in some sort of disguise, no? And I shall be your sister—or your affianced, or the Lady Consuela of Ottavio, whom you escort to the duchess, her Grandmama, and who would be an asset, rather than—"

Someone pounded on the door and bellowed, "All ashore what's goin' ashore!"

Vespa led Consuela to the door saying in a lowered voice, "My little love it will not serve. I have no coach, and may have to ride on a donkey if I can hire one, or travel many miles afoot. To be always responsible for your precious self would be a constant worry at a time I'll need to keep my wits about me. You must allow Paige to take you home so that I can know you'll be safe."

" 'Fraid not," said Manderville. "If you go, Jack, I'm going with you."

Consuela clapped her hands and did a little jig of delight.

Dismayed, Vespa said, "But I can't let her go back to England alone! That would really cause an uproar!"

"I agree. So abandon this foolish plan and you'll find I am in the right of it."

"It is *not* a foolish plan! Don't listen to him, Jack," said Consuela. "We will journey to Rennes, you and I, and find your carpet collector!"

Vespa shook his head. "Whatever the case, your safety must be my first consideration," he said firmly. "I'll take you back to your Grandmama, and then come—"

She gave a wail of mortification, and said she had been so eager to tell him her wonderful news and now that horrid Paige Manderville had spoiled everything.

Manderville looked aghast and hurried off to advise Leggett the decision had been made.

Pierre came back and with a disgusted look at Consuela said, "What? Crying again? What watering pots you ladies are!"

The chevalier told his son to apologize at once, and then sent the boy off to call their coachman to come and get the luggage.

The next few minutes were not pleasant for either of the remaining gentlemen. Consuela wept bitterly and lamented between sobs that she was now the cause of Jack losing Lord Kincraig. Vespa's attempts to comfort her were to no avail, and he could not have been more relieved when de Coligny's coachman and footman arrived to collect the portmanteaux.

The chevalier murmured excusingly, "She has endured much, the little lady."

"She has indeed. There's no end to her courage and resourcefulness, but I fear she is quite exhausted. It is as well she'll be able to rest on the return passage." Vespa took Consuela's arm. "Come, my signorina. I'll see what Leggett has arranged for your cabin, and you can say adieu to your new friends."

The wind was rising when they went on deck. Consuela clung sadly to Vespa's arm, but thanked the chevalier for all his kindness to her, and waved goodbye to Pierre, who had followed the bear's cage onto the quay and was leaping about "as though," said his amused sire, "he went on springs!"

Shaking de Coligny's hand, Vespa said, "I shall never be

able to thank you for taking such good care of her, Gaston. If ever—"

He was interrupted by Consuela's shriek. A chorus of shouts went up, interspersed by squeals and screams and a frenzied scattering of those on the quay.

Consuela squeaked, "Pierre has let that terrible bear out of its cage!"

"*Mon Dieu!*" gasped the chevalier, and ran for the gangplank.

"Oh, heavens!" exclaimed Consuela. "Pierre thinks he can play with the creature!" Vespa was already limping rapidly after de Coligny, and she called, "Jack—do be careful!"

Willy Leggett roared a frustrated, "I ain't a'waiting, Captain Vespa! If we're to catch the tide we must leave—*now!*"

Vespa scarcely heard him; his entire concentration was on the distraught father who, in an effort not to further alarm the bear, was now walking smoothly towards his son.

Pierre was prancing about in great excitement and advising the bear to "cut and run" while he had the chance. Misunderstanding, the bear reared up onto its hind legs. Beside the small figure of the child, the animal appeared enormous.

De Coligny drew his pistol and aimed it.

A shabby looking little man raced up and sprang in front of the chevalier. "What do you intend for my beast?" he demanded with wrathful indignation. "Your child, he release my poor Étudiant with much malice, and in return you seek to destroy the dear soul! My very livelihood! Such wickedness!"

Scanning the bear, who stood at least six feet tall, Vespa thought he had seldom seen a less promising 'student.'

De Coligny said, "If that brute touches my son . . . !"

The little man called, "Come to Papa, Étudiant, my dear. We will not suffer these evil men to harm you. Come!"

The bear snorted and snuffled and threw its head about a few times, then dropped to all fours and ambled to its master, the long nose searching out a likely pocket. Something was withdrawn from the pocket and deposited into a front paw, that was, Vespa noted, well equipped with very long claws. 'Papa' said with some embarrassment, "He likes the currant buns. It is that he have only four teeth, you know."

The chevalier snatched up his son, and snarled something that abruptly dampened the child's exuberance.

Recalled to his own interests, Vespa glanced to the *Saucy Maid.*

She was moving!

"Oh, Lord!" he groaned, and rushing to the edge of the quay made a desperate leap for the vessel. He landed safely, but was unable to hold his balance on the rolling deck and fell to his knees.

In his ears was a beloved voice, shrieking his name.

From the quay!

He clambered to his feet. Consuela, looking far from exhausted, stood beside the chevalier, waving frantically.

Snarling English, French and Spanish curses, Vespa ran back a few yards and again launched himself across the widening band of dark water.

He landed hard, wrenching his damaged leg painfully, which did not improve his temper. Some people who had recovered from their terror of the toothless and now-leashed Étudiant set up a cheer.

De Coligny steadied Vespa while imploring him to exercise some self-control.

Impressed by the Englishman's athletics, Pierre was applauding even as tears of mirth glinted in his eyes. "These English, they move from one place to another very swiftly, Papa," he chortled.

Consuela's mischievous face peeped from behind the chevalier. "I am truly sorry, dear Jack," she pleaded, with not a tear in sight and her eyes alight with laughter.

"Yes, I can see you are," panted Vespa, scarlet with embarrassment and momentarily forgetting how he had grieved and worried for his exasperating love.

"Jack!" Running along the deck to the stern of the *Saucy Maid,* Paige Manderville howled, "What the *devil* are you doing over there?"

"Sorry, Paige," shouted Vespa breathlessly. "But— *No!* You maniac! It's too far!"

It was. Manderville jumped, notwithstanding.

Fortunately, he was a good swimmer.

Ignoring the hilarious onlookers, and Pierre, who had crumpled to the ground and was rolling about, convulsed, Vespa rushed to assist Manderville onto the quay. Such selfless devotion was astounding, and gazing in awe at his gallant but drenched comrade, Vespa said, "My dear fellow! How very good of you! But—oh, egad! Your new coat!"

Manderville dashed salt water from his eyes and peered down at the disaster. "My . . . new . . . coat!" he wailed through chattering teeth.

Vespa took off his cloak and wrapped it about the swimmer. "I must get you out of this wind, before you catch the pneumonia."

De Coligny waved imperatively, and a small carriage drawn by four ill-matched horses was driven to them.

A liveried footman opened the door. Pierre clambered onto the box beside the coachman, and de Coligny ushered Consuela, Manderville and Vespa up the steps, then climbed in to sit beside Vespa. "Shall you wait for the next boat?" he enquired, as the footman closed the door.

Consuela, who was chafing Manderville's icy hands, said, "No! Jack, I will *not* have you lose this chance to find Lord Kincraig, only so as to escort me home! Besides, with that horrid Monsieur Monteil after him the gentleman is in great danger, and must be warned! You cannot turn your back on a kinsman! We are *here!*"

"Y-yes. And dash it all, C-Consuela, we shouldn't b-be!" complained Manderville. "Use your—your wits, Jack! The people on the quay know we're British! We'll be l-lucky to get away from here alive, l-let alone go farther inland!"

Troubled, Vespa turned to de Coligny. "Have I already put you at risk, Gaston?"

The chevalier shrugged. "Long ages past the Bretons migrated here from your land, did you not know it?"

Vespa nodded. "From Cornwall and Wales, I believe."

"Yes. Which is why this peninsula was once called *Petite Bretagne*—or Little Britain. The common folk dislike foreigners, Parisians especially, for throughout our history France has often tried to conquer us. You will think it odd, but I believe my Bretons would be less likely to arrest you, or to blame me for your presence, than they would if you had come from Paris. Still, Manderville is right. To leave my area and travel inland will involve much risk for you, *mon ami.*"

"Perhaps. However, Miss Jones is dark-haired and part-Italian, which would, I believe, guarantee her safety and not endanger you or your family. Gaston—may I impose on you to guard her for me while I go on to Rennes?"

De Coligny looked thoughtfully from one to the other of their anxious faces. He said slowly, "I owe you my life, Captain John Vespa. And as I have said, I am a Breton. Even so, I fought for Napoleon. I will have one thing from you before I answer: your word of honour that your quest has nothing whatsoever to do with this war, and that for France it holds no threat."

Vespa said fervently, "On my honour, and as God be my judge, I swear it!"

"In that case," said the Frenchman with a smile, "my home is but three leagues distant, and I am very sure my wife will be delighted to have Miss Jones' company."

Manderville threw up his hands. "You're *all* mad!" he declared. "S-stark, raving l-loobies!"

The drive to the Château de Coligny was far from comfortable. The road was poorly paved and full of potholes, and the terrain was very ridged. It seemed to Consuela that she was constantly either almost jolted from the seat when the coach was moving down some steep slope, or in danger of having Jack deposited in her lap when they were climbing one of the innumerable hills. The bumpy ride did not disturb Manderville; evidently tired from his impromptu swim, he soon fell asleep.

Vespa wanted to hear more about Consuela's meeting with de Coligny, and the chevalier told laughingly how he had been terrified by her threat to attack him with his own umbrella.

"My lady is an Amazon, *véritable,*" said Vespa, his eyes saying something very different.

Blushing because of that look, Consuela declared, "It was all because of Pierre. He told me *such* a story! He said Monsieur de Coligny was his wicked uncle, who had arranged to have him thrown overboard."

"In order to seize control of his fortune, no doubt," said Vespa, amused. "I wonder you believed the little scamp, Consuela."

The chevalier shook his head ruefully. "He has too much of the imagination, alas."

"He was certainly very convincing," said Consuela. "And one does hear of such things. Only think of the little Princes in the Tower, poor boys. I remember when *Nonna* told me about them. . . ." The words trailed off into silence.

Vespa said gently, "You're thinking of your Grandmama."

"Yes." Her lips trembled. "She is—frail, you know. And she will be terribly worried."

"So I thought, and I left a letter for her with Willy Leggett's brother. With luck it will be in her hands tomorrow."

"Oh, Jack, how *very* kind."

He leant forward to kiss the hand she reached out to him, and said with a smile, "I agree that Lady Francesca must have worried. But as for her being frail—never! She is resilient as steel, and I've no doubt that the moment she reads my letter she will have old Watts drive her down to retrieve Corporal."

"You *found* him?"

"Say rather that he found us, and it is thanks to him that we were able to follow Monteil's coach."

"Dear little fellow! Then *Nonna* will trust you to rescue me once again, for she will assuredly question Mr. Leggett. Thank heaven! Now I may be easy."

She was indeed greatly relieved and her buoyant spirit re-asserted itself. She was with the man she loved, and things were going so well. Her frightening ordeal in Monsieur Monteil's coach had turned out to be a blessing in disguise. Rennes was not very far away, and with luck, between them they would find Lord Kincraig and their troubles would be over.

It was typical of her to be undismayed by the fact that she was far from home, in an enemy country, and without a chaperone; that she had not so much as a toothbrush or a comb for her hair, and only the clothes she stood up in. She was in Jack's hands and he would take care of everything. Within weeks, perhaps, she would be his betrothed. The one shadow to mar her pleasant scenario was the presence in Brittany of Monsieur Imre Monteil. But once the silly man accepted the fact that the Spring Carpet of Khusraw—ah! She'd remembered the name!— Once he acknowledged that it was no longer in existence, he would take himself and his frightening servant away.

She glanced at her beloved. He and de Coligny were engaged in a low-voiced discussion about Brittany and the plans for its development. She listened drowsily, amused by the expertise with which Jack drew out his companion so that the chevalier did most of the talking. They would probably, she thought, become life-long friends. Certainly, de Coligny was convinced that Jack had saved his life on the battlefield, and now he was taking a considerable risk in helping them. He was older than Jack by about a decade probably. He was very handsome and must have been hotly pursued during his courting days. If she had met him when he was single . . . She smiled to herself at such nonsensical thoughts. She liked him very well, but she found him a shade too stiff and rather studiedly dignified. There was no doubt but that he took himself very seriously. She pictured him sitting in judgment in the local *cour d'appel,* if they had such courts in Brittany. He would be grave and distinguished, and look splendid and all the ladies would sigh over him. She wondered what his wife was like, and if she ever did impulsive and reckless things that a lady should not do. Perhaps she was as dignified as her husband.

Glancing at Jack, her heart warmed. He was quick-tempered at times, and might not match the chevalier for looks or dignity, but he was blessed with an underlying strength and compassion. And he had besides a ready sense of humour. How glad she was that he was the man she meant to spend the rest of her life with.

She caught herself up. To be criticizing de Coligny while she sat in his carriage, en route to accept his hospitality, was surely the height of ingratitude. She turned her attention to the window and looked into the grey morning.

She was struck by a pervading impression of emptiness. For mile after mile the land appeared barren, with only sparse vegetation and stunted trees growing in the stony soil. Yet there was no shortage of water, for streams and busy little creeks were rushing about everywhere. Houses were few and scattered, and despite the fact that they were usually situated all alone in the middle of some field or meadow, they were enclosed by low walls with thick hedges growing from the tops as if jealously forbidding the approach of any invasive neighbour. These Bretons, one gathered, liked their privacy. Frequently, a cross loomed up atop some hill, but when she asked de Coligny where so many churches found their parishioners, he replied that most of the crosses indicated only a wayside shrine or small chapel. "They are convenient for travellers or country folk," he said. "But the *bourg,* or village, churches are very well attended on Sundays."

Manderville woke up and mumbled sleepily, "Is it Sunday already?"

They all laughed.

Peering through the window he said, "So we're off on Consuela's wild-goose chase, and my sound advice has been rejected. Much chance you have of catching Kincraig now. Don't say I didn't warn you!"

Consuela shivered. It was weak-kneed and silly, but sometimes she was afraid. Her every hope for happiness rested with a mysterious wanderer who was at the very least eccentric. If he should turn out to be hopelessly insane, or if he refused to acknowledge Jack, *Nonna* would never give her consent. To go through life without him . . . It did not bear thinking of, and she would not dwell upon such terrors. She thought resolutely, 'We will find Lord Kincraig, and he will be a good and sensible—'

"What a jolly fine animal," said Vespa.

A man riding a tall black horse came into view briefly, then was gone.

"He must be going in the same direction as we are," said Consuela. "I saw him soon after we left the port."

Manderville said, "I see three more riders over there."

"Your people, de Coligny?" asked Vespa.

"No." The chevalier looked grim. "They are robbers, most probably. This is not a very safe place to be riding alone."

"Deserters?"

"Some, yes. But times are hard, the crops are poor, and there is little in the way of law and order here. But have no fears, Miss Jones. My servants are well-armed, and we will be on my preserves in but a few moments. I promise there will be wine and a warm fire, and for poor Manderville, a hot bath."

"And some breakfast?" asked Consuela, who had suddenly become aware that she was ravenous.

The chevalier said with a smile, "This, too, there shall be."

～☙～

When first she saw the towers looming on the hilltop Consuela exclaimed, "Oh, my! It is a castle!" The estate road was better-maintained and they passed through wide fields where men and women laboured at weeding or digging out rocks. The men touched their caps respectfully, and some of the women waved, or bobbed a curtsy as the coach rumbled past. She heard Pierre screaming a demand to be allowed to blow up a hail on the yard of tin. His efforts were faint and discordant, and his father chuckled and said that his son's lungs must grow a trifle before they could master the art. A moment later a strong note was sounded, the coachman having evidently reclaimed the horn.

The carriage jolted into a cobbled courtyard and grooms came running to hold the horses and let down the steps. The walls of the château soared upward, grey and cold and somehow disdainful. A manservant, the butler no doubt, and a footman flung open the front doors. As Consuela was handed from the coach, a lady ran down the steps, and with a glad cry of "Gaston! Gaston! At last!" threw herself into the chevalier's arms.

Surprised that such a passionate embrace would be enacted in front of strangers and the servants, Consuela glanced at Vespa. He grinned, and winked at her. The chevalier looked embarrassed. He murmured something to his wife, and ushered his guests up the entrance steps and into a very large hall where he performed the introductions.

Madame de Coligny was a tall lady, slender and beautiful, with great brown eyes and lustrous dark hair. She responded politely, but she was clearly taken aback by the arrival of unexpected company. Her gaze held on Vespa a shade longer than was proper, then she turned to her husband and exclaimed, "But—Gaston! They are *English!*"

"Yes, my love," said the chevalier. "Captain Vespa is the man who saved my life at Vitoria, and—"

"Ah!" She held out her hand to Vespa again and said throbbingly, "Then I must be ever in his debt!"

'Hmm,' thought Consuela.

"I will tell you the whole later, Thérèse," said the Chevalier. "But see, here is our Pierre, come home to us."

He gestured, and the boy, who had been hanging back, came forward and bowed. *"Maman,"* he said politely.

Madame Thérèse looked at him appraisingly, and remarked that he had not grown at all. "Nor did your letters tell us very much," she added. "Did you not like England?"

"More than here," he said, with a defiance that spoke volumes.

It seemed to Consuela that little swords flashed in Madame's eyes. De Coligny looked annoyed and suggested sternly that his son would want to inspect his own room again.

Manderville sneezed and apologized into his handkerchief. Madame edged away from him uneasily. The chevalier gave orders that his guests be shown to suitable apartments and murmured an aside to his butler concerning the preparation of a hot bath.

Following the footman up the winding stone staircase, Consuela heard Madame Thérèse exclaim a shocked, "They are not *wed?*" She paused, frowning, but Vespa's hand caught her own, and she thought, 'She does not understand. The chevalier will tell her what happened.'

En route to the first floor she looked about curiously. De Coligny could scarcely be a poor man, but the château had a stark look; walls were unadorned by paintings, and there were no works of glass or sculpture or pottery. The only decoration appeared when they turned on a half-landing where a large crucifix was hung on the wall. At the top of the stairs a long passage stretched out, silent and chill and grey. Vespa's strong clasp on her hand tightened and she clung to him gratefully.

The bedchamber into which she was shown was small and spotlessly clean, but rather dark, with only two tall narrow windows to admit the light. The bed had a medieval-type headboard that reached to the ceiling and was painted in dark greens, black and browns. The floor was bare of rugs, the walls were an unrelieved stone, and the one painting was a Calvary, the detail so gruesome that Consuela had to look quickly away.

"Good gracious!" she exclaimed involuntarily.

His eyes glinting with laughter, Vespa told the footman to go on ahead with Monsieur Manderville. He murmured as they walked away, "Yes, I know what you are thinking, my little rogue, but you will be safe here. And I may be at ease, for Gaston is a perfect gentleman, and will see that you are well cared for."

"What of his lady?"

"A beautiful creature, don't you agree?"

"A beautiful creature who wishes me at Jericho."

"No, no. Gaston says that she gets lonely here at times, and will be only too glad of your company."

"She looked anything but glad just now."

"I daresay she was surprised to have all of us descend on her with no warning. But did you notice how devoted she is to her husband? I thought it most affecting."

'Men!' thought Consuela. "I wonder if Pierre thought it affecting," she said tartly.

"He's a changeable rascal. One minute trying to have us all arrested as spies, and the next telling his step-mama that he likes England better than La Belle France."

"His step-mama? Madame Thérèse is the chevalier's second wife?"

"Yes. I thought Pierre had told you."

"He told me he was an orphan, the little wretch!"

175

He laughed. "He's full of spirit. The sort of youngster who will grow into a son any man would be proud of."

She stood on tiptoe and kissed him on the chin, and heard a smothered gasp as a chambermaid carrying a pile of clean linens edged past and hurried into the bedchamber.

Vespa whispered, "What was that for, you forward hussy?"

"It was for—for just being you. Oh, see. The footman is waiting."

"So he is, the marplot!" To have found her, to be with her again was unutterable relief. He didn't want to leave her, even for a few minutes. And their minutes would be few, because very soon he must tear himself away. To love so deeply was a blessing, but it carried with it the pain of parting. He lifted her hand and pressed it to his lips, and with a twinge of guilt remembered the promise he had given to a trusting old lady. He sighed and knew he must be very careful, or his honour would be sullied beyond redemption.

In the room he was to share with Manderville a hip bath had been set in front of a hastily laid fire. De Coligny's valet, shaking his head over the crumpled wreckage of the once-magnificent coat, carried it away together with Vespa's garments. A footman came in with a ewer of hot water. He was the first of a continuing line of water carriers so that Manderville was very soon able to enjoy the promised bath, while Vespa washed and shaved.

The fire began to warm the cold air. Another footman brought heated wine and biscuits and advised that Chef was preparing a hearty luncheon. The valet returned with their clothing neatly brushed and pressed, and Manderville's new coat much restored. "Although," its owner said between sneezes, "it will never be the same."

Lost in thought, Vespa stood gazing out of the window and made no comment.

"You're very quiet," said Manderville. "What's churning in that clever brain-box of yours?"

"I was wondering how that rider we saw came to own such a fine horse."

"Because he's a horse thief, of course."

"Perhaps."

"What d'you mean—perhaps? There's no other explanation."

"I expect you're in the right of it. But you know, I've the impression that de Coligny's the principal land-owner hereabouts."

"What has that to say to anything?"

"Only that I looked in his paddocks and stables as we drove in. I saw not one hack to compare with the one our thief straddled. And if it wasn't stolen from here—it would be interesting to know where it did come from."

"Why?" said Manderville. "More importantly, let us collect your lady and seek out this alleged hearty luncheon. After which, you'll be anxious that we continue on to Rennes, I suppose?"

Vespa looked at him from the corners of his eyes.

"No!" said Manderville.

Vespa smiled.

10

"Where is it that you are born?" The shabby and angular wanderer peered at Vespa suspiciously over the slice of dried beef he held in a hand that was lacking three fingers.

Vespa tossed another branch onto the small fire he'd built in the shelter of the woods and took his time about replying. He had left the Château Coligny shortly after two o'clock the previous afternoon, riding the sturdy little piebald mare that the chevalier's head groom had assured him would be more sure-footed in the wilderness country than a larger animal. Parting from Consuela had been wrenching; the sweet girl had tried not to weep, but her trembling lip and tear-wet lashes haunted him and he had made Paige promise to take her home if he did not return within two weeks. De Coligny had provided a razor, strop and soap, together with clothing less likely to attract attention than his own well-tailored garments, and the head groom had drawn a rough map and given him directions that had proven a godsend. He had spent the night in a little hollow, wrapped in his blanket with fallen leaves piled over him, the cold and the myriad night sounds of the open country carrying him back to the Peninsula

Campaign. Up with the dawn, he had travelled all day towards the southeast, walking occasionally to rest the mare, and seeing only a farmer driving a cart westward, and a group of boys gathering firewood, all of whom he had avoided.

He'd reached the lonely little shrine to the Lady of the Sea just before the light failed. It had not been an easy climb, and that he'd found the spot at all was largely due to the fact that the shrine had at some recent date been painted white, and it had shone rather eerily against the surrounding darkness of the trees. A stream ran close by, as de Coligny's groom had said, the icy water clear and sweet. He'd tended to the mare whose name was Bruine. This, he felt was a misnomer, for, as he told the animal, she might be the colour of drizzle, but she was a willing little lady with an affectionate nature. Having built a fire he had settled down to enjoy the now rather stale but still good loaf, and the remains of the cheese and smoked meat Gaston's chef had packed for him. And then this tall unkempt fellow had arrived with his equally unkempt donkey and invited himself to share the fire.

"I was born in *España*," lied Vespa. "Not that it is any of your affair."

Despite his brusque growl the answer appeared to be satisfactory and his unwelcome guest started to slice mould from a hunk of cheese and said with a nod, "That will explain the way of your talk. I knew you were no Breton."

"Nor are you," said Vespa.

The knife stilled. "Why do you say this?"

"Because Bretons like their privacy."

The pale eyes stared unblinkingly. Then, a grin twisted the wide mouth. "A man gets enough of their standoffish ways, I won't argue that point. Me, I like company. That's a nice little beast you have."

"It is. And I mean she shall remain *my* little beast."

"So. You likely have a *pistolet* in that pocket, eh, Monsieur *l'-soldat?*"

"*Very* likely. Why do you suppose me to be a soldier?"

"I saw you walk. You have the limp, but you have the shoulders and the movement of the man of action. You fight for our 'Little Corporal,' eh? Where did you earn your limp?"

"Vitoria. Where did you lose your fingers?"

"Badajoz. Aha—this is the bad word for you, I see. It was a most terrible battle. You have perhaps suffer another wound there?"

"I lost my brother there." Vespa put down his bread and reached out. "I am Jacques."

They exchanged a handshake and the shabby man's face lit up. "Me, I am Paul. It is a good thing for two old soldiers to meet and to talk, no? *Nom de Dieu,* but this Brittany is the lonely place. It cause much discomfort to my poor stomach, which I will tell you is a most delicate machine. How may one talk with these people when one cannot understand what they say even when they *will* speak? At least you have the proper French. What do you here, *mon ami?*"

"Obey my master. He is desirous of meeting with some strange old fellow who goes about buying carpets."

"What, the Crazy Carpet Man?" Paul gave a hoot of laughter. "I wish you joy of him." He tapped his temple. "I think much of the time he knows not where he is."

Vespa's heart gave a lurch. "You've seen him?"

"But—yes. Yesterday? The day before? I forget. *Les enfants,* they like him, you know. I hear them squeak and shout, and there they are, all around his big waggon. And what a grotesquerie!"

His hopes sinking, Vespa said, "The man?"

Paul chuckled. "The waggon—or cart, or whatever it is. People, they laugh and call names. But he is a good-natured old fool. It is sad, eh?"

That sounded more promising. "You have a kind heart, Paul. Can you tell me where I may find him?"

"But of a certainty I can! He is likely no more than a day's journey to the south and you will have but to enquire in Rennes. Everyone knows him and *les enfants* in especial will point you the way he goes."

So his clever little love had been right, after all. 'God bless her!' thought Vespa. 'Tomorrow I may meet my father, at last!'

It rained in the night. He awoke to darkness and a clamorous wind that scattered a flurry of raindrops from the tree above him. *Bruine* stamped about restlessly. Vespa slid the pistol from under the saddlebags that served as his pillow. Moving as silently as a shadow he went to the mare, but his suspicions were unjustified; she greeted him with a soft whicker and there was nothing to indicate that Paul had attempted to appropriate her. The man's bed, comprised of a thick wool blanket that smelled strongly of sheep, was still spread out beside the dead fire. Vespa turned back to his own bed but was momentarily dazzled as lightning's blue glare lit the makeshift camp. The trees seemed to leap up. Bruine gave a snort of fright. Vespa moved quickly to hold her nostrils, for something else had leapt into view: two men stood by the stream. Even that brief glimpse revealed this to be a furtive meeting. Their conversation, evidently conducted in whispers, was quite inaudible, and although he caught a whiff of burning oil, their lamp was now extinguished.

He slipped back to his own blanket and arranged the saddlebags to resemble a man sleeping, then took up a position behind a nearby tree, the pistol gripped in his hand and his eyes fixed in the direction of the conspirators. He was faintly disappointed. He rarely misread his man, but he had evidently done so in this instance. Still, he'd been prepared and had slept lightly. De Coligny had said poverty dwelt here, and poverty had a way of breeding thievery and murder.

Lightning flashed once more, this time followed by a clatter of thunder.

Ignoring his own bed, Paul crept towards Vespa's blankets and reached out.

Vespa's grip on the pistol tightened. He watched and waited for the slash of a knife.

"Monsieur Jacques," called Paul softly, nudging the blanket. "Wake up! Monsieur—"

"I'm over here." Vespa walked forward.

"*Sacré bleu*! You take no chances, eh? I think I am insulted."

"I saw you talking to someone. It is as well to be cautious. *I* think you and your friend are free-traders, but I ask no questions."

"This it is the best way, *mon ami.*" Paul began to roll up his blanket. "You have allow that I share your fire and we talked together. So. Now I must go, for these woods they are become too crowded, which is bad for my poor stomach, you will understand."

"Crowded? I saw scarcely a soul."

"No more did I. But my friend, he says there are strangers about who stop people and ask odd questions. They ask many questions of my friend, which make him most nervous. Paul, he also does not care to be questioned. Perhaps he might not have the right answers, eh?"

Vespa watched him secure the blanket roll across the back of his little donkey. "Did your friend tell you what it was that these men wanted to know?"

"Two of them, they have pretend to search for an Englishman, but this it is not the case, of course. As if even an Englishman would be such a fool as to journey into France while we have this war! Unless he is as demented as the Crazy Carpet Man! So they really look for something else. And with all the uproar over the great robbery causing innocent men to be regarded with suspicion, this Paul he does not wait to find out!"

"What robbery? I've heard nothing of it."

"I thought every living creature must know of it. At some great mint in Belgium it happened, and a young guard most savagely killed. They are saying there was no need to have murdered the boy, and that thousands upon thousands of gold *louis* were made off with. Not one piece did Paul have knowledge of then, or ever will. But—try to convince the police or the military blockheads of it! So I go away from where questions are asked."

Vespa had enjoyed the man's company and was sorry to see him go, and Paul embraced him as emotionally as if they had been old friends. Soon after he had said his farewells the storm drifted away. The little clearing seemed lonely now, and since it was almost dawn Vespa packed up his own belongings and rode out with the first light.

He journeyed more cautiously than ever. That those who trailed him were Imre Monteil's hirelings he had no doubt. The Swiss was the only person who knew he might be in France— aside from the chevalier, of course, who would not have betrayed him. Still, it was odd: Monteil had left the fishing village before him and, with the advantage of a coach and four fresh horses, plus freedom from having to keep out of sight and guard against arrest, he should have reached Rennes last evening at the latest. If Rennes was his destination. Perhaps he was intent upon demanding satisfaction from the man who had knocked him down. Whatever the case, it would be interesting to know what was his business with the Crazy Carpet Man.

The sun came up, setting the clouds afire with pink and red and mauve, and turning the droplets left by last night's rain into countless glittering gems. When the celestial display faded the skies were overcast but bright and although the air was chill it was a crisp cold. Vespa rode with eyes and ears alert for other travellers, but an hour later he had seen only a solitary boy herding some two-score sheep. He was hungry and risked enquiring about a tavern or inn where he might buy food. The boy stared at him with great solemn dark eyes and spoke in the odd Breton tongue that had so much in it of Gaelic. So far as Vespa could decipher, he was being asked the same question as to whether he was from France. When he answered that he was a citizen of Italy the boy evidently understood, because a smile brightened his face, and he pointed to the southeast and said something that Vespa translated as indicating the route to an inn 'with a good wife.'

He thanked the young shepherd and rode on. The boy shouted, and turning back Vespa waved. And far beyond the boy he saw on the crest of a ridge a bright flash, such as might be made by a rifle barrel—or a telescope. Or perhaps merely some traveller's frying pan.

The 'inn' turned out to be a small farmhouse sadly in need of paint. The 'good wife' was a thin, sour-looking woman who stood in the doorway wiping her hands on the apron to which a small girl clung timidly. The woman eyed Vespa with suspicion. He gave her a warm smile and begged that the 'gentle madame' would forgive his poor knowledge of the language since he was Italian-born and could but do his best.

Some of her hostility faded. She sniffed, pushed away the child with one hand and tidied her stringy hair with the other. Her name, she imparted, was Madame Forêt. "It is that m'sieu wants breakfast, eh? When my stove is yet barely warm!"

"And you are very busy, madame. One can see that so sparkling a kitchen must have a peerless lady to rule over it, a lady whose fame as a cook I have heard much of. Might I be permitted to wait? Perchance the little one would care to sit on my lap? I will tell her a story. Your first-born, madame?"

Since the lady was obviously nearing fifty, this was rank flattery, but having been named a peerless cook and housekeeper in one breath, as it were, her hostility was quite gone. She beamed at Vespa. He was permitted to enter her kitchen, the 'little one' flew to clamber on his lap, and at once they were the best of friends.

Vespa told small Anne-Marie the story of Corporal and of his fear of cats and the troubles this had caused. Both the ladies were enchanted and squealed with laughter. As a reward, Vespa was given permission to wash and shave at the pump behind the house. He stripped to the waist and used soap and towel vigorously, the icy water setting his blood tingling. As was his habit, he sang while he washed, taking care to choose a French ballad. Anne-Marie giggled and jumped up and down and while he shaved did her innocent best to teach him how to carry a tune.

Afterwards, he enjoyed an excellent breakfast of a *baguette,* the long round loaf still hot and fragrant from the oven, an omelette served with fresh mushrooms and goat cheese, and a mug of superb coffee.

Madame Forêt washed dishes and hinted gently at his reason for coming to Brittany, and he told her his tale of having been sent to find the 'Crazy Carpet Man.' Both mother and daughter were excited by this confidence. Anne-Marie lisped that the Carpet Man was her especial friend, and Madame said smilingly that the poor depraved one had given her daughter sugared almonds when they had journeyed to Rennes. "If you wish to come up with him, Monsieur Jacques," she said, "you will be wise to swing south of the city, for he was travelling in that direction."

Vespa thanked her and at once made preparations to depart. When he slipped several coins into her hand, Madame gave a little nod as though she had reached some decision, and to his surprise put in a plea that Anne-Marie be permitted to ride Bruine once around the yard. Vespa hesitated; the child was ecstatically eager, but she was very small. He lifted her to the saddle and prepared to walk beside Bruine. However, Madame Forêt insisted that her daughter was quite able to ride without assistance. Clearly, the lady wanted to speak to him alone.

As soon as her little girl was out of earshot, Madame Fôret leaned to Vespa's ear. "You are the good man," she said softly. "But you must beware. You ride a dark path, and you are sought."

He stared at her, but when he attempted to respond she waved her hands impatiently. "This I will say, although I know you are not Italian, but an Englishman, like the crazy one, and the others, who are of a rudeness and speak the so-bad Bretagne."

Taken aback, Vespa said, "Englishmen have been here seeking me? Did they perhaps leave a message?"

She shook her head. "I think they do not wish you well. It is perhaps that you are the spy, and I have too trusting the nature. But my ancestors came from your place called Cornwall. This Bonaparte who calls himself our Emperor, he send his great soldiers to tear all our young men away and force them to go and fight. They have not come back. Not one. And what is he? An upstart! Do I like him? No, I do not! Do I have need of him? Again, I have not! What has he done for Bretagne? Nothing! But you, Monsieur Jacques, you have the kind heart and have made my poppet laugh, who has been sad since her brothers are gone off to the war. And so now I warn you. Guard your back, and keep always among the shadows! And now, be off with you! And *Dieu vous bénisse!*"

Vespa thanked her for the warning and for her blessing and bade an affectionate farewell to little Anne-Marie. An hour later he was still pondering Madame Forêt's remarks, and heeding her warning to be alert for ambush.

He was drawing closer to Rennes now. There were more houses and farms, more people to be avoided, more and better-maintained roads. As far as possible, he kept to by-ways and wooded areas, pausing often to scan the countryside behind him, but detecting no sign of pursuit.

It was as he dismounted and led Bruine to a stream that Madame's warning proved justified. He heard a high-pitched metallic whirr. His reaction was very fast, but even as he crouched and whipped around something jerked sharply at the cape of his cloak. A solid thud, and silence. No following attack; no triumphant shouts; no glimpse of anyone. For a split second he stared at his cloak, the cape pinned to the trunk of a tree. It was a young tree. The bolt had transfixed it. He thought in astonishment, 'Crossbow! Be damned!' And tearing his cloak free, he sprang into the saddle and sent Bruine off at the gallop.

He had not anticipated that Monteil would order his death; in fact, he'd suspected the Swiss wanted information from him. If they'd intended to capture him, a fine marksman could have used a rifle to bring him down without inflicting a fatal wound. But a crossbow—while admittedly having the advantage of silence— offered little in the way of precision, even in the hands of an expert. Whoever had fired that bolt must have known that a hit might very well result in death. And if he died, Monteil would lose the opportunity to either force Kincraig's whereabouts from him, or to make him lead them to the baron. It was puzzling in the extreme—unless the Swiss had already found Kincraig and was determined to keep him away. But in that case—why bother? He was riding alone and would pose small threat to the man, especially if Monteil had his giant servant at his side.

He bent low over the pommel and urged the mare to greater speed. Now that he had been found he must detour, for whoever these enemies might be, he had no intention of leading them to Lord Kincraig. He turned eastward, therefore, and rode for an hour, leaving a clear trail until at length he guided Bruine into a stream and they splashed along for over a mile before leaving the water at a low spot in the bank where the soil was mostly rocks and pebbles and the mare's hooves left no imprint to betray them. Turning in a wide sweep, Vespa headed south once more. Just before noon, he was riding through a copse of poplars at the crest of a rise. It was not a high hill, but it afforded a fine view of the surrounding area. He saw three men riding slowly along the stream he had left and obviously searching for tracks. They were too far away for him to identify them, but as he'd hoped, they were proceeding eastward. He smiled grimly and reined Bruine around. With luck, he'd find Kincraig before the would-be assassins realized their error. With more luck, he'd whisk his lordship safely back to Château Coligny and within a day or two they'd be back on British soil.

"It is the best notion I've heard of for the past two days," declared Consuela, her eyes sparkling. "Of course we should leave! I will—"

Seated beside her in the chill château library, Manderville roared a sneeze into his handkerchief, groaned, and whispered, "Hush! They'll hear you! And I did not say *we*—I said—"

"If you think for one instant, Lieutenant Paige Manderville, that you are going to leave me here with that revolting female—"

He put a hand over her lips. "For heaven's *sake!* Madame Thérèse is very beautiful, and—"

Wrenching away, Consuela said scornfully, "She would agree with you, I am quite sure!"

"Anyone would. And she has been more than kind. Own that she has provided us with food and lodging—"

"Only because her husband insisted upon it!"

"And she gave you a toothbrush and tooth powder, and even loaned you some of her garments—"

"Her garments?" Consuela spread her arms and wailed, "Can you suppose Madame would ever have worn *this?* It is *hideous* and it does not even smell nice! I know I am no beauty, but this rag makes me look absolutely dreadful!"

Manderville eyed the faded brown round gown sceptically. It had seen better days, certainly, many better days; and along the way had been clumsily darned here and there. The colour made Consuela look washed out, and the style or lack of it concealed her ample curves and gave her a dumpy appearance. He was rather surprised that Thérèse de Coligny would offer even an uninvited guest such a shabby frock, but striving to pour oil on troubled waters, he said, "I don't think the chevalier is exactly plump in the pockets, you know; times are hard for these people. I expect that—er, dress was intended to serve only while your own clothes are being laundered. It was—er, probably made for Madame in her youth."

"Stuff! It is from some old cast-offs she had gathered to donate to the poor—I heard her giggling with her maid over it! She said I was not tall enough to wear her gowns, and would look ridiculous if I were to try and do so. Oh, Paige, I am not an ungrateful girl! I do not expect to borrow her *best* gowns, but surely she must have something better than this. I offered to wash and iron my own things, but they were taken away and each time I ask for them I am told they are not drying properly. The truth is that she had a spark in her eye for Jack, and she thinks it will be a grand joke for him to see me in this monstrosity when he comes back." Consuela gave a little sniff and said in a forlorn voice, "I tell you, Paige, she fairly *loathes* me."

"Now why on earth should she do so? I have seen her smile at you most kindly, and she has never by the least hint suggested—"

"Oh, no. She is all polite sweetness to me in front of you and the chevalier, but when I am alone with her, she is perfectly horrid and treats me as though I were a—a fallen woman!"

Manderville groaned. *"Do* try to be reasonable. I know you're worried about Jack, but you must not let your imagination run away with you."

"I have done no such thing! You silly creature, have you not noticed how Madame Thérèse is absolutely obsessed with her handsome husband? I believe she resents anyone—including poor little Pierre—who dares intrude on their privacy."

"You just said she liked Jack, which—"

"She liked him better than she likes me, certainly. And she cannot resist fluttering her eyelashes at any male. But I believe that if she could, she would kidnap her prize Gaston away to a cave somewhere and shut out the whole world!" She scowled and muttered stormily, "There are women like that, you know. It is a form of madness."

Manderville threw up his hands in frustration. "How you can have taken the lady in such aversion is beyond me."

"Yes, because you are a man," she said, rounding on him. "And men are great awkward creatures who clump around in— in china-shops and are blind to everything under their noses— unless it is a woman's bosom!"

With a grin, Manderville said, "Very well, I'll stay here with you, *petit coquin* that you are. Likely my unease is nonsensical and old Jack is going along splendidly." He looked down, but watched her from under his long lashes as he added, "Lord knows, he's faced enough dangers in his life and managed to survive."

Consuela had been preparing to deny that she was a 'little monkey,' but at this she was all contrition and, seizing his arm, demanded, "But you said you have the feeling he needs you. If that is so, we must leave this place at once!"

He shook his head and said reluctantly that he had promised Jack to stay with her and be sure she was safe. "He would never forgive me if I took you into danger, so if you will persist in accompanying me, then I cannot go, do you see?"

She did not see, and when he resisted all her arguments with unyielding determination she flew into a rage and left him. Climbing the stairs to her cold bedchamber, she paused on the half-landing and gazed miserably out of the tall narrow window. It was as grey outside as it was in here, and the leaden skies gave promise of rain to come. Her beloved was out there somewhere, facing who knew what perils, while she fussed and grumbled like a spoiled child about—about trifles, and thus prevented Paige from going to help him.

She sighed. It was all her doing. Jack had not wanted to come here, nor had Paige. She was the one who'd insisted that Lord Kincraig was in Rennes and who had deliberately missed the return voyage of the *Saucy Maid*.

Even so, Madame de Coligny was not a kind person. Contrary, as usual, Conscience whispered that a lady more gently natured than herself would likely have been able to deal with the horrid—with Madame. The fault lay with Consuela Jones, and her wretched temper. When would she ever learn to hide anger behind honeyed words and glittering smiles? Her beloved Papa, striving always to teach her to be more in control of her emotions, had said lovingly but with regret that her nature was volatile.

She'd once asked Jack if he thought her volatile, and he had answered that she had plenty of spirit which would help her over life's rough spots. Darling Jack. She squared her sagging shoulders. Well, she would not let him down this time. She would be meek and humble and behave politely and properly so that Paige could leave her here, and—

Her resolve interrupted by soft laughter, she looked up. The chevalier and his wife were walking slowly towards the top of the stairs. Madame, looking—one had to admit—ravishingly lovely in a pale pink gown of the soft wool called cashmere, was saying that she was sure that Pierre was happily occupied.

"But he particularly asked that I go for a walk with him," argued the chevalier, looking troubled. "I'd forgot the *curé* and Mayor Dubois are to call, and I must be here to discuss the rot in the church roof. Would you object to taking the boy out, my dear?"

Consuela gave an inward chuckle and could not resist waiting to hear the answer before revealing her presence.

"But how should I object, Gaston?" trilled Thérèse. "It is merely that I have so much to do today. I shall find someone to take him, I promise you. Perhaps Captain Vespa's woman can make herself useful."

Captain—Vespa's—woman? Consuela gave such a snort of rage that she wondered flames did not issue from her nostrils.

The chevalier's glance shifted to her. He looked aghast and his face reddened as he stammered helplessly, "Ah—Mademoiselle! I—er, we were just—er, wondering if—er—"

"Yes." Consuela's brand-new resolution shattered to unmourned fragments. She said with her sweetest smile, "I would be overjoyed to repay Madame for her—kindnesses—although I know such deeds are rewarded in heaven. But, fond as I am of Pierre, for he is the very dearest child, surely he would value his mama's company over that of a comparative stranger."

"Very true," said the chevalier, blind to the glare his wife slanted at their guest. "And I have the ideal solution. You can surely spare a quarter of an hour, Thérèse, and if Miss Jones will be so kind as to keep you company, you can get to know one another."

"Oh, that would be lovely, sir," gushed Consuela.

She could all but hear the beauty's teeth grinding, but Madame Thérèse controlled her annoyance and said nobly that she would by all means spare a half hour for the boy's sake.

De Coligny dropped a kiss on her cheek and told her she was all consideration. "If you two lovely creatures will wait just a minute I'll call for wraps for you both."

"Foolish one," purred his wife, secure in her warm gown. "You know I am so healthy I never feel the cold. But we had best provide a cloak for you, Miss Jones. Your nose is quite red, poor dear. It looks as if you might be catching poor Monsieur Manderville's cold."

Consuela allowed that remark to hang on the air all by itself. Surely the chevalier was not so besotted as to miss his wife's spiteful barb, but even if he was that dense she had scored so gratifyingly that she was willing to allow Madame her petty hit.

"Papa said he would go with me," grumbled Pierre, when they walked out onto the front steps.

"I am going with you," snapped Madame, finding that the wind was far more chill than she had anticipated. "Can you never be satisfied?"

"All right," he said. "So long as Miss Jones comes, too."

They set out, following the drivepath, the boy between them. The few remarks Madame uttered were tinged with malice. Away from the constraints imposed by the presence of the gentlemen, Consuela entered the verbal duel, wording her responses in such a way that Pierre would be unaware of the invisible swords that engaged over his head. Soon, he saw a friend in the field and went racing off. Madame Thérèse, whose teeth were chattering, gave a relieved exclamation when a large coach came trundling up the drivepath. She waved to the occupants to stop. This was misunderstood. An elderly gentleman returned her wave, and shouted admiringly that she was the kind *maman* to play with her son on such a day, and the coach went on.

"Imbecile," muttered Madame under her breath. A moment later it began to drizzle, and she declared with relief that they must go back. "It is raining. Pierre! Come here at once. You must not get wet and take a chill."

"This is not rain. It is but drizzle," he called, chasing after his friend's dog. "You go back, *Maman*. Miss Jones doesn't want to go in yet, do you, Miss Jones? Come and meet Henri's dog!"

"I would love to meet Henri's dog," said Consuela, pulling the warm wrap closer about her.

Madame cried angrily, "No! Do you not hear me? I wish to go back!"

"Then by all means you should do so," said Consuela. "I promised the chevalier I would walk with Pierre, and English ladies never break a promise." Pleased with this fallacious sally and ignoring a stamp and a shrill demand that they both come *'at once,'* she hurried across the field and gathered up a stick to throw for the playful sheepdog.

Furious, Madame Thérèse hesitated, then followed them, her commands that they return drowned by the barking of the dog, the happy squeals of the boys and Consuela's laughter.

Five minutes later the drizzle abruptly changed to a downpour and everyone ran for shelter. The field became a sea of mud. Madame's wails were interspersed with expletives that ladies seldom uttered in public, and Pierre began to giggle uncontrollably.

As they reached the château, the front door was thrown wide, and the chevalier, accompanied by Manderville, the *curé* and several distinguished-looking gentlemen hurried outside opening umbrellas.

"My poor drowned ones," exclaimed de Coligny.

"I am *drenched*!" wailed his wife.

"We came back quicker than we went," laughed Consuela, dashing rain from her eyes.

"Wheee!" screamed Pierre at the top of his lungs. "Look at *Maman's legs!*"

Every eye flashed to Thérèse. The charming cashmere gown had succumbed to the assault of rainwater. The hem had shrunk to mid-calf length. It was painfully evident that not only had Madame very skinny legs, but her feet were far from dainty.

The *curé* uttered a muffled snort, threw a hand across his mouth, then hurriedly closed his eyes.

One of the gentlemen let out a quickly stifled guffaw.

Pierre screamed, "What big feet you have, *Maman!*"

Consuela's besetting sin got the best of her and she squealed with mirth.

Madame de Coligny had seldom known humiliation. Aware that she looked both ridiculous and disgraceful, she was shocked and embarrassed, but to be laughed at rendered her livid with fury. In a lightning reaction she snarled, "Revolting brat!" boxed

Pierre's ears, then turned her wrath on Consuela. "You wicked little trollop—this was your doing!" she screeched. "Sharing my husband's cabin like any woman of the streets! Coming here with your lover! You are as shameless as—"

"You forget yourself, Madame de Coligny!" said the chevalier in a voice of ice.

His wife turned to him, her face twisted with passion. The onlookers stood in shocked silence. With an enraged sob, she pushed through them and ran into the house.

11

~~~~~~

Vespa's attempt to elude his pursuers had evidently been successful; unhappily, it also resulted in a considerable loss of time. He turned Bruine to the west and rode as fast as he dared, seeing no one until he came upon a solitary cottage and then a track that led past a farm. Soon, the track was crossed by footpaths; a group of women carrying baskets stopped chattering and stared at him as he passed. They probably knew he was a stranger to the neighbourhood. He touched his hat to them politely, and they subsided into giggles. A man driving a dog cart pulled up and waved his arms violently. Vespa tensed. The man began to shout dire warnings of the dangers lurking on the road ahead. Monsieur must have his knife sharpened and he could give a good low rate—a pittance merely—for so vital a service. Amused, Vespa shook his head and rode on, followed for some distance by howled offers to render scissors, daggers, swords, bayonets or cutlasses razor sharp.

The track widened, more travellers appeared, most passing with scarcely a glance. Vespa slouched in the saddle and kept his head down. There were scatterings of houses now, and the track was replaced by a quite respectable road. Carts and riders were more frequent and soon he glimpsed the sparkle of a river, and beyond it a cluster of spires and towers. Rennes! At last! The old city seemed to be thriving and, at least from this distance, showed no sign of the disastrous seven-day fire that had gutted its centre in 1720.

His nerves tightened when a troop of *cuirassiers* clattered towards him, their steel helmets and breastplates gleaming. He drew aside with his fellow travellers to make way.

It seemed that every eye in that troop was fixed on him; that every soldier must hear the thundering of his heart as the youthful officer in the lead threw up his arm and the troop came to a halt.

The officer stabbed a finger at Vespa. "You. Come here."

The onlookers stared in silence.

Vespa rode forward reluctantly.

"Dismount, and take off your hat."

Had they realized he was British? If they had, was there any way out of this? He could seize this arrogant young bully and use him as a shield. If he had to resort to that his chances wouldn't be very good, but—

"Did you hear me?"

The roar could have been heard in Rennes, thought Vespa. He swung from the saddle and snatched off his hat with a subservient bow.

The officer said jeeringly, "Let's have a look at you."

A corporal grabbed Vespa's chin and jerked his head up, then jumped back as he met the sudden glare in the hazel eyes. "This one is dangerous, sir," he exclaimed.

The officer rode back and scanned Vespa appraisingly. "Age?"

"Five and twenty, sir."

Glances were exchanged among the onlookers.

The officer tapped Vespa on the shoulder with his riding whip. "Perhaps you can explain why you are not in uniform."

"I was, if you please, sir," said Vespa in as humble a voice as he could summon. "I served as *sergent* with General d'Erlon's forces at the Battle of Vitoria and was wounded when we tried to keep the village of Margarita. They sent me home because—"

The officer's eyes had widened. The French defeat at Vitoria was still large in the public mind, and he interrupted peremptorily, "I believe not one word of it! You look well enough to me! Where are these wounds that keep you from military service with the rest of France's patriots?"

"My head, sir. And my shoulder—here. And my leg."

It was ordered that Vespa's shoulder be bared. The officer looked at that scar and the other that ran down his temple. "We will see the leg," he snapped. "All of it. Roll down your breeches."

Incredulous, Vespa glanced around at the spectators. "Here—sir? But—there are ladies."

"He's shy," jeered the corporal. The military men all laughed. The spectators did not laugh. Many of these Bretons had sons and husbands who had been forced into the army, and French soldiers were not popular here. Reminded of this, the officer's grin became a scowl. He barked out orders and his men dismounted and stood around Vespa, providing a human screen. Embarrassed and furious, Vespa struggled with his temper, but complied. The officer bent and inspected the scars that spread from calf to thigh. He glanced up at Vespa's grim face, and stood straight. *"Mon Dieu!"* he muttered in awe. "Were those all bullet wounds?"

There was fear in his eyes now, and Vespa thought, 'He's never been in an action.' He answered, "Grape shot, sir."

The officer had lost some of his colour. He stared at the scars and whistled softly, then as if recalling his wits, he said briskly, "Yes. Well, I am pleased that you are a true patriot who has served France. You may make yourself respectable."

Vespa fastened his breeches.

A sudden salute was offered.

Without another word the soldiers mounted up and the troop rode on looking stern and formidable, bound no doubt for their regiment and the war zone.

Several of the spectators grinned and nodded at Vespa. An older man spat in the direction of the *cuirassiers.*

Vespa could breathe again. It had been uncomfortably close, but another hurdle had been crossed successfully. His resentment faded and he chuckled to himself, wondering what that pompous young ass would do if he discovered he'd named a British captain 'a true patriot who had served France.' Still, he could almost feel sorry for the boy. He'd seen several of that type—all starch and bluster until the first cannonball screamed past, and then as liable to turn and run from the field as to be capable of following orders.

His next challenge came soon afterwards when some caravans approached with two men on dapple-grey horses riding alongside. They moved from one caravan to another and were clearly questioning the occupants. Taking no chances, Vespa turned aside into a patch of woodland, and kept to the trees while staying parallel with the road.

The two men with the caravans were not part of the group he'd tricked into following a false eastward trail; none of those three had ridden dapple greys. Perhaps he was getting jumpy and the caravan pair had no least interest in the affairs of Jack Vespa. On the other hand, he was sure that the solitary rider on the black horse was following him. Why, was another mystery, but at least the fellow kept his distance and did not seem murderously inclined.

If all six were after him—again, why? Had word gone out that he sought the Crazy Carpet Collector? And even if that were the case, why would so many savage but presumably relatively sane people pursue a confused old gentleman? Unless they were witless they must know the poor fellow would never find his 'flying carpet.' And there was Imre Monteil who was very far from witless. For the Swiss to track Lord Kincraig with such determination could only mean that he was after *something* of value; perhaps there really was a fragment of the fabled Spring Carpet of Khusraw still in existence. Such a find would certainly be a treasure that greedy and unscrupulous ruffians would kill for. But it was so unlikely that— He was jolted back to awareness as Bruine stumbled.

For the third time he'd been obliged to detour around impenetrable clumps of trees and undergrowth and now it seemed to be getting dark. He looked up and found that the sky was hidden by dense branches. It was the trees shutting out the light, not storm clouds as he'd supposed. He had been so lost in thought that he'd not paid sufficient attention to his route; as a consequence, he was completely surrounded by trees and there was no longer a sign of the road. It was the sort of lapse that would have provoked him into dealing any of his subordinates a sharp reprimand. Vexed and frustrated, he informed Bruine that she was being ridden by an idiot and reined her to the left, his sense of direction telling him he wasn't far off his route. Instead of dwindling away, however, the trees and shrubs became ever more dense so that he was forced into more detours and had to acknowledge at last that this was no small patch of woodland, but a forest.

Dismounting, he led the mare back the way they had come. They had left no tracks on the thick carpet of leaves and twigs and he saw nothing he recognized as having passed before. The trees met overhead in a dark canopy, and the quiet deepened to a hush that was oddly oppressive. That he should be delayed by this stupid predicament was infuriating, and he was bedevilled by the awareness that unless he found his way out soon, the rogues following might come up with Kincraig before he did. But with each passing moment the more the trees closed in, the more crushing became the quiet.

He was greatly relieved to come suddenly upon a well-worn path. If people travelled this way he would have to risk asking for directions. Preparing to mount again, he saw Bruine's ears perk up and she stood quite still, gazing ahead fixedly. Faint sounds drifted on the air . . . strange sounds; a low bubbling sort of moan, followed by a very soft and chilling ripple of laughter. He saw something from the corner of his eye and, looking up, beheld a pale shape that floated among the branches. The hair on the back of his neck began to lift. For most of his life he had scoffed at tales of the supernatural, but a recent and uncanny experience at his ancient manor house in Dorsetshire had defied all logic and forced him to revise his opinions. Even so, he drew the pistol from his coat pocket and walked forward boldly. "Come down here, else I shall fire," he shouted.

The result was chaos. Howls and oaths rang out. He had a fleeting impression that ruffians were materializing from behind every tree. The pistol was smashed from his hand. He struck out instinctively and a yelp added to the uproar. Brutal fists grabbed him. He twisted free and landed another solid right, but they were too many. Blows were raining at him. Trying futilely to protect his head, he was down. Boots spurned him. A fierce voice yelled "Kill the filthy spy!"

He thought numbly that he had been found out, and for a moment the scene dimmed before his eyes. . . .

They were hauling him up again. Peering dazedly, he did not seem to distinguish military uniforms.

Someone groaned, "Break his accursed nose! He has broken mine!"

Another voice exclaimed, "I have seen him. This, it is the same wild man who was attacking everyone on the *Saucy Maid!*"

Vespa was shaken hard, which hurt his head. A harsh voice snarled, "Speak—curse you! How did you find us? Who sent you?"

But when he tried to explain they were evidently offended by his halting words, and he was shaken more violently.

"He is foreign! Listen to his ugly accent!"

"Kill the *saleté!*"

"Cut his lying throat!"

Glancing up, Vespa saw something white hurtling at him. "Hey!" he croaked, and threw out his arms.

For what seemed a long time, he did not hear them any more. Then, a boyish voice was crying, "But he *saved* me, Papa! He saved my whole life!"

Vespa opened his eyes, and gasped faintly, "Is—is that you—Pierre?"

"It is I. Alain. I was the ghost in the tree. I am a good ghost, but my sheet caught on a branch and I fell. Most bravely you have caught me, monsieur."

He had . . . ? It had been an instinctive attempt to fend off whatever was falling on him. However . . . least said soonest mended. . . .

A great unkempt brute of a man with very long moustachios appeared before him, and growled, "This, it is truth. This *canaille* saved the life of my son. So what now must I do?"

He was the recipient of a chorus of advice on the various and gruesome methods for despatching the spy, and there was no lack of volunteers willing to administer the 'despatch.'

"If you mean to—to kill me," said Vespa faintly. "I think you might at least offer me some brandy first."

This was evidently considered to be a reasonable request. He was dragged to a tree and allowed to lie propped against it while a bottle was produced.

The large father of Alain thrust it at him. "You first, spy. And likely it's your last," he growled.

It was excellent brandy. Vespa's initial conviction that he had been rolled over by several gun carriages began to fade.

The bottle was taken and they all sat down and stared at him while the brandy made the rounds.

Alain's father demanded, "Why were you fighting everyone on the vessel?"

Simplifying matters, Vespa answered, "A rogue stole my lady."

They appeared to accept this as logical enough, but,

"Who sent you to spy on us?" snarled a fierce young man with very black hair and dense jet eyebrows.

"Nobody. I was trying to find—"

A thin bald man cried angrily, "Why do we talk and talk? He will lie, whatever we ask. It is truth that he caught your son, Jules, but he cannot be allowed to go free, you know this!"

There were shouted responses—most approving.

It seemed to Vespa that he was trapped in another of the very strange dreams he'd experienced while convalescing from his war injuries. Here they all sat, in this hushed forest clearing, the birds twittering blithely, Bruine placidly munching at the grass and these men contemplating his murder even as they shared their brandy with him. But it was not a dream, and he knew quite well that his life hung in the balance. He thought of Consuela and prayed he would see her dear face again.

A tall man with a deeply lined face said with authority. "Léon is right. Restore him to his feet for the trial, Jules."

The boy rushed forward. "No! You cannot! Papa! He saved—"

Jules said gruffly, "Go to the tents, boy. This is man's work."

Vespa was pulled to his feet, and the boy was led away, protesting bitterly.

The tall man said, "If you have any last words, monsieur, this is the time."

"I work for the Chevalier de Coligny," said Vespa, and seeing their scowls added hurriedly, "I regret if my speech is confusing. I was born in Italy and my Bretagne is not good."

"How did you find us?" demanded the man called Léon.

"I wasn't trying to find you. I am not here to spy on you, but to try and find the man who goes about collecting carpets."

This drew derisive hoots and the consensus that even a pompous ass like the Chevalier de Coligny would have no use for a lunatic. A husky individual wielding a gory handkerchief reiterated, "He broke my nose, the villain! Kill him!"

"He saved Alain's life," argued Jules, scowling.

"You'll not exchange it for mine!" The eyebrows of the fierce young man met like a bristling black bar across his nose, and he flourished a long knife and glared at the prisoner murderously.

His sentiments won enthusiastic approval. Trying to speak, Vespa was shouted down, and rough hands wrenched his arms behind him.

"Are you all gone mad?" A newcomer pushed his way through the angry group. "I could hear you a mile back. What is all this— *Jacques!*"

Vespa's uninvited overnight guest gazed at him in astonishment.

"Paul!" he said breathlessly. "For Lord's sake, tell these fellows—"

The tall man demanded, "You know this one, Paul?"

"But of a certainty," said Paul. "We fought in the war together. This is the man who shared his fire with me when you found me last night, Raoul. What are you doing here, my Jacques? Did you come seeking me?"

The tension eased, there were mutterings of relief and the bruising hands relaxed their grip.

Vespa said ruefully, "I wish I could say I had. The truth is, I was trying to avoid a pair of ruffians who were following me—at least, I think they were. I dodged into some trees, and suddenly found myself in this forest. I'm no woodsman and in no time I was blasted well lost!"

"They all wanted to kill him, Uncle Paul," cried Alain, wriggling through the onlookers. "And he saved my life!"

Aghast, Paul picked up the boy and hugged him. "This is so, Jacques?"

It did not seem the moment for absolute truth. Vespa said modestly, "Well, I—er . . ."

"He caught me," declared Alain proudly. "I was at that time the ghost of King Arthur, but I fell from the tree, and Monsieur Jacques caught me, and I knocked him down, and then they all tried to—"

"Be still," said his father. "What is your business here, Monsieur Jacques?"

"It is as I told you. I am sent to find the crazy man who collects rugs."

Alain said shrilly, "Ah! My friend!"

"Why?" asked Léon suspiciously.

Vespa shrugged. "I do not know. I think it is Madame who wants him."

"Ah . . . Madame . . . !" Grins, nudges, and knowing nods were exchanged.

"If I don't find him," sighed Vespa, "I shall be in much trouble."

"If Madame wants him and you *do* find him, the chevalier will be in much trouble," quipped Léon.

This was received as a great witticism.

Alain started to jump up and down and, over the howls of laughter, shouted, "I know where he is! He has heard of a flying carpet and is even now on his way to buy it! He promised to take me for a ride in the sky when he gets it!"

"They should clap up that one, before he does someone harm," grunted the bloodthirsty young man, sheathing his knife.

"Indeed, they may do so," agreed Paul. "Those fellows who ask all the questions—I told you of them, Jacques—they also are seeking your Crazy Rug Collector. They mean to collect *him,* I think."

Vespa said, "Then I must find him first. Can you direct me, Alain?"

The boy looked uneasily at his father. "I can tell you he took the St. Just road," he said. "But I cannot guide you out of the forest, monsieur. It is—the ghosts, you see. And there are the menhirs, which I do not at all like." He added solemnly, "One chased me, on a time."

This claim was greeted with scornful laughter, and Jules said with a broad grin that he wished he might have seen a great block of stone chase anyone.

"You must not make up the stories, *mon petit chou,* or they might come true," warned Paul. "I'll show you the way, Jacques. The ghosts do not trouble me."

Curious, Vespa asked, "What ghosts?"

They all stared at him. Jules said, "Why, Sir Lancelot and Queen Guinevere, of course."

Bewildered, Vespa said, "Here? But I thought—" He cut off his knowledge of the British legend hurriedly.

"Long ago, they lived here," said Alain. "And Merlin, also— eh, Papa?"

Jules nodded. "I think Monsieur Jacques knows little of the Forest of Paimpont and of our great King Arthur. But then, I know nothing of Italy, so there you are. Go with Paul, monsieur." From somewhere he produced an intriguing bottle which he slipped into Vespa's saddlebags. "And—thank you for my son's life."

Bruine was led up and, having taken a solemn oath never to betray their meeting place, Vespa mounted cautiously, very aware of the various bruises he had collected. He turned to the individual named Raoul. "When you came to my camp last night Paul told me you'd seen men asking a lot of questions. By any chance did one of them ride a black horse?"

Raoul nodded. *"Mais oui!* There was a man alone mounted on just such a horse. A very fine beast."

"Ah. And the rider also was seeking the Crazy Carpet Man?"

"No, Monsieur. That was two other men—very wicked ones—the kind who would sell their mother for a bottle of brandy! They rode dapple-grey horses; nice, but not to compare with the black animal."

"Then what did the owner of the black horse want?"

"He asked about strangers in the district. But he was a stranger himself. A Parisian, I guessed. So I did not answer, of course."

"Of course," agreed Vespa and, waving goodbye to Alain, followed Paul from the clearing.

Vespa pushed Bruine hard after he left the forest. Soon he could again see Rennes in the distance and was considerably surprised to note how far to the southwest he had wandered. The early afternoon was bleak, a chill wind sent low-lying clouds racing and carried the scent of rain. The road was bustling with traffic. Fretting against all the delays he rode on long after his injured leg had become a relentless ache and his head throbbed as viciously. But he could not ignore the needs of his faithful little mare and, following Paul's advice, he turned off the road at length and walked the tired horse into the yard of a small villainous-looking inn that huddled under a solitary and leafless tree as if trying to hide from the public eye.

The ostler stared blankly and seemed quite baffled by Vespa's accent, but at last shrugged and led Bruine away kindly enough. The innkeeper, a fat little man with crafty eyes and a perpetual smile, ushered the new guest into a spotlessly clean parlour and accepted unblinkingly his explanation of his accent. Vespa relayed Paul's recommendation. The smile broadened, and the innkeeper laid a finger beside his nose and purred that he knew Paul Crozon well, and Monsieur need not be troubled, for it was his habit to ask no questions. There was a fine bed available for Monsieur, in a room he could share with a glassblower who had come from Rome to help with the reconstruction of St. Peter's Cathedral. As Monsieur knew, this cathedral it had survived the great fire only to fall down forty-two years later. "You two sons of sunny Italy will have much to chat about," he said, beaming.

Since Vespa's knowledge of Italian was limited to the phrases used by Consuela and the duchess, he was much relieved to learn that the Roman glassblower was not expected until sunset. He declined the offer of the bed, but followed the host to the tap. When the door was thrown open he was aghast to find the room crowded with men who all seemed to talk at the top of their lungs until he entered, whereupon conversation ceased. In the sudden hush every head turned to him. Fortunately, he had not removed his hat, and he pulled it lower over his fair hair, and kept his head down. The host smirked knowingly and led the way to a corner table far from the window and the glowing hearth. Vespa sat on the high-backed settle and ordered a baguette, cheese and wine. The innkeeper nodded and patted his shoulder. "You may be *à l'aise, mon ami.* There is not an Excise Officer for at the least twenty kilometres!"

This remark was overheard. Grins were exchanged and conversation began again. Thereafter, Vespa might have been invisible. He ate quickly, anxious to be on his way as soon as Bruine was adequately rested, but it was shadowy in his corner, the room was warm and his head started to nod.

He awoke to hear someone grunt disparagingly, ". . . says he is French, but me, I have the French, and his—*voyons*! But it is execrable!"

Another voice muttered, "Well he is no Breton, that I'll wager! It would surprise me not at all if the fellow is a spy! He looks more English than French with that light hair, did you not remark it?"

Vespa tensed and gauged the distance to the door.

The first man said, "I remarked that I do not like him. I do not like his loud voice, or his strange talk, or his manner, which is of an arrogance, and his friends are cut-throats if ever I saw any!"

This bore investigating. Vespa stood and slouched across the room. A serving maid hurried to him, and said his horse was ready, and he paid his shot and went outside.

A large coach and four had arrived. The ostler and stable-boy were busy and nobody seemed to notice when Vespa led Bruine around to the back of the barn. An old rusted bed-frame, some splintered fence-posts, a bucket with a hole in the bottom, a sagging mangle and other debris littered the area which was evidently a home for discarded items. A warped door was propped against the barn. Vespa tied Bruine's reins to the latch and found a knot-hole in the wall through which he could glimpse part of the interior. Three men were in there, arguing loudly in French.

Their horses were led out and while the ostler and stable-boy were saddling the animals the trio moved closer together. They were facing the open doors and Vespa could only see their backs, but they were speaking English now, and he was able to make out the words.

". . . and if that stupid block was right, my unwanted kinsman has wandered into the *Forêt de Paimpont*!"

The voice was unmistakable. Duncan Keith! Vespa swore under his breath.

"Or he followed the old man in there," this suggestion offered in a soft Welsh drawl.

"You're right, by God!" exclaimed Keith. "What better place than a haunted forest to search for a flying carpet?"

They laughed, then a thin nasal voice said, "They'll likely fall foul of the thieves and free-traders who lurk about there."

"Or get lost. They say some folk who've gone into that forest never have found their way out. The little we saw of it made my flesh crawl, I don't mind admitting."

"Either way, we can forget the business and go home."

Keith said silkily, "Can we, indeed? Idiots! D'you think I paid you such a price for anything less than a certainty?"

"You have paid us not a damned farthing yet," the Welshman grumbled.

"The devil! What about the sixty guineas I gave you in London?"

"That was to cover our passage and expenses. We're risking our necks in this business, Keith! And—"

"Keep your voice down, damn your eyes! You'll get the rest of your blood money when I'm sure he's dead! That forest will be a fine place for you to play with your favourite toy, Rand. Perhaps you'll even manage to aim your next bolt accurately!"

There was a nasal curse and mocking laughter, then the ostler called that the horses were ready, and the three hopeful assassins hurried outside.

Vespa gave them a few minutes, then followed. He was in time to see them ride around the bend in the road that led back to Paimpont and the forest.

"Bon voyage," he muttered sardonically, and turned Bruine towards St. Just.

So Duncan Keith was the leader of the group of three. He'd almost had a face-to-face encounter with them. It was pure luck that he'd arrived when he did. Now at least he had identified one enemy; a man who was not above putting a cross-bow bolt through his half-brother. It was curious that the local inhabitants either ignored him or accepted his story, while the real dangers appeared to have followed him from England. The man on the black horse was perhaps another agent of Imre Monteil, who would eventually have to be reckoned with. Who the two riders on the dapple greys worked for and why they sought him was baffling.

He had other things to think about, and with an impatient shrug dismissed the matter from his mind. Alain had spoken with his 'friend,' the Crazy Carpet Collector, only a day earlier. From what the boy had said, the waggon was heavy laden, in which case Kincraig could not be far ahead.

A carriage rumbled past heading north at a spanking pace. The coachman looked vexed and was complaining loudly to the guard about 'mountebanks.' Vespa glimpsed the feathers of a lady's bonnet inside the coach and at once Consuela's lovely and loved face was before his mind's eye. What would she be doing on this grey afternoon? Taking tea with Madame Thérèse and friends, perhaps, or playing some children's game with Pierre. The dear little soul was so kind and warm-hearted, it would be like her to try to amuse a lonely child. He sighed wistfully.

The flow of northward-bound traffic thinned and then ceased altogether. It was not a good sign. There may have been an accident, or a hold-up, or—worse—there might be a military search party ahead, perhaps made up of the 'mountebanks' who had annoyed the coachman. The road skirted a lake fringed with weeping willows and as they rounded the bend his forebodings were confirmed. Several carts, a waggon and a carriage were drawn up blocking the way and travellers were halted in both directions. Voices were raised in anger, and arms were being waved about. Some of those arms were clad in military uniforms. Vespa whistled softly between his teeth and looked about him. A lane led off at right angles to the road and he could see a cross and a small shrine some hundred yards distant. He could stop there, then go back the way he had come without making too obvious a change of direction.

He was turning Bruine onto the lane when a lady's voice rang out over the deeper voices of the men. She was berating them in a mixture of French and Italian. Stunned, he thought, *'Consuela?'* But that was impossible. It *could not* be!

"... are truly a *bruttura!* An imbecile! A great *stupidita!* Have I not say it these three times and more? Unfasten your ears, my good fool!"

212

Vespa moaned, "But it is, by God!" and, ignoring the indignant shouts of the people waiting to get through, he sent Bruine cantering forward.

Gaston de Coligny's smaller coach was at the centre of the dispute. The coachman sat huddled over on the box, a figure of dejection. The door had been flung wide and a small but officious sergeant was arguing with Consuela, who stood on the step, facing him haughtily.

"Never mind about my ears, mademoiselle. You admit you are foreign. How do I know you are who you claim to be? No, it will not do! I *must* have proof of your identity! Since you have none, I've no choice but to detain you."

Vespa's mind raced. This sergeant was far from being a model of a French fighting man. He was sorely in need of a shave, his uniform was ill-fitting and much creased. Probably, a poor man and a conscript. And as such—corruptible. Vespa reached into his saddlebags and took out the bottle Jules had given him.

Consuela was in full cry. *"Non dire cretinate!* Have I not said I am the Lady Consuela of Ottavio? Have I not told you that my *grand-mere* is the Duchess of Ottavio, to whom I now return? Have I not get it through your so dense brain-box that my papers they are carried by my courier, Pietro, who has lost himself? Is it that you are quite *pazzo?* My *grand-mere* is well acquainted with your General Napoleon Bonaparte, and I promise she will be in touch with him about this disgraceful—"

The sergeant was unintimidated. "I will tell you this, Lady Consuela," he bellowed, "that there is a large reward for the apprehension of foreign spies. Your deaf coachman he cannot vouch for your identity. You have no papers to show me, and nobody here has heard of you—or your alleged *grand-mere*! I know my duty, and I demand—"

Vespa's blood ran cold and he spurred Bruine into a gallop, the crowd scattering before him. Two troopers in rather sorry-looking uniforms presented crossed bayonets to halt him.

213

He shouted, "Signorina! My Lady Consuela! Pietro have come! See, I have find the wine!"

Consuela's head jerked towards him and her pretty mouth fell for an instant into an 'O' of surprise. She wore a long cloak and a hood protected her dark curls, and he thought her the loveliest sight he had ever beheld. His mind whirled with conjecture as to how she came to be here, and his heart was torn between the delight of seeing her again, and with fear for her. He did not have to try very hard to appear frantic, and improvised, *"Mi perdoni*? I am—er, *chicchi-richi!" 'Mi perdoni'* he knew meant 'I beg your pardon.' He was less sure of *'chicchi-richi,'* but he'd heard Consuela say it, so thought himself safe, and there were no surprised comments or challenges of his proficiency in Italian.

Consuela's eyes, which had sparkled with delight, now became very round, reflecting an emotion that startled him. He dismounted and bowed before her and, recovering her wits, she burst into a torrent of Italian, while belabouring him furiously with an umbrella.

This behaviour appeared to reassure the onlookers, and one of the soldiers said audibly, "She's Italian, right enough! I've heard about their hot-tempered women!"

Ducking the flying umbrella, Vespa caught a glimpse of the coachman's grinning face. Manderville! If they got out of this bog, he thought ragefully, he'd have a word or two with that hare-brained varmint for putting Consuela at such terrible risk.

A few onlookers were grumbling about his chastisement, and the sergeant seized the umbrella, and bellowed, *"Assez,* signoriny or lady or whatever you are! Have done, I say!"

Turning in an exasperated fashion to the cringing Vespa, he demanded, "Who is—" His gaze shifted. "What is that you have there?"

"A purchase my lady desired me to make," said Vespa. "It is for—"

"A likely story! There has been no tax paid on this, I think."

The sergeant seized the bottle and slid it into the pocket of his cloak. "It is my duty to impound it. You will tell me what the signoriny said."

"My lady is most displeased with me I fear, sir," moaned Vespa, massaging his battered arm. "I have not the very good Bretagne, but—"

"She says you have her papers," snapped the sergeant. "You will now produce them!"

"Do so, you lazy, good-for-nothing blockhead," screeched Consuela. "Do not dare to waste another minute of my time. Show this foolish man what he demands. *Vite, vite!* I shall then see that the duchess will write to his superior *and* to his General!"

The sergeant began to look uneasy. The crowd was losing patience; there were angry demands to be permitted to pass, and that he get done with this terrible-tempered foreign aristo lady. Vespa watched Consuela as if petrified with fear of her and stammered that he had been attacked and beaten on the road and all his papers stolen.

"What?" shrilled Consuela, swinging up the umbrella once more. *"Imbecille!* Dolt! You allowed them to take my papers?"

Dodging the flailing umbrella, Vespa mumbled that there had been five armed men, and he all alone. Sympathetic protests arose from the onlookers, and the sergeant threw up a restraining hand. "This fellow he is bruised, as any fool can see. One might think you would have more compassion for him, Signoriny. *Voilà, qui est louche!* And me I do not like things that look suspicious. Corporal! These people you will escort to that barn over there and guard them until I can spare the time to properly question them."

Obedient to the corporal's gestures, Manderville guided the chevalier's coach and pair into the barn. Vespa, and the still protesting Consuela, escorted by stern troopers with fixed bayonets, were made to follow and the doors were swung shut.

"It wasn't my fault, you bloodthirsty hedgebird!"

Outside, the corporal could be heard arguing with the angry farmer whose barn had been appropriated. Inside, Manderville threw up his coachman's whip to hold Vespa at bay, and dodged around a hay bale.

Consuela hung onto Vespa's coat-tails and cried, "Do not, Jack! Paige is right. It was that horrid female, and poor Paige—"

" 'Poor Paige' is going to eat some hay!" Infuriated, Vespa sprang forward, wrenched the whip away and unleashed his lethal uppercut.

Consuela squeaked and beat at his back furiously. "Oh! How savage you are, Captain John Wansdyke Vespa! That you would attack the good friend who rescued me from—"

His eyes blazing, Vespa turned on her and said through his teeth, "Sit . . . down and . . . be quiet!"

Consuela blinked, backed away and sat on the carriage step.

Vespa bent over the fallen. "You swore to me that you would keep her safe! You know what she is! You *swore* you'd not let her run into danger!"

"I had . . . no choice," moaned Manderville, feeling his jaw tenderly. "Damn you, Jack, you've cut my lip!"

"Why do you just lie there like a limp crêpe?" demanded Consuela, disgusted. "Why do you not jump up and strike the ingrate?"

"Because half Wellington's army knows about Vespa's right," he answered without a trace of shame. "He'd just knock me down again. What I should do, of course, is call him out."

"And what I should do is to cut your feeble heart out," snarled Vespa. "Where the blazes did you think you were taking her?"

"Taking her?" The picture of outraged innocence, Man-

216

derville sat up, sneezed, and said stuffily, "The chevalier sent me after her when she went tearing off—"

Consuela ran to kneel beside him. "You have taken such a cold, my poor Paige. But what else could I do, after that horrid female called me 'Captain Vespa's *woman*—'"

"And said you were a trollop," put in Manderville helpfully.

Taken aback, Vespa demanded, "Why on earth would a well bred and gracious lady like Madame Thérèse—"

"She forgot to be gracious and well-bred when she got wet," said Consuela tartly.

Manderville grinned. "By Jove, but she did! Wet as a whale! But you'll have to admit, Consuela, if you hadn't giggled—"

"I tried to stop myself," she said with a remorseful sigh. "But how could I help it with her standing there in half a gown, while the Mayor and the curé and all those other gentlemen gawked at her—er, limbs."

Vespa gasped in horror, "Gawked—at—*what?* Oh, egad! Whatever did you do to the poor lady?"

"I did *nothing*," snapped Consuela, scowling at him.

"It came on to rain, you see," explained Manderville. "Madame Thérèse was wearing a charming woollen dress—"

"And—it shrank," said Consuela.

"And—*shrank*," wheezed Manderville.

"Up . . . and up . . ." squeaked Consuela, overcome.

For all the world like two naughty children they clung together at Vespa's feet, laughing helplessly. Watching them, his wrath faded. He sat down on the hay bale. "All right, you two rascals. Tell me the whole."

He could not restrain a chuckle when the tale was told and, knowing his lady's mercurial temperament, he could understand her indignation.

"It's too late to change now," he said to Manderville. "But why—once you'd come up with her, did you not take her back to the château?"

217

Consuela said stubbornly, "Because I would not go! And besides, I was so worried about you, Jack." She reached out and he pulled her to her feet. Touching his cheek anxiously, she said, "And I was right, do you see, Paige? Only look at his poor bruised face."

Vespa hugged her tight. "Are you surprised, after beating me so mercilessly with that murderous umbrella?" She smiled and leaned to him. She was soft and yielding in his arms. Gazing down at her, he forgot all about danger and disgrace and jewelled carpets, until an angry shout outside brought him back to earth. Reluctantly, he put her from him, and said, "But it was well done, little meadowlark, and properly fooled our pompous sergeant, I think."

"Then I am glad I was such a shrew. We have told you why I ran away, Jack. Now I want to hear what happened to you."

He gave them a brief account of his journey. "They're not amateurs," he said, holding up the torn cape of his cloak. "This was skewered by a crossbow bolt."

Consuela clung to his hand and said in a shaken voice, "Merciful heaven!"

Manderville's brows went up. "There's a bounty on spies. D'you think that's what they're after?"

"I do not. I think there are several interested groups. Monteil, we know about; the fellow on the black horse, who keeps his distance but is definitely tracking me; two men riding dapple-grey horses, who question travellers about Kincraig; and another three, two of whom are hirelings, and the third—the unkind Mr. Duncan Keith, who has instructed his man with the crossbow to shoot straight next time!"

"Jupiter! Your half-brother?"

"He apparently believes that to be so. Though what he stands to gain by my death, I've no notion."

He went to the door and peered through a crack in the weather-beaten boards. The trooper stood guard, augmented by a farm-hand with a long-tined hay fork. He and Manderville could probably overpower the pair without much trouble, but then the hunt would be up, and Consuela deeply involved. "Monsieur Corporal," he called. "My lady is anxious to be on her way. We must—"

"You must do as the sergeant orders," interrupted the corporal harshly. "If you and your mistress are placed under arrest, you will be taken to the barracks at Rennes."

"Confound it," muttered Vespa. "I *must* get on!"

Consuela said remorsefully, "Were it not for me, you would slip away and find Lord Kincraig. Well, you go, Jack. Paige will take care of me, and—"

"And who's to take care of Paige?" demanded Manderville. "If you mean to abandon us, Jack—"

"As if I would, you great gudgeon. Now tell me how you contrived to pass me by. You must have made excellent speed."

"For one thing we had a pair of horses, and we didn't have to lurk about and avoid roads, as you did." Manderville chuckled. "Consuela was really splendid as the arrogant Italian *grande dame,* and had everyone bowing and scraping."

"I believe that," said Vespa, lifting her willing hand to his lips. "Thoroughly enjoyed your charade, did you not, my rascal? But how did you know where I was?"

"We knew you would most probably ride towards Rennes," she replied, "so we went straight to the city and made enquiries for the Crazy Carpet Man. Every child in the area seems to know him. It was the children who told us he'd gone to St. Just, so we left the city on that road, guessing you'd follow the same path."

Manderville put in, "Good thing you come up when you did. That confounded sergeant was within Ames-ace of flat-out arresting us."

"Yes, and if he were under my command he'd be a private! He was so interested in the bottle I'd brought that he made no effort to verify *my* identity. What a blockhead!"

Consuela said with a saucy glance, "You should thank your stars that blockhead did not know any Italian, Captain Jack!"

"I thought you looked hilarious when I came up," he said. "Doesn't *mi perdoni* mean 'beg pardon' or something of the sort?"

"It means 'will you forgive me?'—which was quite *convenable*. But when you said that you were *chicchi-richi*— Oh, my poor Jack! How I kept my countenance I do not know!"

Manderville asked curiously, "Why? What did he say?"

"Jack said he was—" she gave a choke of mirth "—he said he was 'cock-a-doodle-doo!' "

Manderville howled, and Vespa clapped a hand over his eyes and groaned that he'd never live it down.

A familiar voice was raised. "If you are finished with your quarrelling, may I please have something to eat? I'm fairly starved."

They all whipped around.

Standing beside the boot of the carriage, Pierre de Coligny watched them hopefully.

12

"Why should I not run away?" Pierre said with defiance, "Miss Consuela did. She knows what it is like there! Madame, who is not my *Maman,* hates her. As she hates me."

"Your poor Papa will be frantic," said Consuela, dispensing with insincere reassurances.

Vespa said, "And searching for you."

Frowning, Manderville nodded. "And if he blames us, as he probably will, he'll likely tell the authorities who we are and we'll have every soldier and policeman in France after us!"

"I doubt that," argued Vespa. "Too many people know we were his guests. De Coligny would incriminate himself. Consuela, you and Paige must take Pierre home."

"No!" said Consuela, Manderville and Pierre, emphatically and in unison.

"You've got too many enemies," Manderville declared.

Consuela pointed out, "You may need help. And how can Paige drive me back to the château, when we've told this silly sergeant I am returning to Italy and my Grandmama?"

"In which case, you should be turning east," said Vespa worriedly. "You are heading towards Spain, rather!"

"I wish you will all stop arguing and find me something to eat," complained Pierre.

There arose a sudden flurry of shouts and activity outside. Manderville made a wild leap onto the box of the carriage and Consuela scrambled inside. Pierre ran for the barn door, and Vespa caught him just as it was thrown open.

The sergeant stamped inside and halted abruptly, staring at the boy. "Hello, hello, hello! What's all this?"

"I am the farmer's son," lied Pierre. "And these bad people have kidnapped me."

His accent gave him away. The sergeant said with a chuckle, "Oh, ho! You'll not hoax me with such a tale, fierce one. Your talk is more of Paris than St. Just, and those clothes on your back were never worn by a poor Breton farmer's brat."

Vespa met his enquiring glance and said, "He is Lady Consuela's nephew, sir, and she fetches him from his school in Paris to see his great-grandmama." He added, low-voiced, "He's a rare handful!"

"This I can see." The sergeant's gait was slightly erratic as he moved closer. "Well, he comes by it honestly, I'd say. Now—" he hiccupped, and then called, "Are you awake, Lady Signoriny? I'll have the truth of it all, if—if you please."

There was a strong aroma of brandy on his breath. Vespa gave a mental cheer. His little ploy with Jules' bottle had born fruit. If the fellow was half-foxed, he'd be easier to outwit.

Consuela said, "Leonardo, what have you been telling the sergeant?"

"My name is not Leonardo!" Pierre scowled. "It is—"

"Come, that's no way to talk to your aunt," scolded the sergeant, wagging a finger under his chin.

"If you had but half a brain in your head—" began Pierre haughtily.

"Be still!" said Consuela, frowning at him. "You have my apologies, Sergeant. My nephew is rude."

"He is young, madame." The sergeant rocked on his heels and gave Pierre an indulgent smile. "I didn't know you'd a boy with you. I've sons of my own. Four. And scamps, every one. Now, I feel sure we can come to a quick resolution of our problems. Tell me, young Leonar-ardo. What is the full and real name of this lady, and where do you live?"

Vespa held his breath and from the corner of his eye saw Manderville preparing to leap from the box.

Pierre folded his arms across his chest and said heroically, "I shall tell you nothing, my good fool. Lead me to Madame Guillotine!"

The sergeant's jaw dropped. Then, with a shout of laughter he turned to Vespa. "You were right, *mon ami*. He's a handful. Since you are the Lady Signoriny's servant, you *assurement* can confirm for me her full name and where is her home."

"She is the Lady Consuela Carlotta Angelica of Ottavio, sir. And I escort her to her grandmother, the Lady Francesca, Duchess of Ottavio."

"*Bon!*" The Sergeant snapped his fingers. "At long last we arrive at the answer. So you may be upon your way, and I can get to my own fireside. Do you see how simple it is, Lady Signoriny? Had you but told me the truth to begin with . . ." He clicked his tongue, shook his head at her, and reeled from the barn.

Vespa was inclined to believe Pierre's claim that Madame Thérèse had no love for him. He was sure however, that the chevalier was deeply fond of his son, and he was troubled by the awareness that the poor fellow was probably frantic with anxiety. Even if de Coligny did not at once guess that Pierre had run away, he would certainly by this time have instituted a thorough search. Vespa liked and respected the Frenchman and, under normal circumstances, he would not have hesitated an instant before turning about and taking both Pierre and Consuela back to the château. But the circumstances were far from normal, and he was torn between the need to catch up with Lord Kincraig and his responsibility for the safety of Consuela and the boy.

To an extent she was correct in believing herself protected by her Italian heritage and, if she was apprehended again, the chances were that at worst she would be ordered to leave the country. But if he and Paige should be challenged and it was revealed that she was travelling with two British officers it would be a very different story. The possible outcome made the sweat start on his brow.

As they left the barn and turned onto the road once more, Manderville watched him and called ironically, "Second thoughts, *monsieur le capitaine?* Justified. If we keep on this road much longer you're unlikely to persuade anyone that we're bound for Italy."

"What do you suggest?"

"When we started this journey you told me that your first concern was for Consuela's safety. If you really meant it, we should at once make a dash for the château. That, or turn east towards the Franco-Italian border."

Irritated, Vespa said, "Do talk sense! Every minute we're in France we run the risk of discovery. To travel clear across the country would be madness. And you know very well that to attempt to cross the Alps in winter is unthinkable."

"Why? The really hard winter weather don't set in till after Christmas, and—"

"Very true," interjected Consuela, leaning from the window. "But the terrible mistral can come down without warning, and with a howl like thunder. My dear *Nonna* told me her Mama used to say that one day the duchy would be blown clear across Italy and become a suburb of Padova."

Pierre squeezed into the window beside her and declared

that he had seen the mistral. "I was little then," he boasted. "And the wind it picked me up and carried me off so that my uncle had to run for ten miles to catch me again!"

"What a rasper," snorted Manderville, "But our options are clear. To turn east is unacceptable. To continue towards St. Just is to invite sure disaster, so it's a race for the chateau and the coast."

"No!" shrilled Pierre. "I will *not* go back!"

"We are so close now," pleaded Consuela. "One more day only, and we should come up with Lord Kincraig. It is our future we fight for. Please, *please,* dear Jack, do not give up."

It was true that their every hope to marry depended upon his locating the elusive peer who might be his sire. If only he could in some way get Consuela and the boy to safety. To attempt to reach the Italian border was out of the question, as Paige knew very well. He'd likely only suggested such a ridiculous route because his cold was dulling his wits. As risky as it was to follow Kincraig they *were* close now; he could feel it. They'd risked so much—another day wouldn't make much difference, surely? If they didn't come up with Kincraig tomorrow, they would turn to the west and make a dash for the château.

Consuela's anxious eyes were fixed on his face. He said, "Very well. One more day. But one day only!"

She squeaked and clapped her hands, and Pierre shouted "Hurrah! I am still free!"

Manderville looked disgusted, but whipped up the horses. Vespa reined Bruine beside the carriage and they turned south on the road to St. Just.

The afternoon was well advanced and the chill wind carried a steady drizzle. It developed that Pierre was not the only 'starved' member of the little group. When Vespa learned that in their haste to find him Paige and Consuela had not stopped to eat, he pulled into the yard of the first farmhouse they came to and was able to purchase a cold roasted chicken, the inevitable baguette—sliced and buttered—and a bag of black plums. Pierre ran into the big kitchen demanding to know if there was any cake, and the farm wife laughed and graciously added some bread pudding to their lunch.

She allowed them to eat in her warm kitchen and they were soon on their way again, Vespa riding escort, and constantly scanning the road ahead for any sign of a waggon and an elderly gentleman. They passed a group of the menhirs; the great standing stones that might well have been erected by the same ancient peoples who'd left them in Cornwall and Stonehenge. Vespa pulled back to draw Consuela's attention to the strange monoliths. She was fascinated, but Pierre hid his face against her, crying that the menhirs were well known to be evil men who'd been turned to stone for their wickedness, and that it was very bad luck to look upon them.

The miles slipped away and still Vespa saw no sign of a likely looking waggon. His heart stood still when a young officer in a showy blue uniform rode up and ordered them to pull off to the side. Obeying, but prepared to make a run for it, Vespa was able to breathe again as a troop of artillery clattered past escorting a gun-carriage. Readying for the next action, he thought, that would come in the spring if Wellington could muster the forces and supplies he needed. He grinned faintly, picturing the great man's impotent rage at all the rain.

They were allowed to move on then, encountering tinkers walking by the side of the road with great packs on their backs; ponderous rumbling wains; rickety donkey carts; a brightly painted caravan from which a very old woman leered at Manderville and screeched an offer to tell 'the handsome young citizen's fortune'; a family evidently moving, their goods bundled and lashed to four mules, the husband leading the way and his lady walking beside the last mule, holding the hand of a small girl and keeping an eagle eye on a cradle perched precariously atop the overloaded animal's back.

Vespa's concerned gaze was on that cradle when the inevitable happened: The mule stumbled over a pothole in the road. The cradle slid, but on the far side of the lady, who let out a terrified screech as she made a fruitless grab for it. Vespa had already spurred Bruine. He caught the tumbling cradle in the nick of time, but it was all he could do to keep the infant from falling, and its howls were scarcely less piercing than those of its mama.

The husband ran back to snatch the cradle. The wife retrieved the baby and began to rock it and croon soothingly. Vespa said, "I think that is not a safe place for your infant, madame."

The husband levelled an affronted glare at him, restored cradle and child to their precarious perch and ran back to his place at the head of the column.

As they passed with not one word from the family, Manderville said in French, "That'll teach you to be a knight errant, Captain, sir!"

"The baby might have been killed," said Vespa indignantly. "What would you have done? Galloped over it, I daresay."

"You're in no case to gallop over anything, *mon ami.* Your heroic deed did not benefit your trusty mare. She's favouring her left front leg."

Vespa swore and dismounted at once. Pierre hung from the coach window and informed them that Miss Consuela was asleep. He also spoke without finesse of his own needs which were, it seemed, of an urgent nature. Vespa turned off the road and into a grove of poplars and evergreens. Pierre ran off, and Vespa and Manderville inspected Bruine's damaged leg. Fortunately this only amounted to a thrown shoe but, until she was reshod, she could not be ridden.

Vespa told her she was a good little lady, and unbuckled the saddle, depositing it in the boot. Pierre had left the carriage door open, and he peeped in at Consuela. She was fast asleep, her hood fallen back and an errant curl nestling against her sleep-flushed cheek. One hand lay, palm up, on the seat. How dear she was; how intrepid and resourceful and high-couraged. By Society's rigid standards she was an incorrigible minx, but how many ladies of the *ton* would have taken such risks to help him in this desperate search? How many would have so bravely endured the perils and hardships she had faced with never a whine or a whimper? Aching with love for her, yearning to take her into his arms, he kissed his forefinger and very lightly transferred the kiss to her soft little palm.

Behind him, Manderville sang hoarsely:

> *" 'When is the time a maid to kiss?*
> *Tell me this, now tell me this.*
> *'Tis when the drizzle turns to rain.*
> *'Tis when Pierre's run off again.*
> *Is—' "*

Flushing hotly, Vespa whipped around. "The devil! Have you called him?"

"As you'd have heard were you not so entranced by—"

"Confound the boy! You'd better go and search for him." Manderville sighed and turned away, but Vespa had seen the weariness in his face and the dark circles under his eyes. Catching his arm he said remorsefully, "I'm an insensitive clod, and you've a beast of a cold. I'll bring the young varmint back, it shouldn't take above a minute or two, then I'll drive and you can get some rest."

His 'minute or two' stretched to ten, at the end of which, fuming, he had searched through several thick clusters of fern and shrubs while his calls went unanswered. He was beginning to worry and he climbed to a high point to look about. As he approached the top he heard shouts and squeals, seemingly coming from the far side of this rise. Real alarm seized him. Pierre was the son of a chevalier of France; it was not beyond the realm of possibility that this time he really had been kidnapped! Impelled by visions of enormous ransom demands, a heartbroken father and his own failure to have protected the child, he began to run. At the top of the rise, he halted, and stood there motionless while the raindrops fell unnoticed on his bare head.

At the foot of the slope a large waggon of unusual design was drawn up under a wide-spreading tree, a tent pitched beside it. He could see the smoke of a campfire and he heard a man's deep laughter, but neither man nor fire were visible, for the waggon was surrounded by children. In an oddly remote fashion he wondered where they had all come from. They crowded in, squealing, jumping up and down with excitement, and waving small paper-wrapped objects triumphantly.

'My God!' he thought. 'Oh, my dear God!' Perversely, at the instant of success he was afraid; afraid of discovering that the Crazy Carpet Collector was indeed crazy; afraid of an infuriated denial or of being contemptuously rejected; afraid that—like Duncan Keith—Lord Kincraig might fancy him to be an opportunistic fortune-hunter, or despise him because his mother had married the man he loathed.

Pierre's shrill voice cut through his trance-like immobility. "Here he is, Capitaine Jacques! Here is the Crazy Carpet Person you search for!"

In the midst of the crowd a man stood straight and turned towards him. He said something, and the uproar faded and ceased. The boys and girls began to drift away, some scowling at Vespa resentfully, then running with the quick adaptiveness of childhood, shouting about the rain and home and supper.

The man by the waggon still stood there. A rifle was propped against the wheel beside him, and there was a guardedness in the way he watched the newcomer.

Pierre came leaping up the slope, waving a handful of sweetmeats. "See what I've got, Capitaine! He gave me—"

"Go back to the coach." Vespa did not raise his voice, but the boy checked, gazing up into his stern face curiously. Then he ran off without a word of protest.

Kincraig called in fluent French, "Good day, monsieur. You have been seeking me? What may I do for you? Have you perchance a carpet to show me?"

Vespa limped down the slope. How did one open a conversation under such circumstances? 'Oh, hello, sir. I think I may be one of your by-blows?' Or, 'How d'ye do, my lord? Your bastard son has come to call?' He thought an irritated, 'Idiot!' And drawing closer, realized there was no need for words.

He had expected to confront a much older man, but although Kincraig's fair hair was streaked with grey, his figure was trim, his chin had not sagged, and he looked to be only a year or so past fifty. The features were so similar to his own that it was indeed like looking into a mirror of the future. The cheekbones were slightly more finely etched, the mouth almost too sensitive. There were lines in the face that spoke of suffering, and although he smiled tentatively, deep in the eyes Vespa thought to glimpse a hint of sadness. And it was the eyes that sealed their resemblance; in shape and hue, even to the amber flecks, they were identical to his own. He saw that Kincraig was staring and had become very pale. He said in English, "Good afternoon, my lord."

"Who . . ." croaked Kincraig, "who the—the deuce are you?"

"Until recently I thought I was John Wansdyke Vespa, but—" He sprang forward to support the man who sagged, white to the lips, against the waggon. "And I'm a sorry fool," he added repentantly. "Let me get you out of the rain."

He all but carried Kincraig to the tent and deposited him on a camp bed. Several crates had been piled on their sides to create a makeshift cupboard. Among the objects on the top 'shelf' was a bottle of greenish liquid that he eyed uncertainly.

"Yes—please," whispered Kincraig. "Medicine."

Vespa took out the bottle and following his lordship's signalled instructions measured two inches into a mug and handed it over.

After a minute or two some colour returned to the waxen features, the eyes opened again, and Kincraig said more steadily, "That's better. My apologies, sir. Didn't mean to . . . to throw such a scare into you. A slight nuisance with my health, is all. If you will excuse my crude hospitality, there's . . . some fair cognac in the lower box. I'm afraid my folding chair will have to serve for a sofa."

Vespa settled for both cognac and chair, and having occupied the second and sampled the first, he met Kincraig's searching gaze and said, "I'm so sorry. This has been a shock for you, and—"

"Never mind about that." The baron made a gesture of impatience. "My God, but you've my father's eyes! And mine, of course. To say I'm astonished is a masterpiece of understatement, but there's nothing to be served by tippy-toeing around the issue. Your name and your face tell me all I need to know. The fact that you've come to me says you must know it also. Or— some of it?"

"Not much, sir. But—I think we are—er, related."

"I'd say that is a certainty. Did Lady Faith send you? How is she, bless her heart? How did she know where I was?"

"My mother is well, but she's out of the country at the moment. She never breathed a word of the true state of—of the matter to me. When I learned that Sir Kendrick Vespa was not my father, I decided to try and find out who was. With Mama away, it—er, hasn't been easy."

"I'll wager it hasn't! A tricky business for you, I've no doubt. And you likely judge me a proper rogue." Kincraig waved a hand as Vespa attempted to reply. "No, don't answer. How could you think otherwise? I've no intention to try and wrap it up in clean

231

linen, but I'd like you to know that I was deep in love with your beautiful mother and it was my dearest hope to make her my wife. After she married that— Well, I stayed away at first, of course. But poor Faith was neglected and so unhappy. We began to meet in secret, and I tried to cheer her."

He sighed nostalgically, then went on: "Inevitably, it became an *affaire de coeur.* I won't say I'm sorry. We were as much in love as ever. We belonged together and should never have been separated. Sir Kendrick found out, eventually. I don't know what he said to Faith, but when I confronted him he refused to meet me in a duel—he has a horror of scandal, as I'm sure you know. He was icy cold, and—I'm sorry, but truth is truth—he warned that if I ever came near Faith again, she would suffer a fatal accident. He meant it. And I know he's capable of—"

He slanted a glance at Vespa's enigmatic countenance, and said apologetically, "Well, I must not say more on that head, save that I haven't seen her since. I was too distraught to stay in England and removed for a time to a property I own in Scotland. But it was lonely and when I realized I was sinking into melancholy I began to travel abroad. I blundered into a marriage that was not happy, which spurred me into extending my travels, but whenever I was in Britain the Society pages of the newspapers kept me fairly well apprised of Faith and her sons. I never dreamed one of them . . . might be mine."

He drew a hand across his eyes, then asked, "Well, young man? Now you have my story, are you here to demand satisfaction because of my disgraceful conduct?"

Vespa said with a slow smile, "If my mother did not judge your conduct disgraceful, sir, I scarcely have the right to do so."

"Aha! You've a silver tongue, I see. Which shouldn't surprise me, since I believe you served as one of Wellington's staff officers?"

The voice was clear and incisive now, the eyes sparkling. Lord Kincraig showed no sign of either denial or rejection, and if this was a lunatic, he was indeed a complex one. Heartened, Vespa replied, "Yes, sir. Until Victoria."

"By Jove! How splendid! Then you're no green boy. Still, it was likely a shock for you, as well. Egad, but there's so *much* I want to know! Firstly, how and when did you find out that Sir Kendrick is not your father; and why in Hades wasn't I told of your existence?"

"I believe Mama was frightened into keeping silent, sir."

Kincraig frowned darkly, "Yes. He'd do that, the proud bas—" He bit his lip and cut the words short. "I'm sorry. You are likely fond of him."

Vespa said quietly, "I loved him. He's dead, my lord."

"Great heavens!" Staring in stupefaction, Kincraig gasped, *"Kendrick Vespa? Dead? Recently?"*

"Very, sir. And suddenly."

"But he was always the picture of—Did some public-spirited citizen call him out, or—What on earth—No! Never say it was an accident? Your dear mama was not—"

"My mother was abroad when—when it happened. We wrote to advise her of my—of Sir Kendrick's death."

Bewildered, but trying to take it all in, Lord Kincraig said, "Yet you're not in mourning, and you're—Good God! Where are my wits gone? Do you realize what will happen if you're unmasked as a British officer? You can't go jauntering about France in time of war! Why are you here?"

Vespa said with a slow smile, "I might ask you the same, sir."

"My carpets! Oh, egad! I must see to them!" Distracted, his lordship sprang up and hurried from the tent, Vespa following.

Kincraig stopped, turned back, and asked rather shyly, "May I request an embrace? A man don't gain a fine young son every day, you know."

Vespa's heart gave a joyful leap and he returned a crushing hug. His eyes rather dim, he asked brokenly, "Then—you don't mind, sir?"

"Mind!" Kincraig leaned back and searched his face. "My dear boy! I cannot tell you how—how proud— Oh, Jupiter, the back is open!" He ran to the waggon and Vespa helped pull the double rear doors closed. The waggon was even larger than he'd at first realized, and sturdily built, with a wooden roof and sides so that it resembled an outsize caravan with overhanging eaves. There were many rolls of carpet inside, all neatly disposed, but that would, he realized, constitute quite a weight.

Kincraig said with a proud smile that the waggon had been built to his own design. "I have to keep the rain out, you know. And if I find many treasures on one expedition, the load can get extremely heavy. You see my team over there?" He gestured to where four big cart-horses were loosely picketed and munching contentedly at the contents of their nose-bags. "Strengthy beasts, and there are times—But never mind that. John—may I call you John?"

Sir Kendrick had called him John. He said, "By all means, sir. But I'm Jack to most of my friends." His friends! Dismayed, he exclaimed, "Oh, Jupiter! I've left my coach and my—er, people fast asleep! Forgive, but I must—"

Kincraig looked over his shoulder and said inexplicably, "I think you had best let me deal with this, my boy."

Gaston de Coligny's coach was moving cautiously down the slope, escorted on either side by a rider, each of whom was astride a dapple-grey horse. Manderville was flushed and tight-lipped. From the window, Consuela's eyes flashed an unmistakable warning. 'Damn!' thought Vespa. This was the same pair who had been questioning the people in the caravans and whom the free-trader had spoken of. Seen more closely, they looked grim and dangerous. Certainly they knew their trade, for they'd lost no time in coming up with him. He pulled a low-trailing branch aside and stepped forward as they rode up side by side.

"Good day," called Lord Kincraig. "What have you brought me, my friends?"

"This!" A wolfish-looking individual with a profusion of bushy greying hair reached behind him and dragged Pierre forward.

The boy was white-faced, his eyes big with fright. He said quaveringly, "I did not do anything naughty, Monsieur Jacques."

"But—no," confirmed the intruder, regarding Kincraig with a broad grin. "So you will want him back. He is your grandson, eh?"

Kincraig said in bewilderment, "He was with the children who come for their sweetmeats, but I do not know the little fellow. Perhaps, he is the lady's child?"

The wolfish man shrugged. "You evade. It is of no importance. We will see your waggon now, Monsieur Collector."

"Ah," exclaimed Kincraig, rubbing his hands happily. "You are interested in rugs, is that the case? Come, then! I will show you my harvest! It is always a joy to meet an *aficionado*. But—these beauties they are not for sale, you understand."

He trotted towards the waggon. The two intruders exchanged a slightly perplexed glance.

Pierre struggled and demanded to be put down at once.

"Quiet, scrap," said the leader, and as the boy kicked and wriggled, he added a harsh, "Stop your squirming, or I'll—"

"Ow!" howled Pierre. "Capitaine Jacques . . . !"

Vespa released the branch he still held. It flailed out with a great scattering of raindrops. The dapple greys took the brunt of it and reared with shrill neighs of fright. The man who held the boy fought against being unseated, and Pierre jumped clear. Vespa ran to snatch up Kincraig's rifle. The intruders regained control of their mounts to find themselves staring down a long barrel held in a pair of very steady hands.

Pierre ran to clutch Vespa's coat. "These are very bad people," he cried vehemently. "They are rough with Monsieur Manderville, and they frighten your lady!"

Vespa darted a glance at Consuela.

"I am not hurt," she called. "But they struck Paige and took his pistol."

"Which I will now have back," said Manderville.

"Come and take it," jeered the second man. His face was a mass of pimples and he was shorter and more stockily built than his companion, but looked just as ruthless.

"You will do well to shoot them first, Capitaine Jacques," advised Pierre.

"An excellent notion," said Vespa, taking aim and drawing back the trigger.

Perhaps judging others by his own standards, the wolfish individual cried, "What a bloodthirsty villain! All we wanted was to see the flying carpet."

"A desire we share," said Kincraig with a sigh. "Alas it eludes me, but I have several very fine specimens I will be glad to show you."

His finger steady on the trigger, Vespa said, "If all you wanted was to see this gentleman's carpets there would have been no need to bully my friends and the child. I should warn you that my hand is tiring. And when it tires my fingers tend to cramp. Drop your weapons."

They both glared at him murderously. He allowed the rifle to jerk slightly. With lightning speed two horse pistols thudded to the ground, followed by Manderville's pocket pistol. This smaller weapon had a hair trigger, and the impact caused it to fire. The shot set the horses rearing and squealing and the ball ruffled Vespa's hair, startling him into losing his aim.

Thinking him wounded, Consuela screamed.

Pierre gave a piercing howl.

The two intruders seized the moment and departed at a gallop.

Consuela threw open the carriage door and flew to Vespa's side.

Manderville jumped down from the box and began to gather the weapons.

Pierre demonstrated the benefits of a British classical education by leaping up the slope after the departing ruffians and screaming, "Good riddance to bad rubbish!"

Seemingly bewildered by the sight of a pretty young lady embracing his newly acquired son, Lord Kincraig looked from one to the other, and shook his head. "What a pity," he remarked despondently. "What a pity."

Manderville sniffed, and asked stuffily, "Your pardon, sir?"

Kincraig gave him his gentle smile. "Those two gentlemen," he murmured. "I think they really were interested in my carpets."

Vespa said quietly, "My lord, may I present Miss Consuela Jones: the lady I hope to make my wife."

"Good gracious," exclaimed Kincraig, as Consuela curtsied before him. "Do you say you are travelling together, but not married? What a pretty creature you are, my dear. Your parents must be very broad-minded, but I'm afraid you'll find me rather old-fashioned."

Consuela blushed.

With an edge of steel to his voice, Vespa introduced Manderville, and said, "There is so much for us to discuss, my lord. But our first concern must be to find a safer campsite. Unless I mistake it those two rogues work for an ugly customer named Imre Monteil. I don't know what he wants of you, but he's ruthless and persistent."

"Oh, yes. Monteil. I know of him. A greedy gentleman who collects art works whether or not people wish to sell them. He'd travel to the ends of the earth for a fragment of the Spring Carpet of Khusraw. I can't let him have it, you know. Such a sad waste of his time. But—I suppose it gives him something to do." Nodding to himself, he trotted back into the tent.

Vespa and Consuela looked at each other. She said staunchly,

"We cannot blame him for misjudging us, Jack. Anyone would think the same. I'm sure he will understand when you explain everything."

Manderville asked, "How much have you told him? He must have noted your resemblance, surely? Does he admit your, er— relationship?"

"He was very kind," said Vespa, his chin high. "And seemed delighted to acknowledge me."

"Ah. Well, that's a step in the right direction." Manderville added dubiously, "I suppose. Well, don't glare at me like that. You were warned that he's—ah, eccentric." He chuckled. "He's that, all right."

"Damn you," said Vespa. "Come and help me pole up his horses."

Whatever Lord Kincraig's mental shortcomings, he knew the countryside. At dusk they were snugly settled into a wooded hollow having the benefits of a shallow stream with a level but stony bed along which the horses and vehicles passed without leaving telltale tracks. Vespa had brought up the rear of their little cavalcade and had stayed for twenty minutes on the highest ground, alert for signs of pursuit. He was lured to the campsite by the smell of bacon frying and found Consuela busily cooking over a small fire, and Manderville and Kincraig settling the horses for the night.

Pierre fell asleep when he finished his supper. Consuela could scarcely keep her eyes open and Vespa carried the boy and walked beside her to Kincraig's tent, which had been assigned to them. Pierre mumbled sleepily when he was laid down on the pile of rugs that was his makeshift bed for the night.

Vespa turned to draw Consuela into a long-awaited hug. She snuggled close and with his hand on the back of her curls and her soft shapeliness pressed against him, he yearned with every fibre of his being to kiss her. It would not be dishonourable now—would it? He'd publicly stated that she was his betrothed; she had as publicly confirmed it. Besides, if word got out that she had travelled unchaperoned in his company, the duchess would likely demand that they marry. But the word might not get out, and it would be a shabby trick to take advantage of a possibility, before the fact as it were. The inescapable truth was that he'd given his word to the old lady. To break it would not be the act of a gentleman, and to break it while her grand-daughter was far from home and under his protection would most definitely be dishonourable. Sighing, he forced himself to draw back.

"I think Pierre had better not be undressed. Just his coat and boots. We may have to move again." He looked uneasily at the camp bed with its rough blankets. "This is Turkish treatment for you, Consuela. Will you be warm enough? Shall you be able to sleep?"

She assured him she could sleep through an earthquake, but despite her indomitable smile she looked very tired. He stroked her cheek. "You've been so good through all this, poor sweet."

"Yes," she agreed. "I really think my dear Papa would not be ashamed of me." She caught his hand then, and said urgently, "Jack, I'm so glad you've found your father. But he seems very set in his ways. Will you be able to persuade him to come home now? Grandmama will want to meet him."

"You may be very sure that I mean to try." He pressed her fingers to his lips, and in response to her indignant look, he pointed out, "I gave your Grandmama my word not to try and fix my interest. And even if I had not, I've no wish to trap you into matrimony, little meadowlark."

She said with a sigh, "Sometimes, I wish you had not such a high sense of honour, Captain Jack." And knew that not for the world would she change him.

13

Outside, Lord Kincraig was still sitting by the fire, but Manderville had said his goodnights and taken his cold and his blankets to his assigned 'bed' in the coach.

"You must be worn to a shade, my boy," said his lordship kindly. "Are you sure you're not too tired to talk tonight?"

Vespa assured him that he was not at all tired. "I've waited a long time for this moment, sir."

"In that case, we will not delay it." Kincraig gestured to a nearby crate. "Pull up one of our elegant 'chairs' and we'll try to discover each other."

Their 'discoveries' were at first superficial, both reluctant to put the more harrowing events of their lives into words. Kincraig spoke of his home in Suffolk and his Scottish castle, of which he appeared extremely fond. He was very ready to laugh at some recountings of the youthful exploits of Jack and Sherborne. Soon, however, the conversation turned down a path Vespa dreaded to follow. Despite his denial, he was very tired, but it occurred to him that for all his eccentricities, his lordship possessed a remarkably keen mind. He wanted to know the details of the final tragedy in the quarry at Alabaster Royal. Vespa took refuge in evasions, but it was no use. Always, however gently, Lord Kincraig brought him back to the subject, and at length he capitulated. He kept a tight rein on his emotions, but his brief account and the clipped restrained words painted a clearer picture than he guessed. Kincraig, who had pushed for the truth, had suspected fraud and skullduggery; he had not expected brutality and murder. He saw the sheen of perspiration on the grim young face and for a moment was too horrified to comment.

Vespa slanted a glance at him and said haltingly, "You likely think me a blind fool, but Sir Kendrick was a consummate actor. All those years, and I had not the slightest suspicion that he wasn't really my father. We didn't see him often at Richmond, but when he was there he could scarcely have been more kind—to both of us, although everyone knew he favoured Sherry."

Recovering his voice, Kincraig asked, "You did not resent that fact?"

"Was I jealous? Oh, yes. Of course. But . . . well, you'd have to have known my brother—I expect I should now call him my half-brother. Sherry was such a—a splendid fellow. We were—very attached."

The rain had stopped and the clouds had drifted away. The air was cold and clear, and the moon had come up, throwing its soft radiance over the hills and dappling the ground with the shadows of the trees. Lord Kincraig stood and wandered to where he could watch the horses still cropping at the grass. Seeing none of the pastoral scene, he said in a voice that trembled slightly, "I can scarce credit that even such a one as Kendrick Vespa could have shot you down so callously. It was because he hated me, I've no doubt."

"Not entirely, sir. Quite unintentionally I had discovered his scheme. I didn't know it was his at the time. But I did know I couldn't allow it to go on, and so—well, I stood between him and a great deal of money."

242

"So you implied. But you don't say how he expected to make such a fortune."

"No." A pause, and Vespa said, "I'm afraid I'm not at liberty to discuss that."

Kincraig swung around. "Good God! Do you say you've been *ordered* not to speak of it? Then it must be a matter of national security! Is Lady Faith aware of all this?"

"She knew nothing of it. But if she has received the letter my great-uncle sent off she may be on her way home, and I must be there when she arrives. And now, my lord, it occurs to me that you've very adroitly fished out a great deal of my life history, but have told me very little of yours. Fair play, you know."

His mind still on the appalling events this newly found son had survived, Kincraig hesitated, then sat down again and said with a forced smile, "I've told you most of it. You know that I loved your beautiful mother, and that my own marriage was disastrous. I suppose it was my unhappy home life that drove me to plunge deeper into research concerning my hobby. Eventually, my fascination with rugs and carpets induced me to spend much of the year seeking out rare specimens."

Vespa said carefully, "But you're not really hoping to find a— er, *flying* carpet, are you, sir?"

"That would be a find, to be sure!" Kincraig chuckled. "No, Jack. But it's a useful ploy. When I began my wanderings the news got about that a rich collector was searching for fine rugs. I was besieged by would-be sellers bringing me everything from small mats to very large carpets, and most at ridiculously inflated prices. Since I've spread the rumour that the rich collector is seeking a flying carpet, most of the opportunists have decided I am demented and they certainly have no such item to offer. Thus, I am less overwhelmed with merchandise that is useless to me."

"What about the Spring Carpet of Khusraw? Is that why you continue your search?"

Gazing into the flames, his lordship said dreamily, "Who

knows? As I recall it was Robert Herrick who wrote: 'Attempt the end, and never stand to doubt. Nothing's so hard but search will find it out.' "

"You certainly seem to have found many fine specimens. The waggon cannot take much more weight, I'd think. You must be ready to go home."

"Home. A beautiful word, Jack."

"And you've a beautiful home, sir. Yes, I've seen Lambent Grove. I went there seeking you."

"Did you now." Kincraig turned his head and looked at him thoughtfully. "You likely found the place closed up, which is a pity. It's a nice house."

"Very nice. Your butler was kind enough to show me a few rooms."

His voice expressionless, Kincraig said, "If Barnard was still there, I fancy my son Duncan was in residence."

"Yes."

"And you didn't see eye to eye. Not surprising. I suppose Duncan noticed the family resemblance?"

"Yes."

His lordship's smile was brittle. "You can say a lot with one word, Jack. The boy was offensive, I gather."

"I'm afraid we had a—er, a small turn-up, sir."

"Which you won, of course." Kincraig shook his head and said with a sigh, "Poor lad. Poor lad. It's not his fault. His mother . . ." He shrugged and the words trailed off.

Vespa waited through another silence then said, "You will think this vulgar, my lord, but—I have a small inheritance from my mother's parents. I won't touch the Vespa funds or properties, but I've an old house in Dorsetshire I'm fond of, and I have no need— That is to say— I mean—I am not a pauper."

"Duncan accused you of being a fortune-hunter, did he? What nonsense. I've more than enough for both of you."

"But I don't want anything from you, sir. Except, perhaps, your affection and—and acceptance. If your son could be made to see that—"

"I'm afraid he cannot. To an extent I understand his resentment. You see, when my wife died, I was involved in a rather chancy business. I made a new will, under the terms of which, upon my demise everything would go to my legal heir—Duncan. Although you cannot be named a legal heir, I mean to acknowledge you as my son, and make suitable provision for you. No! Please do not argue. It is my wish, and my right. Duncan knows me. He knows what I will do. His nature is such that— Well, I'm afraid he won't like it!"

No, Duncan Keith wouldn't like it, thought Vespa. Unless perhaps his man with the crossbow shot straighter next time.

❧

The morning dawned bright but cold. Vespa rose early, started a fire and carried a bowl of hot water to the tent. Consuela answered his call drowsily but then demanded that he wait, and next instant her tousled head appeared through the tent flap, and her eager eyes were searching his face.

"What did he say? What did he say? I tried to keep awake so that you could tell me, but I was too tired, and you must have talked the night away! Is he willing to acknowledge you?"

He tugged on an errant curl. "He doesn't seem averse to the notion."

She squeaked and gave a little leap of excitement, causing the tent to rock ominously. "Oh, how splendid! *Nonna* will give us her blessing then, I am sure! Now why must you look troubled? Ah! You think his lordship may not approve of *me,* is that the case? Well, let me tell you, Captain John Wansdyke Vespa, I have done *nothing* of which I am ashamed, and in fact—"

He laughed and tweaked her little nose. "Get dressed,

245

Signorina Fiero! It should not take you above an hour, do you think?"

"Monstrous man! I shall be cooking breakfast in ten minutes!"

A quarter of an hour to complete a lady's toilette, he told her, would break all known records. Her indignant vow to make him eat his words followed him as he went down to look at Bruine, his heart light and his hopes high.

He had ascertained that there were no pebbles or stone bruises on the mare's hoof and was preparing to feed the horses when Manderville joined him, looking flushed and sleepy and speaking in the stuffy voice that accompanies a cold. Scooping oats into a nosebag he said, "Well? Well? Are you the acknowledged son and heir?"

Vespa grinned at him happily. "I am. One of 'em, at all events. Do you know, Paige, the dear old fellow really seems pleased to welcome me to the family."

Manderville slapped him on the back and said he couldn't be more pleased. "This means your path to the altar is clear, at last. Have you persuaded Lord Kincraig to turn for home now?"

"He says he cannot: that he's to meet a fellow who really may have a scrap of this fabulous Khusraw carpet. It's nonsense, of course, but I must tread carefully. Still, I hope to persuade him to change his mind."

While the men shaved, Pierre was assigned the task of being their lookout in case any strangers approached, and Consuela prepared a breakfast of coffee, rolls and omelettes. She was timid with Lord Kincraig until he bowed and kissed her hand with stately gallantry, and told her his 'son' had explained matters. "I gather it is thanks to you that Jack found me, my dear," he said. "I can only hope that my future daughter-in-law will forgive me for my hasty judgment."

She was overjoyed and, to his great delight, his lordship was hugged and a kiss pressed on his cheek. She was, he told Vespa when the two men were poling up the cart-horses, a darling of a girl, sunny natured and full of spirit. "To see the way you look at each other is heart-warming. I think you have found a love that is not given to many. It reminds me of when your dear Mama and I—" He broke off, then finished quickly, "Don't let it slip away, Jack. Guard her well."

"I mean to, sir. And in that connection, I want her back in England as fast as may be."

"Excellent! She can say what she likes about being protected by her Italian ancestry, but she is at high risk here. You must leave at once."

"Very good. Do you think it safe for us to all travel together? Or shall you lead the way while we follow?"

Lord Kincraig chuckled. "Blandly said. But as I told you last night—"

Vespa raised a delaying hand. "Your pardon—father." The word came unbidden to his tongue, and for a minute he was too moved to continue. Then he asked shyly, "Do I—presume too much, sir?"

Kincraig also was overcome, and stretched out an unsteady hand which Vespa took and held strongly. "If you *knew,*" said his lordship. "Of course, you cannot know, but— Consider your little signorina and how deeply you love her."

"More than my life, sir."

"That is how I felt about your mother. To discover that she bore me such a fine son . . . There are no words, my dear boy! I shall be proud to have you name me so!"

Such a display of emotion was an embarrassment to both British hearts, wherefore they avoided each other's eyes and became very much occupied with straps and buckles and harness. As soon as he could master his voice, Vespa said, "Thank you. But—you must know that Consuela refuses to go home unless I do. And I have no intention of leaving until you come also."

Kincraig turned and looked at him squarely. "So soon, you challenge me," he said with a faint wistful smile.

"I have been pursued, shot at and beaten, since I commenced to search for you," said Vespa, meeting his gaze steadily. "It's very obvious that several groups think you have found your jewelled carpet and mean to have it. With all due respect, my lord, I have had the deuce of a time finding you, and I will be damned if I will now run the risk of losing you!"

Kincraig gave a shout of laughter. "I see how it will be. So long as I behave myself I will be 'father,' but if we don't see eye to eye, I am doomed to exist as 'my lord'!"

Vespa reddened. "No, really, sir! My apologies if I spoke harshly. I've no thought to challenge your authority, but—"

"But you demand that I do as you wish."

"Not demand—never that! Only—I do beg of you to reconsider. No carpet ever woven is worth your life—or worth risking Consuela's life. How you've managed to wander about Europe like this in time of war is beyond me, but no man's luck holds forever. It's long past time that you were safe home in Suffolk—or Scotland."

Kincraig looked worried. "The girl presents a problem, no doubt of that," he muttered. And you're quite right. I shall go home. Just as soon as I've met my friend. No—don't argue with me, Jack. I have no alternative, you see. He waits a scant three leagues away. I gave my word to meet him, and I've never broken my word yet."

Vespa's jaw tightened. "Then you leave me no choice but to accompany you, sir."

"Nonsense! Your first thought must be for your lady. Take her home, lad. Take her home."

And so it went, the young staff officer using every wile and stratagem at his command, the nobleman smiling and genial and immovable, until Manderville came to join them with Pierre leap-

248

ing along behind him. "Is this a private quarrel?" he enquired with a grin.

"May I have my sweet?" cried Pierre.

"One only," said Kincraig. "You know where they are." Pierre jumped onto the tail of the waggon and clambered over the rugs to a crate at the far end.

"It isn't a quarrel at all, Paige," said Vespa sharply. "I've merely been trying to persuade his lordship to come back to England with us."

"Jolly good," said Manderville. "The only sensible thing to do. And I think we shouldn't delay. Those are thunderheads unless I mistake 'em."

One glance at the threatening skies and Kincraig scurried for the tent saying in that odd, shrill voice so different from his usual manner, "I must strike camp! If we get much rain it will be difficult . . . very difficult!"

Vespa looked after him uneasily.

Manderville said, "I wonder you convinced him, he seems so determined to go his own way."

"I didn't convince him. Dammitall, he's stubborn as any mule!"

"You resemble him in more than looks, I see," said Manderville with a grin.

"I'm glad you find it so blasted amusing. You won't object to taking Consuela home."

Manderville's response was pithy and profane.

Vespa said intensely, "Paige, you *must!* I daren't leave him— not with that unholy crew at his heels!"

"It appears to me they're at *your* heels. And he has gone on very well by himself these many years, from what I can gather. Come now, own he's dished you. You've done what you could, and he'll have none of it. You cannot compel him to your way of thinking, and if he's given his word of honour—"

"To do—what? Meet some cloth-head who fancies he's found a piece of that confounded ancient rug? It's not *possible,* you know that as well as I!"

"Lord Kincraig don't appear to know it."

Vespa muttered, "Small wonder they call him crazy. I've a damned good mind to take him home by force, if only to protect the dear man."

"You'd catch cold at that, I think." With rare austerity Manderville said, "I for one would have no part in such a scheme, I promise you."

"Confound you," exclaimed Vespa, turning on him angrily. "Then why did you come if you meant to refuse your help when most I need you? If Toby were here, I'll warrant he'd—" He broke off and ran a hand through his hair. "No—forgive me. I don't mean that. You've been very good, Paige. It's just that—I'm at my wits' end. I *must* get Consuela safe home, and I cannot abandon my—my father to his probable death! *Please!* If you will just—"

"Do what?" interposed Consuela, who had come up unnoticed. "Bundle me off again? Paige won't try it, for he knows very well I'd get away and follow you."

"Not if I tied you up and threw you in the coach."

Her blue eyes widened. "Jack! You wouldn't!"

"To protect you from yourself? Oh, my dearest girl, be sure I would!"

"Then it would be a coach you'd have to drive," said Manderville.

Lord Kincraig screamed, "Why do you all stand there? Can you not see there is going to be a storm? Tend to your horses, quickly!"

The clouds were heavier and ominously dark. Even as they all looked up great cold drops began to patter down. His lordship was carrying crates and blankets to the waggon, Vespa ran to help him and Manderville hurried to harness his own borrowed pair.

Jumping up and down, Pierre shouted, "What about Bruine?"

Vespa was reminded that the little mare must be reshod. He called, "Hold up, sir. I'll get Manderville on his way, then ride with you till I can find a smithy."

Lord Kincraig nodded and proceeded to strike the tent. The rain threatened to become a deluge. Consuela pulled up her hood and retreated to the carriage with Pierre. As soon as de Coligny's animals were harnessed and poled up, Vespa went to Bruine who was grazing farther down the slope. He started to saddle her, hearing in his mind Kincraig's words, 'A scant three leagues away . . .' Three leagues; nine or ten more miles of enemy territory for Consuela to risk, and they were not a great distance from the war zone. No, it would not do! She and Pierre must be returned to the chateau immediately. He frowned, thinking that if Manderville refused to help, he'd resort to his army rank and *order* the thimble-wit to take her back. He himself would accompany Kincraig on what appeared to be this last lap, and that was all. His lordship had promised to go home after he met up with his friend, and by heaven, but he'd see that promise was kept, even if he had to resort to dragging the old gentleman back to England by force!

Deep in thought he finished saddling Bruine, and led her up to the camp. It was deserted. Both waggon and carriage were gone. Knowing he would not ride the mare, they'd slithered off and left him to manage as best he could! It was Consuela's doing, of course. The little minx knew he would follow Lord Kincraig and she had no doubt persuaded Manderville to drive out before he could insist that she and Pierre be sent back to the chateau. That blasted weak-kneed Paige! The silly block should have known better, but he was like putty in her hands!

It was as well his beloved was not within earshot as Captain John Wansdyke Vespa voiced his reaction to such dastardly conniving in furious and unrestrained barracks-room language.

He had trudged less than a mile through the now-driving rain when he came upon a commotion. A goose girl hurrying to shelter with her flock had incurred the wrath of a farmer whose load of apples had shifted when he swerved his waggon to avoid the geese. The farmer was bellowing, further frightening the geese; the dray horses were stamping about agitatedly; the girl was in tears as she ran about trying to gather her flock together; and apples were strewn across the muddy road. Vespa stopped to help pick up the apples, and managed in the process to calm the distraught girl and placate the farmer by buying a bag of his fruit. The girl left him with a tearful smile and a blessing, and the grateful farmer directed him to a forge located in a lane "just a scant distance to the south—two hundred meters at most."

For once the directions proved reliable, Bruine was soon being shod by a gregarious blacksmith who had no objection to a foreign accent and in no time Vespa was able to ride out in pursuit of the dastardly conspirators. He came up with them a quarter of an hour later. The carriage was pulled off to the side of the road and barely discernible through the grey curtain of the rain. Manderville had climbed down from the box and was blowing his nose and peering despondently at the right rear wheel.

As Vespa rode up, he said unrepentantly, "Well, it's past time you arrived!"

"No thanks to you, my good and loyal friend! You succumbed to the signorina's blandishments again, didn't you!"

Manderville gave him a resentful look. "You try and gainsay her! I wish—I wish . . ." he sneezed, groaned and finished, "I wish you joy of it!"

He looked quite haggard and was getting thoroughly soaked. Vespa thought 'I'll have him down with the pneumonia if I'm not careful!' He said in a kinder tone, "What's the difficulty now?"

"A damn great blade from a broken pair of scissors or something of the sort has stuck itself in the wheel. I'm afraid it'll split if I don't get it out, so—"

Consuela called from the open window, "Jack! I am so sorry, but we have lost his lordship again!"

He stared at her then asked Manderville, *"Lost* him? How the deuce could you lose him in bright daylight?"

"It ain't all that bright. He drove around a bend in the road and when we came up, there was no sign of him. He's slippery as any eel, and could have hidden himself in any of a dozen spinneys we passed."

"Stay here," said Vespa tersely. "I doubt you'll be noticed in this deluge. I'll come back as soon as I can."

Manderville grunted, and from behind his handkerchief enquired, "What does that mean? A sennight from Wednesday?"

Ignoring him, Vespa reined Bruine around. Consuela watched him penitently from the open window. "I know you are cross, dear Jack. Have you decided to abandon me?"

"Yes," he said, fighting the urge to kiss her rosy but drooping lips.

She giggled and clapped her hands. "Your eyes give you away! I am very naughty, but you still love me. Where are you going?"

He had remembered that when he'd left the forge he'd noticed some deep ruts in the lane. Lord Kincraig's waggon left just such marks. He said, "I passed a lane where his lordship might have turned off. Keep out of sight, and do please try to be good."

"For a change?" she prompted mischievously.

He nodded. "For a change."

"Be careful," she called after him.

He rode fast but not so fast as to draw attention to himself. Traffic was lighter in the rain but he scanned each coach and rider going south, alert for a fine black horse, or two dapple greys, or Duncan Keith's unlovely trio. The wheel tracks were still visible when he reached the lane and he turned Bruine down it. Paige had been right about his lordship hiding; there was a spinney ahead and the tracks led right in amongst the trees. It was rough going for Bruine; for the big cart-horses to haul the heavy waggon over such muddy and rock-strewn terrain must be downright murderous. Why on earth his lordship would come this way was—

Vespa's irritation was banished abruptly. The waggon was just ahead, balanced on the two left wheels and tilting crazily against a tree. His first dismayed glance told him that Kincraig had been driving along a narrow track when the weight had caused the ground to give way under one wheel: probably a rabbit warren or some such thing. The horses did not appear to be harmed and were standing patiently, but there was no sign of Kincraig. Vespa rode up quickly, calling his father's name. He thought he heard a faint response from under the waggon and he threw himself from the saddle to peer underneath. His lordship lay sprawled a few feet from the tilting side. Vespa raced around the horses, his eyes flashing to the tree that was the only thing keeping the waggon from toppling. It was a young birch and it was leaning perilously. At any instant it might snap under the weight, or be uprooted, and Kincraig would be crushed. He fell to one knee beside the inert figure. "Sir—I must get you out of here! Are you hurt?"

Kincraig blinked up at him, then smiled weakly. "Found me, did you? Found me . . . in a pickle. No, don't move me. I was thrown clear. Not—not hurt, but I think I'll—just rest here for a—"

A root of the tree was torn from the earth. The waggon jerked with an ear-splitting creak.

"I think you won't, sir," said Vespa and, gripping Kincraig by the shoulders, dragged him clear and propped him against a boulder. "Now you can rest," he panted. "I'll get the horses unhitched in case the waggon goes down."

It looked to be in imminent danger of doing just that. He worked feverishly to get the team un-poled and led them off to the side. Securing the harness straps to a low branch, he ran back to the waggon. It was even more tilted now. He knew how heavy it was and that to venture onto the far side and try to push it up would be not only useless but likely suicidal. Even if he found a sturdy fallen branch and tried to lever it erect, he'd never prevail. The ground to the right of the track sloped down a little but it wasn't impossible. He led the two leaders to the waggon and tied their harness straps to the two right-hand wheels, then guided the horses down the slope. They were fine big animals, but their combined strength failed to do more than shake the waggon. Frustrated, Vespa thought, 'The wheels are too low, dammit!'

An idea occurred to him; the kind of crazy idea that his army comrades would have expected of him. He tore open the rear doors of the waggon, praying Kincraig would be carrying what he needed. His prayers were answered; on one wall hung a neatly coiled length of rope. "Excelsior!" he exclaimed and appropriating it, tied the end to the harness of one animal. Holding the rest of the rope, he climbed cautiously onto the driver's seat. The waggon let out a sound like a groan, and shifted. He hung on, watching the tree and holding his breath. The birch was young and supple and held firm. Moving cautiously, he clambered onto the roof, trying not to notice how the waggon lurched under him. The surface was wet and slippery, and too slanted for him to stand upright, so he lay down and fed the rope around the back of the tree trunk.

Climbing down again, he secured the free end of the rope to the harness of the second horse and set the pair in motion again. He had to stop them twice while he adjusted the length of the rope so that the pull on the tree would equal that of the harness straps secured to the wheels. The third time he started off again, the horses leaned into their collars and strained their powerful muscles with, at first, little apparent effect. Suddenly, there was a jolt. The waggon had shifted slightly. Elated, Vespa urged the pair on. The waggon jerked. He could only pray the tree would not snap. The waggon swayed and began to tip. Gradually, the roof moved upward, the tree straightened. Then, with a crash, the right wheels hit the ground and the waggon bounced upright. "Whoa!" cried Vespa, and the cart-horses halted.

There came a burst of applause. Lord Kincraig, still lying against the boulder, exclaimed admiringly, "Jolly well done!

Flushing with pleasure, Vespa praised and petted the pair, then poled up the team again. "You've got some splendid cattle here, sir. Now, what may I do to help you? You said you weren't hurt?"

"No. Not at all. The wheel went down into a pothole I suppose, and I was hurled from the seat when the waggon tipped. Must have knocked the wind out of me for a minute or two."

Despite his cheery manner he was pale, and made no attempt to get up. Vespa asked anxiously, "Why did you go off like that? It's too dangerous for you to jaunter about alone. You could have been badly hurt and with no one near to help."

"Pish! I'm as fine as fivepence. If I could—er, just have my medicine."

"Oh, egad! Of course, sir."

Vespa hurried to the waggon, Kincraig calling instructions as to where his medicine could be found. The accident had resulted in the contents of the interior being scattered about haphazardly. Vespa righted two crates before he found the bottle and reached for it, relieved that it wasn't broken. Something cold touched the back of his neck. He stood rigidly still, thinking that it was either a pistol muzzle or a knife. He was struck lightly, this time on the head. There followed an odd chinking sound.

He said harshly, "Well? Who is it?"

Silence; followed by more metallic chinkings.

He withdrew his hand and the medicine from the crate, and this time was hit squarely on the wrist.

He stared down at a gold piece. A French *louis*.

"What on earth . . . ?" He looked up, then ducked aside as a veritable rain of the coins showered from a wide crack in the roof.

He set down the medicine bottle and a glance at the rolls of carpets made him gasp. Gold glinted everywhere. He scooped up two handfuls and realized he held the equivalent of thirty guineas. There must, he deduced numbly, be at least another hundred *louis* scattered about. Frowning, he thought, 'The old fellow is *really* out of his mind to carry such a sum with him!' He remembered then and, tossing down the coins, took up the medicine and hurried outside.

There was no sign of Lord Kincraig. He had wandered off again. But had this latest disappearance anything to do with accident or illness, or had the old gentleman simply slipped away to meet his friend? If that were the case, out of simple courtesy he might at least have said something before he left. Irritated, but still uneasy, Vespa searched about for some time, dreading to come upon his lordship lying collapsed somewhere. He made no such sad discovery, nor were his calls answered and he concluded at length that wherever his father had gone, he would return at his own convenience. It was, he thought glumly, another instance of Kincraig's eccentricity.

He climbed back into the waggon, and scowled up at the roof. No more coins were cascading down, but something else could be seen. He climbed onto the carpets, crunching gold pieces under his boots. A piece of sacking hung down. He gave it a tug and it came away together with several more gold pieces. Evidently, his lordship carried his purchasing funds concealed in a sack in the roof. It must have split from the impact with the tree— or perhaps when the ceiling boards had ruptured.

He began to gather up the scattered coins. It took quite a few minutes and when they were all collected, he had counted out two hundred *louis.* Murder had been done for much less than this! His lips tightened into a thin, determined line. If anything had been wanting to convince him he must force his father to return to England, this piece of folly turned the trick. The very thought of Kincraig jauntering about all alone in an enemy country, with a great bag of gold hidden in his waggon, made his blood run cold.

He piled the coins on the torn sack, but there was no way to tie it securely. If his father had purchased all these rugs there might be an empty sack he could use. He stood on the carpets again and reached up. The splintered board gave slightly when he tried to move it aside and another hard shove opened a loose section he was able to slide back. Now, he could reach inside. He groped about, and he had guessed rightly, for he felt another sack. Only it wasn't an empty sack. It was solidly heavy. "Jupiter!" he gasped. "However much is the old fellow hauling about?"

Tugging and struggling, he could feel two more sacks, but how many were up there he couldn't tell. He was really alarmed now, for such a risk must surely be unwarranted even for a gentleman who was slightly unbalanced. He sat on the carpets and stared blankly at the golden glitters all around him. And unbidden and unwanted came the memory of the free-trader Paul who had shared his camp and told him of the robbery at the Belgian mint and the young guard who had been needlessly murdered.

Disgusted with himself, he muttered, "Nonsense! He is an honourable gentleman! As if he would do such a thing!" Besides, Lord Kincraig was a rich man. He'd said, "I have more than enough for both of you." But how had he amassed his fortune? Could it be that this was the real reason for the years he'd spent roving about Europe and spreading his silly rumours of jewelled and flying carpets? Had Duncan Keith tried to put a period to his unwanted half-brother not because he coveted the entire Kincraig fortune, but because he was afraid Jack Vespa might discover that their father was—

Such disloyal thoughts were disgraceful. It couldn't be true! It *couldn't!* But his eyes were as if drawn back to the sack. And he saw that it was indeed the kind of sturdy container that money houses tended to use. Struggling to dismiss the suspicions that were so horrible and yet so inescapable, he found that he was gathering the coins together once more. He stood on the carpets and began to stuff the *louis* and the torn sack back through the aperture in the roof. He tugged the splintered board as far closed as he could, then jumped down from the waggon and closed the doors.

The rain had stopped. Lord Kincraig was nowhere to be seen. He walked to where Bruine was grazing and secured her reins to a shrub. And he thought wryly that it would appear he might have exchanged a sire who was a murderous traitor for one who was a murderous thief. The duchess would be a great deal less than delighted to welcome him into her proud 'royal family' if that was the case. The only hope would be that his lordship had some perfectly logical explanation.

With a cynical shrug and a heavy heart, he sat on the tail of the waggon to wait.

14

Perhaps because he was so troubled, Vespa found the wait intolerable and after some minutes had passed he went in search of his father. The rain had given way to a misty overcast that did nothing to lighten his spirits. He left the spinney but Lord Kincraig was nowhere in sight. About two hundred yards to the south another copse of trees bordered a stream and he started in that direction. As he drew nearer, he heard men's voices. His lordship, it would seem, had met someone. A comrade in crime, perhaps? He swore under his breath, and moved cautiously into the trees.

There were two of them and they were conversing in English, but so softly that he could detect only a word or two: ". . . damned chancy, but worth . . . if we can bring it off!" That was Kincraig, and speaking with an irked briskness quite unlike his often vague ramblings.

His companion muttered, ". . . hot after you . . . I'll try to find out where . . . Don't like . . . no choice . . . *con Dios!*"

It was the farewell, and in Spanish. Vespa sprinted forward, his steps muffled by the pound of hooves, and was in time to catch a glimpse of a fast vanishing rider. A rider mounted on a splendid black horse. 'And that,' he thought bitterly, 'properly drives me to the ropes!'

He walked quickly back to the waggon, not much caring whether Kincraig saw him or not. He was adjusting the team's harness straps when Kincraig joined him.

"Been looking over my fine fellows, have you?" he said, resting a hand briefly on Vespa's shoulder.

"I can find no injuries, sir."

"Thank goodness for that! I was sure the waggon must go down. Only thanks to you it did not. Where did you learn that trick?"

So it was to be all lightness and business as usual. Somehow, Vespa found a grin. "Army training, I suppose. We were very often obliged to be inventive so as to win free from some tight spot or other. Do you still want your medicine, sir?"

Kincraig stared at him vacantly.

"You had asked me to get it for you," he reminded. "But when I brought it out, you'd gone. Are you feeling better?"

"Oh—yes. Much better, I thank you. Sometimes, you know, I become a little confused, and I suppose the fall rattled my poor brains a trifle."

Vespa's lips tightened and with an ache of the heart he entered this sad sparring match. "I shall have to keep a closer eye on you. I expect you'll want to inspect your waggon, but I think it's no worse for the accident."

Kincraig glanced at him obliquely then went to the rear of the waggon, peered about inside, and closed the doors. "You're right. No harm done that I can see."

"Then if you've completed your business here, we can go on. Consuela and Paige likely think we're at Jericho!"

Kincraig said ruefully that his joints seemed stiff after his fall, and Vespa helped him onto the seat and handed him the leathers.

Kincraig enquired, "What business?"

"Eh?" Mounting Bruine, Vespa said, "Oh, I thought perhaps this was where you were to meet your friend."

A pause while his lordship guided the team expertly into a wide turn. Then he replied, "He said he might leave a message here if he was delayed. There's an oddly shaped boulder in those trees over there. It serves as our post office. I walked over, but there was no message."

"Ah. Then your friend has not been delayed and will be waiting for you?"

"I hope so." For just an instant Kincraig's expression was very grim, then he said brightly, "Let's go and make sure."

They returned to the lane, Vespa riding beside the waggon and trying not to abandon all hope. After a while, he tried again. "Don't you have locks for your doors, father?"

Kincraig turned and smiled at him. "No, my dear boy. I've never felt the need."

'Good God!' thought Vespa.

"These people are very honest, you know," his lordship added. "And what are they going to steal? My carpets?"

"You did say that some of them are very valuable. And thieves who know of your collection would also know that you must carry funds to pay for whatever you decide to buy."

"No, no. I carry very little cash. All my purchases are by bank draft. I've an account at the Bank of France in Paris—" He saw Vespa's astonished expression and said roguishly, "under another name, I'll admit, but all perfectly legal. So you see, I've little to fear from robbers."

Vespa thought miserably, 'Except for a waggon roof that is practically solid gold!'

They did not speak again until they came up with the chevalier's coach. Manderville and Consuela had waited inside and hurried to meet them. Pierre shouted from the branch of a tree that he had found a bird's nest, but there were no eggs inside.

Vespa dismounted and took the hand Consuela reached out to him. "No uninvited guests?"

She shook her head. "You were gone so long, I was worried to death."

"We were just about to go in search of you," said Manderville, scanning Lord Kincraig narrowly. "Had some trouble, have you, sir?"

"A small *contretemps* with a wheel." His lordship shrugged. "Luckily, my enterprising son was able to solve the problem. Shall we proceed?"

Consuela was watching Vespa, and as he handed her back into the carriage, she asked softly, "What is it?"

He assured her she was finding trouble where there was none, but although he smiled there was an emptiness in his eyes that she had seen all too often during his convalescence and had prayed never to see again.

They resumed their journey. Kincraig led the way, and Vespa, who was driving the carriage, stayed a good quarter mile back, so as not to give the impression they were together. When they stopped at a wayside tavern to rest the horses Consuela and Pierre went inside to buy lunch, and Manderville complained that he was unable to sleep and might as well drive, because the boy was not still for an instant. When Vespa, lost in thought, made no comment, he asked, "Well? Now what are you mulling over?"

"You wouldn't believe me," answered Vespa shortly, and limped across the cobbled yard to where the cart-horses were being fussed over by an elderly ostler with whom his lordship was chatting earnestly. It struck Vespa that the old man's French was unusually faultless, but it was broken off as he came up, and the ostler hurried into the stables.

Vespa went in search of Consuela, wondering if the ostler was in league with the gang of thieves, and which of them had so viciously murdered the young guard at the Mint. To think such evil of the father he had just found and to whom he was so deeply drawn brought a pang of anguish. If only his suspicions proved to be unfounded. Heaven grant that was the case, and he was letting his imagination run away with him, and shooting at shadows.

They left the farm with baskets of bread, cheese and pickles, and a bottle of wine in each vehicle, plus a jar of milk for Pierre. Of necessity Lord Kincraig drove out first. Manderville volunteered to be coachman and, since the rain had stopped, Pierre sat on the box beside him, so that Vespa was able to join his lady for their 'luncheon.' He ate sparingly, but he cherished these moments when he could hold Consuela's hand now and then. She chattered happily about their marriage and their life together, and he gazed at her, responding appropriately and adoring her, even as he railed helplessly at the Fate which had dangled the promise of a joyous future before his eyes, only to snatch it away again.

He was watching her profile, framed by the opposite window, when he realized they were turning through a broken-down gate and into what appeared to be an abandoned farm. There was a grove of sycamores beside the gate, and a stony track led across a field that looked as if it had never produced a crop of anything but weeds. The carriage bumped along the track which gradually sloped downward, ending in a yard shaded by dense trees much in need of trimming. It was a gloomy and silent place. Vespa felt an odd shiver between his shoulder blades. Consuela's hand tightened on his. He opened the door, said, "Stay here, love," and jumped down.

Some tumbledown outbuildings clustered near a wreck of a house sadly out of plumb and looking as if a strong breeze would topple it. Kincraig's waggon was drawn up outside a large and crumbling barn.

Pierre was already leaping off to explore the house.

Vespa started towards the barn, and Manderville howled, "Wait up, Jack! I'll go with you!" as if he were a mile away.

Vespa glanced at him but walked on and into the barn.

His lordship was there. On his knees. A man lay sprawled before him. One look told the story. Momentarily speechless with shock, Vespa halted. Then, he took off his hat and said curtly, "He's dead, sir."

"Yes." Kincraig bowed his head into his hands. "Poor fellow! Oh, the poor fellow!"

Manderville ran up. "Oh—Egad! What happened?"

Vespa bent over the dead man. "Shot. But he was beaten first: savagely. It's murder, Paige."

They had both seen death in many terrible forms on the battlefield but like Vespa, Manderville had a reverence for life. "Poor devil!" he exclaimed, paling. "This was your—er, friend, my lord?"

Kincraig nodded and said brokenly, "My very good friend. Known Ivan . . . all my life. God! I didn't bargain for . . . for anything like this."

Disgusted, Vespa thought, 'Well, you should have!'

Manderville said, "He's been dead for some hours, I'd guess. We'd best have a look round. The killers may have waited for us."

Kincraig shook his head. "They'd have attacked when I drove in. No, I fancy this brave gentleman sent them off on a false trail, bless him."

"If he came in a waggon, whoever did this has made off with it." Vespa added ironically, "And presumably, his fragment of the Khusraw Carpet. There are cart tracks leading away to the south."

"What do you mean to do, sir?" asked Manderville.

Kincraig looked very shaken. "I—don't know yet. I must—"

"Have done," interrupted Vespa harshly. "This fiasco has gone on long enough! You've led me on a merry chase, my lord, but I am not so blind as you appear to think, and I'll brook no more of your devious little games."

Kincraig sighed heavily, but did not respond.

Manderville said a bewildered, "What fiasco?"

"The one I have foolishly drawn you into," said Vespa, "for which I apologize. But it is over now and I'll not subject Consuela to one more unnecessary hour of peril. We will turn west at once, and make a run for the nearest port."

"What d'you mean—west? If we're to restore Pierre to his home, we'll have to strike north!"

Vespa was driven by two emotions: the oppression of this gloomy place, and a strong premonition that time was running out. He said tersely, "Too far. We'll find a boat and a captain willing to sail around to the *Golfe de St.-Malo.* I want Consuela off French soil by tomorrow!"

"We'll still have about a thirty-five mile journey overland," said Kincraig glumly. "Two or three days, at the least."

"If we push the horses hard we can get there in half that time," rasped Vespa.

Staring at him, Manderville said, "I don't pretend to guess what bee you've taken into your bonnet, *mon Capitaine,* but you can't push horses hard when they're hauling a load like his lordship's waggon. They'll have to be rested and—"

"Whoever murdered this poor fellow is after what Lord Kincraig is carrying," snapped Vespa. "They'll be searching for the waggon so it must be abandoned. You'll not object, my lord." His smile was humorless. "Since your late friend here evidently failed to bring you his piece of the legendary carpet."

Lord Kincraig met his contemptuous gaze wistfully. "You're perfectly right, my dear boy. The waggon must be abandoned."

"What?" gasped Manderville.

Vespa had been sure his father would protest, and waited for the next stratagem.

"But it must be carefully hidden," appended Kincraig.

Vespa muttered, "I wonder why that doesn't surprise me. First, we'd best find some shovels."

While Manderville and his lordship went in search of these necessary items, Vespa hurried to the carriage and warned Consuela. She was horrified by the new tragedy, and hurried to the house to find Pierre and keep him away from the grim scene.

They buried the dead man under a small apple tree. The soil was soft from the rains and very soon their task was accomplished. Heads were bowed while Kincraig offered a reverent prayer for his friend, then Vespa and Manderville left him alone by the grave to say his last farewells.

Walking over to the waggon, Manderville said low-voiced, "What a ghastly thing. What kind of ghoul would kill a fellow like that?"

"The kind of ghoul in search of information—at any price."

"I suppose so. Poor Kincraig blames himself, that's clear to see. You were beastly short with him, Jack. He's hit hard, and you might at least have tried—"

"I'm trying now," said Vespa. "Trying to guess how he'll manage to hide his damned great waggon."

Consuela hurried to them. She was pale and shaken, and to turn her mind from its horror of the murder, Vespa told her of their latest problem. She gazed at the waggon and said hesitantly, "It will be very difficult, I think, because it is so big." Lord Kincraig came up, and she asked, "Perhaps there is a cave or—or gully nearby where we could conceal it, sir?"

"I wish I knew of one, m'dear. But as you suggest, there must be a hundred likely hiding places; I'm sure we'll come upon one."

"What are we going to hide?" asked Pierre, approaching with a hop and a skip.

Consuela said, "We can't take the waggon any further, dear. Bad men are trying to steal Lord Kincraig's carpets."

"Oh." The boy raced off and ran twice around the waggon, then came leaping back to announce that he knew just where to hide it.

Manderville ruffled his curls. "Tuck it in your coat pocket, eh, scamp?"

"Don't be silly," said Pierre, jerking his head away. "It's the best hiding place in the world! If I tell you, will you buy me some sugar cakes?"

"What you are, my lad, is a rogue! Sugar cakes, indeed!"

"We must leave at once, your lordship," urged Vespa. "If this was the work of Monteil's bullies, they may very well come back. You'd best get your personal effects together."

Kincraig nodded and went over to the waggon.

Pierre tugged at Vespa's coat. The boy had taken to regarding him with hero-worship in his eyes, and now said anxiously, "I'll show you, *mon Capitaine.* Please do come; it will only take a minute. One minute, only!"

Vespa could not resist that pleading look, and exchanged his irritated frown for a smile. "If it's a good hiding place you shall have a dozen sugar cakes," he promised.

"Wheee!" squealed Pierre, and taking his hand led him to the house, then stopped.

"Around the back, do you mean?" asked Vespa. "I'm afraid it would soon be found, Pierre."

"No it wouldn't, *Capitaine,* because this farm was accursed, and people do not come here. But I don't mean that we should hide it *behind* the house. I mean *in* the house!"

Vespa hadn't really expected anything much, but this piece of folly caused his brows to lift, and he said, "Oh, you do! Have some sense, lad. How do you suppose we could get that monster inside? Through the front door?"

Pierre giggled and tugged him at the run around the side. There had once been a sort of wooden lean-to at the back that had evidently served as a wash-house, but a big branch had fallen and caused part of the outer wall to cave in. Vespa frowned at the ruins thoughtfully.

Consuela had followed, and she slipped her hand into his. "I'm sorry, Jack. Pierre means well, but this is silly; houses are not built to accommodate waggons."

"Exactly so." He lifted her hand and kissed it absently.

"Which fact might work strongly in our favour. I judged it mad at first. But do you know . . . it just might serve. I'll go in and have a look."

He climbed over the branch and, brushing away webs, made his way inside. Pierre went after him eagerly, but Consuela waited, saying she would forego the delights of mould and mice and spiders.

They emerged in a minute or two, and a look at Vespa's face caused her own to brighten. "It will serve?"

"I think it may! It's a dirt floor, so there's no fear of boards collapsing from the weight of the waggon." He patted the exuberant Pierre on the back. "Jolly good work, young fellow! If you were under my command, you'd get a promotion out of this!"

"I am a sergeant!" the boy howled. "Monsieur Manderville! Your lordship! Your problem it is solved by Sergeant Pierre!"

Kincraig and Manderville were incredulous at first, but Vespa pointed out that if they moved the branch and cleared away the buckled rear wall they could back the waggon inside, then replace wall and branch so that the waggon was concealed from view. "If we take care to cover any betraying wheel ruts," he said, "who would ever think to look inside a house for such a vehicle?"

Manderville pursed his lips. "To abandon his lordship's beautiful carpets is too chancy by half, in my opinion."

"It is," agreed Kincraig. "And if I could but think of a better solution, I would take it. The pity is—I cannot. I have lost my— my dear friend, and the most important thing now is to get Miss Consuela and Sergeant Pierre to safety."

With strict instructions to keep out of sight, Pierre once again became their lookout, and went skipping off full of his own importance. Consuela reconnoitred the front of the house to be sure that, once inside, the waggon would not be visible from either of the small windows, and the three men set to work. The fallen branch was heavy, but between them they were able to move it aside. They took down the rotted wall in sections, and then dragged an old tub and a rusted mangle into what had been the kitchen/parlour. Much accumulated rubble had to be cleared from the lean-to before the waggon could be backed through the gap in the wall. It would be a tricky manoeuvre for there were scant inches between the roof and the top of the waggon. Kincraig knew his horses and spoke reassuringly to each one, then stood beside the leaders, assessing the gap they must negotiate.

Vespa said, "We're fortunate that the ceiling is so high. Even so, once inside it will be a tight fit. The tail will be right against the far wall. If there's anything more you need to take with you, now would be the time to get it, sir." He waited cynically for his father to reclaim at least one sack of the stolen gold, but Kincraig said he had already removed his "necessaries" and that Manderville had been so kind as to store them in the boot of the chevalier's coach.

Consuela clung to Vespa's hand nervously. "It's going to be terribly difficult to back it into such a narrow space. If only he could just drive it in."

"Even if he could, the inside door is on the wrong wall, and we wouldn't be able to get the horses out. But they're fine animals, and if you will be so good as to guide him from this side, and Paige from the other, I think his lordship will manage."

She was only too glad to be given a chance to help. Vespa watched as the challenging process began, then slipped away. He went quickly to the carriage. Kincraig's belongings had been packed into two boxes. He inspected each item, even feeling in the pockets of the garments. There was not a single *louis*. So all the gold was to be left in the waggon. To be retrieved, of course, either by his lordship or an accomplice; probably, the man riding the black horse.

There arose a deafening screeching sound as he closed the boot, and he limped rapidly around the side of the house. The waggon was backed halfway into the lean-to, the horses rolling their eyes in alarm and Kincraig trying to calm them. Vespa was struck by the incongruity of the scene—the giant waggon look-ing for all the world as though it was being extracted from the house.

Manderville was on the top, struggling to break away a por-tion of the roof of the lean-to that had sagged down, blocking any further progress. "Where did you get to?" he demanded irritably. "The waggon is fairly stuck! Can't budge it back or forward, con-found it all!"

Vespa retrieved two of the shovels and handed them up, then climbed to join him. The sagging portion of the roof had scraped across the top of the waggon, leaving deep gouges before it dug in, halting any further progress. He said, "If we use the shovels as levers, perhaps we can raise the roof enough for the waggon to move." He called down to Lord Kincraig to be ready to back the team again, then he and Manderville attempted to lever the roof up. It was hard going and he wondered cynically what would hap-pen if the pressure of the shovels broke through the top of the waggon. He was denied that scene as the obstructing section of the roof suddenly buckled and broke off. He and Manderville cleared away the debris and climbed down and Kincraig once more inched his team backwards. Within minutes the waggon was inside and halted by the far wall.

The cart-horses were lathered from their efforts and Man-derville walked them away to allow them to cool down.

Consuela, his lordship and Vespa stood gazing at the remains of the lean-to.

Kincraig said, "It's very tight, but once we replace the wall and that big branch, I do believe it will show not a sign."

"Except for the pole, of course," said Vespa. "It will have to come off, and should slide underneath—or is that not poss-ible, sir?"

"The work of a few moments, merely. When I designed my waggon, I tried to anticipate any predicament, you see."

"You did indeed." Vespa met Kincraig's gentle smile but did

not return it and wondered how many 'predicaments' his larcenous sire had surmounted these past few years.

Consuela exclaimed, "Oh, my goodness! What about the horses?"

At last that dilemma had been mentioned. Vespa thought with bleak irony, 'Well? Speak up, my lord!'

Kincraig said, "Oh, they'll fend for themselves well enough. We'll simply turn them loose."

"If we do that, sir," argued Vespa, "anyone coming upon them will surely realize there's a cart or a waggon somewhere about."

"Or steal them," said Consuela. "They're beautiful animals."

Kincraig made light of such objections. He would leave instructions with a peasant who dwelt nearby. The old man would be glad enough to earn a few pence in exchange for making sure that the cart-horses were taken care of and kept from the hands of thieves.

Vespa thought, 'And kept available for your friends!'

The roof and walls were propped and nailed more or less together again, the branch hauled back in place and another branch added to brace it and conceal a hole in the wall. Manderville and his lordship led the cart-horses off to the peasant's hut, and Consuela worked beside Vespa to obliterate the ruts left by the heavy wheels.

"When people conceal things, my Captain," she said, wielding a large rake industriously, "other people are apt to imagine much worse things."

It was true. And it would be kinder to tell her now than to let her go on dreaming her dreams of their happy future. He slanted a quick glance at her face; none too clean after this hectic day, the wet dark curls straggling about her flushed cheeks, and her blue eyes watching him with such trust and devotion. No complaints that she was tired and cold and her clothes wet from the rain; no moans about missing her Grandmama, or the need for her maid and a comfortable bed and a chance to bathe and change clothes.

She was the bravest and loveliest creature he had ever known, and he loved her so much it was an ache inside him.

His jaw set, and he went on raking with swift angry strokes. How could he tell her their last hope was gone? How could he bring her such grief—especially now when her beloved *Nonna* was not here to comfort her? Besides, he did not really *know* that his suspicions were justified. Suppose it developed that his lordship was an innocent dupe? After all, he'd been ready enough to leave the treasure waggon—perhaps he wasn't aware of what the roof contained. But that was grasping at straws, of course, and a foolish attempt to delude himself. There were too many pieces that fit the puzzle, too many coincidences for there to be any—

Consuela leaned on her rake and pushed back a curl that had tumbled down her forehead. "What has he done, Jack?"

Startled, his eyes flashed to her face again.

"My poor dear," she said tenderly. "Don't you know yet that you cannot hide your sorrows from me? Oh, I admit you do very well at concealing your feelings from others. But when you are distressed, I can feel it. And you have been deeply distressed ever since Lord Kincraig's waggon almost fell over. Something happened then, I know it. Won't you tell me? Perhaps I can help."

A lump came into his throat and his eyes blurred. He said brokenly, "My precious little Signorina . . . I don't deserve—"

"*Capitaine! Capitaine!*" Pierre galloped down the slope at reckless speed, knees flying. "Bad . . . people! A great black coach with . . . with the coachman and a footman in black livery. The coachman was that seasick pirate from . . . the ship!"

"Ti Chiu!" whispered Vespa. "Then Monteil's found us! Outriders?"

"*Oui, mon Capitaine!* There are two other men besides."

"The same pair we chased off yesterday?"

The boy's eyes became very round. "But—yes, sir! With the grey horses. How did you know?"

"They're coming here?"

"No. They went on past, but the great giant coachman looked this way. Oh, but my heart it stand still! And the black and white man he put his head out of the window and give a shout, and the great giant slowed the coach. But then he saw it, and I saw his face, and I thought, 'No, Sergeant Pierre! He is very afraid. He will not come here!' And I was right! He drove on. Fast. Just as I knew!"

"What did he see?" asked Consuela curiously.

The boy led the way from the yard and pointed up the slope towards the lane. "There! That is what frightened the giant! I did not see it when first we came, but it is why this farm died and why nobody comes here!"

Vespa said, "It's another of the menhirs."

"Where?" asked Consuela, "I do not see it."

"There, by the sycamore trees. And it's one of the larger specimens."

At first, she could only discern the trees, but then she realized that the shadows in the centre were not shadows, but instead one of the great standing stones left by the ancient people. "How fascinating they are," she said.

"And how lucky we are that Imre Monteil's coachman is superstitious," said Vespa. "But he's much too close. We daren't give him another chance."

He managed to imbue them with his sense of urgency, and very soon they were back on the lane. This time Kincraig had volunteered to drive the carriage, noting kindly that poor Manderville was worn out from his cold and lack of sleep. He had obtained excellent directions from his peasant friend, he said, and now knew the quickest route to the coast. "A most excellent fellow! He was even able to tell me where a likely fishing boat lies at anchor."

Riding Bruine beside the coach, Vespa said, "Was he, indeed. And did his excellence cost you enormous largesse, my lord?"

Kincraig laughed. "What a cynic!"

275

"What's a 'cynic'?" asked Pierre, who had claimed a seat on the box.

"I am," said Vespa dryly. "And we should put 'em along now, sir. It's liable to rain again at any minute, and there's little enough daylight left."

Kincraig cracked the whip, the horses leaned into their collars and the coach bounced and jolted over a surface poor to begin with, but made worse by potholes and mud.

The afternoon was drawing in and Vespa's hope to drive through the night had to be abandoned when the clouds darkened and an icy rain began to patter down once more. He shouted, "Hold up a minute, sir. Our sergeant must go inside, else we'll have him down with a cold also!"

The boy was wet and shivering and raised no objections. Vespa swung him from the box and handed him in to Manderville. Consuela looked wan and tired, but she had a smile ready, and set to work at once to dry Pierre's curls.

Vespa asked, "Are your pistols loaded, Paige?"

Manderville nodded. "Trouble?"

"Perhaps not, but I've twice thought someone was behind us."

"We'll have to stop, even so, old fellow. Won't be able to drive after dark. Not one of us knows these roads."

Another half hour and Vespa saw a ribbon of smoke rising above a rolling hill some distance ahead. If it came from the hearth of an inn, it might be their last chance of shelter for the night.

He called, "My lord, are there are any inns or *pensions* along—"

There came a high-pitched metallic twang. It was an evil sound, and one he knew. For an instant of stark terror his mind warned that a crossbow bolt could go right through the back of the carriage! Dreading to hear a scream, he heard instead a choking cry. His gaze flashed to the box. The reins had slipped from Lord Kincraig's hands and he was slumping forward.

Rage seared through Vespa. He leaned perilously from the saddle and caught the leathers. Drawing the team to a halt, he turned Bruine and rode to the window.

"Help his lordship!" he shouted, then drove his spurs home.

It was a hurt the little mare had not expected from this man. Ever faithful, she sprang into a gallop. Vespa crouched low over the saddlehorn, retribution in his heart, pistol in one hand, the wind whipping at his face and his narrowed eyes fixed on the distant rider who had left the lane and now plunged at reckless speed across the meadows.

15

There was no doubt in Vespa's mind but that the fleeing assassin was one of Duncan Keith's hired bullies and that he was now making a frantic dash to rejoin his comrades. The awareness and with it the knowledge that he himself might very well be riding straight into an ambush did not for an instant weigh with him. All that mattered in the white heat of his fury was that he bring down this cowardly murderer.

His quarry left the lane and headed across country. Vespa followed, not slackening his speed. The assassin turned and glared back at him. It was a costly move for at that moment his mount stumbled. He was a good horseman and retained his seat and the animal recovered almost at once, but the distance between them had shortened. A moment later the useless crossbow was flung aside. Again, the assassin turned. Vespa saw the flash before he heard the shot, followed by the hum of a bullet whizzing past. They topped a rise and he saw the gleam of water below. The other man was looking back to see if his shot had gone home, and he turned too late to avoid the lake.

With a howled curse, he wrenched at the reins. Frightened

and confused, his horse tried to change direction only to flounder and go down with a tangle of legs, a shrill neigh of fright and a great splash.

Vespa was on the bank then, pulling Bruine up and hurling himself after his adversary who had been thrown a short distance from the shore.

The water was like ice. It was hip deep when he reached the assassin, but the man seemed dazed and was evidently finding it difficult to stand.

"Murderous cowardly swine!" Vespa pushed his head under the water.

Strengthened by terror the assassin fought and struggled madly. He succeeded in breaking free and his head shot from the surface. Vespa grabbed his hair and forced him down again, avoiding the arms that flailed in frenzied attempts to beat him away. The desperate struggles weakened, and then ceased. Vespa let his head come up and he sagged, choking for breath and gasping out faint pleas not to be drowned. The temptation to deal him just such a fate was strong, but Vespa wanted information. Dragging the half-conscious rogue by the hair, he waded to shore. His prisoner tried feebly to crawl out, but he was too weakened. Vespa hauled him onto the grass and kicked him onto his back.

The face was pale and half covered by strands of wet hair. But even in the fading light there was no mistaking him.

"You accursed fool," panted Vespa. "You've just murdered your own father!"

"But—m'sieu," wailed the proprietor, wringing his bony hands and trotting along the narrow passage beside Vespa, "you both are very wet! And it is that I have floors, you comprehend! And rugs, m'sieu! They will be ruined, m'sieu!"

"Where are my friends?" Vespa had tied Keith's hands and

now used the crossbow he'd retrieved to prod him towards the stairs of this small hedge-tavern.

"I cannot," moaned Keith, swaying drunkenly. "I shall . . . fall down."

"Then I'll have the pleasure of kicking you until you get up," said Vespa grittily. "I saw our carriage in your yard, host," he added. "Don't make me drag this carrion up your stairs to no purpose!" He flourished the crossbow and the host recoiled eyeing the weapon in horror.

"No, m'sieu! I mean—yes, m'sieu! The poor gentleman is above-stairs and my girl but a minute ago finished washing the blood from the floor, and now, m'sieu—"

"You will be well paid."

At these magical words the host brightened. "It will be the second door to your right hand, m'sieu. Madame Lannion, my wife, is with the young lady."

Vespa nodded and urged Duncan Keith on. "Move, dog's meat!"

The stairs were steep and winding. At the top the second door in a short passage was partly open and Vespa shoved Keith inside.

Manderville and a tall middle-aged woman, Madame Lannion no doubt, were bending over the bed. Kincraig lay on his side with his eyes closed, the crossbow shaft still transfixing his right side just below the armpit. Consuela, pale but composed, was taking his lordship's shirt as the woman cut it away. She looked up when Vespa entered, and said unsteadily, "Thank God you've come!"

"Is he still alive?" asked Vespa.

She nodded, staring at Keith.

Vespa experienced an overpowering sense of relief, but there was a lot of blood and, remembering his lordship's medicine bottle, he knew death lurked nearby.

Manderville turned his head. "Caught the bastard, did you?" he said, forgetting the presence of ladies. "I wonder you troubled to fetch him back, if—" He broke off, staring at Keith. "Good Lord! It wasn't *him?*"

"My murderous half-brother." Vespa shoved Keith hard and the man staggered to the wall and slid down it to sit sprawling on the floor.

Consuela gasped, "Oh! How wicked!"

"Yes. A new low point in depravity, would you say?" Advancing to the bed, Vespa asked low-voiced, "How bad is it?"

"The poor gentleman is not so bad as wouldn't be better without all the evil words and violence," said Madame Lannion severely. Glancing at Vespa, she saw the crossbow and uttered a muffled shriek. "Ugh! Take that wicked machine from my house!"

Pierre, who had been perched in the window-seat, jumped up and volunteered to take the crossbow away.

Vespa handed him the weapon and looked up to find Kincraig's eyes on him. "I'm very sorry, my lord," he said gently, bending over the bed. "I knew we were followed. I just didn't think it was this particular group of ruffians."

Manderville sneezed and went into a bout of coughing, and Madame Lannion eyed him uneasily, then handed another strip of cloth to Consuela and stood straight. A handsome woman with a proud face and a splendid bosom, she met Vespa's anxious gaze levelly. "This I do not at all like," she said. "I help the Gentlemen where I can, but—" she shrugged, "This young man is ill, and—"

"Who—me?" Manderville wheezed indignantly, "Sound as sixpence!"

"—and I will not be responsible for the death of the Carpet Collector," Madame swept on. "You must tend him yourselves."

She had said 'the Gentlemen'—the widely-used term for free-traders. Vespa took a chance. "I was counting on you, ma'am. Paul said if I came this way I must stop and say good day."

She checked. "Paul? You know Paul Crozon?"

"I but left him two days since. He was with Jules and Léon and the rest, and his nephew sends you his love."

"Ho!" she said with a flash of her dark eyes. "That one! A rascal is what, and will grow up to be as foolish as his Papa. Ah, but this changes matters, Monsieur . . . ?"

"Jacques, Madame."

She smiled. "No last names, eh? It is as well. I will do what I may. With luck our farrier is in the tap. He is a finer doctor than most who have the title, and he will know what is to be done. Try to keep your poor friend quiet." A nod, a swirl of voluminous skirts, and the door closed behind her.

Kincraig whispered, "Crossbow . . . Then—then it was—" His gaze fell on the sullen features of the man on the floor, and he groaned, "Duncan—did you . . . hate me so much?"

Vespa said quickly, "He didn't mean to hit you, sir. It was me he aimed at. Missed again, didn't you, Keith!"

"Oh, no," sneered Keith.

Kincraig's wound was bleeding sluggishly. Bathing it as best she might, Consuela exclaimed in horror, "You really meant to kill your father?"

Kincraig tried painfully to lift himself, but Vespa eased him back down. "You must lie still, sir. We'll have help for you in only a minute or two."

Keith laughed. "No, you won't, fool! You can't push the bolt through, nor pull it back. He's as good as dead."

"Shut your mouth," snarled Vespa, turning on him in a fury.

"No," gasped Kincraig. "I want to know . . . *Why,* Duncan? I'd have left you a rich man, even . . . even allowing for Jack's share of the inheritance."

"Well, now I'll be a *very* rich man, won't I? You won't live to acknowledge him as your bastard, or to change your will, and, more importantly, you won't have time to enjoy a son who'd suit your antiquated notions better than I do. A gallant soldier, a fine athlete, a man of noble principles. What pitiful stuff! And only look at what's left. The gallant soldier has been discarded. The fine athlete is now a cripple. And his ridiculous principles will keep him from enjoying the Vespa fortune and estates—if there are any left."

Manderville started forward, fists clenched. "Why, you filthy wart! I'll—"

"No!" Pale with fury, Vespa held his friend back. "We'd as well hear it all."

Keith grinned, and added, "On the other hand, there is your legal son, Papa, who is hale and whole and has done quite well in the Trade. Didn't know that, did you? I've been a smuggler for years. Brandy, scent, guns—right under the noses of the stupid Excise men."

Manderville said stuffily, "What you mead is that in addition to your other revolti'g qualities, you're a traitor!"

"Not to myself," said Keith, laughing.

Vespa saw the glint of tears in Lord Kincraig's eyes. He said, "My apologies, Consuela," and crossed to where Keith sprawled. His half-brother's bravado vanished, and he cringed against the wall, babbling, "You can't hit me! My hands are tied! You must play fair!"

Bending over him, Vespa said softly, "One more word out of you, disgusting whelp that you are, and when we get that bolt out of my father, I'll use it on your own slimy hide! And you had better pray he lives, for if he dies—be assured that I'll do it anyway!"

Keith saw death in his eyes and recoiled, whining that he was freezing cold and sure to become a victim of pneumonia.

Madame Lannion hurried back into the room carrying a tray of medical implements and followed by a stoop-shouldered nondescript-looking man wearing a knitted cap and clutching a bottle of brandy. "This is our good Monsieur Aunay," she said. "He will help the poor gentleman."

Frowning, Vespa reached for the bottle. "I think you won't need this, monsieur."

"No," said the farrier in a deep boom of a voice. "But—he will!" He poured a generous portion and said, "Lift him. A little. No, not you, monsieur! You're soaking wet!"

Vespa drew back and Manderville and Madame Lannion raised Kincraig to the point that he could sip the brandy. Clearly, he was in much pain, but he didn't utter a sound while the farrier inspected the wound.

Leading Vespa aside, Aunay said, "We have two chances, monsieur."

"You m-must cut it out," said Vespa, through chattering teeth.

"That is our second choice. The first is a seldom-used tool of surgery." The farrier nodded to Madame Lannion, and she brought him a pair of heavy pruning shears. "Do not look so appalled, monsieur," said the farrier with a smile. "Fortunately for us, the bolt has the cruel steel barbs, but a wooden stem. If it were a steel bolt, I would have no alternative but to cut it out."

Vespa eyed the shears uneasily. "If it's wood, couldn't you just saw through the beastly thing?"

"I could try, but I had rather not. It would be more trying for my patient. With luck, one or two hard snaps with these, and we can pull out the bolt. One thing in our favour is that it is so far to the side. I think it has not touched the lung, but the gentleman—your father, sir?"

"Yes. He is not young, is that what you're th-thinking?"

"He is, I can see, a brave man. But it will be a shock. You accept that I am not a *bona fide* surgeon, monsieur?"

"You come highly recommended. I am sure you will do your best."

"As you wish." Aunay looked pleased. "Then—we proceed.

The young lady she must leave while we remove your papa's garments, and I wish you will swiftly find dry clothing, or I will have two patients on my hands!"

"Th-three," moaned Keith.

Vespa ignored him and turned back to the bed. Looking into the haggard face of the injured man, he knew suddenly that whatever his crimes, the bond between them was deep and binding. He said, "No tricks please, father. I want you to dance at my wedding."

Kincraig said nothing, but his eyes brightened and the white lips twitched into a smile.

It was still dark when Consuela ran down the stairs. A fire was burning on the hearth of the tiny coffee room and breakfast had been set out on a table. Vespa stood with one hand on the mantel, gazing down at the flames, and she ran to him, saying anxiously, "What is it? When I left you last night he seemed peacefully asleep at last."

He turned with a smile and took both her hands. "And how incredibly brave and kind you were, to stay with us as you did. Our clever amateur apothecary had given him some laudanum, so he slept through much of the night."

"Which is probably more than you did." She touched his tired face worriedly. "Have you seen Monsieur Aunay this morning?"

"Yes. He looked in just now and told me my father goes along nicely. I wish to heaven we could leave him here, but we must be on our way at first light." He led her to the table and pulled out a chair.

She sat down and said, "You never mean to take him with us? Jack, you cannot! He endured that dreadful ordeal very bravely, but the poor man is in no condition to travel."

Vespa had already snatched a hurried meal, but couldn't resist the chance to share these few minutes. He poured her coffee and moved the butter and jam and the bowl of hot rolls closer, then sat beside her. "He will be in worse condition if we don't get away from here quickly." With a grim look he went on, "My delightful half-brother won free in the night!"

"Oh, never say so! I thought you had him securely tied in the cellar?"

"I did. Like a fool! I should have kept him under my eye. He managed to persuade a gullible kitchen maid to loosen the ropes, and was free in jig time. I came down on the run when I heard her screeching. Keith had turned out all the the horses. I tried to stop him but he went off at the gallop on a fine hack."

Dismayed, she said, "And will bring back his nasty friends, I suppose."

"No. When I hauled him out of that lake yesterday afternoon he was in a rage because his hirelings have deserted him. Apparently, there are dragoons out searching for us, and his men were English and decided the risk was too great."

Spreading jam on a roll she asked, "Then—why must we leave so quickly? You and Paige could deal with Keith, surely?"

"Most assuredly we could. But the unnatural varmint promised to find the dragoons and send them after us. He's sure to implicate his lordship. It would present an ideal way to be rid of him."

"Oh, what a *horrid* creature he is! But surely they'll not believe what he says? Lord Kincraig has wandered about the continent for years and everyone knows—forgive me, Jack—that he's more a joke than a threat."

"They'd change their minds in a hurry if Keith should fabricate some tale about my father being a British spy." He thought, 'or a ruthless bank robber!' "And I've your precious self to consider." He ran a finger down her cheek lovingly. "I dare not risk it, Consuela. We must make a run for the coast. Paige is poling up the horses. Poor fellow, he really has a brute of a cold. Madame has been changing my father's bandages. I'm going up now to help him get dressed. Will you see about young Pierre?"

She nodded, but said worriedly that it might be as well to leave the child here so that he could be restored to his family. "The Lannions seem to be good people."

"Yes, I'm sure they are. But the boy is my responsibility, you know."

"Indeed he is not! I was the one who gave him the chance to run away."

"And it is thanks to me that he was not sent back at once. Besides, if we leave him, like as not he'll run away again and try to find us, and get thoroughly lost in the process. No. I must deliver him to Gaston myself."

Consuela had to admit the logic of what he said, but much to her exasperation, she was unable to fulfill the task he had set her. The truckle bed in the room Pierre had shared with Manderville was empty and the boy was nowhere to be found. She gathered her few belongings together and carried them down to the stables. The carriage was ready, the horses harnessed and stamping impatiently. A yawning ostler said that he had seen young Master Pierre carrying the crossbow "like a soldier," but didn't know where he was now. Consuela asked him to put her bag in the boot, and wrapping her cloak tightly around her, went outside.

Dawn was brightening the eastern skies, the air was wintry but, at least at the moment, it was not raining. She went around to the side of the tavern and called, but there was no sign of Pierre. Vexed, she muttered, "Wretched child. Where have you got to now?" Jack was so anxious to get an early start, and he certainly would not leave without the boy. She walked up the lane a short way, calling, and peering through a swirling ground mist for a glimpse of a small figure carrying a crossbow.

She heard Pierre before she saw him. His answering calls were broken by sobs and she began to run, fearing he had fallen and hurt himself. She traced the cries to a cluster of yew trees some distance across the field. No sooner did she enter their shade than Pierre sped to throw himself into her arms. He was still clutching the heavy crossbow, but raised no objections when she removed it. The defiant warrior had vanished, and he was just a very frightened little boy who clung to her whimpering a plea to go home to Papa.

"But of course you shall, my dear," she said, holding him tight. "Captain Jacques is even now preparing to leave. Why ever did you not come when I called you?"

"Because . . . because of—*them.*" He half whispered the words, his big eyes peering around in terror.

The hedge tavern was out of sight. Consuela thought of the wicked Duncan Keith and his scoundrels, and of Imre Monteil and his terrible coachman, and tried not to look frightened. Lowering her voice she asked, "Who, dear? I cannot see anyone."

"There!" He pointed impatiently. "And there, and—there! Oh, but they are all around! I didn't see them when I came in here to practice with the crossbow. But it began to get lighter and there they were. Watching me!"

Consuela saw also. An impressive circle of the megaliths with the trees as if clustered to conceal them. With a sigh of relief, she said, "But they are just some menhirs, Pierre. Nothing more than great slabs of stone. They cannot harm you. Only think how clever the ancient people were, to manage to bring them here and make them stand upright."

He shook his head vehemently. "This, it is not possible! People today cannot move them. I know, for my Papa and some of his friends tried once. They were big and strong, but it was no use. And if modern men who are clever can't do it, how could cavemen who were stupids? It was magic, Miss Consuela! And they are here, weaving evil spells all—all round us!"

In his abject fear his voice had risen shrilly. Consuela said with decision, "Nonsense! That is just silly superstition. Now come and—"

"No," he wailed, tightening his hold about her. "Only look at the bad things that have happened. Yesterday the Carpet Collector went to meet his friend, and found him killed stone dead near that great big menhir. And then the old gentleman was shot and is going to die—"

"But—no, Pierre! Lord Kincraig is much better this morning. Only come and you will—"

"No! I cannot! He is brave, the old Carpet Man. But he will die, and I like him and it was only because we came near these menhirs it all happened. Do you see how many there are? Oh, I tell you, they are demons, and—"

"That's enough!" The note of hysteria in his voice caused her to say sternly, "Whatever would your papa and Captain Jacques think if they saw you blubbering like a baby over a silly old piece of rock? Pick up your crossbow like a brave boy, and come with me at once." She had to pry his arms away and he struggled and looked up at her piteously, his face tear-streaked and his eyes reddened. Hardening her heart, she said, "Hurry, now. We are going to find a ship to take us back to the village near your papa's château. If you don't want to come I shall have to go without you."

He gulped a sob, but took up the crossbow and walked as close to her as was possible, trembling with fear at every step.

Consuela rested a hand on his shoulder, and as they stepped out of the circle of yews, she said comfortingly, "there now. That wasn't so bad, was it? And we are quite safe in spite of those silly menhirs."

But glancing up she saw that she had spoken too soon.

Manderville was dismounting as Vespa rode at the gallop into the yard, and the two men exchanged shouts of "Any luck?" The host ran from the tavern and looked from one troubled face to the other. "The luck there is not," he mourned. "But you have been searching for three hours, *messieurs*—how can they have gone so far?"

"How, indeed." Vespa handed Bruine's reins to the ostler. "There has been no letter for me, Monsieur Lannion? No message?"

The host shook his head.

Manderville looked at Vespa sharply, but said nothing, and sneezed his way up the steps.

The host trotted along beside them. "My spouse she says we should perhaps restore your papa to his bed, Monsieur Jacques. Elegant as it is, he does not rest so comfortably on the sofa."

The window shades were still drawn in the small parlour, and the room was dim. There were no customers at this hour and a maid hovered about dusting half-heartedly.

Fully dressed, propped by several pillows and with a blanket thrown over him, Kincraig lay on the sofa that only a determined optimist could describe as 'elegant.' Vespa scanned the drawn white face and, as if the injured man sensed his presence, the hazel eyes opened. The glow of affection dawned at once. Vespa knew too well the after-effects of wounds, and he took up the glass of water on the occasional table and offered it. Kincraig drank gratefully. Vespa asked, "How can we make you more comfortable, sir?"

"By leaving." The voice was weak but clear. "You should— should have gone at sun-up."

"If you mean, without you, that is not to be thought of. I'll confess I've a heart of stone, sir. I'd have packed you in the coach and driven out long ago. Unfortunately, the boy and Miss Jones have wandered off somewhere. The lady has a habit of—of disappearing."

His lordship's head jerked up, he flinched painfully and lay back again. "You never think . . . Duncan?" he gasped.

"Your son spoke of dragoons, sir," said Manderville, carrying in two mugs of coffee. "But we've seen no sign of military."

Vespa accepted one of the mugs with a nod of thanks. "They were on foot," he said, his eyes bleak. "We searched every area they might conceivably have reached. Pierre's an enterprising rascal. He doesn't want to go home and he might well have led Consuela a merry chase, but—"

He broke off as the ostler ran in, flushed and excited and waving a note. "This it is left for Monsieur Jacques!"

Vespa was across the room in two long strides, and tearing the letter open.

Manderville asked, "Who delivered it? Did you see?"

The ostler shook his head. "I walk the little mare to cool her down and when I come back, the letter it is stuck on a nail on the stall. I see nobody."

As if turned to stone, Vespa was staring at the paper he held.

Manderville asked hoarsely, "Well? What does it say?"

Vespa neither moved nor spoke.

Manderville took the paper from his hand. The writing was neat and clear:

This time your lady visits me by invitation. You have one hour to exchange her for the location of the waggon. If you prefer to keep the waggon, I will give her to the dragoons who are everywhere now, and collect the reward for foreign spies.

Do you think she will be shot—when they finish with her? Or guillotined?

How sad it would be for such a pretty head to fall into the basket.

My coach will wait by the shrine on the west side of the lake.

I. M.

Manderville swore and handed the note to Lord Kincraig.

Deathly pale, his mouth set in a tight line, Vespa walked to the door.

Manderville sprang to seize his arm. "What are you going to do?"

Tearing free, Vespa said harshly, "D'you think for one instant that I'd trade Consuela's dear life for that damned waggon?"

"You mean to tell him where it is?"

"Be assured of it!" He started for the door again.

"No!" Coughing, Manderville sprang to block his way and said breathlessly, "You cannot!"

"Like hell I can't! Stand aside!"

"You don't understand! The waggon holds more than carpets! The roof—"

"Is full of stolen gold. Oh, yes, I knew. I didn't think you did. Perhaps that explains your 'devotion' to my search, eh?" Vespa said bitterly, "I should have guessed. But if you think I'll exchange the life of my precious lady for a few hundred gold *louis*—" he shoved Manderville aside and reached for the door handle.

His lordship, dragging himself to one elbow, panted, "Jack! Wait . . . you don't—"

"Sorry, sir. But you'll have to get along without your ill-gotten gains!"

Manderville seized his shoulder, wrenched him around and struck hard and true.

Vespa measured his length on the floor.

Dazed and astonished, he gasped, "Why, you . . . damned blackguard!" and started up, only to pause as Manderville's small pistol was levelled at him. Even now, he'd not expected this. "You . . . wouldn't," he said.

"I will. If you leave me no choice."

Staring into his friend's unwontedly stern face, and noting the blurred look to the eyes and the high flush, Vespa muttered, "You . . . really are ill!"

"No. But I daren't take the chance you might level me with that confounded right of yours."

"You'd shoot me—for a few filched bags of gold?"

Lord Kincraig said faintly, "We'll have to . . . tell him, Paige."

"You're in it together," said Vespa, sitting up and wiping blood from the corner of his mouth. "My God! Well, nothing you could tell me would make a difference. You'll have to pull that trigger, Paige, because I'm going after my lady."

"The gold wasn't . . . filched, Jack," said Kincraig. "I—I rather suspected you thought it was."

Manderville said, "And it's not a few bags."

"I'd guess about four hundred *louis,*" said Vespa contemptuously, kneeling and watching for his chance.

"Try guessing about forty thousand," said Manderville.

Staring at him, Vespa gasped, "You're out of your mind! The roof wouldn't hold that much weight."

"No, but the waggon also has false sides and a false bottom."

"And some of the carpets have—have gold sewn into the backings," said Kincraig.

"Great heavens! How long have you been in the bank-robbery business, sir?"

Manderville sat down wearily and blew his nose. "Wrong business, Jack."

Kincraig explained, "I am . . . by way of being a—a courier, you see."

A courier? Vespa thought, 'What kind of courier would take such a fearful risk as to haul a fortune in gold *louis* across France?

Towards Spain . . .' And it all fell into place at last. He groaned and slumped back on his heels. "Oh—my God! *Wellington?*"

Kincraig said weakly, "The Field Marshal hasn't been able to pay his men and—he is desperately in need of funds. Without them, he faces sure defeat in—in the spring."

"And you work for him?"

"Not exactly. I—at present—work for Nathan Rothschild, who—who made the loan. We had to get the gold to Wellington somehow."

"And I'm under orders." Manderville stood and put up his pistol. "Have been from the start." He reached out and pulled Vespa to his feet.

Manderville's stubborn insistence that Lord Kincraig was not in France, his persistent attempts to turn them aside and then his determination that they keep together made sense now, and Vespa exclaimed, "Damn you, Paige! Why didn't you tell me?"

"Sworn to secrecy, old boy. I wouldn't have broken my word now, if this hadn't happened. You can guess the need for it to have been kept so desperately quiet. We had to ship £800,000 in gold under Bonaparte's nose, you might say."

"Eight . . . hundred . . . *thousand?*" Vespa tottered to the end of the sofa and sat there, trying to take it all in.

"I am but one of many couriers," explained Kincraig, holding his injured side painfully.

"Your father has taken some really horrendous risks." Manderville broke into another spasm of coughing. Wiping tearful eyes, he wheezed, "He was supposed to rendezvous with a British warship off Belgium, but a trap was set and he had to make a run for it. Afterwards, he took the chance of trying to get through to Wellington direct. When you began to sniff around in search of your family tree, Wellington was horrified, and assigned me to try and head you off."

"*Head me off?* Why in hell didn't he just *order* me off?"

"I don't pretend to know, dear boy. He's been heard to remark that you were one of his finest staff officers. He knew about—er, Sir Kendrick, and that you'd been wounded again. Perhaps he sympathized, or perhaps he thought you'd never get this close. At all events, Hasty Adair said the great man's hand was over you. To an extent."

Vespa was briefly silent. Then he said slowly, "You've been splendid, sir. And I've been a proper fool. I am so sorry!"

"Nonsense. You reacted exactly as—as you ought. I knew you wouldn't blame me . . . once you learned the truth." Kincraig held out his hand.

Vespa took it and held it firmly, then he stood and offered a short and rather shy bow. "I'm very proud to be your son, sir. But—I'm afraid I must leave you now."

Manderville, who had moved back to lean against the wall, stepped forward. "I'm with you, Jack. What d'you mean to do?"

Vespa smiled. "Why, I'm going to tell Monteil where the waggon is, of course."

"No!" Aghast, his lordship protested, "You *cannot!* I—I know how much your lady means to you, Jack, but—if Wellington loses this war, Bonaparte will enslave all Europe, and Britain! The prospect—"

"Is terrible indeed, sir. But, tell me, if you will, do you think it possible that Imre Monteil knows what you carry in the waggon? Or is he drawn by the lure of your legendary Spring Carpet?"

Kincraig hesitated, then replied slowly, "I really believe that the only men who know the truth of it are Rothschild's people, who are, I would stake my life, incorruptible; and Field Marshal Lord Wellington."

"Yet—Manderville knew. Who else, Paige?"

"Prinny, of course. Cannot very well keep our next monarch in the dark. Hastings Adair, and one or two other high-ranking officers, probably."

Vespa frowned thoughtfully. "You said you were one of many couriers, sir. Have the others run the gauntlet successfully?"

"I've no idea. The reason I failed was that, as Manderville said, I was prevented from keeping the rendezvous with our warship."

"You were able to keep other rendezvous, though." Kincraig looked puzzled and Vespa said, "The fellow who rides the black horse. I think you had a chat with him after the waggon toppled. One of our people, is he?"

"We have him to thank for leading Monteil astray," said Manderville. "Otherwise we'd have had him and his Chinese juggernaut on our heels before we ever reached Chateau Coligny."

Vespa nodded. "And your friend who was killed at the meeting place, sir?"

"Poor Ivan . . ." Kincraig sighed. "Such a good, brave man. A ship has been despatched to take me up. Ivan was to tell me where to meet it."

"He was badly beaten, sir. Did he know what you carried?"

"You mean—might the secret have been forced from him? I think not. He was of the Intelligence Service, and those poor fellows are seldom given the full story, you know. He—er, he did manage to leave me a message, however."

"He did?" Startled, Manderville asked, "How?"

"He must have still been alive when his murderers abandoned him. He'd managed to scratch a sign in the mud. An arrow. Pointing southwest."

"By Jove, but here was gallantry!" exclaimed Manderville, awed.

"Gallantry, indeed," agreed Vespa. "One last quick question, Father. You said there were *louis* sewn into some of the carpets. Would that constitute a great sum?"

"There are fifty in each of two rugs."

"A hundred pounds, roughly. Hmm. Well, we must be off or the hour will be up." Vespa gripped his father's hand once more.

"Don't wait for us, sir. Get to the coast and a ship as soon as you're able."

Lord Kincraig said fervently, "Come back safely, my dear boy. God be with you both."

As they hurried to the stables, Vespa outlined his plan. Manderville said dubiously, "It's not much of a plan. D'you really think it will work?"

"It *must* work! I'll get Consuela out of that bastard's hands, or—" Vespa paused, looking very grim.

"Yes, of course," Manderville cuffed him gently. "Sorry, old fellow." And he thought wearily, 'We might have a chance—if only we can get rid of the juggernaut!'

16

A bitter wind had come up by the time Vespa approached the lake. The tree branches were tossing about and a few remaining leaves scattered down. On a distant hill a great castle loomed majestically against the flying clouds, the slate rooftops of a village clustering about it.

He rode fast, praying that he could bring this off and wondering if Paige, who was beginning to look quite pulled, would get through. Ever alert, his eyes searched for Monteil's coach, but before he reached the lake he was surprised by two men astride dapple-grey horses who charged from a hollow, drew rein at the last possible instant, causing Bruine to shy nervously, and then pulled in on either side. It was the unlovely pair they had encountered before. They had probably hoped to unseat him, but he was a consummate horseman. He stroked the mare's neck to quiet her, and watched them in a contemptuous silence.

"Mark you, Bertrand," jeered the bushy-haired individual, looking as wolfish as ever. "Is he not the strong and silent soldier boy?"

His friend seemed to have acquired even more pimples. He

giggled, and said, "He is—now, Étienne, but monsieur will have him chattering like a magpie in jig time." He added tauntingly, "If he wishes to see his lady again."

Vespa said, "Doubtless, Monsieur Monteil is accustomed to wait while you two exchange clever witticisms."

Étienne laughed and brought his whip down hard across Bruine's nose. The mare reared with a shrill neigh of fright and pain. Bertrand swung the grip of his horse pistol at Vespa's head, smashing him into a blurred world of echoing voices and laughter.

In a remote fashion it dawned on him that they were moving again. The old head wound and the side of his jaw throbbed with pain. He slumped forward over Bruine's mane as if barely able to stay in the saddle, while gradually his mind stopped spinning and confusion was replaced by rage.

They were slowing. The bushy creature—that would be Étienne—called in his nasal voice, "Wake up, Monsieur-the-so-dashing-Capitaine!"

Bertrand sniggered, "I'll dash him!"

Vespa was ready. As a heavy riding whip flailed at him, he ducked, caught the thong and heaved. Bertrand uttered a surprised yelp and disappeared under his horse. Étienne cursed furiously and swung up a pistol. Vespa spurred Bruine straight at him so that he had to rein aside.

A harsh voice rang out: "Enough! *Imbeciles!* Did I not say that I wanted him unharmed?"

Imre Monteil's luxurious coach waited beside a grove of trees. His Chinese coachman, arms folded across his massive chest, was at the heads of the leaders. On the box, a liveried guard held a musket aimed steadily at Vespa.

Watching frowningly from the open window of the coach, Monteil said, "My apologies, Captain. I had hoped we could deal as civilized gentlemen, but I see my men have been rough with you."

Vespa said coldly, "Never send an animal to do a man's work."

Bertrand crawled to his feet, his narrow eyes glaring hatred.

Monteil shrugged. "You appear to have dealt with my 'animals'—what is it you English say?—deedily? And now, Captain, you and I must deal together. Where is the waggon of your illustrious sire?"

So the Swiss knew Lord Kincraig was his father. Vespa countered, "I will tell you after Miss Jones and the boy are released and I have your word they will be allowed to leave."

The Swiss called, "Ti Chiu!" and the Chinese coachman trundled to the far side of the carriage and swung open the door.

Vespa started around the coach, but the guard on the box shouted, "You will stay where you are, monsieur!"

Halting, Vespa said angrily, "If you think I'll tell you anything until Miss Jones is beside me, you're all about in your head, Monteil!"

The white hand resting on the window gestured.

Vespa heard a low growl of rage followed by running footsteps. He flung himself from the saddle in time to catch Consuela as she rushed into his arms. He held her close, and she half-sobbed, "Oh, Jack! Oh, Jack! They have hurt you! I did it again, didn't I?"

"You're safe," he said huskily. "Just at the moment that's all I care about."

Ti Chiu came around the coach, limping slightly, and growling at Pierre as the boy ran past, sticking out his tongue with gleeful derision. The coachman made a snatch for him and Pierre squealed and hid behind Vespa. "I kicked him. Hard. And I am not sorry," he declared, and keeping a wary eye on Ti Chiu, he went on: "And it was not Miss Consuela's fault. She came to help me, Capitaine Jacques, because I was captured by some terrible menhirs. I am a brave boy, but I was very afraid, I will say it!"

"You were well justified." Vespa gripped his shoulder comfortingly while slanting a glance at the Chinese. Stark horror was written on that usually inscrutable countenance. "And Miss Consuela was very brave to go to you." He looked steadily into Consuela's eyes. She managed a tremulous smile that wrung his heart and that faded as he added, "Because I know how very much she fears those megaliths."

She had never said such a thing, but she sensed that this was not a joke, and answered cautiously, "You do not like me to be superstitious, but—"

Pierre interrupted excitedly, "Everyone knows they come to life at night! They wouldn't let me go, and they made evil spells round and round us. That's why these bad people caught us! But Miss—"

"Enough!" said Vespa. "Did these varmints hurt you, Consuela?"

She shook her head. "They wanted me to tell where Lord Kincraig left the waggon, but I didn't know how to direct them properly, so they were angry and made all kinds of horrible threats."

"Harsh words," said Monteil with a sigh. "And when I have with much patience allowed you the friendly little talk. I find your conversation not entrancing. We will now drive on."

It was exactly what Vespa had expected, but he protested indignantly that Monteil had promised to release Consuela in exchange for the location of the waggon. "You did not stipulate that I was to lead you there!"

"But you see," explained Monteil with the thin smile that never seemed to reach his dull black eyes, "People are so sadly devious these days. You will surely not expect me to release the lady until I am sure you have kept your part of the bargain. Besides which," his smile broadened "you are so much outnumbered, *mon ami,* and you must bear in mind that you have incurred the displeasure of my men. They would be pleased, I am sure, to help you understand my point of view."

His two bullies expressed their willingness to make things

clear to the Captain. They were so willing, in fact, that Vespa felt Consuela shiver. He said, "I think you have an exaggerated notion of the worth of that waggon. I'll take you there, but then Miss Jones and the boy go free. It is agreed?"

Monteil nodded and purred blandly, "But by all means, Captain Vespa."

⌒⌒⌒

The last time Vespa had ridden this road, Lord Kincraig had led the way and his own mind had been preoccupied with other matters. As a result, it was as much as he could do to recall the route, and he was relieved when the road narrowed as it wound through a ravine-like break in the hills, which he did remember. After that, for a while memory failed him, but he was again reprieved when they came to the river, crossing it at length over a tall-sided wooden bridge whose strange construction made it quite a landmark. And so he went along, feeling his way as it were, from one vaguely familiar spot to the next, until they came at length within sight of the broken gate leading to the abandoned farm.

Monteil had insisted that Consuela and Pierre return to the carriage, and Étienne and Bertrand rode on each side of Vespa. His nerves were taut as he rode onto the stony track and past the grove of sycamores. There was no shout, no sign. He sent up a fervent prayer that his plan would not fail; Paige had been right, it was so appallingly simple it could not really be termed a plan. If he could just get Consuela safely away . . . if he could just keep the waggon from falling into Monteil's greedy paws . . . if only Manderville was in place . . . His father would never forgive— There was a dispute behind him. His heart leapt. He thought, 'Aha!'

Monteil howled. "Vespa! Halt!"

The carriage had come to a stop. Ti Chiu was climbing down from the box. Through the open window Monteil raged at him. "You bovine idiot! What d'you think you're about?"

His henchman strode back onto the lane and stood there, facing away from the farm, arms folded across his chest, massive, forbidding, immovable: for all the world like another menhir. His master's commands were as if unheard; insults, curses and threats were completely disregarded.

Vespa called innocently, "Is this far enough, Monteil?"

"How do I know, curse you? I see no waggon!"

"You'll find it further along this track. You'll come to—"

"We will come nowhere without you lead the way! Guard! You drive on."

"But—what about Ti Chiu?" enquired Vespa.

Monteil's response made Consuela cover Pierre's ears. One gathered that Ti Chiu refused to go any farther towards a farm that had been abandoned because of the menhirs who dwelt there. He was an ignorant dolt, an imbecile, and he could stand there like the block he was until they took him up after they'd found the waggon! "And it had better be here," snarled Monteil.

Riding on, Vespa was cheered by the thought that the first step in his plan had succeeded. For the moment, at least, the greatest menace was out of commission.

When they stopped in the yard, Étienne ran into the barn. He came out a moment later to report that there was "no waggon, monsieur," and leered hungrily at Vespa.

Monteil said softly, "I warned you, Captain!"

"And I warned you. The waggon is here. Let Miss Jones and Pierre down and I'll show you."

Bertrand picked at his unlovely countenance and said, "He make the big bluff, but I will beat the truth from—"

Monteil stepped down from the carriage. "You will keep the lady here, while our captain fulfils his part of the bargain. Étienne, you come with me."

Consuela and Pierre left the coach and stood together, holding hands.

Tearing his eyes from his beloved, Vespa said, "This way."

Monteil and the wolfish Étienne followed. When they reached the back of the farmhouse, Vespa paused, astonished. He'd not dreamed Paige could have done so much in such a short time, but the branch and the smashed wall had been moved aside, the waggon was out of the lean-to, and the pole connected once more.

Monteil exclaimed, *"Sacré bleu!* Kincraig he is crazy indeed! He leave his treasure of carpets standing here like this? Unguarded?"

Vespa gathered his wits. "As you know very well, my father was shot by your killer with the crossbow. We had to get help for him quickly."

He was afraid the Swiss would realize his answer made little sense, but Monteil was too eager to inspect the waggon to analyze the remark and the reference to a killer with a crossbow disturbed him. "I have no such person in my employ," he said, with an uneasy glance at the dismal farm and the distant menhir. "Open the door of this ugly cart."

Praying, Vespa threw the doors wide.

A French *cuirassier* in all the glory of luxuriant whiskers, great steel helm and breastplate, a sabre in one hand and a musket in the other, leapt from the waggon, howling at the top of his lungs, "Traitors! Murderers! Thieves! Now I have you caught in my fist! I arrest you in the name of *l'Empereur!"*

There was a concerted gasp. Impressed by Manderville's resourcefulness, Vespa whipped around, and his right jab sent the gawking Étienne into collision with his employer. Monteil thrust him away and they retreated at the gallop. From the corner of his eye Vespa saw another *cuirassier* hot after Bertrand, whose knees had a fine fast action. Although puzzled by the reinforcements, Vespa was not one to let opportunity pass by. He snatched the bugle that hung about Manderville's neck and blew a fairly creditable 'Advance at the double' on the dented instrument. The retreat became a rout. Carriage, Swiss and Bertrand tore up the stony track, Étienne running weavingly after them, with the second *cuirassier* in hot pursuit.

Laughing, Vespa said, "Paige, when I asked you for a diversion, I never dreamed—" Turning to his friend, the blithe words died away.

The musket was still aimed at his heart. The *cuirassier* who held it so steadily was scarlet with wrath.

Whoever he was, he was not Paige Manderville.

"Whoops!" said Vespa.

"You have blow on my bugle!" the *cuirassier* roared, putting first things first. "You are not of La Belle France! You, I arrest as the English spy!"

"I apologize for your bugle, monsieur," said Vespa politely. "But—who is this?"

Instinctively, the *cuirassier* turned his head. Into Manderville's fist.

"Gad," said Vespa, easing the Frenchman down. "What happened? And how on earth did you get the waggon out of—" Again, his sentence went unfinished.

The four cart-horses were being shepherded across the field by a solitary rider.

"Damn!" exclaimed Vespa, and snatched up the *cuirassier*'s musket.

"Easy, Captain, sir! Easy!" croaked Manderville, pushing the weapon aside. "I'll own I've been tempted from time to time, but . . ."

For the first time Vespa had a clear view of the man on the black horse. Incensed, he curtailed his lusty swearing as Consuela ran to join them.

Her reaction was quite different. "It's *Toby!*" she cried joyously. "Oh, how lovely! We are all together again!"

Vespa took her outstretched hand, his eyes softening, but he said, "Of all the bacon brains, Broderick! Trailing me all over Brittany! Why didn't you identify yourself? I thought you were one of Monteil's ugly crew. I'd have blown your head off if you came close enough!"

"Exactly why I kept at a safe distance, my tulip." Grinning, Broderick dismounted, clapped Vespa on the back, and flushed shyly as Consuela hugged him.

"That'll be enough of that," said Vespa, pulling her to him. "I allowed it only because I am told you kept Imre Monteil off our heels for a while."

"Then I'm entitled to another hug," said Broderick. "I've found us a short-cut to the Lannions' hedge-tavern."

"Have you, by Jove! Jolly good, Toby. But there's no time for more rewards. Our French friend here is probably part of a scouting party. The rest of his troop is liable to come calling at any moment! We must be least in sight, but *vite!*"

The men worked swiftly to pole-up the cart-horses. Consuela and Pierre bound the hapless *cuirassier* and he was dragged, barking out ferocious threats, into the house. Within five minutes the waggon of the Crazy Carpet Collector was speeding along under wind-whipped trees.

Broderick led the way, following a rutted track that he assured them would bring them onto the road leading to the hedge-tavern. Vespa rode Bruine, keeping close to the waggon, and Manderville drove, with Pierre and Consuela perched on the seat beside him. There was little talk, even the boy sensing their tension although nobody voiced the fears that were uppermost in all their minds: that the French military were much too close on their heels; and that Imre Monteil knew exactly where they would go.

Broderick's 'quickest route' began to seem very much the long way round. The heavy waggon bumped and jolted over the uneven surface, and the wind became a near gale, blowing a cold drizzling rain into their faces, and sending branches and leaves flying.

They'd been travelling for half an hour when they turned

west onto the road to the Lannion hedge-tavern. The river was running high now, the water roiling and full of debris. Vespa realized belatedly that the oddly constructed bridge was a comparatively flimsy wooden structure. If it could not bear the weight of the heavy waggon . . . He glanced uneasily at Manderville, and saw apprehension on the handsome features. "Hold up!" he shouted.

Manderville pulled up the team.

Vespa sent Consuela and Pierre across the bridge on foot. Broderick and Manderville rode, and Vespa—over Manderville's hoarse but indignant protests—drove the waggon. The cart-horses trod onto the timbers and began to snort and toss their heads uneasily. The bridge creaked and it seemed to Vespa that it swayed. He thought, 'Please God, we're so close now!' If the waggon crashed into that muddy boil of water below it would be the end of his father's brave struggle and he would have failed his General. On the far bank he could see Consuela looking pale and frightened, watching him and clinging to Manderville's arm. The bridge creaked even more menacingly. There was a sudden loud crack and the off wheeler neighed and pranced in the traces. Vespa's heart jumped into his throat. A large carriage approaching from the west stopped, and pulled off to the side of the road. Rain sheeted down blindingly. 'Nothing ventured,' he thought and in desperation whipped up the horses. They plunged forward and the bridge definitely swayed, but then there were shouts of triumph, the wheels thudded onto solid ground, and he could breathe again.

Consuela flew to climb onto the waggon seat and hug him. "Wretched Englishman," she half-sobbed. "As if anything was worth taking such a chance! I had rather see the stupid waggon swept away than have you go down with it!"

"To say truth, love, so would I," he admitted, kissing her forehead. "But Wellington and England are desperately in need of my father's 'Spring Carpet!' "

He ordered Consuela and Pierre to travel inside so that they could keep dry, and then they were off again, this time with Manderville bringing up the rear. The afternoon was wearing on and the wind seemed ever stronger. After a while Manderville galloped to the front of the waggon, and tried to shout, but his voice was now quite gone. He gestured urgently to the east. Vespa leaned to the side and peered back. Far off he saw the glitter of light on metal.

Breastplates and helmets.

"Here comes the cavalry," he muttered grimly, and cracked the whip over the heads of the team.

The cart-horses leaned into their collars and responded gallantly, but they were handicapped by the bulk and weight of the waggon. Each time Vespa glanced behind them it seemed to him that the troop of *cuirassiers* was closer. It was a race now, and one they had little chance of winning unless in some way they could give the French military gentlemen the slip.

Their chances shrank when they reached the section of the road that wound between the steep walls of the ravine. A group of travellers had spread themselves across the narrow road. They plodded along at a snail's pace; there was no room to pass, and they showed not the slightest inclination to move aside.

Guiding the cart-horses as close as he dared, Vespa hailed the individual bringing up the rear of the train. The face that was turned to him looked familiar. The man screamed something, and the people ahead halted and glanced back. There were children, and riding the lead mule was a lady with an infant in her arms. It was the same family whose baby had almost fallen from the mule two days ago.

Vespa called urgently, "Sir, your pardon, but we are in great haste. Could you be so kind as to let us pass?"

The man stared at him expressionlessly.

Pierre stuck his head through the small door behind the driver's seat and shouted, "The soldiers! They are catching up—"

Vespa snapped, "I am aware."

The eyes of the man standing in the rain became very round. He craned his neck, looking back. Then he looked up at Vespa. He ran to the front of his straggling little column and called orders in a Breton dialect so broad it would have been better understood by a Scot than by a Frenchman. In a trice the mules were all at the farthest edge of the road. Vespa drove the team on carefully and as they passed, called his grateful thanks. Nobody said a word in reply, but the lady nodded and waved the infant's tiny hand at him, the little girl smiled shyly, and briefly, on the face of the head of the house was a broad grin.

Looking back a few minutes later, Vespa saw that the family and their mules were all over the road again, and scarcely moving at all. 'God bless 'em,' he thought fervently. 'They've repaid the favour!' Now, the troop of soldiers would be so delayed that he might, after all, have a chance to collect his father and find a hiding place somewhere along the coast road. A slim chance, but at least a chance.

The cart-horses were going along well. The short wintry afternoon was fading, but a distant thread of smoke wound upward. It was lighter than the darkening clouds, and soon dispersed by the wind, but his hopes lifted because it meant they were within sight of the Lannions' tavern.

Consuela opened the small door behind the seat and tugged at his coat.

"Almost there, m'dear," he said with a triumphant grin.

"We must stop," she cried in distress. "Look! Look!"

He looked back. Manderville was huddled over the pommel and appeared to be in imminent danger of tumbling from the saddle.

"Toby!" howled Vespa, pulling up the horses.

Broderick turned and waved and Vespa gestured urgently. Reining back, Broderick called, "Now what's to do?"

"Paige is done! We'll have to get him in the waggon. Give me a hand."

Manderville was quite unconscious and breathing in an alarmingly rasping fashion. Between them, they carried him to the waggon and Consuela's care.

"Silly chawbacon," muttered Broderick. "Why didn't he say something?"

But they both knew why Manderville had held out for as long as he could, and that they would have done the same.

As they closed the back doors Vespa slanted a glance up the road. It was impossible to see very far in the fading light, but for as far as he could determine there was no sign of any *cuirassiers*. Climbing up to the driver's seat, he could only pray they would not reach the tavern and find Monteil waiting for them. At least the road from here was fairly level and there were few travellers on this cold afternoon. He urged the cart-horses to greater speed and promised them they would very soon be in a warm barn. The waggon rumbled along and the minutes slid past, and at last they were turning into the Lannions' yard.

The host ran out, waving his arms excitedly. The ostler hurried to the heads of the lathered horses.

Climbing down from the seat, Vespa was stiff and tired. He'd had little in the way of sleep these past two nights, but there was no time for rest now, nor time for them to summon the skill of Monsieur Aunay, the farrier-apothecary. Before he reached the waggon doors Manderville swung them open and disdaining assistance proclaimed himself a blockhead but well-rested. It was a courageous attempt but he stumbled over the front steps, and Consuela, looking weary herself as Vespa lifted her down, whispered that she was afraid that Paige might have the pneumonia.

"And you, my brave girl, are exhausted," he said, tightening his arms about her.

"No, no," she lied. "I am very hardy, you know. But Pierre is

311

fast asleep. I suppose we had as well leave him in the waggon. We shall have to press on at once—no?"

Vespa had already made up his mind that the boy must stay at the tavern, however, and that word should be sent to de Coligny. Broderick volunteered to carry the sleeping child, and Vespa and Consuela followed Manderville inside.

Lord Kincraig, fully dressed, lay on the parlour sofa. He started up eagerly as they came into the room. He looked pale and haggard but insisted he was 'doing very much better,' and was delighted to learn that not only had Consuela and Pierre been rescued, but the waggon was safely in the barn.

"Bravo!" he said, watching Vespa proudly. "You've done splendidly, my boy!"

Madame Lannion hurried in and, after a shocked look at Consuela, said a chamber was ready and that the young lady would want to wash and rest after her ordeal. Longing to offer such luxuries to his beloved, Vespa dared not, and said reluctantly that they must leave at once. "Are you able to travel, sir?"

"But no, he is not!" interjected Madame, outraged. "No more is that one!" She stabbed a finger at Manderville who had sat down on the first chair he encountered and fallen asleep. "Only hear how he breathes—as if someone in his lungs was sifting wheat! More journeying, and you will be burying them both! Nor are you yourself but a step from the grave," she added, taking in Vespa's drawn face and the dark shadows under his eyes. "Come, Mademoiselle, you at least shall wash your poor self and have a hot cup of coffee, if only in my kitchen!"

"I'll be very quick," promised Consuela.

Vespa nodded and smiled at her, then pulled a chair close to the sofa and sank into it gratefully.

Kincraig asked, low-voiced, "You are pursued?"

"Yes, sir. A troop of *cuirassiers*. At most, a mile or so behind. We've some friends along the road who will, I think, do their best to delay them but—"

"Jupiter!" Dismayed, his lordship exclaimed, "We must not fail at this stage of the game! Lend me your arm, Jack, and we'll be on our way."

Vespa helped him to sit up, watching his face anxiously. Kincraig was obviously in pain and momentarily bereft of breath, but he declared staunchly that with a little help he would go on nicely.

Vespa left him to rest for a minute and went out to check on the horses. Toby had not yet brought Pierre inside and he was quite prepared to find his friend snoring beside the boy in the back of the waggon.

He stretched wearily as he walked across the yard. It was dark now, and raining again, but the wind had dropped and it was very still. There was no sign of Broderick or the ostler.

The sense of danger was sudden and strong. His hand blurred down to the pistol in his belt.

Pain seared across his forearm and the pistol fell from his numbed grasp.

Amused and triumphant, Duncan Keith said, "My, but you're fast, brother dear!"

A strong hand shoved Vespa between the shoulder blades, sending him into violent collision with the side of the waggon. The horses snorted and stamped nervously. The shutter on a lantern was opened, releasing a bright beam of light.

Supporting himself against the waggon, Vespa blinked at a squat individual with a pouty mouth and sparse red hair under a sodden hat. The man glared at him and demanded, "What did you do with my crossbow, curse you?"

"Threw it . . . in the lake," lied Vespa.

The squat man swore and started forward.

"Not yet, Rand!" Duncan Keith flourished a crimson-stained sabre. "First, we talk."

Horrified, Vespa cried, "My God! What have you done to the boy?"

"Nothing as yet," said Keith. "This is all yours."

Vespa glanced down, shocked; his sleeve was wet with blood.

From his temporary sanctuary under the waggon Pierre called fiercely, "You didn't have to cut him!"

"No." Keith grinned. "But you must not deny me life's simple pleasures, child. And before you ask, Captain, sir, your comrade in arms is in the waggon. We got him when he tried to carry off the boy."

The muscles under Vespa's ribs cramped. He endeavoured to keep his voice calm. "Dead?"

"He will be. Unless you cooperate. I met up with my man Rand, as you see. And Rand found out that Monsieur Monteil has been following my father. Now Imre Monteil is a greedy man but he is also very shrewd. He would follow this stupid cart only if it contained something of great value. I have come to relieve you of it. And—" he stepped closer to the open waggon doors "—and I do not propose to wait."

Vespa said curtly, "I take it you've already searched the waggon?"

"And found only some moth-eaten rugs. Don't attempt a delaying war of words, Vespa. You know what the old man is carrying. Tell me—and fast. My patience is short at the best of times." He grinned broadly. "No one will miss Broderick very much, and there is always the boy—if all else fails."

"All right, all right! You heard about the Belgian Mint robbery?"

Keith stared at him.

"I have." Rand grunted, "A fine haul they made. Lovely fat sacks of gold!"

Incredulous, Keith said, "Do you say my so-high-and-noble father was involved in that piece of lawlessness?"

"Yes. And not for the first time, I'm afraid."

Rand laughed, and Keith exclaimed, "Why—the old fraud! So *that's* why he's wandered about Europe all these years pretending to search for valuable carpets!"

314

"They're valuable when gold *louis* are sewn into the backings," said Vespa.

"Aha!" cried Rand and darted for the waggon doors.

Broderick's limp figure was pushed out and dumped on the ground. Vespa gritted his teeth with rage and started towards him, but Keith shouted a furious, "Stay back!" flailing the sabre about so menacingly that Vespa had no choice but to obey.

From inside the waggon Rand shouted, "There's nothing in this one but moths and dust. . . . I can't feel anything solid, here, either. . . . I think. . . . your bastard brother was lying in his— Wait! Yes, by God! Here it is, Mr. Keith! And—in this other also!"

Keith gave a yell of triumph. "How much?"

"Lord knows. There's just these two, so far as I can tell. We'll have to tear them apart to find out!"

"Not here! We'll take them in my coach! Get over there and help him, *mon Capitaine.*"

The gold-filled rugs were heavy and the cut in Vespa's arm made the transfer of them a painful business. It was all he could do to lift the second heavy rug. As it was loaded inside his half-brother's coach he heard hoofbeats.

Rand cried shrilly, "Horses! Coming fast. It's those damned dragoons, like as not!"

Keith made a sudden dart and snatched for the boy.

Whipping the pistol from his pocket, Vespa shouted, "Let him be, or I'll fire, Keith!"

Rand sprang onto the box of the coach.

Under no illusions as to the loyalty of his hireling, Keith howled, "Wait, you cur!"

Broderick, who had crawled nearer, shoved a rake at Keith's feet. Keith tripped, cursing furiously and swung the sabre high. Broderick ducked lower and flung up an arm to shield his head.

Aiming carefully, Vespa fired.

Keith staggered, and grabbed at his arm.

"Damn you, Vespa!" He dropped the sabre, ran to his coach

and clambered to the box, snatching the reins from Rand. "You lose, even so," he shouted "The *cuirassiers* know you're English spies! I hope you all go to Madame Guillotine!"

Vespa sprang for the box, but he was slow. Keith whipped up the team and with a shrill vindictive laugh turned his coach onto the road and disappeared into the night with a rumble of high, fast wheels.

"Never—saw you miss—such an easy shot," said Broderick faintly.

Crawling from under the waggon, Pierre wailed, "Oh, sir! He got away!"

"And—with all the . . . blasted loot," said Broderick.

Vespa's smile was mirthless. "Enough, at all events, to hang him," he said, and blew out the lantern.

Scant seconds later there came the pounding of many hooves, the jingle of spurs and harness and a French voice upraised in command. "There they go! After them!"

At a thundering gallop the troop shot past in pursuit of Duncan Keith's coach.

Vespa knelt beside Broderick. "My poor fellow, are you badly hurt?"

"Bent . . . brainbox, I think. Jove, but . . . you're a real slyboots, Jack! You *meant* that . . . that wart to take the carpets!"

Actually, Vespa's initial plan had been to foist the two gold-laden rugs off onto Imre Monteil. Fate had decreed differently, but his plan had not gone to waste. It had, in fact, come in very handy.

Broderick was staring at him.

He said with a smile, "What a thing to say!"

17

"*A*re they all going to die, Capitaine Jacques?"

Somewhat bewildered, Vespa looked down at the boy who sat so close beside him on the seat of the waggon. He recalled the Lannions' adamant refusal to keep the boy with them, but he couldn't seem to remember Pierre waking up and climbing out to him. Nor did he recall the coming of the streaks of light that were now painting the eastern sky to announce the arrival of dawn.

When they'd left the hedge-tavern it had been necessary to go along with caution, for it was so dark. Gradually, however, as if relenting, the rain had eased to a drizzle and then stopped, the clouds had begun to unravel and a full moon had sailed into view to light the heavens with its glory and to show him the road ahead. He had driven all night, torn by the conflicting needs to race on and attempt a rendezvous with the ship and to stop and seek out an apothecary for his father and his friends.

The constant jolting had wrought havoc with Lord Kincraig, who had insisted, even as he stifled a groan of pain, that they keep on, no matter what happened. Manderville was no better:

burning with fever and coughing rackingly but whispering that he was starting to feel 'more the thing.' Broderick was deathly pale, tight-lipped and silent, his clenched fists a mute testimony to his suffering, yet able somehow to muster a grin when, it having been necessary to stop and rest the horses, Vespa had twice looked in on what Consuela called her 'field hospital.'

Distraught, he knew that he had no choice. As a British officer, his first duty was to his country. Through that long night, it sometimes seemed to him that he could see Wellington's fierce dark eyes fixed on him. He knew quite well what his Chief would expect of him. To fail that expectation was unthinkable.

So here he was, driving with three very sick men being bounced and jostled about in the waggon, who should have been in bed and under a doctor's care."

"Are they?" the boy repeated now.

"Eh? Oh—no, of course they're not going to die. They're just—just a little bit out of curl, but they'll be better when they've rested and had something to eat."

"So will I." Pierre watched his face anxiously. "Are you out of curl too, sir? If your arm is very bad I can take the ribbons, you know."

The cut in his arm was a continuing nuisance, but only one of several. His various bruises ached and his leg nagged at him ceaselessly, but the worst thing was the very odd feeling that his head was no longer in its proper place, but drifting along beside him. The temperature had plunged after the rain stopped, the cold helping him to stay awake, but he dreaded that he might fall asleep and the waggon would go off the road and get stuck in the mud, or tumble from one of the bridges spanning the rivers and streams that abounded in this region. To hand the reins over to someone else, even for half an hour, would be bliss, but a small boy, however willing, could not tool a four-in-hand. "Thank you, Pierre," he said with a smile. "I shall keep it in mind. Meanwhile, you can help by making sure I stay awake." He peered at the road ahead. "I wonder if we are anywhere near the coast yet."

"I don't know, but I am cold, and this is not a good place, Capitaine."

Vespa looked at him sharply. "Why do you say that?"

"They're all around us." Pierre lowered his voice. "I think they have gathered here, to catch us!"

Startled, Vespa scanned the surrounding countryside, and in the brightening light he saw menhirs, which indeed seemed everywhere and were of all shapes and sizes, some towering towards the heavens, some balanced horizontally one above the other, but all mighty.

They were on a broad heath and ahead was a village looking very ancient and peaceful in the early morning. They must stop now. The horses were ready to drop and must be baited, and everyone was hungry.

He said something to Pierre about the menhirs; he wasn't sure what. The boy seemed reassured, however, and a moment later was pointing out the sign on a tiny inn at the edge of the village.

Vespa turned the team into the yard and climbed from the seat. He had to cling to a wheel for a moment, as the inn ebbed and flowed before his eyes, but the dizziness passed and he went to open the back doors of the waggon. Consuela had fallen asleep holding Manderville's hand. She woke when Vespa called to her, and came at once to him. Shocked by his haggard appearance, she exclaimed, "Oh, my dear! How terribly tired you are."

He kissed the cool soft fingers that caressed his cheek and, looking in at the casualties, asked, "How do they go on?"

"Your father has slept much of the night. Toby, I think, must have a concussion, and has been in considerable pain. He has only now dropped off to sleep. Paige has been delirious at times. He is full of fever, poor soul. I'm afraid. . . ." The words trailed off, then she said a touch too brightly, "Dare we go in and command some breakfast? Just a cup of coffee would be heaven!"

He agreed and sent her off with Pierre to see what they could buy.

A wizened little ostler came out of the stables pulling on a coat and yawning, his breath hanging like a small white cloud on the frosty air. In later years the one thing about the inn that stood out in Vespa's memory was the scorn on the face of that solitary ostler. "Monsieur," he said acidly, "is doubtless aware he is killing his horses. Monsieur is no doubt on a mission of supreme urgency that he would so ill treat these fine beasts."

At this point Manderville began to mutter wildly. The ostler viewed the waggon suspiciously.

"Mon Pére," said Vespa, tapping his temple. "Poor old fellow."

The ostler led the team towards the barn, the curl of his lip conveying his belief that monsieur's papa was not the only one in the family with a brain-box full of maggots. "Poor beasts," he grumbled. "I shall take off your harness and walk you until you have cooled a trifle, then—"

"No!" Feeling the ultimate villain, Vespa said, "Rub them down and water them, if you please. But keep them poled up, and they can have no feed. I must press on as soon as possible."

With a dark scowl the ostler observed that monsieur's accent it was not that of a Breton. Vespa repeated the tale of his Italian birth.

Staring, the ostler said, "Monsieur have the bad injury."

Vespa glanced down. There was a dark stain on his gauntlet; the bandage around the cut on his arm had been a very makeshift affair and must have slipped. "I was—er, chopping wood," he said.

The ostler met his eyes steadily, then began to lead the team up and down and around the yard.

Very sure that the man had not believed a word of his story and that the moment their backs were turned they would be reported to the authorities as suspicious foreigners, Vespa stamped up and down trying to get warm while he kept watch.

A very young and sleepy fire-boy was the only person yet stirring in the kitchens and the most Consuela was able to bring away was a bowl of chicken broth and some stale baguettes. When she carried these provisions outside, Vespa marvelled because, in the miraculous fashion of creatures feminine, she had brushed out her lustrous curls and washed her face, and looked as bright and pretty as though she was a happy young girl setting forth on some carefree excursion. Pierre trailed after her, carrying a pan of water, and the ostler's curiosity reawakened when they both disappeared into the waggon.

It was growing lighter with each passing minute, and as soon as he dared Vespa guided the team out onto the road once more, followed by the incensed ostler who stood shaking his first after them. For the next few hours they travelled through increasingly populated areas, skirting little towns and picturesque villages, halting occasionally at some secluded spot for a brief rest, and coming at length into a richly forested area, and then a succession of green gentle valleys.

They had not once been challenged nor had there been any sign of Monteil or soldiers, and Vespa was half asleep when Consuela asked, "Where are we going, Jack?"

She was sitting beside him. He looked at her blankly. It seemed a very foolish question. Where were they going? He replied, "I've no idea. Except . . ." he racked his brain "except that we're heading to the west. I hope."

"Yes, dear." She reached up and pushed the damp hair back from his forehead. "But do you know where we are to meet the ship?"

Of course he didn't know where they were to meet the ship. He said severely, "You know we don't know. They know we don't know. *They* must find *us,* you see, but they can't sail on French soil." That didn't sound quite right, and he paused, frowning.

Somewhere, somebody shouted. Consuela slid to the side and looked back. "We are being followed! Oh, Jack, they're coming very fast!"

"Is it those blasted *cuirassiers* again?"

"No. I think it must be Monsieur Monteil!"

"Devil take him," moaned Vespa, whipping up the team. "Does he never give up?"

They raced at a thundering gallop along the road. The reins must be soaking wet because they were so heavy it was all Vespa could do to hold them up. Now, something was blinding him. Blinking, he realized it was sunlight. Pale winter sunlight on water. There was a beach—a long beautiful beach. The sand was white, and glittering.

Pierre screamed, "Look! Look! A great ship!"

Vespa muttered, "I see a sort of lagoon—are those all ships?"

Consuela looked at him worriedly. "They are islands, dear. The ship is far out and at least five miles to the south. It will never find us."

Peering from the small window behind the seat, Broderick called weakly, "Someone has! See there!"

"Soldiers!" cried Pierre. "And they're coming right for us, Captain Jack!"

Vespa was concentrating on trying to lift the whip. It was incredibly heavy and he was so very tired. He'd just close his eyes for a minute. . . . His head nodded and he jerked himself awake. This wouldn't do! He must keep on—he *must not* fail his General and his country. But why couldn't he hold onto the reins? What on earth . . . was the matter with him?

And then came another pair of hands; strong little hands that took the reins from his failing grasp, and a beloved voice that said, "Let me help, my love. Can you see the soldiers now?"

He shook his head hard. Yes, he could see them now. Coming from the south. Straight for them. At the gallop. A troop of—of what? The uniforms seemed to be red, but he couldn't distinguish the brass plate with the imperial N and the crown that would brand them Lancers. And now they were clad in dazzling white—like Carabiniers but minus the easily identifiable tall helmets. Why on earth had they changed their uniforms?

Consuela wailed, "Oh, my heavens!"

She was staring to the east. He turned his head slowly, and saw a coach and four and two outriders on dapple greys bearing down on them. Monteil! Pox on the wretch! But if that was Monteil, then who was behind? More *cuirassiers,* perhaps? At all events, he thought wearily, there was nowhere to turn now, but into the water. Could the cart-horses swim? That thought struck him as hilarious and he chuckled foolishly.

Consuela was pulling up the team.

He said feebly, "No, love. No—we mustn't give up yet."

Pierre shrieked, "Papa! Papa!"

Clinging to the side, Vespa managed to look back again. The coach and the escorting riders approaching from the north looked murderous. Small wonder, if it was de Coligny. And he had given the poor fellow his word of honour that in seeking Lord Kincraig he did nothing against France. Nothing against France . . . Except to provide Lord Wellington with part of the means to continue the war! His word of honour . . . "Oh, Gad!" he muttered.

"What did you say, my dear?" asked Consuela.

"Nothing that—makes sense. Pierre, get down, lad. Hurry to your father. And—God speed!"

The boy looked at him, suddenly tearful. To Vespa's astonishment, his hand was seized and kissed. Then Pierre was in the road and running back to the slowing coach of the chevalier.

The military troop was less than a mile to the south.

Monteil's carriage was bearing down from the east.

De Coligny was behind them.

'A touch ticklish,' thought Vespa.

Consuela had managed to whip up the team and they were

charging straight towards the soldiers. Bless her brave heart. He tried, not very successfully, to encourage her. Monteil's coach became a blur that seemed to swerve suddenly. Consuela was crying out. She needed him! He pulled himself together and took back the leathers and in a burst of strength, cracked the whip over the horses' heads. The waggon seemed to fly. Those French troopers had best get out of the way, by God, for he was going right through their centre!

There was a lot of shouting and noise.

The troopers were scattering in all directions.

Consuela was screaming.

Lord Kincraig was cheering.

Someone howled, "He's done it!"

If he had done it, he could go to sleep.

Grateful, he sighed and his head sank onto Consuela's shoulder. He wondered vaguely if they had crossed into Spain.

It seemed to him that he heard shots.

The man who stood at the window was young, and a colonel. The window was round, and the floor was moving up and down. So this must be a ship. How he came to be aboard ship, and why he was in bed at what appeared to be late afternoon, Vespa could not imagine, but he had a vague sense of having made a horrible bumblebroth of something. After two attempts that were inaudible, he managed to ask, "Am I under arrest, sir?"

The man at the porthole turned and approached the bed.

"Oh," said Vespa. "It's you."

"It's me." Colonel the Honourable Hastings Adair sat on the end of the bunk, his handsome face grave. "How do you feel?"

"Puzzled. How long have I been here?"

"Two days. We had a rendezvous to keep before we turned for home."

Vespa knit his brows, trying to sort it all out.

The young colonel asked, "What's the last thing you remember before you dozed off?"

Dozed off . . . ? Was that what he'd done? Not during an action, surely? Lord! He said slowly, "I seem to recollect a road, and— Great heavens!" He started up and found it such an effort that he lay back again, panting. "My father! Broderick and Manderville! And—Consuela! What—what . . . ?"

Adair sighed. "I was afraid you'd remember Consuela."

"Hasty, you villain! You're teasing the poor fellow!" Broderick came in, clean and shaved and with a neat bandage around his head.

"I'll point out," said Adair, "that I am a colonel, and despite that romantical bandage, you, Broderick, are a lowly lieutenant!"

"An alive lieutenant!" exclaimed Vespa, greatly relieved as Broderick came to grip his hand. "Toby, is my father—"

"He's not quite as alive as this impertinent cloth-head," said Adair. "But he's going on very well and should be up and about within a week, so the ship's apothecary tells us."

Broderick said mournfully, "Poor old Manderville is in a bad way."

"Oh, blast the luck! It was the pneumonia, then?"

"Yes. He's through the worst of it, apparently. But—" Broderick winked "—poor sailor, you know."

Vespa grinned, then said apprehensively, "Does Wellington know what happened?"

"He does." Adair said with a sober look. "He's going to demand an explanation, Captain, of why you disobeyed orders, and—"

"What orders? I never received any orders!"

"—and why you blithely gave away one hundred *louis!*"

"That ain't fair," exclaimed Broderick. "Against all odds he got the rest of the loot through!"

"I—did?" said Vespa hopefully. "But—how on earth—"

Someone was knocking at the door. Adair sprang up and opened it, then bowed, and Consuela hurried in.

"Oh!" she cried in delight. "He's awake! And you didn't call me!"

Broderick pulled a chair beside the bunk and she flashed him a smile as she ran to occupy it and take the hand that Vespa tried, and failed, to reach out. Nursing it to her cheek, she asked, "How are you today, dearest Captain Jack?"

"I feel very well," he answered, smiling at her adoringly. "Except—I cannot understand why I am still so pulled."

"You great clunch," said Broderick. "You drove all night without tightening the bandage round that cut on your arm. It's a wonder you ain't bled white!" He settled onto the side of the bunk and went on: "There are some very interesting studies being undertaken on blood. For instance, did you know that the body of the average male contains about five litres of the stuff? And that although a fellow can lose a considerable amount without turning up his toes, at a certain point he will go into shock—which is likely what happened to you only you were too dense to—"

"Go away," murmured Vespa not taking his eyes from Consuela's radiant face.

"Well, of all the—"

Adair took Broderick by the collar. "This way, Lieutenant," he said firmly, propelling him to the door.

"If that ain't the outside of—"

"The outside of Captain Vespa's cabin," said Adair, and closed the door behind them.

"Alone at last," sighed Vespa. "Now, if I only had the strength . . ."

Consuela pointed out, "I am very strong."

"And I swore an oath not to try and fix my interest—"

"Whereas," she murmured, leaning closer, "I am very interested, and I have sworn no oaths. . . ."

326

After a delightful interlude he asked dreamily, "Did we really get the gold through?"

"No. *You* got it through, dearest!"

"Never! Paige and Toby helped, my father was superb and you—you were a real heroine, my signorina! How you hung onto the reins with those precious little hands while I was totally useless—"

"How you kept going for as long as you did was a miracle, my poor darling. And when you broke the ranks of that troop . . ." She chuckled. "There was no stopping the team. What an uproar!"

"I can guess. And if I know Frenchmen—"

"They weren't French, Jack."

He stared at her, bewildered.

Tidying her hair, Consuela said, "They were British dragoons."

"British?" he gasped. "A troop—of *our* dragoons—in *Brittany?* You're roasting me!"

"No such thing. The captain of the warship had been told to rendezvous with us between Lorient and Quiberon and that we would signal by lantern—which we did not know, of course. He tacked about offshore, waiting, then sent an intelligence agent in to try and trace us."

"The poor fellow we found killed at that abandoned farm?"

"No. But the intelligence officer had met that gentleman and told him where we could meet the ship. You'll recall that he had managed to draw an arrow in the dirt, pointing to the southwest. When we didn't keep the rendezvous, Hasty Adair, who was aboard the warship, demanded that a troop be landed."

"Good Lord! They'd come to help and I charged—"

"Right through them, dearest."

He groaned. "When am I to be shot? Were any of the poor fellows hurt?"

"Only their pride. But they've forgiven you. In fact, they seem quite proud of their encounter with the Flying Captain!"

He looked at her amused face uneasily. "What a thing to do—after they'd taken such a chance for our sake. I wonder they didn't have to fight every inch of the way!"

"Yes. It was a desperate venture, but Lord Wellington had said nothing was to be left undone that might get the waggon through. I suppose nobody expected a troop of British dragoons to be there. Luckily, we met up with them fairly soon, and the war-ship changed course and sailed back to us."

"But—I distinctly recall seeing a great lagoon—with ships that you said were islands."

"So they are." She stroked his cheek gently. "And you are talking too much and must rest now. Is your arm very painful?"

"A little stiff merely, I thank you. But how could a warship put into a lagoon?"

"It didn't, my love. The water was shallow when the tide went out. We drove across to one of the islands and two longboats came with a landing party, and all the gold was loaded, and rowed out to the ship. We left the poor waggon and the cart-horses behind."

"The French did nothing while all this was going on?"

"Hasty thought that at first they were taken by surprise. Then there seems to have been a panic—the local people thought Wellington had broken through Marshal Soult's lines and was invading."

Vespa laughed. "What—with one troop? But I was sure I heard shots."

"You did. The chevalier restored order and rallied the people, then led an attack on our little island. He really was magnificent, Jack, and I'm very sure he will be given a medal or some sort of honour."

"Still, he didn't prevail."

"No, thank the Lord. And we were safely away before those fierce *cuirassiers* came charging to help him. Now, go to sleep."

He yawned drowsily. "Then Wellington will have his funds.

And my father is a fine brave gentleman . . . Consuela—my beloved one . . . your Grandmama won't deny me now . . . do you think?"

But before she could answer, he was contentedly asleep.

<hr>

It had been snowing all day. The village of Gallery-on-Tang looked like an artist's depiction of Christmastime, with smoke curling from the chimneys, thatched roofs buried under a white mantle and people bustling about the slippery street, bundled in their winter cloaks and scarves, exchanging cheery greetings.

Some two miles east of the village the ancient manor house at Alabaster Royal also wore winter white, and lights from many windows painted amber glows on the snowy lawns. The steward, Hezekiah Strickley, and Harper, the groom, were busily at work in the stables; rotund Chef Henri sang uproariously in his kitchen; Mr. Thornhill, the statuesque butler, issued a constant stream of orders; Peg, the stout head housemaid, trotted about happily, picking up the various items she dropped along the way, and encouraging her rather ill-assorted retinue of assistants to make haste because "all the rest of 'em is coming today!"

In the great drawing room Captain John Wansdyke Vespa paced restlessly, glancing often to the front windows, and running a nervous finger around the neckcloth that Thornhill had adjusted with, it would seem, an eye to strangling him. At his heels Corporal trotted patiently, and Manderville, strolling in from the stairs, observed that the little dog must have walked miles this last hour. "By George, but you look impressive, Jack. Regimentals, eh? Jolly good touch."

Vespa turned to face him. "I'd hoped they might help my cause a little. The ladies love a uniform, you know. Is my father coming down?"

"Said he'd be at your side in time to welcome— But I think he won't. Someone's arrived."

"Oh, Lord!" moaned Vespa, paling. "Paige, do you think the duchess still will have none of me?"

Manderville pursed his lips. "Hmm. Well, she might very well, of course." And thinking that the old lady would be short of a sheet to even consider rejecting his gallant friend, he thought also of the scandal that seemed to grow more lurid every day and had so tarnished the name of Vespa. Stifling a sigh, he added: "Best to be prepared, dear boy."

The doors were thrown open. Thornhill announced in his great dramatic voice, "The Duchess of Ottavio. Miss Consuela Jones."

Vespa's eyes flashed to his beloved. She wore a gown of white velvet trimmed with pink embroidered flowers, and a silver fillet was threaded through her dusky curls. He thought she looked virginal and adorable, but there was worry in her blue eyes and his heart sank as he bowed before her grandmother.

The diminutive Lady Francesca, regal in dark red brocade with gold piping around the high-standing collar and down the front openings, and an undergown of gold silk, allowed him her hand to kiss. "It is taking the unfair advantage to wear that uniform munificent," she said, tapping him on the wrist with her fan, and passing on to Manderville. "I see by your so impudent grin that I have said something not right, Lieutenant Paige. But I will forgive you because it is agreeable that you will not die, after all."

Under cover of Manderville's laugh, Vespa whispered, "Has she made up her mind?"

Consuela murmured, "Have you seen the newspapers?"

It was no more than he had expected, but his hopes plummetted. London had been seething with rumour this past week. The Society columns had named no names, but even the most naive of their readers must guess who was the 'late lamented diplomatist' they pilloried.

". . . It has been learned that this once greatly admired gentleman had intended to abandon his wife . . . "

330

". . . the inamorata who was young enough to be (and almost had become!) his daughter . . ."

". . . the sudden and violent demise of a famous and hitherto much respected gentleman of diplomacy . . ."

". . . One can scarce wonder that the late Sir K——— V——'s faithful wife fled the country, or that his son, Captain J—— V——, a popular young officer of impeccable reputation, has not yet gone into mourning. . . ."

And all this when they knew only a few of the true facts. If the whole should ever be revealed . . . ! Vespa pushed that fearsome prospect away and ushered the duchess to the most comfortable fireside chair while Manderville drew up another for Consuela.

Stroking Corporal, Lady Francesca said, "Thank you for your welcome, small dog. Although you are not the one I expected would be here to receive me."

"Lord Kincraig is a little delayed." Vespa darted a pleading glance at his friend, and Manderville drifted from the room. "My apologies," Vespa went on, "but he will be here directly. Had you a—er, very cold ride, ma'am?"

"We will dispense with a discussion of the weather, if you please."

He bowed and stood before her silently, as if in tribunal.

At her most formidable, the duchess said, "I hope I need not tell you, Captain Jack, that I have much admire you. It would have been exceeding easy on this latest escapade of my naughty grand-daughter for you to force my hand. This, you have not doing, which is the reason I am here today. You brought her home safe, and nobody is knowing she is running about Brittany with you, so her reputation is still contact!"

Consuela said, "Yes, but—"

The duchess quelled her with a glance. "Even so," she resumed, "the gossip mongers they gabble and twitter all over London Town about Sir Kendrick's wickednesses. I know, I know," she said cutting off his attempt to speak. "For this you are not to be blamed, and you are not his son. But London *thinks* you are. Your name, every day it drags lower in the dust, Captain Jack, and my little meadowlark is of a proud and, er—" She paused, and murmured to Consuela, *"Senza macchia?"*

"Unblemished," supplied Consuela, looking mutinous.

"Si. An unhenriched royal house. It is with real regret, my dear Jack, that—"

"My deepest apologies for being tardy." Lord Blair Kincraig came briskly into the room, and paused on the threshold.

It was an entry Thornhill could not have bettered for dramatic effect, and there was a momentary hush.

His lordship was a vision of the sort of sartorial splendour that might be attempted when attending a great function at Carlton House, or some other London palace, but was seldom seen in the country. In formal evening dress, his black coat hugged his shoulders to perfection; his waistcoat was faultless; peerlessly tied, his neckcloth gleamed no less brightly than the snow on the lawns; and knee breeches and silk stockings displayed his shapely legs to advantage. Jewelled Orders flashed on his breast, and a great emerald glowed on one hand.

Awed, Vespa performed the introductions.

Kincraig bowed over the bony little claw the duchess extended, and with exquisite grace occupied the chair nearest her. "I must tell you, ma'am," he said, smiling into her cold eyes, "that I am a great admirer of your granddaughter."

"Under the circumstances which were then, I find that remarkable," she said tartly.

"But—no. She is a very brave girl. Were it not for her, we none of us would be sitting here today."

"I could wish, sir," said the duchess, leaning forward. "That we were not!"

Thornhill relieved this awkward moment by leading a small procession into the room. Two housemaids, one struggling with a uniform that was at least two sizes too large, and the other wear ing an eye patch, carried laden trays. Tea was poured and passed around, and little cakes and pastries were offered.

When the servants left, Vespa tried again. "My lady, I may have small cause for pride in the man I believed to be my father. Lord Kincraig, however, is willing to acknowledge me."

"Say 'proud' to acknowledge you, rather," said his lordship warmly. "Forgive if I become vulgar, but I am a rich man, Lady Francesca. I will be happy to have my man of affairs lay my son's expectations before you and discuss the matter of a dowry, if you give your sanction to the match."

"Easy said! But under what name would my granddaughter leave the altar? London is fairly rocked by the scandal Kendrick Vespa have left behind."

"It is my wish and my intention to adopt Jack. Legally. He can be wed under the name John Wansdyke Keith."

"*San Pietro* aid me!" The old lady gave a crow of mirthless laughter. "A fine mare's nest that would stirring up!"

Vespa put in quietly, "No, sir. I thank you, but I cannot change my name without shaming my mother, and that I will never do."

"My dear boy," said his lordship. "People will only have to see us side by side and our tale will be told."

"Just so," agreed Lady Francesca. "And there will be more of the horrid scandals! No! I will not have my granddaughter tainted by murders and treasonings!"

Consuela looked frightened, and said in desperation, "*Nonna*—I love him! I owe him my life! Have you no gratitude for—"

"Child, child," said the duchess, distressed, "I know what I am owing to our fine Captain Jack. But can you not see that I must be guided by what your sainted mama would wish? Would your fine English father be proud if I permit that you carry the name of a murdering philanderer, who—"

Corporal was barking, voices were in the hall and, belatedly, Vespa realized that Manderville stood in the doorway beckoning him frenziedly. He sprang to his feet, then stood gazing in astonishment at the latest arrival.

Clad in a magnificent robe of black satin with an overskirt of black lace, a black lace cap on her luxuriant light brown hair and stark horror in her big blue eyes, Faith, Lady Vespa, tripped into the room.

"Jack! What on earth—? How can you be *entertaining* at such a time? And—*heavens!*—why are you not in mourning?"

Recovering his wits, Vespa hurried to take her hand and drop a kiss on her cheek. "Mama! How glad I am to see you! When did you come home? Had I known you were on the way— Oh, Gad! Forgive me! I must present you! The Duchess of Ottavio, Miss Consuela Jones and Lord . . . Blair . . ." His words trailed off.

Lady Faith had bobbed a curtsey to the duchess and nodded in obvious perplexity at Consuela, but it was clear that the final introduction was not required. As if mesmerized, she stared at Lord Kincraig, and he, equally affected, gazed at her.

She whispered disbelievingly, "Blair . . . ? Oh, Blair, is it *really* you?"

In a voice ineffably tender, his lordship said, "Yes. It's me, my dear."

A soft blush crept into her pale cheeks. Watching her, Vespa thought that never in his life had he seen her look so radiant.

The Duchess of Ottavio regarded the little tableau thoughtfully. "Bless you, my dear *San Pietro,*" she said with a sudden beaming grin, "I do believe you have sent us the answer!"

Epilogue

~⚬~

The February morning was very bright but bitterly cold, giving Vespa the excuse to keep his lady's hand tucked very tightly in his arm as they walked across the frosty meadow together, a small and happy dog frolicking along more or less with them. When they came to a spreading old oak tree, Vespa pulled Consuela even closer.

"Jack Vespa!" she said primly, when she could say anything at all. "That was naughty, beside which it is the third time you've kissed me this morning!"

"I have to make up for lost time, you see."

"And *outside!* In full view of—of . . ." she glanced around the deserted meadow.

"Of Corporal? He likes it when I kiss my future wife. Sweetheart, you didn't answer me. Shall you mind living down here at Alabaster after we're married?"

"Oh, no. I love the old place. But—I must confess, your house on the river is very beautiful."

His face became closed. "My mother's house."

"Yes, but your mama will be Lady Kincraig next year, and living up at Lambent Grove or in Scotland much of the time. She won't need the Richmond house."

"Then I'll close it."

"And what about that very nice butler who tried so hard to help you when you were searching for clues to your real papa? I suppose he will be cast carelessly into the street to starve?"

He chuckled. "You mean Rennett. I suspect many gentlemen would try to lure him into much more exalted houses than Richmond if he chose to leave me. But, d'you know I think I'll see if he wants to come down here. Thorny really prefers to valet, and I don't think he'll object if Renett takes over the tasks of butler. There, does that satisfy you, future Mrs. John—" He hesitated.

"Mrs. John Wansdyke Keith," she finished merrily. "Oh, Jack, I do like that name. And I love your kind papa! Only . . . it would be nice if we could spend a *little* time in Town each year. During the Season, you know."

He tilted up her chin and kissed her again, then with his lips brushing hers, murmured, "You would hate the Season."

"But *Nonna* would love it. And she has been so good, Jack, keeping in the country with me all these years. And I *would* like to shop—and shop—and shop! I never have *really* visited all the Town bazaars and warehouses."

"Heaven help me! I'll be ruined!"

"Within a week," she agreed. "Oh, look, here comes Paige, and riding his precious Trouble at the gallop."

Vespa sighed. "Now what?"

"I bring news," called Manderville, flourishing a letter. "The great man has sent you a communiqué!"

"Wellington?" Vespa took the letter and broke the seal apprehensively.

"Likely means to have you shot on a charge of donating one

hundred *louis* to the enemy," said Manderville, but also looking concerned. "Jove! Have you read it already?"

Vespa said with a grin, "It's not lengthy," and showed the letter to Consuela.

She laughed and handed it up to Manderville, who read aloud, " 'Well done!' Is that all? I suppose it constitutes rare eloquence, coming from old Nosey!"

Feeling as if he'd been given a medal, Vespa said, "The allied army is advancing again. He must be in high fettle. I wonder he could spare the time even for so short a note."

"He finds time if he is really moved." Manderville said, "Speaking of moving—you've received a gift, old lad. Best come up to the house and see."

Always excited by a present, Consuela exclaimed, "Oh, how lovely! Hurry, Jack!"

"Who sent it," asked Vespa. "Do you know?"

Manderville said airily, "Oh, yes," and with a grin sent Trouble cantering back to the Manor.

He was outside the barn, and taunted them for being such a pair of slowtops when they walked up the drive. "Stay there! I'll bring out your gift. It's from poor old de Coligny."

Startled, Vespa exclaimed, "Stay back, my love! It's likely a mine!"

Manderville laughed and, returning, said, "I rather doubt that."

Vespa stared. A soft muzzle pushed against his ear and an affectionate whicker sounded. He reached up to caress the firm neck. "Bruine!" he said, deeply touched. "Oh, how very good of him! Is there a letter—or a message?"

"A message, only. A rascally fellow brought the mare up from Villy Leggett's *Saucy Maid*. He was to tell you that Gaston de Coligny is grateful because you took such good care of his son. And that when the war is over he will come and knock you down!"

Vespa laughed. "Nor would I blame him, poor fellow!"

He patted the mare and told her she was a very welcome enemy agent.

Then, holding his lady's hand tightly, he walked up the steps and into the great house that was his birthright, and that they would share through all the shining years to come.

12/98

MOR

WITHDRAWN

THE

BRIGHTEST

SUN

THE

BRIGHTEST

SUN

ADRIENNE BENSON

PARK
ROW
BOOKS

PARK
ROW
BOOKS

Recycling programs
for this product may
not exist in your area.

ISBN-13: 978-0-7783-0776-1

The Brightest Sun

Copyright © 2018 by Adrienne Eve Benson

For questions and comments about the quality of this book, please contact us at CustomerService@Harlequin.com.

ParkRowBooks.com
BookClubbish.com

Printed in U.S.A.

My parents, who cracked the world open for me so stories could spill out. My brother, who somehow made them all seem funny. And TCKs everywhere, who grow wild in the spaces between. This is for you.

THE

BRIGHTEST

SUN

PART I

FROM A DIFFERENT TRIBE

One of the old women severed the umbilical cord and passed the tiny body, slippery and warm, up into Leona's arms. It felt unnatural to hold the baby; the infant seemed too small somehow, almost weightless. Leona rolled carefully onto her side and settled the baby next to her. The brand-new hands splayed and stretched blindly in the dim air. Dust motes floated in the crack of light coming through the one palm-sized window cut from the mud walls. Leona watched as the dust swirled. She wished she had a bigger window. She craved light and air. For the first time in the almost twelve months she'd been in Kenya, she yearned for things she'd left home in America. She wanted clean lines and shiny surfaces, nurses in sensible shoes and the comfort of hospital machinery whirring and clicking and dripping around her. For a minute, she even wanted her mother.

The small body wiggled beside her and a sound came out— staccato like the bleating of a newborn goat. It was a tenuous sound, hesitant, an experiment with an uncertain outcome. The tiny lips pursed in anticipation of what only Leona could give. It was a girl, Leona saw. She squeezed her eyes against the coming tears and tried to roll over onto her stomach. She wanted to bury her face in darkness. She was so tired. She felt a sob in her throat and then a sound filled the dark room. It was her scream, she understood, although she couldn't feel her mouth opening or the reverberation of air. She only heard the sound of keening fill the space around her head and saw Simi and the Maasai attendants jerk their faces up and look at her, then glance at one another, concerned. Simi reached across the baby's back to take Leona's hand, but Leona shook her friend off and brought her hands to her face. She tried to press them over her mouth tightly enough to stop the sound. Her insides were glass, shattering in the shell of her skin. This baby was born of loneliness—the desperate kind that arises in people who live among foreigners; who don't share language or gestures.

Leona arrived at the manyatta in a little, dented Renault 4 she purchased, with cash, from a departing French expatriate who she'd met her first night in Nairobi. She drove the distance between Nairobi and Loita hesitantly. It was her first time in Africa and the small car didn't feel like it would offer protection from lions or elephants or any other wild game that might lurk in the yellow savannah grassland she drove through. The drive terrified her so much that she promised herself to stay in the manyatta and only use the car for emergencies. But after a few weeks the dry dust made Leona's skin itch, and the nearest water source, a little tributary of the Mara River, was low and thick, too muddy to bathe in. Leona didn't miss much from home, but she did miss the feeling of a shower, the water soaking her hair and skin. She couldn't stand the way her skin felt, the way her body stank. She wanted a hot shower. She wanted to immerse herself in soap and water, to scrub her hair and fingernails and wash the spaces between her toes. Her yearning to be clean was visceral.

So, only six weeks after her arrival, she packed an overnight bag and drove to Narok to spend the night at the Chabani Guest House. The hotel was small and cheap, mostly used by safari guides and the occasional shoestring tourist or traveling Peace Corps volunteer. But it was clean, and with electricity, running water and a real, if old, mattress, it felt luxurious to Leona. The sky outside was darkening and cool when she arrived. The purple dusks in Kenya were short; night came quickly. Leona turned on all the lights in her room, and laughed at how easily they flicked into brightness. The manyatta had no electricity. After she scrubbed the dirt from her skin and scalp and stood under the warm, rusty water until it ran cold, she dressed in clean clothes, the one set she hadn't worn yet, saved in the bottom of her suitcase. Until now, she'd only smelled it occasionally. The scent of the American detergent lingered in the fibers and reminded her of home.

She felt new and lighter somehow, cracked free of her dusty shroud. With the smell of floral shampoo still lingering in her hair, Leona went down to the hotel's café to order a drink.

The bar was wooden-walled and dark. The only light came from a string of colored Christmas tree bulbs—the big ones people back home wrapped around outside tree branches—and a disco ball revolving slowly above a central space where people could dance. There were no dancers that night. Maybe it was still too early.

Leona chose the bar stool farthest away from the only other customers, a white couple, both about her age, maybe a little older. Leona didn't like small talk so she avoided making eye contact with the two. But she hadn't seen other white people for weeks, and she found herself unable to keep from glancing up at them. The two were clean; both neatly dressed, which made Leona think they might be tourists. But the woman turned slightly, and Leona recognized the logo of a well-known antipoaching foundation on the front of her T-shirt. The woman was pretty. Petite and blonde with a sunburned spot on her nose and rosy pink cheeks, she watched the man intently as he spoke, his body movements fluid as he gestured with his arms, acting out the story he was telling her. The man was attractive, square shouldered and blond with large, tan hands. Leona forced herself to look away and focused her concentration on gathering the right collection of Swahili words to order a beer. She felt the sudden lightness of joy when the barkeep slid a sweating, brown Tusker bottle her way. She didn't bother asking for a glass.

The beer—after so long without alcohol—made her feel luminous and unencumbered. The couple laughed loudly and Leona glanced at them again. The blonde woman was standing, holding out a bill, which the man waved away. He turned to the barkeep and said something in rapid-fire Swahili. Then he turned back to the woman and laughed again. Leona heard him say, "Now you'll have to meet me again, next one's on you."

Leona watched him watch the woman walking out of the bar. She wondered if anyone had ever watched her with that intensity.

Halfway through her second beer, she found she didn't mind when the blond man slid his stool closer to hers and offered to buy her another drink. As they talked, the ease of English after the weeks and weeks of only rudimentary Maa made Leona giddy. Normally a reserved, quiet person, she felt almost drunk with the millions of words she could so easily pluck from her head and toss out, like confetti.

"You're a flirt," she said. "Your girlfriend barely left."

"I am a flirt." He nodded, smiling. "But you're wrong. She's not my girlfriend. I met her here tonight. Interesting girl, though. Working on antipoaching—elephant protection."

They purposely avoided names. It didn't come up at first, names hadn't mattered, and anyway Leona, after weeks of being a curiosity among the Maasai, wanted the anonymity. As an anthropologist, she constantly had to study, observe and ask questions. Now, with this man, she wanted to suspend words and curiosity and talk. Later, alcohol erased the curiosity of names, and the next morning, slow and headachy, Leona felt exposed. She wasn't new to sex, she'd had a couple of boyfriends during her college and grad school years, but they drifted into, and then out of, her life like ghosts. She'd never, though, slept with someone she'd just met, and under the weight of her headache and nausea, she was ashamed of what she'd done. She wanted to disappear. Sex was a fraught thing. Hard for her to indulge in, an unsettling mix of pleasure and fear.

The man was breathing evenly and heavily next to her, and she had to very carefully slide from under his arm and out of bed. She found her clothes and dressed quickly. But the door creaked when she opened it, and she heard his voice, sleepy and rough. "Going to leave without a goodbye?"

"I have to go back," she whispered.

"You mean you have to come back to bed," he said, patting the empty mattress beside him.

Leona turned back to the door and grasped the handle again, pulling it open. When it clicked shut behind her, she raced down the hall to her own room and tossed her shampoo, razor and yesterday's clothes in her bag. She'd planned to stay in Narok for the day. She wanted to have the hotel do her laundry, and indulge in a big breakfast with coffee. But now she changed her mind. She was embarrassed. She hated feeling out of control, and she was ashamed of herself for letting it happen. She lived by the mantra that it was best to be alone—less difficult, less complicated. She didn't want to see the man again, or look him in his eyes. She thought she'd see her own shame there, reflected back at her.

Outside the hotel, the morning street was almost empty, but already the air smelled like wood smoke, frying dough and rotting produce. She opened the trunk of her car and tossed her bag in.

"Is it me, or are you running out on your hotel bill?" a voice called, and when Leona turned, he was there. He was dressed and his feet were shoved into unlaced boots. "I have to go up to Solai today. Can't put it off. But I'll come to the manyatta as soon as I'm done there. I'll find you."

Leona felt the bubbling up of terror deep inside her. It was always this way. Even in college, and graduate school, it wasn't the sex that made her most frightened, but the aftermath. The first time she'd seen a therapist, it only took thirty minutes of talking through her background before the therapist said, "It sounds like you're not sexually frigid, but emotionally cut off." She'd never gone back for another appointment.

"No," she said, "don't bother with that." She inhaled consciously. The panic made her breathing shallow, the imaginary walls that closed in around her made her lungs tense and ineffective. The man was standing close, looking down at her. His eyes were calm, and his face open. She could smell him— warm skin and sleepy breath.

"No, I want to," he said. "I had fun with you last night. No reason we can't see one another again, is there?"

There was always this dread when a man wanted to get to know her. She wasn't normal in this way. Other women her age wanted boyfriends, wanted to marry. The idea set off an alarm in Leona's mind. It always had. She could share physical intimacy, but the notion of allowing herself to want anything else, to be vulnerable in any other way, tore her in two—yearning and revulsion. She wanted to be normal and allow someone to love her, and to return love, but the fear was always too great, and it always won.

She couldn't look at the man's face when she answered. Instead, she glanced sideways, pretending to watch a mangy dog rolling in the dust. "I'm not interested in a relationship," she said. It was her typical line, worn thin from use. She wondered if it sounded as implausible to him as it did to her.

"Who said anything about a relationship?" the man asked. His lips turning up into a grin that made Leona's pulse quicken. "I'm just talking about seeing you again. Maybe reprising our night." He raised his eyebrows suggestively. He was flirting. Leona felt that hollow ache she always felt at moments like this; the ache of wanting something she was far too terrified to actually reach for.

"I have a boyfriend." That always worked. Even so, Leona didn't wait to see if his face changed, or if his voice hardened into understanding.

She turned, climbed into her car and slammed the door shut. She might have heard him calling, but she couldn't be sure. She sped off as fast as she could toward the manyatta. She didn't look back. She didn't glance into the rearview and see him standing next to his truck watching her leave. She didn't want to think about how she'd feel if he never really came looking for her.

Now, with the baby beside her in her little mud-walled hut, she had no desire to speak. She wept with fatigue and terror as the dark women hunkered at her side, murmuring and running their rough fingers along her arms and across the new baby's head.

"You must let her nurse," the Maasai midwife said. She reached over and pulled Leona's T-shirt up, freed her aching breast and clasped it firmly, rubbing the nipple on the baby's new mouth.

"Now it's empty, but the baby will bring the milk."

Leona wanted to cringe at the unfamiliar fingers on her breast and at the mewling little thing next to her. The baby was blindly flailing, her mouth open hopefully, trying to burrow into Leona's flesh like a chigger. Leona closed her eyes. She only wanted to sleep. The midwife grasped Leona's breast again, flattened it in her hand and inserted it firmly into the baby's mouth. Leona felt a strange sensation and opened her eyes. The baby was connected to her and its desperate little mouth was pulling on Leona's flesh. A shudder of alarm rippled through her and she bit her lip against the scream she could feel rising in her mouth again. She couldn't be a mother.

At first when Leona noticed her missing period, she was relieved. The task of finding enough privacy and water to wash herself—let alone driving all the way to Narok to buy supplies—was something she dreaded. When the bleeding didn't appear, as it should have, Leona was happy. It was all the changes in diet and the syncing with the other women, she assumed. But then it didn't come again, and again.

When it dawned on her that she was pregnant, it was like she'd been diagnosed with a fatal disease. Her thoughts obsessively circled back to it, again and again. She couldn't concentrate on work and she couldn't sleep. Every time she closed her eyes, the tide of dread and distress washed through her. She spent hours flipping through the medical manual she'd brought with her in a desperate search for a remedy. The book offered no way to flush this thing out of her.

By the time she sought out the *laiboni*, the witch doctor and spiritual leader of the community, she hadn't slept for nearly a week. The *laiboni* was a wizened elder who sucked his few remaining teeth when he saw Leona and never seemed to understand her halting Maa. As the village doctor, he had a special role here and knowledge of traditional medicines Leona was dying to include in her work. But he was a stubborn interviewee, and Leona suspected he was wary of her presence in the village. She'd been delicately trying to gain his trust, not asking too much of him yet, instead hoping that the other villagers would assure him of her intentions. Being too direct with the old man might cement his unfavorable opinion. But now Leona was desperate.

"*Sopa,*" she greeted him, ducking her head as a gesture of respect. He was sitting alone under an acacia tree just outside the village enclosure. He lethargically waved a bead-handled cow tail in front of his face to keep the flies from setting into his eyes. He murmured his own greeting back but said nothing else. Leona lowered herself to the ground in front of him and crossed her legs. She batted a few lazy flies away and tried to decide what to say. Her phrase book lay in her lap, and she flipped through it. Where were the words she needed?

"Hello, my friend." A voice above Leona pulled her from the book. Simi stood above her, smiling. Simi was the third and youngest wife of the secular village leader's son. She had been educated in the local school up to sixth grade, and was the only woman in the village who spoke English. Simi wasn't absolutely fluent, but had enough for most basic conversations and, more important, had the curiosity and dedication to interpret Leona's explanations and hand gestures. Simi had a sense of the things Leona needed to learn to live in the manyatta, and was never shy about teaching them. She'd been the one, early in Leona's stay here, to grasp Leona's hand and guide her outside the village to the shallow riverbed, dry now, and indicate that Leona should come to this spot when she needed to relieve herself. Simi helped Leona buy the few kitchen items she needed—the large pot, or *suferia*, for boiling water, the frying pan, the tins of sugar and tea—and taught Leona how to keep the embers in her fire pit alive all day. She was the one who Leona talked to like a friend. But Leona couldn't bear to be honest now. Not about this. Especially not about this.

"*Sopa, Simi*," Leona said. She used the Maa word for hello, even though Simi preferred speaking English whenever possible. "I am researching the doctor's work today. Can you help translate?"

Simi hunkered and spoke quickly to the old man. He nodded and waved his cow tail faster.

"What do you want to know?"

Simi relayed Leona's question without a blink. Leona was surprised. Maasai looked askance at premarital sex, and Leona knew her situation might cost her the relationships she'd built here.

"It's for my book," she assured Simi. And then she asked her to translate the detailed questions she had about the plant, where it was found and how much was used. Was it ingested or topical?

Later, when the old man stood up and shuffled home for tea, Simi turned to look at Leona. Leona tried to tell if Simi's eyes held anger or sadness and, if so, for whom?

"You should have asked only me. I could tell you this information. Now it is possible that the others in the village will discover your secret."

"Simi, it's not for me," Leona whispered, suddenly on the verge of exhausted tears. "It's for the book."

But Simi's face was serious now, and she leaned close to Leona's ear and whispered, "You have a baby...inside?"

Leona started as if her friend had slapped her. She looked down at Simi's slim fingers resting on her arm. She glanced up at Simi's face and then away again. What should she say? Knowing that Simi might disapprove or, worse, that she'd be reminded of her own pain made Leona frantic with embarrassment and anxiety.

"The man," Simi whispered, her eyes serious and steady, "did he force you?"

Leona couldn't stop the tears. Her eyes filled up and she used the heels of both hands to press into her eyes. "I'm sorry, Simi, I'm so sorry."

Leona considered two things: it was not acceptable for unmarried women to have children out of wedlock and, because of that taboo, her status as a foreigner would be the only thing to prevent the community from banishing her. She thought of the precarious position Simi herself was in—married for three years with no children of her own. Would Simi's desperation and the irony of the situation make her angry? That was a risk. Leona's work here was going well, and she couldn't bear the idea of leaving. She couldn't bring herself to claim rape, but she could lie.

"My husband," she said. It was not unusual for Maasai spouses to live apart.

"You never told me you had a husband," Simi stated. Her voice was quiet, but Leona felt it like a warm current deep below cool water. Simi knew she wasn't married. Simi knew this baby belonged to nobody, but she wouldn't betray Leona's secret.

"Your husband, he must be a strong man." Simi smiled a small, sad smile. "He is living so far away in America, and still he can give you a baby!"

"Simi, I can't have a baby." Leona searched for a reason that Simi would understand, a lie to cover a truth that Simi would never really be able to understand. "My body is broken. It's dangerous for me to deliver a child." This was a reason a Maasai woman would see as reasonable. Not the other, not the choice Leona made to sleep with a stranger.

Later, after the village was quiet and dark and most families had settled around their fires in their little huts, Simi slipped through Leona's door. She held a blue plastic bag filled with leaves.

"I found this for you near the river. Put some inside where the baby is." And then she slipped outside again.

The leaves were rough and uncomfortable, and Leona worried they would somehow make her sick, poison her for her stupidity. But she slipped a few inside herself several times a day and waited for the relief of blood. It never came. Instead, her breasts began to hurt, she found herself thirsty and her jeans grew tighter and tighter. It was too late.

Leona considered driving to Nairobi to check herself into the hospital for the birth, but it was easier for her to force forgetfulness, and eventually she lost track of the days. There was work to do here. It had been a dry year and the year before had been dry, too. The Maasai in Loita were worried; cattle and goats had begun to get thin. Some of the baby goats had already died, their mothers too emaciated to produce enough milk. Years ago, the Maasai were free to go wherever the good grazing land was. In times of drought, they moved their herds a hundred and seventy miles to Nyeri, in the central highlands, where grass stayed greener and rains were more common. Under British rule, though, the government limited their movements and, with British settlers setting up their own farms, Maasai land was reduced further. The final nail in the coffin of the traditional Maasai way of life was the wildlife preserves. In the 1970s, citing the need for land and wildlife conservation, great swathes of Maasai land were designated as game parks. Grazing was prohibited.

Leona's work was centered on discovering and mitigating the effects of the government-imposed strictures on the traditionally nomadic Maasai people in Western Kenya. She had the idea that if she could prove that the Maasai culture was changing, and that those changes would negatively impact Kenya in general, it would add fuel to the argument that the government should allow the Maasai more movement, more chances to keep herds healthy and more chances to survive. Her study was vital, life and death, and Leona took it that way—without the option of other grazing land, this culture could disappear as fast and as easily as the rivers and streams were drying.

She had no idea how pregnant she actually was. Thinking about how much time had passed made her panic, so she forced herself not to think about it, let alone plan for it. She hadn't seen a doctor; she hadn't had checkups. She spent the months trying to ignore her growing belly and forcing all thoughts of the future out of her head. She felt sick when the movements started—the tugging and sliding of her insides felt like a punishment. She watched Simi watching her grow, and when she let Simi place a hand on her moving belly, she wished fervently that the roles were reversed. After a while, the other women around her noticed, and that was a relief. They offered to help carry water and sent their own children to collect wood for Leona's fire. And so it settled in—the silence, the forced ignorance. Leona worked constantly: watching the people around her and taking careful notes. The people in the village knew that she was there to observe their culture and way of life so she could write about them, maybe help them with the grazing problem. They knew her research meant she observed them and wrote in the notebook she always had with her, and that she asked questions incessantly about everything she saw. Leona began to draft what she planned to turn into her book, an academic study of the shifting cultural norms of the Loita Maasai brought on by laws limiting their nomadic heritage. She concentrated all her efforts on looking outward, and purposely pushed away what was happening inside.

That's why her baby was born in the way of Maasai babies—in her dim *inkajijik*, the small hut made from thin branches covered with mud and dung. Only the embers in the fire pit lighted the birth, and when the baby's eyes opened, they opened to a halo of wood smoke. The first face the baby saw was brown and wrinkled and adorned with strings of beads sewn onto strips of leather. The first sounds she heard were the women ululating four times to alert the village to the birth of a girl, their calls echoed by the lowing of cows.

Three days after the baby was born, Leona was curled around the infant on her bed. She was still so tired. She must have dropped off because the sound of a car engine and the shouts of people greeting one another outside slipped through her sleep. She lay still, for a moment forgetting everything, and grasped at the feeling of peace. It evaporated the moment she recognized one of the voices outside. When the tall blond man dipped his shoulders and neck to fit through her little door, she wasn't altogether surprised. If he heard the story of an American giving birth, he'd know who it was. A white woman having a baby in a Maasai village would be big news. There was nobody else it could be. That he came, though, shocked her. She assumed he'd avoid further contact, eschew responsibility. But there he was, and for a moment Leona was stunned into silence.

"How are you?" he said. His English words, though flattened by his British-Kenyan accent, were startling in their familiarity. Leona tried to discern his reaction to the birth from his voice, whether or not he was angry. She concentrated hard, but her vision felt fuzzy and her thoughts flipped too quickly to pin down and consider. He was so handsome, and she remembered how her body stretched toward him that night, like a plant craving light. Even now, a part of her pulled toward him. She thought of how it felt to be pressed into him, how her head had spun with alcohol and need and how she'd wanted him, and how he'd wanted her, too. But the person she was that night in the Chabani Guest House, the woman who'd used flowery shampoo and worn her tightest jeans, the woman who had not walked away when the blond stranger spoke to her...that wasn't the real Leona. It wasn't her, she reminded herself as she looked up at the man. Her cheeks reddened and she wished, for the millionth time, that she could erase the previous months and erase that night and erase that rare, stupid version of herself.

The man leaned down and studied the sleeping baby.

"A girl?" he whispered, and reached out as if he wanted to touch the baby with his fingertips to check if she was real, but he stopped before finger met cheek. He glanced at Leona's face and then away again. She couldn't read him. He folded his lanky body and knelt on the dirt floor next to where she lay, up on the raised bed of rawhide stretched and dried to stiffness on a frame of sticks.

Watching the man now, here, in her home, Leona realized that although she had no idea what he was called, she knew a lot of other things about him. He'd grown up on a cattle ranch in Solai—close to Maasailand—and had a profound understanding of the Maasai and a fluency in their ways. He knew many of the elders in Leona's manyatta. This was what had impressed Leona the night they met and caused her to feel that unfamiliar yearning stretch through her. He made her feel comfortable, so she didn't hesitate when he gently picked her hand up off the bar and told her to follow him to his room. She liked his coarse blond hair and his sunburned, peeling arms that wrapped around her in the night, and his wide, calloused fingers rough on her breasts. While it was dark and they were breathing together that night, she let herself think about how it might be to have a man of her own—one she wanted—to lie with every night. She hadn't wanted that before, but under the darkness of that night the thought was as exciting as it was terrifying.

In the weeks after she'd met him, though she knew she'd been clear to him, brutally so, perhaps, Leona found herself hoping through the hot, still days. She couldn't shake the suspicion that something was different. In the golden evenings when the sun pulled colors out of the sky and turned the landscape soft and blue, she scanned the horizon around the manyatta for the telltale clouds of dust a Land Rover would make if it were hurtling up the track toward her.

She hated herself a little more each day when it grew dark without him coming. And she hated him for causing her to hope that he'd ignore the way she'd brushed him off in Narok and come find her, anyway. The multiplying cells inside of her—his baby—had nothing to do with her confusing feelings about the man himself. This was her usual pain: wanting to be seen and loved but being utterly unable to let herself allow it. She accepted being alone, she liked it, but there was the occasional wondering. How would it be to share a life with a man? Maybe with this man? How would it feel to see him and to allow herself to be seen? Each evening when he didn't appear, she nursed her disappointment by listing the reasons it was better to be alone. She knew them by heart—and she knew that however many items she listed, there was really only one reason: her own fear. This made her hate herself, too.

The dust gathered in her hair and made her itch, but she

didn't go back to Narok to shower. She lived with it, like the Maasai did. She was adjusting, she convinced herself, to the life of an embedded anthropologist. When she really understood she was pregnant, and it was long after she could do anything about it, she felt too paralyzed to make the effort to find out who the man was, exactly, and to let him know. She couldn't imagine the conversation they'd have to have, or the decisions they'd have to make. It was too much. She told herself over and over again that she didn't want a relationship, she preferred being in a place where everyone was different from her, where she could restrict her interactions and be just an observer. The man—the baby's father—wouldn't allow her to limit herself. He would require more than she felt she knew how to give. More than she wanted to give. Intimacy was a risky thing.

Now, here he was.

A Maasai woman, squatting in the shadows by the low embers of the fire pit, reached out and handed him a chipped enamel cup of chai. He took it and thanked her in Maa. He looked perfectly relaxed, happy even, to be there. Leona was grateful Simi had gone to the river; surely she would have noticed Leona's discomfort. Surely she would have fit the pieces of the puzzle together. And what then? Leona felt a sudden anger burn in her chest—here was another man who walked in without permission, who settled in her space with no regard to whether she wanted him there or not.

"Were you going to tell me?" the baby's father asked now.

Leona shut her eyes tightly. She answered in Maa.

"Go away. It's not your child."

"That's bullshit, and we both know it." He paused, then spoke so quietly Leona could barely hear him. "I didn't have a good father myself, but I think I'd like to try to be one."

His voice cracked slightly. "Whether or not you want me in your life, the girl deserves a father in hers."

"You had a shitty father? Well, so did I," she said. "What makes you think you'd do a better job?"

She saw the man wince. His expression hardened. She knew she'd hit a nerve—she'd hurt him. She wasn't happy about that, but she sensed a shift in his attitude and felt relief. If she had to hurt him in order to get him to leave her alone, so be it.

To her surprise, he spoke again. "Give me a chance to be a better father than mine, or yours, apparently."

She felt hemmed in, strangled. Why wouldn't he just go? Like a trapped animal, she bit hard. "A father is the last thing this baby needs. I didn't tell you because I didn't want you to know, because I don't want her to suffer through a terrible childhood like I did. You're not going to change my mind."

Leona grew up watching the rain fall on the green, green grass in the yard of her parents' home in Beaverton, Oregon. Her father was a surgeon—never around during the day—and her mother was only a shadowy presence, less a mother than a waft of perfume in another room, always on the way out, always saying goodbye. Leona was left home with a housekeeper who lazily vacuumed the Persian rugs and huddled on the back deck in her blue uniform smoking secret cigarettes and blowing rings into the wet sky. Leona had no siblings, and was never encouraged to bring friends home or to go to parties, so she was ignored at school. Not bullied, not sought after, but invisible.

If she were ever asked to sum up her childhood in one word, she would have said *silent*. Silence was forced on her. Her father's infrequent presence was a dark thing, covered by night and a sleeping house. The crack of her bedroom door opening and the memory of rough skin pressed against Leona's cheek, the dank smell of his breath and his wet lips hissing in her ear, "Don't tell your mother. Don't say anything to anyone. You'll ruin it…you'll ruin me." Those nights Leona bit her soft inner cheeks bloody and raw to keep from making a sound.

Only once did she try to break the silence with her mother. Her father always left the house early, and at breakfast one day Leona unlocked her voice. Her mother smiled at her over her toast, and Leona whispered a phrase she'd chosen carefully, the canary in the mine. "Dad came into my room last night." The coffee bubbled loudly in the percolator, and Leona found that forever after, the sound made her anxious.

Her mother's pause lasted a lifetime. Leona dragged her fork through the egg yolks on her plate, afraid to look up.

"Your father is under a lot of pressure at work," her mother finally answered, and when Leona glanced up to explain what she meant, to spill it all out like a liquid from a broken bottle, she caught her mother's eye. There was a tiny flicker there, a lit candle, and then the curtain snapped tightly shut over it. A shutter firmly closed against a possible storm.

After that, Leona kept the secret locked away from everything else. In the daytime she sat through classes at school, concentrating hard, always finding the correct answer. In the evenings, she sat at the kitchen table doing homework while the maid ironed. Her mother came and went, came and went, off to Ladies Auxiliary meetings or the Junior League. Leona's insides turned to stone, but she never wondered if her mother noticed that her father couldn't look Leona in the eyes.

The invisibility—the pressure not to speak—became a habit. It saw her through high school and college and, later, through her doctoral program in sociocultural anthropology. Leona grew a jagged space—a broken section deep inside. She learned that people, especially the ones closest to her, weren't to be trusted.

She declared a major in anthropology because she felt she'd never learned to understand humans; her childhood had given her no great notion of how her own species worked. She was desperate to go as far away from her parents as she could. Leona wrote with skill and conviction and her Fulbright application was chosen. Three months later she was ensconced in a bathroom-sized mud-and-cow-dung *inkajijik*, in a manyatta filled with identical *inkajijiks*. They all circled the central livestock corral and were protected from lions and elephants by thorny acacia branches piled in a ring around the whole cluster. In the rare letters to her parents, Leona referred to her new home as a "gated community."

Dusty and crowded, the manyatta was noisy with the grunting of livestock that lived inside the circle of thorny branches, and the sounds of hyenas, wildebeests and the occasional lion from outside. The small door to her hut was open—as they all were—and she loved the voices she could hear almost always, even brighter in the night, from the tiny huts all around her. She loved the constant scent of other humans and the way the livestock made the air smell tangy. It surprised her at first that she even loved the lack of physical space in the Maasai culture and how a child climbed into her lap every time she sat down and how the other women included her without question in their daily lives. For the first time she felt seen. Eventually she realized her comfort came from the fact that she was foreign. The language barrier and the cultural differences gave her the perfect excuse to feign misunderstanding, to keep people at a manageable distance—not physically, perhaps, but emotionally. At home she couldn't hide this way. Her unwillingness to be vulnerable was an obvious thing, a scarlet letter people read as standoffish, odd. Here, her days were filled with sound and the presence of people, and she felt warm in it, relaxed, fully in charge of the depth and frequency of any emotional exchange.

But through everything—the meals she shared with the villagers, the long walks to the spring to collect water in her bucket, the rare rainstorms that saw her side by side with the other women in the village slapping fresh mud and soggy cow dung on the leaky *inkajijik* roof while rain poured down her back—she remembered the first rule of the anthropologist, Participate Only to Observe, and she held back the one thing she could: herself.

Here in Loita, people expressed curiosity about Leona. Women and children crowded into her little *inkajijik* to watch her. These women wanted to know about her father and her mother and her old life. It wasn't lost on Leona that her first experience of bonding with other women was in a language she didn't speak fluently and in a place half a world away from where she'd come.

She liked the questions the women asked, she liked the way they wanted to know her; it was novel and pleasant. Mostly, she loved that she could pick and choose her answers, and that they could never know what she held back—they couldn't force intimacy against her will. When she spoke to them about herself, she chose her words like picking fruit from a tree, selecting wisely—concentrating on telling them things that didn't hurt. She painted a picture of her life up to now that was simple and easy, a life that didn't make her sad. Mother, Father, school and work. She deflected the conversation when she had to. It was easy to edge away from dangerous memories by changing the subject to the differences between a Maasai home and an American one, or how American people dressed and what they ate. Only Simi pressed. Her curiosity was relentless, and she asked endless questions about life outside the village. Her brief education had given her a rare glimpse into the world, and she drank Leona's stories like water. Simi was different from the other women. She didn't loiter by the river gossiping, or tease the other women to make them laugh. She had several books, children's primers, really, that she'd kept from her days at school. Once she showed them to Leona. She proudly lifted them from a small basket tucked under her bed. She could read, she told Leona proudly—none of the other women in the village could.

After that, Leona selected a couple of novels she'd brought with her—beloved classics. *The Call of the Wild* was Simi's favorite. Simi poured over the book. She'd sit under an acacia reading for hours, oblivious to the annoyance of the other women who called her lazy and proud. Her innate intelligence broke down the urge to judge things. She'd ask Leona to explain the words she didn't understand, like *snow*. She said she liked the way the dog was in charge, the loyalty he showed. She said she'd never thought that even Americans could be cruel to each other—in Kenya, America was seen as a perfect place where only good things happened.

It suited Leona to be emotionally removed from the commotion around her and to have the freedom to be on the outside looking in. Here, nobody expected any more than that from her. Back home, when another person did something Leona didn't comprehend, something that hurt or confused her, she felt a terrible sense of bewilderment, of sinking beneath the surface into a place where she couldn't breathe— the fear of not understanding what she felt she should have understood. Here, that panicked sense was gone. She didn't want to cross that line, to feel confused and misunderstood without a reason again.

Leona knew that in Maasailand, babies weren't recognized until they were three months old. Children are loved, but utilized, and the utility is treacherous. She'd seen babies die of disease before they took their first steps; she'd observed death rites for teenagers bitten by snakes, toddlers who fell into cooking fires and the bleeding body of a seven-year-old fatally mauled by a hyena while tending goats outside the village. It was prudent, Leona thought, to hold your children at arm's length when you lived the hard life of the Maasai. Anything could happen, after all. Life out here was fragile; you had to be tough. This was what she told herself when her baby was born. These were the thoughts in her head. She convinced herself it was good to keep distance between herself and the baby. She wrapped her leaky breasts tightly with a *kanga* and let another nursing mother in the village feed the baby. She let Simi take the baby to her house to sleep, and she let Simi carry the baby on her back during the walks to the river. This was the line that she drew between herself and her child.

Simi loved the baby. With no children of her own, she was free to adopt a baby who couldn't, for whatever reason, be cared for by its own mother. Leona knew that Simi was more of a mother to her child than she was. She also knew Simi's place in the village, as a childless wife, was precarious. She said yes when Simi asked to make it official; she consented to an adoption ceremony—the *laiboni* slaughtered a ram and both women ate the fat. That was the traditional process. Leona knew, in her own head, that her daughter would never really be Maasai, that she was, by her inherited DNA, privy to the perks of being American, but she felt better in an unexpected way. Her child had two parents now.

The Maasai elders gave the baby her first, sacred, name. The name only used by the parents, nobody else. *Nalangu*, they whispered to Leona, which meant "from a different tribe." And that's what the little pale baby looked like. A different tribe, an alien being that Leona observed; who she watched learn to roll over on a rawhide blanket, who she watched nurs-

ing from another woman's breast, who took her first steps in
the red dust and dried dung of the manyatta. Leona watched
the baby grow in the same way she watched all the babies of
the village grow. She allowed her baby to go to Simi for comfort, and not come to her. She spoke to the baby in English,
but she spoke to all the kids in English—their parents wanted
them to learn. She convinced herself that nothing was different, that the nine months of her pregnancy never really happened and the terror she had felt through it all was just a bad
dream.

At night, though, Leona often woke up sweating and terrified, her nightmares alive in her mind. She dreamed of her
baby disappearing into a puff of smoke, or being carried away
in the mouth of a lion, the wide tawny shoulders heaving as
it leaped over the thorny fence, the shaggy blond mane curling slightly over the cold, yellow, animal eyes. Those nights
she'd sit bolt upright and reach over to check for her baby's
presence. The baby was never there. When she was awake,
Leona hated the version of herself she saw in the nightmares;
it wasn't the smoke or the lion that caused the frantic heart
beating and the suffocating breath, but instead it was the vision of herself, just standing there watching, calmly stirring the
chai in her dented enamel cup with her metal spoon, in con-
centric circles, over and over again, while her child vanished
before her eyes. What kind of mother did nothing but watch?

Leona found peace and freedom in concentrating on her
work. It was important, not just to her, but to the community. When a Maasai member of parliament gave a speech in
Narok, Leona pulled him aside afterward and told him of her
work, of her idea to convince the government to allow grazing
privileges, at least during droughts. He'd been trying to forward a similar idea and asked Leona to send him her research.
This forced Leona to focus more fully on her observations of

specifics; current grazing patterns versus the ones the elders had known, old ways of dealing with drought versus the new ones. Leona began to visit other manyattas in the area, gathering observations and stories from the largest sampling she could. Those trips away from her baby didn't upset either one of them. Nalangu was perfectly content with Simi and her wet nurse; Leona was perfectly content not being a mother.

When Nalangu was one, it came time for her to be given a real name—one that could be said aloud, a name that she would keep. Leona allowed Simi to choose that name, and when the girl's hair was washed with milk and water, and then shaved, Leona watched, notebook and pen in hand. The new name Simi selected was *Adia*, gift. Like all the kids in the manyatta, she was the child of everyone—free to eat and sleep with any of the mothers, and so Leona's connection to Adia remained the same as her connection to all the babies around her; affectionate but removed, seen through a telescope, detailed but remote.

Since Maasai fathers played only a tiny role in the lives of their children, Adia's lack of one was barely a detail worth considering. By the time Adia turned three, Leona didn't think much about the girl's father. She'd succeeded in keeping him away. Leona was relieved, frankly, to let it go.

It was easy for Leona to concentrate on her work with all the mothers available to her daughter. And, because of that, it was easy for the days to slip into months, and even years. Occasionally, Leona drove to Nairobi to meet with her government contact. She provided him with the information she'd gathered, and he began taking it to the halls of parliament. Leona liked her trips to Nairobi. She was beginning to crave a city again, the intellectual stimulation of others like her. And she was finally making a name for herself. Other local anthropologists sought her out; she was becoming known in her field. And she rarely thought of Adia. She knew her daughter was safe in the manyatta under the watchful eyes of Simi and the other women.

During one trip to Nairobi, she was introduced to the head of the anthropology department at the University of Nairobi. He'd requested a meeting, and after they talked awhile, he offered her a position on his staff. Leona was thrilled. Now that she had evidence to support her theory that imposed grazing borders were disproportionately damaging to Maasai communities, she could take that to the lecture halls. She could talk to students about the way their own society was changing, and maybe help inspire a new generation of people committed to the work of helping nomadic people.

Leona thought of her daughter and considered her choices. She could mother the girl alone in Nairobi without the benefit of the village women. She thought back to the nightmares she'd had early on and how casually her nightmare self watched as the baby vanished. What an unsuitable mother she was. It occurred to her that she could leave Adia in the manyatta and come to Nairobi by herself. The manyatta was Adia's home, after all, and she had Simi.

Leona harbored a smoky vision of Adia as a teenager, bent over books in a real high school. That vision, she understood, would require her involvement as a mother. But that was a distant problem. Adia was too young for school, and she'd be safe and happy in the manyatta, at least for a while. She was barely three—far too young for Leona to have to worry about educating her.

The thought niggled at her mind and made her heart beat fast in her chest. She told the department head she needed time to think, to tie up a few loose ends in her research, but she knew her decision was made. The whole drive back to Loita she imagined the way it would feel to teach, to make more contacts in the higher realms of Kenyan government. She could feel excitement in her blood. She could do this; she could use her work, her skills, to help the people she'd come to love so much she'd practically given them her firstborn child.

She stopped for gas a few hours' drive from the manyatta, and, on a whim, decided not to wait. Leona liked to be resolute after making a decision. While the attendant washed the windshield, Leona asked to use the phone. The connection was fuzzy and unclear, but the department head understood. She accepted the position. She'd move to Nairobi soon. The new semester was only a few weeks away, and as she drove the final miles to the place she'd called home for over four years, Leona listed the things she'd need in her new life: a place to live in the city, clothes to wear for teaching (her old, torn jeans and cotton blouses wouldn't do); a bank account; an office with a decent computer. These thoughts distracted her as she rolled to a stop outside the manyatta enclosure. She registered the presence of more people than usual milling around but didn't think about why they might be there. Her mind was full of other thoughts. In her *inkajijik*, Leona looked around. She'd probably leave most everything here. Simi could use it, and Adia. Absently, Leona reached for a small pile of mail someone—Simi probably—left on her bed. The mail came from Nairobi via Narok, and then to a shop that doubled as a post office nearer the manyatta. Usually, when she received mail, the shopkeeper would send his son to deliver it to her directly. This mail must have come while she was away.

When Leona wrote to her parents, she selected her words carefully. She didn't keep Adia a secret, but she didn't write much about her, either. In the letters, she explained only that the father was not present and that the baby—a girl—was happy and safe. As Adia grew, the letters Leona received from her parents became insistent. They'd started a bank account for the girl; they'd rewritten their will. Her father, in particular, couldn't imagine life in the manyatta. He couldn't stomach the idea of his only grandchild—a little girl, for that matter—growing up in the dirt, as he said, without the civility of nearby doctors and things like electricity and running water. Leona forced herself to open all of the letters and to read them. But each time a fat, white envelope—half covered with stamps—appeared in the manyatta, she felt her breath quicken and saw sparks of light behind her eyes. She felt she was sinking. She wondered why she'd bothered to tell them about Adia in the first place.

When she read the letters they wrote to her, the pain of her childhood came back like the feeling of a phantom limb, or the flashes of her remembered nightmares. But something surprised Leona, too. Underneath the anger she had for her parents, and the resentment, she fought an unexpected jealousy. The idea of her parents showing concern for Adia when they had never shown much for her was a notion that cut her. She planned to never let them meet her child. She planned to never go back to the wet silence of those Oregon skies or to the dead feeling of being alone in a house with only the ticking of clocks and the hum of the refrigerator to remind her she was alive.

"And who is the father?" this most recent letter asked. "You must know. If nothing else, a girl deserves a father." It was this that forced a crack in Leona's long-held conviction about keeping a distance from the white Kenyan. The cruel joke that her own father—simultaneously brutal and absent—should imply that his granddaughter needed something he'd never given Leona sent a shiver up into a hidden spot in her brain. She pushed the thought away and tried to bury it. She told herself that Simi and the village were all Adia needed, at least for now. And yet the thought grew in her mind.

Her father, her parents, made Leona what she was—silent and isolated. During the torturous moments when the worry couldn't be pushed away, Leona wondered if she was giving her own daughter the same relationship her parents had given her—disconnected and cool. She hated the idea of that, and the guilt it filled her with, but she didn't know how to be different. Knowing she'd fail was why she'd never wanted to be anyone's mother in the first place. She was torn. When she watched Adia with the Maasai children, laughing and playing games, never alone and never silent, she was happy. Adia always had Simi. Leona told herself that Adia's childhood was better than her own. Adia would grow up with age-mates and friends, and the constant activity and watchful eyes of the entire village. It helped Leona to realize that, if her daughter grew up here, she would be nothing like she herself was. Leona tried to convince herself that giving her child a community, a feeling of belonging somewhere, was far more important than giving Adia herself as a mother.

This most recent letter, the one Leona read now after accepting the position at the university, was no different from the others. Leona crumpled it into the tiniest ball she could, tossed it in the fire pit, and went to find Simi.

As she stepped through her doorway and into the light, she noticed again the number of people in the manyatta. There was the *laiboni*, the spiritual leader, surrounded by the young *moran*, warriors, in the central area between the small houses. Newly initiated warriors crowded the manyatta. Their faces and their long braids were slicked with a mixture of bright red dirt and sheep fat. It made Leona feel light-headed when she realized that in the faces of these brand-new men—most only thirteen or fourteen—she recognized the rounded faces of little boys she'd first met four years ago. Now they were men. She'd been here for so long. She hadn't considered how it would hurt to leave them all behind. To leave Simi. The thought made her feel dizzy, and she wandered over to sit with the elders in the shade of a scraggly acacia tree.

"What's happening?" she asked one wizened woman.

"Emurata," the woman answered.

When Leona first came to the manyatta, she forced herself to watch everything, all the rituals and ceremonies. Her work was to observe, without emotion, the daily life and events that reflected the beliefs of the people she wrote about. Her least favorite ritual was the girls' coming-of-age rite, the *emurata*. She found it impossible not to wince at the cutting of the flesh, and she found herself unable to keep from feeling a harsh judgment against the entire idea. Her resolve to observe everything without critique was tested every time she was audience to an *emurata*. After watching three of them, she convinced herself she had all the information she needed about the practice and stopped going to the ceremonies at all.

The ceremony had started and the *moran* began to dance. They stood in a circle, impossibly tall and impossibly thin, backs as straight as the spears they held. When they began their singing, they chanted *uh-uh-uh-uuuu-huh* and the straight-bodied jumping made their braids slap against their backs and the iron of their spear tips glisten in the sun—Leona knew the circumcision was about to start. She stood up and walked past the dancing *moran*. She wanted to be outside the village, far enough away so that the wind in the acacia trees would fill her ears instead of the sound of the rites.

Vaguely, as she made her way through the crowd, she glanced around for Adia. It was rare that she was alone with the girl, but she wanted that now. It occurred to her she would miss the daily interaction—as unsubstantial as it was—with her daughter. A tingle of worry nibbled at her from somewhere deep and hidden. Her parents' letter, the guilt it made her feel, pressed into her mind. She wanted to hurry, but she was caught between the desire to leave and the unfamiliar feeling of maternal responsibility leaking through her. Where was Adia?

Leona could tell the instant the knife met flesh by the sound of the deep-throated cry of the girl that rose from the squat dung-and-wattle structure and hovered in the air. An image flashed into Leona's mind of Adia, sprawled and bleeding. It couldn't be her, Leona knew. At three, Adia was far too young, but the image of her daughter being cut, now or years from now, set Leona's heart pounding. Someday Adia would be thirteen. Someday, if Leona did leave her here, Adia would think of the cutting as normal, as necessary. This would be her world. Maybe her father was right. The idea of giving him credit for parenting advice made Leona sick, but she couldn't ignore it. This was her daughter, after all. And then some tiny, unwelcome shoot of a poison plant took root in her mind—a thought she didn't want to think. As much as she hated them, there was a part of Leona that desperately wanted her parents' approval. They were happy to have a grandchild. It was the first thing Leona had done to inspire their pride.

Leona's head throbbed, and she felt a trickle of sweat beading down her back. Her heart was beating too fast now, she wanted to sit down, to be able to breathe slowly and pull her thoughts back to where she could contain them, control them.

Then the girl screamed again. Of course she screamed. Of course she writhed against the knife. And Leona, alert and wild with panic, bounded across the dusty paddock.

The quick absence of light when she bent into the ceremonial *inkajijik* made her stop and rub her eyes, but when she opened them, through the haze of smoke, she saw her small blonde daughter sitting ramrod straight in a gaggle of little girl age-mates, watching intently as the bleeding almost-woman curled in pain under the glinting blade. Leona's eyes watered, the wood smoke thick in the air. Through the tears, she thought she could see blood in the dust, little bands of soft flesh left behind.

In one fluid movement, Leona leaned over the embers in the fire pit and pulled her daughter up and out into the light, hissing through the smoke that choked in her throat as she dragged Adia, "You can't watch this. This is not for you... Not for you. Not for us."

Through her panic, Leona didn't see Simi approach, concerned, and when Adia turned away from Leona to pull herself toward the other woman, who grasped the girl's other arm, Leona responded by pulling harder. Flickers of her life as a child popped in her mind. It wasn't all bad. There was the summer camp she loved, the elderly neighbor lady who bought all her Girl Scout cookies one year after Leona admitted to being too shy to go door-to-door, the ice-cream truck in the summer, the smell of the Christmas tree in December and the Thanksgiving dinners they shared with friends who always brought Leona little presents. Was she stealing that life from Adia?

"You are not Maasai," Leona hissed. She saw Simi then, and their gazes held, both women clutching the girl who stood, sobbing, in the dust between them.

"I adopted her," Simi said.

Leona remembered the ram, and the fat she had eaten and the relief it brought her to know she wasn't solely responsible for the baby. Simi had helped her. Surely, though, she hadn't meant forever? Surely Simi knew that Leona didn't really have to obey the traditions of a culture that wasn't her own?

"You are her second mother," Leona said, watching Simi's face carefully—there was nothing but alarm in her eyes. Adia twisted, trying to release herself, but instead stumbled.

"I am her first," Leona continued. "She has a family in

America." She thought of the letter, of her parents' concern that Adia be educated, be allowed to live like an American. Leona wished there wasn't a minuscule part of her that didn't agree with them. She hated that, on some level, she knew they were right.

Adia jerked backward and fell. Leona kept her grip, but Simi, in an instinctual moment, leaned forward to break Adia's fall. In that second, Leona pulled Adia out of Simi's reach.

"Simi, she can't be a Maasai. I can't let that cutting happen to her."

Then her own daughter's voice, thick and raw, hysterical, rose above the manyatta like the call of an exotic bird, out of place, far from home. Whether she was screaming from the pain of Leona's tight grip around her upper arm, from the humiliation of being dragged out of the ceremony or from fear of the sudden and uncontrolled presence of a mother she hardly knew, Leona didn't know. She didn't care. Leona pulled Adia up and held her up against her hip. She knew that she had to get Adia away from here quickly, while the conviction was strong. She stumbled as fast as she could to where her car was parked.

"This is not your real life, Adia," Leona said over and over again. "You are not Maasai. You are like me. You are like me."

Leona's car was dented and rusted to the point of being colorless. Now, she pulled the back door open, grateful it was unlocked—her shaking hands could never have managed a key—pushed Adia into the back seat and clicked the child's seat belt firmly. She didn't say goodbye to the people she'd lived with for so long, she didn't let Adia say goodbye. She was frantic to leave, driven by the thought that if she didn't go now, her own fear would force her to change her mind again and leave Adia behind. Simi was screaming frantically on her knees in the dust, other women gathering by her, and one began running toward the car. Leona slammed the driver's-side door shut so violently that the window slid down into the door frame, off its track, rendering it useless. She managed to fit the key into the ignition and start the car. She popped the brake and hit the gas pedal. Adia screamed and screamed, crying out for Simi as the car bumped wildly on the lumpy, dusty road. She banged on the window with her small fist and kicked the back of Leona's seat.

Leona felt like a kidnapper.

It was getting dark when the lights of Narok emerged on the horizon. Leona hated driving at night. There were too many hazards—broken-down trucks in the road you couldn't see until it was too late to avoid them, elephants wandering, antelope shocked into stillness right in front of you by the flash of your headlights. Leona knew of too many car accidents to take it lightly, and when she reached the cluster of buildings that made up the Narok town, she shuddered the Renault to a stop in front of the Chabani Guest House. She hadn't been here since the night of Adia's conception. She felt a flutter of nerves. What if he was here? What would she say? But the lobby was empty, and when the attendant showed Leona to the nicest room—one of only three with an en suite bath and more than one light to read by—the hall was empty, too.

That night, Leona avoided the bar. Instead, she walked a teary-eyed Adia to a café down the street. Adia, over and over again, asked for Simi, for her mother.

"I want to stay with my mother," she said once. "Not with you."

Leona lied and told the girl they'd go back home soon. She ordered Adia french fries, grilled meat and ice cream. The novelty of the ice cream worked. This is a vacation, she told her daughter. Back in the hotel, Adia consented to a shower and laughed at the feeling of water pouring over her head and down her back. When she climbed into bed, wet hair slicked against her neck, looking as small and pale as a grub, she asked Leona what the sheets were for? The pillow?

Her own daughter had never slept on a mattress. The thought shouldn't have been a surprise, but it shocked her. Leona flicked off the light and lay in the dark. She remembered her own childhood home, her father distant and silent, with hard, hard hands. She remembered what it felt like when she was a child and a stranger in her own life. She thought of the man who gave her Adia, a gift that terrified her into numbness for so long. The girl lay in the bed beside her, so close Leona could feel the rise and fall of her breathing, the tiny lungs; the warm air she expelled.

When Leona finally fell asleep, she fell asleep with Adia's soft hair under her chin and her arm wrapped around Adia's shoulders. There wasn't a nightmare that night. Leona's sleep was calm. She dreamed about the sky, clear and calm and infinite. It was the kind of sky she remembered from one long-ago summer when she was a child, and the darkness hadn't bloomed inside her, and the endless rain hadn't come.

When Leona woke up it was barely light. A centipede trailed along the polished floor and Leona watched it disappear and reappear through the shadows. She absently smoothed back Adia's hair with her palm. They were in Narok now. The white Kenyan came here, Leona knew. He lived nearby. If they waited long enough, asked the right people the right questions, they could find him. Leona was sure of that. She felt a twinge inside of her somewhere, a place so deep she'd almost forgotten, silent and still but, finally, shivering with potential. The sky was getting lighter outside the window and there were squares of light on the wall opposite the bed. Leona twisted her back so she was facing her baby. She traced her finger along the small nose that looked like hers, the ears that reminded Leona of her own mother's. Then she recognized the feeling that was so tiny and so deep down between her bones. Hope was a seed inside of her.

A WOMAN LIKE A WILDERNESS

Simi's earliest memory was one she wished she could forget. Mostly she pushed it to the back of her mind and kept it trapped there in the dark. Sometimes, though, mostly while she slept, it slipped out of its confines and floated, ghostly, into her consciousness.

The details were no longer clear. In her memory, the *inkaji-jik* was chilly. That didn't make sense, Simi knew, because her mother was a good Maasai woman who always kept burning embers in her fire pit. She would never allow the fire to burn out or let the air chill. There would have been fire. But still, in Simi's adult mind, the memory was cold. It was a typical evening, happy and calm. She and her mother and brother sat by the fire. Simi and her brother were telling their mother about their day at school. Their mother loved hearing about school and was proud that she was sending both her children, not just her son.

Simi's family was rich in cattle and children. Her mother

was her father's fourth wife. This was a lucky thing for Simi because by the time she was born he'd grown accustomed to the demands children placed on his time and his money. Mostly her father kept away from the children, and he only visited Simi's mother's house when he needed something. He spent his time with other elders under the shade of an acacia tree. One of his wives made honey beer, and he enjoyed that and spent most nights in her hut. Sometimes he liked the honey beer so much his speech slurred and his walking became erratic. Before the night when everything changed, Simi thought her father was funny when he was drunk. Afterward, it made her hate him.

Simi's mother was quiet and thoughtful; she didn't spend much time with the other women. Instead, in her free time she sat alone and made intricate beaded jewelry. Her designs were delicate and unique. They were so beautiful that people from other manyattas, some two or three days' walk away, began to seek out her creations. Sometimes they would trade a goat for a piece, sometimes they would pull a faded wad of shillings from their wraps. Simi's mother allowed the animals to wander with the others. She made no secret of them. The money, though, she hid. She saved it in an old tobacco tin she kept hidden in the dark space under the bed. When Simi turned seven, her mother bought a used school uniform and sent Simi to school. Simi's father didn't notice, or didn't care, that Simi left the manyatta each morning, dressed in a uniform she carefully kept pristine by washing it each week in the river and hanging it to dry over a small, thornless bush.

As the years passed, her mother earned enough money to buy Simi a new uniform, and she provided Simi with a clean exercise book each year. In all her eight years of school, Simi never missed a day. She walked in rain and dust, and through the torrent of taunts and names the boys tossed her way as she went. In the early years, she walked with other girls, but one by one they all left. They were circumcised, married and sent to live in their husband's villages. Every time another girl left, Simi fought dread that she would be next. But her mother kept sending her. Every evening when it grew dark and all the people withdrew to their houses, Simi and her brother showed their mother letters; they taught her how words were written. They taught her addition and subtraction and times tables. Those years, in Simi's mind, were the happiest. But, in the way daylight follows a dark night, the dark follows daylight, too.

Simi couldn't remember the details anymore. When her father entered, her brother was in the middle of speaking. What story was her brother telling? Simi only remembered that he stopped, mid-word, when their father burst into the hut. This was where her memory skipped from a feeling of contentment to one of fear.

"Where is the money?" Her father's voice. Angry and urgent. "You have been stealing money." His voice stank of honey beer.

Simi's mother was a good wife. Simi knew that. She'd never seen her mother disagree with her father. But now, Simi's mother turned to him and said quietly, "I have not taken your money. I have given you many sheep and goats."

Simi remembered sliding closer to her mother. She remembered the warmth from her mother's skin, and how suddenly it disappeared when her father leaned down and pulled her mother up.

"You are a liar, wife!"

Simi watched as her father dragged her mother from the hut. She couldn't move. Her brother jumped up and disappeared through the door. There was scuffling outside. Simi heard her mother make a guttural sound and then she heard a thud. Suddenly her father was back, standing above Simi. His red eyes, foul breath and the angry quivering of his lips made him look inhuman, like a monster or a wild beast.

He leaned down slowly and, when his face was only inches from Simi's, he growled.

"You, child, find me my money."

Later Simi would cry and wonder why she did what she did. But at that moment, her monster father took all the thoughts from her head. It was just an empty cave.

"It is there," she whispered, pointing under the cowhide bed.

Her father pivoted, still leaning low, and stretched a long arm out into the space under the bed. His face instantly changed when his fingers felt the tin box. He smiled wide, stood up, tucked the box under his arm and was gone.

Simi crept out of the hut. She thought her mother might be there, but she wasn't. It was dark and she could hardly see the sleeping cattle. Not even the stars were shining. Simi kept the fire alive, and knowing her mother would want something warm to drink when she returned, she put a pot of water on the fire for tea. She added the sugar and milk and took it off the heat when it boiled. The tea grew cool, and the milk formed a skin on top, and still her mother didn't return. Finally, unable to keep her eyes open, Simi curled up on the bed and fell asleep. She woke again when her mother returned and climbed into the bed next to her. Simi listened to her mother breathing for a long time. She was ashamed of what she'd done.

The next morning, Simi woke up early. Her mother was stirring chai in the pot and ladled out a hot cup that she handed to Simi. Her face was calm.

Simi watched her mother's face carefully, desperate to know if she was angry with Simi or if, Simi hoped, she understood the choice Simi made. She found it impossible to refuse her father. Surely her mother understood.

"It was your school money, Simi."

Shame bubbled up in Simi's mouth. It was impossible to drink her tea.

"I wanted you to learn so when you married, you could be smarter than your husband. A husband can beat his wife, he can take what she has, but he can never take the things she knows."

Simi stood up. It was almost time to leave for school. She glanced at the hook where her uniform hung. It was empty.

"Your father wanted that, too. I gave it to him."

The loss was a blow to her chest. Simi fought to find air to breathe.

Her mother continued, "He has also told the *laiboni* that you are to be cut."

How fast everything changed then. Simi was fifteen. Many of her age-mates were already women—circumcised and married and gone from her manyatta. The last several years were dry; Simi's father's herds had thinned, and the land grew hard. The bushes and trees the women cut for firewood and building were less and less plentiful. They had to walk farther to get them and, without tree and grass roots to hold the soil together, when it did rain, it merely turned the land to mud. All the seeds and tiny grasses were gone. Money was harder to find and, therefore, food less plenty. Simi would bring a bride price of at least two cows and two goats and one less mouth to feed.

Her mother changed. In the evenings, she didn't ask Simi's brother about what he was learning in school. Simi didn't ask him, either. She tasted bitterness every time she thought of him writing in his exercise book and learning things while she cut wood and washed clothes in the trickle of water that used to be a river. Instead, each night they sat quietly, staring into the fire and sipping tea.

The night before Simi's *emurata*, though, her mother took her hand and said, "I was a weak wife." Then she reached up and unlatched her favorite necklace from her own neck. It was a stunning piece, wide and flat and shimmering with beads in all shades of blue and green. Simi remembered watching her mother make it, painstakingly selecting the perfect bead to sew on next. It was the only piece she'd refused to sell. Simi felt her mother's rough hands slide the necklace around Simi's neck and fix the clasp shut.

"You are my daughter," her mother told her. "And now you are a woman and soon a wife. Your life will be like mine, but maybe not your children's. Maybe they will have a wider sky."

Simi looked at her feet. She knew her mother was still bitterly disappointed in her, in the way she'd ruined the dream her mother had had—to send Simi to school and delay marriage. This was a gesture that her mother had forgiven her, maybe, but had not forgotten.

Simi was resigned to marriage. Even with her schooling, it was inconceivable that she wouldn't follow the path of all the other women before her. She was lucky that the man who chose her was the son of the village elder, the one whose opinion mattered and to whom others paid respect. Her husband was a pleasant man and had an easy rapport with all his wives and his children. Simi was the third wife.

Simi was married for one year before her husband began asking if she was unlucky. He asked with pity in his eyes— a childless woman is a sign of chaos; disorder in the way the world always works. After all, of what importance is a woman without a child? A woman is to provide children; if she cannot give babies, what can she give?

There were things to be done in this situation. The week-

long silent praying to N'gai, the eating of lambs, the visit to
the *oreteti* tree in the forest, the slaughtering of the ox, the
dousing with milk and the eating of fat. For two years Simi
consulted with the village doctor. Four times, she hoped. And
four times the babies, unformed, left her. The other women,
especially the other wives, looked at her through eyes tinged
with suspicion. An unlucky woman could veil the whole village with her curse. And what was unluckier than a woman
who couldn't bear children? God only made perfect things;
imperfections were doled out in life only to the people who
deserved them. A childless wife was an imperfection of the
highest degree—a stunning slight from God. Some husbands
cast out their infertile wives to save themselves from the stain
of bad luck she might bring to the family. Some villages refused to allow unlucky women to stay.

Simi's husband didn't tell her the American was coming.
She found out through his first wife, Isina, when the women
all gathered at the river to wash their clothes.

"Why is the *muzungu* coming here?" someone asked. "To
steal our men?" The women laughed.

"How will she live here when she cannot speak to us?"
someone else asked.

Nalami, Isina's daughter, turned to Simi. Her hands were
soapy with lye, and her palms red and chapped. She paused and
then said slowly, "Simi, you will be the only one who will be
able to talk to her." The other women nodded and murmured.

"Ooh, Simi." Loiyan cackled. She was the second wife, and
although she often kept the women laughing with her jokes
and her brassy interactions with the men, she had a meanness
that could flare up with little warning. In the beginning, Simi
was frightened of Loiyan, but she wasn't anymore. Still, she
didn't like Loiyan—she thought of her as she did a snake, more
dangerous because the strike was often unexpected.

"Ooh, Simi." Loiyan stood tall and tipped her head back. "You will be too important. You will be an American yourself." Loiyan pranced in place, pretending to be a white woman.

"You don't look like an American," Simi said, "you look like a sick hippo." All the women laughed, and Loiyan sucked her teeth and hunkered down again to rinse her pile of clothes in the slow-moving river.

Simi was excited by the news of the *muzungu*. When her husband came to her the next night, Simi handed him a cup of chai and asked him why the American was coming.

"She wants to study us, the way we do things."

Simi was surprised. She couldn't imagine why anyone would be curious about the lives they led in the manyatta. She couldn't imagine why an American would come all the way here just to watch them.

She had seen white people before, but never up close. Usually she saw them behind the glass of a vehicle window, through a film of dust billowing from under the slow-rolling tires as she stood by the side of the road. Often, the white faces on the other side of the glass stared at her, too, with eyes as wide and curious as hers. Sometimes, if the windows were open, the white people would lift their hands and call "Hello!" It always thrilled Simi when this happened. English was her best subject at school, and hearing words she'd practiced over and over again coming from the mouths of strangers was exciting. She loved the way learning a different language had made her feel free—like she had a key to a new life. When she waved and called "Hello" into the van's dusty wake, she felt important. English was her connection to the world outside, and now, though her school days were long past, she was proud of her knowledge. Her mother was right; nobody could take away the things she knew.

In the early days, the American hardly spoke. She wandered like a ghost through the dust in the manyatta and started at the movements of the cattle. Simi watched her closely. She felt too shy to talk to the white woman at first, but she also worried that if the American stayed frightened and out of place, she would leave. Simi desperately wanted her to stay. She watched how the other Maasai women crowded into the American's little house—one they'd constructed for her the day she arrived—and just sat there, watching the strange woman and gossiping among themselves. Finally Simi slipped in with them one afternoon and watched the white woman trying to light a fire in her fire pit. There were no embers there, and Simi quickly got up and fetched a bright coal from her own house and brought it back. She sifted it into the American's fire pit, added a few twigs and dry grasses and blew it all into a flame.

"You must keep some fire alive all the time," she said quietly. "We let it burn, just a little, even at night. We must always have our own fire, miss."

The white woman smiled. "You speak English! Thank God! I've been needing you!" Simi felt herself flush, and she knew the other women were watching. She thought she heard Loiyan sucking her teeth.

"Please," the American said, "tell me your name. Mine is Leona."

From that moment, Leona was always near Simi. "Help me, Simi," Leona would say, and the questions that followed were endless and wide-ranging—from how many handfuls of tea to toss into boiling water for chai, to how a man selects a wife. Simi grew bolder in her English, and lost her shyness with Leona. She scolded Leona the time Leona forgot to dip her head when greeting an elder, and warned her never to walk far from the manyatta in the evenings, when the shadows grew long and the hyenas and leopards stirred from their dens. With Leona next to her at the river, washing their clothes together, Simi found Loiyan left her alone. It wasn't enjoyable to tease Simi anymore when Simi had a friend to speak to in a language Loiyan couldn't understand.

Simi came to understand that Leona's life back in America was completely different from the life they all lived here. Leona showed them photos of enormously tall buildings, expanses of grass so green it almost hurt their eyes to see it.

"Where are the cattle?" Simi asked when she saw the grass. "They must be too fat to walk!"

The images were breathtaking—it was hard to imagine they were real. Leona explained to Simi that not only did America look vastly different from Loita, but that life there—everything from clothing to speech to thoughts themselves—were unlike those here. Simi knew that some of the other women, ones who had never gone to school and seen a photo in a book, didn't understand how to grasp the images and ideas Leona introduced them to; their minds were so firmly here that they could not see things differently. Simi could, though. She'd read stories about people different from herself and knew that the Maasai way wasn't the only way people lived. The images in the pictures and the stories Leona told were like dreams. They flickered in her mind and flashed against the reality she saw around her constantly, two worlds—one inside herself, and one outside, like hot flames that burned blue and orange and red all at the same time.

In the evenings, Leona would come to Simi's house. Her Maa was improving. Often, they practiced together. Leona would look through her notebooks and ask Simi questions about things she'd seen that day, and note ages and names of the people in the village. In return, Leona would teach Simi American slang. Simi loved the feel in her mouth that the new words gave her, and took to peppering her Maa with "That's cool!" and "For real?" Other nights they'd drink tea and just stare into the fire quietly. One night, after Leona had been in the manyatta for several weeks, she sat on a low stool next to Simi. Simi threaded beads onto a strip of leather for a bracelet. It was dark outside, and chilly. "You don't have children," Leona stated.

Simi was relaxed in Leona's presence but this statement—vocalized so clearly and directly—shocked her. It was unexpected, too bold for Simi's comfort. She started and spilled some tea in her lap. It was hot and it stung. Her eyes welled, and she glanced across the bright embers of the fire and saw Leona watching her. There was no malice in Leona's face. Part of Simi wanted to bury the subject forever, but another part was desperate to talk about the pain, release it to someone else in a way she couldn't with the other women. Leona's face was clear, her eyes blank.

"How long have you been married?" Simi heard Leona's question and shifted uncomfortably.

"Three years," Simi answered.

"It's a problem to be a wife without a child?" Leona was speaking as if she had her notebook and pen with her, but Simi saw she had neither.

Simi answered in English. To say the words in her language made them hurt more coming out. "We say that a woman who hasn't given birth is like a wilderness. A woman or a man with children to remember them can never die. But a person like me? When I am gone, nobody will remember."

"In America people can choose to have a baby or not," Leona said. "But even so, there are people who want to but can't. This is something that happens everywhere, Simi. Have you seen a doctor?"

Simi didn't answer. She was tingling with discomfort now. There was no way to explain it all to Leona. Her pain was not something for an American notebook, something to be inscribed with a pen on paper. Simi's bitter frustration about not having a child, and her fear of the repercussions, were not something she would ever let see the light of day. She tried to keep herself from even thinking of them. How could sharing the story in words even scratch the surface of Simi's disappointment and terror at the way her own body betrayed her? She was grateful when, after a long silence, Leona smiled and said she was tired, and then stood up to leave.

With Leona in the manyatta, Simi's daily life changed. Her ability to communicate was a link between the American and the others. She had a certain power she'd never felt before. Even the men saw it. They approached Simi carefully with their questions about Leona, and the conversations Leona had with the villagers all happened with Simi hunkered close by, interpreting for both parties, not just the words themselves, but the ideas and feelings behind them. For the first time since Simi understood the fact of her infertility, she felt her fear loosen. Leona was her anchor. Even with her bad luck, they couldn't send her away while they needed her so much. They were grateful for Simi's education now. There were educated men in the village who spoke English, but because Simi was a woman, she had easier access to Leona. A man couldn't spend so much time with a woman who wasn't his wife without eyebrows being raised.

Leona joined the women daily at the river, and the women taught her to bang her clothes against the rocks and rub the bar of White Star soap until it frothed. It made the hours of banging and rubbing and rinsing clothes go faster when Leona was there. Simi was sorry, in some deep way, that she wasn't the only woman who could have a companionship with Leona. Leona was beginning to make friends with many of the other women, but she was grateful that Leona seemed happy here, content. She wanted Leona to stay for a long time.

"Simi," Leona whispered one day when they were resting their soapy hands. "I think Loiyan is pregnant."

It was something Simi knew already, but she glanced up at Loiyan, anyway. The folds of the other woman's wraps strained a bit under the swell of her belly. Simi swallowed a hot ember of jealousy. Loiyan already had three children. Two of them boys.

"Isn't it true that a childless wife can adopt a baby of another woman?" Leona was whispering her words, but also speaking in English, not Maa. The conversation, Simi understood, was one Leona wanted to keep secret.

"Yes," Simi answered simply. The possibility had crossed her mind a thousand times. To be regarded a mother didn't absolutely have to mean bearing your own child. "It happens often." Leona opened her mouth to speak again, but Simi already understood the subtext of Leona's question, and answered it before Leona could clarify.

"Unless the reason for the adoption is that the mother died, the women have to be as close as sisters."

Later the thoughts of adoption—and the seeming impossibility of it—crowded Simi's mind like the scuffling cattle in the paddock—pushing against each other and refusing to let her sleep. Her husband was rich with children. Loiyan's three and seven from his first wife, Isina. Now another baby was coming, and still, she herself had nothing.

A few months after Leona arrived, Simi found her squatting next to the *laiboni*, struggling to make conversation. Simi offered to translate, and when she heard the questions Leona asked, she felt herself shaking. Her skin went cold, and her vision blurred. She recognized a feeling of deeply embedded anger, but there was something else, as well—a sense of betrayal. N'gai had betrayed her, and now Leona had, too, by so easily achieving, and not even wanting, the one thing Simi desperately desired.

That evening Simi left the enclosure. She walked until she couldn't see the acacia tree fencing, and she couldn't hear the sounds of people. It was near dusk, and this was dangerous. Simi didn't want to be seen, though. She needed time alone, and she didn't want to talk. She stood at a place where the land dipped down toward a stream, now dry, but where shrubs and grasses were thicker. She saw a family of zebra, munching calmly, and she felt safer—they didn't sense a predator nearby. Near where she stood, she saw a young green shrub, the one they used to treat stomachaches. They always needed this plant, so she began plucking leaves, tying them up in the end of her *kanga* as she did. It was later, when she returned home to heat up tea, that she had her idea. Leona hadn't learned to tell one plant from another, so Simi tossed a handful in a crumpled plastic bag and made her way to Leona's house. These leaves would do nothing, Simi knew. And as she handed them to Leona, she imagined the baby clinging tightly to the dark insides of Leona's body. Simi's own muscles clenched at the idea of that fullness. If only. If only.

It was early one morning—before dawn, even the cattle and goats were still asleep—when Leona's cry broke the dark sky into two. Simi heard it. It woke her from her dream and sent a rushing shiver down her spine. It was time. She wrapped her *kanga* around her shoulders to stave off the cool air and crossed the enclosure to Leona's house. The midwife was already there, and some other women, too. Everyone loved to participate in a birth. There was Loiyan with her own new infant—another boy—snuggled fast asleep in a wrap tied tightly against his mother's back.

Leona was lucky. The birth was an easy one, and the midwife had no trouble releasing the baby from Leona's body and into the world. The cord was cut and the new baby—a tiny, pale girl—was placed in Leona's arms.

There were women who didn't take to their babies. Simi had seen it happen before, but never with someone who didn't also have the wild-eyed look of the cursed. Leona's reaction frightened Simi. After the baby was placed in Leona's arms, Leona made a wailing like an animal. Her mouth opened, and her eyes closed, and the cry was from a deep place Simi never suspected Leona had inside of her.

Leona tried to nurse the infant, but within days she pushed the baby away and wrapped a *kanga* tightly around her breasts to stop the milk from coming. It wasn't uncommon for mothers to be unable to nurse—it happened on occasion, and another nursing mother could always step in and help. But Leona could nurse. The few times she tried, her milk came strong and plentiful. Simi could see that the baby was able to drink her fill and that Leona's breasts were swollen and ripe. Simi never heard of a woman who could nurse but wouldn't. There was a sharp feeling in Simi's belly when she saw the way Leona treated the baby.

Simi told herself she was helping Leona when she began caring for the baby herself, and when she arranged for a wet nurse. The wet nurse had five other children, one only a few days older than Nalangu, so she didn't mind when Simi handed her the pink baby for feedings. A few weeks later, when Leona's interest in her baby hadn't increased, Simi asked her husband for a ram to make the adoption official. His wife's adopting Leona's baby was a good thing, and although he found Nalangu's color unappealing, he was happy to provide the animal. All his wives should have children, and this would bring luck to Simi and the community. Even if the child was the color of a bald baby aardvark. Simi divided the ram's fat into two portions. Leona was still gray and quiet, and Simi told Leona the fat would make her body strong again after the depletion of pregnancy. After all, that was the truth. Leona never asked why Simi bundled off the other portion of fat. Simi told herself that Leona must know the procedure for adopting. She'd been here for so long now, taking notes on everything. Surely they'd talked about this.

Simi loved being a mother. Her place in the village was cemented. Loiyan didn't tease her anymore, and her husband no longer looked worried when he came to her at night. Simi was part of things now—safely protected from the wilderness of a life without a child.

Simi didn't choose Nalangu's name, but it sounded like the hand of fate reaching out to give Simi what she'd wanted for so long. Until now, she'd felt like a member of a different tribe herself. Now she and this new person were together, they had each other and that would allow them both to be included. Simi knew Leona watched Simi and the baby together with a sense of relief. Leona's skin grew pink again, and the hollowness in her eyes filled out. She seemed happy. By the time Nalangu turned one, and it was time to give her a proper name, Simi didn't ask Leona what she thought. The mother could decide this one, and Simi chose Adia, "gift," because that was what this child was.

Later, Simi wondered why the clouds came that particular day, and what it was she'd done to deserve renewed punishment. She was a good person, a good mother to Adia. She took all the necessary steps to ensure that N'gai—God—was satisfied with her. Leona had been going to other manyattas often lately. She also traveled to Nairobi. Simi could sense that her friend's attachment to the village was waning. Simi was ashamed that the notion of Leona leaving brought her relief. There were times she wondered if her baby would feel more like hers if Leona were gone. The link they had—Leona and Adia—simply through the color of their skin, was too obvious. People outside the village, people who didn't know, assumed the wrong connection. When Leona was gone, it would be easier.

It was a day like any other, hot and clear and dusty. They needed rain, but they always needed rain. It was a special day, too. The *emurata* was a glad day for the village, and the *moran* were gathering. There was no way Simi could have known that Leona's mothering urge, so long dead, would choose this day to rear its head and strike.

It was past noon, and the sun was flat and hot and stared down at the village with its burning face when suddenly Simi heard Adia's scream. She recognized her girl's voice like her own and, with her heart pounding in her chest, she leaped up from where she'd been sitting with some other women and raced across the village. She expected to see a snake or a leopard or some terrible creature hurting her daughter. Instead, she saw Leona dragging her baby—*her* baby—from the *emurata* hut. Leona's face, usually blank, was a riot of clouds like the darkest of rainy seasons. Her eyes were glassy—those of a cursed woman—and they lit upon Adia like flames. Leona's English was fast and rough and too angry for Simi to grasp completely, but her intention was clear. She was taking Adia away.

Instinctively, like any mother would, Simi reached out to pull her daughter back from the abyss. Adia shouted her name, "Yeyo! Mother!" She clutched at Simi's hand.

Adia screamed, *"Tung'wayeni!"* at Leona, "Don't touch me!"

And the girl tried to wrest her arm from Leona's grip. Simi saw the terror in her daughter's eyes and tried to make Leona look at her—she tried to get the American to calm down, to speak in a way Simi could understand.

But when she did, her words echoed Simi's darkest fear. "Adia, you are my daughter!" Leona said in a cold and measured voice—finally speaking so that Simi could take it in.

"You are mine. You are mine."

Adia stumbled, and Simi's muscles fell slack with shock, and her grip released from Adia's arm. Then the girl was gone. Simi fell to the ground. The other women gathered around her, but she couldn't answer their questions.

Simi watched her daughter's anguished face through a screen of dust and then through the smudged window of Leona's car as it pulled away. As the car grew smaller and smaller, Simi gathered her energy and drew herself up from the ground. She chased after the car, kicking up dust and cutting her feet on the sharp stones. She followed Leona's car until she couldn't anymore, and then she fell to earth like a rock. She looked up once to see the tiny car far in the distance, and then, like all the white people she'd seen before, they disappeared.

When the dust died away and the earth beneath her grew cold, Simi lifted her head. The evening was coming, and she could hear the sounds of the village far behind her. The *emurata* was finished, and the children were bringing the goats and cattle back from their grazing. Something—she couldn't name the motivation, because every cell inside her wanted to die—forced her to stand and shuffle back through the enclosure and into her house. It was dangerous to be outside the manyatta at night. She could be attacked by a leopard, a lion, and eaten. It was the smallest part of her that pushed her to avoid that by retreating to her home. She bent to enter and fell into her bed. The fire needed tending, but she couldn't make herself care. Simi's longing for her daughter came in painful waves that made her feel as if her body was burning on the inside.

How could this be real? She was desperate to relive that last moment when she held Adia's arm and watched as the terrified girl was pulled from her grasp. How could she have let it happen? How could a mother let her child—her only child—be taken? God was right not to bless her body with her own children—she was not fit to be a mother.

Over the next few days, Simi was broken. She could only lie in her bed. The other women—even Loiyan—came into her hut to see how she was. They kept watch, boiled chai in the *suferia*, and tried, constantly, to make Simi open her mouth to drink, to swallow, to take the small sustenance that the sugar and tea and milk might give her. The women whispered to each other as they watched her. Simi didn't speak. She couldn't open her mouth, not to answer the women and not to drink the tea; she could hardly open her eyes.

She remembered the time after Adia's birth, and how Leona had sunk into herself, barely speaking, barely eating. A thought crossed her mind that this was Adia's mark—that her mothers were destined to share a kind of darkness. And then she remembered that Adia had been pulled away from her; she was nobody's mother—not anymore. It was that thought that made her stomach heave, and she leaned over and retched. Because she hadn't eaten for days, it was nothing but bitter, sticky foam she coughed out. She watched as it disappeared, slowly absorbed into the dirt of the floor. The women in her hut tsked and sucked their teeth.

Late that night, Simi woke up. Her hut was empty. The other women had gone home. That was a relief. Her stomach growled. Her mouth still didn't want food, but her belly called for it. She stretched her weak legs and slid off the bed. Even though she'd barely sipped water in the last few days, she had a desperate need to urinate. The cattle in the manyatta enclosure lowed softly and shook their great heads as Simi slipped past them. There were fewer than there used to be, Simi noted. The drought was bad again. It seemed the pattern was changing—a year of good rains and hope, followed by several years of dry land and dry skies, starving animals and hungry people. It struck Simi just then that nothing was certain. Not ever. Not even the continuation of the life she'd always lived. More and more Maasai men were abandoning cattle herding and moving to Nairobi to seek work. There were manyattas where no men lived at all, only women and children, all the husbands and sons having left for new opportunities. Everything was changing.

Simi squatted down and felt the relief of emptying her bladder. It felt good to be outside, to breathe the cool night air and look up at the stars. It was a clear night, not one cloud to tease her with the possibility of rain, but none to obscure the universe above her, either. The moon was new. It was a curved edge, as sharp and clean as a scythe. The Maasai myth said that the sun and the moon were married. Olapa, the moon, was short-tempered and, during a fight one day, she wounded her husband. To cover his wound, he began shining more brightly than anything else. To punish his wife, he struck out one of her eyes. Now, Simi thought, as she slowly stood up, her body weak from lack of food, the sun was punishing all of them by shining too hard, never allowing rain clouds to form.

The moon, the wounded wife, was lucky, Simi thought. She'd only had an eye taken. Simi remembered her mother always said nobody could take an education from her. That was true, but her mother never told her that everything else could be taken; a body part, grazing grasses for the cattle, a way of life and a daughter.

WATER IN A DRY PLACE

Nairobi lay in the highlands, but Narok was on the floor of
the Rift Valley, and when Jane's plane cruised over the valley's
edge and the land fell away in a great crack, she stared out the
window and searched for her first glimpse of the elephants.
Kenya was red. The terrain was rusty and volcanic—the dust
made from layers and layers of ancient lava, dried to a crust and
ground down by time. The earth looked like gaunt stretches
of skin seen through a magnifying glass—gray-brown and
pocked, with the scabby outcroppings of rock and the dried
blood of the barely damp riverbeds.

Kenya was new to Jane. Africa was new. Her flight from
Washington had come in for its bumpy landing at Jomo Ken-
yatta Airport in Nairobi less than twenty-four hours ago, and
now she was about to touch down in her new home. Her eyes
were raw with fatigue, and her skin felt dry and grimy. She
pressed her face to the tiny plane window and tried not to
blink. She didn't want to miss any of this first introduction

to her new home. She didn't know what she was supposed to see. She'd been told that the drought was severe, that all of eastern Africa was drying out, dying. The rivers were low and water was precious.

Jane traced her interest in elephants back to a day at the National Zoo. She was six, and her brother, Lance, was four months old. Her mother had Lance strapped in a front pack, snuggled against her chest. This made her walk slowly under the weight of the baby. Jane wanted to hurry, to run from one animal to another, taking everything in at once. She knew if Lance weren't there, they would have been able to walk faster, and it made her angry with the baby. Her mother led Jane over the zoo's winding pathways, and when they reached the elephant enclosure, she let Jane step up onto the lowest rung of the metal fence. The elephants had just been fed, and they rooted through the bales of hay and grasses with their trunks. They waved their enormous ears gently, like the tails of the tropical fish her father kept in the tank in his study. Jane heard her mother sigh with pleasure. The gentle motion of the animal's trunks up and down between hay and tiny mouth, and the rolling motion of their jaws, gave them a delicacy that made Jane laugh and clap her hands. Jane's mother wrapped her arm around Jane's shoulders, and her breath was warm and sweet in Jane's ear. Jane could feel her mother's joy at the sight of them.

"Aren't they lovely?" she asked. "They're very maternal creatures. I read that somewhere." She leaned down and kissed the top of Jane's head. "Very maternal, just like I am."

Jane's mother was sick for a long time before she died. Jane was ten when the diagnosis came, Lance was four. At first nothing changed. There were doctor's appointments and days when her mother was too tired to cook dinner so her father brought home McDonald's instead. But mostly it was the same as it always had been, and Jane began to believe it would always be this way. On the tired days, Jane would come home after school and curl up on the couch next to her mother and do homework. Lance would lie on the carpet watching TV and eating Cheerios one by one from a plastic bowl. But by the time Jane was twelve, there were more and more tired days. She turned thinner than any grown-up Jane had ever seen, and she was always cold. She began coughing and spitting up blood into a bright green bandanna she kept shoved up the sleeve of the nubby brown sweater she always wore. The sounds of the wet coughs scared Jane, and she found herself avoiding her mother; instead of sitting next to her on the couch, Jane spent the hours between school and dinner in her bedroom. Once she heard her mother calling her in that thin, weak, dying voice. When Jane came down the stairs, her mother was standing at the bottom of the flight, clutching the newel post to steady herself.

"I understand it's hard to watch me, Jane," her mother said. "And I know you love me and if you need this time alone, take it. But we have to talk about Lance. You're his sister. That gives you some responsibility." Jane didn't hear what her mother said next, because she'd already turned and raced back up the steps. She slammed her door as loudly as she could, and after that, she always pretended she couldn't hear when her mother called.

There was an open casket at the funeral. Jane's father left Lance with a babysitter and wanted to leave Jane home, too, but she begged and cried and finally he relented. Her mother's body was ravaged by disease, but someone had put foundation on her face, blush on her cheeks. Jane thought she looked beautiful, and that she would like the blush and the rosy color of the lipstick they'd put on her. But it struck Jane that just under the powders and the creams her mother's face was gone. That is, it was intact and Jane could see it all—eyes, lips and the familiar way her mother's ears curved and the diamond studs in her lobes that she wore every day. But they didn't add up to her anymore. Her mother was an empty shell—like the ones cicadas left behind in late summer, only this one resembled the person Jane loved most in the world. The unfairness of that moment, the trickery, made Jane burst into sobs so loud and incessant her grandmother had to lead her away.

The house was quiet after her mother died. Jane hated it. She missed the singular sounds of her mother's movement, the way she slowly climbed the stairs and shuffled along the hallways in her slippers. Jane even missed the ugly sounds of the coughing. Most of all, though, she missed how it felt before she hated herself. She replayed all those recent afternoons when she'd avoided the sounds her mother's sickness made, and instead closed her bedroom door. She would do anything to have those afternoons back. She didn't bother with homework, but she did take up her old place on the couch—napping there after school and then, again, after dinner. Sleep was the only way she could turn off her mind.

Her father must have noticed that Jane didn't do anything except sleep, and one evening, a few months after the funeral, he looked at her across the dinner table and he said, "Life goes on. She'd want us to be happy." As far as Jane could remember, that was the last they'd spoken of the grief they all stumbled through alone.

Lance grew silent. Far quieter than a boy his age should be. He spent hours draped in an armchair in the family room, watching TV. He barely spoke to Jane.

Her father started smoking and spent evenings in his study, watching his fish and blowing rings of smoke up toward the ceiling. "You shouldn't be near all this smoke," he'd say when Jane was lonely after dinner and wanted to be near him. "I'll come and find you later, tuck you in. We can talk then." But he rarely remembered, and Jane eventually stopped trying. She felt like a shadow, visible, but of no substance, and it frightened her. It felt like fading away. Some days she thought she might just disappear.

Two years later her father was married again, and the only thing Jane had left of her mother was a pile of photos and some ugly antique furniture that traced the maternal line back for generations. Her father's new wife was kind to Jane and Lance, but she hated to "wallow," as she said, in the memories of their life before, of Jane's father's other wife.

When her father remarried, Jane and Lance lost their mother all over again, in Jane's mind; by picking a new wife, he erased her mother further. The new wife moved into their house, opened the windows, banished the fish tank and aired out the smoky study in favor of a guest room and a small, barking dog. Soon, all the photos that included Jane's mother were gone, piled into boxes in the attic with her books and the antique furniture Jane would inherit when she grew up and had a house of her own.

It was true that her father was happier, and his new wife was kind and funny and cooked dinners every night so they could sit around the table "like a family should." Lance watched TV less, and smiled more, and all of this made Jane grateful. But she couldn't push past the notion that this woman was an intruder in their house, in their lives, and that this new family they had formed was just a weak facsimile of what it should have been.

Jane was in graduate school before Lance began showing signs of his own sickness. Her master's program in conservation biology was difficult. Jane struggled with math—the tricks of statistics and probability eluded her. She had to work hard, and this gave her a ready excuse to ignore her father's calls, to listen to, but not return, his messages saying that Lance was seeing things that weren't there and talking to empty corners. One message sounded as if her father were about to cry—a depth of emotion Jane hadn't even seen from him after her mom died. That was the message saying that Lance was sent home from college because of a violent outburst and was under psychiatric care.

She'd never mentioned the conversation her mother tried to have about Lance, the one where Jane was supposed to agree to be a good big sister. And now she never would—being a responsible sister to a normal little boy was one thing, but Lance was an adult man now, with psychological issues. The calls and the urgency in her father's voice made Jane increasingly desperate to flee.

Within days of arguing her thesis, Jane applied to the Elephant Foundation. Her adviser knew the foundation's director, and Jane was hired. She went home for the first time in months to tell her dad. Lance was at home at the time, but Jane remembered the message her father left her, telling her they might have to put Lance in a home, right before her thesis was due, and how she'd listened to it once and then deleted it. Now she saw that her father's face was pinched. He looked older than he should. At dinner one night, when his new wife was in the kitchen, filling plates with dessert, Jane told him she was leaving, soon, for Kenya.

"Wow," he said, nodding. "That's far away...but you'll be happy."

His blasé attitude made Jane illogically angry. It was her choice to leave, to go as far away from home as she could. She was the one leaving him, leaving Lance and the new wife. He should be angry, or sad. But he didn't seem to care, and he didn't beg her to stay. She'd always be just a small, annoying shadow in his smoky study, or a child with grief so big it made his new wife uncomfortable. Jane wasn't surprised by his reaction, but the vicious rush of anger and the grief she tasted on her tongue stunned her. She'd almost forgotten it was there, secret tinder she kept hidden away.

"Before one, two years ago...this was green," Muthega, the Kikuyu guide hired by the Elephant Foundation, told her when he parked the Land Rover and fumbled for the keys to her new front door. He'd waited on the airstrip of the tiny Narok airport for her plane to land, and he was standing there, in a khaki shirt with the foundation's logo emblazoned on the chest pocket holding a handwritten sign with her name on it, when she'd disembarked. It made Jane laugh; there was only one other passenger on the little plane.

"Are you sure you're here for me?" Jane had joked, but Muthega just nodded solemnly and hoisted her suitcase onto his shoulder.

Jane's house in Narok was a two-room building, low and squat and slapped together with rough, gray concrete. Just to the south were the dusty streets and the warren of other flat-topped concrete buildings of Narok, but north was nothing but dry grassy savannah edging the Maasai Mara game reserve, and the distant line of trees that clung to the bank of the Mara River. The yard space around the house was bare dirt, with a little dry scrub grass and one lone pink bougainvillea that climbed the wall next to the front door and grasped the earth below it in a constant struggle for water.

Now Jane looked around the dry patch of land that was her new yard. The high concrete wall surrounding her plot of land distracted her. It was at least six feet tall, and the top edge glinted with shards of broken bottles.

"For thieves," Muthega said, following her eyes with his own. "It can be dangerous for you here."

Jane thought of the dingy little town they'd driven through

to reach this house. It seemed quiet and charming, in a dusty way, not particularly dangerous. Anyway, she'd keep the gate locked, she told herself, and better to be safe than sorry. She didn't dwell on the thought; she was desperate to get out into the bush.

Muthega's job was to drive her to where the elephants were. He did his best to track their movements. Elephants are creatures of habit and in the dry season their daily range is somewhat limited. Once Jane tracked them long enough, she could calculate the specifics of different groups. And once she and Muthega had figured that out, they'd situate bush cameras in the areas the various elephant groups were likely to congregate. Timing was critical; once the wet season came, the elephant groups would migrate much farther afield and be nearly impossible to track. Muthega smoked cigarettes that smelled like burning rubber, but Jane was glad to have him around because he had watched the elephants in this area for years, and because he wore a rifle slung over his shoulder. It was for people, not game, he told Jane. It was the people who made her uneasy; it was people who she was here to combat. The presence of Muthega's gun was comforting.

The foundation's war on poaching was waged in three ways: the collection of DNA samples from elephant dung, which would help other researchers pinpoint sources of illegal ivory; the logging of traps, poacher sightings and slaughtered elephants on a GPS; and the placing of elephant cams in areas most heavily used by the animals. The foundation hadn't tried the cameras here before, but there had been a successful pilot program in Sumatra, where faces of three poachers were caught so clearly on the cameras that within days of posting Wanted posters promising financial rewards, they'd all been jailed. Jane brought ten remotely operated cameras with her from the foundation headquarters in Washington. She was responsible for safeguarding the expensive equipment, and because the elephant cameras would bring a high price if stolen and sold, Muthega's gun was necessary.

Jane and Muthega followed the elephants by tracking their footprints in the dust. Often they saw them at the edge of the Mara River, where the water was low and groggy and ran thickly, more solid than liquid. The edges of the river were gray with silt, and the elephants had to lumber farther and farther from shore to find spots deep enough to settle into and drink from during the hottest hours of the afternoon. This left them exposed for Jane to count and study, but exposed, also, to the poachers.

Smaller streams and tributaries, and the springs far from the river, had dried up to nothing more than trickles. The last good rainy season was two years ago, and now crowds of eland, gazelles, zebras and giraffes migrated off their habitual feeding grounds, away from their usual watering holes. The river teemed with game in numbers it couldn't possibly sustain, and daily Jane and Muthega saw the dead—gazelles dropped in their tracks, bony and starving, set upon by hyenas and eaten alive, their bones and gristle left behind, fodder only for the vultures and the marabou storks who held their ground as Jane and Muthega drove by.

Muthega and Jane didn't talk much. He smoked constantly, and scanned the horizon. It kept him busy, and to make conversation, Jane felt, would be too distracting. She told herself he needed to keep his focus on the signs of elephants and hints of poachers. Jane put her feet on the dashboard and studied the unfamiliar landscape. When they did speak to each other it was brief exchanges about the land, the animals they saw, how the lack of water affected the game, and the dead. The dead, always the dead, in little leather piles of hoofs and bones, the only parts left after the feasting and the incessant sun.

Jane had a cistern at home, filled up biweekly by a water truck. She had no idea where her water came from, and never wondered. She conserved it as much as she could, bathing only every two days. It never occurred to her to ask Muthega about his family, if they had enough, or if the people in the town worried about the endless drought. Jane only thought of the thirsty, skeletal game. She saw the women of Narok clustered daily by the drying river, washing clothes and filling up cans and buckets and calabashes to carry home. Often when they crossed the river at the low, wooden bridge closest to town, Muthega slowed the Land Rover for the women who thronged there. They gathered in groups, their heads weighted with basins of clothes to rub with bricks of lye and then rinse in the sluggish river. There were always tiny children with them who splashed in the water and flickered like dark flames in the mud. Muthega greeted the women in Swahili, his smile breaking open and his tongue clicking his teeth to punctuate his words. The throngs of women around the car made Jane uncomfortable. They watched her during the exchanges, and sometimes they gestured at her, and Jane knew Muthega was answering questions about who she was and why she was here. None of the women spoke directly to Jane. They just watched her.

Sometimes, when they crossed the river in the evening, returning to town for the night, Muthega stopped and let some of the women climb up in the back seat with their basins of laundry, which smelled like the sun, and the buckets they'd filled. It felt too crowded then. The women pushed and laughed behind Jane, their knees bruising her through the back of her seat and their joking, singsong voices saying things Jane couldn't understand. She wanted to tell Muthega not to pick up the women, but she didn't know how to phrase it in a way that wouldn't seem unkind. How could she explain that the women made her feel unseen all over again, or that watching the toddlers walk home in the care of older siblings made her sick with guilt? It was seeing these little children take care of each other that made her guilt unfurl. She'd flown halfway around the world just to escape her family, her obligation to care for her brother.

One morning, less than a month after she arrived in Narok, Muthega tapped the Land Rover horn outside Jane's gate. He always came early and today was no different. The sun hadn't risen. It was a navy blue dawn, cool and clear.

"The poachers were nearby last night. The dead one is just by the river. I will show you," Muthega said.

The sky lightened as they drove, silently, into the scrubland on the opposite side of the river. But still, when Muthega waved his hand to indicate the body was nearby, Jane saw only a dusky gray, curved rock. It looked like a boulder lying there in the flat grassland. Then she saw the carrion. Vultures circled the sky and marabou storks stood by, as still as fence posts but for the way they tipped back their heads to swallow their mouthfuls of meat. They didn't scatter when the truck rumbled up next to them, but merely stepped back a few paces on their backward-kneed legs, more annoyed by the presence of humans than afraid. The sky-hung vultures retreated to the upper branches of the nearest acacias. Muthega jerked the Land Rover into Park and reached behind him to pull his rifle from the back seat. He double-checked it was loaded and climbed out. Jane assumed he suspected the poachers were still close.

"Coming?" he asked, slamming his door. "We must gather the evidence."

The flesh that burst from the bloody hacked holes in the animal's face was bright pink. Against the sullen brown of the earth it looked unreal, plastic. The dead elephant was young, Jane could tell instantly, in the prime of his life. Likely he'd only recently left his family clan to find a mate. He'd been shot first and then hacked through with machetes to harvest the parts poachers would sell—tusks, tail and feet. The rest of him was left for the feeding frenzy of hyenas, jackals and wild dogs that slunk out of the underbrush, and the rancid-beaked vultures and storks that floated in from wherever they'd been lurking to feast on fresh meat.

Muthega climbed up onto the elephant's shoulder and pulled the giant ears up to search for a tag.

"This one I think is Twiga," he said.

They had seen Twiga just days before, feeding on the bark of a baobab tree a few miles to the north of here. When Muthega told Jane his name that day, she had laughed. "He's named 'giraffe'?" she asked.

Muthega complimented her on a new Swahili word learned, and told her that when Twiga was younger, still in his mother's clan and unnamed, he'd been seen stretching his trunk as far as he could up the side of a nearly bare tree to pull down the few remaining leaves.

"Like a *twiga*!" Muthega explained.

Jane closed her eyes and pulled her bandanna from the pocket of her shorts. She tied it tightly around her nose and mouth. The flesh wounds on the animal were fresh, the blood on the ground still sticky, and the iron smell of raw meat hung in the air.

Muthega laid a calloused hand with wide, flat fingernails on her upper arm.

"Miss Jane," he said slowly, as if she hadn't been trained in this already, "you must photograph the body for the records, collect samples for the DNA and measure him."

Then he let go of Jane's arm and left her standing, dizzy, next to the body. She watched him walk out into the surrounding scrub bush so, she assumed, he could look for tracks or evidence of the people who'd killed Twiga. But instead he set his gun down under an acacia and hunkered on his heels. He pulled a cigarette from his shirt pocket.

Jane glanced down at the raw place where Twiga's face used to be and it felt like looking at someone she once loved. She'd seen photos of poached elephants before, of course, and had worked on collecting DNA samples from elephant dung and tusk fragments during an internship in Sumatra. But this, the reality of a healthy, beautiful animal in the midst of the drought that was killing so many others...felled by the brutal force of humans, stunned her more than she thought it would. A rage swelled up in Jane. "Goddammit!" she muttered. "What the fuck is wrong with these people? What kind of abhorrent subhuman asshole does this?"

Jane reached down to pull a tiny flake of severed tusk from the ground. She placed it carefully in a plastic vial. She gathered a skin scraping and a marble-sized piece of dung. She took measurements to determine the rough age of the animal and the size the tusks might have been. She did her work—what she'd come here to do. She could feel that her face was twisted and hot, and tears and snot were soaking the bandanna. Flies, awakened by the rising sun and attracted to the smell of blood, buzzed in waves around her head, settling on her arms and cheeks, licking thirstily at the tears hung in the corners of her eyes. Jane waved her arms fruitlessly. It was getting hot, and the meat was beginning to smell. Muthega's cigarette smoke caught in a gasp of the breeze and mixed with the smell of meat. Her stomach rolled over in her belly and she bit her lip, forbidding herself to vomit.

Sweat dribbled down her forehead, and when she rubbed it with her hand, a flake of dirt fell in her eye. It hurt and she cursed and cried out. Muthega hunkered and smoked, just watching her. She hated him then. The way he just sat there, emotionless. He didn't care, Jane thought, and she wanted to smack him, to see him feel pain, to watch him cry. She felt the flicker of that angry ember she had forgotten was in her, and the rage spilled out like blood.

"Goddammit, Muthega! At least get off your ass to get the fucking measuring tape! There's one in my bag—in the trunk. Sample collection jars, too. Jesus Christ!"

"Okay, Miss Jane, okay," he said laconically.

Jane pulled her small digital camera out of the pocket in her shorts and pointed and clicked, pointed and clicked through her tears. First she photographed Twiga, what remained of him, for the foundation's records. Then she pointed the lens at Muthega as he rummaged through the trunk of the car for the measuring tape. He'd placed it on Twiga's hind leg, and then he'd sat down again. She would go to her boss in Nairobi. She would have Muthega fired for not even trying to trail the poachers, for avoiding the responsibility of helping her get the information they needed from the body. Jane snapped picture after picture of him hunkered there, in the dust, a calm look on his face and smoke circling his head.

He smiled up at her as she clicked and cried. He said in a voice so calm it made Jane want to kill him, "Anger will not bring Twiga back to life, Miss Jane."

Then he stuffed the end of his cigarette into an anthill and stood up. "If you have finished with the work, we can go now."

Jane watched the body as they drove away. The vultures and the storks slipped back through the sky and began their feast. There would be nothing left soon, Jane thought. "Take me home again, Muthega," she said. "I need to deal with the samples." She wanted to be alone now; she didn't want to have to talk to Muthega or watch him sucking on his cigarettes. She didn't want him to see her crying.

That night she climbed into her little wooden bed early. She wanted sleep to blot out the day. It was late when the smell of them woke her, the African smell of wood fire and meat, dust and sweat. She kept her body still but cracked one eye. Her front door was open and she could see the sky, a shade lighter than the dark of her room. She heard the low murmur of their voices through the dark. They'd come for the cameras, she thought. She kept them in a tin trunk locked with a padlock. Her heart choked her and panic took over. She wished she had Muthega's gun.

In a single movement, Jane pulled herself from under her sheets and ran. She had no desire to fight or to defend the few things she kept in the house; even the cameras weren't worth her life. She made for the open space beneath the sky. She thought the air might save her, or the land. The wall around her garden was tall and too smooth to climb. She turned and ran for the gate.

Jane was halfway across the bare yard before she was caught. Dry, calloused hands jerked her forearm and she fell. The voice attached to the hands grunted and spoke rapid-fire Swahili, and then she felt fingers around the back of her neck, pressing her face into the ground. She couldn't understand the Swahili. It was too fast and her vocabulary too small. Jane thought there was a familiarity to one voice, though, a growl, a shudder of smoke in the throat.

It seemed like hours before they were gone. She heard them rummaging through her little house, going through her things. She heard the smashing of glass—the outdoor elephant cameras, she knew—on her concrete floor. But why had they broken them? The thought occurred to her that they'd be of no value to sell now. So, what did they want? There was nothing else to steal. Even her little digital camera, which would bring the men a couple of hundred dollars in the market, wasn't in the house. It was in the truck. Jane kept it in the glove compartment so she'd have it if she ever needed it. Finally, they crossed the yard to leave. One voice spoke to Jane in halting English. "Next time we kill you, too." Jane lay there for a long time. She was terrified that if she moved they would come back, or that if she looked up, she would see nothing but the flash of a blade slicing toward her.

The light came in the Kenyan way—quickly, like a shade pulled up. Jane finally sat up. Her whole body hurt. She wondered if she was bleeding. There was a puddle of her own saliva in the dirt where the men had pressed her face. Jane felt bits of dirt on her tongue.

Jane pulled herself up, knees cracking as she bent them straight. She focused only on her next step. She thought of nothing else. She was frozen and terrified that, if she stirred her mind in any direction, what had happened would crush her.

Luckily, there was space on the afternoon flight from Narok to Nairobi. When the plane landed, Jane took a taxi from the airport directly to the Elephant Foundation's main office on Wayaki Way. She focused on reporting Muthega to the regional director, a large Kenyan man called Johnno, famous for his lifelong dedication to elephants and his harsh indictment of poachers.

Jane hated that she cried, again, when she told Johnno the story.

"Muthega and his friends, they were the ones," Jane sobbed.

She described the smell of the bodies, the rough hands and the familiar phlegmy voice. She showed them the photos on the tiny screen of her camera. There was Muthega, how guilty he was! Just sitting there.

"It had to have been him," Jane said. "He obviously doesn't care about the elephants and he is in league with the poachers. He wanted the cameras destroyed."

Johnno answered, "We cannot have criminals working for us like that. Sorry, so sorry we had to learn this way."

Jane thought she would feel stronger when she reported Muthega, when she set in motion the wheels that would punish him for what he did to her, to the elephants. Johnno told Jane it had happened before—poachers bribing protectors to look the other way. Ivory was a lucrative trade, and it paid to hand out bribes for easier access to the animals.

"But Muthega," he said, "Muthega surprises me. He's been an excellent, trustworthy employee for years. We've only recently given him a substantial raise. This drought, though… Everyone is desperate. People's children are dying."

He shook his head, disappointed, as betrayed as Jane was.

Later that afternoon Johnno drove Jane to the US Embassy to file a report. The marine who inspected her passport looked like a boy from home. The carpeted hallways, the smiling portraits of the president and the familiar accents Jane heard around her made her dizzy with longing—how she wanted to go home.

It was a man about her age who helped her fill out the paperwork to lodge a criminal complaint. He was tall with dark hair, and when she told him what happened, his brow furrowed and he winced. Jane thought she heard him curse under his breath. When the paper was filled out, he pulled a business card from inside his desk and reached over to hand it to Jane. Under the seal of the United States was his name in gold letters—Paul O'Reilly.

"I don't know if you were planning to go back to Narok to work, or back to the States, but you'll have to stay around Kenya for a few weeks, maybe a few months," he said. "Authorities will want to question you. Don't worry, I'll help you. Call me." He smiled and Jane felt dizzy again. She slipped the card into her backpack.

Jane stayed in a hotel in Nairobi that night. She showered until the water turned cold, scrubbing and scrubbing and wishing to turn herself inside out to be able to clean every part of her of the memory of those men. Then she crawled into bed and she slept and dreamed about her mother. In the dream, Jane was an elephant and her mother was chasing her, and every time Jane turned around to see if her elephant mother was there, she saw the flash of a machete through the dust she'd kicked up behind her as she ran.

The hotel phone woke her.

"Muthega," Johnno said immediately. "Are you sure he was among the men who assaulted you? Did you absolutely see him?"

"I heard him," Jane said. "I thought I did."

Jane remembered the smell of the men, meaty and smoky. She wondered if Johnno ever smelled that way.

"Is there any way, any way at all—" he said this gently, apologetically "—that you could be mistaken? You see," he went on, "the Narok police have found a body. They think it may be him, but it's too maimed to tell. Hacked with a machete the same way the poachers hack apart the elephants— face and feet and hands."

Jane listened, both to Johnno and to her own heart, banging in her chest. Johnno kept talking, his voice small and sharp through the phone, a needle to her brain.

"Some of the other locals are saying Muthega was targeted. He'd made enemies of the poachers recently—instead of staying away like he'd done before, letting them do their business unimpeded, he'd been watching them closely, taking photos of suspects in the town while they drank beer. He'd been taking names."

Jane thought of Muthega the day they watched Twiga through the barren trees, the way his voice softened when he told her Twiga's name and the reason for it. Jane thought of how he always spoke quietly and made little clicking sounds when they drove together, slowly, through the herds of Thomson's gazelles because they were too fatigued to move like they should have and he didn't want to scare them. Jane thought of his smile and his easy banter with the women by the river, the bits of hard candy he'd sometimes hand out to the children. She thought of his possible wife and how she had never asked if he had one or if she could meet his family. She'd never treated Muthega like a colleague, not like the people she'd worked with in offices back home.

Then she remembered that tiny, critical word—*too*. Jane heard one of the men say "too"—he spat it at her like a stone. "Next time we kill you, too." Jane hadn't forgotten that word when she told Johnno her story. But it referred to Twiga, the elephant. Jane had been sure of that. "Next time we'll kill you as we did the elephant." That's how she'd explained it to Johnno. She hadn't considered any other angle. She was angry and scared and wanted Muthega punished.

The rain came that night. It beat the windows and dimmed the streetlights. When it moved on and left nothing but heavy, dripping trees, cool air and pools of water in the streets, the winged termites released themselves from their subterranean caves and spun through the air in frantic, pale clouds. They beat against Jane's window in a desperate attraction to the bedside light she had turned on. Jane watched them flicker and dive, flicker and dive, until finally they fell away when the sky turned to dawn.

In the morning, she called her father. She had no idea what time it was back home, but the phone rang only twice before his new wife answered, sleepy but happy to hear Jane's voice.

"Jane? Your dad's been wondering when we might hear

from you! We're dying to hear all about it, let me get him…
he's in the bathroom."

Jane heard what sounded like the phone dropping from her
stepmother's hands, and then a voice calling through the halls
of the house she remembered so well.

"Honey, it's Jane! Come quick!"

Then her father's voice, low and soothing, said, "Janie! So
glad, so glad to hear your voice! We miss you. We've been
gathering things to send you in a care package. But we haven't
finished. Is the address you gave us still the right one?"

Jane imagined the house. The warm kitchen with the old
blue table where she always ate breakfast—weekdays cereal and
every Sunday waffles that Jane and Lance would pool in syrup.

Jane tried to keep the tears out of her voice when she spoke.
"I miss you, too, Dad. I miss you both. How's Lance?" This
time, when her father described Lance's progress, and how
the new medication helped with his moods, and how his new
psychiatrist was brilliant, Jane listened. In her mind she saw
Lance at five or six, sitting at the dining room table alone, eating the peanut butter sandwich she'd slapped together for his
dinner so quickly that the slices of bread didn't line up. She
thought of how he looked up that evening and asked her to
read to him. Had she even bothered to answer before leaving
him there, alone, and shutting herself back in her bedroom?
Even then, when he was just a regular kid, she'd been a terrible sister. She'd made him a shadow, a vague annoyance, as
she thought her father had done to her. How unfair that was.

"Dad," Jane said when her father paused. "I called to ask you
something. It's important. You've made a will, right? You've
made me his guardian if something happened to you? I'm next
in line. He's my brother, and I want to help."

Jane flew to Narok that afternoon. She was terrified to go

back to the place where she had been both victim and perpetrator, but she had to—one more time.

She slipped the card out of her backpack and studied it again. Paul O'Reilly. She assumed she'd still have to be questioned in the case. She'd have to go back to Nairobi and meet him again soon—tell him the whole story and maybe help find the people who did this to Muthega. There were no papers to accuse the faceless men she didn't know, but she'd do what she could to find them.

The tiny plane cruised over the edge of the Rift Valley, and the earth fell away below. The scroll of the land spread out below Jane, empty and pale. The rains had swelled the river and its banks were dark with dampness. The plane banked steeply and suddenly the land swung out of Jane's view, replaced with nothing but sky, darkening into evening, and another storm's arrival. When the plane tipped back and leveled, Jane looked down again. The land was too dark to see details now. It had turned into shadows and long, ill-defined shapes where the river once was. Jane thought of the local women standing in their muddy courtyards, holding their faces and their buckets to the sky. The plane was a winged termite, released from the dry, tight earth. And Jane was one, too—flinging herself into the darkening sky, desperate for softening earth, desperate for light.

NAROK

Leona had lied to the white Kenyan, and now it was time to tell him the truth and ask him to help her. She hated needing help, and with every breath she fought the instinct to give up, to go back to the manyatta and let Adia have her old life, no matter what that meant for her future.

The expression on Simi's face when they left the manyatta that day flashed in Leona's mind. What on earth had she done? Simi was the one who'd mothered Adia all these years; she was the one who protected the girl. Leona felt weak. No matter what, she would go back, she would tell Simi that she was sorry, she would let Simi know that she'd always be a mother to Adia, even if Adia lived in Nairobi or Solai or somewhere else. She vowed to keep the connection between her daughter and Simi alive.

Leona felt frozen somehow now that she'd made the sudden decision to move out of the manyatta. She wasn't Maasai, and the white Kenyan wasn't, either. Leona thought about the white Kenyan's family, and in her imagination he'd had the perfect childhood; one foot in the customs of his European heritage, and the other firmly in the ways of this place. Leona couldn't think of a better solution for her girl, but her thoughts were unsettled, confused. She felt unable to make a decision bigger than what to eat for dinner or when to make Adia take a shower. Narok was a small town—most people knew each other at least by sight—but it was far bigger than the manyatta, and that allowed Leona the illusion of anonymity. That, for now, was a relief.

In the manyatta, Leona was peripheral to Adia. The girl had moved with a constantly shifting school of manyatta children, all between the ages of two and seven, who swirled in and out of the individual *inkajijiks* like tides. All the mothers there were fine-tuned to the concept of benign neglect; that was the Maasai way.

In that sense, Leona knew, her version of new motherhood was vastly different and perhaps completely opposite to that of her own mother's, who birthed Leona in a bright Portland hospital while Leona's father drank coffee in the lobby. Leona's maternal grandparents lived an hour's drive away, but Leona was told, later, that they never came to stay after she was born; they never helped Leona's mother ease into the first days with the new baby. Being a mother was immediately a lonely thing. Leona's mother hadn't taken to the role, or the isolation. As soon as she could, she hired the nanny and the housekeeper. She'd never had another baby. The similarities Leona was beginning to see between herself and her mother made Leona feel bruised deep inside. She'd never wanted the comparison. It was the main reason she hadn't wanted children of her own. She was from a long line of mothers who didn't mother. And now, here she was.

In Narok, motherhood became central to Leona for the first time. It became a lonely and alien way of being. She was uncomfortable directing Adia's every move, and she wasn't used to being the girl's only source of entertainment. Time stretched out thin and slow, and even Leona's body seemed to move as if through deep water. The daily ritual was her job, while her position in Nairobi sat waiting. She wouldn't leave until she made a decision about Adia's father. She'd called the department head and assured him she still wanted the job, but lied about why she'd have to delay her start. There was a new piece of information she was tracking down—old stories of days when Maasai crossed into Tanzania for grazing. She didn't know if he believed her, but he said he'd hold the job for one semester. The university could wait.

Now, since they arrived in Narok less than two weeks ago, every day was the same. Breakfast at the café next to the hotel was first. Adia ate piles of sweet dough in the form of greasy, fried *mandazis*, and Leona drank cup after cup of hot chai. She hoped that if she drank enough of the sweet tea, the caffeine would eventually bring her back to life; speed up her blood again, throw a spark into the damp ash she'd become. Without her work, she didn't know who she was, and she could feel that the absence of purpose was making her depressed, empty. But she had to push that aside. She had to find Adia's father. Everything else had to wait.

For the first two weeks in Narok, Leona went to the bar daily. She described what she remembered of the white Kenyan to anyone who would listen. Often her audience were at their most unsuspecting, tired from their day and only wanting to order a beer, and when she pulled at their shirtsleeves or nudged their shoulders, they looked at her askance, suspicious. She knew someone, eventually, would know who she was describing, and also that her behavior would be talked about, but she kept her voice low; she murmured like a spy. Rumors blew like the dust around here, and she didn't want the white Kenyan to know anything before she could look him in the eyes.

She wondered if she'd recognize the man if he walked in. She'd only seen him twice, after all. The drunken, sweaty night of Adia's conception and then again only days after Adia's birth three years ago, when she was exhausted and terrified and had lied to him to make him disappear. She wondered if Adia looked like him and if, when she saw him, she'd know it instantly.

It was an aid worker's driver who finally gave her what she needed. One morning at the end of their second week in Narok, Leona saw a set of waxy Chinese crayons and a lined exercise book in the window of Narok's only stationery store and, on a whim, she pulled out a small wad of shillings and bought them. Leona didn't know what was normal for a three-year-old American, but she knew Adia missed her manyatta friends. She'd never been without a gaggle of age-mates, and Leona hoped the crayons and paper, which Adia had never used before, would help make the sitting and waiting more bearable. Back at the bar, Adia proudly showed the bartender her new gifts, and just as Leona was instructing the child on how to hold a crayon, she felt a tapping on her shoulder.

"Madam." The voice was gruff and wrapped in the scent of beer. "You are looking for Mister John?"

Leona spun around so fast the crayon she was holding flew across the room and rolled under a distant table. Adia screeched and hopped off her stool, then scrabbled on the floor to retrieve it. The speaker was a tall, muscular man around her age, she figured. He had scarification marks on his cheeks that told Leona he wasn't Maasai. Perhaps Kikuyu, she thought. He wore a khaki safari suit with a badge that said, "The Mara Lodge—Driver."

"Mr. John?" Leona tried to keep her face impassive. Suddenly she was frightened. Maybe it was a mistake to find him.

"Yes, Mister John, from Solai. Wilson—" here the man

indicated a bar regular, slumped in a chair in a dark corner "—Wilson told me you were looking for Mister John. I know him."

"Is he here?" Leona asked, her voice unintentionally high.

"No. I am also from Solai. I can tell you how to go."

He nodded at the bartender, asked for another Tusker and, when it was slid across the polished surface to him, tipped his dusty hat toward Leona. She would pay.

He used Adia's blue crayon to draw a rough map in the little exercise book. Then he ripped out the page and handed it to Leona.

"You can go there by car in one day. But the road is bad, so if it is raining, you cannot make it." He swigged back a long drink of beer.

Leona was grateful for the checks her parents enclosed in their letters. Her Fulbright fellowship was long expired and the stipend from it had dried up. The only money she earned anymore was the pittance her articles received when they were published, and the promise of an advance on the book. In the manyatta, money hadn't mattered. There was nothing to spend it on. But in Narok everything cost. She fished a two-hundred-shilling note of her father's money out of her wallet and handed it over to the dusty man standing next to her. He answered with a solemn nod and placed the blue crayon carefully back in the box. Leona folded up the paper with the blue crayon map and slipped it into her bag.

Occasionally, Kamau, the guide who had drawn the map, came back to the bar she still visited. She didn't ask after the white Kenyan, John, anymore, though. She had the information she needed and now only had to decide how to deal with it. Those days she watched Kamau across the room, and when he looked over she always waved. She didn't want to talk to him, wasn't attracted to him in any way, but Kamau's presence gave her a connection to John. John. His name. She could hold it in her lips and write it down on paper if she wanted to. She could give it to Adia. But it felt unnatural to say it out loud, slightly uncomfortable, like wearing a heavy jacket on a warm day. The tenuous connection to Kamau was the only kind of relationship she could manage right now. Her thoughts were too ragged and her indecision was a living thing inside her, like cancer.

One afternoon Kamau caught her by the arm as she made her way out of the ladies' room.

"Have you followed my map, madam? Have you gone to Solai?"

"No," Leona lied easily. "My car is in the garage. Have to wait."

Then she felt a shiver of terror when he answered, "I can take you there. I am going to visit my father. I can take the car of my boss."

Kamau turned and waved at a friend across the room. As he walked away, he shouted back to Leona, "I will find you here in two days, and we can go to Solai."

It was late that night when a pounding on the door woke Leona from a dead sleep.

"Miss, you have a call," the yawing night attendant said.

Years ago, when she first arrived, she'd given the Guest House phone number to her parents. For emergencies only, she said, and she assumed they'd never call, or that if they did, she wouldn't even get the message. As Leona stumbled sleepily to the lobby, she realized this phone call was the first she'd ever received here.

Leona hadn't heard her mother's voice since she left the US. The familiarity—even after all this time, surprised her so much she almost didn't hear her mother breaking the news.

"I wasn't there," her mother's voice echoed over the phone, the time difference and bad phone service making her sound tinny and strange, like she was phoning from a distant planet.

"Why didn't you tell me he was dying? You've been writing me letters—you've been in contact. You just decided to tell me now?" Leona asked, wondering if her voice sounded odd to this woman she hadn't spoken to for almost four years; wondering if she should be crying. She didn't feel like crying. She didn't feel anything, except far away.

"He didn't want to speculate if you'd come or not," her mother answered, blunt to the core.

She added, in case it hadn't been clear, "He thought you wouldn't come anyway, and he didn't want to spend his last days watching for you and hoping."

Leona wondered how she was supposed to respond.

"In any case, nobody was there at the time of death. It was just after 2:00 a.m. He'd sent me home. Either he wanted to die alone, or he didn't expect it to happen so fast. Who can say?"

Leona wondered how it would be to die alone. If, with your last intake of breath—knowing the darkness was closing in—you would yearn to reach out, to feel your hand touching someone else's, to have your last sight be that of a human face, someone who knew you. She wondered if her father felt regret and wanted to make a deathbed apology. But maybe he'd just pushed the memory of what he used to do to her so far back in his brain that he couldn't retrieve it anymore. She felt a flaring up of terrible joy when she realized that her absence at his deathbed meant she wasn't there to forgive him. She couldn't have stood looking in his eyes and seeing anything—remorse or, worse, lack of it.

"Anyway, we need to plan a funeral. He's cremated, so there's no real hurry. We want to schedule it when you can come. You and the girl. It's time to come home, Lee."

For a second Leona was stunned by the use of her childhood name. Nobody had called her that for so long. She felt her eyes fill with tears. That place wasn't home. It never had been. She thought of the bed where her daughter was now, stretched out crossways, fast asleep. Adia's skin was nut-brown and her hair a halo of knots and golden curls. She looked nothing like Leona. She wore only a pair of little boy's underwear. A goatskin bracelet hugged her tiny wrist. Her small bare feet were thick with calluses and grime. Leona bought her a pair of rubber-tire shoes in the Narok market, but Adia hated wearing them, and when the left one went missing under suspicious circumstances, Leona didn't bother replacing it.

In Leona's memories, her childhood home was a cool, gray and silent place. It was a place of carpets and leather-bound books, meals around a table with the sound of scraping silver. She tried to picture barefoot Adia in her old school, following rules. She tried to see wild-haired Adia at her mother's dinner table eating with antique forks and knives, drinking from a crystal glass. She couldn't imagine it. She wondered if maybe where you were born informed your cells or if the air your mother breathed while you swam inside her contributed to your body, to your mind. Maybe the place in which a person was conceived set in motion that person's own unique history. If so, Adia was a child of dust and the smell of wood fire and livestock. Leona could never make her leave this behind.

Now, she hung up the phone and went back to her room. She lay down in the hard Chabani Guest House bed with her daughter curled up next to her. She had a sensation of spinning away.

Leona didn't sleep after the conversation with her mother. When Adia woke up just as the sun was breaking over the horizon, Leona's head felt as heavy and unwieldy as a boulder. She desperately wanted to stay in bed with her eyes closed. She was exhausted and filled with spinning thoughts about her father, but she was also uncomfortable going to the bar now that Kamau had offered to drive her up to John's farm.

She didn't want to see him, to have to brush off his offer of
the drive or, worse yet, work up the courage to tell him the
truth—that she was too scared to see John. But Adia had gotten used to their daily task, had befriended the bartender and
the cooks and insisted, after breakfast, that they go about the
day as they always did. Leona tried to rouse her brain and
her body by showering in cold water, but she still felt slippery somehow, greasy both inside and out. She felt sad, too.
And that was unexpected. She wondered if she'd miss her father, his presence on the planet, even though it had been so
long since she'd seen him, and even though she recognized
she didn't feel tenderness toward him, nor love. But she saw
she was fatherless now.

It rarely rained those days. The bottom of the Rift Valley
was desolate and dry. It was the sound of wind through rough,
yellow grasses and a constant film of dust on sweaty skin. That
year, though, the drought was worse than usual. It had gone
on too long. The previous two rainy seasons were sparse. The
deep water tables never completely filled, and the Mara River
and its tributaries lagged low and thick, the usual waterline
nearly forgotten. A storm a week or so ago brought rain that
fell hard. The children danced and laughed and drenched
themselves in it. As she watched them, she thought it meant
hope. But it was a one-off storm. Heavy and solid, but too
hard, and it had washed away the topsoil and left little behind.
Then it disappeared again, and the mud dried back to dust
and the rivers—dangerous with flash floods for a few days—
shrunk to trickles again. Another storm was expected, though.
Soon, the people said. Leona assumed it was only wishful
thinking, because the sky looked like it always did to her.
The locals said they saw something different in it, a heaviness
maybe, a slight deepening of color in the clouds that looked
promising. People were waiting. All along the slogging rivers

women waded deeper and deeper to wash their laundry, the gazelles and elephants coming closer and closer—their fear of humans mitigated by their desperate thirst.

When Leona finally got out of her shower and dressed and gathered the energy to take Adia back to the Chabani bar, she noticed there were more people standing in the streets than usual. It seemed more crowded somehow, more active. People called to each other from open shop doors and children buzzed past with intent.

"Maybe today's the day it'll rain," Leona said, leaning down to take hold of Adia's hand. "Maybe people are excited."

Leona had never seen Adia scared, and it dawned on her suddenly that Adia was alone, too. Fatherless, like she was now or, she thought grimly, "father-lost" in Adia's case. Nothing stood between the girl and the world but she herself, the reluctant mother. The enormity of that was more of a shock than her father's death.

"Lee, he left you everything."

The phone again, late at night. Her mother. By Leona's watch it was 3:35 a.m. and the knocking at the door pulled her from a dark and murky sleep. She blinked her eyes and rubbed them.

"I can wire some money to you for the tickets. When are you coming? We have to move forward with arrangements.

"I'm sorry, Lee." Her mother hummed through the phone, when Leona began to cry. She assumed Leona's tears were ones she shared. "It must be hard to be so far away from family now. At this time."

Her father's service would be formal, everyone in black, and everyone speaking in hushed voices. The priest would stand in his bright white robes among the enormous flower arrangements. Leona remembered the smell of her grandmother's service. She'd never forget the urns full of lilies and roses. She'd loved those flowers before that day, but the cloying smell in the church made her so sick with their heavy perfume that she still couldn't bear to be near them.

"I can't come." Leona couldn't make her voice any louder than a whisper. She felt that if she said it quietly enough, she could imagine that she hadn't said it at all. She could imagine away this conversation; this severing of ties. If she went there now those rainy skies would cling to her. She doubted she'd be able to escape and come back to Kenya; she'd get stuck. Adia would be foreign there, foreign and fatherless.

"Lee." Her mother's voice was hardening like mud left in the sun. "You will regret not coming. No matter what went on between the two of you. Please."

When she hung up the phone and padded back to her room, she didn't try to sleep. She knew she wouldn't be able to. Instead, she walked over to the window. Her mother's words shocked her. What her mother said meant that she knew. She knew the whole time Leona was being violated by her father. She knew and she'd never done a thing to stop it. Leona bit her lip so she wouldn't scream and wake Adia. She wanted to open the window and scream and cry and shake the night with her anger and her hopelessness. She would never be able to punish him now. His death clipped her tongue, forced her silence.

The window was barred on the outside, so thieves and monkeys couldn't get in. Glass louvers on the inside could be closed against rain or dust. Burgundy strips of cloth hung from a wooden rod, the limp fabric masquerading as curtains. Leona pulled the cloths aside and turned the rusty handle that opened the louvers wide. She needed air. Outside the wind stirred the branches on the flame tree and made the petals on the bougainvillea flutter. There was a moon, and it was bright and perfect, and it turned everything—the dry grasses, the walls of the buildings, the roofs and the cars out there—

a mournful gray. It wasn't silver, but instead the shades of a black-and-white film, color drained away but everything as visible and as lit as at midday. Leona felt a shift in the air and noticed a cold edge to the night. Yes, she thought, the rain is coming again. The rain would come and it would make the air wet and heavy and delicious for the plants and the people, but it would make the road to Solai impassable. Her little car wouldn't be able to manage flooded roads or deep muddy ruts. It had to be now. Time was short.

She pulled her jeans off the dresser and slid herself into them. She wrapped her hair in a bandanna and went to the bathroom to wash her face and brush her teeth. She packed the toiletries she'd purchased into a plastic bag and added Adia's crayons and paper, and the few pieces of clothing she'd bought in Narok to replace what they'd left behind.

It would be light soon, and they would have to go immediately. Her shoulder bag sat on the chair next to the dresser and Leona retrieved it. As quietly as she could, she dumped the contents on the end of the bed and felt through it all, putting the things back in one by one. Her wallet, her keys, a hair clip, a small notebook. There wasn't much. And then she felt the scrap of paper. It was folded over and over and she walked to the window to see it better in the moonlight. The line drawings didn't look blue now, the crayon Kamau used may as well have been black, but there it was, the map he'd carefully drawn.

Leona put the map in her pocket and then sat on the bed, legs stretched out in front of her. When the moon went down again, when the sun came up, the lines on the map would be blue again. She'd be able to follow them. She'd hurry, before the rain came.

JUJU

Liberia sits on the curve of West Africa's spine. Ocean currents fold and twist around the coast that stretches from the tropical jungles of Congo all the way up to the dry desert sands of Morocco. The year before, pushing opposite those ocean currents on a night flight from Washington, DC, Jane and Paul moved here. Monrovia was Paul's second Foreign Service post.

Liberia was bright with a sun that pushed down on everything below it, a sun that burned in an instant, a sun that made Jane light-headed and even chilled her to the bone if she sat in it too long. Liberia was sweat that rolled down her back, tacked her shirt to her skin, filled up her ears and dripped into her eyes. Liberia was tropical storms that would suddenly bunch up the sky in huge, black clouds to crumple what had been a flat hot day into a driving rain, which, just as suddenly, would stop. Liberia was the constant taste of salty ocean air from the surf that roiled on the sand just on the other side of the garden wall, the incessant drone of the air conditioner. It was the constant motion of living things: mold, centipedes, beetles and plants that grew up thick and green and so fast Jane could almost see them moving, fed by the sun and rain. It was sitting, day after day, waiting for Paul to come home. Liberia was mystery, too. It was black magic and juju and things that sounded like they could never be true, but which were, things as true as a finger on a trigger, things as true as blood.

She should have known. There were times early in their courtship when Paul and Jane barely saw one another. They started dating at the beginning of his Foreign Service career, when Jane was finishing her work with the Elephant Foundation—training her replacements, a husband and wife team, to take over where she and Muthega left off. When Paul's new assignment came in—Washington, DC—Jane moved back with him. Jane's father gave her away, and her stepmother was the matron of honor. Even Lance attended the wedding, sitting quietly the whole time, a dazed look on his face.

Jane remembered falling in love with Paul at a specific moment. She would always remember it. After Muthega's murder, Paul was the one who helped her file the report; he was the one who helped her pack up her little house in Narok. It wasn't those things, though, that made her love him. Instead, it happened the day he drove her to see Muthega's family's little house, tightly built with mud bricks and a shiny new tin roof. As they parked the car, Paul mentioned the nicer-than-average construction was probably thanks to Muthega's western, nonprofit salary. The home's tidy profile belied the tangle of dogs, undergrowth and runny-nosed children that wrestled for attention in front of it.

"Baba Muthega ni wapi?" Paul asked when an elderly woman shuffled out of the house to greet them. Jane was impressed at the way Swahili simply rolled off Paul's tongue. She nervously

poked at the dust with her shoe and shifted her bag from one shoulder to the other.

The inside of the house was murky and bare. An old man sat curled on a mat in the corner, and the woman invited Paul and Jane to sit on a pair of low stools under the tiny, empty window.

Jane toyed with the hot cup of chai the woman—Muthega's mother, she assumed—handed her. Paul drained his cup of tea and began to speak.

Jane watched him talk, his language sure and fluent. She had learned enough Swahili to basically follow where he was in the narrative by noting the reactions of the old couple. They nodded and winced, whispered acknowledgments and wiped tears from their eyes.

"They know already, someone sent word last week."

Paul knew Jane would be relieved that she wasn't the one breaking the awful news.

"In fact, Muthega's wife and children are in Narok now, gathering his things and applying for a scholarship for his eldest daughter to go to the school there. A better school than the one here in Solai. Apparently she's smart—they want her to be educated."

"Paul, tell them I have money. She doesn't need a scholarship. There is money for them."

"Money?"

"It's money the foundation pays in…instances like this one. His back pay and some life insurance. Plus some I'm donating. I want his family to be okay… I know they relied on him."

Paul turned to Muthega's mother. *"Yeye ana fedha kwa ajili yenu. Katika benki katika Narok."*

"Not in the bank, Paul. I have it…here." Jane pulled her bag from her shoulder and rummaged through it, finally pulling forth a wad of dollar bills.

"Jane, that's a lot," Paul said quietly. "It's more cash than Muthega would have been able to get for them in his whole life. Sure you want to do that?"

"It's foundation policy," she blustered, but the look on Paul's face told her that he knew the bulk of the cash was her own.

Muthega's mother reached past Paul and plucked the money from Jane's hand, then turned and tossed it to the man lying prone on the mat.

They drove silently away from Muthega's house.

"You know his murder had nothing to do with you, right?" Paul finally said. "He's not the first to be murdered out here, and he won't be the last."

"I should have tried harder to get to know him," Jane answered. "I shouldn't have yelled at him, accused him... I should have been smarter. I was so..." She began weeping.

"It's just unfair. And now his whole family has to suffer."

Paul stopped the car then, and turned to face her. His face was serious. "Don't carry that guilt. You can't live in Africa—or anywhere in the developing world—if you feel guilty about what it is you have versus what it is the people around you have. You won't make it." His voice was almost angry. "This work, my work and yours, requires you to be tough. If you feel guilt for everything, you'll burn out."

Jane loved how Paul was voracious in his appetite for his work. He took every short-term assignment the State Department offered him, especially the ones nobody else wanted. He was a wonderful diplomat. He could talk to anyone. He could make anyone feel important, and he loved entertaining groups.

"Send me to the seventh circle of hell, and I'll have the devil lapping from my palm in no time," he'd say at events between swigs of beer. His bravery was attractive to Jane then. She didn't mind that his travels left her to attend parties alone and, in fact, she loved telling their friends where he was. "Paul? Oh, he's in Syria."

Jane and Paul had barely returned from their honeymoon when Paul accepted an unaccompanied yearlong tour in Angola, then he went to Mozambique, where land mines still studded the earth, and Jane worried every day that went by without a call from him. They wrote each other letters. He had R & R in Spain and made enough money to fly Jane out to meet him and book four-star hotels and order expensive wines at dinner. In the spaces between these visits, Jane concentrated on her own fledgling career as a biology teacher in a private high school and on the friendships she was forging. She spent long weekends with her father and stepmother and took turns visiting Lance. Life didn't change for her much, really. She preferred, in some regards, the way their new marriage was structured, and the long stretches of time she had to live alone. Her job was time-consuming, and often she graded tests into the night and felt relieved that there was nobody there to interrupt her. Marriage was a theoretical thing at that time in her life, a daydream. Even the ring on her finger didn't seem real.

In college, Paul minored in art history, focusing particularly on sacred African carvings. When he was offered the post in Monrovia, where Jane could finally join him, his first reaction was excitement at having a chance to see, in person, examples of carvings from the region.

"You can get a job there, if you want," he told Jane. "We'll meet people, have dinner parties." He made it seem like a partnership. But at the dinner parties they threw in Monrovia, he crowded their table with local intellectuals and foreign development workers who drank wine and ate the expensive imported cheeses Paul kept hidden in the fridge. Jane sat at the foot of the table patiently as he held court, regaling the guests with the stories he'd learned when he studied the sacred art—tales of the Leopard Society and the masks they used to frighten other tribes, and the masks he wanted to see, and the ones he was desperate to buy. She found it hard to edge the subjects into areas where she was an expert, where she could contribute. Nobody cared that she was a biologist, that or that she'd been an excellent teacher. Paul and the others were passionately worldly and could talk for hours about international politics and the issues of doing development work in third world nations. Jane knew little about those subjects.

Jane assumed that she would find a job in Liberia. People told her international schools were always looking for teachers, and that finding work would be easy. She even contacted an elephant conservation NGO that worked on antipoaching efforts in the Sapo National Park. But somehow after she arrived here, she felt sapped. She drove out to the American school once to meet with the principal, but their talk was awkward. She'd felt ill that day but forced herself to go. The whole time she sat in the office, making small talk and trying to seem capable and prepared, her head pounded and the vague feeling of needing to vomit hung in her belly. Later, the principal called her to say that although there were no full-time staff vacancies, she would be number one on the list of potential substitutes.

"Don't worry," he said. "This is tropical Africa, teachers will be calling in sick all the time." School had been in session for two months already. Jane knew that. He hadn't called her once. She wished she cared, but she didn't. The heat here weighed her down, drained her motivation. Occasionally she thought of Kenya, and she remembered how crisp the morning air was when she and Muthega would begin their day and the way the mourning doves cooed the sky awake just before dawn. She saved the details of Narok, of the Mara, in her mind, pulling them out now and then to examine. On some level, she realized that when they came to Liberia she'd expected it to be more like Kenya. The utter difference was a bruise of disappointment, and the hope she'd felt before they arrived here turned to lethargy. When she missed her period twice in a row, she felt vindicated. This had to be the reason for her exhaustion.

Holding her secret close, Jane spent her days reading and walking along the wide stretch of beach in front of their house. Occasionally, she'd slip into her bathing suit and sit in the sand on a towel, watching the surf. In the late afternoons, showered and changed, she'd dab perfume behind her ears, and wait for Paul to return. She was never alone; Mohammad was there, too. Silently wiping dust from the framed pictures on the wall, organizing the kitchen or chopping things for the dinner he'd cook for them. Evenings were Jane's favorite time of day. When Paul was home, he'd always turn on the stereo and the house would be filled with jazz. She and Paul would sit down for dinner, and Mohammad would light the candles and place their plates in front of them. Jane felt like royalty when Paul was there and it was just the two of them. And dinner was a time of anticipation, too, because Jane knew it was always then, in the later evening, when the Charlies would come.

The "Charlies" were roving groups of folk-art sellers that fascinated Paul. Jane never figured out what their name meant. Even Paul couldn't tell her. The Charlies bought their goods cheaply from villages in the densely forested up-country, packed everything into market bags and came to the capital city to sell them door-to-door to foreigners. They brought West Africa and all its dark secrets out of the jungles right up to Paul and Jane's back porch, rapping softly at the back door.

When the Charlies came, Jane and Paul slipped out the kitchen door, closing it tightly behind them to keep the air-conditioning in. The Charlies set low wooden stools on the polished concrete floor of the back porch. The things in the

Charlies' bags were new to her, mostly unattractive in her opinion.

"I'm looking for a passport mask," Paul said one night, and the Charlies dug through their bags to draw out some examples of the small carvings, dark and delicate and as compact as shells.

"What are they for?" Jane asked.

The Charlie sitting nearest her turned and said, "The juju can come to you wh'n you are sleeping."

He was tall and had long fingers. He held a cigarette in one hand, and tipped his head back to spout white smoke into the darkness above their heads. It hung there like a ghost.

He continued. "If you can see the forest spirit, Gle, wh'n you are dreaming, you can tell the carver how that Gle was looking, and he will carve it for you like making a photo. When you dream, juju can come. It can tell you things you must know."

Jane looked at the masks Paul held; they were hardly bigger than his palm. One was a woman's face topped with intricately carved braided hair; the other was a man's with a pattern of tribal cuts fanned out across his wooden forehead. Jane wondered what those dreams whispered to their owners, and where the people who had commissioned the masks were now.

Paul went straight for the dark heart. He didn't turn away when the Charlies mentioned that one wooden figure had been placed under a dead body to help usher the man's spirit to a better place. It didn't faze him when they told him the mask he was holding had been steeped in the blood of a sacrificial goat and that's what gave it its strange, dark patina. Jane was different from her husband in this way: she liked the new things better. The freshly carved pieces that seemed unfettered by a history of use, those were the ones that Jane would have chosen. She was afraid of the darkness.

Mostly the Charlies concentrated on Paul—his authority and masculinity made Jane invisible—but that night one of them gave something to her, as well. He murmured, "Madam, just take a look." He pressed a necklace made of smooth, brown seeds into Jane's palm, then a carved wooden doll a little girl would have carried and dressed and named.

"It's nice, isn't it?" Jane ran her finger over the small wooden face, and felt the strands of fabric hair.

Paul glanced over and chuffed a small laugh. "Hon, that's nothing more than a village Barbie doll. It's not even old."

Jane smiled apologetically at the Charlie who'd offered her the doll and handed it back.

Nights when Jane sat next to Paul, watching him work, she felt she didn't understand him at all. When he'd stopped traveling without her, when they'd finally settled into a marriage where they were together more than they were apart, Jane assumed they'd cement the closeness they felt when they were first dating. In those early days, they'd sketched out a future together, they'd built the scaffolding of a marriage, and Jane hoped he would be one of her best friends, true partners and lovers. But somehow, after they came to Liberia, they kept missing each other. Each was visible to the other but untouchable, like the images on a movie screen to the audience: she could see him, she could hear him, but he couldn't see her back. She waited for the right moment to tell him he was going to be a father. It would change everything, she knew. Put it all right and Paul would see her again.

Days were too quiet and too long, and when Paul came home in the evenings, she was too eager to see him. She had no stories to tell him about her quiet days, and instead she pelted him with questions. She was desperate for attention, and it made her ashamed. She'd never been like this before, and she didn't want to tell him about the baby while she felt so weak. If she did, he might worry, and that would risk cementing her like this in his eyes; a dependent, weak wife cast in the amber of his mind. At night she dreamed of Narok. Of elephants that walked on hacked and bleeding legs, of babies reaching their trunks up to nurse and sucking on nothing but blood. She woke from those dreams sweaty and terrified. She wanted nothing more than to protect this baby, her baby, the way she hadn't been able to protect Twiga or Muthega or her mother.

In Liberia there were tales of up-country tribes who lived by the rules of black magic and curses. There were stories of how drummers could talk to each other over miles of air, through miles of thick forest, with the drums they pounded. There were the masked stilt walkers who danced in the streets and stopped passersby to ask for money. If you didn't give them what they were looking for, they would use their juju against you. In Liberia it was impossible not to believe these stories. It was impossible not to believe in magic. Jane felt the juju would hurt her.

One night as Jane sat in the dark next to him, she heard Paul whistle low, through his teeth, "Oh, that's a fantastic piece!" She saw what he was reaching for and then shut her eyes tightly, but the mask couldn't be unseen. Two roughly carved eyeholes pierced a piece of dusky, gray wood. The nose was wide and straight, and the forehead split slightly, so that a scar ran down the hard, angry-looking brow. The crack had been mended with bits of wire that gave the effect of crude stitches. Under the nose was the slash of a mouth, stiffly open as if the wooden face were trying to scream, and embedded in the mouth were six or seven yellowed, cracked teeth.

"*C'est les vrai, vrai dents des gens, quoi,*" one of the foreign Charlies murmured proudly. Jane noticed another salesman edge away from the wooden face, refusing to look in its direction.

"It's a Dan mask," he whispered to Jane in a voice that made her quiver. "When the witch doctor must put on curse. That one be the mask for killing someone." Paul didn't see the man leaning away from the mask. He didn't put it on and tease him with it, or tell him he shouldn't believe what he did.

Jane hated the mask. She hated Paul for buying it. She wondered how it was that he could look at the masks and the carvings the Charlies brought to them and say exactly when they were carved and by whom, and even why. He could spin stories of up-country ceremonies that made his friends at their dinner table gasp with glee and revulsion. But lately, when he looked at Jane, she didn't know what he saw. Jane knew he missed her independent self, the strong, curious scientist he'd fallen in love with. But she didn't know how to retrieve that old version of Jane. It scared her that Paul wasn't curious about her anymore.

The morning after Paul bought the mask, he excitedly installed a hook on the wall between the bathroom and the guest room. He stepped back to make sure it was centered and straight. This time, he didn't ask Jane if she thought it would look nice there. At night, when Jane got up to use the bathroom, she edged past the mask with her eyes closed. During the day she avoided it as much as possible. She didn't want the hollow eyes to follow her; she didn't want to see the real teeth. She thought about the mask constantly. She wondered if the teeth had been plucked from a dead person or, worse, if they'd been broken out of someone alive, someone whose mouth would have filled with blood and empty spaces.

The president was shot in his sleep just before dawn and dismembered by his own army. When the static on the speakers cleared and the radio announced the *coup d'état* in shouts and chants, the army had already declared victory. *"In the cause of the people,"* the voices on the radio shouted from the kitchen, *"the revolution continues."*

After the president's murder and the coup, the Charlies stopped coming. The army enforced a strict curfew—dusk to dawn, penalty of death. From the balcony overlooking the beach, Paul and Jane watched soldiers in their camouflage pants and torn T-shirts sleeping in the sand. Even during the day, when he went to work, Paul advised Jane not to walk down the beach.

"It's not that they want to hurt Americans," he assured her. "This is a local thing—it's not ours. But they're drunk and armed and not to be trusted."

He wanted this to make her feel better, safer. He smiled when he said it, even held her hand. But it made Jane feel even more foreign to this place, like a ghost that nothing—not the juju and not her husband—could see. She was an interloper—as foreign and displaced as a broken bead on the forest floor.

A week after the coup, thirteen ministers and cabinet members of the old ruling party were sentenced. The accusations were shouted on the radio, and the announcer's gleeful voice said, *"Justice will be served."* The announcement sent a shiver down Jane's spine, and she told Mohammad to turn the radio off. She didn't want bad news today; she didn't want to be sad or anxious. She'd been to the embassy doctor, who confirmed what Jane already guessed. She wasn't alone in her body. She held the secret close. She wanted to think of a special way to tell Paul the good news. She wanted this to be a moment that would make him really see her again—as his wife, as the mother to his unborn child.

In the predawn darkness the next morning, the shouts of soldiers on the beach woke Jane up. She tiptoed to the bed-

room window and peeked out. By the slashing beam of flashlights, she saw a line of men unloaded from the back of a truck.
They were led, single file, over the gray sand by a sinewy-
armed man who wore his mirrored sunglasses even though
the sky was dark. Waving a heavy-looking gun, he shouted
at them to be quiet, to kneel where he pointed.

The sun rose and the telephone rang. Paul's boss needed
him at the office; documents had to be secured, loose ends
tied up. The political situation had turned, the army in charge
was angry; they were murdering dissenters in the streets. Any
minute there might be evacuation orders for Americans.

"This could go up in smoke," Jane heard Paul say into the
phone, and she begged him not to leave the house. The day
slid dangerously in front of her—too long for her to be alone
with the terror she felt and the chaos outside—the drunken
soldiers and the guns. The iron garden gate, and the elderly
guard who sat in front of it all day, seemed too thin a line of
defense.

"Just stay in the hallway," Paul implored Jane before he
left. "Stay away from the windows—stray bullets!" He didn't
want her looking out at the beach or sitting on the balcony
where she could be exposed. She slid to the floor and leaned
against the windowless wall. She could hear the radio on in
the kitchen. Mohammad was listening to the news again. He
was afraid, as well, and that made Jane even more frightened.
Jane took a deep breath and rubbed the place where, inside
of her, she imagined cells splitting and multiplying, and she
was glad she hadn't told Paul. She didn't want the idea of the
baby spoken aloud in the world yet. It was better for now, she
thought, to keep even the words tucked safely in her mind.

Jane sat in the hallway, waiting for Paul to come home. It
was hot and not light enough to read. Her muscles ached from
not moving, and her skin felt sticky. The mask was there in the

dark, inner hallway, too. She felt it staring down at her. She didn't want the mask near her baby, didn't want its empty eyes boring into her belly. It was an evil thing. The anger surprised her. It was drawn like water up a tree's roots; filling her veins with heat, making her heart beat faster and her face flush hot.

After the dim hallway, the sun was sharp in her eyes. She blinked and squinted and crawled out the balcony doors as quietly and as slowly as she could. She kept her body close to the floor. She didn't want anyone on the beach to notice her. The soldiers were everywhere. Some lay in the sand, others stood smoking in groups. When the breeze shifted, Jane could smell the acrid smoke. A few soldiers took turns pulling what looked like large tree branches out of the back of a truck.

None of the soldiers engaged the thirteen men still kneeling silently. They'd been in the same position since before dawn, and now the white sand glistened like ice under the high, hot sun. The ocean had shifted from the deep black of the early morning to jade green. The thirteen men waited, hunkered down and sweating.

Jane slid on her stomach away from the sliding balcony door and past the wicker chaise she loved to sit in and read. She didn't want Mohammad to walk by the doors and see her. Edging her body under the rustling leaves of the potted palm, she watched the men on the beach through the decorative openings in the balcony's brick wall.

While she sat, thirteen thick tree branches were pulled from the truck and whittled into posts. The posts were set upright, anchored deeply in the sand. The thirteen waiting men were ordered in loud voices to peel off their shirts. The men were tied with green plastic rope to the posts. None of the men tried to escape, none of them screamed or begged for mercy. They simply stood, their hands tied to the wooden stakes behind them. They seemed tired, even bored. Jane imagined the terror they felt and how it could make them listless.

Jane was shocked by the sudden snap of thirteen bullets— one after the other, *BAM, BAM, BAM* in even intervals of split seconds. The bullets sounded distant to her, sliding high above the noise of the tide coming in. It was over quickly. Each bullet hit its mark. The bodies slumped, one by one, crumpled in upon themselves in puddles of blood that spread out in the sand and were absorbed into it. Jane couldn't breathe; she couldn't move. She sat there in the sun, her heart shattering in her chest. Her body shook involuntarily and her breath was short and ineffective. She clenched her palms over the beginning of the baby in her belly and she felt a new sensation of fear physically. It forced its way inside her; it coursed thickly through her blood; she felt it curling around her organs like a writhing, headless snake.

She must have screamed. It was Mohammad who found her. Mohammad who put his arm around Jane and helped her shaking legs find their way back inside to that shadowy stuffy hall. Mohammad who brought her a blanket and a glass of water, and Mohammad who held Jane's secret closely tucked away so that it never saw light. When Paul finally came home that evening, Jane was curled like a snail on the floor, eyes tightly shut. She felt him crouching next to her and heard him breathing quietly as he tiptoed away. She wished he'd sit next to her and stay, that he'd smooth back the sweaty hair from her cheeks and tell her it would all be fine, just fine.

That night Jane and Paul picked at a cold dinner of leftovers at their dining room table. They kept the light off and lit candles. Throughout the meal, fear coiled in Jane's belly. She started at every loud sound and avoided making too much noise. She listened to Paul talking with one part of herself, and with the other part Jane listened to the silence beyond their walls, beyond their locked gate, beyond the sounds of surf on the beach, out to where the sun was sinking into the horizon in a puddle of disappearing light and the dark was rolling in.

Jane told Paul about the baby a few days later; she just blurted it out at breakfast, nothing special. He was thrilled; he couldn't wait to be a father. But he still didn't stay inside with her after dinner to watch a movie or talk. In the following weeks the government stabilized, the curfew lifted and the Charlies returned. They came up the steps and waited. Mohammad whispered, "Sir, they are here." But Jane didn't join Paul on the back porch anymore. She sat in the living room pretending to read, plugging her ears and forcing herself to breathe when she thought she heard the sound of bullets whizzing through the air on the beach. Before Jane drifted off to sleep at night, she didn't think about the mask anymore. Instead, she saw herself watching silently through the railings as those men in their droopy pants, with their glistening skin and bewildered eyes, were shot.

Jane didn't go to the beach anymore, either. On clear Saturdays, Paul would try to tempt her with the suggestion of ocean swimming, picnics on the sand, kite flying. She never agreed. She used the pregnancy as her excuse—she didn't feel well, she wanted to stay inside. He didn't know what she knew: that the ocean had licked blood from the shoreline, that the blood swirled in the water now; there were bullets; there were beads of flesh rotting under the sand. The beach was a decaying thing, marked by violence, and Jane didn't want any part of it—any molecules of sea or silica or even the air off the waves—to melt through her skin or lungs and dissolve into her baby. She had to be a wall now, between her baby and the tragic world they lived in.

GOD IS THE RAIN,
GOD IS THE SKY

The air was cooler in the hills, easier to breathe. Simi concentrated on that, the rhythm of her breath. She kept her eyes cast downward and tried not to think about the distance she'd come from the manyatta, or the length of the return journey. She walked as fast as she could, but she was still weak and empty and her legs felt heavy and slow. The prospect of a night out in the bush, alone, wasn't one she relished, so she didn't stop to rest her legs or to drink water. The path was rocky, and a long-ago rain cut a deep track in the dirt. It was too narrow for her to walk in, so she tried to straddle it. Occasionally one foot would slip, causing her to stumble.

Around her, the world changed. Her path led upward, away from the yellow savannah spread out below her and up into the Loita hills. The scrub gradually became taller, and greener, and the plant life changed. After a while, Simi noticed she couldn't see down the escarpment into the savannah anymore.

The trees along the path were too thick now, too tall. Even the sun was hidden behind them. Far above her tree branches rustled and shook with the weight of colobus monkeys that leaped between them, hooting warnings to each other as Simi crossed under them. Once, Simi looked up to see a mother colobus launch herself from one branch to another, the long, white fur stripes along her sides and tail streaming out behind her, while a tiny baby clung bravely to her breast. Even when the branches were still, Simi could feel the peering eyes of monkeys all around her. The forest breathed, and its heart beat; it was a unified body that lived and moved, its cells the countless creatures and plants that made it, and the rocks and the dirt and the air.

The part of the forest body Simi looked for was the large *oreteti* tree she'd visited six years ago when she first realized she might be barren. That time, she'd come with other women. They'd eaten fat and cleansed themselves with milk. They danced and sang songs and then each woman left an offering at the tree. Some of the women left calabashes of milk; one left a tin of sugar. Simi couldn't remember if all of the other women had later given birth, but she knew some had.

Even after six years, it was easy to find the tree. It was as wide as Simi's hut and stretched so far up that even when she tipped her head all the way back she couldn't see where the branches met the sky. This was an old tree. The *oreteti* begins as a seed dropped into the branches of another tree by a bird or a monkey. The seed breaks open and tiny roots grow. As the roots gather nutrients from their host, they grow bigger, and longer, and more plentiful, wrapping the host tree in python-sized roots that seem to descend from the sky itself. The host tree struggles to survive the *oreteti's* embrace, but eventually dies and rots away, leaving an enormous, intricate lattice of great roots that curl and crawl over one another as they push themselves higher and higher from the earth to the sky.

Simi knelt down in the soft earth at the base of the tree. She stilled her breathing and licked her dry lips. The *oreteti* commanded respect and reverence. It was through an *oreteti* tree's roots that N'gai handed the cattle from heaven into the care of the Maasai. The roots could also take prayers to N'gai, who shares a name with the rain and also the sun. Years ago, Simi put her faith in this tree. She danced and sang and made her own offering. But the tree hadn't taken her prayer to N'gai. Or N'gai hadn't wanted to give her what she sought. Instead, he'd only taunted her—giving her a full womb and then emptying it again and again, like water poured from a calabash. Then a baby had come. Not one grown in her own body, but a baby all the same. But that was a taunt, too, and now, like all the others, that baby was gone.

Simi stood. The tree loomed above her, its countless arms snaking in and around and over each other. In between the woven roots, Simi knew, was a dark, empty space where the host tree used to be. Last time she was here, her desperation made her brave. The other women implored her not to—there were surely snakes hiding there, they'd cried, maybe a leopard. But she'd slipped in between the roots and entered the tree's middle space. Now she remembered the feeling of peace that came over her then. She wasn't frightened that day. The other women chatted nearby, and their voices had been comforting. She was safe, she felt, in the belly of the sacred tree, and she lowered herself and sat on her haunches and prayed there, in the dark. The women's voices faded, and all she could hear was the sound of the leaves so far above her in that dark hollow. When her prayer ended, she'd reached up to her neck, unlatched the necklace of blue and green beads her mother had given her and laid it on the ground. Six years ago she'd offered her most valued possession in the hope that N'gai would bless her with children. She'd placed it directly in the heart of the *oreteti*. But N'gai hadn't blessed her. And now she wanted her offering back.

In the time since she was here with the other women, the tree had grown many more winding roots. The space she'd slipped through before was now crossed over by new growth that barred her entry. Simi carefully examined the tree. The side that faced the path was covered tightly, and around the other side, a tangle of undergrowth obscured the tree's base. Simi slipped her machete from the leather band around her waist. Her heart beat painfully in her chest. The forest was full of animals, from snakes to leopards, and any of them could be hiding in the bush. The bravery she felt with the other women was gone now.

Slowly Simi picked her way around the tree, sliding the branches and leaves out of her way with the blade of her machete. She examined the tree as she moved, looking for an opening she could access. It didn't take long to find one. It was off the ground, though—she'd have to sidle up the large roots, slide into the opening and then drop back onto the ground in the middle of the tree. It wasn't so high that the drop would hurt her, but it might be difficult to climb back out.

An image of the car, carrying her daughter and disappearing into a cloud of dust that choked her, flashed through her mind. What did she have to lose, anyway? Who would miss her? She told nobody she was leaving just after dawn that day. She told nobody where she was going. It didn't matter. Now, childless again and far past hope that she could ever conceive, she wouldn't be missed. In fact, she wasn't sure her husband wouldn't cast her out, anyway. An unlucky, cursed woman like her.

Simi took hold of the tree, one serpentine root in each

hand, and hoisted herself up. She was weak from days without eating, and her arms barely held her. But she found footing on a lower root and pushed herself upward. The opening she wanted was just above her head. Once Simi grasped the root that formed the bottom edge of the space, it was easy for her bare feet to find secure places to stand, and slowly she worked her way up until her chest rested on the bottom of the open space. She leaned over and peered down into the center of the tree. It was quiet. No sound of an animal breathing. No dry rasp of a snake slithering below her. Dim light entered from the spaces between the filigree of roots, but there were puddles of shadows she couldn't see into. She wished she had fire to illuminate the space, but she didn't want to take the time to find the wood to make a spark. She knew if she found the necklace soon, and hurried back through the forest, she could be down the escarpment before dark. She could ask to stay at the nearest manyatta for the night.

So she moved quickly, pushing herself up and sliding the front of her body forward, then grasping the top edge of the opening and pulling her legs up so she was sitting on its edge, her back to the forest and her feet dangling into the darkness. She slid forward and dropped into the space. Her feet hit solid ground, and she braced herself for the sharpness of fangs in her ankle, or the slipping of a centipede against her toes. Nothing. She stood for a second, letting her eyes adjust to the minimal light, which fell in soft shafts, echoing the shapes the tangle of roots made all around her. She leaned her head back and looked up. The tree was taller than she remembered, the top invisible to her. The original roots, born in an upper branch of the host tree, were thicker than they were at the base, and so closely entwined they allowed no light to enter.

She waited to see if the feeling of calm she'd felt the first time she slipped into the heart of this tree would fill her again.

Her head, whether light from lack of food and the long walk up the escarpment that day or from the dizzying effect of the light through the tree, spun. She knelt down in the dirt to steady herself and took a deep breath. The spinning slowed, and Simi looked around, hoping her eyes would adjust to the low light. She didn't think the necklace would be hard to find. She'd only placed it on the ground, not in a hole or in some divot of the trunk that would have grown taller and taken the necklace with it. Slowly, Simi leaned forward and stretched her arms out, carefully patting the ground all around her. Six years of dust had gathered here since last time, as a hopeful young wife, she came here in an act of faith. She'd assumed the offering would work, and that soon enough her empty belly would fill with children and her life would spin out the way she, her mother, her father and everyone else expected it to.

Remembering that hope, and the way it slowly gave way to disappointment, made Simi feel weak again. It had been upsetting enough to be unable to bear a child, but shouldering the expectations of generations of ancestors who expected her life to unfold in a certain way made it worse. It wasn't simply the absence of a baby, but also the absence of a place. Before Adia, Simi had lived with a constant undercurrent of fear. She never knew if she'd be forced to leave; if the others would begin to see her bad luck as catching—as a curse on all of them. And when Adia came to her, the fear vanished. She had a baby to love and a secure place in the community. She'd been just another mother, not someone to look at sideways and wonder about. Adia. Simi remembered the weight of Adia's infant body in her arms, the way Adia curled next to her as she slept and the way her little voice sounded when she spoke. Grief rolled over her with the force of a beast attacking her. She felt her chest collapse into the dirt. For an instant she thought it really was a big cat, and she imagined she could feel the creature's hot, fetid breath on her neck and its claws tearing her skin. She couldn't breathe. Her lungs constricted and terror filled her. Light popped behind her eyes, and heat flashed like fire across the surface of her skin. She thought she was dying, and she tucked her body around itself and held her head in her arms, the instinct for self-preservation too strong to deny.

She must have faded into sleep, because when she opened her eyes, it was completely dark. Every light had faded into blackness. She wiggled her toes, and felt the sensation along her legs, and stretched her arms wide. Everything moved just as it should. Simi was tired. Too tired to make the effort to rise. If darkness had fallen, she couldn't risk a walk back through the forest, anyway. She let her body relax again. Every piece of her was still. She made no movement except for the rising and falling of her breath. The panic was gone now; the fear had left. She only felt resigned. Her life wasn't what she'd planned. The children weren't coming. Adia was gone. There was nothing she could do about it. Her husband might or might not shun her, and she might or might not be mauled by a lion on her way to the river one day. Things happened all the time that were out of anyone's control.

She thought of the moon she'd observed the night before and how, underneath it, she'd noticed that the animals were dying again, the drought slowly killing them off, and how the women had to go farther and farther to collect firewood and how men were leaving their traditions behind to find work and money in Nairobi. Her life wasn't the only one that didn't continue the pattern of all the lives that had come before. Nobody's future was written from the past. She remembered when Leona first arrived, she told Simi she wanted to help the Maasai hold on to their traditions by figuring out ways to graze their livestock in places the drought hadn't reached.

Thinking about Leona threatened despair, and to quell those dangerous thoughts, Simi shifted her body, just a bit, to relieve her hip bones of the ache the cold ground had sown in them. As she shifted, her left arm, still stretched out its full length, shifted, too. The fingers on her left hand moved, and under them Simi felt something that wasn't dirt. The dark was too thick to see the colors, but Simi felt the details. All the beads were there. The clasp still seemed to work. Simi sat up and fastened the necklace around her neck. Her mother had wanted Simi's life to be different. That's why she'd worked so hard to get Simi to school. She couldn't imagine her daughter not marrying or being cut, but she'd wanted her daughter to have a modern mind, to go one step further than the women of her own generation. How odd that a *muzungu* was working so hard to try to preserve their way of life, while Simi's own mother had injected change, however small.

Simi was grateful for her mother's vision. She thought that, if she'd had a daughter, she would have taken one step even further into the future. Her daughter, the one she didn't have, would get an education and Simi would make sure she finished. That's how she would keep her mother's vision passing into the future.

Simi wrapped her *shuka* tightly around her shoulders and, within the secure confines of the *oreteti*, curled herself into a ball. One last thought flipped into her mind before she drifted off—if she had that daughter and if she encouraged that daughter to finish secondary school, when would that girl be cut? Cutting signified a girl's readiness to marry, and usually she became a bride quickly afterward. Would she still be cut at thirteen, but wait to marry? Would a husband be willing to wait? Or, would the girl be cut after secondary school? It made an extraordinary picture in Simi's mind—an older girl, one of seventeen or eighteen, educated, having *emurata*. It didn't make sense; you might as well have a man nurse a baby or an old woman become a *moran*.

In the morning, the slow sun found its way back through the pattern of roots. Simi opened her eyes and the bits of light were like stars. The forest around her was already awake, the colobus monkeys were busy searching for breakfast and the birds called to each other, gossiping in the chilly air. Simi's back hurt from the way she'd curled up to sleep, but she was rested. She felt an emptiness that she hadn't felt in the previous few days. That is, she didn't feel happy, but she felt an absence of the deep grief Adia's leaving gave her. It was still there, she knew, but it had settled into a deeper place, the way a stone, after it's tossed into water, settles on the river's floor, leaving no traces of itself when the ripples smooth out.

It wasn't as hard as Simi expected to climb back out of the space in the tree, nor for her to start walking back toward her manyatta. And once she passed the outer edge of the forest and broke back into the open sky with the wide savannah stretched out below her, she paused and sat on a large stone. She unclasped the necklace and examined it. The beads were dirty—all those six years of dirt clustered in the spaces between them—but, as she had thought the night before, they were all there. Simi used the bottom edge of her *kanga* and rubbed at the beads, dislodging the dirt bit by bit. She rubbed until she could see the colors of the beads, blue for the sky and rain that should have come, green for the way the land would look if it did. When it was clean, she clasped it back around her neck and began her long walk home.

CHILDREN BECOME
THEMSELVES

There was a kind of unease stalking Jane, and it grew daily as her pregnancy bloomed. She couldn't decide whether to blame the mask, the murders she'd borne witness to or the history of her own blood. Thoughts of Lance and his disease haunted her. It was genetic, and the idea that it might infect the cells she was giving her baby terrified her. Without warning the feeling would leap on her back and dig its claws in, a jungle animal weighted with muscle and teeth and driven by an instinct not to let go. Jane didn't know how to fight the thing off and, instead, began to hide all day in her darkened bedroom, curtains drawn against the Liberian light, the air conditioner rattling on its highest setting to drown out the sounds of the surf and the world going on—without Jane—outside.

For weeks, Mohammad slipped inside the bedroom only to place bowls of soup and bottles of boiled, filtered and chilled water on the bedside table. Jane would eat the things Mohammad cooked. She trusted him and his fastidious adherence to the rules of cleanliness. But she ate little else. Nothing fresh, nothing raw. The potential to make her baby sick by eating diseased produce or ingesting even a drop of untreated Liberian water hung over Jane constantly. Even her desire to shower was outweighed eventually by the terror that the unpotable tap water would somehow pass her lips. In the late afternoons, Paul returned from work, and when he was home, Jane climbed out of her bed and sat at the dining table with him to nibble dinner. She tried to be calm and happy around Paul, but the fear kept leaking out. All day long Jane counted squares on her calendar, calculating the day of conception and the day she was due. She wondered what her baby looked like week to week, she obsessed over the growth of her baby and was frightened to lose track. She compulsively checked off the days as they slid past. At thirty-two weeks the embassy would send her to the States to wait until Grace was born. Jane only had to hold on until then. At home, things would be clean and safe, and she would be able to breathe the air and drink the water again.

"I'm worried," Paul said one night. "You aren't doing well." His face was scared, and the concern Jane saw there was a chisel to her fear and broke it all open.

"I'm scared," Jane cried. "I can't stop being scared, and I keep thinking this is how my brother started." She couldn't stop crying, and the bursts of emotion kept her in tears until Paul finally convinced her to get back in bed. He curled next to her, stroking her hair until her sleep came.

Jane refused to leave the house at all and missed two appointments with the embassy doctor. Finally Paul arranged a ticket for her to fly home. He knew the albatross of a wife suffering the kind of mental distress Jane was experiencing would impact his career. The State Department would limit his choice of future posts, and he'd be a far less attractive employee to ambassadors if they found out. Unwilling to risk that, he told his boss that Jane wanted her mother to help with the preparations for the baby. His tour in Liberia was almost finished, anyway. He would join her just before the baby's due date. His next post was assigned—Washington, DC. They'd settle for a while.

"Back from Africa!" Those were her father's first words when she exited customs and saw him. He looked older than the last time she'd seen him. Older and somewhat fragile. Jane hugged him, and he said, "And pregnant! Sure it's not a voodoo baby?" He laughed.

Jane could still smell the salty Liberian air in her own hair, and when she opened her suitcase later, it released the scent of her Monrovia house—the slight tang of mildew she'd become used to and hadn't realized was so pervasive.

That night, Jane woke up sweating, breathing heavily. She lay completely still, eyes tightly shut, and listened hard. In her dream, someone was there in the room with her. Someone was watching from a corner as she slept. Someone's breath mingled with hers in the darkness of the bedroom. Slowly she gathered the courage to open one eye, then the other. The curtains were gauzy against the windows and since she'd kept them open for the air, they billowed out a bit with the night breeze. The streetlight, a few houses down, sent a cool white glow into the room. Even still, it took Jane a few minutes to remember where she was—in the guest bedroom of her parents' house in Fairfax. There was the heavy wooden dresser between the two windows and the chintz-covered armchair piled with things she'd begun to unpack. There was the cat, curved and silent as a comma in the bed beside her. They weren't touching, but Jane sensed the weight of the little body, the slight heat the cat gave off.

Jane tried to shake the dream from her head, but it left her breathless, with little shocks of terror that burst in her veins like fever. She wished her father hadn't joked about her "voo-doo baby." Jane's genes were tainted; she knew that. Her father knew that, too. It wasn't something to joke about. The baby slid inside her and the movements were a comfort. This baby would be fine, Jane whispered to herself. Her brother was her brother, not her, and his demons wouldn't infect her or her baby. Jane told herself this over and over in a mantra of her own design. Finally, she turned onto her left side and the cat stretched her legs and purred, then shifted into a furry ball. Jane pressed her right hand to the stretched dome of her belly. This was how she held her unborn daughter and this was how she banished the nightmare and finally fell asleep once more.

She woke to an overcast sky and the promise of rain. For June it was cool in Virginia. She could hear someone in the kitchen downstairs, and a sudden memory of her childhood struck her. When Jane's mom was still healthy, she'd make a pot of tea and a pile of cinnamon toast for Jane every morning. Jane would sit at the blue kitchen table and eat. Jane's friends thought it was weird to drink tea. None of the other kids did. But Jane's mother made it sweet and milky, and Jane had a favorite cup, which she used every day. Jane couldn't remember what happened to that mug—dark blue with white flowering vines trailing around it.

Later that first morning, Jane joined her dad and stepmother in the kitchen. She poured herself a cup of coffee. "If I can borrow the car, I think I'll go today," Jane said. She'd showered and dressed but still felt bleary and light-headed from the jet lag and disturbed sleep. She hoped the coffee would help. "To see Lance."

Jane's father didn't answer. His face changed slightly—his mouth slid into a line, and his jaw clenched just enough that Jane noticed. Jane wanted to force the conversation, poke her father with words. This was the chasm between them now. Her father and stepmother kept a strict schedule of visits to Lance—they had to draw lines, they'd explained once, in order to protect themselves from pain. Jane knew that was true theoretically, but in her heart she had never understood how her father could turn his back on his only son. Although Jane had come to appreciate—even love—her stepmother, she also silently blamed her for the boundaries erected between Lance and their father. Her real mother would have done anything for Lance.

It was disconcerting to drive along streets that were wide and clean and empty. They were so different from the crowded and colorful streets in Monrovia. There she'd have to navigate puddles of oily water and stray dogs wrestling for scraps, and she'd have to share space with children selling single cigarettes and ladies hawking vegetables or dusty packages of biscuits and noodles. At every stoplight someone would rush to slap a wet soapy rag on her windshield in the hope of earning a few cents. There was a loneliness to these empty American streets. Jane was shocked to feel a tiny wave of nostalgia unfurl inside her. She never ever thought she'd find things to miss about Monrovia.

The place her brother lived now tried hard to look homey from the outside. There were bright flowers in pots on a wide front porch and cheerful green shutters on all the windows. But you had to sign in at a front desk where a man had a dozen screens that all showed different views. In them you could see hallways, people shuffling in grainy black-and-white. The people looked like specters. Jane signed the book the man indicated, and then she was buzzed through a metal door into one of the hallways. She thought the man at the desk was probably watching her now. She was a specter, too, like all the others.

After two years away, Jane was shocked by her brother's appearance. Thin and pale and hunched over in a metal folding chair, he stared up at a TV screen affixed high in a corner of the common room. Jane could hardly tell the women from the men, as slouched and hunched as they were, dressed nearly identically in dreary, loose cotton clothes that puddled around them. But she knew her brother, and at her first sight of his back, she recognized him out of all the others. Something about the lines of his body, the way he sat, the shape of his head. It all made him, the little brother she grew up both resenting and adoring in the years before her mother's death. He'd been a distraction in those early days when she wanted nothing more than to have her mother to herself. Later, he'd been a symbol of the reality that her mother was really dying—one she dodged by avoiding her mother's desire to talk about Jane's responsibility to Lance. But things changed again when Jane's father remarried. Then, Jane saw him as her ally, the one person left who connected her directly to her mother. As he'd gotten older, he'd made her laugh and dared her to climb trees and helped her, slowly, move past the heaviness of her grief. He was smart and funny and athletic. He was handsome, too. When, in the middle of his sophomore year in college, he'd had his first schizophrenic episode, the whole family was shocked. They racked their memories for signs they'd missed, quirks of moods, silent periods, brief moments of deep confusion. They never agreed on whether or not the signs had been there, and after a few years, it didn't matter anymore.

"He's okay, you can go to him," an orderly in bright green scrubs told Jane. She tried to ignore the other patients watching her as she crossed the room and knelt down on the linoleum next to her brother's chair.

"Hi, Lance, it's me. I'm back."

She didn't expect a reply, and she didn't get one. He was often quiet. The drugs kept his hallucinations at bay, but they also sent him spinning in a different direction—into a completely internal world. After his first breakdown, Lance moved home and began a strict regimen of medications and therapy. Her father watched him closely, hired the best psychologists and sought innovative treatments as he researched endlessly.

Her dad and stepmother poured money and time into Lance at just the time when they wanted a new kind of freedom. Lance's sickness took over every aspect of their lives for years. They couldn't leave him alone, couldn't travel and couldn't trust him to take care of himself. Lance didn't always respond to the medication, and when he forgot to take it or it stopped working, he could grow violent in an instant. By then, Jane was away at college. One day, not long after she'd come home to tell her dad she was leaving for Africa, she'd witnessed Lance switch from calmly eating lunch to grasping his father's head in a tight lock, only letting go when Jane and her stepmother leaped upon him, scratching and screaming and pulling him back. The next day, her father had Lance committed again.

"We can't put you in the face of that danger," he'd said. "You shouldn't have to be afraid in your own house." But Jane hadn't been afraid of Lance. Not ever. Instead, she felt only anger. She remembered the fight she'd had with them after Lance was gone. The things she'd accused them of—of using her as their reason to finally get rid of her brother.

Jane sat with Lance in the common room, with other patients watching them for several silent hours. Once, when she felt the baby moving, she grasped Lance's hand and pressed it to her belly. "That's your niece or nephew," she said, and she watched his face. His expression didn't change at all.

"He didn't talk," Jane said later that night at dinner. "Not even a word." She mentioned it only as something to say; she knew they didn't want to hear about Lance. They had locked him away in a mental compartment they only opened during their twice weekly, one-hour visits. But Jane wanted to talk. She still obsessed over her own mind and moods. The anxiety that had weighted her down for the last few months fed off the deep-seated fear that her own brain was as diseased as her brother's. Or, worse, that this baby of hers would inherit Lance's sickness. She was terrified of that and even more terrified that if that did happen, she would end up doing what her own father had—sending the child away and barely looking back.

Paul returned to her just in time. He'd packed the Monrovia house up and had all their freight directed to the States. He was exhausted when his plane landed, and Jane let him go right to bed. She opened his suitcases, though, and pulled out a couple of books he'd packed, a shirt or two and his toothbrush. She sniffed everything closely, both wanting and dreading a whiff of the place he'd come from.

Barely two days later, Grace was pulled from Jane under bright lights and a rush to the operating table. It wasn't what Jane expected, and she lay shivering with surprise and terror as the doctors cut her open. Paul's face was mostly hidden behind a neat blue mask, but Jane noticed the way his eyes looked— as if, for the very first time, he had no understanding of what was happening. There was nothing he could say, no way to control the outcome of the birth. Through the fear and the chill in Jane's body, she saw his eyes and they made her feel a bubble of sympathy under everything else. Paul was not in charge here. This was not his element, and even though Jane never wanted Grace born this way—she'd imagined a natural birth, free of drugs and scalpels and fear—she was oddly relieved to see Paul in this moment of vulnerability. This wasn't his to manage, none of it was. He wasn't in control, and for the first time in their relationship, Jane felt fear like heat from his skin. She'd never seen him raw like this. It made her feel vindicated, somehow. *Now you know*, she thought. *Now you know.*

When Grace was in her arms—wet and red as meat—she felt elated. Paul leaned down and kissed her temple, awe in his eyes replacing the fear. He hadn't looked at Jane with that expression for so long. She was new again for him—strong and capable. Already baby Grace changed everything.

For the first six weeks of Grace's life, the new family lived with Jane's parents. Paul spent days at the State Department, settling into his new position. Occasionally, Jane left Grace with her parents so she could visit Lance. He never spoke to her. He was a shell; the dark breathing creature of his brain, his real self, was hidden so deeply it couldn't come out.

One evening, a few days before they were set to move into the little house they'd rented in Arlington, Jane and her father packed Grace into the stroller and walked slowly through a nearby park. Together they watched the little children dig holes in the sand and shout from between the bars of an elaborate jungle gym. Mothers sat on benches, watching closely, occasionally offering up juice boxes and packets of pretzels or Goldfish crackers to the kids who buzzed back and forth to them, bees to flowers.

"I miss those days," Jane's father said. "When you and Lance were little and it was so very simple. It all changes fast. You just can't predict."

Jane didn't answer. She was stunned her father had said Lance's name. She hadn't heard it from his mouth in so long. The stroller wheels clicked against the seams in the sidewalk, and Jane's father breathed deeply. "It's not perfect, nothing ever is. Kids aren't yours to keep, in the end, Jane. You can't control every outcome. I tried to make a place for Lance, but I couldn't. It was too hard. We had to accept him the way he is. The Lance you knew? The Lance we loved? He's gone forever. It was our gift to him to finally acknowledge that. Children become themselves. You can't force an outcome just because you want to."

A few months later, Paul and Jane took Grace to get her passport photo. They didn't know when, but they would be posted overseas again, and even the baby needed official papers. Because Grace couldn't sit or stand for the photo, Jane had to hold her up. The photographer directed her to stand behind a thick, blue drape and push her hands out—still draped—to lift the baby up for the camera. Behind her dark curtain, Jane held tightly to Grace's wiggling body. Several weeks later, Paul brought the passport home with him from work. When Jane looked at it, she saw the beautiful round face of her beloved daughter. It was a good picture, and Jane filed it away with her own passport and Paul's and didn't think of it again.

Months later, when they were packing up for their next post, Paul pulled the three passports out and laid them on his dresser where they wouldn't be forgotten. This time, when Jane opened Grace's, her eyes were drawn to the space beyond Grace's soft, round head to the undefined, almost ghostly shape behind the blue curtain. For a second Jane thought maybe it hadn't been her back there, not her at all who lifted the baby's body dutifully up to the camera's eye. It couldn't be her who'd agreed to take this new and delicate thing so far away. And she felt the sensation of slipping on ice, uncontrolled and dangerous; there was no way to stop from falling. For an instant, she didn't even recognize herself.

SOLAI VALLEY

There it was again—a puff of dust.

Ruthie's heart beat fast. She licked her bottom lip, and wondered if she should put her boots back on. If it were John coming back, she'd want to meet him at the turnoff. The sun was sliding low, a pure white smudge in the pale blue sky. Twilight was coming. She should put the kettle on. John would want his tea.

Her eye had caught something out beyond the screen door, out beyond the paving-stone walkway that led from the house to the two concrete posts marking the entrance to the property. The front field was out that way, hardly a field now that the drought had erased the grasses and shrubbery bit by bit, leaving only the bones and hides of the cows she used to help tend.

She knew what it meant, that puff of dust. In the distance, where before everything went bad, trucks would rev their engines up that last hill, making for the barns where they'd load their beds with fresh milk and meat. No trucks had come for so long now.

She opened the screen door and stepped out onto the terrace. The stones were curved and warm under her stocking feet. How long it had taken Martin and the Kikuyu to make this terrace. Ruthie remembered the endless lines of sweating workers, bent under the weight of baskets filled with river stones Martin had them dig and then lay in the cement he'd carefully mixed. Every day the project grew. First, Ruthie agreed to have a small patio there, just enough for guests to stand on while knocking at the door. But then she had an image of them all sitting in wicker chaises on a large stone terrace, drinking Pimm's Cup in the evenings while the children played in the garden and the sun set—all the colors they would see in that wide-open sky where evening was short-lived but beautiful.

The chaises were gone, long ago rotted through and never replaced. So instead of sitting, Ruthie wrapped her arms around herself and stared out at the rutted dirt road, where the cloud of dust had become a small car.

Fifty years ago, when Martin proposed, the Solai Valley was ripe. Ruthie didn't hesitate when he asked her to marry him and move to the farm he'd bought here. Nairobi and the Club, her life in her parents' house, it all made Ruthie tired. She craved the land to the north and the way the space and the overwhelming sky made you feel small and free. It was in her bones, she argued to her parents, as both of them had been ranch children raised by British *émigrés* in the expanses of the Rift, and Ruthie herself spent her childhood summers on the farms in Loita and Nyeri where each pair of her grandparents had, at that time, still worked—eking out livings that sustained them until they died. And then the farms were sold. Her parents hadn't wanted either of them, and there was nobody else to pass them down to. The money Ruthie inherited from each sold farm was, in fact, the seed money for the house behind her now, for the barns, for the sheep dip and the Kikuyu school they'd built at the back of the acreage. Both were empty now, the concrete lining of the dip and the foundation of the school each as dried and cracked as the land.

What hope they'd had then, what visions of a beautiful earthbound life filled with cows and milk and children of their own that would come back to farm on school holidays and work side by side with Ruthie and Martin and the Kikuyu.

They had had a few good years. At the beginning Ruthie was strong, and they had the patience to wait for the land to blossom with the corn they planted, the bananas and beans, and of course her daisies and herbs and the passion fruit vine she was training up a trellis in the back. They had that patience, and they had the open faces and clear eyes that made talking to each other so easy.

They had expected to work hard for the first few years. They had also expected that, eventually, things would be easier. That the rain wouldn't stop for so long, and that then, when it finally did come, it wouldn't be in such great deluges that it washed away topsoil and seedlings. They hadn't anticipated the darkness that fell into Ruthie after their first baby was born. How she would look at the tiny body asleep in her arms and have visions of leaving him under a bush for a hyena to eat, or the guilt she was racked with when the visions subsided.

"There's another one dead in the front field." Ruthie spoke quietly to herself now. "Another dead cow. This drought will be the death of all of us."

So deep in her own memories, Ruthie was startled enough to gasp when she heard a car door slam.

"Hello?"

The greeting came from a woman who stood beside a small and very dusty, dented car. Her accent was American, Ruthie noted, and her dark hair was pulled back into a long ponytail, but her head and face, well, all of her, was covered in a veil of the ochre dust the dry roads had spun up under her car tires. The woman wore jeans and a T-shirt, also covered in dust, and the same sandals made of car tires that the Maasai wore.

"Well, you're a right mess!" Ruthie couldn't think what else to say. She hadn't seen a *muzungu* stranger on her land for so long, for years and years. She swallowed the sudden bitter taste of disappointment that flooded her mouth. It wasn't John come back to see her. It wasn't John, just some lost aid worker or tourist needing directions.

"Are you John's mother?" the woman asked as she began approaching the stone terrace.

The words made sense. Ruthie understood each one separately, but strung together in this way, they confused her. She let the question sit. She did have a son. Was his name John? It was.

"Yes." Ruthie was suddenly aware of how alone she was. She couldn't afford the house staff anymore, not to mention the farmhands, so only Samuel had stayed on. He was as old as Ruthie was and, over the years he'd worked as their houseman, had married three wives one after the other and built a small house at the back of the land. Ruthie was glad he stayed; he and his son were the ones who helped Ruthie now, a few hours a week, with the house. Samuel still did her shopping, as well, down at the market. But she couldn't expect them to hear her if she screamed, not from this distance.

"My name is Leona. I'm wondering if your son is here? I met someone in Narok who told me this is where I might find him."

For a moment Ruthie felt her brain whirring in her head,

trying to find the traction to organize the storm of thoughts blowing around like leaves in a windstorm. *Which son?* Ruthie wondered first, then she remembered, and then the confusion subsided.

"He's not here anymore." Ruthie spoke in a voice that wavered a bit, and then she cleared her throat. "What is it you want with him?"

The woman didn't answer Ruthie right away. She only stood there in her dusty jeans and rubber tire shoes and looked as perplexed as Ruthie felt. Then she turned and walked back to her car. Ruthie thought maybe she would get back in and drive away again, without another word. But instead, the woman opened the back door and leaned down. When she turned, in her arms, Ruthie saw, was a sleeping child.

Though covered with the same dust the mother was, and dressed only in a red *shuka* and several strands of beads, Ruthie could see the child was young—only three or so.

"What on earth have you got there?" Ruthie asked. "Why is this child dressed like a villager?"

Ruthie knew children were fragile. How often had she watched the Kikuyu children succumb to malaria and dysentery? It was common. But a white child? Ruthie felt her neck prickling with sweat. She squeezed her eyes closed. This couldn't happen again.

"No, no, no!" she scolded herself, pushing away the demon thought in her head. "This is not that. This is not that."

She opened her eyes and saw the younger woman's stricken face. Had she spoken aloud? It was so hard to remember anymore, what was in her head and what was outside. She spent the days speaking to nobody, and sometimes the words broke free from her mind and flew out into the world like birds from her mouth.

"She's not sick," Leona said. "She's only sleeping. It's been a long day. We drove from Narok. The road is worse than I expected. We didn't bring food for the trip, only a little water. It's gone now. I came here…" She paused, considering. Ruthie saw her eyes close and open again, shifting down to gaze at the grass. "I came to talk to your son. I wanted him to meet his daughter."

Ruthie's heart might have stopped just then. Her mind did. She could feel her thoughts, her lists, the memories she flipped through, even her ability to move, to speak, drain out of her. She turned into something frozen, instantly not a living thing. She forgot to breathe.

The American woman turned to look out at the road behind them. The dust had settled, and the horizon was clear and empty. The day sky was lifting itself up, tucking the final folds of light away and drawing out the colors of the land.

It was out of her control, this body was, Ruthie thought. As quickly as she'd been drained of life, she filled back up again. She didn't want to. She wanted to stay a stone thing, to die, to disappear from here.

Leona resumed talking, as if she hadn't noticed that Ruthie had died and come to life again right in front of her.

"I'm sorry, but are there villages near here? A town? I didn't see one on the Narok road, but maybe beyond here? Close?" Ruthie saw Leona looked worried. "I can't bear to drive back to Narok tonight. It's too dark—my daughter is too hungry. We need to find a place to eat and sleep."

"You'd best come in," Ruthie said, glancing down at the smooth face of the child. It was a girl. She couldn't remember when she'd last seen a white child that age. She yearned to reach out and touch the girl's cheek, her hair. Leona shifted the girl in her arms so that the small blond head was nestled in the crook of her neck, and her hands were clasped under the child's legs. Ruthie turned, and Leona followed her back across the stone patio and up the steps into the house.

Ruthie hadn't had guests for years, and she felt herself becoming flushed and nervous when she glanced around and saw how her house might look to a stranger. The tight foyer, the faded chairs in the sitting room and the cobwebs that traced the upper corners of the walls. She felt a flash of annoyance at Samuel and his son. They had gotten lazy, hadn't they? Not bothering to do their best for an old woman.

"Sit," Ruthie said curtly, her annoyance shifting to the strange woman. Who was she and why had she come? "I'll make a pot of tea. I'm afraid—" Ruthie knew the lie was coming and did nothing to stop it "—the servants are off today."

Martin had designed the house so that all of the rooms in the back looked out over the garden. Ruthie wanted a garden desperately. In her parents' Nairobi house, there were always fresh flowers in vases, newly plucked herbs hanging to dry in the kitchen, and enormous jacaranda and flame trees that burst into bloom and filled the windows with lavender and crimson. When Ruthie moved here, to this house, her first order of business was to create a garden in the back. She had it all in her head. She took her time to sketch out her plan, carefully labeling her drawings with the correct genus and plant names, and using her oil pastels to plan where the pinks would go, the gladiolas, the roses and the herbs. She wanted it to be perfect. But a drought that year had slipped its fingers one by one across the land.

At first Martin told her it would be best not to water the bougainvillea she was trying to train up the front of the house, between the windows, or the stands of glads she'd painstakingly transplanted from her mother's garden to soften the look of the entryway. How sad she'd been to watch them die. Then he said she should forget the garden entirely. "We don't have the resources now," he warned, "not the manpower or the water. We've got to put everything into the farm, the cattle."

Now Ruthie stood in her kitchen. The polished concrete floor was cold under her feet, and the window looked out over nothing but more scrub. A lone acacia in the middle distance was a flat smudge against the darkening sky. One or two stars emerged above it. It would be a clear night.

She heard sounds from the sitting room, a rustle and then voices—one small and thin, the other a woman's voice. The child was awake and the knowledge of that sent a frisson through Ruthie. She felt both terrified and thrilled at the opportunity to sit near a little one again, to watch the tiny hands move.

Only two tea bags left, but Ruthie used them both. Samuel would have to go to the market tomorrow. Only a tiny bit of milk, as well. Children liked milk. She wondered if she should pour it into the teapot or into a glass for the girl. She chose to save it just for the child and found a packet of digestive biscuits in a cupboard she hadn't opened in days. When had she put them there?

The girl was a dirty thing curled up like an animal next to her mother on Martin's chair. They shouldn't sit there, Ruthie thought. It was Martin's chair and he wouldn't like it. But she held her tongue.

"So, can I ask you where John is?" Leona looked up and sipped her tea.

Ruthie's teacup shivered in her hand, almost tipped.

"It's important that I speak to him." Leona glanced at the child when she said this and reached out to touch the girl's head. "He needs to know."

Ruthie paused. The edge of her cup grazed her bottom lip and she couldn't remember, for a second, what she was doing by holding it there, so close to her face that she could feel steam. What was that for?

Sometimes Ruthie knew she was sliding into forgetfulness. She would notice that she'd left the tap on and that precious water was escaping down the drain. She would wake up to where she was and turn the water off or close the refrigerator door or pull the ant-covered butter from the cupboard where she'd left it days before, having forgotten, for the moment, that butter should be kept where the ants couldn't get it. She watched this happen to her father, and she wasn't surprised by the lapses in memory she had, the confusion. She tried hard to think of only one thing at a time, to concentrate on what she was doing. She couldn't always, though, and the moments of lost thoughts were increasing.

The splash of milk from the child's cup broke into her thoughts. She'd dropped the glass and had leaped back from it while her mother fussed. "God, be more careful!"

"It's all right, girl, it's all right. There's a rag in the kitchen, down the hall," she directed Leona. "She's just a child, no need to scold."

It was much later, after she showed Leona to an empty bedroom and gave the girl some blankets to curl up with on the armchair that she realized she hadn't answered Leona's question.

Ruthie sometimes wondered when things changed. Was it watching her garden die? Seeing the parched land suck the life out of every living thing it could hold? She remembered clearly that it was around that time when the life, the smiles and jokes, had slid out of her Martin. He changed the same way the land did those first years. But when the rain came—finally, after three years—and things grew green again, Martin never turned back. His face was set by then. His eyes were tired, his arms were burned the color of dirt, and his anger at the land, at everyone and everything, never left. His anger would have come again anyway, Ruthie knew, just as the drought came back. They had two years of normal rains and then season after season that were dry as bones. They were doomed from the start of this farm; the weather never settled back into the patterns they'd depended on.

So they rarely sat on the wide terrace in the evening, having drinks and watching the children. Instead, Martin sat in his chair in the sitting room, where he drank whiskey, not Pimm's, and Ruthie learned to be quiet near him, to keep the babies from crying. She learned to watch the way he clenched and unclenched his hands, the way the new muscles in his forearms rose and fell like breathing.

Ruthie woke in the earliest part of the morning. The windows in her bedroom were thick with darkness and, way out there, somewhere, she could hear the whoop of a hyena. How she hated them. After the first baby was born, her blood turned thick with constant dread and terrible thoughts pushed into her brain like worms through dirt.

It was always a hyena. A hyena that snuffled the dirt for the new baby smell and sidled on his bloody paws up to where, in her mind, her baby lay, naked and prone, innocent and perfectly unaware. In the beginning, she had no control. The pictures in her head would flicker on—the hyena would come closer and closer and she would watch as it stopped, sniffing the baby's head and soft hair. Later she learned to force the images away by shouting. She'd let her anger take over instead, and that cut the visions short. The hyena stopped in his tracks, turning tail and slinking back into the underbrush. But her anger made her children slink, too. They would eye her warily, close their mouths and cry. How she hated herself then. How she wished she could find the words to explain that her temper was her only way to let them live.

In the end, it wasn't a hyena at all. But still, the sound of them, even after all these years, drove a spike of despair through her heart.

Leona woke after the sun was already above the horizon. The narrow bed Ruthie showed her to last night was hard, and the mosquito net had holes in it. All night she'd heard buzzing in her ears, and now she could see several mosquitoes resting on the interior of the net. They were thick with her blood. She turned her head and stretched her arms and legs. Her muscles hurt from hunching over the steering wheel all those long hours yesterday, fighting the bumps in the road. She sat up and pulled the useless net out from under the mattress. At least she could trap the creatures in here, hope they would die before the net was used again. And when would that be? The house looked like nobody ever came. The woman, Ruthie, seemed like she hardly ever saw another person.

Leona noticed as she threw her feet to the floor and stood up that the room was nearly empty. There was only the bed and the net, a small table with a lamp on it and, across from the bed, a white dresser. The dresser looked wildly out of place in the simple room in this derelict house. It reminded Leona of the kind of things in her parents' house, back in Oregon. It was shiny white, with curved edges, and perfectly round glass pulls on the drawers. There were painted flowers, faded now, but visible, along the drawer faces.

Curious, Leona walked to the dresser and slid her hands across the empty, smooth surface. The tips of her fingers remembered the feel of this kind of furniture, even though it had been years since she'd seen anything like it. The memory pulled something in her. She opened the top drawer, expecting to find nothing but dust or maybe silverfish. But instead she found it full. Tiny linen clothes, all folded perfectly in even piles, interspersed with the smallest pairs of shoes Leona had ever seen. There were three little brown pairs of soft leather, and one little white pair with ribbons for ties.

Leona picked up each pair of shoes one by one. She touched the soft fabric of the clothes and the delicate stitches in the knitted hats and sweaters. She never had clothes like this for her daughter. She had left all that behind when she moved to Kenya. Leona shoved the drawer shut and opened the next one. This one was empty except for a large photograph, framed in silver, turned facedown. Leona didn't hesitate to pick it up, to turn it over, and when she did she saw two little boys. One about three, she guessed, and one younger, barely sitting up. They were dressed in the things the drawer held—the linen overalls, the tiny shoes. Leona could clearly see her daughter in one of the faces. That must be him, she thought, as a baby.

Leona flipped the photograph back on its face and shut it in the drawer again. She remembered that she'd told Ruthie the truth, that it had escaped her mouth without her realizing it until it was too late. She wondered if Ruthie would even remember.

Ruthie lay still in her bed, listening to the air in the house around her. Strange how even the silence changed when someone else was in the house with her. She imagined she could hear the child breathing. The child. She pulled the thread of a vague memory in her brain, and like a magician's multicolored scarf pulled from a hat, the thought loosened and broke free. Her grandchild.

Ruthie sat up in bed and turned so her feet could find the floor. She had to see the child.

She didn't bother with the lights. She'd lived here long enough that she knew each divot in the concrete floor by heart. She padded down the hall and into the sitting room where the girl curled, fast asleep, in Martin's chair. A line of mosquito bites studded the girl's cheek. Should have made sure she had a net, Ruthie scolded herself. She grasped the edge of the blanket she'd directed Leona to cover the girl with last night, and tugged it back up to the child's chin. She paused with her hands on the blanket and lifted a finger to stroke the girl's cheek just above the reddened bumps. How soft it was, how curved. Ruthie quietly pulled a stool from the corner of the room and perched upon it. She watched the girl's eyelids shiver with dreaming.

Leona had said John was the father, and of course that was true. Of course. But deep down in Ruthie's bones, she recognized the imprint of her other son on this girl's face. The set of the eyes, the particular placement of the ears, the way the eyebrows swept gracefully up in the middle. She hadn't been able to look at the one remaining photo of Thomas for years and years, and watching the sleeping girl was nearly as painful. Had he been this age? Ruthie wondered. She couldn't remember; she wouldn't let herself remember. She slid off the stool and went to the kitchen to heat water for tea. It was only after she filled the kettle and turned on the flame that she remembered she had no tea. Shame. She'd have to see if Samuel had some. She had to feed her guests, of course.

So she left the kitchen to dress. She thought she could hurry to Samuel's little house and be home before the girl woke, but as she crossed the sitting room she caught sight of two blue eyes, wide-open and peering around the room curiously.

She didn't want her granddaughter to be frightened, so she spoke in a whisper. She held out her hand and said, "The sun's nearly up, girl. Come, I'll show you where I watch it being born." Without a word, the child slipped from under the blanket and stood up.

★ ★ ★

The sitting room was empty when Leona wandered through. She'd left her daughter curled on the chair last night fast asleep. Ruthie had given her a blanket to put over her and then shown Leona to bed. But the girl was gone, the blanket neatly folded, the chair vacant. Leona felt dread pour through her like a liquid spilling down her back.

"Hello?" she called down the hall toward where she assumed the other bedrooms were. There was no answer. Leona just heard the hiss of the kettle and, in the kitchen, found the stove on, the flame from the burner so high it licked halfway up the sides of the kettle, almost to the handle. She turned the burner off and glanced up to where the large window looked out over the yellow savannah. In the distance, she saw two figures walking slowly up a small hill. Ruthie was bent at the waist, leaning toward Adia. Leona saw her daughter reach up and take the old woman's hand. "Thank God," Leona thought, as she looked around the kitchen for the teapot, the tea and something to eat.

She found the teapot sitting on the windowsill, the cold dregs of last night's brew in the bottom. The box of tea bags was empty, however, and when Leona began opening cupboards to look for more, she found almost nothing. The wrapper from the biscuit package they'd eaten last night was in one cupboard, next to a quarter bag of flour infested with black weevils. In another cupboard was a full set of cups made from delicate china, painted with the softest pale pink flowers. There was a matching teapot and sugar bowl, too, and a curved milk pitcher of china so fine, Leona thought she could see through it. But that was it. The other cupboards held a few rough pottery mugs—the ones they used last night, still dirty, Leona noticed, and a few plates and random pieces of cutlery. The fridge was nearly as bad. In the back were a couple of slices of bread in a bag and an empty jar of marmalade.

Leona was starving. They'd left Narok yesterday just after a breakfast of *ugali* and chai, and stopped a few hours later in a tiny, unnamed town for *mandazis* and more tea. But then, apart from the weak tea and the biscuits they'd eaten here last night, they'd had nothing. Well, Leona thought, she'd simply fill up the water bottles and head out. It would only be a couple of hours until the next town, or at least a village, where they could ask for food.

She couldn't see Ruthie and her daughter anymore, but around the back of the house she found the path up the hill where she'd seen them last. The air was cool, and she heard a hoopoe in an acacia tree nearby calling its own name. God, she thought, how amazing it would be to live here, to have this empty space be the backyard, the hills in the distance your daily view, the sounds of the creatures all around you. Nobody, no people for miles.

Leona walked up a long bare track that meandered from the house up a steadily rising hill through the grasses—someone had used this very path so many times that the foliage just here had stopped growing. Leona wondered whose feet had worn it down.

At the top of the hill Leona saw her daughter and Ruthie. They were sitting on a stone bench under a spreading baobab larger than any Leona had ever seen. The tree's broad branches were thick with green leaves, and the shadow it threw was dark and wide. When she neared them, they both turned, and for an instant Leona saw them in each other; the way Ruthie's lips curved at the edges was in her daughter's face, the way each of their necks rose, long and elegant, from their shoulders.

Leona scooped her daughter up, and sat down on the bench in her place, the girl in her lap, facing Leona's chest, small arms around Leona's neck. There were headstones at her feet, Leona saw. That's what Ruthie was showing the girl.

"Who are they?" Leona asked Ruthie, tightening her hold on her daughter.

"It's her family," Ruthie answered. Leona's heart skipped. It was too late to pretend anymore. Ruthie had heard; she knew.

"Where is John?" Leona asked again. In her imagination, she'd come here and found him, they'd talked it all through and he'd accepted, happily, his role as a father. On the drive up yesterday, Leona daydreamed a joyous reunion of father and daughter, of settling her daughter into a new home where John could raise her as Leona expected he'd been raised—in a family of happy ranchers, connected to the earth and each other. And then, Leona had imagined, she would be free again. Free to settle into academic life in Nairobi with nobody to worry about but herself. She wanted Ruthie to tell her John was coming back, that he lived in this beautiful place and they could wait for a while and then he'd be here.

Ruthie tried to answer. She worked to make her mouth move in the way that would tell Leona what she needed to know. But instead she heard the sound of the snuffling animal, smelled the rotten hyena breath on her face, saw the baby under the bush, unknowing, still loving her, his mother, still instinctively connected to her, still unaware of the ways a mother could betray her child.

Her head filled with pictures she couldn't organize, and among them was the one she dreaded the most, the split hairbreadth when she'd tried to run from Martin, and his breathing muscles, his stony face, his whiskey and his rock-hard fists. She'd run from the house that night; it wasn't dark yet, but where did she think she would go? She couldn't remember that, but she remembered how she'd flipped on the engine in the farm truck and revved it loudly. She remembered the hysteria she felt that night, the desperate need to fly away into another world, away from the desolate land and the sullen man she found herself with. She remembered that she left her children behind. She threw the truck in Reverse, hit the gas and only then looked back.

It was little John's face in the rearview mirror that she couldn't forget. The O of his mouth, the fear in his eyes. For the shortest second, Ruthie thought his rapidly approaching figure was running after her because he didn't want her to leave him behind, didn't want her to leave. He'd only just started walking, was unsteady on his feet and slow. But Thomas was older. He'd darted out after her when the only thing she could hear was the whooshing of desperation in her ears, her need to escape.

She didn't see him running behind her to help John, she didn't see him. She saw John's eyes, those saucers of terror, before she felt the bump under the truck tire.

Everything had changed the day Thomas died. It all had changed that day, like an earthquake that jarred everything out of position, and nothing ever went back right. She didn't attempt escape again. Martin finally succumbed to cirrhosis, and although she tried her best, the farm was left to decay. John had moved to Nairobi by then, and one by one the servants and farmhands had drifted away to jobs that would pay.

In her head Ruthie opened her mouth to tell Leona the truth.

She heard herself say, "John is dead."

Leona felt it physically; the news hit her in the solar plexus. She winced at the pain and gasped. The door she'd counted on being opened slammed shut. John was the family she'd counted on for Adia, and the aunts and uncles and cousins she imagined him having. But there was none of that, just this doddering old woman. Adia couldn't stay here. Leona wanted to ask how John had died and when, and whether he'd left behind other children or a wife, but she couldn't form the words. Ruthie's face was pinched and sad. Leona didn't want to prolong the suffering of making the old woman remember. What did it matter, anyway?

"What will you do?" Ruthie asked. She wanted to hold the girl's hand again, walk with her down the hill and take her home.

Leona shook her head slowly. She had no idea what to say. She had no idea what she'd do. "Go home, I guess," she answered, and a blank page spread out in her mind. The ease of moving back to the manyatta tempted her. She could leave the girl there. Simi would be thrilled, would mother her better than she could herself. Then she could forget everything. But she knew she wouldn't do that, and so the question went unanswered. Where would home be?

"Home to America," Ruthie stated. That was a good idea. It would be better for the child there, she expected.

They didn't stay under the baobab much longer after that. Leona helped Ruthie walk back down the track through the grasses and reminded her not to leave the kettle on, the flame up too high. Leona was torn, she told herself over and over again as she fought the road back to Narok, about leaving such a fragile woman alone in such a wild place. But she couldn't possibly stay. She was stung with disappointment and hemmed in by the hot breath of indecision. What now? She'd made a plan; she'd tried to execute it. Now there were too many new decisions to make, too many new things to consider.

Ruthie had watched the dust die down on the road after Leona drove away with the girl and she was alone again. She stood by the window long after the car had disappeared and her hips began to ache with the strain of standing. She couldn't decide if what she'd told Leona was what she'd really meant to say.

Samuel came that evening with her groceries. He came nearly every day to check on her, and sometimes brought fresh food with him. He told her not to try to cook by herself; in her hands, the food ended up in the wrong places, burned or rotting, improperly stored or cooked. He would do it, he implored. And so he came that evening laden with bags from the market, and he placed the milk and eggs in the fridge and the biscuits and tea in the cupboard. He was sweeping ants off the counter when Ruthie thought to reach out and grasp him by the arm. He turned and looked at her, and she noticed the film over his eyes, the gray curls in his hair, his thin, old voice.

"I've misled her, Samuel. The American woman."

"Madam, sit please," Samuel whispered. "You are tired. There is nobody here, no American."

Ruthie knew he hadn't seen Leona, hadn't seen the little girl, her granddaughter. The house Samuel lived in with his family was beyond the hill, out of sight.

"They were here, Samuel. My granddaughter and her mother. I've told them John is dead. He's the girl's father. She looks like our family, exactly like Thomas." Ruthie took a deep breath.

"But you must tell them I meant my Martin is dead, my Martin and my Thomas. They are the ones who've gone. John is the one she wanted, of course. John, in Nairobi. I don't know why I said what I did. You must help me. You have to remember to tell her if she comes back, or to tell him. You must."

When the dark fell, Ruthie watched Samuel leave her house. He'd made her tea, fried an egg for her and laid it carefully on toast. The house felt more empty than usual. She wished they had stayed, her granddaughter and the American.

That night, late, Ruthie watched from her bedroom window as the moon slid up the sky. It would be a bright night. The moon would illuminate the open land behind the house; it would keep hyenas in the shadows. It would spill on the gravestones under the baobab and shine down on the faces of her dead.

She thought about Samuel telling his son to go into the market tomorrow to call John in Nairobi. She needed him to come. John would come. He was a good son; the one who lived.

CHILDREN ARE THE BRIGHT MOON

Leona drove without stopping. The dust from the road billowed thickly through the windows and covered Adia, who was stretched out and sleeping on the back seat. Leona glanced at her hands on the wheel. They looked like clay—as if she was a still, carved statue. She felt like one, too—still and cold and unable to think. She just drove. Even the potholes and the bumps and ruts in the road didn't concern her. She let the car bounce and dip and bang, and she didn't slow down until she saw the buildings of Nakuru town in the distance. She wished it wasn't so close, and she regretted not driving more slowly. In Nakuru the road split—the southeastern route led up the edges of the Rift Valley escarpment to Nairobi, and the southern route led back to Narok and, beyond that, to the manyatta. Nakuru meant a decision.

Leona lifted her foot off the accelerator and let the little car stop. It seemed so silent when the engine died. She watched the dust sink from the air around her, and then opened her door and stepped out of the car. Her legs felt rubbery and weak from the combination of sitting still for so long and the constant vibrations of the engine through her muscles. She shook one leg, and then the other, and then walked up the road a few steps. The sky was empty and clear, and Leona had the sensation she might be able to just walk into it. She could pull the blue around her like a blanket and sleep. The image made her smile. How long had it been since she last felt relaxed?

"Mama?" Adia's voice was small and sleepy through the space between them. Leona felt her heart seize up—just the tiniest bit—when she heard the voice. Were mothers supposed to feel that—what was it, disappointment?—when they heard their babies call to them? Simi had always looked thrilled to see Adia. Leona thought hard, but couldn't remember ever seeing Simi look tired or annoyed when Adia wanted her. "Yeyo." Adia called Simi "mother." Although Adia called Leona mama, when the girl said them, the two words for the same thing sounded different to Leona's ears. When Adia said *yeyo*, the word was softer somehow, less foreign to Adia's tiny lips.

Leona walked back to the car and opened the back passenger door for her daughter to climb out. "Go pee if you have to," she said, and then the choice was made without her even making it—the words just came out—so easily they surprised her when she heard them. "It'll be another couple of hours driving until we see Simi." Adia's face, still sleepy and layered with the fine, red dust of the road, lit up as brightly as Leona had ever seen it. She couldn't take the words back now. She settled behind the steering wheel again. Her legs still felt stiff, and her neck was sore, though Leona felt lightness in her chest she hadn't felt before. There were solutions to every problem.

They'd been gone just over two weeks. A tiny amount of time, but Leona thought the manyatta looked different. As they drove closer, the light began to darken in the sky, and the silhouettes of the squat, curved houses looked cold and shadowy. Leona knew that inside the huts fires were crackling and hot, sweet tea was boiling. But the image didn't make her feel warm and secure as it had before. Instead, she thought of the dense smoke in the huts and the low chairs that made her knees ache when she lowered herself onto them.

Adia, however, became more animated as the village drew closer and closer, and when Leona finally brought the car to a stop, Adia flew from the back seat like a bird and was off— just a tiny figure silhouetted against the darkening sky—and then disappeared into the enclosure.

Leona sat in the still car. The windows were open, and the air was filled with the smells she'd loved and lived with for so long: wood smoke and cattle and meat roasting on a fire and, underneath it all, the sharp smell of dust in the grasses and the wind; a distinctly African smell. The wave of emotion she felt suddenly took Leona by surprise. It was the exhaustion, she told herself as the tears came. Leona hardly ever cried. The heavy feeling in her chest and the tears themselves were a shock to her, but more of a surprise was the feeling of longing. She wondered how it was possible to long for something you hadn't left yet. Preemptive nostalgia, she decided. She was ready to leave—she wanted to leave, but in so many ways she would miss this life, this manyatta, these people. She would miss Adia. She drew in a deep breath and wiped her eyes on her sleeve. The car door, slamming shut behind her, sounded too sharp for this soft place.

First, Leona went to her old home. Nobody was in the central corral, just the lowing cattle, methodically chewing their cuds. They shook their heads as Leona threaded her way through them. Of course her fire was out. She couldn't remember if she'd extinguished it before she left that afternoon, or if it had gone out naturally. Either way, the hut was dark and chilly, and the coals in the fire pit sooty and dead. She fished her key fob out of her jeans pocket and found the tiny flashlight attached. Its light was too small to make out much, but she ran it over the contents of the little room with the hope she'd see a box of matches. She usually kept some, but she couldn't see any now—not on the little wooden shelf she kept her cups and plates on, not on the overturned box she used as a bedside table. She was wary about fumbling around in the dark too much. Snakes were always a possibility since the place had been empty of people for so long, scorpions, too. Instead, she swallowed her dread, and turned to head back toward the corral.

It was hard for Leona to think about that afternoon. On one hand she accepted that, at least in her mind, she'd acted in Adia's best interest. She'd wanted to provide a different life for the girl, one her own parents would approve of, and one that might be more secure. But shame rose in her chest now. The look on Simi's face haunted Leona. Simi, who had been a friend and confidante; really, her only friend and confidante. Simi, who had loved Adia in a way that Leona hadn't—couldn't. How could she have hurt her friend that way? Dreading the confrontation, but needing fire, and wanting to get it over with, she crossed to Simi's house and ducked in the door. The air inside was acrid and stale. Simi hadn't been taking care of the fire, or cooking much. That was obvious. The embers glowed tiny and orange in the very bottom of the fire pit, they would die soon, but in the pale glow they gave, Leona could make out two figures twined together on the rawhide bed across from her. One thin woman, wrapped in a *shuka* and shaking with sobs, and one little blonde girl.

Leona knelt on the dirt floor and blew into the coals; she tossed in a few bits of kindling she found there and emptied Simi's bucket of water into the *suferia*. She busied herself without speaking; finding Simi's tin of tea, the sugar in a twisted piece of newspaper and a small jug of milk someone had recently left.

When the tea was ready, Leona ladled it into three cups. Only then did she clear her throat and speak. "I've made tea. Simi, Adia, we have to talk."

She handed a cup to both Adia and Simi, and then sipped from her own. She wished she knew what to say.

"Simi, I'm sorry." It was a good start, a necessary one. "Adia loves you, and I love you, and you're an excellent mother to her. Much better than I am."

Simi stayed quiet. Leona noticed how comfortable her daughter looked, curled in Simi's lap, the mug held carefully in her hand. Leona wondered again, for the hundredth time, how on earth she could have pulled these two apart.

"I am her mother, too, though. And even though Adia lives like a Maasai and thinks she's a Maasai, she isn't. The fact is..." Leona grasped for what to say next.

"The fact is that she is an American, and that brings good things, good opportunities." And here her voice veered into pleading. "I haven't been a mother to her, not like you have. I can only really give her two things—education and an opportunity to be American if she wants. I'll probably never be as good a mother as you are, Simi. That's why I hope we can agree to both be mothers to her. You for here, and me for Nairobi, and one day maybe for America."

Simi looked down at Adia, who had drained her cup and now lay with her head in Simi's lap, her legs stretched out to the side.

Simi was quiet. Leona felt a rustle of panic. If Simi refused, what would she do?

But then Simi shifted Adia off her lap and stood up. She knelt down and pulled a box from underneath the bed. From that, she lifted a traditional, wide necklace. In the firelight, the beads glinted and shone. It was beautiful. Even to Leona's untrained eye, it was obvious the work was delicate and perfect.

"When I knew I couldn't have my own baby, I gave this to N'gai. I hoped he would accept it and make me pregnant, but he didn't."

She looked up and Leona saw that Simi's eyes were clear and her gaze unapologetic. "I gave you leaves that I knew wouldn't work to make you bleed your baby out. I knew that she would live inside of you. I wanted her here more than you did."

Leona hated to cry, and the threat of a sob made her want to escape back into the darkness of her own little hut. Simi had never spoken to her this sternly, and maybe anticipating Leona's instinct to run, she placed her hand on Leona's arm.

"I took the necklace back from him. I lied to you and I stole my offering back—all for this child."

Leona didn't like the way the shame felt on her skin, like an itchy heat rash. But she forced herself to stay still, to endure the words she knew were true.

"You ask if we can both be her mother? I have always been her mother. If you wish for my daughter to go to school in Nairobi or in America, I will find a way to let her go."

Leona didn't answer. She was exhausted. Her body felt weak and worn out. She took the last swig of tea and tried not to catch Simi's eye as she stood up. She didn't want Simi to see how upset she was.

But Simi reached over again and touched Leona's pant leg. "Look at her," she said. When Leona looked up, Simi's eyes were gentle. "Two mothers can be better than one." Leona sighed deeply and tried to shake away her sadness.

"Look at our daughter," Simi said in a voice more proud than Leona had ever heard her use.

Leona looked down at the blond head of her child. She was

surprised that when she opened her mouth and said, "She's fast asleep," her own voice was warm and hopeful.

Leona woke the next morning in her cold, fireless house to the sounds of children playing a game, and she heard Adia's laughter. Leona stretched, rubbed her eyes and looked around the house where Adia was born. Then she pulled on her jeans and left. She didn't know when she'd be back.

Simi was up and different from the shadow she'd been last night. Leona, too, felt a sense of calm she hadn't felt in weeks. She was relieved she'd made this decision. Simi had already been to the river for water and had a pot of *ugi* boiling over the fire.

"Eat," she commanded Leona, handing over a bowl of the hot porridge. "It's a long drive to Nairobi."

Leona didn't wait long to leave. She found Adia playing outside the manyatta and gave her a hug. The little girl's body hummed with energy, and Leona knew she was desperate to escape back to her game. She released her daughter and watched as the girl bounded out of sight. Simi walked to the car with Leona and the two women stood together for a long, silent moment.

"I'll come back on as many weekends as possible, and holidays. When she turns six, I'll take her with me and enroll her in the school there. The one where she'll meet other American children," Leona said. She needed to watch Simi agree to this again in the light of day. She needed to make absolutely certain the other woman understood. "So, when she turns six, she'll come live with me."

Simi nodded. "Leona," she said, "you know I wanted to finish school. I would never stop my daughter from being educated."

"And no talk of *emurata* for her—ever. I don't even want her attending them." This was most important.

"Even though I'll take her to Nairobi when she's still too

young, she'll be back and forth here a lot as she gets older, and I don't want her ever thinking she'll be cut. She cannot ever begin to want it, to think she needs it."

Leona had to trust that Simi would not put the notion in Adia's mind. The girl needed to know, all along, that she would never be joining her age-mates in that ceremony.

"Simi, you'll have to make it clear, not just to Adia, but to the elders."

Simi hadn't reconciled the image she'd had of an older girl, one who'd been to school, being cut. She had no idea how that would work, or if she could keep Adia from feeling the weight of that tradition. But her mouth opened, and she said what she needed to say.

"I swear to you, Leona, she will never think it's going to happen to her. She will never think she needs it."

Leona climbed in her car and closed the door. The window was still broken—permanently rolled down—so Leona stretched out her hand and clasped Simi's. The women looked at each other and Simi said, "Sometimes a child needs two mothers."

Leona didn't answer. She was ripe with more sadness, but also she felt a sense of relief. She was doing her best with what she had. Adia needed a family, and now she had one. Simi needed a child, and now she had one. Leona, well, she needed her work and her freedom, and her solitude. At least for a while longer.

As she shifted the car into Reverse, she leaned out the window one more time and waved at Simi, who still stood, her hand shading her eyes, the silver on her beaded necklaces glinting in the morning sun. It was a Kenyan sun; the kind she loved best—the brightest sun Leona had ever seen. Leona turned the car toward the road, and then she was gone.

THE BAOBAB IN SOLAI

John wasn't expecting anything other than the usual weekly update. "How's the old girl, then, Daniel? Still hanging on?"

But Daniel, the houseman's son, didn't assure John that his mother was okay, still forgetful, still confused, but okay. Instead, he sighed into the phone and clucked his tongue.

"Your mother, she is telling stories now, Mister John. My father is worried. Yesterday, your mother told him that an American *memsahib* came to the house. That she had a small girl with her. She said it was your daughter."

John lowered his coffee cup. His hand shook.

"An American was at the ranch, Daniel? In Solai?" His voice was rough in his mouth. "She had a girl with her?"

"Mister John, that is what your mother told my father when he went to cook her dinner last night. He told me that she was very firm. She was clear. *Tell John the American came. Tell John she brought his daughter.* But I am telling you, Mister John, this cannot be true. I think your mother's mind is almost finished.

We saw nothing. We saw nobody." The phone line crackled. Despite being less than two hundred miles away, the phone connection from Solai to Nairobi was tenuous at best.

"No worries." John managed to hide the catch in his throat. "I'll come to see Mum. I'll check that she's okay."

Almost four years ago, he was well on his way to being drunk when the American woman entered the bar. The place was a dark, wooden-walled room lit primarily by Christmas lights strung all around and looped across the ceiling over the bar. The woman seemed comfortable, like she'd been there before. She wasn't a tourist; John could see that from the way she greeted the barman in a familiar way and the quiet mix of Swahili she sprinkled on her English.

He'd liked the way her slim legs looked in her faded jeans and the way her straight brown hair was pulled back from her face in a tight ponytail, but how one piece, slightly shorter than the rest, kept falling back across her forehead. He liked the clear and steady gaze she gave the bartender when she ordered her beer and the way she didn't seem at all self-conscious of being in a bar, a woman alone in the middle of southwestern Kenya.

But mostly, he had to admit, he was drawn to something else about her—the air she had, the way she sat in this still pool of just herself and the way her face was so clear and plain and yet… He'd recognized something in her, a kinship of the broken. She was not whole, somehow. She resonated with echoes of spaces inside her that he knew too well. She wasn't beautiful, definitely not the kind of woman he normally found himself attracted to, but she was of his kind. He knew her without speaking a word.

When the blonde American he'd been flirting with came back from the restroom and stood behind him, sliding her sunburned arms around his shoulders and pressing her breasts against his back, he slid loose and turned to face her.

"Now you'll have to meet me again, next one's on you."

The way her face fell punished him a little. He didn't like hurting women's feelings, but it was better, he figured, to rip the Band-Aid off as quickly as possible. He stood up and walked down the bar to where the brunette sat. He slid onto the stool next to her.

"Nipe bia ya Tusker, Matthew."

She made no movement to acknowledge him, even when he surreptitiously edged his stool closer to hers. She made no half turn so that her knees would brush his, gave no sidelong glance as she tipped her glass of beer to her lips. He'd never met a woman so unaware of his presence. He raked the fingers of his right hand through his thick, blond hair. He kept it just slightly long, curling over his ears and at the nape of his neck. Women loved to toy with it—pulling gently at the curls over his temples and brushing it back from his eyes as if he were a child. They liked to feel as if they were helping him, taking care of the handsome and hapless man-child.

Not this one, though. She didn't move a muscle when he pulled his fingers through his hair or when he deliberately laid his hand down on the bar just an inch or two from the wet ring her glass left there. Instead, she flagged the barkeep and ordered another beer.

"It's on me, Matthew," John said loudly. "Get the lady a drink."

That's when she turned to face him. Her face was slender and she wore no makeup. Her eyes were clear and her gaze completely steady, no guile, no sense of nervousness or needing to flirt.

"Thanks," she said. "But you don't have to buy my drink."

"No worries. I saw you come in. You're not a tourist are

you? What... Peace Corps? Development worker? Christ—"
he paused and tipped his head back, squinted his eyes at her
"—don't tell me you're a bloody missionary!" He grinned as
he said it.

Women told him all the time that with his looks, he could
call a person a bastard and it would sound like a compliment
if he smiled when he said it. He registered the tiny movement
in her brow, the slight softening of her mouth. It worked.
She dipped her head and the errant tendril of hair fell from
behind her ear and slipped across her cheek. Before he could
think what he was doing, he lifted his hand to slide it back
into position for her.

"Are you English?" she asked.

"Not for generations. Born in Nakuru, actually. Kenyan all
the way back to my great-greats. They came here from England to farm and to fuck. The farms mostly went to shit, but
they drank enough that they stopped caring." He flashed the
smile again. "How about you? American?"

She nodded. "Pacific Northwest. Oregon."

"Well, we've established that I am home and that you are
not. So what's your story? What brings you to the armpit's
asshole here?"

"I live south of Narok. In Loita. I'm living in a manyatta
there. You know..." She paused, and he watched her finger-
ing the label on the bottle. Peeling and unpeeling the same
corner, over and over. "I'm an anthropologist." She smiled
and turned to face him straight on.

"So it's you, then? You're the *'muzungu Maasai'*? I've heard
about you."

He took a deep drink from his bottle and waved at Matthew
to bring a couple more. "I've been to your manyatta before.
Hired *moran* from there. Years ago, before I hired a permanent staff of guides."

She smiled. "I have to admit, it's amazing to speak English like this. It's been forever since I've had a conversation in a language I know fluently."

She blushed and he watched the light—so tiny—click on behind her eyes.

He could hold his alcohol easily. His father's son. But hours later, when he laid his hand over the woman's and pulled her from her bar stool, he planted his lips on hers as she stood and he felt dizzy. Maybe that's why he'd not thought of his usual protections. It didn't occur to him. In his dank hotel room, he'd not thought at all. They were both just bodies being swept away down some fast-moving river, clinging together, trying not to drown. They were just movements, not thoughts and not words. They didn't speak once, but he felt her underneath him, her dark interior shifting and rising, turning itself over and outward, desperately seeking whatever light he could shed for her. His body, too, betrayed the usual spaces he liked to keep between himself and his women. He fell into her when he was finished and found himself drifting off to sleep, unable to move his arm from around her shoulders and not minding how close she was—her hair across his face and one naked breast rising and falling, all night long, under his palm.

They hadn't even exchanged names, he and that woman in the bar. It was something of a game they played. Flirtation. He asked her, and she'd answered with a series of Maasai nicknames, words that described her but didn't name her. He laughed, but when he asked again—seriously this time—she said she would tell him the next time they met. If there was a next time. He had to leave early that morning to drive up to Solai. It was time he checked on his mother, made sure the water was still on in the house and that Samuel hadn't given up and moved away. The woman, though, left even earlier.

He woke to see her fully dressed with her ponytail tightly in place, trying to slip from his room.

He followed her outside in nothing but his jeans and his unlaced boots. The cool air made the hair on his arms prickle. He couldn't stand to see the woman leave. He wanted to kiss her again. He told her he'd track her down and for the first time with a woman, he meant it.

He told her that she'd be easy to find, even without a name she stuck out like snow in Tsavo.

Now, as he hung up his phone and replayed what Daniel had told him, he remembered the look her face had taken on when they stood there. It stilled, her eyes shuttered themselves and she'd looked up at him and said firmly that he shouldn't try to find her, that she wouldn't want to see him if he came to the manyatta. He nursed the feeling of having been stung all the way up to Solai.

So he didn't try to find her. The rejection he'd felt that morning was the one thing he'd always tried to avoid in relationships. He was the one who rejected, not the other way around. But then, months after their nameless tryst, he found himself back at the Chabani bar. Matthew slid a beer to him and laughed. "Did you hear about the *muzungu* lady with the baby in Loita? A pure white Maasai baby!"

And the blood in John's veins ran cold for an instant, and then he felt his heart slow—he breathed easily. Something bloomed inside of him like a flower.

He found her easily, just as he knew he would. It was curiosity that drove him there, and the easy excuse of needing to hire more *moran* to take a group of incoming tourists into the Nguruman forest. Part of him couldn't imagine it would really be her, that it would really be his child. A gaggle of kids led him across the dusty paddock, and then he ducked through a tiny door frame into a smoke-filled *inkajijik*. Her face surprised him. He tried to stay calm, and he accepted with a grateful smile the hot cup of chai a Maasai woman handed him.

But he was frightened. The woman on the rawhide platform barely resembled the woman from the bar. This woman's hair was lank and unwashed; it hung behind her ears like eucalyptus bark. Her skin was sallow and sunken. She looked unwell, he thought with some alarm, and he wondered what he should do. He felt responsible for her condition.

It was her eyes that frightened him the most. When he saw her first, they seemed blank, dead somehow. But as she registered his presence they shriveled and became as hard and brittle as glass. He stared into them, and asked the only thing he could think to ask, "Were you going to tell me?"

Because there was no question that the baby was his. His body was alive with the vibrations of instinct. His nerves and veins and bones all shifted toward the tiny, red-faced thing wrapped in a *kanga* and lodged firmly next to the woman in the bed.

"It's not your child." She sounded cold. Her voice wasn't just angry but also absolutely dismissive.

It was a tone he recognized. It was the way his father spoke to him, and he felt himself instinctively turning away, as he'd learned to do. He felt physical pain in pulling the pieces of himself back into place, but he forced himself away, back out into the sunlight again.

Before John was born, his mother was beautiful, lean and graceful with gentle eyes and a delicate smile. His father was tall and well built with a wide smile and blond curls like John's own. There were photos in the house of these younger versions of his parents. Only Samuel noticed them, and only to dutifully pick them up every week, dust them carefully and put them down again. The people in the photos, the beautiful, happy, young people, were completely disconnected from the people John knew as his parents. His parents weren't happy. He'd never known them happy. There were photos of John, too, a few at least. But only one of the brother he once had, and that photo was hidden away in a drawer. John found it once accidentally. He was tiny when Thomas died and never thought to wonder why the hidden photo wasn't displayed.

Often John wondered if being the child of desperately unhappy parents was worse than being the child of merely uncaring ones, or even of being the child of no parents at all. Being orphaned, John suspected, would be freeing. Orphans, he assumed, could breathe. Not him. His breath was squeezed out of him by the suffocating triangle he and his parents formed. He found space only away at school and in the expanse of his parents' ruined farm where his playmate was Daniel, the houseman's son, and he could spend the day pretending Daniel's small concrete house was his, the chickens and the goats and the laundry on the line, too. He could pretend Daniel's mother was his and that she loved him like a second son, a white son.

Times he'd spent at home were regimented. He always woke up early and joined his mother for a silent cup of tea in the kitchen, the floor cold under his bare feet and the sky outside a deep gray. When he heard his father stirring—padding heavily down the hall to the bathroom, clearing his throat and coughing while he pissed, long and heavy, and never quite in the bowl, John glanced at his mother. Every day at that time he saw the softness of her sleepy features gel into something hard, the shell covering the body of an animal too soft for the world.

"Bye, Mum," John always whispered, and then he was out the door, running barefoot over the still-cool dust, leaping over the shadows of anthills. He ran fast so he'd hear nothing but his breath growing more and more ragged as he ran, hard, toward the flickering lights and the smell of wood fire in Samuel's *shamba*, way, way back at the farthest edge of his parent's land.

When he was older, living in Nairobi and building his business, his father began to die. John dutifully returned to the farm to see him. Standing at his father's bedside late one afternoon, John watched the old man struggle for breath under sweaty sheets and a veil of skin gone gray and thin as a curtain over his bones. John couldn't think what to say. He merely listened to the wretched breathing, the sound of his father's struggle against death.

Samuel hired a couple of Kikuyu to dig the grave up on the hill under the enormous baobab, but John made a point of taking the shovel from one and jamming it into the earth himself, over and over again. He wanted to know how it felt to dig his father's grave. He dug until his shoulders burned and his eyes stung with sweat. The Kikuyu stepped back and watched. After some time they laid the other shovels down and hunkered on their heels, whispering to themselves and smoking. John finally stood straight, leaned the shovel against the trunk of the baobab and wiped his face on the tail of his shirt. The earth was pulled open, a wound that wouldn't heal, and next to the bleeding pile of red dirt was the tiny mound and miniature headstone that marked his brother's grave. John swallowed a desire to kneel down on the little grave and whisper a warning. If the dead could commune with one another, Thomas should prepare for the imminent arrival of his violent grave-mate.

At the funeral, his mother, Samuel's family and a few local farmers stood with the priest at the top of the hill behind the house. The day was overcast, and under the spreading branches of the baobab it was chilly and damp. Nobody cried. The grave was refilled, flowers placed on top and headstone installed. Now there were two grave markers—father and child.

When John was a boy, there were so many nights he lay awake in his bed and listened to the erratic thumping sounds of knuckles on flesh, punctuated by his mother's soft weeping. Once, when he was a teenager, she told him that she tried hard to make herself soft, to allow her body to absorb the blows, to relax enough that it would be quiet. Her great concern was only that the beatings not disturb John.

When John was thirteen, his maternal grandparents died, and his mother inherited a little stone house in the Nairobi suburb of Karen. At the time, she told him firmly that she would never sell it—she wanted him to have it when he was grown. The place stood empty for years, but John tried time and again to convince her to leave his father, move to the Karen house and let his father rot out here alone. The last time he tried to make her leave was during one of their early morning teas. It was a cold Christmas and the night before his father had flung the decorated tree into a wall, sending delicate antique ornaments smashing onto the floor.

"Please, Mum," he said, gripping her hands over the kitchen table. Neither he nor his mother had slept, and both were bleary and nervous from lack of rest.

His mother jerked her hands from his. There was anguish in her eyes he'd never seen. She looked terrified, as if, this time, he were the one beating her.

"I tried to get away once, John. It killed your brother. I'll never leave that baby again, and he can't come with us, can he?"

Her voice was ripe with secrets, and John was afraid to ask her what she meant. She stopped talking, poured more tea and they never again discussed the idea of her leaving.

After John finished school, he moved to Nairobi and started

his photo-safari business, which earned him good money. He let a woman or two stay around for a while. There were two in particular he lingered over. Both had wanted to marry him; they dropped hints and introduced him to their parents and joked to their friends—with him in earshot—that he better not get used to the milk if he wasn't planning to buy the damn cow. It wasn't marriage that frightened him away from the women, ultimately. It was the expectation of children. His own mother was all he knew of motherhood, and he couldn't, he wouldn't turn a girl he loved into that. He considered it kinder to break their hearts than their spirits.

And now. Now he'd gone and had a kid, anyway. And the image of the broken woman lying in the dark *inkajijik* with her glass-hard eyes and glass-hard voice haunted him. Had he poisoned her with the presence of his genes in her body? He didn't consider looking for her after that day. He tried to put the fearful new-mother face and his own craving to see his baby out of his mind. He purposely avoided the area anywhere near that manyatta. Instead, he hired *moran* from much farther away. He thought of the baby and the woman less and less over the years. How long had it been, three years? He did the math in his head, Christ, how time had flown. The girl would be three. Not a baby, but a walking, talking person. He wondered what her name was, if she looked at all like him.

Daniel's phone call left John anxious and unable to sleep, so long before dawn the next day, he loaded his bag into the cab of his truck and left Nairobi. He stopped for lunch in Narok, gassed up the truck at the BP station on the main road and then drove to the Chabani. He needed a beer. He told himself he needed a beer, needed food, needed to stretch his legs. But somewhere inside him a tuning fork was resonating, softly but clearly. He didn't want to admit he'd stopped here in the hope he'd catch a glimpse of a blonde-haired girl, a child with his face, maybe, one that might catch his eye and know—instinctually—just who he was.

"*Imekuwa ni muda mrefu,* Mister John," Matthew, the bartender, greeted John as he took a seat at the bar.

"It has been a long time, my friend," John answered. "Too long."

John wondered if Matthew knew why he was here, if he'd seen his daughter. He didn't have to wait long. Matthew popped the cap on a Tusker, and placed it on the bar.

"Your girl, my friend, she is looking like you."

John's heart beat fast. He didn't know if he was ready to see her, to face the nameless woman. But his blood streamed faster in his veins, and his heartbeat was so quick it was almost painful.

"Matthew, are they still here? In Narok?"

"No, Mister John. They were here for so long. Maybe two, maybe three weeks. Every day they would come here. They would sit just there." Here, he indicated a booth tucked into a dark back corner.

"*Memsahib* would drink tea all day long, and the child would play. The *memsahib* was looking for you. But now—" Matthew paused and popped open another beer "—they are gone. I haven't seen them for days."

"Well," John said, "I'm headed up to Solai to speak with my mother. Hope she'll tell me where they've gone."

The stars were blooming in the sky when John finally saw the lights of his mother's house on the horizon. He felt himself inadvertently slowing down, barely pushing the wheels of the truck through the ruts and pits in the road. For the last few years, every time he came here, there was a part of him that feared finding his mother's body stiff and cold on the floor of her house. He knew, theoretically, that Samuel and Daniel checked in on her faithfully, kept her fed and the house clean.

He sent money to them from Nairobi every month to cover the expenses and to pay them for their time, but in his heart he couldn't believe they'd stay.

The truck shuddered to a stop outside the house, and he pulled the key out of the ignition, then leaned back and closed his eyes. He used to regret his childhood. He used to wish he could pretend it all away and grow up normal in a family that smiled at one another, talked about things, a family that wasn't marred by absence.

He thought of his family like a photograph—all of them in a row, in outdated clothes with outdated haircuts and a big black scribbled-on space where Thomas would have been. A permanent deletion whose ink stained all of them, long beyond the quick moment that marked the moment the family was ruined.

He opened his eyes and sighed, then pulled himself out of the truck and grabbed his duffel. The front door was open, and light spilled out through the screen. Moths and beetles buzzed and banged themselves against the door. He waved them away as he slid through the door, knowing most of them would find a way inside regardless. The edges of the screen were pulling out of the frame, and there was a large hole near the bottom. He sighed. Every time he came here, there was something to fix.

"Mum?" he called.

He was surprised not to see her in the hall, waiting, or asleep in the faded flowered chair in the living room. God, was this the time he'd find her body? His breath shortened, and he felt a chill climb through his veins.

"Mum?" His voice was shrill, and he took a breath. "Mum!"

She was nowhere. Her bed was made, the bathroom was dark and empty, the kitchen light was on, but there was no sign she'd been there, either.

John banged out the screen door again, paying no attention to the large rhino beetle that flew past his ear and into the house.

"Mum!" he called again.

Maybe she'd gone to see Samuel. It was not unusual for her to walk back across the field, over the hill and to the houseman's little compound. They'd all told her not to go at night, but they all knew her mind was failing, and whether or not she remembered the warnings was anybody's guess.

"Dammit," he muttered, opening the door of the truck again. He'd drive there.

His headlights bore down on the dusty ground, illuminating the sparse grasses and wizened acacia trees. Now and again tall crusts of chewed earth rose like towers—the anthills he used to leap on and crush underfoot, trying to destroy them before the ants could swarm his legs and bite.

Just ahead of him now was the hill. The family burial ground with the two headstones—one small and one large. The truck bounced over a rut and the light of his headlights leaped up for an instant and shone on a tiny, ghostly figure— his mother, her white puff of hair and pale housedress. She was so small, hunched there on the stone bench under the massive baobab—she was just bones, really, bones and skin under her long flowered dress. When did she get so old?

He stopped the truck but left the engine running and the lights on. He didn't want to spend the time retrieving his gun, and the lights would help keep hyenas and snakes at bay.

"Mum, you gave me a scare!" He walked up behind her and she turned to look at him, her face a tiny, white moon.

"I killed you both," she said.

John knew his mother was suffering from Alzheimer's or senility or some such thing that had slowly been erasing her mind. It was more than the incessant forgetfulness or the conversations she had with nobody but herself. Her mind was deteriorating; he had to face the fact that she was no longer able to care for herself enough to get by with only daily visits from Samuel. He could hardly bear to watch her speak this nonsense and act in ways that were both confusing to him and pathetic.

"You didn't kill anyone, Mum. You're having a spell."

"Do you remember your brother? No, he was too young."

"Don't remember, really. And there aren't any photos to remind me."

"I couldn't bear to look at his face in a photo. I only kept one, but I hid it."

John was horrified then that his mother began to cry. Her face folded in upon itself, and tears slid down her cheeks. Had he ever seen her cry? Even when his father hit her, even on the most miserable days, she was a stone.

"I never told you. I never told anyone. The only one who knew was your father. That's why he punished me. I deserved it."

"Jesus, Mum, what are you saying?"

"You are a father now. You know that, right?"

Her brain seemed clear. Her eyes, even through her tears, were wide-open and lacked the clouds that usually marked her moments of confusion.

"Don't do what I did. I tried to run away and it killed Thomas. I still feel the bump..."

Her breath heaved, and a cry rose like a night bird, a scream so deep inside her that he could almost see it pulling itself up through her body. She clenched her fingers into fists and pounded them on her knees.

"Mum, shh! It's okay..."

He put his arm around her shoulders. He hadn't touched her in so long, and her skin felt like paper, her bones like twigs.

Her face was tipped up toward the stars, which, unhindered by any ambient light, spread out endlessly.

She paused in her cry for a breath, and then she shook her head and said calmly—he would always remember how calmly she spoke the secret out loud. It was a voice he'd never heard her use, strong and clean and honed to a sharp edge by the force she used to get it out.

"I have to tell you before I die. You have to know. I killed Thomas when I tried to run away. He came too close to the tire… I didn't see him. It was the farm truck, so high up, I couldn't see…" She trailed off, her voice spent and the tears rising again.

John's body felt frozen. His skin was cold and he shivered. His brother's death was always a shrouded thing, mysterious and frightening, and never spoken of. He hadn't ever wanted to know the details. He still didn't. How could she have lived with this?

He didn't say anything. His own heart throbbed in his chest.

"Now you're a father and I've killed you, too."

Startled, he glanced at her face. Tiny clouds were forming behind her eyes. She was disappearing again. This time, he felt relieved for her. Maybe in these moments she could forget or she could conjure another life in her head, one that wasn't so painful.

"The American came to give you your daughter. She tried to find you. She came all the way here with the girl."

"Yes, Mum, and I've come now, too. I want them to find me. You can tell me where they are, and I'll go there. Or maybe you told them to come back here? That you were calling me to come and meet them?" His voice was hopeful—he felt a flicker in his chest, a star fallen to infuse him with light.

"No, you see, that's what I mean. I killed you, as well. I told her you were dead. That she could never find you."

The star turned to ice in his neck. He glanced at her, not wanting to believe what he heard. Had she really told the woman he was dead? He couldn't bear to think he'd missed out on knowing his daughter forever just because of the lie his mother told. Dammit! He wanted to accuse her, to shout at her, to tell her that she had no right.

"How did you leave it with her? Did she say anything about where they might go?" He knew the anger in his voice, the urgency, might scare his mother into silence, but it colored his words, anyway. He'd never felt so desperately in need of an answer.

"To America," Ruthie whispered. She was sure this was what Leona said. She was sure she was right this time.

"Right, the northwest. She told me. Did she say where exactly, by chance?"

But when John looked over at his mother again, she was gone. Her body was still there, his frail mother in her too-loose dress, but her eyes were clouded over completely. She'd disappeared back into herself. He was alone.

He had made mistakes in his life. He knew that. He'd treated women badly, he'd not always been a good son and for most of his childhood he'd been filled with churning lava of hatred for his father and jealousy toward his dead brother. But he couldn't remember feeling worse during any of those times than he did now. This was a brutal itch of regret that strangled his insides and made him jump up from the stone bench and hurtle himself at the wall of baobab bark. Before he could think, he'd slammed his right fist into the tree trunk. The pain soothed somehow, and so he did it again and again. Finally he stepped back and clasped his right hand in his left. The bones throbbed and the tattered skin was slick with blood. He was too tired to care.

He sat on the bench until the horizon showed a thread of

gray that gradually seeped into the night, turning the sky from darkness into dawn. A mourning dove cried from the branches of the baobab above him. A breeze shuffled the leaves above their heads. His mother still sat beside him, leaning her body into his, her head on his shoulder. She'd fallen asleep at some point in the night, and he was conscious that her nightgown was damp with dew. He'd need to get her home, warm and into dry clothes.

He realized he couldn't leave her here alone any longer. Not even with Sam and Daniel looking after her. She needed him now. He thought of his house in Karen and how she could have a little bedroom there and sit in the garden and, finally, relax in a place that was far enough from the ugly reminders of her marriage so that she could forget.

John stood up and lifted her into his arms. With every movement, his hand pulsed with pain. He ignored it. How light she was. Like a child. The truck's headlights had dimmed now, the battery dead. He couldn't drive her back to the house. He'd have to carry her. He paused for a second, shifted her in his arms and began walking. Making his way slowly, carefully, down the hill to home.

PART II

KHAMSA

Where Liberia hid in the shadows under the curve of western Africa's lower edge, Morocco was out in the light, pushing forward like a face upturned toward the sky. The boulevards were wide and flat, and the whole place felt bright and airy, clean. Jane didn't miss the moist breath of Liberia's jungles, which crowded too close to the city. She didn't miss the tangled bushes that, even in the city, could hide snakes and insects. Monrovia was hidden things that lay in wait and whispers from unseen sources. Rabat was the five-times-a-day call from the mosques whose distinctive square minarets dotted the skyline and the clear-as-glass skies that made the walls in the old city shine pink and gold.

When their plane landed in Rabat, the embassy expediter met them at the airport. He held a sign with Paul's name on it. Jane's shirt was damp with water Grace had spilled just before landing, and her eyes felt sandy from lack of sleep. Grace was a good flier. Even though she was only ten, she'd been on so many planes she couldn't count them. When she was one, Paul was assigned to a three-year stint at the embassy in Mexico City. After that, it was Lima, Peru, then Kathmandu, Nepal, where they'd stayed for four years. Grace loved the takeoffs and landings, but this had been a long trip, and by the time they taxied across the runway to the airport, she was tired and sullen. In the last twenty-four hours, they'd flown from Washington, DC, to Paris and Paris to Rabat, with nearly ten hours spent wandering Charles de Gaulle Airport in between.

"Salaam a lekum!" Paul said loudly and slipped in front of Jane to grasp the expediter's hand and shake it vigorously.

"Mehreba!" the man answered. "I'm Tarik."

Jane smiled at Tarik and nudged Grace to say hello. "You can shake his hand, Grace," Jane murmured. Grace dutifully reached out her hand and greeted the man under her breath. Jane noticed her daughter's grimace, slight as it was. She wondered if the wet spot on her chest was obvious. She felt dirty, and the bright light of midday made her more conscious of the fetid, sweaty airplane smells that rose from her skin and clothes. Tarik drove them from the airport to the house the embassy assigned them. The boulevards around the old city were wide and smooth. Jane sat behind Paul next to Grace, who leaned her head against the window and appeared to fall asleep. Jane mindlessly stroked her daughter's arm and watched the city slide by outside the window.

This was their first posting back in Africa, and Jane couldn't help but dredge up memories of the last time they were posted together on this continent. In Monrovia, the trees and bushes all blended together in a smear of green. Jane was never curious about the flora there. But Morocco seemed more like Kenya, a place she remembered with mixed feelings but entirely without the anxiety Liberia pricked in her. Here, she could pick out familiar plants—thick stands of lavender lining a sidewalk, purple clematis climbing a streetlight and enormous carob trees that threw their deep shadows over the little tables of an outdoor café where men sat drinking from tiny cups. The car rolled to a stop at a red light, and Jane watched as a crowd of kids in matching school uniforms crossed the street in front of them. One little girl, no older than Grace, glanced in their direction and smiled. Jane thought of the girl's parents, somewhere in the city, who kissed their daughter goodbye this morning and sent her off to school—trusting the world to bring her back safely that afternoon. The idea of Grace being alone in the world like that made Jane's heart beat faster, and a wave of heat passed over her.

The house was large and airy, the outside painted the color of dried grass and surrounded by a large dusty garden. Jane envisioned lavender there, a carob tree that would shade their own patio table. Paul pulled their suitcases from the trunk, while Jane and Grace slid out of the car, dragging their purses and carry-on baggage behind them. Tarik fished through his pockets for the house keys and, when he found them, smiled and presented them to Paul. The door was thick wood, carved into intricate patterns. It was beautiful. As Paul slipped the key into the lock, Jane noticed a shiny piece of etched metal just above the door frame. It was the shape of a hand with two fingers stretched to each side, and three fingers in the middle pointing down. The etchings on the hand were detailed and flowery, abstract, but in the middle of the palm was something Jane recognized—the outline of an eye, wide-open with a tiny dot of black pupil in the center.

Jane turned to Tarik and gestured up to the metal hand. "What's that?" she asked.

"It's Khamsa...the hand of Fatima." He smiled sheepishly, as if he were embarrassed to explain the meaning to her.

"Some people, like the old people, believe it helps make you safe from djinn, the witches."

Jane thought of Liberia and the juju that killed the president and the evil that lurked in the mask she hated. "What do the djinn do?" she asked.

"They cause madness," Tarik answered simply, and then grasped the handle of a suitcase and hoisted it inside. Jane felt the sensation of ice sliding down the back of her neck. She turned to watch Grace standing in the driveway, rummaging through her backpack. As Grace grew older, Jane became more watchful of the signs that her daughter might share Lance's disease. The notion terrified her.

Turning back to the door, she reached up and ran her finger over the etchings of the Khamsa. They were worn and smooth. It must be old. Who put it there, and why? She wondered if the hand was supposed to be hung and forgotten, as if its protection would swirl in the door frame and cover everyone passing under it, or if it was something like rosary beads or prayer wheels that had to be touched in order to work. Jane thought she shouldn't risk making the wrong decision, and so she reached out and placed her palm on the metal shape. She closed her eyes and imagined her daughter. "Be safe," she whispered, "be safe."

It was her job to control the world around Grace, her job to keep Grace sheltered from bad things and as far from the possibility of tragedy and darkness as she could. Maybe her own father couldn't have helped Lance, but maybe he didn't try hard enough. For an instant, Jane wondered if her cloud of anxiety was a gift—the wild animal on her back, claws drawn, a spirit animal, given to her for a reason. Her job was to embrace it, to pull all the bad things inside herself, like a sponge, and thereby keep them from Grace.

"I can take it down for you," Tarik said as he passed her again on his way back to the car. "It's just an old superstition."

"No," Jane said, turning to look Tarik in the eyes. She needed all the assistance she could get. She spoke slowly, clearly. It was important that he heard her. "No. I want it to stay."

Fourteen years into their marriage, there were times Jane wanted to bite Paul, times she couldn't stand the sight of him. She wondered if other wives felt this way.

And even though she could still easily remember that first moment she fell in love with him—the feeling of it, the intense, visceral way her heart filled up when she pulled back and looked into his eyes—she couldn't conjure that anymore.

Sometimes her anger at him took her by surprise. She didn't know where it came from, or where inside her the angry spring's source hid. She had a happy life, privileged. After Muthega, she hadn't wanted to track elephants anymore, so she pushed that dream away and, instead, followed her dream of motherhood, and she took hold of the end of Paul's dream, too. They'd travel the world, he'd rise through the ranks and, one day, be an ambassador. She could keep herself occupied with the children they would have or the jobs at each embassy specifically set aside for "dependent spouses." The title was something of a joke; it was all wives. Dependent wives. Paul never pressured her to take one of the jobs, which Jane was grateful for. She had a masters in wildlife biology. One she used for less than a year, but still, she didn't want to work if she wasn't working in her field. There were days, though, after Grace got older and started school, that Jane felt she was wading through deep water or like a snake had wound its way around her neck and was slowly suffocating her.

Jane got pregnant only the one time. They tried for more babies, but none came. Jane didn't mind as much as she thought she might. She liked having only one child. She loved that the child was a girl. It didn't bother Jane when she and Paul and Grace arrived in some new, strange nation and woke up in a house they'd never seen before, and then had to make their way in a new city, meet new people. Since Grace was born, Jane always had her as a partner in adventure. When Grace was a baby, Jane sought out the English-language playgroups and made friends with the other women and their babies. When Grace started school, it was easy to meet the other international moms at events, through the parent-teacher association, on the soccer field, at scouts. Jane found she liked the life they'd created. The one Paul gave them. Somewhere along the line there was a shift. Jane thought about it a lot, but she couldn't pinpoint where it began. Slowly, though, her gaze turned from Paul to Grace. Grace became the one she orbited, and Paul took a secondary role.

As Grace got older, she spent nights at slumber parties or afternoons playing at her friends' houses. Jane used that time to catch up on reading, go for lunch with friends or dinners out with Paul and other embassy couples. Grace always came back, and she always needed Jane. Grace wanted to be with Jane more than she did with her own friends. The early afternoons after the slumber parties were Jane's favorite times. She would pick Grace up and help her unpack her overnight bag, and then they would curl up on the couch with cocoa and Grace would giggle and tell Jane the things they'd eaten at the party, how late they'd stayed up and which girls fell asleep first. Sometimes she'd drift off and Jane would feel Grace's weight on her legs. Grace relaxed into sleep so deeply that Jane could shift her over and not wake her up. Just like when she was an infant and, after a night nursing session, Jane could carry her back to the crib, lean over and lie her down on her back and watch her eyelids, fluttery and as pink as the inside of a shell.

★ ★ ★

It was a Sunday evening when Paul and Jane told Grace they were moving again. It was time. They'd been in Rabat for three years already, and Paul's tour here was finished. Grace had spent the day swimming with a friend at the club, and Paul and Jane picked her up and drove out to their favorite café, one with outdoor tables on a patio that overlooked the Boure-greg River. It was a quiet evening, still warm, and the breeze that blew off the water smelled like the fish the men hauled off their brightly striped boats in nets the color of the sand.

"Grace," Jane said, just after the waiter set a sweating, icy glass of Coke in front of her daughter. "We're moving to Nairobi, where your dad and I met!" Jane's tone was happy because she was happy. Their family moved—that's what they did, what they'd always done. This was their life. Jane and Grace would, as always, set up the house, hire a cook, a houseman, maybe a gardener. Jane would go with Grace to school the first day, meet her teacher, scope out the other moms. Jane and Grace were a team, still connected, if not literally by blood and flesh anymore, then by mutual devotion and shared interests. Jane had fond memories of Nairobi. The wide streets, the rows of jacaranda trees along the sidewalks and the cool, crisp air. That would be nice to return to. She thought about what it would be like to see the Rift again, to see if the rivers were full. She wasn't sure she wanted to see Narok again or the places she and Muthega had explored in that rattling Land Rover, but she pictured the silhouettes of elephants against the red evening sky, and suddenly she felt a surge of real joy.

So when Grace looked back at Jane and her eyes said instantly that she was angry, Jane was surprised.

"Hey, hon, you knew we would eventually—we always do," Paul said, and then, "Get this, your old man is going to be second in command! Whaddaya think of that?" Jane smiled at him vacantly, and a slip of a thought fluttered through her mind: Grace was thirteen now; she was growing up, turning away. Jane still saw her as the main character in their family play, but maybe Grace didn't see Jane—or herself—that way anymore.

Jane glanced back at Grace. "We're women of the world, Gracie! Right?" But a switch flipped in her daughter's face and she sat there for the rest of the meal, poking at her pizza, her mouth drawn, her eyes empty. That night Jane ducked into Grace's room to kiss her daughter good-night. She tried again to cajole Grace into seeing the excitement that she saw, that Grace had always seen before. But Grace began to cry. "I don't want to go somewhere new. I want to stay in one place. I want to stop. Don't you understand? I want to stop. I want a real home for once."

After that, Grace stayed silent, sullen. The days they all spent packing her Rabat bedroom were tear-filled and angry. As annoyed and hurt as Jane was by her daughter's shift in behavior, she was also terrified. She racked her memory to compare Grace's actions to her brother's at this age. He wasn't diagnosed at thirteen, but maybe there were signs? Maybe Grace was showing those signs and Jane just had to recognize them.

Jane was a nuisance to her daughter for the first time, and Jane's bewilderment and anxiety made her lash out at Paul in misplaced retaliation. The three of them spun like eddies in a pond, separate, divided, dragged down.

On Grace's first day of school in Nairobi, Jane woke up early, edged the new houseman aside and made Grace's favorite breakfast: French toast and potatoes pan-fried in butter. When Grace appeared, she was wearing the outfit they had assembled together the night before: a khaki knee-length skirt and a floral blouse opened over her favorite lavender T-shirt.

"You look darling!" Jane told Grace. The truth was, though, that Grace looked like a different girl. Her eyes were dull, her hair seemed limp, even though the night before Jane had washed and dried it, pulling it straight, long and shiny with a big, round brush.

"Eat up, baby!" Jane said in a voice as happy as she could make it, because Grace's sadness shocked her. Jane wanted to push her own optimism into her daughter, make Grace's eyes light up again.

Grace cried herself to sleep some nights. She never let Jane see it. She pretended to be asleep if Jane poked her head into the bedroom, and she never cried when Jane was with her in the car, or even at dinner when Paul and Jane chatted about their days. They both tried to draw Grace into their conversation, but Grace only nodded quietly, barely speaking. Jane told Paul to let it go, that she'd come around. Jane thought she would. It was unlike Grace to hold a grudge, to be so withdrawn.

It was curious, too, that Grace's emotional absence changed the dynamic between the three of them. Without her as the central force for each parent to focus on, Jane and Paul were thrown back together in a strange way. For the first time in years they mostly talked to each other at meals. After dinner, when Jane and Grace would have worked on homework or watched a DVD together, Grace disappeared into her room. She didn't want help; she didn't want to snuggle with her mother on the couch and watch a movie. Instead, Jane and Paul circled each other warily in the evenings, trying to decide how to be alone with one another. After a while, they began talking to each other more, pouring glasses of wine and sharing the space more comfortably. It was nice, Jane thought one evening, to have this back. She hadn't missed it at all when it floated away from their marriage, when a distance neither of them understood or knew how to clip back had blossomed between them. Grace did it for them. When she ducked out of her place at the center, the two ends grew closer.

It didn't mean Jane didn't worry. She did. Constantly. She researched early symptoms of schizophrenia and kept Grace as close as she possibly could. She met with Grace's teacher to share her concerns, considered going to the school nurse. She didn't do that, though, because one day when she picked Grace up from school Grace had a smile on her face. She didn't want to talk much, and she was still sullen every night at dinner, but when Jane went out to the balcony after dinner to watch the sky darken, Grace came out and sat with her. It didn't last long. Something she said upset Grace, who then flounced back to her room. But the nugget of information Grace gave her that night made Jane want to shout with relief. A friend. Grace had finally made a friend at school.

RIPTIDE

The unraveling started with an early-morning phone call. It was Thursday, a school day, and Adia was awake. She never slept in. Her life in the manyatta had trained her from birth to wake by dawn, and even though she and her mother lived in Nairobi now, that habit didn't change. The house was perfectly still. Adia could tell it was almost dawn because the stars were fewer; most had already flicked themselves back to wherever they lived when the sun came up. Adia always woke up early. Her mother didn't, though, and Adia knew to creep around the house silently so as not to wake her. This morning, just as Adia stepped up from her bed, the phone rang. Adia startled. Their phone never rang much: sometimes Leona's colleagues called, but their manyatta family, the ones Adia would love to talk on the phone with during the weeks she was here in Nairobi, didn't use phones. This early in the morning, the sound was both unexpected and harsh. Adia tiptoed out of her room and up the hallway toward her mother's bedroom, and by the time she reached the door, the phone was clatter-ing to the floor. Her mother's voice through the door was harsh and annoyed.

"Hello? Hello? Who is this?"

Adia couldn't imagine who would call this early, and she leaned close to her mother's door to listen. There was a long pause. Adia wondered if her mother had fallen back asleep.

"What? Here? Mother...no."

Adia startled again. Her mother was calling someone else "mother." This was a revelation. At thirteen, Adia knew, of course, that everybody had a theoretical mother and father, but she'd never, not once, heard her mom talking about family. Adia assumed that she and her mother had that in common—without a father of her own, it wasn't a stretch to imagine her mother with no parents at all.

Through the closed door, Adia heard the phone slam back into the cradle and her mother whisper-shout, "Shit!"

Then the creaking of the bedsprings sent Adia racing, as quietly as she could, back to her own bed. She didn't want her mother to know she'd been listening.

Usually, Adia dressed herself for school and had breakfast alone. Gakaki, the houseman, always set a cup of hot tea, a boiled egg and a piece of buttered toast in front of her, and she'd eat while he sat on his haunches on the stoop outside the kitchen door slurping his own tea and smoking a cigarette.

This morning was different. Adia slid on a pair of jeans, which, she noticed, were feeling tight in the butt and ended an inch or so above her ankles. Adia didn't care about how her clothes looked, but she hated the feeling of being con-strained. Too-tight jeans and T-shirts that tugged awkwardly made her feel conscious of herself, made her feel like she was a dog on a leash. Today would be more uncomfortable than usual. She pulled on her favorite hat—leather with a wide brim that her mother had worn for years and then passed on to her. Her boots were by the front door; she would put those on at the last possible second before running out of the house to catch the bus. She hated shoes and wore them only because her school didn't allow bare feet.

When Adia walked into the kitchen, her mother was already at the table. She held a large teacup and breathed the steam into her open mouth slowly, evenly. She didn't acknowledge Adia. Gakaki sidled in quietly; he knew, too, that Adia's mother would be grumpy this early and that he should do what he could to be unobtrusive. He gently set Adia's plate on the table and then her tea, and then he stuck his tongue out at her and crossed his eyes, and Adia had to push her palm over her mouth, hard, to keep from giggling.

"We'll be having a visitor next week."

Adia glanced at her mother, who now had her eyes open and was sipping her tea through pursed lips. She winced a little when the hot liquid hit her tongue. Gakaki always boiled the tea just a little too long.

"Your grandmother—my mother. She wants to get to know you."

Adia paused with her fork halfway between her plate and her mouth. There were so many things she wanted to talk about, to ask her mother. But through the sudden chaos in her brain, only one question slipped out.

"Wait, what?"

Even though she heard her mother address the phone caller as "mother," she still couldn't quite believe she'd heard correctly. "I have a grandmother?" The thought that there was family in America never occurred to her. Her curiosity had only one focus—her father. This new information was a revelation.

At school that day Adia was distracted. She wondered how

long her grandmother had known about her. From birth? If it was that long, why hadn't she come sooner? The idea of a family—people connected to her outside of the tiny, cool orbit she and her mother made—excited Adia. She quivered with the possibilities.

The school cafeteria was nothing but a small canteen that sold sodas and chips, attached to a large, open-sided *rondaval* filled with picnic tables and benches. Most of the other kids at her school had parents who were diplomats, and their lunch boxes were full of imported cheeses, peanut butter and cookies and chips not available to people without embassy commissary privileges. Adia unwrapped her sandwich without thinking. Usually she was careful about her lunch and how she ate. She never knew what might end up in her lunch bag. Once Gakaki packed her a little plastic container of scrambled eggs. That day, she hunched low over it, because she didn't want the other kids to see. It was such a weird thing to have for lunch. He'd also forgotten to pack a fork, but she was so hungry she picked the pieces up with her fingers. She propped a book up on the table and pretended to read, but the book somehow tipped off her desk and when she reached out to grab it, her eggs spilled out of the container and onto the table. The girl sitting next to her shouted, "Gah! That's what was smelly! Adia's eating eggs!"

The other kids laughed and made retching noises, and one of the teachers on lunch duty peered over the top of his glasses and told her to make sure she cleaned it all up. Adia spent the next five minutes wiping egg into her palm, making sure she retrieved every bit. The rest of the afternoon her stomach grumbled. After that day, she tried to skip lunch entirely, ignoring her hunger pangs and trying to get by on just an orange or banana. She ate bigger breakfasts and drank a lot of water to keep herself full.

Today's lunch was a chapati, leftover from dinner the night before, rolled around a hunk of cheese. The chapati was torn and the cheese poked out the end a little. Adia sized it up and weighed her chances of eating without attracting notice. At least it didn't smell. Maybe nobody would notice. She was hungry.

"Is that a penis?" a boy nearby whispered. The kids who heard erupted into laughter.

"Adia's eating a penis!"

This time, the teacher didn't look up at all. Adia shoved the mess back into her lunch bag and opened her book. She didn't read it, though. She couldn't concentrate on the words at all. Instead, she tried to will the red flush from her cheeks by thinking about her grandmother. Her grandmother wanted to meet her. Her grandmother had wanted to meet her since she was a baby; her mother told her that this morning. Her grandmother would love her.

Adia didn't question the basic facts of her life. She didn't wonder why she and her mother lived in Nairobi or why she went to the international school with the sons and daughters of diplomats and development workers rather than a local school with kids more like the ones at home in the manyatta. She never wondered at the notion that her father was long dead, or if there were surviving family members of his that she could meet. She accepted those things without question. She accepted that she lived here with her American mother, but that she also had a Maasai mother in Loita. She accepted the things her mother told her about her father—he was a descendent of colonial Kenya, a "Kenya Cowboy"; he'd grown up in Maasailand like her. And he died when Adia was small.

She sometimes wondered if not having a father was the thing that made her different from the kids at her school. They were not like her. They came and went as their parents transferred into and out of Nairobi like migratory birds. She was a chicken that never went anywhere. Adia had plodded through the school since kindergarten—she was one of the few students who'd been there that long—but it didn't matter. She still never knew any of her classmates for more than a year or two before they disappeared forever. She was the silent, invisible ghost always left behind.

After a while she realized that her clothes and her food and her lifestyle made her too different for them to be friends with her, anyway. The other kids dressed in clothes brought from Europe or America. They talked about movies and TV shows they watched back home. They had mothers who brought cake or cupcakes to class for birthdays. They referred longingly to places far away from here, places they called home. Adia didn't have any of those things. Her clothes were from the market or made by tailors from cloth her mother bought on Biashara Street. Her mother never came for birthdays or awards ceremonies or even for parent-teacher conferences.

Leona let Adia skip school the day her grandmother arrived. They drove together to the airport. Waiting in the meeting area, Adia watched the people come through the door from customs. There were so many. She had never seen a photo of her grandmother, so she had no idea who to look for. Instead, she alternated watching her mother's face and watching the crowds of people dragging suitcases behind them. Her mother's face was calm until, suddenly, it wasn't. Adia watched her mother's mouth curve into a forced smile and saw the natural light cloud in her mother's eyes. She was here! When Adia turned to see who her mother was looking at, she was stunned. This was not the person she imagined. The tall woman striding toward them with her own stiff smile pasted on her own stiff face was exactly the opposite of who Adia imagined was her mother's mother.

Her grandmother Joan arrived in a flurry of suitcases and a flapping safari jacket covered in pockets. She was tall and thin with perfectly white hair that started at her chin on one side and went all the way around to the other side without getting higher or lower. The ends were all exactly the same length. Adia wondered if she used a ruler when she cut it.

"Hello, dear!" Joan said as she stuck her face forward to give Leona a kiss. Adia noticed that the kiss never actually met Leona's cheek.

"Hi, Mom," Leona answered. And then she pulled Adia by the arm in between herself and Joan. Adia felt like a shield.

"Mom, this is Adia," Leona said.

"Well, there she is! Aren't you a tomboy!" Joan said. Adia couldn't tell if being a tomboy was good or bad in her grandmother's eyes. Joan leaned over to kiss Adia's cheek and, once again, Adia noticed that the kiss never made contact.

Her grandmother smelled like flowers and the pockets of her jacket were filled with hard candies and tissues. She had hands so pale that Adia could see bones and blue veins through them, and one of her fingers had a sparkly ring the size of a Band-Aid on it.

The best thing about her grandmother's coming was that the morning after she arrived, they all left for Mombasa. They didn't take the train, like Adia and her mother did when they went. Adia was relieved. The train was slow and hot, and mosquitoes billowed through the windows and feasted on them all night long. Adia didn't like the close feeling of breathing in the little four-person compartment they always had to share with two strangers.

Her grandmother bought tickets for them to fly to Mombasa on a little plane, and the lurch in Adia's belly when they sped down the runway and up, up, up into the air was exhilaration and fear and intense joy and it tickled her inside all over.

But even better was the hotel. Usually Adia and her mother stayed in a little thatched hut near the water. The huts were plain but had a place to cook and take a shower and electricity and running water. Adia loved them because it felt like playing house and she could race between the ocean and the little porch all day.

The hotel Joan booked for the three of them was more beautiful than any place Adia had ever seen. The hallways were large and open, filled with enormous chairs covered in cushions, and everywhere were potted palm trees and ceiling fans that made the palm leaves flutter. The hotel employees all wore bright white uniforms and perfectly white sneakers and moved quickly but so silently Adia imagined they were not really touching the glassy polished floor at all.

A bellhop pushed their luggage on a wheeled cart. Adia's grandmother's suitcases were clean and unscuffed and made of fabric that had pink flowers all over it. Adia wished the suitcase she and her mother shared was made of that fabric, but instead theirs was brown and lumpy and had a zipper held closed with a twisted paper clip. Grandmother Joan was not like her own mother, Adia thought. She was more like the embassy moms she saw at school sometimes. The bellhop, even, was more elegant than her mother, and his air of sophistication was alluring to Adia.

"When I grow up, I want to work here," Adia said, imagining the luxury of spending all day in that beautiful place.

Her grandmother stopped in her tracks and tipped her head back and laughed a laugh that was like silver bracelets clinking together in her mouth.

"Leona, darling, did you hear that? Your daughter aspires to be a maid in an African hotel!"

Adia smiled, but inside she felt shaky. She didn't understand the joke her grandmother found funny. Adia watched her mother turn and glance at Adia, and then at her own mother.

"She can do whatever damn well makes her happy, Mother."

Joan pursed her lips and shook her head so that the chin-length hair moved ever so slightly across the back of her neck.

"Leona, darling, lighten up! Of course we want our girl to be happy, but she's an American girl...with options!"

Joan turned to Adia and placed her hand on Adia's arm. Her fingers were soft and a little squishy, like the banana slugs that took over the garden when it rained, only with long bright red nails pointing out from the ends.

"You'll see," Grandmother Joan whispered to Adia. "When you get home, you'll see. There is a world of things a girl like you could do." Adia wondered what her grandmother meant. She had two homes—one in Nairobi with Leona and one in Loita with Simi.

The bellhop halted, and they all stopped in a little cluster behind him. He fumbled with a large key, and then rolled the cart into a room that would easily fit, in Adia's estimation, the entire *inkajijik*. She thought if she stood with her back against one wall, she couldn't even throw a ball hard enough to hit the opposite one. There were two big double beds and a shiny, glinting bathroom behind a tall, heavy door. The bellhop crossed the enormous room and pulled open a set of drapes that exposed sliding doors and a balcony. Adia gasped. The ocean stretched out brilliant and blue as far as she could see. It looked so close. She wondered if she could jump off the balcony and splash right into the waves.

"Well, I'm connected..." Joan said, opening a door Adia had thought was a closet, but instead led to a different room, equally big, with two more beds. Joan fumbled in her purse for a handful of bills and pressed them into the bellhop's hand.

"Just leave the pink suitcases in there, dear."

Joan looked at Adia and said, "They only work for tips, darling. You don't need to do that. You have options. When you're home, you'll see."

Leona turned from where she'd been examining pamphlets on the desk and leaned in close. She poked a finger toward Adia's face and said coldly, "Goddammit, Mother, she is home. Nairobi is her home. She's only ever lived here in Kenya. This is what she knows, and it's a perfectly wonderful place to call home, by the way."

Adia watched as her grandmother's face turned pale. Joan said nothing, but she turned and disappeared into the other room, closing the door firmly, but quietly, behind her. Leona went into the bathroom and slammed the door shut. Adia could hear her cursing under her breath as she peed. Adia's stomach was twisted into an unfamiliar knot. It made her think of the giant centipedes that curled into black shiny balls if you poked them. That was how they protected themselves, but her stomach didn't feel protected. It hurt. She wanted to smack her mother for being so rude to Grandmother Joan. How dare she push away the only family Adia had. Adia glanced at each of the closed doors, each with someone she loved behind it. She didn't open either—she wanted air. On the balcony, she leaned over the railing and watched people in bathing suits below. She wasn't used to hearing people argue. She wasn't used to seeing her mom angry, and she wondered why, from the moment Joan came into their house, the air around the two women felt stiff, like cardboard. It scared her that Joan might leave again.

Later in the pool, underneath the surface of the water, it was quiet. The space around her body felt soft and exactly the right temperature to match her own—there was no border between her skin and the water. Only when she pushed her feet hard on the bottom of the pool and thrust herself upward to break the surface and breathe in gasps of air did she feel her own skin again, the breeze chilly and sharp against it. Those moments of breath and air were as short as she could make them. Push up, break the surface, exhale, inhale, exhale, inhale, hold it in and down again, back through the water to the quiet, perfect space below.

In the brief seconds Adia was in the air, she could hear her mother's and grandmother's voices alternately scratching and pounding like the surf from the ocean just beyond the pool patio. Their voices made Adia's heart beat faster in her chest and it hurt. She could tell her mother was angry. Her words were quick and short and spiky, and her face hard and dark.

"I want to take Adia out into the bush," Joan said. "I want to see where she grew up, where you lived."

"Mom, you'd hate it out there. Dust and heat and no dry martinis."

"I don't mean I'm going to take her to live in a village somewhere. I mean on safari. There are safaris you can book. Nice ones with hot showers and sheets and, yes, even cocktails." Joan pulled her sunglasses up and squinted into the light. "There were brochures in the lobby. Some look quite nice."

Adia was at the far side of the pool, standing with her hand outstretched across the surface of the water. She was making tiny splashes with her palm. Then she disappeared below. Once, when Adia popped out of the water, she stayed up a little longer than it took to catch her breath. It was quiet, and she heard her grandmother say, "Lee, we have to talk about why you're so angry with me. I came to you. I came all this way to see you and to meet my granddaughter. I thought my making this effort, even after so long, would begin to bridge the gap. I want to bridge that gap. I'm old, and I don't want to die without repairing our relationship. Can you give me that?"

★ ★ ★

Leona's bathing suit was faded and stretched out. She'd been picking gently at the little fabric pills that clustered on the suit where it stretched across her chest. Her mother's words made the skin on her arms and legs bead with goose bumps. She felt exposed and pulled the large hotel towel around her. She pretended to watch Adia bobbing up and down in the water. This conversation was the opening to the dark tunnel of her past. Her breath quickened and the words she'd practiced in her head, over and over again through the years, scuttled away like sand crabs. She searched for a way to say what she wanted in a measured way, but all she found in her mouth was anger. It stirred and frothed, a rabid dog in her throat.

"You knew," she rasped. She never imagined that she would ever have this conversation with her mother. She'd fantasized about it but never thought the reality of it was possible. Now it felt like she wasn't thinking about anything at all, but that the words were pushing themselves out of her by their own power.

"You let my father do those things to me. I tried to tell you and you ignored me. You let him ruin me. I wanted to die. I wanted to cut myself into pieces. You destroyed my childhood. I watched you do nothing to help, and then I finally escaped. I escaped halfway across the world and made a life for myself without any help from you. Now you're here? Now you want to talk? Well, guess what? Fuck you!"

Joan's mouth was an open black hole in her face, and the sunglasses had slid back down all the way onto the tip of her nose. She was perfectly still. For an instant Leona thought she'd killed her mother or turned her into stone—maybe she was a medusa with snake words. Leona's blood was streaming with adrenaline, and her heart beat wildly. During her speech, she'd felt separate from the body she inhabited, just a mind floating somewhere far above the quivering, angry woman spewing out feelings like pus from a wound. Now, watching her mother, Leona's two parts slowly seeped back together. She looked around. She must have been shouting. She hadn't meant to, hadn't thought she was, but people around the pool were watching them. Leona had the feeling of eyes on her, and then she saw that Adia, too, was standing stock-still in the water, staring at Leona from under her slicked wet hair.

Suddenly, Leona felt sad. This wasn't how she'd pictured it. She wanted to hurt her mother, yes. She wanted to punish Joan for the complicity she'd shown all through Leona's forty-two years. But it didn't feel good to finally shout what she'd held in for so long. There was no relief, no burbling up of happiness to fill the now-vacant space. Nothing like that happened. Just emptiness. A heavy emptiness. Leona didn't like all the eyes on her; she wasn't one for dramatic scenes, and the idea that Adia might have heard, that she would know…it was too much. She'd taken such care to construct a relationship with her daughter that would never allow light to shine on Leona's earlier life. Leona stood quickly, shoved her feet into her flip-flops and walked away before her mother could say a word.

The lobby was cool and deserted. Leona felt faint and dizzy. It wasn't like her to get emotional. She saw a chair tucked into an alcove and sat down. She wanted to hide, and it felt good to be folded up in this deep chair with its large, winged sides that hid her from view. Leona closed her eyes and forced herself to think about something besides the words she'd just spoken.

She focused on the bush. Should she let Adia go on safari with Joan? Her first reaction had been to say no. When Adia was born, Leona swore she'd do anything rather than expose Adia to her parents. But really, with her father dead, the danger was gone. Joan had been complicit, but never cruel. And Adia seemed happy to meet her grandmother. Leona prickled with a surprising jealousy when she saw how Adia hung on to Joan's every word, desperate for the old woman's affection.

Leona opened her eyes and saw that the lobby was still empty. The shelf of brochures was just across the hall. She knew there were safaris her mother would be comfortable taking. She'd heard of the luxury some of them promised, but she'd never known details. Leaving her flip-flops behind, Leona padded over to the display. There were plenty to choose from. Looking past the ones for parasailing in Lamu and exploring Mount Kenya, she pulled out all the ones that looked suitable. Once gathered, she brought the whole pile back to her chair and curled up in it again.

They were all just variations of one theme: game watching from the air-conditioned comfort of safari vans, and sleeping on Egyptian cotton sheets in tents more Beverly Hills than bush. Most of the safaris went into Tsavo and Amboseli. If Joan wanted to go closer to where Adia was born, those wouldn't be good options. Leona noticed only one that went closer to Loita. It was a photo safari based out of a luxury camping site near the Nguruman forest. Adia might even know some of the Maasai guides; it was close enough to the manyatta that some of them might work there. She could even escape and make her way to the manyatta if she had to. Leona opened the brochure to study the itinerary. Before she saw anything else, she caught sight of a face in the upper right-hand corner, a photo of the proprietor, she assumed. She looked closer and blinked to clear the flashes of light that were exploding in her head. She tried to steady her breathing, but the flashes in her brain were so violent she thought she might throw up.

He wasn't dead. Even if the brochure was out-of-date, it couldn't be that old. When had she met his mother? Ten years ago? And his face in the photo was different—he'd clearly aged.

He wasn't dead and he wasn't far away. The whole time he'd been in plain sight. Maybe they'd crossed the same street in opposite directions. Maybe they been at the same bar one night, just hours apart. Had she seen him once and not recognized him?

There was a noise next to her and she looked up. Her mother stood there, her face a closed window.

"I just need to tell you."

"Jesus!" Leona said loudly. Her mother standing there was a surprise, and an unwelcome one that pierced the shock. But Leona was too exhausted to argue, or to refuse and stand up and walk away. The photo left her stunned in complete inaction. Her mother, now, was the least of her concerns. Leona nodded in the direction of another chair and watched as her mother, thin as a stem, struggled to pull the chair close.

"I was a bad mother," Joan said, lifting her hand against the argument from Leona that didn't come.

"I knew I was bad from the moment you were born. It didn't ever come naturally to me. I was terrified all the time when you were a baby. I could hardly leave the house for the first year because it all scared me too much. My mother didn't even come to help for the first couple of weeks, but then she had to go, and by the way, she was a bad mother, too." The words scraped Leona's skin. She didn't expect this—a plea for mercy, and she didn't want it. Seeing her mother as vulnerable now upset the entire balance of Leona's memories. But the older woman's words kept coming. They were a wave Leona was pinned under, and the only way to keep from getting sucked out to sea was to let it pass over her.

"Your father was a stern man. Not at all affectionate. He was always desperate for order, for things to be just so. He got mad one spring when the rows of tulips I planted along the walkway came up red and pink. He wanted only pink ones.

He made me pull the red ones out and then go to the florist to buy replacements in little pots. Can you imagine? But I did it. I did everything he asked because I had nothing else. Where could I go? My parents would have been horrified if I'd gone back to them. I had no job, no skills. And then there was you, this daughter I felt completely unable to manage. We hired nannies and, after a while, I relaxed a little… I had to keep busy all the time, had to be out of the house as much as possible. That's where my freedom was. Yes, I knew. I knew but I didn't want to believe it. I couldn't allow myself to be-lieve it, because if I did, and still I stayed? What would that have made me? A monster.

"Once I even asked him. I hoped that if he knew I knew, he would stop. He told me I was wrong, that I was imagin-ing things, and that the depression was back and making me think things that weren't there."

She paused, and Leona looked up. There were tears in her mother's eyes, but Leona pushed back a pang of sympathy. This didn't change anything. Her mother could have mustered up the courage to help and she didn't. But somewhere, some-where Leona couldn't identify or pinpoint, there was some-thing new. Being a mother was confusing and hard. Children sometimes took things from you that you wanted or needed. She came from a long line of bad mothers. She hadn't yet bro-ken the streak, and she saw, now, that her mother was noth-ing but a flawed human who, in the sea of motherhood, was weighed down by her own albatross. This feeling was new. Maybe not the burbling up of relief she'd wanted, but maybe a pinprick of light.

"When you escaped to college and grad school and then all the way to Kenya, I was relieved. I was glad for you. But, by the way, you didn't do it without help, did you? You've been living off the account he left you when he died. I'm glad."

Leona breathed deeply and exhaled. She couldn't believe that her mother, her reticent mother who hardly spoke more than the basic exchange of pleasantries while Leona was growing up, was saying all of this. She didn't know her own mother at all, she realized.

"When your father died, I missed him. I grieved. But I also felt a weight had been lifted from me." Here, Joan reached over and touched Leona lightly on Leona's hand—the one still holding the brochure.

"I saw a therapist. Can you believe that? It took me that long...all these years, to gather the courage to come to you."

Leona glanced away. Seeing her mother so exposed, so raw, made Leona feel as if she'd been dropped into a new country where she didn't understand the customs or the language. She couldn't meet her mother's eyes. This conversation was too big to consider now. She needed to let it absorb more slowly. Her mother was still leaning in close, watching Leona. Leona noticed the tight network of lines on Joan's cheeks, and the drapey quality of the skin across her neck. In her memory, her mother's face was smooth and expressionless, her constant makeup a mask, her thoughts always unreadable behind it.

"Well, Mom, I'm not sure how to react," Leona said, and her voice came out more sharply than she'd planned. Her mother's eyes flashed in surprise, and she leaned back, pulled her hand from Leona's arm. Instantly Leona knew she'd offended her mother somehow, and a bewildered feeling overtook her. Why was she feeling guilty for hurting her mother's feelings? It wasn't equal, not in the least, to how her mother had hurt her. Still, that she admitted she'd made a mistake somehow made Leona flush and, as a way to deflect the feeling, she separated out the brochure with John's photo in it and thrust the rest into Joan's lap. She slid John's into the space between the side of the cushion and the chair's arm. She stood up.

"I think you and Adia should go on safari together. I'm sorry I insulted you before. They do look nice. I want her to spend time with you."

The next time Adia popped up from under the water in the pool, she saw that both her mother and grandmother were gone. She was glad. Hearing them fight made her insides loose and scratchy, and when her mother cursed at Joan in that shrill voice that didn't seem like her mother's at all, Adia felt like she was tumbling in space. She'd barely gotten a grandmother and she didn't want to lose her so fast. Now the chairs where they'd been sitting were empty. The sun was pulled back and settling down on the other side of the sky, and the pool, which had been sunny and bright, was now shaded and cool. Adia climbed out of the water and stepped off the patio's cement steps and onto the warm, soft sand. Down at the surf, a few little kids were running back and forth along the frothy line where ocean met sand and up to where their parents stretched out on brightly colored beach towels. Adia walked as close to the little family as she could without their noticing and sat in the warm sand.

"Don't go in the water too far, kids!" the mother called at one point. "There may be riptides."

The oldest-looking child, a girl of about seven, plopped down on the edge of her mother's towel.

"What's a riptide?" she asked.

Adia knew. She'd studied them in science class. She whispered to herself, "A narrow stream of water traveling swiftly from shore out to sea."

She heard the mother say, "It's most important that if you get caught in one, you don't fight. The real danger is not in being in one, but in how you react to it."

Adia remembered that her teacher told the class that rip

currents were caused by the shape of the shoreline itself, not by the moon or the sun or the particular undulations of the seafloor. The tides reacted to the particular way the shoreline behaved. The shore was in charge of the whole dynamic.

Adia watched the kids and their parents for a long time, trying to discern the pattern the children made between water and family. Who responded to whom? Which were the shoreline, Adia wondered, the kids or the parents, and which the tides? If she had a father and a mother together, like those kids did, Adia knew what she would be. She would be the water that answered the shoreline of her parents. She would swirl around their edges, delighted to be the third in their dynamic of two. They would be happy together—just like these parents seemed to be. Adia's parents would laugh and hold hands and be as steady as land. Adia, then, would be free to drift and return, drift and return, always knowing she had a safe, dry place waiting for her.

Later, at dinner, Adia watched her mother's face closely when her grandmother said, "I'm going to book a safari, the one that Adia liked the most." All three of them were rosy and exhausted from the sun and the water. Adia's eyelids drooped and she could hardly eat the hamburger the waiter had set down in front of her. Joan and Leona sipped wine and picked at their fish.

"Which one did you choose?" Leona asked Adia, briefly pushing the fatigue away and concentrating on her daughter's face.

"I forget the name," Adia said quietly, "but I picked it because grandma wanted to see our manyatta, and this one was the closest."

"What?" Leona asked, her voice shrill in the quiet restaurant. "I didn't see one anywhere closer to Loita than Amboseli."

"Really?" Joan said. "It must have dropped out of the pile you gave me. I found it sticking out of the chair cushion after you left this afternoon. It looks wonderful. Perfect for us. Adia, you've held on to it, right? I'll need the number."

Adia nodded. Earlier that evening, while they waited for Leona to shower and change for dinner, Adia and Joan sat on the balcony off Joan's room and looked through the various offerings. Adia picked the one closest to the manyatta, it was the only criteria she used. She'd been looking at the pictures when Leona called to them, saying she was ready and should they go down to the dining room? Adia needed her shoes and found them under her bed. She dropped the brochures on her bedside table. "Good girl. Give it back to me tomorrow and I'll try to book us in next week. Adia will miss a few days of school, but never mind. Of course, you're welcome to come along."

Leona felt her whole body shaking. She felt both cold and as if she needed big drafts of fresh air in her lungs.

Adia fell asleep fast, her dreaming mind full of ocean currents, pulling and pushing away from a wide shoreline. When she woke suddenly, she blinked into the dark and felt her body was a long piece of seagrass, waving in the depths of some dark body of water.

The voices came from behind the closed door leading to her grandmother's room. Adia couldn't hear words, just the rise and fall of quick, angry speech. She lay still for a moment, wondering if it would stop. When it didn't, she slid out of bed and crept to the door. She learned a lot of things by creeping up to doors lately, she thought. She pressed her ear lightly against the wood, holding her body stiff, not getting too comfortable, ready to spring back to her bed if she heard footsteps on the other side.

"No, you listen to me…" her grandmother hissed. "You can't keep everyone from her. Not me, not him."

Then her mother's voice. "I wasn't keeping her from him. From you, maybe, but not from him. I thought he was dead! I looked for him. I wanted to give her to him. But he was dead. This is as big a shock for me as it will be for her."

"But maybe this is the best way for her to meet him. Casually, not some big to-do."

"Jesus, Mom, I'm not sending Adia on safari to meet her dad. How would that work?" She mimicked a young girl's voice and said, "Thanks for a great experience, and by the way, I'm your kid!"

Adia's body stiffened with the word, the feeling of waving, dizzy, underwater rushed over her again. *Dad.* She said *dad.* At the sound of footsteps, Adia pulled herself away from the door. She leaped back under her sheet and pinched her eyes closed. She heard her mother rustle in the bathroom, turn on the light, flush the toilet. Then Adia heard her mother's bed creak, and the room was dark again and quiet. Adia was so used to being alone with her mother's silence that the idea of trying to pierce through it had never occurred to Adia. But that small word lingered in her brain—*dad.*

The idea of a father felt electric, and it kept Adia awake for hours. She stared up at the ceiling and watched the shadows bend and curve. When she was certain her mother was long asleep, she pulled the brochures from her side table, and slipped them under her pillow. When she finally fell asleep, the shoreline stretched out in her mind, infinite and pale against the dark waves swirling and churning with deadly riptides. *Drift*, the water whispered to her in her dream, *drift.* And the shoreline grew farther and farther away.

Adia woke. Her hair was tangled over her face and her skin felt warm and clammy. Her breath was hard and fast with fright, and in the dark she could barely see the last remnant of her dreaming self, almost invisible now in the vast sea, sliding out, alone, beyond the horizon line.

NAKURU

The first time they met, Grace didn't know what to think of Adia. She was strange, that was obvious. The only seat left in class on Grace's first day—already two months into the school year—was next to Adia, who looked totally different from the other kids, from all the kids Grace had ever known. She had long messy blond hair and wore a lot of jewelry—beads and beads sewn onto leather bracelets and necklaces. She must have had six or seven around each wrist and around her neck, too. Grace had never before seen a white girl with so many beads. The other kids all looked up at Grace when the teacher introduced her, but the blonde girl just stared out the window and twirled a clumpy strand of hair around her finger. When Grace sat down, she noticed the other girl's fingernails were dirty and cracked in places, and that she chewed on the skin around them, so her fingers were covered in tiny cuts, bleeding a little. "I'm Adia," the blonde said when she caught Grace staring at her beaded wrists. "My Maasai family named me."

At lunch that first day, Grace sat at an empty table toward the back. First, she was alone, but then she saw the strange girl coming toward her. "I usually sit here," the beaded girl said. "I don't mind if you sit here, too, though." Grace hesitated—she understood already that Adia was an outcast in the school hierarchy and that by sitting with her Grace might be painted with that brush, too. She'd never been anything other than popular in her schools before. But now she didn't care. She was tired of all of this, the moving, the new houses, always being the new kid. She couldn't be bothered to get up and sit somewhere else. So what if the other kids thought she was weird?

Grace didn't talk much at that lunch. Instead, she listened to Adia. Adia talked as if she'd been holding words inside her like air in a balloon that popped. She couldn't hold back. Grace was annoyed at first. She wanted to be alone. But as Adia talked, she became more and more intrigued with her story. Finally, she stopped eating altogether and just listened. Adia was practically Maasai. She and her mom spent holidays in the manyatta. Adia had learned to herd the goats and start a fire using only sticks and her own breath. She'd learned how to grasp a goat by its feet and flip it onto its back so a man could slit its throat. She learned to drink the nourishing fresh cow blood the Maasai way—by piercing the skin of the cow's neck with a sharp spear, and then, after drinking her fill, pinching the skin back together so the cow could walk away with just a trickle running down its neck and the feeling of a bee sting. Both her parents were white; Adia said her dad was a Kenyan cowboy from a long line of white Kenyans. But Adia, as she said herself, was Maasai. By the time the bell rang for class to start again, Grace knew that Adia was the most interesting person she'd ever met and made up her mind to be her best friend.

★ ★ ★

Evenings in Nairobi were cool, mostly because of the alti-
tude, and Jane often brought a cup of tea out to the balcony
after dinner, wrapping up in an old gray throw and watching
the bats leave their upside-down beds in the banana trees and
go flitting around above her while the stars blinked awake.
The rare occasions when Grace joined Jane made Jane want
to cry with pleasure. Tonight Grace lay in the chaise next to
Jane's and stretched her hand toward Jane.

"Can I share that blanket?" Grace asked, and Jane would
have given Grace her own skin if she thought it would draw
Grace closer again. Jane handed Grace the blanket and felt for
her fingers as she took it. Jane wanted to touch her daughter,
to trigger a desire in Grace to make her want to climb over
next to Jane and huddle together under these foreign stars. But
Grace just leaned back and curled up with the throw piled
on top of her.

"Adia says people like us try too hard to make America
wherever we go. And it's true, right?"

Jane was cold without the weight of the blanket on her,
and the bats suddenly sounded like mice scratching the sky
for food. Jane didn't like Adia. She didn't like the furtive way
Adia glanced out from under her slack bangs or the awful
clothes she wore.

"I know you're still new at school, and it takes time to settle in, but is Adia the only friend you have so far? She isn't
like any of the girls you knew in Rabat. I mean...she seems,
I don't know, so different from you. Like she needs to run a
comb through that hair, and what's with the jewelry?"

Jane wanted Grace to giggle with her. She would have before. Jane knew her Gracie—Grace and Jane were the same.
But Grace didn't giggle.

"I like her, Mom. She's different and cool, and she's nice.

And I don't care about her hair and neither should you." Then she got up, tossed the blanket back on her mother and went inside.

A few days later, Jane offered Nakuru as her olive branch.

"Let's go for the day, Grace," Jane said. "I'll drive. We'll let your dad sleep in."

And then Jane added, "Bring your new friend. We'll pick her up on the way out of town. A girls' road trip."

Grace's face brightened, and Jane thought, who is she? But Grace never wanted to be alone with Jane anymore. Adia was the only hope Jane had of spending time with her daughter.

When Jane and Grace picked Adia up on the way out of town, it was early morning, and the girl sat in the half dark, hunched on her heels at the end of her driveway.

"Where's your mom?" Jane asked before Grace could even say hello.

"She's asleep," Adia said. "She hardly ever gets up before nine." Adia reached down and grabbed the straps of a lumpy, green, canvas backpack.

"My Maasai mom is meeting me at Nakuru. I have stuff to give her." She opened the back door of the car, tossed her bag in and climbed after it, snapping the door shut behind her.

"Doesn't your mom want to meet me?" Jane asked, ignoring her instinct to add, "Your American mom? I was looking forward to meeting her." Jane was stunned by a mother who would sleep in and let her thirteen-year-old daughter wait in the dark for a stranger to pick her up to take her away for the day. *Feral*, Jane thought, *she's like a feral child*. Adia's pants were dirty at the cuffs, and her T-shirt was stained and at least one size too small. Her ropey hair was shoved up into a large, leather hat that looked like it had seen more than a few dust storms. Jane watched Adia settle into the back seat next to Grace who, with her clean, brown ponytail, jeans and white sneakers, looked like a different species compared to Adia. When the girls threw their arms around each other, Jane shuddered.

They drove out of town quietly. The girls were still sleepy, curled up with their heads tipped against opposite windows. The sun was just crawling up the lower third of the sky when the road rose and suddenly seemed to drop out below them. Jane turned off onto the shoulder and they all got out to stretch their legs. The road wound steeply down and down and down, switchbacking all the way—hundreds of feet—into a huge great bowl in the earth.

"You guys never saw the Rift Valley before?" Adia asked, sensing Jane's and Grace's awe. Jane didn't correct her. Even Grace didn't know she'd once lived on the valley floor. She was vague about that period of her life—she didn't like to think about it much anymore. Adia waved proprietarily toward the horizon. "My Maasai family live out there." Jane looked over at Adia, and she saw the sun on Adia's darkly tanned arms and her dusty clothes. In this context, she looked of this place. Her clothes and hat and hair and jewelry made her look like a sliver of the savannah below them sprung into human form. For an instant, Jane wondered if she would have come to look like that if she'd stayed. If she'd met someone else here to marry and Grace had that man as a father, would she look like that, too? The road was rough and deeply pocked, and sometimes the edge just fell away. Jane gripped the wheel tightly and slowed to a crawl. But now and then Jane glanced up into the rearview mirror to watch the girls. Grace had closed her eyes again and leaned her head back against the headrest.

Adia directed Jane to a small road that seemed to lead to and from nowhere. "They'll be coming up this road," she said. "If you park here, we'll see them." They were close to the lake.

Jane imagined she could smell the brackish water, the scent of feathers and guano. She was anxious to get there, to show Grace what she expected would be a magical sight and to tell her daughter how long she had waited to see it. But when they reached that spot in the road and Adia told Jane to stop, Jane was in equal parts stunned and awed. She saw Grace gaze at Adia with admiration as Adia hopped out of the car and used the front bumper to climb on the hood of the car, her lumpy rucksack next to her.

Jane leaned against the driver's-side door, drinking lukewarm water from her Nalgene bottle, and Grace lay across the back seat, her bare feet sticking out the window and her forearm slung over her eyes.

The Maasai women finally appeared through a break in the dust. It was like they unzipped a tent flap and stepped out—suddenly there they were. There were four of them, all with shaved heads and bare feet. All wrapped in loosely draped cotton cloths tied at the shoulders and wearing masses of the same beaded jewelry Adia wore. One of the women had an indolent toddler tied to her back.

"There they are," Adia said as she hopped off her perch. Then she strode up the road toward the women.

When they were close enough, Adia took off her hat and bent her head to each woman and they touched her hair, murmuring smoky, low words like a humming. Adia spoke to them in their language and untied the baby from the woman's back and held it like a mother would as she chatted—the baby perched naked on her hip, Adia's tan arm looking pale and angular against the baby's curved, brown bottom. Grace climbed out of the car and watched Adia with the gathering of women.

"Hey, Grace, bring me the pack." Adia glanced over her

shoulder as if she'd just remembered that Grace and Jane were there.

Jane watched as Grace knelt in the dust, tugging open the straps and pulling things from the pack to hand up eagerly to the Maasai women, greedy for their attention. There was sugar, tea, tins of milk powder, OMO detergent and what looked like a large tub of Crisco. The women murmured and nodded, and one by one all the goods Grace brought out were tucked away in the folds of their wraps. Adia handed the baby back to its mother, who tied the girl deftly to her back again. Grace stepped back and watched as Adia and the women grasped each other's hands and said their goodbyes. Adia stood, her hand shading her eyes, and watched as the little band of women disappeared up the road, back through the curtain of dust.

Jane shut the car windows and flipped on the air-conditioning. She heard Grace's quiet voice say, "Are those the women you told me about? Your Maasai mother and the other wives?"

"Yeah," Adia answered, and her voice didn't sound strong anymore, but sad. "Simi is the one I told you about. She's my Maasai mom. I lived with them until I was six. Now I just spend summer vacations with them. Sometimes long weekends or when my mom is traveling. I wish she traveled more."

Jane thought of Grace's relatives—her grandparents, aunts, uncles and cousins on Paul's side, and silent Uncle Lance on hers. Grace had never met Lance and only saw her other relatives for a couple of weeks every other summer. Grace barely knew her American family, and unlike Adia, she had no other tribe. Jane thought that she and Paul never stayed long enough anywhere for Grace to make those kinds of connections. In a way, Jane and Paul had stolen something from their daughter that they could never give back. They flew away from everything. Grace had no one besides her parents, no place but where they were, and that was always temporary.

It wasn't like Jane pictured. Her imagination had it all wrong. Or maybe it was just too late. The drought had been too long, people said. It was entrenched all over Kenya now. People were hungry. Livestock was dying. *Shambas*, the family gardens people depended on, were nothing but rocks and dust, and when rain did fall, it fell too quickly and too hard to be absorbed into the bare soil. There were no grasses to hold on to the water, help it seep into the earth, so it spilled away, leaving nothing but volcanic rock and limestone—the earth's underbelly that could grow nothing of substance.

When Jane and Grace and Adia finally reached it, Lake Nakuru was shallow and dank, and it spread out at their feet like spilled paint swirled into browns and dark greens and grays. It seemed the flamingos were dying in great, pink waves. It was beyond what Jane imagined from the articles she'd read. The bodies of the dead lay half-submerged in the fetid water, their exposed backs baked by the sun, their lifeless necks, long as flower stems, drifting slightly in the gentle, shallow currents, their unseeing eyes watching over those forgotten eggs below them. The ones still alive were desultory and disappointing. They fitted themselves exactly in the drying shallows above the ancestor eggs. The earth was changing under their feet, water turning to mud, mud turning to dry land. But these birds stayed anyway, rooted to their home.

The dust that muted their pink feathers saddened Jane; the plastic water bottle she saw bobbing in the muddy edge; the cigarette butts half-buried in the slimy green algae that lined the shore. Jane had the sudden memory of her father standing near the jungle gym at the park so many years ago and telling Jane about acknowledging the moment they realized that Lance was gone. Things disappeared. Moments died, maybe her father was right to move on. Now Jane wanted to wave her arms and shout at the dreary flamingos left behind, to see them take to the air like the ones already gone, to imagine a new place for themselves. This wasn't what Jane had expected; it was not what she wanted to happen.

A group of European tourists climbed out of a zebra-painted pop-top minibus. They littered themselves along the path, red-faced and cameras clicking. They looked alien to this land-scape. Fleshy, pale, breathing hard, like grubs plucked from under rocks, blinking into the sunlight. Jane wondered if she looked like them in the eyes of those Maasai women, or if Grace did with her shiny hair and fresh clothes?

"Comme c'est beau!" a woman in a wide-brimmed straw hat said to herself, breathing deeply in satisfaction, clasping her manicured fingers. Jane wondered just what the woman was looking at. Nothing here looked beautiful to her.

Jane lifted her hand for an instant, wiped the dust off her forehead, and when she glanced back, Grace had stretched out flat, barely visible beside Adia. Adia, who hunkered, bored and blank as a shell, picking at her fingernails, her hat throwing her face into shadow, the skin on her arms as dark and dry as the dust at their feet. Adia—the only one who belonged to this earth. Jane felt a stab of resentment. She was happy that her daughter was feeling better and gave credit for that to Adia. But what did her daughter see in this girl? She was like no-body Grace had known before. She wished she could under-stand what her daughter saw in this strange girl.

Standing there, by the changing lake, she sent a prayer to the sky that her daughter wasn't really disappearing. "Don't let her leave me," she murmured. "Not like Lance, and not in a way that will never, ever change back."

It was a mistake to come to the lake, to the floor of the Rift. The landscape was so familiar it made her ache, and the memories came too fast. It hurt to remember Muthega and the women by the river and the dusty kids. It hurt to remember herself back then and how much stronger she was. But she'd still been too weak to stay, still too weak to swallow her fear and continue her work. After Muthega's murder, she told herself, and she told Paul, too, that what she admired most about the elephants was their deep maternal instincts. She said she'd lost her desire to work in the bush with them, and only wanted to emulate them.

It felt true at that time, and she hadn't missed the work in the years since. She'd followed another path—to be a mother to her own baby, to keep the child close, folded safely in the curve of her arm, her metaphorical trunk. Elephant daughters lived with their mothers for life, though. Human daughters didn't. They grew apart from their parents, up and away, and the mothers had to open their arms wide and release them. It took strength. Jane wondered if she would ever be strong enough to let Grace go.

FOREST OF THE LOST CHILD

The son of the shopkeeper always yelled his messages long before his feet reached the manyatta. Simi and the other women, gathered by the muddy trickle of the river, heard his voice and looked up from their washing. They could see a small billow of dust moving toward them.

"That boy has the voice of an elephant in pain," Loiyan muttered. She didn't smile, although the other women laughed. Simi noticed Loiyan's pinched face, and realized that she hadn't heard Loiyan enjoy her own jokes recently. Simi wondered if the other woman was pregnant again. She had three sons who were already *moran*, and a newly married daughter pregnant with her own first baby. Loiyan also had four children who still lived in the manyatta. All girls, two were toddlers, one was a serious girl of seven and the last was a baby, barely weaned. During the early pregnancies, Loiyan blossomed. Her cheeks grew round, her belly blossomed like a flower and her skin shone. Each of the first three babies was born quickly and easily. Loiyan was good at bringing babies into the world.

Then there was a tiny boy born too soon to live, his body perfect and waxen and far too still, and it was then that Loiyan shifted. Just a bit. Her humor, Simi thought, was always a bit sharp. Her voice was always a little too loud, and her opinions a little too important. But there was always a brightness behind her barbs and her actions. She was quick and tough and never afraid. After the stillborn son, though, her personality grew uneven, a little darker, a little angrier. Some of the brightness had faded. Simi knew the pain Loiyan felt—she could remember her losses like they were still happening. But instead of that making it easier to talk to Loiyan, it became harder. Loiyan and Simi were never close, but the terrible thing they had in common seemed to drive them apart further. Loiyan no longer teased Simi; she didn't address her at all.

The pounding of footsteps came closer, and with it a cloud of dust that descended on the women. The boy bent over, breathing hard. He lifted water from the stream into his mouth with one hand and wiped his forehead with the other. "Simi," he huffed, "Adia is coming to Narok town tomorrow. She will have things for you. You can meet her there at midday."

He splashed water on his face and rubbed it hard. The sun glinted off the droplets like tiny shards of glass. Simi smiled at the boy and thanked him. "Go to my house and wait. I'll come soon and make you tea. You shouldn't go back to your father hungry and tired."

The phone in the little shop where the boy's father worked as both postman and shopkeeper rang often; so many husbands and sons were in Nairobi now that every day someone would call, asking the boy to deliver a message to one of the manyattas nearby. Simi, though, was the only one who had a daughter who called.

Simi turned back to the river to rinse the few items that were still soapy. She noticed Loiyan staring at her sideways.

Even with all her children, she'd never be happy, Simi thought. Loiyan was a jealous woman. And for some reason she couldn't begin to explain, that made Simi feel sorry for her. Before she knew what words were going to slip from her mouth, she said, "Loiyan, come with me tomorrow. Adia will have things for all of us." Loiyan looked down at the slow-moving water and sucked her teeth, but Simi knew she would agree.

Simi laid her wet clothes on bare, hot rocks and hurried home to make the shopkeeper's boy tea. She knew his family had little these days. The drought lingered, and there were children born now who couldn't remember ever seeing the land green—the descriptions their parents gave them were nothing more than fairy tales. But the families who still had livestock were doing well enough to feed themselves. Leona had kept her promise to the Maasai—in certain situations, for prescribed lengths of time, people could take their cattle and goats to feed in the highlands, where there was still grass to eat and water to drink. In the driest months, this left manyattas full of only women and children. Women and children who didn't have money to buy things from the shopkeeper. Women and children who did without sugar in their tea anymore and whose bellies often grumbled in the dark hours of the night.

Simi was the lucky one. Her Nairobi daughter never let a month pass without bringing soap and tea and sugar and fat to cook with. Adia was generous, and everyone in the manyatta benefited. This made Simi proud.

The next day, Simi and Loiyan began the walk to Narok. First wife, Isina, came, too, as well as her grown daughter, Nalami, who was visiting her mother. Both the other wives missed Adia almost as much as Simi herself did. The walk from the manyatta to Narok was long, and it was hot, and Loiyan carried her smallest baby on her back, wrapped in a *kanga*. Still, though, Simi was surprised at how slowly Loiyan

walked, how heavy her breathing was, and wondered again if
Loiyan was pregnant. She worried that they might miss Adia.
By the time the sun was almost directly overhead, Isina had
taken the baby from Loiyan and tied it securely to her own
back. Loiyan hadn't argued—she gave up her burden word-
lessly. This alone made Simi worry. Loiyan wasn't someone
who easily kept from arguing.

The women stopped to drink water from a trickling spring
just outside of Narok. Isina handed the baby to Loiyan, who
sat, slumped and breathing hard, on a flat rock. The baby was
hungry and wanted to nurse. Loiyan clasped her daughter to
her breast, but even as the baby pulled and suckled, Simi could
tell she wasn't getting much milk.

"Loiyan, are you sick?" Isina asked. It comforted Simi,
somehow, that the other women noticed, too. Simi noticed
beads of sweat dappling Loiyan's hairline, gathering together
and sliding down the sides of her face.

"I'm just tired," Loiyan answered, and she stood, a little
unstable, on her feet. She handed the baby to Isina. "Help
me carry her."

It wasn't much longer until the women noticed the outline of Narok on the horizon, the squat buildings, the uneven
rooflines, and then there was a white car, new and shiny under
the film of dust. There were two figures Simi could see: one
sitting on the hood, one leaning against the car. Simi squinted
to catch sight of Adia, and then she saw her daughter sliding off
her perch and striding toward her. Her daughter. How lovely
Adia always looked. And then they were standing together,
talking. Even Loiyan looked better. She'd always had a place
for Adia in her heart. All the members of the manyatta did.

"Yeyo, I have things for you," Adia said as she took the baby
from Isina. Adia held the baby against her hip, and the child
reached up and grasped a handful of Adia's hair and laughed.

"My mother's worried about the grazing. Are the men back yet? She wanted me to ask you. It's important for them to stay there only for the time allowed. If they're still out there, if they stay past what they're allowed, they may not be allowed to go back next time."

Isina answered. "They're still there. None of them has come back yet. We only have a few goats here for us to eat, no cattle. We cannot sell them or we'd have no meat, so we cannot buy the other things we need." Adia turned then and waved her arms. "Hey, Grace, bring me the pack." Turning back to Simi, she said, "I have soap and milk powder and sugar and *kimbo*. Some tea, too. And my friend. I want her to meet you, Yeyo."

The other girl began pulling items out of a backpack and handing them up to the women. Simi watched her carefully. She was similar to Adia—the same color skin, the same texture hair, but also so different. Her face was pale, and her eyes big and rounder, somehow, her fingernails were clean and white. Simi thought the girl looked a little frightened.

"We can't stay long," Adia said in Maa, and Simi felt a pang of disappointment. She'd have to say goodbye again so soon.

"Grace's mother is waiting. She's impatient." Adia smiled when she said it, but it made Simi angry with the other woman, that still figure in the distance, leaning against her car. She wondered if that woman had ever experienced any sadness at all. As Simi watched, the faraway woman put a bottle of water to her mouth and tipped her head back, drinking a long drink. Simi could imagine the feeling of cool, clean water in her mouth. It had been so long since the rivers were clear and cold.

"But I'll come again soon, Yeyo." Adia kissed the baby on her little cheek and handed her back to Isina.

Simi watched the car drive away. She thought she saw the round, pale face of Adia's friend pressed against the window, staring back at her. But then Loiyan made a small sound and sank to her knees. She was so close to Simi that her hair grazed Simi's calf as she fell.

"Loiyan!" Nalami shouted, and she knelt to hold Loiyan's head in her lap. She felt Loiyan's cheek and said, "She's too hot. It's a bad fever."

Simi wished they had some water, even a little, to wipe Loiyan's face, cool her down a bit, and to squeeze into her dry, hot lips. But the drought had made the smaller sources, the ones they might have found nearby, dry up and disappear.

Simi carried Loiyan on her back the same way Isina carried Loiyan's baby. Nalami was weighed down, too. She had the tins of *kimbo* and the butter and all the other things Adia had brought. The women walked slowly, and Simi had to stop often and gently slide Loiyan down to the ground and then stand up straight, catch her breath and stretch her aching back. Nalami's manyatta was not far, but the walk was slow, and the afternoon was hot and still. Worry weighed on Simi, too. She'd never seen a person faint and not revive quickly. Loiyan was still limp, her heart was beating and her breath was even, but her eyes were open and unfocused, and her jaw was loose and slack.

When the women finally reached Nalami's manyatta, it was evening. The sky was purple and the sun a dull red. It looked like an unhappy sky, a worried and bruised sky. By this time, Loiyan's baby, having slept during most of the walk, was wide-awake and hungry—crying for milk. Nalami's husband had three wives, one largely pregnant and another with children beyond weaning age. The pregnant woman might have milk. Otherwise the baby would have to eat *ugi* and maybe a little cow's milk, if some could be found. That would be a problem for Nalami to fix. Simi, meanwhile, carried Loiyan into

Nalami's hut and laid her out on the bed. The *laiboni* would help now.

Simi didn't sleep well. It was too dark for her and Isina to make the walk home, so they slept on the rawhide bed in Nalami's mother-in-law's house. Simi wasn't used to sleeping that close to another adult, and every time Isina shifted, the movement woke her. It was still night when she gave up. Outside the hut, the sky was beginning to shift from darkness into dawn, and a pale, almost imperceptible orange light was the only indication of where the earth and the sky joined.

Simi and Isina left for home before the sun was fully up. Simi carried Loiyan's baby, who, still hungry from her sudden and unwelcome transition from mother's milk to gruel, fell asleep immediately, her cheek pressed against Simi's shoulder. She thought of Loiyan's other children, who waited for their mother to return. They would be sad and frightened. But Isina was carrying all the things Adia had given them, and maybe Simi could cheer the children up with sweet tea. None of them had had sugar in their tea for so long.

Two days later, Simi lay with Loiyan's baby in the shade of an acacia. The baby had begun to get used to eating *ugi*. She was a happy little thing. Simi had been caring for all of Loiyan's daughters for the last two days. Loiyan's older children had left the manyatta, the oldest daughter was married, and the three older boys were *moran*. These four little girls needed care, though, and Simi stepped in to provide it. The baby slept next to her at night, and the three younger ones slept nearby, like a pile of puppies cuddled together near the warmth of the banked fire. Simi loved hearing their sleeping breaths whenever she woke.

Now the baby was sitting next to Simi and running her chubby hands in the dust. Simi began to sing a song she'd made up when Adia was a baby. She was trying to pull the words out of her memory when she heard a shout. She sat up and shaded her eyes with the palm of her hand. There was dust, lots of dust in the distance. It was movement. A child darted from behind a nearby tree and raced past Simi to a large rock outcropping that had a view over the valley. From there he might be able to see what was within all that dust. Other women, other children, appeared next to Simi. They gazed out at the brown cloud. Then the boy on the rock shouted. He jumped up and down and shook his fists in the air. It was a victory dance. He'd seen the cause of the dust and it was the men and boys, the livestock. They were coming home.

That night a cow was slaughtered. The *moran* danced and, after so long being so quiet, the manyatta was filled with noise and movement, people and animals and activity. Simi watched the dancing with Loiyan's baby in her lap, the two toddler girls leaning on her thighs. She couldn't remember when she'd last felt this happy, this full.

Several days later, Simi and some other woman were at the river again. The children milled around them, some help-ing pound soap into the dirty clothes, some splashing water on themselves and laughing. Simi was happy to see that Loi-yan's seven-year-old was playing with a friend and that the toddler girls were splashing in the water. They asked about their mother sometimes, and each time Simi told them not to worry. Their mother was coming but, until then, she would care for them. "Don't worry," Simi told them, "I will care for you like you are my own until she comes. Don't worry."

Then the shout again, the pounding of a boy's feet, and the shopkeeper's son appeared, breathing hard and bending over, hands to knees.

"The *laiboni* sent news," the boy said. "It's Loiyan. She's dead."

Simi looked up to see if Loiyan's daughters had heard the

boy and was relieved to see that the children were outside hearing distance; they'd moved to play farther down the river. *Etwaltwa*, death—a bad omen for someone as young as Loiyan to die.

"They took her outside the *inkajijik*," the boy continued. "The *laiboni* saw that death was coming. They didn't want to bring bad things to the manyatta."

Simi nodded. It was common. To have a death in your home meant having to move the whole manyatta to a different place. Often this was avoided by moving the dying person a distance away.

"Where is the body?" Simi asked the boy.

"It is there," the boy answered.

Simi didn't accompany her husband or co-wives to Nalami's manyatta. She stayed behind with Loiyan's children. She didn't want to see Loiyan's body rubbed with fat and taken to the forest. She didn't want to remember Loiyan that way. Tonight, when it just started to grow dark, hungry nighttime animals would come out of their lairs. If Loiyan was lucky, and enough fat was used to prepare her body, the hyenas would come first. They would feast. Hyenas, like the *oreteti* tree, were messengers between N'gai and the people, and they would return Loiyan's body to nature. For her part, Simi would keep Loiyan alive in the best way she knew how, by caring for her girls. A woman with children, after all, would live forever.

JACARANDA

Adia shivered with anticipation and a desperate need to pee. Her body's movement made the branches shake, and the feathery jacaranda leaves fluttered. A few lavender blossoms flickered past her as they fell to the ground. Adia caught one and rubbed it between her fingers until the petal turned to purple juice, and then she dabbed it on her lips. Sometimes the stain lasted for a while, like lipstick, unless she forgot and let herself chew her lower lip—a habit she was trying to break. Adia leaned forward and craned her body as far as she could without falling out of the tree. From this exact spot she could see the road. Right now it was empty. Grace wasn't here yet.

She'd never had a friend come and visit her before, and she couldn't wait. She'd imagined what it would be like to have someone else there, someone besides her mother and Gakaki. But instead of spending her weekends with friends, she'd climb the jacaranda tree and stay high up among the leaves and lavender flowers for as long as she could. Some days, after she'd been in the tree for hours, Gakaki would wander out to the garden and call her name.

"Miss Adia!" he would call. "Are you here?" But he never saw her up in the tree. He never looked very hard. He'd call once and then go back inside. If Adia climbed high enough, she could see into the window of her mother's study. She had to lean her whole body onto one large branch and rest her chin on her arms. It was comfortable like that and she could watch her mother typing her papers—or was it a book now? Often her mother would pause and lift her fingers off the keyboard to think, and twirl a particular strand of hair through her fingers. Adia tried staring at her mom really hard—letting her eyes bore into her mother's head. She tried not to blink and she concentrated so hard she shook—but it never worked. Her mother never felt Adia's presence. She never turned, sensing the eyes on her, to find her daughter's face.

These days, though, instead of trying to stare her mother into noticing her, Adia imagined her father. She had his face always in the back of her mind. She memorized the photo on the brochure, and she went over and over it, trying to see herself in him. She kept the brochure hidden in the biggest pile of clothes in the deepest of her dresser drawers.

Her mother still hadn't told her the truth. Right after her grandmother left, Adia purposely brought her father up in conversation. She'd asked her mother if he had hobbies. Did he paint? Ride horses? Take photos? At the time, she felt it was bold for her to ask these questions. Too bold, maybe. Surely her mother would see through what she was doing. But her mother answered with an abrupt adherence to the story she'd always told.

"You don't have a father, Adia. He died. I didn't know him long enough to know if he had hobbies."

When she was little, Adia's mother told her that her father

was Kenyan, a rancher, or "Kenya Cowboy" as descendants of the British colonials were known. That made Adia proud. After that, she'd imagined her father often. She made him a brave man living in the landscape that she loved more than anything—the scrubby land near Loita. She imagined a man who would take her out on safari where they would sleep in tents and watch together as the sky turned orange and the enormous sun sank behind the horizon. They would light a campfire and let the glinting eyes of the curious animals not scare them at all. She wanted to be as brave and wild as this father she imagined, and she wanted to imagine him as the opposite of her mother. He wouldn't be taciturn or silent or always working. He would shout her name and climb the tree with her. He would smile every time he saw her. He would look at her when she came into the room. He would be interested in what she had to say. Now, Adia had a real face to think about. Her father was a safari guide—a man of the land, just as she hoped.

It was only because of Grandmother Joan that Adia knew the truth about her father. But Joan never spoke about him, either. Not when she and Adia went on their safari in Tsavo—about as far from the manyatta in Loita as they could get. To explain, Joan had only said that the other safaris were already booked up. This was the only one that had two spaces for the dates they needed. "Next time," Joan assured her, "next time we'll go to your neck of the woods." She and Adia had weekly phone calls since Joan left, but her father never came up in those conversations, either. That he was really alive, somewhere out there, was a secret they all carried separately.

When Grace came over to her house the first time, Adia was surprised to see her mom with her. Adia's own mother expected Adia to get where she needed to go on the city buses or the cheap overcrowded *matatus*. Adia felt a flush of shame when she saw Grace's mother get out of the car, slam the door behind her and then stand, looking the house up and down, slowly turning to take in the view of the dried-up garden, the patches of dirt, the old broken bucket on its side and the wicker table and chairs. Adia was in the jacaranda then, and she felt too stunned to move when she saw Grace and her mother approach the front of the house and then disappear from her view. She heard them call out, and then she spied her mother through the window. From this side of the glass, Adia couldn't hear if her mother said anything in reply, but she did see her look up, annoyed, and rise from her chair. Adia scrambled from the tree then. She didn't want Grace's mother to meet hers.

When Adia rounded the house, she saw Grace's mother was tipped forward, her leather sandals' toes barely over the threshold of the front door, and she was craning her neck around the doorsill. "Hello? I've brought Grace to play with Adia."

Adia was breathless when she reached them.

"Hey, Grace! I was up in the jacaranda tree. Come on, I'll show you."

"Wait." Grace's mother put her hand out to touch Grace's arm. "I want to meet the adult in charge first. Adia, please get your mother."

"She's working."

"Well, maybe I'll bring Grace back when I can meet her. Grace, come on…"

"No, Mom!" Grace tried to twist away, but the hand on her arm gripped tightly, her mother's fingers turning her skin white.

"No!" Adia pleaded. "Don't go. I'll get her."

Adia left Grace and her mother at the door, and disappeared into the darkness of the house. She thought about lying, telling them her mother was gone, that Gakaki was in charge, that he was babysitting. But she heard her mother's study door open and the sound of footsteps in the hall. Adia had never considered her mother's appearance before, but now she looked critically. Her mom's hair was dark brown and streaked with silver. She wore it in two messy braids with a halo of escaped hair standing up in a fuzzy patch at the crown. Her face had tiny lines clustered around her lips and the corners of her eyes. She was barefoot and wrapped in a cotton skirt, topped by a white T-shirt that had a tiny drop of coffee exactly where her left nipple was. She glanced at Adia as she passed, smiled faintly and continued to the front door. Adia rushed to catch up.

"Hey," Adia's mom said. She smiled and used the back of her hand to rub at a smudge on her cheek.

"I'm Adia's mom. Leona. Nice to meet you."

She waved her hand vaguely around in the air. "Grace is welcome to come in. I'll be here the whole time." Grace's mother stood stiffly, her hand still on Grace's arm.

Grace's mother made Adia look at her house differently. Grace's house was neat, and Adia's house was anything but that. When you walked through the front door, it was into a hallway piled with shoes and boots and slippers. Three Cape buffalo skulls were nailed into the wall, their horns used as lopsided coatracks with piles of old jackets and flannel shirts and key fobs hung over them. Sometimes there were clumps of dried red mud from the garden that would crush under your feet if you stepped on them and then cover your heels with fine, red dust.

Leona didn't clean the house much. She didn't think about it. Gakaki ("That name sounds like a cat coughing up a hairball," Grace said with a giggle that first day when she met him) was supposed to clean, but he never seemed able to make a dent in it. Little cobwebs decorated the corners of the ceilings, and papers and books were piled on every surface.

It was more comfortable for Adia to go to Grace's. Even though Grace's mother and her stiff face and her questions made Adia nervous, she loved going to Grace's house. She felt, when she walked through the front door each time, that she was an anthropologist stepping into a whole new world, and it made her see the appeal in the work her mother was so passionate about. Being different, entering an unknown and exotic culture, was exciting.

Every time Adia went to Grace's, she found new mysteries—the stacks of brightly colored boxes and packages of commissary food imported from the States, DVDs with television programs and movies that showed Adia the parts of American life she'd never even imagined before: happy families gathered in kitchens so shiny they looked unused, big fluffy dogs with no sign of mange that slept in special beds, piles of snow that kids threw at each other and made statues with. She could hardly believe the way people looked in the videos—perfectly clean, perfectly dressed and perfectly happy.

The biggest mystery, though, the biggest draw to Adia, was Grace's father. He wasn't there most of the times she was. He traveled a lot, Grace said, and he worked into the evenings most days. But when he was there, it fascinated Adia to watch him. He didn't look the way she pictured her own father. He wasn't broad shouldered or blond. He didn't have scars on his hands from bushwhacking, or a burned red neck. Grace's father was slight. He looked a lot like Grace, with his dark hair, narrow, straight nose and slanted cheekbones. He wore crisp white button-down shirts with shiny glinting cuff links. In the evenings, the few times Adia was there when he came home, she noticed that the first thing he did when he walked through the front door was set down his briefcase, then unbutton his cuff links and toss them in a little ceramic dish on a table in the hall.

He hugged Grace and her mom a lot. At first Adia found it uncomfortable. She wasn't used to seeing families interact this way. But then she noticed the TV families in the States were like that, too—smiling and talking together, hugging and kissing. She added that to the list of what her own father would be like. He would hug her and kiss her cheek hello and goodbye. He would look at her as if she was the most wonderful thing in the world. That's how Grace's father acted with Grace.

When they all sat down for dinner, he would ask Grace questions about school, about the things she was studying and what she liked best. The first time Adia ate dinner with the family, Grace's father poured the water from the carafe into all the glasses and said, "Gracie, honey, how did that math test go today?" Adia couldn't remember when, or if, her mom had ever kept close enough track of her schoolwork to know to ask that kind of question. She glanced at her friend. Grace rolled her eyes.

"Come on, Grace." Her dad seemed awkward, still standing behind Grace with the sweaty carafe in one hand. He leaned down to put the other hand on Grace's shoulder. "I know you were having trouble with multiplying fractions. Did the stuff I showed you help?"

Grace gave her shoulder a violent shrug and her father's hand flicked up like a bug. "God, Dad. Can we not talk about math now?" She kicked Adia's ankle under the table and made a face. Adia understood that she was to sympathize with her friend over the annoying, interfering parents, the myth she'd heard of but never experienced personally. Adia glanced at Grace's father and saw that he was stung. He caught her eye, though, and smiled.

"Our nickname for her lately is Grumpy Gracie."

Adia burst out laughing, and laughed a little harder when she caught Grace's dark expression watching her. Adia knew she'd crossed a line with her friend; she should have sided with Grace, not her dad, but it served Grace right, Adia thought. She had a father. She had an interested, kind father who asked her questions and smiled at her. She should treat him better.

Grace liked to have Adia spend the night at her house, but didn't like sleeping at Adia's. Adia didn't blame her and wished, actually, that she could spend more time at Grace's house. She wished she could stay there forever. Even Grace's mom eventually became less scary. She took them on road trips sometimes, on long weekends, and let Adia and Grace sing at the top of their lungs as they whipped along the highway down to the Rift, the back seat windows wide-open and the wind hitting them hard, forcing them to shut their eyes and pulling the words from their lungs.

At night, when Adia slept over, Grace's mom would have them shut the TV off at 11:00 p.m. and get into bed. Sometimes Grace grumbled and muttered curse words under her breath, but she always did as she was told. She'd find her parents in the living room, where they would be curled up at opposite ends of the couch, each reading a book. Grace would lean down and let each parent give her a kiss good-night and a hug. Adia would stand next to the coffee table and wonder where to put her hands. It wasn't the affection her friend received that made her uncomfortable, but rather the desperate ache she felt inside. Her father would do that, too, once she found him. It was on the list now, in her imagination. He would hug and kiss her good-night every night. She would sleep well, knowing he was in the house, watching over her.

One night, Grace was talking about a boy from school that she liked. It was late, and Grace was laughing about some-

thing the boy had said, and so Adia heard it before she did—
the rise and fall of Grace's parents' voices from another room.

"Shh," Adia whispered from her nest on the floor. "What's
that noise?" In the dark Grace's voice trailed off and she was
silent. The Morse code of Grace's mother's voice tapped a constant discourse while her father's interrupted with deep in-
termittent thumps, his words like things thrown against the
wall, thudded and mean.

"I guess it's my parents talking," Grace mumbled. "They're
just talking."

"Sounds like they're fighting to me," Adia answered. She
couldn't help but feel at once terrified that her perfect idea
of a family included parents who fought, and gleeful that the
shine of Grace's life at home might have a ding, after all. But
she hid the possibility of relief that Grace's life wasn't perfect,
and she sat up. She found Grace's hand and squeezed it.

"Grace," she said, thrilled with the thought that had only
just occurred to her. "If your parents got a divorce, maybe your
dad would marry my mom. Then we'd be sisters!"

Grace was silent. Adia could hear her breathing, and she
could hear, too, that the angry voices from the distant room
had quieted. The argument was over, presumably. Adia let
go of Grace's hand and lay back on the floor. She hugged the
pillow and pulled the sleeping bag close. She was just drifting
off—listing in her head, as she did every night, the attributes
she knew her father would have—but she heard what Grace
said. She heard the tiny, choked voice from under the covers
in the bed above her, and she let the message settle around
her like dust. She didn't reply. She hoped Grace assumed she
was asleep, that she hadn't heard.

"I would rather be motherless than have your mother."

In the dark, Adia was filled with the shame of knowing
that she understood exactly what Grace meant.

She knew Grace was angry, and it scared her. Adia loved having Grace as a friend and she didn't want to lose her. She flipped through her mind for something she could say to make it better—to make Grace like her again. And then it slipped out; the secret she wasn't sure she was ready to tell. "My father's not dead, anyway. He might marry my mom. I know where he is."

It worked.

"Holy shit!" Grace flipped over to face Adia and leaned over the edge of her bed. "How did you find out?" Her face was so close to Adia's that Adia could feel hot breath on her cheek.

Adia shifted her body away from Grace and sat up. The sleeping bag slid down her back and pooled on the floor. The air was chilly, and Adia pulled it up over her shoulders again. She hesitated to explain. She knew the story made her mother look dishonest, and she didn't want to give Grace fodder that would deepen her distaste for Leona. But she couldn't think of a lie that would work. "I just heard my mom and grandma talking about him."

"And they said where he lives?" Grace was breathless. "Why didn't your mom tell you sooner?"

"My mom saw his picture in a brochure. He runs a safari business. She didn't know before now, either—she thought he was dead."

"I wonder if they would get married? If they met again?" Grace asked. And the idea of that made Adia shiver with wishing.

Grace turned over onto her back and was quiet for a minute. Adia wondered if she was asleep already. But then her voice rose again, quieter now, but firm, less breathless.

"You have to find him, Adia! I'll help you!"

Adia didn't sleep well, and when she saw that the sky was lightening, she got up slowly. She didn't want to wake Grace.

She put her clothes on and shoved her pajamas into her back-pack. She went to Grace's desk and scrawled a note: "Forgot! My mom wants me home for breakfast! Call me later!" She wondered if Grace would believe her lie. She thought they both knew that Adia's mom would be asleep until noon. That she never ate breakfast anyway, let alone worried if Adia had.

Adia crept past Grace's parents' closed bedroom door and down the stairs. She hoped Selestenus wouldn't be in the kitchen yet; she didn't want to risk Grace or her parents hearing them converse. But she was lucky—the whole downstairs was still and empty. No coffee percolating yet, no smell of eggs and toast.

Adia shifted her pack on her shoulder and slid back the bolt on the front door. There would be a night guard on duty; she'd have to get past him, but if she greeted him quietly, nobody inside the house would hear. She opened the front door and was about to step out into the chilly morning air when she caught the glint of something on the table by the door. Just where he always left them, Grace's dad's silvery cuff links lay in the ceramic dish. Adia looked at them for a minute; she picked them up—just to feel the smoothness of the metal, to run her fingers over the carved design on the face, to touch the place where they might rub against Grace's father's wrist.

She heard a noise and turned. From the kitchen the coffee-pot gurgled into life. The back door opened and shut again. Selestenus's footsteps echoed softly down the hall. Not wanting to be seen now, she slipped out quickly and quietly shut the door behind her.

The night guard was at the gate. Someone—Selestenus maybe—had brought him a steaming cup of chai, and he sucked it loudly as he opened the gate for Adia. He nodded his greeting and smiled like there was nothing unusual, nothing at all, about a young white girl walking up the road alone at dawn. Adia turned once to look backward, to see if there were lights on yet in Grace's house, if there was anyone who might know she was gone, who might worry. But the windows were dark. Even the night guard had disappeared back into shadows. Adia turned to the road. She slipped her hand in her pocket and felt the cool metal of the cuff links, smooth and firm. They felt good under her fingers. If she ever did find her father, maybe she'd give them to him. She was certain he would like them.

By the time Adia saw Grace again, early Monday morning at school, Adia had almost forgotten the secret she'd shared. But Grace hadn't. Adia was sitting at a table in the open-sided cafeteria when she saw Grace's mom's car pull up the circular driveway in front of the administration building. The car had barely come to a stop when the back door flung open and Grace leaped out. She shouted goodbye to her mother and slammed the door behind her. When she saw Adia, Grace broke into a run.

"Adia, I have the best idea!" Grace slammed her backpack down on the table next to where Adia was sitting and took a deep breath. "I'm pretty sure it'll work."

She paused to catch her breath and noticed Adia's blank expression.

"Your dad!" Grace said. "For when we go find your dad."

Adia loved having a friend. A best friend. Mostly, she felt she'd do anything to keep Grace happy so the friendship would stay intact. She never wanted to go back to eating alone, to having the other kids roll their eyes when she walked past. She didn't notice those things anymore, not since Grace came. But, for the first time since she'd known Grace, Adia regretted being open. She didn't know if she wanted to find her father now. Not yet. And she was pretty sure she wanted to do it alone—or even with her mom—when she did. But here was Grace, so eager and so excited, she'd planned the whole thing out.

"So," Grace said, "I'll convince my mom to let me spend the night at your house... I think she's getting used to your mom enough to say yes. And then we'll sneak out and get a bus to your dad's house. You can find out if there's a bus, can't you? You know all that stuff."

Grace's face was shiny and hopeful. Adia couldn't bear to disappoint her friend.

"Well, I know the bus to Narok." Adia hesitated, thinking. It would be fun to introduce Grace to Simi. "Then I usually take a *matatu* from there to Loita. I don't know where my dad lives. But he runs his safaris kind of near Loita. They may have heard of him, anyway." Adia knew this would buy her time. Maybe by the time they got to Loita, Grace wouldn't want to go farther. Maybe nobody in the manyatta would know how or where to find her dad, anyway. There was always that possibility. "We'd need more than just one night, though," Adia told Grace. "Ask your mom to let you stay with me for the whole weekend. Friday after school to Monday."

Adia could have told her mom the plan—not the whole plan, but the part about taking Grace to meet Simi. Maybe her mom would even have given them a ride to the manyatta. The secrecy Grace imbued the plan with, though, deterred her. What would her mom care, anyway? She might not even notice—Adia had taken herself to the manyatta plenty of times.

It was dark when Adia shook Grace awake on the chosen morning a few weeks later. They needed to catch the early bus in order to make it before dark. She'd let Grace have her bed, and Adia had curled up on the bedroom floor in a sleeping bag. She knew Grace wouldn't be comfortable on the floor, although Adia knew well that any spiders or beetles in the house could just as easily crawl into the bed. What Grace didn't know didn't hurt her. Adia wondered what Grace would think of life in the manyatta—it made her feel nauseous to think that Grace might hate it, might find it too dirty and different. If Grace was uncomfortable there, Simi would be hurt, and the one person Adia wanted to hurt less than Grace was Simi.

They'd both slept in their clothes, so when Grace finally woke up, stretched and crawled out of bed, they didn't have much to do before tiptoeing down the stairs and out the door. It was dark and chilly, and the girls were silent as they trudged down the street outside Adia's house to the closest *matatu* stand, where they could get a ride to the bus depot. Miraculously, or maybe simply because it was so early, the *matatu* they found wasn't crowded. The girls each had a seat, and not long after they sat down, the fare taker swung himself into the van, banging the side to alert the driver, and they were off.

Grace didn't seem to mind the *matatu* or the crowds at the central bus park where Adia bought tickets for the Narok bus and then found a stall selling chai and *mandazis*.

"We have an hour," Adia said, waving Grace toward a low wall where they could sit. She handed Grace a cup of the sweet tea and newspaper-wrapped *mandazi*. "It's like a doughnut," she said. "You'll like it."

The girls didn't talk. It was still too early. They swung their legs against the wall and sipped their tea. Adia wondered if her mother was awake yet. If she would notice the girls were gone.

The bus left on time, which Adia assured Grace was highly unusual and extremely lucky. It was crowded, though, and Adia pushed Grace on through a throng of people and then shoved herself in, directing Grace to a window seat and then flinging herself down. The aisles would be full, too, with people and possibly livestock and poultry, she explained to Grace, so by sitting in the window seat, Grace would be pro-

tected from the possibility of having a chicken in her lap, or
a runny-nosed baby.

"I see why you told me not to bring anything that wouldn't
fit in my backpack," Grace said as more and more people
filled the bus. There was no room to move. Adia was pressed
against Grace, who was pressed against the window. Both girls
clutched their backpacks to their chests.

"This is why I brought so much stuff to Simi when your
mom drove us down here. When I'm on the bus, I can't really bring anything."

By the time the sun was directly overhead, the crowded bus
had wound down the Rift Valley escarpment and was bumping along the pitted tarmac toward Narok. Grace had fallen
asleep, her head bumping against the window every time the
bus hit a pothole. Adia vacillated between excitement at seeing her friends and Simi again, and introducing Grace to all
the people she most loved, and terror that it wouldn't go well.
She didn't let her mind wander to the reason for the trip. Finding her father, meeting him in person, seemed so outrageous
a notion that she couldn't even bring herself to imagine how
it would unfold.

Grace remembered Adia's Maasai mother from the time
they met in Narok. She was waiting at the fork in the road
about a mile away when the *matatu* from Narok dropped them
off. Grace couldn't understand how she knew when the girls
would arrive, but Adia said she'd probably been waiting for a
while. When Simi saw Adia, her face filled with an expression Grace couldn't imagine seeing on Leona—it was a face
full of complete devotion. Grace noticed that Adia's own face
matched. It was obvious Simi and Adia adored one another.

Grace ducked her head when Adia introduced her, the way
Adia had told her to, and Simi touched the crown of Grace's

hair and then said in English, "You are welcome here, like another daughter." Grace knew why Adia loved Simi so much; there was something about her. She made Grace feel immediately welcome and safe. Even in this completely unfamiliar world.

Grace woke up in the pitch-black of a thick, predawn night. The night before, the family, Simi's husband and some other people—Grace couldn't figure out the connections—cooked a goat to celebrate Adia's visit. Adia helped. She held the goat's four feet so when it was on its back and prone, it couldn't kick and escape. A man had delicately slit the animal's throat, and then held it upside down so the blood emptied into a large pot. Later, the same man removed the goat's skin in one whole piece, and cut rectangular pieces of it out. He then slit the rectangles in the middle, and slid one on Grace like a bracelet. She could still smell wood smoke in her hair and when she moved her arm, she could feel the goatskin clinging to her wrist. When she reached down to touch it, she could tell it was still slightly damp and malleable. When it dried it would tighten and stiffen, and it would hug her wrist. It was bad luck, Simi told her, to cut it off. Goatskin bracelets had to be worn until they broke off on their own.

Grace stretched and pulled the thin cloth *shuka* over her. She and Adia slept on the rawhide platform in the little hut where Adia was born. Grace hadn't slept well. Adia had fallen asleep instantly, and her heavy breathing and the sounds of the livestock just outside the hut kept Grace awake. She could have sworn that sometime deep in the night, she'd heard lions, too.

The people in the little village started their day early. Before the sun gripped the sky and dragged itself upward to illuminate the Loita Hills and the early spring grasses, Grace heard movement outside the hut. There were voices and sounds of someone herding the cattle out of the enclosure to graze. A baby cried, and there were clanks of metal pots being filled with water for tea. Grace couldn't bear to open her eyes; she was too sleepy still. But then Grace heard her friend's voice out there, too. Adia was a different person here. Grace couldn't believe how seamlessly Adia merged into the Maasai language and Maasai life.

"Hey, Grace! Morning!" Grace rolled over at the sound of Adia's voice.

"Come on, Simi's making tea."

Grace sat up and rubbed her eyes. She slipped a rubber band from her wrist and made a ponytail in her hair. Then she followed Adia out into the morning sun.

Simi's house was smoky and warm. Grace could see Simi through the murky light. She was blowing on the embers of last night's fire, and tossing handfuls of tea leaves into the big, dented *suferia*. When the fire grew hot, she added fresh milk and sugar to the boiling tea leaves. Next to the fire was a little pot full of white porridge. As the tea boiled, Simi scooped out spoonfuls of the paste into enamel bowls and handed one to each girl. Grace watched Adia dig right into it. She used her fingers to scoop out the stuff and roll it into golf ball–sized portions she then flicked into her mouth. She made eating with her hands look elegant, easy. Grace tried to mimic her, but the porridge was sticky and it ended up all over her hands.

"Did you ask about your dad?" Grace asked. Then slurped at the tea Simi handed her; an attempt to cover the unpleasant flavor of the porridge.

Simi looked up from ladling tea into Adia's cup. Her eyes were wide.

"Adia," she said. Her words were hesitant. "Your father, he is not alive."

Adia spoke in Maa. Grace wanted to tell her to speak in

English, so she could understand. Instead, she interrupted. "He's not dead. He runs a safari business. Adia thinks he may have hired guides from here. Do you know?"

Adia looked stricken. She and Simi locked eyes and then, slowly, each turned to look at Grace. Grace was suddenly uncomfortable. Had she broken some cultural rule she didn't know existed?

Simi reached out and grasped Adia's arm. Adia looked like she might cry. They spoke to each other quickly in Maa. Grace sat back. She sipped her tea again, trying to pretend she wasn't there. Obviously her question was unwelcome.

Adia glanced at Grace. On one hand, she was angry with her friend. It wasn't Grace's place to get involved in this. Adia consented to bringing Grace here because she figured she could tell her that nobody knew of her father and then they could head back to Nairobi. But a small part of her, deep down, was excited. Grace pushed her to this, and now, maybe, it was the right thing to do.

"Grace, I had to explain to Simi that he isn't dead." Relief washed over Grace. She hadn't broken any rules, just good news. She thought Adia had told Simi already—Adia couldn't blame her for not knowing, especially when Adia and Simi mostly spoke Maa to each other.

"Anyway," Adia continued. "She does know a few *moran* who worked for a *muzungu* man a couple of years ago. She doesn't know if it's him or not, but she's going to find the guys and introduce me."

Leona hated the telephone. It always meant bad news. Especially when it rang this early in the morning. She opened her eyes. Jesus. It was only nine thirty. And a Sunday, too. Fuck. It was probably her mother. Joan never seemed to remember the time difference. Mostly she called in the middle of night, which was okay since Leona stayed up late, but every now and again there was a wake-up call.

"Hello, Mom?" She coughed and told herself, again, she had to stop smoking. The voice on the other end wasn't her mother, though.

"Leona? Hi, this is Jane. Grace's mom."

Leona rubbed her eyes and sighed. It was a mother but at least it wasn't her mother.

"I'm just calling to check in with Grace. To see when she wants me to pick her up."

"Um. Okay." Leona sighed. She suspected it would be easier to just do what Jane was asking rather than trying to put it off, or ask if Grace could call her later. "Let me see." She put the phone down and shuffled down the hall to Adia's room. The door was closed and the room was quiet. Leona knocked and listened. Nothing. Expecting to see the girls fast asleep, Leona cracked the door open. Sun was pouring into the window, and the room was still. Adia's bed was unmade, as always, and the sleeping bag was piled on the floor, but nobody was sleeping. The girls were gone.

"Shit," Leona muttered. She wasn't worried about Adia and Grace as much as she was worried about what Jane would say.

Grace couldn't take her eyes off the men who crossed the ground in long strides—it looked like they were floating—to speak with Adia about the man they once worked for. Adia translated sporadically, but Grace barely listened. She watched the men's long fingers play on the pale ends of the *rungu* they each carried, a smoothly polished wooden throwing club they wore tucked into a leather belt around their waists. The men were each wrapped in bright red cloths—two pieces, one tied at the shoulder, like a sideways cape, and one wrapped around their waists. Their shoes were sandals made from strips of car tires, and they all wore bright beaded strips of leather around their wrists and necks. Grace had seen Maasai in books before, but the pictures had no smell, and the men were heavy with the scent of mud and ochre in their tightly braided long hair. When they first approached, they laid their spears down and Grace saw how sharp the tips were, how long the ebony handles were. She heard Adia say, "Yes, yes, John." And then the men unfolded their long legs and floated off again. Grace wished they would stay longer—having them so near was thrilling, like living in an exotic book. Grace felt a heavy emptiness in her chest as she watched them go.

"Okay, I think it's him." Adia sounded tired. "If we're going to go, we should go now. The bus for Solai leaves from Narok this afternoon."

"I can't put Grace on the phone now, unfortunately. The girls left already." Leona spoke firmly into the phone. She wanted to convey an air of authority, of confidence in her ability to survey a situation with her daughter and know everything was fine. Jane didn't seem convinced. In fact, she melted into a panic with a swiftness that startled Leona.

"Oh, okay," Jane answered. "Where did they go?"

Before Leona could think of a good lie, she told the truth. "I don't know—Adia has a whole litany of places she goes."

"You don't know where they are? When did you last see them?"

Leona realized she didn't know. She thought they'd been at the house the evening before. When she was out in the yard last night, curled in the wooden chair she'd dragged out there so she could stare at the stars and smoke, she thought she'd heard them. Hadn't she?

Leona assured Jane she'd call back soon. But when she hung

up the phone, she had no idea how to proceed, no idea what to do next.

A few minutes later, while pouring herself tea in the kitchen, Leona saw Gakaki emerge from his room. His quarters were set against the side of the house, a two-room concrete addendum to the house built when it was common for household help to live on-site. Leona had offered him the rooms when she first moved in. Adia was too little to stay alone then, and she wanted him to be there when she needed to leave—alone—on short notice. She rapped a knuckle on the window and waved him over.

"Adia was packing things to eat," he said, when Leona asked when he'd last seen the girls. "She was putting food in her backpack. And water bottles."

Leona was relieved. She knew what that meant. Adia often woke early on weekends to take the bus to Loita. When she did, she foraged in the kitchen for snacks to eat on the bus. "Ah, they went to Loita," she said out loud.

"Miss Leona, I heard Adia and her friend talking of the father. Of Adia's father."

Leona's head swam and her hands began to shake. How on earth did Adia know? And why hadn't she realized this could never be kept a secret? Leona called Jane back and kept her voice light. No reason to worry this other mother who seemed to worry over nothing no matter what. "Yeah, they just went to meet Adia's friend. Yes, yes, they're fine. I'll have Grace call the minute they get back."

"Gakaki, if they call or come back, tell them to get in touch with Grace's mom." Leona didn't take the time to pee or fill up a water bottle. She just jumped in her car and started driving toward Solai. If she paused to think, even for a second, she would lose her courage.

BUFFALO

Sunday was shopping day, and John had paid the Muslim shop-keeper for the supplies and was loading them into his truck. The basics—milk, eggs, tea, a bit of sugar—and some luxuries like beer and Scotch whiskey.

He turned to push open the shop doors with his shoulders, but stumbled a bit when the door opened from the other side.

"Sorry, John!"

It was Daniel's wife's brother. John had met him several times before, but couldn't remember the man's name. He was successful, though—owned a beautiful plot of land just outside town where, rumor had it, he was planning to build a safari lodge. John had been meaning to speak to him about cross-pollinating—bringing his clients to Solai for discounted hotel fees. He couldn't begin that conversation now, though, because the man stepped into the shop and said, "I saw you have a visitor up at the house. I just drove past your gate and saw a *muzungu* woman there. A relative, perhaps?"

Startled, John fumbled one of the bags, and the shopkeeper's young assistant rushed to his side, "Mister John, *pole, pole...*" he murmured as he slid a few of the plastic bag handles from John's wrists onto his own.

John looked up and saw the man still smiling at him.

"Yes," John said, not knowing what else to say, "a cousin. Distant. Lives in Uganda."

He set the bags in the bed of the truck, lodging them tightly with the spare tire and an old tarp so they wouldn't slide around too much on the way home. *"Muzungu,"* the man had said. A white woman. Who on earth could it be?

John never intended to stay in Solai. After the night his mother confessed the truth about his older brother and about the fact that she'd told his daughter's mother he was dead, he'd shuttled back and forth from Karen to Solai every couple of weeks. The constant need to return to Solai made running his business from Nairobi hard, and so, eventually, he'd just stayed here. He'd transferred the business to Solai, and divided his time between that and taking care of his mother.

The road up from town to the house was pitted and pocked with hillocks and holes carved out by the recent rains. John's bottles of beer and whiskey rattled louder and louder in the back of the truck, the road growing worse the closer to the farm he got. And the louder the rattle, the more nervous John grew. He knew who he wanted the woman to be. But what were the chances? She was in America, had been for years. God knows he hadn't been with many other women since he'd moved here, and the ones he had found time to seduce were clients. All safely back where they'd come from, America or Europe. Too far away to make him feel hemmed in. This visitor was probably just a Jehovah's Witness or some other do-gooder. John reached up and felt the stubble on his chin. He glanced at his reflection in the rearview. The last time he shaved, he'd seen white hairs between the yellow ones. An image of his father flipped into his mind…pure white hair and beard. He'd looked like a child's image of God.

The afternoon was waning, and shadows were just beginning to lengthen. John pulled up next to a car parked in his usual spot. It was a Renault 4, a common car here. But he had to catch himself as he climbed out of the Land Rover; he almost stumbled and fell. This was a dusty, dented one, old and worn. His breath and heartbeat sped up. He leaned over and placed his hands on his knees. He felt he might faint. Or vomit. He remembered this car. He remembered watching it speed off, leaving him standing alone and choking on dust outside the Chabani Guest House. Now it felt as if every cell in his body were shivering. He'd thought of Leona often. He dreamed about his daughter, and he yearned to see her. But the hope that that would ever happen had died in him a long, long time ago.

John rarely locked the house, and he was surprised when he found the place empty. "Hello?" he called, just to make sure.

Ruthie had been dead over six months now, but the silence still seemed new to John. She hadn't made much noise in her decline, but the feeling of another human in the house was something he'd felt. He missed it.

The car's driver, whoever it was, was nowhere in the house, and there were groceries to unload. Passing the dented little car again made his heart beat with anticipation. What was it doing here, and where was the driver?

He gathered his bags and the boxes and the Scotch and piled them on the kitchen counter. They were heavy, and he paused and looked up. In the distance, up on the hill with the baobab, he could make out the shape of a figure. There was a person up there, a person sitting on the bench overlooking the headstones.

It didn't take long for John to stride up the hill. But as he got closer to the figure, he felt himself becoming more and more nervous. He was almost near enough to touch the person's back when he stopped. Should he speak? Simply sit down on the bench, as well?

Then the woman turned. John felt a jolt. She didn't look the same. Her face was smooth and curved into high cheekbones; her eyes were clear. But the way her mouth was set; the movement of her hand to her chest when she saw him—John knew she was equally stunned to see him. She stumbled from the bench and stood. She was almost as tall as him, and John rarely met a woman he could look in the eyes without bending his neck.

"John!" the woman said, and her American accent softened and rounded out her vowels.

"What are you doing here?"

His question was a stupid one, he scolded himself. There were days when the fantasy of meeting her again played out lovingly; they saw each other somewhere and she was apologetic, regretful. She'd made a mistake, she said in those daydreams of his, and she wanted to make it right. Other days his imagination was clouded with anger and he'd see her somewhere and shout; he'd demand answers and shake her if he had to. He had played out every possibility there was. Except for this one. He was utterly empty of emotion and it rendered him speechless.

"I visited your mom here, years ago. I hoped she still lived here," Leona said. Her voice sounded like cigarettes. It reminded him, vaguely, of his father's. He felt a tinge of emotion then—anger. Resentment.

"You're about six months too late." He nodded sharply toward the newest headstone, still pale and bright, not licked by lichen or time.

"I hoped she still lived here so I could ask her where you were. But I saw a man when I drove up—Daniel, he said he was—he told me about her and said you'd be back soon, that I could wait."

"Well, you found me. Why are you looking for me?"

"Your daughter, Adia, she has run away. I thought she might have come to find you."

John felt his mouth go slack and his skin prickle. He didn't know how to stop his spinning thoughts enough to formulate an answer. "No," he finally managed, "I haven't seen her."

Leona sighed.

"She must have gone to Simi, then." Leona's voice was clear—she didn't seem at all upset, or shocked, by these circumstances. First, John wondered how she managed to be so controlled. Then he felt the bubble of anger rising in his throat, and the shout came quickly and loud, "I wouldn't even know what she looks like. I haven't seen her since she was a newborn."

"Well, she looks like you," Leona said. Still cool, still firm. "I need to find her. She's with a friend, and the other girl's parents are anxious."

She looked down, rummaged through a leather bag slung over her shoulder and pulled out a beaded key fob.

John was stunned by the heat that rose in his face. Was she kidding? To see each other after all these years and the only thing she could say was, essentially, hello and goodbye?

"Jesus, woman. You're just going to disappear like that again? I've wanted to see you—to see her—for years. I didn't even know you were in the country anymore, but even still, every time I see a girl who could be her age…every time I see a white woman who could be you, especially around here…" He paused. He hated being this emotional. He swallowed back a combination of tears and anger. "I'm not going to let you walk away. I want to meet my daughter."

She looked up at John. Her eyes were dark and rimmed with tiny lines. He wanted to touch her cheek. Or slap her silly. He still couldn't decide.

"Well, then, I could use your help. I need to drive to the manyatta, see if she's there. Will you come?"

John still didn't know what to think. He hadn't settled on the emotion that matched the situation. But he knew he didn't want to let Leona go away again, not without some answers. And if he could meet Adia? The notion sent shivers down his back. He'd waited for so long.

"We'll go in my truck—it'll be better on the roads."

By the time they were outside the farm gates and on the way, the sun was just low enough in the sky that it glared directly into the front window. It was impossible to see, and John went mostly on instinct.

"I thought you were in America," John said. "And if you weren't, then why did you wait so long to find me?"

"She told me you were dead," Leona said simply. John glanced over at her profile.

He saw her start and then she screamed.

"Shit! Watch out!" She threw her arms up, instinctually reaching for something to grab onto.

John was shocked into alertness and he slammed on the brakes, bringing the truck to a screeching, quivering halt. There, less than twenty feet in front of them, was a large Cape buffalo. It stood stock-still in the middle of the dirt track, its enormous head low and heavy. It held one front leg slightly aloft, delicately. John noticed the leg was bleeding.

The buffalo grunted and shook its great, heavy horns. Then it was running and in seconds had thrown its full weight and battering-ram head into the front of the truck, shaking the frame, causing Leona to scream again.

"Fuck!" John shouted, and he flipped the engine off. He watched as the buffalo turned and galloped—fast for having a hurt leg, John thought—back to his starting point and then turned again, head lowered for a second run at the truck.

John twisted and reached for his rifle behind his seat. In one swift motion, he ensured it had a bullet in the chamber, cocked it and slid out of the truck.

"What are you doing?" Leona cried.

"Stay put."

He strode forward to meet the buffalo as it raced again toward them.

John was an excellent shot. It was the one thing of value his father had given him. It was necessary out here. His parents forbade him to be out on the land without his rifle, and John had used it plenty of times before. Never for the pleasure of hunting, which in fact brought him no pleasure at all, but for his own safety. He'd shot the heads off snakes and killed a hyena that approached him too fast one afternoon. He'd even come close, just once, to shooting his father. He remembered how powerful he'd felt as he held the older man's head in his sights. He knew he could hit him in one shot, and he knew that he'd be okay if he did—self-defense wouldn't be a lie. But in the end John lowered the gun and, instead, ran fast to Daniel's, leaving his mother alone at home to bear the brunt of his father's mood.

The first bullet hit the buffalo's chest, tearing away a chunk of flesh and causing the animal to stumble, grunt in agony and turn in the direction of the pain. He must have seen John moving, and John heard Leona scream as the animal, fueled by pain and fear, hurtled away from the truck and toward John.

John backed up as quickly as he could manage. He recocked the rifle—Christ but how he wished he'd counted the bullets in the chamber while still in the safety of the truck—and fell backward. He saw a wall of black buffalo descending on him, close enough that later he found the animal's blood on his boot. He fired again, and the buffalo fell. Immediately there was a thick silence. The only sound was a breeze through the grasses and the faint echo of the gunshot where before there had been hooves beating the ground and John's and the buffalo's terrified breathing.

The buffalo was beautiful. Huge and healthy, but for the broken leg. It was a shame he had to die.

Leona appeared next to him. She stood at the buffalo's head, looking down.

"Fuck! I thought I was going to see you trampled to death."

John looked up and saw Leona's hands were shaking. She had her sunglasses perched on the top of her head, and her eyes were wide-open and round with shock. She knelt down and stroked the buffalo's ear. "It's a beauty, though."

"Did you see its leg?" he asked. He hoped his voice would steady soon. In his mind he could still feel the ground shaking beneath him as the heavy animal came barreling toward him. Fear and adrenaline made his muscles weak and his blood pounded in his veins. He could hardly believe he'd felled it with that last shot.

"It was broken. He would have died soon anyway...a lion would have gotten it, a hyena. It would have been eaten alive..." He stopped. Leona already knew. She'd been in Kenya long enough to know. Life was hard out here for the unfit, the unhealthy. A quick death by bullet in the brain was far better than the alternative. He didn't need to tell her that in his own life he'd learned that death is often the kindest thing.

In this drought, the dead buffalo would give all the scavengers a rare meal. Tomorrow it would just be bones. Maybe he would go back and retrieve the skull as a reminder of the afternoon. He'd start a future soon, one he would write for himself. He was alive, and for the first time in ages, that felt like it might be a lucky thing.

The bus from Narok to Solai was far more crowded than the one they'd taken down the Rift from Nairobi the day before. Adia climbed on first and stood in the aisle, looking around for two seats together. Grace stepped up behind her, and stood so close Adia could feel her breath on the back of her neck when Grace said, "We can sit separately. I don't mind."

The bus was crowded. Only a few seats remained, and with the dozen or so people behind Grace, trying to board, Adia knew they had to grab any seats they could. They'd be gone in minutes.

"Okay, you sit up here." Adia pointed to a window seat just behind the driver. A prim, middle-aged lady sat along the aisle. Adia knew Grace would be safe from errant hands—men who thought it would be funny to pinch a young woman. "I'll take that one in the back."

Grace slid into the seat and adjusted her backpack on her lap. "No prob," she said and flashed Adia a brilliant smile. "I'll see ya on the other side!"

Adia squeezed into an aisle seat at the back of the bus. A large woman in a vivid pink dress and pink plastic shoes occupied the window seat. She held a baby, swaddled in a *kanga*, on her lap.

"*Jambo,*" Adia greeted the woman in Swahili, and then leaned back and closed her eyes. She didn't want to get into a conversation. For this reason, she felt grateful that Grace and she had to sit apart. Adia wanted to think, to calm her nerves and try desperately to figure out what to say if, when, she saw her father.

The bus rattled and bounced along the heavily pocked road to Solai. The lady in the pink dress fell asleep and her head lolled onto Adia's shoulder. Adia opened her eyes then and glanced down. She smiled at the baby who stared back at her with big, shiny eyes. Adia looked up and saw Grace's long brown ponytail waving in time to the bus's jolts. She was proud of Grace. Grace hadn't complained once about the buses or the *matatus*, and she'd seemed comfortable in the manyatta. Adia had been terrified to introduce Grace to that part of her life, and the relief she felt now, knowing that it had gone so much better than she could have anticipated, was warm. She looked out the window at the golden land sliding by. She couldn't be down here, at the bottom of the Rift, without feeling lucky. This was her home. The most beautiful place in the world.

Suddenly, Adia saw the pink-dress woman's head jerk forward and smack the seat in front of them, hard. Adia saw the baby bounce and, without thinking, she flopped her head and chest and arms down, covering the baby and pinning the tiny body to the mother's bright pink lap. She felt a pain slice through her skull and vaguely realized that her head, too, had slammed into the metal bar at the top of the seat in front of her. She registered the glass flying over her head, and the horrible, uncontrolled movement of the bus, but, oddly, she didn't feel fear. Later, she'd play this moment over in her head until she could name what she felt—utter acceptance. She was going to die. It was this that frightened her most in the weeks and months to follow. The ease with which she gave up. Then the movement stopped as suddenly as it had started. The air, the people, the vehicle, Adia's thoughts were all completely still and silent. Nothing moved.

Adia tasted blood and ran her tongue over her teeth. One was jagged and broken, and her mouth filled quickly with blood. She watched the blood fall to the dirty bus floor and make a little pool. No one spoke; no one breathed. Adia looked up and saw the green lights on the dashboard flicker and dim. She couldn't see Grace's ponytail. She hoped Grace wasn't scared.

She looked over at the pink-dress lady and saw that she was still, too. Her head thrown back and resting on the cracked bus window. There was blood on the window. Then the panic rushed in, a tsunami of terror, and Adia could hear herself screaming. Underneath her arms, something moved. There were those shiny eyes and there was that baby's mouth, open like Adia's own, screaming and screaming loudly and long out the broken window and over the pitted dirt of the road and over the dry grasses waving in the wind as if nothing had happened at all. Then Adia realized they weren't the only ones crying and screaming, but that others, too, from where they were, were moaning and sobbing into that clear, wide-open Kenyan sky.

The baby's mother moved then, she slowly lifted her head from the window and Adia watched her eyes as they made a shift from dazed and unsure to horror as she realized what had happened, and then how they slid into relief as she noticed Adia leaning into her lap, still clutching the baby. Adia sat up then. Her head hurt, and her back did, too, and so did her still-bleeding mouth. She managed to reach down and pull her backpack out from where it had wedged under the seat in front of hers, then she picked her way gingerly toward the front of the bus. There were bodies she stepped over. Broken ones and bleeding ones. Some moved a little, some made terrible sounds, but the worst were the ones that were completely still. Adia couldn't see Grace at first. She saw the prim woman Grace sat next to. There she was—she was a still one, flopped like a doll over the seat clear across the aisle from where she'd been. Her eyes were wide-open, and she looked perfect, but Adia noticed the slight off-kilter look to her back. Backs didn't bend that way.

Then Adia saw Grace, curled like a bug near the driver's seat. Her silken ponytail gliding across the dirty bus floor. Adia knelt down to tuck Grace's hair over her shoulder. She leaned down and whispered in her friend's ear, "Grace! Grace, it's okay. I'm here." Grace's eyes were closed. Maybe she was sleeping. Adia felt like escaping into sleep, too. Adia bent herself over her friend as she'd done the baby. The baby had survived. The baby was all right. She ran her palm across Grace's cheek, and then she closed her own eyes. Maybe none of this was happening at all.

The bus shook and the voices of the people wove themselves around Adia's consciousness. Men were shouting, people were lifting bodies out of seats and carrying them past Adia and Grace. The bus was crowded now, so crowded and noisy. After a while, a man leaned down and grasped Adia by the shoulders. He said something. His hands were rough, his grip strong. Adia pulled herself from him and clutched at Grace again. She wouldn't leave Grace. This was not Grace's world; she'd be scared when she woke up surrounded by unfamiliar faces and a language she didn't understand. The man said something else, he wrested Adia away from Grace and lifted her up, high above her friend and the dirty bus floor and the broken people who still littered it. He lifted her down the bus steps and into the sunshine.

"You are lucky, *toto*! You are lucky because you lived." Adia heard his words, but they rattled in her brain without finding footing. They didn't make sense at all. She tried to push past the man and board the bus again, but he was large and had long arms and a passive face. He gestured to a woman who stood nearby, and the woman came closer and took Adia's hand.

"Come here to sit with me. Help will come soon."

Adia let herself be led away. She was tired. More tired than she'd ever been. She wanted to sit under a tree with her head in this kind woman's lap and fall asleep until everything was normal again.

Adia and the woman sat. Adia was thirsty and tried to open the straps of her backpack to get her water bottle, but somehow she just couldn't make them work. Her fingers had forgotten how to function. Another woman approached. It was the mother in her pink dress holding the baby. One of the mother's eyes was crusted over with a thick layer of blood.

"They need *kangas*," the mother said to the woman next to Adia. "The flies are too bad now. They have to cover the dead."

The dead. The dead. Those words, too, flipped into Adia's brain without taking root. They echoed and echoed and she looked up and saw that, yes, there were lines of people lying on the earth as if they were sunning themselves on a beach. Those were the dead. A couple of women had gathered extra *kangas* and market bags and were carefully covering the bodies to keep flies from licking up the drying blood. One of the women who'd just draped a cloth over someone stood up and moved, and in the space she'd vacated, Adia saw a pale arm peeking out from under a plastic bag. No. That was wrong. She stood and walked to the line of people and pulled the bag off the girl who lay underneath. It was a mistake. Grace wasn't dead. Grace wasn't dead. Grace wasn't dead. Adia sank down and stretched out next to her friend.

"Jesus!" John cursed loudly, and Leona pulled up her sunglasses and looked in the direction he was pointing. Up ahead in the distance, the road was crawling with people. There was a crowd. Where did they all come from? Leona wondered for a split second, until she registered the black smoke billowing up and heard the people shouting and crying. By then, they were close enough to see that a large, crowded bus had collided with a truck loaded down with supplies headed from Nairobi to Narok and too heavy to be easily maneuverable. Both vehicles were badly damaged. The front of the bus was crushed and the windshield shattered. There was blood on the glass, and the swarms of people, the survivors, were frantically pulling bodies from the bus—some seemingly alive, some dead, all broken.

John swerved the truck to the side of the road and jerked to a stop. Leona and John flew out of the car and ran toward the bus. They saw the *muzungu* body. Then another. A young girl, her hair matted with blood and her limbs completely still, and a blonde girl lying so close to the first, and so still, that together they looked like a carving. Something like electricity snapped in Leona's brain and a deep shock of fear tore through her so violently that she stumbled and fell. She couldn't gather the strength to stand, and so she just watched John stride ahead of her, speaking in rapid-fire Swahili, demanding information, asking if someone had called an ambulance. Leona had been a distant mother, unemotional, but she knew the singular curve of that blonde girl's shape, she knew that body almost as well as she knew her own. John didn't know, Leona thought. He didn't know that girl was his girl, that the way her expressions folded on her face sometimes reminded Leona of him. That the blood on her face, the salty blood he was dabbing at with a handkerchief, was as much his as it was hers. That girl was the two of them, swirled together. Leona didn't pray. She was impatient with the concept of God. But just then, at that moment, she closed her eyes and murmured a wish. "Please let them have a chance to know each other. Please don't let her die." And she imagined the wish, her breath made into whispered speech, floating up to the outer limits of the sky, where maybe, just maybe, God would hear it.

GIRL IN THE SHAPE OF
AFRICA

Letting go a little was Paul's idea, but Jane agreed. Part of her knew she had been holding Grace too tightly for too long. Paul and Jane had both had mostly regular American childhoods; being independent was part of that. Their parents hadn't been their friends, like Jane was with Grace. When she and Paul grew up, they taught themselves to ride bikes and spent whole weekends only seeing their parents for meals. That's the way it was for all kids back then. Jane told herself she was more protective of Grace because they lived overseas—Grace was not at home, and dangers were different here. But Jane knew, somewhere inside herself, that that wasn't really the truth. This was Grace's home, after all. Jane was the one in strange territory. Jane clung to Grace because she needed her daughter more than her daughter needed her.

When Adia began spending the night at their house, coming over after school to do homework, Jane felt like she was doing a service for the girl—feeding her nutritious food, making sure she minded her manners. She didn't entirely trust Adia, who'd foraged in the pantry for food without asking permission, and Jane still wondered if it had been she who'd taken Paul's cuff links, but Jane thought it was better, much better, to open her home to Adia, rather than have Grace going to Adia's house more than she did already. Jane's skin crawled at the thought of that grotty place.

But when Grace finally did beg to spend the weekend with Adia, Jane said yes. Jane knew there wouldn't be as much supervision as she herself would provide. She'd seen Leona's distracted parenting, the way she let Adia traipse around the city on *matatus*. And Grace had even mentioned that Adia caught buses into the Rift Valley to visit her Maasai friends sometimes. All alone. Jane couldn't imagine doing that as an adult, let alone allowing her child to. But she told herself to trust Grace. She'd raised her right, hadn't she? Grace would make responsible choices over the weekend because she was a responsible girl.

It was evening and the balcony was cool. Jane was sitting in the chaise, trying not to worry over the fact that she still hadn't heard from Grace, and that Leona hadn't called back, either. Paul had stepped out onto the balcony, too, and handed her a glass of wine. "The bats," he said, and Jane nodded—they were blooming from the innermost branches of the banana trees like velvet flowers and speeding across the sky. Paul reached down and caressed Jane's shoulder. They were rarely alone anymore, and even through her fear, a tiny ember of gratitude lit inside Jane. She didn't want to cry now, not from fear or thanks for her husband's gentleness. When the ringing phone jarred the silence, Jane started so violently that Paul's hand was flicked off her shoulder. "You're as nervous as a cat," he said. "I'll get it."

The noise, the gasp-turned-cry her husband made, would,

for years, visit Jane in her dreams, shocking her awake at least once a week, stealing sleep for the rest of those nights. She always thought that if there were one moment in her life when she would have chosen to be deaf, it would be that moment. She'd never heard Paul sound so helpless, so broken. It was as if she were an auditory witness to the second his life dipped into darkness.

Someone ran to the nearest village to find transport to Narok. Luckily, someone there had a motorcycle and sped off to alert the clinic that wounded and dead were coming. Another flatbed truck appeared from the horizon and had room for the bodies. The dead were gently laid in the truck; the wounded that could sit hunched in the truck bed, too. Then a smaller car, a tourist Jeep, pulled up. John was busy guiding the remaining survivors into the spaces on the truck, so Leona just gestured at him, called in a voice scraped raw that she would take this girl to the clinic in the Jeep. He didn't need to know. Not now. For the first time since Leona had pulled Adia from Simi's grasp all those years ago, Leona wanted her daughter to herself.

The two tourists in the Jeep, and their driver, were silent. The tourists had ashy, shocked faces, and their staring eyes kept returning, time and again, to the odd and bloody girl. Leona had to close her eyes because she was afraid that she'd suddenly leap up and smack them. Their sad faces and their pity. She hated them. Now and again Adia became overcome and leaned down, face in hands, and keened. A whistling breath escaped her lips, and she rocked back and forth, not sobbing so much as moaning. It was a dry, heaving call, something from another world.

It was dark by the time Grace's parents arrived. They came with a little team of people from the American embassy. By then, Adia was curled in a corner of the crowded clinic's waiting area, fast asleep. Leona sat on a bench that rocked on uneven legs and occasionally stood, forced herself outside to buy tea from a stall, where the milk was boiled over a charcoal brazier that gave the tea a smoky taste. Leona had just returned to the bench with a fresh cup and sat, exhausted, with her head tipped back against the wall and her eyes closed. She wondered where John was.

A woman's voice, strained and raspy from sobbing, cut through her thoughts.

"This is what happens…this is what happens when you aren't careful!"

Leona lifted her eyes and saw a face hanging above her, big and red and raw as meat. It took her a moment to recognize the face as the one belonging to Grace's mother. Now the face was as swollen and haunted as Adia's was before she drifted off.

"This is what happens!" The woman sobbed through the gasping of her breath and the tears and mucus that slicked over her face and choked her words so they were staccato, hemmed in by quick, ineffective breaths. The sounds felt like stones pounding Leona's ears. Leona stood up, her legs shaking. She saw that the noise had woken Adia, and now the girl was trying to stand, her face stricken and gray.

"They were too young to have that kind of freedom. You may not care about your daughter, but I care about mine. I'm a real mother!"

Adia pulled herself up off the floor and moved to Leona's side. She took her mother's hand and squeezed it. The squeeze was welcome but unfamiliar. They didn't hold hands, Leona and Adia. They hardly touched at all. There was a man behind the screaming woman now. Dark and slight, he wasn't crying but looked as empty as a shell. Leona thought he must be the husband, Grace's father, whom she'd never met. His face was slack with shock, his eyes red-rimmed and bewildered. Still, he was calm. He pinched the woman's shoulder blades and whispered into her ear until she turned and stumbled away through a doorway into a room behind her. The people who'd come with her followed. Later Leona discovered they were the embassy doctor, the consular officer and the duty officer.

Once Grace's parents arrived at the clinic, there wasn't a reason for Leona and Adia to stay. Instead, Leona led Adia through the nighttime streets to the Chabani Guest House. Leona couldn't quite believe they were back here—and stranded—after all this time. Without a car, they'd be dependent on the same bus to Solai that Adia and Grace had ridden. But Leona couldn't parse out their options or make a plan. She was too exhausted. Instead, she tucked her daughter into bed and went to the bar for a beer. Matthew, the barkeep, was there, and his familiar face was comforting. After she emptied her bottle, too fast and on an empty stomach, she told Matthew that if he saw John, to tell him she was there, too. Then she'd climbed, light-headed, off the stool. She was not in control anymore. She didn't want to be, either. It was too hard and too lonely. Under the fluorescent light outside the door to their room, Leona looked down and noticed there was blood—Adia's blood—on her shirt. She fought the urge to lift it to her lips and taste it.

In the morning, John was there. Leona stepped out of the shower and dressed quietly. She didn't want to wake Adia, who had slept fitfully, once even waking herself up with sobs. Now, although relaxed in sleep, her face was still swollen and red. The light tapping on the door startled Leona. She pulled her dirty T-shirt over her head and cracked the door an inch, not knowing who to expect. John's face was scrubbed clean and pink, his hair combed with a wet comb. The look of hope on his face told Leona everything she needed to know.

"I'm sorry," John whispered as Leona stepped into the hallway and pulled the door closed behind her. "It never crossed my mind that it was her." His face looked as excited as a boy's. "I immediately went into emergency mode and it never occurred to me. Matthew told me last night. I couldn't sleep. Is she okay?"

Leona was prepared to be, she expected to be, annoyed by this early-morning visit and its emotional impact. But instead she felt a ripple of relief shiver through her. This was what it was like to share the burden of something heavy.

"She just wants to sleep," Leona whispered. "She's been sleeping on and off—mostly on—since we found her."

"What a crushing thing to happen to a kid." John's eyes were dark with sadness. "She'll be grieving this for a long time. What about the other girl? Her parents…" John trailed off. Then he said, "I just can't imagine." In his mind he thought suddenly of his own mother, who had also lost a child. How did she get through it? How would the parents of the dead girl he'd loaded into the back of the truck yesterday get through it? The body he'd carried was so light, the face, bloodied as it was, so smooth and young.

John looked at Leona. Her hair was wet from her shower, but her clothes were rumpled and dirty and a little bloodied.

"Of course we'll go back to Solai today," John said. "She'll recuperate at my house. Nairobi is too far to take her in this condition."

The ride from Narok to Solai was quiet. Leona was right; Adia curled in the back seat with her eyes closed and didn't say a word the entire time. John didn't know whether she was asleep or just hiding from the bone-crushing pain of her new reality. He understood that desire to hide. He'd felt it himself a time or two.

John slowed down when they passed the buffalo's body. Had that only happened yesterday? It felt like years ago. He didn't stop—there was still flesh on the animal's bones, still vultures feasting. He didn't want the skull anymore. Today was the real beginning of his life.

When John pulled the Land Rover up the last hill, Adia roused.

"Where are we?" she whispered.

"Home," John answered.

Leona turned in the passenger seat to look at her daughter. She watched her daughter's face, the tanned cheeks, the strong jaw and the hollow sad eyes. The saddest eyes Leona could remember seeing. They were a puzzle, the two of them—two pieces that never seemed to fit. It was her fault, she knew that. She'd never really tried to be a decent mother. She took a deep breath, and she felt the familiar feeling of guilt sliding under her flesh like bits of broken glass. She wasn't, she hadn't been, brave enough to be a good mother. She hoped she was brave enough for it now.

Leona closed her eyes tightly. She was aware that John was still there with them, his wide shoulders almost brushed hers. But he was their third, her daughter's father, and he had a right to be there when she told Adia the truth. "I've been keeping a secret, Adia," she said.

"I already know, Mom," Adia said quietly. "My father's not dead. Grace and I were trying to find him."

Leona reached out and clasped Adia's hand. "You found him, Adia." Adia's face was calm, and she turned to look up at John, who'd shifted so he could face her. Adia didn't move her hand from under Leona's, but her lips curved up in the barest feather of a smile and she watched John as she said, "Grace and I were coming to find you. She would be so happy." Then her face crumpled again, and she began to cry. "I just can't believe it."

Leona sat there holding her daughter's hand tightly. She wished she knew what to do.

"Let's go inside and eat." It was the only thing she could think of to say.

Leona remembered where the kitchen was, and soon began opening cupboards and taking things from the fridge. She pulled out a frying pan and eggs and was cracking them, mixing them with a little milk.

That's how John found them. Adia sitting at the table, and Leona at the counter.

"How's her cooking?" John asked Adia.

Adia looked at him, and then at her mother, who she'd never seen acting quite so maternal.

"I don't know," she answered. "I can't remember the last time she cooked."

John smiled at her and pulled three glasses off a shelf. Then he bent down and retrieved a bottle of whiskey from a cabinet.

"Then we'll probably need a drink."

He poured two glasses half full of whiskey and placed one on the counter for Leona. He splashed a bit of whiskey in the third glass and then added water. He set it on the table in front of Adia. "It'll help a bit," he said.

The sky outside the window was golden. Leona watched shadows playing on the grass underneath the magnificent baobab. "I sat under that tree with your mom," she said. "Years ago. She told me you were dead. I believed her."

"She was confused like that for ages before she died. Alzheimer's," John answered. "She told me that she told you I was dead. She said you went home after that, to America. I never looked for you. I never thought I'd find you. But still…something…something made me do a double take, get my hopes up, every time I saw a woman or a girl who could have been you and—" now he turned to Adia "—Adia, a good Maasai name."

Then Adia spoke. "We've been in Nairobi the whole time. Mom found out you were alive recently, a few months ago. Your brochure was in a hotel. She didn't tell me, though." Leona winced and flipped the eggs onto plates John had set beside her.

They sat together at the kitchen table and ate the omelets and toast in silence. Afterward, Adia said she wanted to go to sleep. John led her down the hall to a little guest room and showed her where the bathroom was.

"I hope you sleep well," he told her. "Tomorrow, or sometime when you're ready… I look forward to beginning to get to know you."

Leona washed the dishes and wiped the table of crumbs. She was surprised at herself—she didn't usually like doing domestic chores, but here, in this house, with the wide-open savannah outside the window and no sound but the tinny chatter on the radio she felt relaxed.

When the last dish was washed and placed in the drainer by the sink, Leona stepped out the kitchen door. She remembered, years ago, walking up this path to the baobab, watching Ruthie and Adia holding hands and walking together in the distance. Now Leona walked alone up the hill to the tree. The breeze was cool and just strong enough to make the grasses whistle. She crossed the crest of the hill where the headstones were casting their evening shadows.

"I think we need another drink." Leona started when she heard John's voice behind her.

"Didn't mean to scare you," he said, "but there's been a lion around here in the evenings." Leona saw he had a rifle under one arm and a bottle in one hand.

"Guns and drinks," she said. "That's a combo."

Underneath the baobab, the bench was cold and the light dim and green, like being underwater. When they weren't speaking, the silence fell thickly around them.

"We'll have to share," John said, and twisted the bottle's top. "Scotch."

He opened the bottle and handed it to Leona. They sat side by side on the bench, and the cool of the concrete seeped through John's pant legs. It was always chilly here, and the light was always murky. Leona nudged his shoulder with hers and passed him the bottle. He registered, again, the fact that their shoulders were almost the same height and that he could see her eye to eye with no effort. He liked that about her.

They drank quietly, watching the leaves above them turn blacker as the evening collected around them. After a while Leona stopped shuddering after each taste, and he stopped being shy about gulping it down. The bottle was more than halfway finished before they spoke.

"So these are your dead," Leona finally said.

She stretched one leg in front of her and, with her foot pointed, tapped the larger gravestone with the tip of her shoe. John knew the alcohol was working its magic on her brain and her tongue. She smiled a little at the three gravestones at their feet.

"There's a tiny one and two big ones. It's so sad to have a tiny one."

John cleared his throat. Again, he found himself speaking words he'd never uttered aloud before.

"The largest is my not-so-dearly-departed father, the newest is my mother, and the smallest my older brother, died in early childhood. I hardly remember him."

He thought about biting back the rest of the story, but he

kept going, piercing through the shell of secrets that marked his life.

"My mother killed him, actually. I only recently found out. It was an accident. Ran him over in a truck."

The alcohol stirred the horrible absurdity in his brain. It wasn't funny. Nothing about his childhood was funny. It was one fucking nightmare after another, he thought. But he felt a laugh in his chest. It was all so awful.

"Oh, God. It's not funny, is it?"

Leona watched his face closely. She looked so kind then, so young and open. He wondered if she'd looked that kind when he first met her. She hadn't the last time he saw her. Not even close. He'd never told anyone about his childhood before. Not even the women who'd wanted to marry him. But this woman was different; this was the woman who had his child. And now he wanted nothing more than to drain the sickness from himself, to pull it all out from the darkness and fling it into the world. He didn't want it anymore.

"She hit Thomas—that's what my brother was called—because she was frantic to leave my father. He was a terrible, mean drunk. She was so desperate to leave that she was going to leave the two of us, Thomas and me, behind."

He took a final swig from the bottle and then hurled it as hard as he could. It shattered on the largest of the three headstones. He felt Leona wince beside him.

"It was, needless to say, an unhappy childhood."

He glanced at Leona and saw that her eyes were steady and serious. She wasn't recoiling in horror, as he thought she might. She smiled gently at him, and her teeth were brilliant white, even in the gathering dark, and perfectly straight. American teeth, he thought. She reached out and touched John's hand.

Her hand on his brought him back to where they were. It

sparked a yearning in him that made him feel lonelier than he'd ever felt. The women he'd been with lately, the shiny, doll-like tourists, they were only scratching an itch. He didn't know them, and they seemed more interested in him as a novelty. He'd been in Solai for years now, and apart from the groups of tourists he met at the airport and took on safaris, he hardy saw anyone else. Not anyone he hadn't grown up with, anyway. He'd pushed his need for touch, and for understanding, behind him in service to his mother.

"Yes, and we're drunk, girlie. But not to worry…this place has seen more drunks than it can count."

He paused and then continued. It felt important to tell his story, to get it all out. He wanted Leona to know him, the dark parts, the sad parts that had never before seen light.

"Before my dad was put in the dirt here, when I was still a kid, I used to come up here all the time. I'd curse my dead brother for being the one who got away. I wanted to be the dead one. I wanted to be the one who didn't have to see my dad breaking my mother's bones, or see how my mother let it happen time and again. I didn't want to think that my mother was the kind of person who'd have left me if she could—I was just a baby—with that bastard. I thought he was the lucky one—lucky dead Thomas.

"Then my father died. I dug his grave myself. I wanted to put him in the ground. It made me happy to know he was dead."

John thought of his father's slow death, how relieved he'd been when his father was buried in the ground, unable to hurt anyone anymore.

"I was happy my dad died, too." Leona's voice was clear and free of guilt. "He was a bastard, too. In a different way." She didn't elaborate. This was a subject still too uncomfortable to talk about. She didn't talk about it. Not at all. But she wanted to give this to John. A gift of understanding.

Talking to Leona was easy this time. John saw what he'd recognized in her all those years ago—they were both broken people. Broken in ways they could understand in the other. They could see the pieces of each other lying deep on the other side of the walls they'd put up. As in a foreign country where the language is utterly incomprehensible to those who'd never heard it before—they shared an understanding none of the other people in their lives did. They were the sole inhabitants of this land, speakers of a unique tongue. They could see each other's failings and potential. It was inevitable.

John felt like talking. He felt like the words he was sharing, finally, would find a home, a place to settle and then blink out, like ash. They weren't hard and permanent. They could escape into the night sky and never bother him again.

It was late when they walked back to the house. Leona stood outside Adia's door for a moment and then opened it slowly, wanting to check in on her. She assumed Adia was already asleep—wrung out and exhausted by tears and terror. Leona doubted she'd have come in if she'd known Adia was awake; she felt she wasn't qualified to guide her daughter. For so long Leona prided herself on keeping her own grief contained, boxed up and reserved. All her emotions were controlled, most of the time, anyway. She crept across the dark room to Adia's bed. She sat on the edge of the mattress and then lay down next to her girl. She was so close she could feel the Maasai bracelets on Adia's wrists, feel the bones just under her skin and even feel the pulse of blood through her daughter's veins.

"Adia," she whispered into the dark. "I love you."

Leona was surprised when Adia rolled over and burrowed her face into her mother's arm. She wasn't asleep, after all, and Leona felt embarrassment. She wasn't sure she'd ever said those words to her daughter. She wasn't sure she'd ever felt them as keenly as she did now. At this moment, she would have lived through all of it again for the chance to be a different kind of mother.

Leona squeezed her eyes shut tightly and saw lights shooting across the insides of her eyelids. The silence that had infected her since childhood was a habit now, ingrained in her blood, written in her DNA, embedded in her flesh. She didn't want her daughter to live this way. She wanted Adia to find comfort in connections, to feel, always, the warmth of sharing time and space, and her deepest self, with others. To make that happen, Leona realized, she had to let her own silence leak out. She had to break herself open so her daughter could see inside.

That night, Leona lay in the same bed she'd slept in before. She didn't sleep well. Her mind spun with images of John. She was surprised at how she remembered his smell. He smelled like dry dust and sun and sweat, a heady combination. Her head filled with memories of the first time they met, of the sensation of his arm brushing against hers while they cooked earlier that evening. She turned over and over in her head the secrets he'd told her under the baobab. She rarely found herself physically drawn to men, but John was different. The whole time they'd sat together under that tree earlier, she'd wanted to touch his skin, to feel his warmth on her fingers.

PART III

MOFFAT'S WIFE

Death in Kenya—in all of Africa, really—is common. After years on the continent, Jane knew that. Livestock is trotted to the butcher and, without preamble, right on the sidewalk in front of the shop, the animal's neck is slit and then the carcass is hung upside down to bleed out. Shopping in the open markets means walking on blood-slick ground through rows and rows of skinless heads and headless bodies lined up on tables, flies laconically licking from the dead beasts' empty, staring eyes.

Just after their arrival in Nairobi, Jane was out in the suburbs with another embassy wife. The other wife told Jane about a shop she loved and how she had to show Jane the tradition-ally dyed fabrics you could buy there. The other woman was driving and she drove much faster than Jane normally did. Suddenly a dark shadow flashed in front of the car and Jane heard a thud.

"Christ," the other woman muttered, "damn dog came out of nowhere."

Jane turned and saw the bloody spot on the road where the dead dog lay, his fur burst open like a too-ripe fruit.

Jane wasn't naive. By the time Grace died, she had been in Africa long enough to know that animals weren't the only living things that blinked out of the world so easily. Humans died constantly, too. They died of disease, of hunger, of age, of a million different things. They died in *matatu* accidents and on airplanes. They died at the hands of other people like all those men she'd secretly watched on the beach in Liberia. Life, especially here, Jane knew theoretically, was fleeting and fragile. But she never thought that it would happen to her.

The days and weeks after Grace died were blurred. Jane didn't remember those days when the ghosts came to her— was that her own stepmother? Her father? Was that shadow Jane's oldest friend? Who had told them the news? She couldn't imagine dialing a phone, let alone speaking the terrible words aloud. They slid their palms down Jane's cheeks, smoothed her hair, asked if she was hungry—how could Jane be hungry when her baby was dead? How could her body need food or water or sleep? Jane couldn't imagine wanting anything ever again. She was dead, too. The weeks turned to months; they went to the States for R & R and returned. Nairobi wasn't home, but Jane didn't care. Home didn't exist for her anymore.

After they had Grace cremated, Paul wanted to take the remains to America. That way, he said, she'd be at home.

"We can visit her grave," he'd said.

Jane couldn't eat, wasn't sleeping, barely speaking. She wanted to disappear. But she was firm in this: home was no set place for any of them anymore. They'd been nomads for too long. Grace would stay with them.

During the long afternoons when the sun slanted through the flame tree at the edge of the garden, illuminating the dust in the air, Jane often found her heart racing and her breath choked in her throat. The anxiety came almost daily, but still it surprised her. The tingle in her limbs rushed up from her fingers to her shoulders, her toes to her thighs, and blossomed into popping flashes of light behind her eyes. She'd struggle up from her chair, clasping the edges of the table for support and for the feeling of hardness under her fingers. Gripping the table seemed to draw her back to earth, back to reality, and then, as suddenly as it came, the panic disappeared. She'd sit back down, arrange her legs under the chair, take a sip of lukewarm tea and stroke the edges of the saucer.

Worse than the attacks that found her in the afternoon, though, were the dark breaths of despair that crept up on her while she slept curled like a leaf around her husband in the middle of the night. They gripped her out of nowhere, her dreams tossed up into the darkness, and she'd wake strangled for breath. She still couldn't believe that Grace was gone. Jane supposed it was better to have the anxiety wake her from her sleep than the other possibility—the times right after Grace died when Jane would be asleep and then wake up feeling calm, happy even, because she'd forgotten. The crash of memory, when she realized again, was devastating. This was better, marginally. But the nights she woke up like this were so dark, so long. She hated hearing Paul's even breathing in those moments, so content and relaxed he was. She hated how he slipped into sleep so easily.

When she was asleep, she could escape reality, but upon waking it crumpled her like paper. It was a physical pain she lived with constantly, a feeling of bone-deep agony.

"Let's go to Nakuru," Paul said one evening at dinner. "Have a safari, see the lake again." A distraction from the grief, he'd said.

It was a year since Grace had died, and her ashes were the one thing Jane would take if there were a fire. People always used to ask that question. It was even one of the choices for the application essay for her college. She'd answered it but couldn't remember what she said. The days of having to think—really think—what the choice might be were over. Now her answer was ready-made, always at the tip of her tongue. She'd leave everything else behind, even Paul, and take only her daughter.

She'd hated the lake when she was there with the girls. But maybe it would help, she thought, to see if the lake looked healthier now, if somehow it had changed for the better. Maybe it would help to see the birds again. The lonely way they floated above the eggs they'd lost reminded Jane of herself.

Paul stood behind Jane at the edge of the soupy water. She heard him clear his throat and shift his boots in the dirt. Jane had hated him every day since Grace died. Hated the way he tried to comfort her and how he wouldn't lay blame. Jane wanted to be punished. She should never have ignored her instincts. She'd been right all along—the world was a dangerous and terrible place and anything could happen. She cursed herself daily for letting down her guard, but Paul refused to hurt her.

"I want to be alone a minute," Jane said, and she heard that her voice was shriller than she'd intended, anger always too close to her surface.

Paul didn't answer, but he shifted away. Jane could hear the change in the air behind her and felt his absence. She hadn't wanted to leave their home to come here. Not even for the day, as Paul had planned. She was a snail ripped from her shell, too soft and exposed. Jane hated Paul for finding it easier than she did to get on the Rift Valley road and drive away, to trade the comfort of grief for the distraction of this wild, desolate place.

There was a flat rock nearby and Jane sat down on it. It was warm beneath her. She felt like lying across it and letting it absorb her so she'd disappear. But as brackish as it was, the water beckoned. Jane unlaced her boots and pulled them off. She peeled her socks from her feet and rolled her pants up to the knee. The mud under her toes was slimy and colder than she'd expected. Jane shuffled her feet carefully, half expecting to feel the smooth roundness of eggs underneath, and not wanting to crush them. The living birds clucked and cawed nervously as she edged closer to them.

A flash of pink caught Jane's eye and she looked up. A lone bird near the edge of the lake had raised it wings. It stood still for a moment, and then began running, its spindly legs and the knuckles of its knees carrying it fast across the shallow water. Then a split second of stillness and it seemed to hang in the air, its long legs now gracefully stretched behind it. And it was off, wings silent in the sky and powerful. In seconds the escaped bird was nothing but a dark spot, too high, too far to see anymore. Jane wondered if that bird had left anything behind.

She turned to catch Paul's eye. She hoped he'd seen the bird in flight. It was beautiful. He grinned back at Jane from the shore. He'd seen it. Jane waded a little farther into the murky water. Paul was the kind of bird who'd have the courage to fly away. He knew how to spread his wings and hang, silent, in the air. Jane wondered if he'd leave her behind, preserved but empty. There were times, in the months after Grace's accident, when she wished he'd leave. She'd been a ghost, and like a ghost, she'd wanted to be invisible, to nurture her pain alone, to let it cover her like mist so she could disappear into it.

Now, in this place, the water licked Jane's calves. She felt nothing but the physical sensation of the sun on her shoulders, the slight wind that flicked a hair across her cheek. She took off her hat and tipped her head back. The sky was white and flat. There was no rain there, just high, thin clouds and somewhere, somewhere far enough away that it could look only forward not back, was the flamingo she'd watched leave.

Suddenly, Jane wanted to run through the water as fast as that bird had. She wanted to wave her arms and shout at the limp, left-behind birds until she scared them into flight. She wanted to see them take to the air, drink the newness of the sky and imagine a new place for themselves.

She wished she'd brought the small silvery urn with them. She thought of it, sitting on her bedside table next to her books, her reading glasses and a vase filled with roses from their garden. She thought Grace would like it here, to be sprinkled on the surface of the water and to sift, slowly, down to nestle into the silt below. She'd rest among the other lost eggs and be watched over by the birds. Maybe, soon, the rain would come back and spill down the sky for days and days on end. If that happened, Nakuru would fill. The flamingos that hadn't left yet would shake the rain from their feathers and raise their necks so their beaks would point skyward. Grace would swirl around their feet and they would watch over her.

Africa had, in Jane's mind, cemented itself into a shadow land—dark and veiled and seething with things that frightened her. Insects and snakes and newsreel images of civil wars and starvation, of guns and hunger and disease—of accidents that happened in the blink of an eye, ones that changed everything. But she was linked to this place, now, deeply and irretrievably, and she couldn't face going back to the States. She told Paul, when it was time for him to transition to a new post, to bid on another African country. Jane knew they couldn't stay in Kenya forever—Paul's job wouldn't allow that—but she wasn't ready to leave Grace's place behind, either. Grace was Africa now, too, and Jane wasn't ready to make the continent nothing but conversation for cocktail parties. She was trapped, linked to the place by the worst moment of her life. So when Paul was offered Lusaka, they didn't hesitate to accept.

But Jane didn't expect the shock to her system the move caused. She didn't expect the anxiety, the visceral instinct she felt, her body, veins and tissues all leaning away from here, cringing away from this strange place, pulling her thoughts back toward the familiar, always. Like the way a plant in a gloomy room curves and stretches toward the distant band of light it craves. Jane felt physically the yearning toward her daughter, toward the past when things were still okay. She was not moving on; she was not beginning to accept. She was in danger, she knew, of being cemented in this, a beetle cast in amber, forever preserved in a terrible moment.

She tried to explain her feelings to her husband; she tried to tell him how stunned she was by the unfamiliarity of everything she encountered. Everything was different now that she didn't have Grace to explore the new place with her. The air itself smelled repugnant to her, and every morsel of food, every sip of water, tasted dusty and old. She didn't know if it was the new country or her grief that colored everything here. Paul smiled sadly when she told him all of this. He'd held her hand and said, "You'll get used to it. It will become less hard. I promise." And what choice did Jane have? His work was here now. It was a distraction for him and it was working for him. His feet were finding ground. If she left, she would leave alone.

The other American embassy wives were so different from her. They had kids or jobs to go to, things to wrap themselves around. They seemed breezy and confident and comfortable here. They spoke of Lusaka like they spoke of their children—pesky and frustrating, but beloved. Jane tried to socialize at the beginning; she tried hard to conjure the person she had once been, but when she went to the spouses' teas and to the meetings of the International Women's Group, she found her words stuck behind her lips. Her roots had been clipped; she had nothing here—no job, no friends, nothing that was hers alone. Even her words had been pruned. She was aware that some of the other embassy families knew about the accident, about Grace. Embassy communities were tight-knit, and even though the people within them moved around constantly, that meant that all of them knew people in common—news of tragedy spread fast through the expatriate grapevine. Jane never spoke of it to anyone, though, and nobody brought it up with her. Paul encouraged her to speak with the embassy doctor; he could arrange counseling, maybe an antidepressant. But Jane couldn't imagine crying and talking about it with a stranger.

Jane's whole purpose while Paul was at work became avoiding the houseman. The houseman's name was Moffat. Moffat sounded like soft old slippers shuffling along through the rooms of the house. Moffat's mannerisms bore a disconcerting similarity to Muthega's—he spoke in the same way, and he provided a similar service—helping Jane with things she didn't necessarily need help with. He was kind, too, like Muthega was—giving rides to the women and candy to the kids who thronged around the truck. Moffat's kindness made Jane angry. Sometimes people would come to the door selling fruit or fish, and Moffat always opened the door. Jane never gave him money to buy any of the things, but he always crouched in the doorway and chatted.

Although Jane and Paul had always had household help in every post they'd taken, Jane realized that she'd never been home so much. She'd been busy, out and involved, helping at Grace's schools, working out at the embassy gyms. This was not how she'd been since Grace was born, terrified to leave home, forced inside by fear, like an animal too used to captivity to find the courage to escape, even when the cage door was wide-open. For the first time, Jane found it disorientating to have a stranger underfoot all day. She tried to avoid him, but it was hard.

The house had only two levels: the bottom one was a wide-open swath of living room, dining room and kitchen, and the top was just a line of three airy bedrooms and a bathroom laced like beads along a wide, empty hallway. Moffat seemed determined to dust and mop in every nook. Jane wanted to make herself invisible when Moffat was in the house, so when he arrived each morning, she acted busy and distracted and greeted him while hurriedly gathering up books and papers and pens and a large mug of tea. When she scooped up all she could hold—books and papers in one crooked arm, mug of tea clutched in the other hand, she escaped to the backyard table, where she sat shuffling her pile of novels and books on native flora, or she hunkered down in the weeds and poked at the dirt with her trowel and tried to force away the image of a pair of tiny hands in hers. Grace had helped in the garden since she could sit up.

One day, Moffat didn't come. Jane felt his lateness without looking at her watch. She sensed she'd waited longer than usual to gather up her books and her tea; she noticed a slight difference in the intensity of the light that streamed through her kitchen window. She wondered what happened. She thought she should try to get in touch with him. But how? Jane had been to his house only once when she and her husband dropped him there in the car one rainy afternoon when his bicycle chain was broken.

It was late morning when Jane heard the familiar click of the gate latch and then the scrape of metal against the concrete walkway. She stood up from her patch of weeds in the yard, laid her trowel aside and wiped the dirt from her hands. She saw Moffat and a woman she didn't recognize walking slowly up to the front door.

The woman was tall and sinewy, and under the puffed sleeves of her blouse her bare forearms were lean and muscular. She wore a piece of colorful fabric wrapped tightly around her waist like a skirt, and it hugged the hard bloom of her pregnant belly tightly. Jane walked around the side of the house to meet them. "Come in," she said, gesturing to Moffat like he was an expected guest. She wondered how one was supposed to talk to the houseman when he appeared at the front door, late and with a guest. Should she be stern? Beatific? She led the pair into the living room and sat down in an armchair. She was embarrassed about the mud smeared on her legs and under her fingernails.

Moffat and the woman huddled on the couch. "This is my wife, madam," Moffat said. Jane was surprised. Moffat looked ancient and mousy. His wife looked elegant and clear-eyed, and sitting ramrod straight on the couch, she towered over Moffat.

There was a pause, and Jane wondered if she should offer the couple tea. She thought yes, she would, and moved to get up. Just then Moffat and his wife rustled and spoke to each other in hushed voices. They looked at Jane expectantly and she sat down again.

Moffat's wife leaned over to rummage in a small bag at her side and then drew out a white envelope. She handed the envelope to Jane and sat back. Suddenly Moffat's wife looked tired. Jane had a flash of empathy. She'd never been so tired as when she was pregnant. She could have slept and slept.

Jane held the envelope in her hands for a moment. It felt empty except for a small lump in one corner.

"Madam," Moffat began, "we had a thief in our house last night." Jane listened while the story unfolded, the envelope cool between her fingers.

A pair of robbers had slid into Moffat's house before dawn that morning. They came in through the plastic sheet that covered up the unfinished part of the roof. Jane wondered what the robbers were after. She'd seen Moffat's house herself.

There was nothing to steal there. "My wife heard the thieves before I did, madam—she fought with them." Jane glanced at the tall woman on her couch. "There was a fight, madam, one of the thieves, they bit my wife." Moffat pointed to the envelope in Jane's hand.

"Oh, yes," Jane breathed, and slit it open with a finger, dumping the contents into her palm. Moffat's wife sat still and calm on the couch. Her thin body, straight but for the round stomach and the knot of brilliant cotton on her head, made her look like a wilting flower.

Jane looked at what lay in her palm, confused. It was a small mushroom, no bigger than her thumb tip and the color of warm earth. She wondered what to say. Why would they give her one brown mushroom? And what did the mushroom have to do with their story of the thieves? She raised her head to ask, and when she did, she saw Moffat turn to his wife and nod abruptly. Moffat's wife pulled aside the colorful fabric of her head scarf to reveal her upper neck. It was streaked with blood. Moffat said, "Her ear, madam." Jane looked at Moffat's wife and then back at the mushroom in her own hand. It wasn't a mushroom at all. It was the smooth fleshy lobe of Moffat's wife's ear.

Jane swallowed and tried not to recoil as she shuffled the bitten-off ear back into the envelope. Her hand felt as if it had been burned in the place where the ear had sat for those long seconds. She wanted to cry.

"Madam, we need a ride in your car to the hospital. My wife needs to see a doctor. In the fight, we think the baby could be hurt."

"Why did you save the ear?" Jane's thoughts were jumbled; she couldn't make sense of what Moffat was asking. She thought of the flesh in her palm and swallowed, tried not to blanch.

"The ear is proof of this fight, madam. I can show the police. I can show you so you know I was not lying when I didn't come to work this morning on time."

"Um…and the baby?" Jane asked, swallowing her tears of horror and longing for her chair in the yard, her trowel and her weeds. She rubbed ineffectively at the dirt on her hands.

"Yes, madam, my wife is worried about the baby. The thieves, they kicked her."

"Oh, my God!" Jane said. Her voice sounded too loud. Moffat and his wife were so calm. She, on the other hand, felt completely out of control—like she was shaking from the inside out. She'd just held someone's ear in her hand. She tried to measure her response, to calibrate her voice to match those of her visitors. "Of course," she whispered, "let me get my keys."

The teaching hospital lay on the outskirts of Lusaka. Jane drove hesitantly. She hated driving now. She was nervous; the streets were rutted with deep holes, and people, animals and other cars tended to appear without warning. How easily accidents could happen. She sat stiffly and gripped the wheel tensely, leaning forward with concentration.

The sun was in her eyes, and she fumbled to pull down the shade. She crawled along through the traffic, unsure where to go, which turns to make. Occasionally Moffat leaned forward from where he sat in the back seat with his wife, and pointed one way or another, and Jane dutifully turned.

The halls of the hospital were filled with people. Jane felt nausea rise—this place was too similar to where she'd seen Grace, broken and gone. She didn't think she could stay. But Moffat guided Jane and his wife to a space on a wooden bench set against a wall. He motioned to them to sit. "I'll try to find the doctor, madam—you can sit here." Jane and Moffat's wife sat. The space on the bench was small. Moffat's wife was pressed up against Jane on one side, and on Jane's other side was an old man with a shriveled arm. The man appeared to be asleep, his head lolled back against the wall, his mouth slightly open and his eyes shut. Jane sat stiffly, trying not to feel the closeness of Moffat's wife's pregnancy. She couldn't bear to think of the hollowed-out space in her own body.

As other people sat down, the space between the women got smaller and smaller, and Jane felt herself being squished. The old man's wilted arm lay like a flower against her leg, Moffat's wife's elbow was almost in her lap. The hallway grew hotter and hotter and the air grew thick and smelled of unwashed skin and the fetid breath of the sick.

Jane felt herself growing light-headed and angry. This place was making her anxiety raise its head. This wasn't good for her—to be reminded. Why did Moffat make her do this? Why was she stuck in this horrible hospital hallway pressed skin to skin with all these strangers? These Zambians were staring at her unabashedly, probably wondering—as she herself was—what she was doing here. It occurred to Jane that she should be frightened—Africa was dangerous, after all—but she felt too annoyed to be scared.

Jane was distracted by a fluttery touch on her arm. Moffat's wife was looking up at her, wiggling her fingers lightly on Jane's arm to get her attention. "Yes?" Jane asked, more sharply than she'd intended.

The women spoke words that Jane couldn't understand. "I'm sorry," Jane muttered, "I don't speak Nyanja." The woman motioned to the bench they were sitting on, and then made a gesture of leaving and returning. "Oh, yeah, you want me to save your seat. I'll try." Jane couldn't think of a way to do that. She shrugged. "I'll try," she said again.

Jane spread out when Moffat's wife left. She slid down and let her knees fall open. She pushed her elbows back so they touched the wall behind her. She made herself big. It suited her mood to poke the old dead-armed man in the side and to glance up angrily at the lady standing nearby with a sagging toddler in her arms, eyeing the vacated space with big, glassy eyes. It was a side effect of grief—this anger, this self-involvement. Before, she would have felt sad to watch this woman and her sick child. Now, though, she couldn't spare the emotion on someone else's pain. She hurt too much herself. But she felt an odd sort of kinship with Moffat's wife, whose ear she'd held in her hand and who had entrusted her with her valuable spot on this bench.

Just when Jane thought she couldn't hold off the press of people anymore, she saw Moffat's wife returning. She edged through the crowds belly-first and caught Jane's eye. She smiled and held up her hand. In it was a smooth, ripe orange, a bright blister of color in the dark hallway. Jane smiled back and folded herself smaller so the woman could sit next to her again.

Moffat's wife began to peel off the skin of the orange, sending light sprays of scented spritz into the air. It smelled delicious. Jane tried not to stare, but her mouth watered. She was suddenly thirsty and hungry. Moffat's wife nudged her with an elbow. Jane looked up and saw the peeled orange in her outstretched hand. Moffat's wife smiled.

"No," Jane said, hesitating, "you go ahead, pregnancy makes you hungry." She knew the woman couldn't understand her words, but it seemed worse to stay silent. Moffat's wife pulled back her hand and in one swift motion split the orange in two right down the middle. She pressed half into Jane's hand. Jane looked down at the plump, cool half she held. She wondered if the orange was dirty. She watched Moffat's wife use her thumb to dislodge a section from the half she held, and slip it between her lips. Jane could almost feel the sweet juice and pulp sliding down her own throat as Moffat's wife swallowed. Moffat's wife reached out and, before Jane could refuse, grasped Jane's hand and pressed it, palm down, on the tight rise of the flesh of her stomach. Jane closed her eyes and felt the baby thump. When she opened her eyes again, Moffat's wife was smiling up at her.

"I had a baby, too," Jane said. She knew Moffat's wife couldn't understand, but it helped to say the words out loud, to claim them again, after so long.

"I lost my baby." Jane's eyes filled, and her breath shortened. The panic rose in her body again, setting off the flashes of light in her head and the breathless feeling of drowning. Jane closed her eyes and tried to count her inhalations and her exhalations, regulating her breath. She felt Moffat's wife pluck the orange half from Jane's hand. Then she felt the soft edge of a section against her lips. Moffat's wife held the piece of orange up to Jane's mouth, her slim, dark fingers so close to Jane's face that when she opened her eyes, she could see the rough skin on her knuckles.

The orange was cool and sweet. It filled Jane's mouth with juice. She opened her eyes and tried to smile. "Thank you," she whispered.

Just then Moffat pushed through the crowd and reached out to take his wife's hand. Moffat's wife stood, and Jane saw the way the two looked at one another. Had she and Paul ever had that expression? That look of instant understanding and devotion? The moment, so many years ago, when she sat in the car sobbing as Paul held her flickered into her mind. He did then. There was a time, not so long ago, when they'd understood each other.

Moffat spoke quickly to his wife in Nyanja and then turned to Jane. "Madam, they will see my wife now."

Jane shucked the sleeping old man's flaccid arm off her leg, where it lay, heavy and immovable. She stood up. Like water pushed into a void, all the bodies on the bench slid over to fill the space she'd vacated. She took a deep breath to dispel the fear that bubbled up at the thought of exiting the crowded hospital and finding her car and then her way home without Moffat and his wife to help her.

Moffat's wife looked up at Moffat and whispered something to him.

"Madam," Moffat said, "we can take you to the car. Maybe the doctor will wait for us."

Jane smiled in relief and nodded. She wouldn't have to push through the throngs of people in the hallway alone. But when she turned, she glimpsed Moffat's wife's neck, the bare brown expanse of skin and the stain of dried blood visible under the colorful headscarf. She caught the look of worry on Moffat's face. She remembered the feel of the unborn body sliding under her hand when Moffat's wife pressed her fingers to her belly, and she remembered, with a spasm of sadness, how thrilled she'd been when she felt the butterfly wing of her own baby's movement deep inside her, and how that baby grew up to be her daughter—who would always be her daughter. She thought of Moffat's wife, so pregnant, fighting off the thieves in the night. How brave she was.

"No, I can manage." She looked Moffat straight in the eye. She thought it was the first time they'd had eye contact. His clear eyes belied the old-man slope of his shoulders, the wrinkles on his forehead.

After the smells and crowds of the hospital, Jane's car was quiet and still. She took a deep breath and closed her eyes. Her heart beat fast, and she felt sweat sliding down her back. But she was a grown-up. If Moffat's wife could fight robbers, she could drive herself home. She could do this. She drove slowly and concentrated on not getting lost; she registered the garbage on the streets, the animals wandering past and the grubby barefoot kids with streaming noses. She was careful; she edged around the possibilities of living things darting out from any corner. When she finally pulled into her driveway, she felt like celebrating. She raised her fingers to her nose and inhaled the scent of the orange that lingered there. It was such a familiar and beautiful smell.

Jane locked the car and followed the path around the house to her backyard. She didn't bother to go inside the house. She didn't want to lurk in the dim rooms right now. The sun felt good on her shoulders, and the air smelled sweet. The weeds still choked the flower beds; the bare patches of lawn still looked mangy in the late-afternoon light. Jane's books and her teacup still sat on the outdoor table. But she didn't sit down. She felt a sense of energy she hadn't felt for years. She pulled her clippers from their case, slid her gloves onto her hands and breathed deeply the scent of the rich, perfect earth into her lungs. She knew Moffat's baby would be all right. She'd felt it under her own hand, and she wanted to make sure to have flowers to bring when the baby was born.

It would be slow, she knew, pulling out all the weeds and preparing the soil. Gardening was a process; you had to go through it one step at a time, like being pregnant, she thought, or like grieving. It took the time it took. But she would make this garden grow, and later when Paul came home from work, he wouldn't find her caught inside. He would find her out here and he would look at her like she was real, like he knew her and was welcoming her back to him. This time she would see it. She would let him look deeply at her, and she would look back at him that way, too.

A ZEBRA TAKES ITS STRIPES WHEREVER IT GOES

"They're sending me away."

Adia and Simi sat together under an acacia.

"My grandmother thinks it's time for me to live in America, to learn to be an American. But it's not even near where she lives. It's the place where she went to high school a million years ago. On the east coast. So I won't even be near the one person I know in the whole country." Adia picked up a pebble and tossed it away. "She's worried because I haven't been going to school since Grace died."

Saying this out loud made Adia's eyes fill, tears threatened. "I couldn't go back to school, not without her."

Simi knew the story already. Leona wrote from Nairobi, weeks after the accident, asking Simi what to do, telling her that Adia wouldn't get out of bed, refused to go to school. For a few weeks, Adia had come to stay here, in the manyatta. A change of scenery would be good—they all thought so.

But Leona had called Joan, too, who suggested a more drastic change of scenery—a whole world of change. Even John, when Leona mentioned the possibility of sending Adia away, had been positive.

"I can't see how it would hurt," he said, but he was reticent. He didn't know if his vote would even count, and he was relieved when Leona said that Adia would come back for holidays, that of course she'd come to Solai. She wanted John in Adia's life. That wasn't a question anymore.

Noni, the baby, now eighteen months, sat in Adia's lap, chewing on Adia's hair. Not far away, the toddler twins, Naeku and Naisiae, drew in the dirt with sticks.

"She told my mom to use my dead grandpa's money. I guess he left Mom a lot, and she has a bunch left. My grandma convinced her to use the money for my education."

Since her visit to Kenya, Joan called Adia every week. "You're my only grandchild, and I want you in my life," she said almost sternly. But Adia felt warmth under the formality, and she looked forward to the calls.

"You'll get used to America," Joan said. "You'll meet lots of new friends and you'll love the school, it's absolutely gorgeous." She told Adia stories about how it was when she was a student there, years and years ago, and tried to convince Adia that it would be fun.

Naeku screamed, and Simi and Adia looked up in time to see Naisiae pulling Naeku's stick away.

"Children are a blessing," Simi said wryly. And Adia laughed. "You love it, Yeyo!" This adoption was never made official. After Loiyan died, Simi just continued caring for the children. None of the other wives minded—they all had children, too, and even grandchildren, of their own.

Today, Kiserian, the eight-year-old, was at school. Simi didn't wait to enroll her. She didn't ask her husband—she simply walked the child to the school building a few days after Loiyan died and paid the fees. It was a story Simi hadn't even told Adia. She was determined to send the girls to school and didn't want to ask her husband for money because that would allow him the chance to refuse. Simi made a promise to herself in the heart of that *oreteti* tree so long ago. She found the necklace that night, and she wasn't bitten by a snake or eaten by a leopard. N'gai had encouraged her. She would not risk having her husband forbid her dream from coming true. Instead, she left the girls with Isina early one morning. She didn't have money to pay for school. She had only one way to get it.

Two hour's walk down the Mara River was a *muzungu* hotel. Simi had seen it several times before from a distance. It was a large building that spread along the river like a snake. There were more glinting glass windows than Simi could count, and a large stone terrace on one end with lots of tables and chairs. That's where Simi went. She walked until she was close enough to see the terrace with the tables and the chairs and the tourists eating things she'd never seen before. They drank colored drinks from tall glasses. Simi stopped. The *muzungu* tourists sat at those tables, and people brought them things to eat and drink. She wasn't sure she'd ever seen so many *muzungus* in one place before. Any bravery she'd felt that morning was gone. But she couldn't let fear stop her. She knew this hotel had a shop inside. Years ago, she'd spoken to some women who lived near here and they'd said that the shops even sold jewelry. They laughed when they told her that they could spend just an hour making a bracelet or a necklace, they could use the cheapest beads and create the simplest designs, and these shops would give them money. They'd set the ugly necklaces and bracelets on little tables and then the tourists would buy them.

"The *muzungus* don't care if the thing is cheap and badly

made." One of the women laughed. "They will buy every-thing."

Simi desperately hoped that was true. Not looking up, and trying to pretend that none of them could see her, Simi walked quickly around the stone terrace. The tourists' voices were loud. Around the other side of the building Simi found her-self standing on a large, circular road with zebra-striped vans parked in a row. These were the vans she remembered from her childhood, the ones she'd wave at, hoping the faces in the window would see her, call out to her those English words she'd craved so much then. Two men dressed in khaki uni-forms stood smoking in a shaded spot next to the building. They greeted her in Swahili.

"I am here to sell something in the shop," Simi said. "Can you tell me where to go?" One of the men chuckled. "They won't like you to go in there, sister. But I can tell the shop-keeper to come and see you."

The men dropped their cigarettes on the ground and crushed them under their boots. Then they turned and walked toward a huge glass door, one shaded by trees and flowers in pots bigger than any Simi had ever seen. One of the men turned back to Simi, motioned for her to wait and then they opened the great door and disappeared.

Simi waited. She squatted in the shade where the men had stood and examined the vans parked so neatly on one side of the driveway. Beyond them, in the distance, were purple hills that hid the horizon. Simi wondered how far away those hills were. She waited longer and felt herself getting sleepy. It was midday. She thought of Loiyan's girls back in the manyatta, and this thing she wanted so badly to do for them. Just then, the door opened and several people came out. There was one of the men she'd spoken to coming through the front entrance and leading several tourists across the driveway. Two of the tourists were women, both with nut-brown skin the same shade as Simi's own, two were men and then a boy about Kiserian's age.

Simi called to the man. He glanced over at her, and then spoke to the group of people. She couldn't hear what he said to them, but then he turned back and called to Simi, "They don't want to buy anything today. You should go home."

Simi stood. She wasn't sleepy anymore. She was hungry and thirsty and she was here for a reason. She wouldn't leave until she had what she wanted. The man and the tourists were beginning to get into one of the vans. The driver held the door open, and the young boy climbed in first. Simi didn't want the man to leave before she spoke to him. She hurried over and he looked up. One of the women looked at Simi, too. She said something to the driver, and he answered her.

Then he turned to Simi and said, "I am taking these people on a game drive. That is what they came here for. Don't waste our time."

Simi looked directly into the man's eyes, but she chose her words, and her language, for the woman standing just behind him. She spoke in the clearest, boldest voice she could find, and said in English, "I have a rare necklace to sell. My mother was the best jewelry maker in the manyatta. The necklace is old, and it's more beautiful than anything in that shop. If you haven't told them I am here, then you are a bad employee. This will be the best necklace in the shop."

She'd hoped the man would be struck by her words, maybe ashamed. She knew he was lying. He grinned, though, and only said. "Go away, woman. This is not a place for you."

"Wait a minute, Jackson." The woman spoke to the driver, who looked surprised. But her eyes were on Simi.

She continued, "Did you try to see if they'd sell this woman's necklace?"

Then the man looked annoyed, not ashamed. "They do not sell this kind of thing here." He spoke in a loud voice, mimicking authority.

"I've seen the jewelry in there." The woman's voice reminded Simi of Leona's. The woman smiled at Simi. "Can I see the piece?"

Simi reached up and unhooked her mother's necklace. She held it up. It was warm from where it had lain against her neck. The woman gently took it from Simi's hands and looked at it carefully. "It's beautiful," she finally said. "Your mother was an artist." She smiled warmly. "It must mean something to you. Why do you want to sell it?"

Simi hoped the woman would understand the reason she gave. She was being a dishonest wife by not asking her husband for the school money, and maybe this woman would disapprove.

"I have four daughters. They are mine now because their own mother died. You see, I want to send them to school, but I need money for the school fees. If I ask my husband, he may refuse. Then my daughters will never get an education." She looked away. Sharing all this with a stranger made her feel exposed. But she was desperate. She examined those distant purple hills and pretended she was far away from here.

"What is your name?" she heard the woman ask. She answered.

"Simi," the woman repeated. "Simi, I think your daughters are lucky." The woman turned and poked her head into the van where the other tourists sat. It crossed Simi's mind that the woman would jump in the van and drive away—her mother's necklace still in there with them. But the woman wasn't getting into the van. She was speaking to the men. Simi could hear her own story being recited in the woman's voice. Then one of the men spoke. Simi cold hear his gravelly voice, but she couldn't make out his words.

"Okay," the woman said, and pulled something off one of the van's seats. Then she reappeared again and stood smiling at Simi.

"I want to buy your necklace," she said. Simi glanced at the driver. He'd gotten into the driver's seat, and Simi could see his face through the window. He looked angry.

The woman spoke again. "Can you tell me how much the school fees are?"

Simi did a quick calculation in her head. "Two hundred shillings for one year," she said.

"And there are four girls? That's eight hundred shillings for one year. That's…less than a week's groceries at home in Atlanta." The woman opened a wallet and looked inside. Then she leaned back into the van and spoke to the others. Simi saw them rustling. They gave something to the woman.

When the woman turned back to Simi, she was holding a handful of money. "We'll pay for five years for each girl." Simi looked at the money. It was a lot.

"Is it an okay price for the necklace? It's four thousand shillings." The woman looked a little worried. Simi felt faint. It was more money than she'd ever seen. She'd hoped to sell the necklace for the two hundred shillings needed for Kiserian's first year. Now she could send all the girls for five years. She felt dizzy and looked in the woman's eyes. She wanted to assure her.

"This is too much," Simi breathed. "It is so much money."

The woman smiled. She looked happy. "It's a beautiful necklace. And I want those girls to go to school. Please take it."

Simi tied the money into a knot of her wrap.

"I can help you put it on," she said, and the woman handed the necklace back to her and turned, lifting her hair out of the way of the clasp. Simi fit the necklace around the woman's neck. She'd never touched a foreign person other than Leona and Adia. The woman's skin was soft, and though her hair was straight, Simi noticed little curls of hair just like her own at the woman's nape. When Simi secured the necklace, the woman turned around to face her. The blue and green beads looked beautiful.

"Thank you," the woman said, "I'll take good care of it." Then she smiled once more and climbed into the van next to the others. She slid the door shut and the driver, still annoyed, Simi assumed, roared off with a squeal of the tires.

Simi walked home quickly. She was excited and happy, and also terrified that someone would rob her. But she couldn't stop smiling. She would miss the necklace, but when she'd given it to N'gai the first time, he didn't want it. He gave it back to her for a reason. She had to make sure that dream came true.

Now, sitting under this tree with Adia and three of her other daughters, Simi felt a deep sense of pride. She looked at Adia and said, "You are brave. And you are lucky. You have this chance to go to America and get a good education. It's a chance the other girls will never have. You have to take it. But you are not going alone, Adia. We will be in your head. You will be learning all those American things for us, too. Bring it back to your yeyo and your sisters."

"It's not just that," Adia said. "I'm scared to go. I'm not brave. I've never been anywhere but here. And I just barely met my father. If I go, I won't see him for a whole year…" She trailed off, and then said, "And Grace." Adia's voice cracked and her eyes filled. "I feel like if I leave Kenya I'm leaving Grace, too."

Simi patted Adia's arms and murmured. "You know that

the dead cannot die if we remember them, Adia. Grace will always be with you, too."

Later that afternoon, two goats were slaughtered. Adia was going to America, and that was a reason to celebrate. Adia sat with the other manyatta children. She was the oldest one now. The Maasai girls her age had mostly been circumcised and married; the boys she grew up with were *moran* now. Simi watched her oldest daughter helping Kiserian with her homework. They bent their heads together over Kiserian's exercise book, Adia showing Kiserian how to form the letters of the alphabet. Simi felt deeply proud. There were times, years and years ago, that she could never imagine she'd be blessed with one child, let alone five. There were times she thought she might not even be allowed to stay in the community, a barren woman like her. But all those years were over, and now everything was different. Everything had changed. Sometimes Simi woke thinking it couldn't possibly be real, that this must be a dream. But it was a dream tinged with sadness. Simi never thought Loiyan would be someone she thought fondly of, but she found she missed her. The twins didn't speak much about their mother, and Noni would probably never remember her, but Kiserian talked about her mother with love and sometimes tears. Loiyan had been a dedicated, loving mother.

The younger girls fell asleep early, their bellies full of meat. Simi and Adia sat by the fire. They didn't talk much. The fact that Adia was leaving tomorrow, back to Nairobi and then on an airplane to America, hung between them. Simi thought about what she'd said to Adia earlier that day—that she should welcome this change, that she should be happy to get such a good education. The truth was muddier. Adia hadn't come from Simi's body, but her existence, from the moment she was born, altered Simi's life in ways she'd never have anticipated. She hated knowing she wouldn't see Adia for so long, and that she would be so, so far away.

"Yeyo," Adia said. "I'm really sad to leave. I'm going to miss you and everyone here. I'll miss the Loita Hills and the sky and the way the grass smells. I lost Grace and now I'm losing everything else."

Simi stood up and gestured for Adia to follow her outside. She walked to the edge of the manyatta, where light from the fires in the little homes couldn't reach. The air was chilly. The stars were out. It was a clear night, and the moon was almost a perfect circle. The air smelled like livestock mixed with dust, wood smoke and charred meat.

"I love that smell so much," Adia said. "I never want to forget it."

Simi sighed. "You cannot worry about that," she said. "You know they say 'A zebra takes its stripes wherever it goes.' You don't ever really leave your home behind. It is the stripes of the zebra...it will follow you like your own skin does."

Simi looked up at the moon and remembered again the way her mother told her an education could never be taken away. She remembered the sad time after Leona took Adia and how she stared at the moon one night and felt that, even though she had that education, everything else had been taken from her. The moon was watching her again tonight, and this time, she wouldn't be sad. Adia was her oldest daughter, but not her only one anymore.

In the morning, Simi and the girls walked Adia up the road to where she could catch the *matatu* to Narok, and then the bus to Nairobi. Simi felt the wait was far too short, and too soon, Adia was wiping her tears and saying her goodbyes.

Simi pushed her blonde daughter up into the open door. She'd made a promise to Adia's other mother, and she would honor it. It was hard, though, feeling Adia's spine through her thin T-shirt, knowing she was pushing her daughter into something neither of them really wanted. Then Adia was on the van, perched in a window seat, her face pressed against the glass. Simi saw the pink splotches on her girl's skin, and thought she might die from the weight of sadness.

Adia thought she might die, too; she fought the desperate need to tell the driver to stop, to let her off. Instead, she watched Simi and her sisters through her smudged window and waved until she couldn't see them anymore. Then she just watched the landscape flying by. She wanted to drink it, to ingest it. She wanted to tuck the whole sweeping savannah into her cells, into her brain, where she could remember it forever.

A couple of hours later, as the bus chugged up the side of the Rift Valley, she turned and looked back at the wide expanse of land far below her. The light was pearly in the late afternoon, and she could barely make out the smudge of greeny-gray that marked the Nguruman forest, and just below it, the place where the manyatta was. Adia sighed and turned around to face forward, toward Nairobi. She wanted to be like the zebra, carrying this home with her, wherever she went, in the very pores of her skin.

CAPTIVITY

The animal was wild. Adia knew that immediately, though she'd seen nothing exactly like it before. It was bigger than a serval cat, maybe the size of a cheetah, but thicker, somehow, leonine, with a wide yellow face and white fur lining its ears. It was a predatory cat—it moved like a lion through the foliage; shoulders rolling purposefully with each step, eyes focused straight in front, head slightly down so the spine was a line, flat as a horizon. Adia took in the details without really thinking. As a child, her Maasai friends taught her how to share space with untamed creatures. She'd been close enough to lions and leopards to reach out and pet them if she'd been stupid enough to try. She'd been close enough to hyenas to smell the rotting meat on their breath and sense the damp blood of zebra on their chins. Adia instinctively slowed her own breathing, taking in air carefully, making herself as motionless as she could. She knew how to behave in the wild.

The animal stilled. It was watching something Adia couldn't

see. It flattened its chest into the earth, leaving its backside still as a stone and showing Adia it had a thick, long tail. It was stalking something. Adia had seen kills before; she'd killed animals herself, in fact. The Maasai only ate goats and cows occasionally, but when they did, they slit the animals' throats, collecting every drop of blood and every scrap of meat—utilizing every part. Even the smallest bits of wet skin were slit down the middle and worn as bracelets that dried to a fuzzy rawhide around the wrist or ankle. Adia wasn't squeamish about that sort of thing, so it was with curiosity, not horror, that she watched the tawny creature leap up suddenly and pounce. The bushes were too high for Adia to see exactly what it killed, but she could hear the grunts the cat made and the struggle of its prey.

The bushes stopped moving, the sounds quieted and the cat emerged again. A large gray rabbit was clutched in its jaws. The cat didn't stop to eat. Adia was surprised. She wondered if it was more like a leopard. They liked to drag their conquests up into trees before feasting. The rabbit was huge, and the cat paused to drop it and reposition it in the grip of its teeth. It was close to Adia now, just a few feet away. The breeze was in her favor, and the animal didn't sense she was there. She was invisible. With a perfect view of the animal's profile, Adia could see clearly that its sides heaved with the efforts it had put forward. Adia saw the telltale drooping of its underside, the way the belly widened and stretched. She saw the cat's swollen teats. Whatever the animal was, it was female, and it was pregnant.

"Are you Adia?" the woman who picked her up at the Philadelphia airport asked. But she pronounced it "Ay-die-ah." And the way her thick lips curled into a smile made Adia swallow her correction. "No, it's Ah-dee-ah," she wanted to say, but couldn't. She didn't correct the woman—the dorm mother, Adia later understood—at all during the forty-five-minute drive to the school, and so the name stuck. Here in America she immediately understood she wasn't herself anymore; the name assigned to her was strange and ugly to her ears. She'd never been shy about speaking up before now; she didn't know what it was, exactly, about the unfamiliar place that made her feel mute. She only knew that she was different here, too.

"You're from Africa?" a group of girls she met that first day asked, their eyes wide with curiosity. And then the co-coa-colored girl who was her roommate asked, "Then how come you're white?"

The question made Adia stammer and she hated the apologetic way strings of words she'd never even said before stumbled from her mouth. "I'm American. My mom is American... that is...my dad is Kenyan... British Kenyan... He's Kenyan but, you know, white... I have an American passport...even though I've never been here before. I've never been to England, either. My real home is Nairobi, but I like it better with the Maasai. In the manyatta."

"The *manyatta*?" the cocoa girl asked, and her voice made the word—the word that Adia loved most in the world—sound ugly in her mouth. "What's a *manyatta*?" But she threw back her head and walked away, laughing, before Adia could explain.

Her name wasn't the only thing that was different here. The light in America was different, too. It was thin and hard, somehow, like a pane of glass. Adia was used to a different kind of light, a softer version. Back home, the light cupped around you like a palm. It held you near, but was yielding. You could push your way through it, you could pull it around you, consider it a comfort. This new light, this American light, didn't look at the people it illuminated. It didn't move like the Kenyan light did, which always changed and shifted like a living thing.

The sounds were also different. Adia was used to silence. Sometimes, back home, Adia climbed the jacaranda tree and heard nothing but rustling leaves and starlings. This boarding school was never silent. The wooden hallways echoed with footsteps and voices from early morning until lights-out on the dorms at 10:00 p.m. And then there were other noises, too. There was the noise of her roommate shifting in the upper bunk and causing the bedsprings to squeak, and the uneven legs of the bunk shaking and thumping the floor. There were late-night bangs and clanks from the radiator and the vague traffic sounds from the road outside the school's gate.

These new sounds—the shouting of laughter from other rooms, the scratching of pencils in notebooks during study hall, the faint, muted voices from the dorm mother's TV slipping through the wall—they all made Adia feel lonely and stranger than she felt already. The sounds made her hate the sources a little. She didn't want to get used to these people, these lives, these shiny, clean girls. She didn't want to become one of them. And yet, she was lonely.

She heard Grace's voice in her head, always, and cried herself to sleep with the ache of missing her friend. She hated the way the memories wouldn't loosen their grip. And she'd learned something that Grace was wrong about, something important, and it deepened her grief that she couldn't tell Grace—that she'd never be able to tell Grace what she finally knew to be true—that it wasn't really better to be motherless than to have Leona as a mother. Adia would have given anything, now, to be high in the jacaranda tree watching her mother through the window, or listening to the quick tapping of her mother's keyboard through a closed door. She would have given anything to see Simi now, to curl up next to her in her dark, smoky house, listening to the far-off sounds of hyena and Simi's heavy, sleeping breath.

It was hard to be away from home, and making it worse was the silence that blanketed her from the inside. She could barely make herself open her mouth; she felt herself melting into the walls and the floor and even the air. People looked past her; they didn't hear her or notice her absence or her presence. Only the letters from her mother and John, Simi and even Joan made her seen. When a letter arrived, if only for the time it took her to read it, Adia felt like herself.

In the free time between classes and meals and study hall, Adia escaped outside. She was more comfortable without the walls around her, or the waves of other people. When she first found this path down to the little lake in the woods abutting campus, she thought it felt like swimming the way she did in Mombasa. The air in the woods was like water swirling her hair around her face, and the silence a good silence—a heavy and infinite thing that pressed on her like arms holding her tightly. Here, the air smelled wet and cool, and the light was cloudy and green. She could hear the breeze in the treetops and the calling of unfamiliar birds, she could smell decaying leaves on the path and damp earth that she pressed into with her boots as she walked. She could put aside the feeling of being invisible and, instead, reach out and touch things that didn't recoil from her: the rough bark of the trees, the pine cones that smelled sharp and soapy. She could breathe here without the chaos of all those eyes and voices that never looked at her or spoke to her.

Three weeks in, Adia woke before dawn one Saturday and lay in her bed, watching the rectangle of sky out the window. She traced her finger across the wool blanket she'd painstakingly packed from home. She could hardly bring anything with her—just two suitcases—but she'd insisted on this. She'd had it her whole life, and in its fibers she smelled smoke and the faint scent of sheep. She loved that it smelled like her manyatta home. She'd heard her roommate complaining to another girl about how Adia and her stuff "smelled like a barn," and once she came back to the room to see her school supplies, the folders and stapler and blotter she'd bought from the school store, pushed way over to one side of the long shared desk that stretched across the wall under the window. Embarrassed, she sniffed and sniffed everything she owned, but couldn't figure out what smelled bad. She tried to make her things and herself smaller, even more invisible, so her presence wouldn't bother her roommate. She crammed all of her clothes into her dresser, and left the shared closet empty of her things. She meticulously stored her books and papers in the drawers at her end of the desk and kept them tightly closed. She kept the offending wool blanket folded as tiny as she could make it and pushed far under her pillow.

Careful not to wake her roommate by jostling the bed frame, Adia slipped out of bed and into a pair of jeans and a sweatshirt. She picked up her boots and closed the door quietly behind her. The wide dorm hallway was empty and still and Adia took a deep breath and padded silently down the stairs to the outside door. It opened when she pushed it and a surprising surge of happiness jolted her into a smile. She slipped the boots onto her feet and ran. She was free. She sprinted past the playing field and down the path toward the lake.

The trees made the dawn darker but Adia wasn't frightened. She ran until she couldn't breathe without gasping. Then she stopped and looked around. Her breath was loud in the early silence of the woods. To her left, the lake shimmered under the barely rising sun. Adia turned and found a tree with roots large enough for her to sit comfortably between. She leaned back against the tree and closed her eyes. She wanted to imagine herself into a different place. By the time the cat appeared, Adia had been sitting between those roots for hours.

When she saw it, Adia stood slowly, gripping the tree trunk for balance. That's when the cat made its kill. Now the dust-colored animal held the rabbit tightly in her jaws and began her slow, shoulder-rolling walk down toward the lake and slunk between two bushes and out of sight. The leaves closed behind her like a door. Adia knew it was stupid, especially since she was alone, but she was bored now, and achy from sitting so long. Plus, the animal had made her kill already, and big cats were less dangerous when they weren't hungry. Adia crept along the same path the animal took. She tracked it easily. The late stage of the cat's pregnancy made her slower, less agile. Adia stayed conscious of the breeze, and shifted as the wind did, ensuring the animal wouldn't smell her. Adia forgot about her roommate and the silence inside her and the feeling of being completely invisible. By the time she heard shouts, the sun was high in the sky.

Adia pushed through the underbrush in the direction of the voices. Judging by the screams, something terrible had happened. The lake was calm and smooth, the sun dappling the surface. A few kids in canoes slipped across the water, trailing tiny splashes that glinted in the sun with each stroke of their paddles. The long dock and the boathouse were frantic with bodies. The few teachers on weekend duty were herding the kids not already in canoes to the farthest end of the dock. One teacher stood waving her arms above her head to signal the canoes across the lake to come back. Adia wondered why they all seemed scared. When the teacher on the dock saw her, he yelled, "There's a mountain lion! Get out of the woods."

"Did you hear?" her roommate asked her that night, just before lights-out. She was breathless. "There's a lion in the woods. A bunch of people saw it by the lake."

Adia looked up from her book. She hadn't heard her roommate speak to her—at least not without sneering or clipping
her words angrily—before, and she wondered if this change
was a cruel trick. Like someone holding out a cookie to a child
and then snatching it away again.

"Yeah, I know. It's pregnant."

"Pregnant, how do you know?"

"I was out there really early this morning. I saw it make
a kill, and then it got closer and I saw it. It's really pregnant,
too. Like any day now."

"You saw it? You got close? You're fucking crazy. Crazy
or lying."

There it was—the cookie snatched from Adia's hand. She
should have known. But talking to her roommate—to someone—
surprised Adia by feeling good. Her voice liked the air it slid
through, outside her body, and her face liked being looked at.
Something deep inside her blinked awake.

"I can take you to find her if you can wake up early enough
tomorrow. She's not hard to track."

It was odd being out in the woods with someone else. Adia
found it slower going; her roommate stumbled in the dark and
kept grabbing Adia's arm in fear. She made too much noise,
and Adia imagined how her Maasai friends would mercilessly
tease this rustling, stumbling girl.

"How did you learn how to do this?" she asked once, and
Adia was about to answer when she heard a slight sound, a
muffled sort of huff. The sound of breathing.

"Shh!" she whispered as quietly as she could. She held her
finger to her lips and motioned her roommate to stop, to stay
where she was. The huffing was clearly audible. Adia tested
the wind with her finger. She knew it would be unwise to go
any farther. The Maasai, as brave as they were, weren't foolish, and tracking a predator in the dark like this would never

happen back home. She suspected the animal was feeding, which was both good and bad. It wouldn't be hungry enough to see the girls as food, but it would be protective of its kill.

"We should turn around. It's right beyond this bush." Adia said the words under her breath.

"What the fuck, Adia? We came all the way out here. Are you wimping out or bullshitting me?"

Adia felt her roommate's moist breath on her ear. Something deep within her pulled taut at her chest and Adia had the feeling of a rush of cold water through her blood. It was that feeling that made her ignore her instincts, take a deep breath and push forward as slowly as she could.

"Fine, come on." Adia slipped carefully through the branches, spreading them with her hands and moving her body slowly.

"Look! There!" Adia was on the other side of the stand of bushes now, and she had a clear view. Her roommate sidled closer to her, and, to Adia's surprise, reached for Adia's forearm and squeezed it.

"Holy shit," her roommate whispered.

The lion was roughly thirty feet away, and in the shadowy light the dawn was bringing, they could see her clearly. The cat was lying prone in the hollow base of a rotten tree. Her head was resting on the ground, and her legs were outstretched. The sounds were not the huffs and grunts of a cat enjoying its kill, but rather the sounds of pain. The cat raised her head and chuffed. She rolled over and struggled to a standing position. She stood, trembling, head down, legs splayed.

"I told you, she's pregnant. She's having her babies."

Her roommate's eyes grew wide and the two girls knelt in the dirt and clutched one another's hands as they watched.

In America, there were rules Adia had to learn. There were rules about when to be certain places, when to eat, when to study and when to turn off her light at night. Adia had to clean her room in a certain way on a certain day, and she was forbidden from leaving the grounds without permission. She had to ensure she remembered the rules the school imposed. Forgetting meant she was singled out and reminded, or given extra study hall or a demerit as punishment. The official school rules were hard enough to understand and follow, but the unwritten social rules were far more complicated and dangerous. There were certain invisible lines that shifted and moved that you had to keep your eyes on. Crossing these lines meant the punishment of sidelong looks and the subtle shifting away of sweatshirted bodies in the halls or cafeteria, and the pervasive sense that made you feel your own body, any touch from you, was poison to everyone else.

After watching the lion together and slipping safely back into their room before the dorm mother caught them, Adia felt a sense of camaraderie, of having shared a danger and survived, with her roommate. When the bell rang for breakfast that morning, Adia was eager to finally have a place to sit, to chat with the other girls and actually eat hot food, drink cocoa and orange juice, instead of escaping the cafeteria with pockets full of bread and fruit. She hadn't eaten a hot meal in days. She followed the crowd of girls into the enormous room and wove herself around the chairs being pulled out and the plates of eggs and pancakes being carried precariously between tables. There she was! Adia made her way toward the table where she saw her roommate just sitting down. There was even an empty chair. Adia reached for it and gripped the back, ready to pull it out and sit down. A thin-faced girl with sleek blond hair looked up.

"Not so fast, lion tamer. That chair is reserved."

Adia glanced at her roommate, who sipped her glass of juice and smiled into the middle distance, refusing to look at Adia.

"This table isn't for zookeepers," the blonde said. Adia's roommate laughed.

Adia froze with embarrassment, all the hope and the flicker of happiness drained out of her. She made herself turn; she bit her lip to stop any tears and didn't even try to grab a yogurt or a bottle of water. She only wanted to leave. At the door of the dining hall, she turned once to see if anyone was watching her go. Just then, the dean of students stood. Spoons tapped glasses and a hush fell. Now it was too quiet for Adia to open the creaky door unnoticed.

"Some of you know that a cougar was seen in the woods. Everything is fine, nobody was hurt and these animals don't want to hurt you. They're way more scared of you than you are of them. That said, we're responsible for your safety so, for now, no one, absolutely no one, goes to the lake or the woods until the animal has been caught," the dean said loudly. "We've called the Park Service, and they're going to do what they can to remove the animal."

Adia wondered if that meant they would hunt the cat down to kill it, or simply catch it and take it elsewhere. The lion had brand-new babies. Four had been born while Adia and her roommate watched, three healthy and one stillborn. Adia's eyes welled up and her breath constricted.

The lake was shiny under the clear sky and the moon was almost full. Adia was grateful. She'd forgotten to bring a flashlight, and although the lion didn't really worry her, she did think about the possibility of snakes. She wasn't sure how many poisonous ones might be in this part of the States; she didn't like the idea of chancing it. She found the dock and walked all the way out onto it, her footsteps on the wooden planks dull and hollow. She lay down on the wood and looked up at the stars, wondering what time it was in Nairobi, in Loita. What would everyone she loved be doing? She shivered. September was cool here. She sat up and pulled her backpack close. She wanted her blanket.

The shot was loud, close enough to make Adia shriek in surprise. She stumbled to her feet, but kept her body low, and still. Another shot rang out. Then she heard footsteps and a voice from the woods just behind the dock where she hunched.

"Got it!"

Adia's heart pounded in her chest, and adrenaline surged through her. She didn't think at all. She pulled her pack onto her shoulders and ran toward the sound of the guns and voices. She felt fingers grabbing at her forearm and felt the nearness of bodies as she passed the thin beach into the low bushes that bordered the lake. She shook the hand off and kept running.

She scrambled through the thickening trees, heading in the direction she'd last seen the mother cat. She was grateful, again, for the moon illuminating the tree roots and rocks, and she leaped over them, running all the way to the hollowed-out tree.

Her breath was ragged and painful in her chest, and she stopped just beyond the small clearing where the tree was. There was no sign of the mother cat. She kept her eyes wide and tried to look in all directions at once. If she was wrong, the mother could attack. Nothing was more dangerous than a mother with babies, and she could be lurking anywhere, ready to pounce.

The three cubs were snuggled into a little pile of kitten fur in the farthest curve of the tree trunk. They were still blind from birth, and they mewed and stretched their tiny arms, paws splaying with needle-sharp claws. Adia knelt down and reached into the tree. Their fur was so soft. One cub blindly took the tip of her pointer finger and began to suckle it. Wishful thinking, Adia thought.

The men found her quickly. She'd only been there a couple of minutes when they crashed loudly through the bushes nearest her and said, "You could have been killed!" One of the men pulled her up by her shoulder and she saw they wore uniforms. Matching hats and jackets, matching badges on their chests. Their flashlights cut the gentle darkness like knives.

"You killed her! You killed her and she has babies!"

"What, now?" one of the men said, and the other knelt down on the ground and shone the beam of his flashlight into the hollow tree.

"By God, would you look at that?" he said quietly. "Kid's right. We've got ourselves a couple of cubs right here."

"Better take 'em out. We'll have to deal with them. Make some calls when we get back."

He looked at Adia and added, "Yeah, had to get her out of here, so you kids can have your woods back. Been a problem around here lately, anyway. Couple of dogs got taken last week up at the houses down the street. Don't want you all getting hurt."

The light was coming up slowly, stretching out above the trees, filling in the spaces between the dark branches and coloring the woods a watery gray. The light here, in the midst of these trees, wasn't the hard-as-glass light Adia still hadn't gotten used to. This was the kind of light she understood, malleable and soft. Adia watched as the men pulled heavy gloves over their hands and reached in to grasp each of the cubs, one by one, and carried them to the truck parked on the lake road. One of the men pulled a small, empty cooler from behind the passenger seat and opened it wide. The two men nestled the kittens all together in the bottom. When they opened the back of the truck to load the new cargo, Adia saw the body of the mother lion slack on a tarp. She stepped close enough to see the scars pitting the short fur on the lioness's cheeks and around her wide-open, bead-green eyes.

"We'll take 'em somewhere nice, girl," one of the men said. "They'll be treated well, I promise."

Adia thought of those cubs growing up motherless, and she started to cry. Once the sadness was exposed to the air, she couldn't turn it off. Huge, painful sobs rushed through her like waves. She thought she'd never cried so hard and so suddenly and so loudly. She hoped the babies wouldn't be taken to some zoo or animal sanctuary. She hoped they would be let free. Wild. She hoped they would never come back here, but instead find a place far, far away from people. She pawed the tears from her eyes, wiped her face with her sleeves, but the sobs kept coming.

"They'll be fine," one of the men said, shifting his weight from one booted foot to the other. He glanced uncomfortably at his partner. "You just take care of yourself now, girl."

"Wait," Adia said, and her voice was ragged and cracked. "Let me wrap them up."

She slid her pack down her arm to the ground and pulled the blanket out. It smelled like everything she loved, and she knew she'd miss it. The men watched as she leaned into the truck and carefully tucked the rough cloth around the little cats. They wiggled and mewed and nestled together. They would need to be fed soon.

Adia watched the men climb into the truck and disappear up the dirt road, away from the lake. When she couldn't hear the engine anymore, Adia picked up her empty pack and walked slowly up the wooded path to the large empty lawn that stretched out across the length of the school's main building. Lights were turning on in windows; she could hear voices and other sounds, hair dryers and laughter. She turned her back to the building and sat down in the damp grass. They would find out soon she wasn't where she was supposed to be.

The open green extended all around her, up to the imposing building behind her and down all the way to the woods where the sun was cracking the sky open now, and the rays were long through the trees.

Her face was raw and pink, and she knew the tears weren't yet gone. She didn't care. She was tired of invisibility. She stretched out on her back and watched the sun continue to rise. She was cold without her blanket, but she didn't need it anymore. She pressed her bare palms against the grass, and dug her fingers into the dirt beneath her. She bit her lip and tasted blood. It mixed with the leftover tears that crowded her throat. The sobs came again and she didn't try to stop them. She didn't care who saw her. She didn't care who heard. She was a wild thing, testing out her fangs.

A FATHER, FOUND

Leona loved that first moment she could see the curve of the hill up to the house in Solai. How long ago it had been since she'd come here first, but how satisfyingly familiar the land was. There were the chipped concrete posts that marked the driveway; there in the distance was the hill and the silhouette of that massive baobab. After all these years in Kenya, Leona was still impressed with its size. She'd never seen one as big.

They rounded the last curve of the track and pulled up next to the stone patio.

"Here we are." Leona flicked the engine off and wiped her sweaty palms on her jeans. "Your dad's probably inside."

"It feels weird." Adia spoke hesitantly, but with a smile that belied her excitement. "So weird to have a dad."

All that year, while Adia was in America, she lived for the letters she received from her mom and Simi, Joan and John. John's were her favorite. He wrote her funny memories of his boarding school life and descriptions of the tourists he took on safaris. Adia wrote back about how much she missed Kenya. She saved every letter she received from Kenya. She tucked them in a box she hid at the very back of a dresser drawer. The idea that her roommate might find the letters and read them made her nauseous with fear. When she felt most alone, Adia took the box out and carried it down to the lake. Sometimes even in the middle of the night. She read and reread the letters so often she could almost recite them. John's were the ones she reread first.

Now, though, with him bounding out of the house and across the patio toward Leona's car, Adia felt shy. She opened the door and stepped out hesitantly. John didn't feel the awkwardness. He flung his arms around Adia so tightly Adia's feet left ground.

This is what it feels like. The thought flashed into her head without prelude. *This is what it feels like to have a father who loves you.* And she sent up a silent thank-you to Grace. All of this was because of Grace, and Adia never, not once, let a day pass without thanking her friend.

That night, tucked into the narrow bed she'd slept in twice before, Leona couldn't sleep. She'd grown used to Nairobi and the urban night sounds. Here, it was all different. She heard elephants growling low and deep as they lumbered up the hill, and the whooping of hyenas somewhere in the distance. Finally she slipped out of bed and down the hall to the kitchen. Maybe tea would help her sleep, or warm milk. She loved the view from this window, how wide and open the world looked from here. In the silvery dark of the half-moon, the grasses and trees, the anthills that rose narrow and as tall as a man from the earth, all looked magical. Leona had been feeling restless recently. Her teaching job was not as exciting as it had been in the early years, and the work she'd been passionate about—preserving Maasai herds by increasing grazing land—had gone as far as it could go. Things were still very bad—the land was still dry and the animals still hungry, but there was nowhere else for them to go, the green lands were shrinking as the dusty ones were growing.

She stirred her tea in her cup and thought about Adia, how she'd been pulled from Kenya and sent to make a life somewhere as foreign to her as the moon. She wasn't sure, if their roles were reversed, that she'd be able to do the same. When she got back in bed later, she curled up under the blanket, and in that second between waking and sleep, she had a flashing thought—she'd never been as brave as her daughter. She'd lived her whole adult life hiding from the things that scared her most. Not animals or loneliness, but the far more dangerous risk of connection—of allowing herself to know and be known, all the way through, even the darkest parts.

The next morning, bleary from lack of sleep, Leona padded across the patio to a wicker chaise. The paving stones were smooth under her bare feet and she clutched a mug of coffee in her hands. She hardly ever woke up early, and she wanted to take the opportunity to see the sunrise. She didn't see John until she'd settled herself down. When he spoke, she jolted in surprise, sending a splash of coffee down her sweater.

"Ah, fuck!" He apologized, "I didn't mean to scare you. I thought you'd seen me!" He rummaged in his pants pocket, pulled out a handkerchief and handed it to Leona. Then he leaned back in the chair and was quiet.

Leona watched the orange orb slip from behind the horizon and climb up the sky, tossing orange-and-yellow light across the wide-open land as it moved higher and higher. It stunned her, and without pausing to think, she said, "I saw a photo of you once, that time I first came here. It was in the dresser in the guest room. A photo of two little boys. I assumed one was you—it looked just like she did when she was a baby. But maybe it was Thomas. I didn't know about him then."

"You saw that picture?"

"It was in a dresser in the guest room. There were baby clothes in there, too. Lovely things." She paused and looked at John, and then down the hill to where giraffe were beginning to nibble their breakfast of acacia leaves, and a tawny eagle called from somewhere she couldn't see.

"Where's that photo now? Adia might want to see it. She should know about her family."

John nodded, but didn't answer. Leona continued, pushing hard against her own reticence to talk, her own discomfort at probing the deeper parts of other people with her questions. She was good, so good at this in her professional life, but it terrified her when it meant something personal. Still, she was determined to pave the way for her daughter to have a real relationship with John, and since Adia didn't know what questions to ask yet, she had to ask them.

"If possible, I'd love for her to see that photo. Or any others that you might have of you as a kid, or of her relations on your side."

"I have all that stuff somewhere. I packed it up when Mother was dying. I didn't want to look at it then, and I assumed I would take the sentimental stuff to the Karen house. Never occurred to me I'd stay here."

"Why did you stay?" Leona asked. "The business?" She knew he'd done well, and the town of Solai had become a bustling place, with markets catering to the tourist industry that, though not as big as elsewhere, was all due to John's work.

"No," he said. "The business is good, yes, but it would be better in Nairobi, or elsewhere, Tsavo maybe, Amboseli. I stayed because, once I got here, once I learned about my mother and the awful life she lived here... I didn't want to leave her alone again. The way she stayed for Thomas? I think that's why I stay, too. For her."

Adia woke late, a combination of jet lag and adolescence, and when she made her way to the kitchen to find breakfast, John was sitting at the table, buttering bread for his lunch.

"You're awake!" He grinned. "Sleeping beauty."

"Where's my mom?" she asked. It was one thing to read John's letters and write letters back to him, and to imagine what it would be like to be with him, father and daughter, but now, here, Adia felt shy and awkward. The only father she'd ever really seen being a father was Grace's dad. And he and John were not the same at all.

"In Solai, gone to pick up groceries and put gas in her car. Make you some toast?"

Adia's stomach was empty. She was starving, but it felt weird to sit here, just her and John. She didn't know what to talk about.

"I'm okay. Going to go for a walk, I think." She motioned out the window. "Maybe up to the tree."

"Perfect," John said. He popped the last bite of bread in his mouth and wiped his hands on his shirt. "I'll come along."

Adia didn't try to make conversation as they walked, and John didn't, either. Not really. Now and again he'd tell Adia some memory from his childhood, how he'd climb anthills and race to his friend Daniel's house and try to beat his record every time—counting steps out loud to scare any animals out of the way and taking bigger and bigger leaps across the red earth. Adia didn't answer, but she listened, and she tried to imagine this man as a boy—younger, even, than she was now.

At the top of the hill, though, Adia turned to John and smiled, "I love this tree," she said. She ran her fingers across the pulpy wood. The baobab, the "tree of life," was as porous as a grass stem. Its roots absorbed water in otherwise dry places from deep within the ground, and the fibrous wood held it tightly.

"I love it, too," John said. "It's one of the biggest I've seen. When I was at boarding school I had dreams about this tree. And when I moved to Nairobi to start work I missed it. Every time I came back to visit I'd take a photograph. I must have a hundred now, all taken at different angles, different times of day. If I can find them, you can take the ones you want with you when you go back to school. It'll help you remember, like it did me."

After his mother died, John felt inert. He'd expected the opposite—to finally feel free from all obligations, no family left, just him. He'd imagined himself moving back to the city, starting to meet women again, maybe even finding one to fall in love with. He felt maybe he was ready for marriage. But it didn't happen like that, and instead when Ruthie died, he'd felt as if his insides were nothing but an empty hole. Hollow and static. He was pulled under waves of grief that rose and fell like the ocean, and couldn't be predicted. On safari one day, with a family of Brits here on holiday, he'd felt strong, in control. But then he watched the little boy look up at his father with an expression that made John feel as if he were breaking into pieces.

"I thought I'd leave here," he said. Adia was still standing next to the tree, picking at the bark with a finger. "But right around that time was when your mother came, when I found you."

"When Grace died," Adia said.

"When Grace died," John confirmed. "And that's the kind of thing that makes life so damn confusing, doesn't it? Because here's this awful tragedy—your being hurt and losing your best friend, but me finding my daughter. The one I'd wanted ever since she was born."

Adia turned away from her inspection of the bark and faced John. "I wanted you, too. I imagined having a dad forever."

"And there you have it." John smiled. "We wanted one another and we found each other. It doesn't erase the fact that Grace is gone. Nothing will ever do that."

He patted the cool, stone bench next to him. "We have a lot to learn about each other, don't we? I've had no practice being a dad, no role model, either."

He smiled, and put his wide, warm hand on Adia's shoulder. "But we'll work out how to be with one another."

Adia felt a tightness in her chest uncoil, just a little, and felt her back relax. Her stomach growled loudly, and John laughed. "I'm already failing! Any dad worth his salt would have made sure his daughter ate something before dragging her out on a walk and giving her a lecture!"

It was almost dark when Leona's car bumped back up the driveway. She'd stretched her errands out for as long as she could; she stopped and had tea at a bakery, browsed at a tiny shop that sold books and wondered how Adia and John were managing. She hadn't told John she would be gone for so long or why she was really leaving. But she wanted to spend time alone, quiet. And she thought John and Adia would be able to talk more easily if she weren't there. Now, as she pushed the car door shut and hoisted her bags out of the trunk, she wondered if it was a mistake to leave them alone together. Maybe they'd avoided each other all day, not talked at all. Worse, maybe they'd discovered that they had everything in common, maybe they wouldn't want her back, wouldn't need her at all.

Leona piled her bags on the patio. She wasn't ready to go inside just yet. Instead, she walked around the side of the house and partway up the hill. The gathering dark made it too dangerous to walk far alone. In the near distance she heard a hyena. There were animals out now; this was their time. She turned toward the house again, and saw that, through the darkness, the brightly lit windows shone.

She had a sudden memory of her childhood home and how, sometimes, after school in the winter, she'd walk up the street from the bus stop and wish to see the windows in her house lit up, warm and welcoming and with someone there to take her in.

She stopped and turned to look back up the hill, where the baobab was silhouetted against the sky. The sky folded itself around the enormous tree and grew darker and darker until Leona couldn't see anything anymore. Not the branches, not the leaves, not the lonely headstones. Even the sky itself, for that moment, was invisible to her. It lifted itself like a lid, and air rushed in.

Leona turned back to the house. In the light of the kitchen window, she saw John and Adia. They were sitting at the table. John had a box at his feet and what looked like photos, some framed, some not, spread across the table between them. Adia was holding one, large and in a gilded frame, and John was pointing at it. Leona imagined him telling his daughter the stories of these people, her family, and his. She only knew the saddest stories of John's life, but surely he had happy ones, too. And if not, maybe it was because the happy moments in his life were still ahead, spreading out like the sky. Maybe the same would be true for her, too. She hugged herself against the chill air and began walking back down the path. She had come a long way, so had Adia, and Simi, and so had John. They all had. There were pieces of all their lives that were broken and ugly, but new ones were emerging. Adia had two mothers and a father now; Simi had more daughters than she'd ever dreamed she could have.

Leona considered herself and her daughter and John, in that moment the three of them inconceivably together in the wide-open land they all loved so much. Things slipped into the places where they were supposed to fit, and despite her fears and her refusal, time and time again, to love, she was here. She was here and she could feel herself opening. It took courage to relearn everything, to let her darkest spaces crack open to the light. It took bravery.

Leona smiled into the dark and quickened her pace. She let out a deep breath. She was ready to be brave.

★ ★ ★ ★ ★

BEHIND THE BOOK: HOW NOSTALGIA BROUGHT *THE BRIGHTEST SUN* TO LIFE

ADRIENNE BENSON

At the end of the movie version of *Out of Africa*, when Karen Blixen is leaving Kenya, she says, "If I know a song of Africa, of the giraffe and the African new moon lying on her back, of the plows in the fields and the sweaty faces of the coffee pickers, does Africa know a song of me?"

I always cry at that point, because I know exactly what she means. Clichés about Africa aside, the landscape in Kenya is arresting. It changes with the seasons and with the mood of the sky. My family left the US when I was four, and with only one brief stint back there, we'd been in Africa for a total of ten years by the time I returned to the US from Kenya at sixteen because of my dad's job as an international aid worker with the US government. We'd lived in two other African countries—Zambia and Liberia—but Kenya was where I lived the longest (five years) and it was the place I felt most connected to. It was where I began the adolescent individuation from my parents, where I first claimed experiences for myself and where I began to see the very tender and tiny shoots of the adult I'd later become. All of this meant that Kenya, and her dramatic landscape, was the place lodged most firmly in my heart when I returned to the United States to begin a life in a "home" I didn't really know.

People like my characters Grace and Adia and me are Third Culture Kids (TCKs)—kids who spend significant portions of their formative years outside their parents' countries. They are not immigrants—they are always expected to repatriate to their passport country. In the world of the TCK, good-byes and leaving are not only par for the course, but are also something to be excited about. TCK culture swallows grief. Moving somewhere new is considered an adventure, not an end that should be mourned; grieving is discouraged. Well, as I learned, when grief is sublimated and memories age, nostalgia flourishes.

In the way Adia was born of the special kind of loneliness expatriates can feel, *The Brightest Sun* was born of a nostalgic ache I've wrestled with for the thirty-one years since I left. The word *nostalgia* itself is a hybrid of the Greek words for *homecoming* and *pain*. As a writer, my therapy of choice for mental pain is to catch the things that hurt and put them on paper. I find it helps to clear the darker spaces inside me and empty the little throbs that collect in my mind like dust bunnies under the sofa. So when I heard Leona's voice in my head, I knew that she was only the eye of a needle, and that the thread she'd pull through the story was one that would also empty me of the nostalgia I'd harbored like a phantom limb for so long. So I set her in that same stunning landscape I couldn't forget, and I gave her a baby, Adia—a little TCK to watch growing up in between two cultures.

I knew kids like Adia, clearly foreign but allowed to root for an entire childhood in a single setting. Even though they knew they'd have to leave, and that they'd still face the struggle to find place, they displayed a deeper sense of belonging than those of us who moved more frequently. Adia's story isn't mine, so once I'd conjured her, I saw a place for something more like my own story. That's where Grace came in—her TCK experience is more closely aligned to mine. But you don't have a TCK without a parent who chooses to uproot. Grace gave rise to her mother, Jane, who has pushed aside her own needs and given up a career in order to accompany her husband, a diplomat, to his various international postings. Further, you can't have expatriates without a foreign nation for them to live in, one peopled with individuals who each have a deep and complex history and culture of their own. That's Simi—the steady one who never chooses to be foreign, but instead grows foreign simply because of her inability to be what her community demands.

The struggles the three women and two girls in *The Brightest Sun* face is really the struggle to define, and it's a universal struggle: to define yourself as a mother or daughter, to define yourself in relation to where you live and to define your place in the world—literally and figuratively. It's that struggle, ultimately, that I undertook and it's that struggle that inspired the book.

I'm not Karen Blixen. I know that Africa doesn't have a song of me. I know that the deep nostalgia I feel for aspects of my childhood are not reflected back by the places I lived, or by shadows underneath the baobab trees, or by the delicate dawns when the grasses glitter with dew. Any trace of me in Kenya, or Liberia, or Zambia, or Côte d'Ivoire is long gone.

But fusing those memories and nostalgia and imagination into this novel was part of my personal journey. I knew I needed to claim that space in between—the little sliver of Venn diagram where "American" and "other" meet. That's my place. I knew I wanted to bring the life of that "in-between" expatriate child to the page, to set it down and introduce it to people who don't know it. Those kids, and the adults they become, are my people, after all. And though Africa will never sing of me, I'm okay with that—my song isn't purely an African one anyway, nor is it American. Instead, it's the anthem of the sojourner, of all the placeless kids whose home is everywhere and nowhere. It's the song of kids who dream foreign smells and foreign tongues and who, when the plane taking them away banks and turns, trace on the window the dark shapes of hills they may never see again.

ACKNOWLEDGMENTS

People say writing is solitary. But writing a book for publication, and making that book into a real, tangible thing with a good story, believable characters, correct spelling and commas all in the right places takes a village. I'm lucky to have, somehow, been adopted into a literary village full of creative, smart, dedicated and kind professionals—people without whom this book wouldn't exist.

I've wanted to write a novel since I was seven, but it wasn't until the summer I turned forty that I tried. That summer, I accidentally opened an envelope addressed to my houses' previous owner—an inadvertent act that changed my life. The flyer was stamped with the George Washington University logo, and advertised the university-sponsored Jenny McKean Moore Community Workshop, a writing workshop led by actual, working writers. I applied, I got in and I was so nervous the first night I almost threw up.

The Brightest Sun was born in that first JMM workshop, and honed in a second workshop I took three years later. It was born because of the encouragement my two instructors—the first real writers I'd ever met—generously gave me, and the faith they had in my ability. Their support sustained, astonished and inspired me. I also met and stayed in touch with another participant, Terri G. Scullen. Over the course of the next four years, Terri read draft after draft after draft of this book, and not only had the kindness to remain my friend, but also gave me invaluable ideas, helped me attack the story and cheered me on. Terri, an amazing writer herself, was this book's most constant and most exuberant supporter.

Writers need readers for those first drafts, readers with critical eyes who can see the good and help point out the bad. I was lucky. I found a group of smart women who called it like they saw it, were generous with their time, gave excellent feedback and always had good snacks—Lisa Burke, Justine Hedgepeth, Laura Kaiser and Heather Prichard, I owe you multiple margaritas. Sharon Samber, I owe you Scotch (and probably money). Carol Hawk, friend since third grade and hawk-eyed reader, for your patience and insights, I owe you, too.

Finally, the pros that pulled me into the club I'd yearned for so long to join. Matt DiGangi of Bresnick Weil Literary Agency took a chance on me, made me feel like a professional, helped me keep the faith through the submission process, made me laugh and, ultimately, sold the book to the incredible (and possibly magical) editor Liz Stein of Park Row Books. Liz saw what the book should grow into and gently led my writing there. I am deeply grateful to her for the countless hours of work she put into this project. I'm also grateful to the rest of the team at Park Row for so professionally and seamlessly doing all the other hard work necessary to bring a book into the world—from copyediting to printing, from marketing and publicity to designing a cover so beautiful it made me gasp. This is a dream come true for me. A dream that took buy-in and faith from lots of other people and that is what stuns me the most—the willingness of so many others to help make this happen. I'm more grateful to all of you than you may ever know. Thank you. Thank you. Thank you.

QUESTIONS FOR DISCUSSION

1. Leona, Jane and Simi all have their own approaches to motherhood. In what ways are they different? Is there a commonality in how they assume the role of mother? Are there aspects of each mothering approach that echo ways in which you mother or were mothered?

2. The book discusses global issues like female genital mutilation, poaching, climate change and how laws impact traditional lifestyles. How important are these to the development of the characters? Do they enhance or detract from the story?

3. Landscape plays a prominent role in the book. How is sense of place a critical element in the telling of the story? In what way does landscape or place impact your own life and your personal life story?

4. The book centers on mother/daughter relationships. The mothers are very different from each other, and they judge

each other and are judged—often harshly. Is this a reflection of the reality of motherhood? Do we tend to set a certain standard, or expect certain things from mothers that may not always be reasonable?

5. The parents in the book are all flawed, some dramatically—there is child neglect, incest and domestic violence. In what ways do these parenting flaws impact the children in the book?

6. Adia grew up in an unconventional way and had a strange—and sometimes tragic—childhood. What do you see her doing as an adult? Would she choose to live in Kenya? Where would someone like her be at thirty?

7. Leona struggles with attachment and childhood trauma, and this is observed in her inability to form romantic relationships. But toward the end of the book, we see a shift. Do you think she would ever be comfortable in a partnership or marriage?

8. The main characters in the novel are all outsiders in their communities in some way. Are there benefits to "outsiderness?" Leona, Jane and Paul are outsiders by choice. Why would someone choose to live outside his or her community, or set up homes in places where they are foreign?

ABOUT THE AUTHOR

Adrienne Benson's earliest memories include roasting green mangoes over bonfires in Lusaka, Zambia; climbing walls to steal guavas from the neighbors; and riding in the back of a VW van for weeks on end, watching her mom and dad navigate African border crossings and setting up campsites among thieving monkeys and vocal lions. A USAID worker's daughter, she grew up traversing sub-Saharan Africa, finding homes in Zambia, Liberia, Kenya and Côte d'Ivoire. At sixteen, she made the hardest border crossing of all—the one that brought her "home" to America—a country she barely knew. She's been a Peace Corps volunteer in Nepal, lived in Ukraine and Albania, slept in more airports than she can count and is now happily ensconced in Washington, DC, with her three kids. Her writing has appeared in Buzzfeed; the *Foreign Service Journal*; *Brain, Child*; the *Washington Post*; the *Huffington Post*; *ADDitude* magazine; and several anthologies. *The Brightest Sun* is her first novel.